GOLD FEVER

SECOND EDITION

DARK SAVIOR SERIES
BOOK 1

JIM CLOUGHERTY

NOTE TO READER

If you enjoy *Gold Fever*, join the newsletter and receive free side stories set in the Dark Savior Series world! You'll get all side stories released up to this point, including *Slaying the Beast*, *Ground Into Dust*, and *The Seer's Game*. As more are released, you will receive those for free as well!

https://www.jimclougherty.com/subscribe-fantasy

For Noah and Allie

CHAPTER 1
TRAPPED

A Savior descends, dark as night
He brings us treasures, ever bright
It is not enough, you must have more
This is the will of our merciful lord
Shining black will show you the way
To a place where your Dark Savior lay…

Dalton Rayleigh awoke with a start. He rubbed his eyes and glanced around the dimly lit cave. The luminous blue rocks on the walls gave off a unique glimmer that in different circumstances would have filled him with wonder, but he had grown to hate everything about them. They faded in and out, slowly; repeatedly; and it made him sleepy. His men were all huddled in different corners, trying to stay warm. It had been some time since they last saw daylight.

'Stay away from the mines of Mt. Couture,' had been a mantra often repeated by the oldest and wisest in Dalton's home village, Faiwell. It had been common knowledge, in fact, that going there could only bring needless pain and death to the unfortunate souls ensnared in its grasp. However, as a mining settlement, Faiwell lived and died by its precious metal trade. A shortage of such metals in the surrounding mountains had the Village Elders worried for everyone's future. Faiwell's farms were not meant to feed the entire population, and if the shortage were to continue, a famine might occur.

These worries led Mining Guild president Drake Danvers to step in with a new solution: Attempt to mine the precious metals of Mt. Couture for the first time in over a hundred years. Not only was it the last mining site within a day's travel of the village, but the well-told legend of the *Gold Pit* at Mt. Couture's center enticed the Village Elders and convinced them that it was worth the risk. Besides, Drake had reasoned, the threats of the mines might have been mitigated by now.

So much for that, Dalton thought with a snort. From the very moment he and his team of 49 had entered the mines, it felt as if everything had been trying to kill them. A tunnel collapse had killed four, while six more had perished at the hands of wretched creatures who called Mt. Couture home. Most disturbing of all, five of the miners had disappeared without as much as a word or trace left behind. Some of the men were beginning to go stir-crazy, and, with the collapse having blocked their only known exit, they'd been wandering for long enough that thirst was becoming a concern.

Dalton wrung his hands, thinking of ways to ration out the remaining food and water. He hated playing the role of leader, but his zeal in trying to impress a Village Elder's granddaughter had seen him agreeing to the Mining Guild's odd request that he take charge of the first team sent in. As a battle-hardened warrior, he had little experience in mining. To make matters more awkward, he was a man of action and had often found himself at odds with the other miners, who were used to proceeding with caution. Soon, he thought, there'd be more conflict between him and the team. Tough decisions loomed on the horizon, and they wouldn't be popular ones.

"Sir, could I have a word?" a tall, stringy man asked, snapping him out of his train of thought.

Dalton looked up to see Baltr shuffling over to the cave wall where he was huddled up. He plopped down next to him as if a lack of strength in his legs had made him sit. He wore brown, ragged clothes underneath an oversized miner's apron. It was hard for Dalton not to smirk at such silly garments.

"What's on your mind, Baltr?" Dalton asked.

"A lot, sir," he replied with crossed arms.

"You don't have to keep calling me 'sir'. I think we're past the point where anyone cares about their title."

Baltr ignored him and continued, "We have officially run out of markers meant for the incoming team to find us."

"Another problem to add to the list…" Dalton muttered as he picked a crumb out of his dark beard.

"Morale is low, supplies are dwindling, and some of the workers…" Baltr trailed off, staring off into the distance.

Dalton eyed him. Thanks to soot and the brim of his mining helmet obscuring it all, he could barely make out his sharp face in the subtle blue light of the rocks. Yet, the white in Baltr's wide eyes struck him as he slowly looked his way.

"They're acting peculiar."

"Hard to blame them in a situation like this," Dalton said with a sigh. "Since that tunnel collapse, we've been wandering in circles. This place is more like a *maze* than a mine. If we don't first succumb to our thirst, then I'm sure that horrid *Nightcrawler* will finish us off."

Baltr narrowed his eyes. "Sir, just because you came up with the name of the beast, doesn't mean you must bring it up in every conversation. We haven't seen that monster in *at least* a day, I would say…"

He brought up a finger and wagged it. "Ah-ah-ah. Don't forget why I called it *night*-crawler. It only hunts us after sundown. It's impossible to tell the time of day in this shit-heap, but I'm sure nightfall approaches… and then, there will be nothin' we can do. That thing ate my sword for dinner… our weapons are useless."

"Can we circle back to the condition of our men, sir?" Baltr asked, leaning in. Dalton nodded. "They are acting the same way *Ollie* did before he disappeared. Appearing sickly, becoming defensive over the treasures they've found, rambling on about a 'Dark Savior' and how we must-"

"'Dark Savior'?" Dalton interrupted with urgency on his tongue.

"Yes, sir." He paused for a moment. "Very little of what Ollie said before his disappearance made sense, but he'd been mumbling about a 'Dark Savior' of some kind. Now, more of our men are doing the same, and I worry for their safety."

The warrior flashed a knowing smile. "Ollie's disappearance eventually led to you becoming my second-in-command. How do I know you aren't planting the seeds for my 'disappearance'? So that you can take over as leader?"

Baltr groaned. "Please take this seriously, won't you?"

Dalton looked away, holding in a laugh. He had come to enjoy Baltr's company for all the wrong reasons. It was fun to get reactions out of him whenever he tried to make serious conversation. Befriending *anyone* in this hellscape meant that they'd probably be the next to fall, he thought with a sigh. Perhaps he would indulge him and take the conversation seriously while he still could.

"'Dark Savior', eh?"

"Sir?"

"Have you had any strange dreams, lately?" he asked with a sudden focus in his brown eyes.

"Nothing comes to mind. Why do you ask?" Baltr said, cocking his head.

After a few moments of hesitation, Dalton said, "No reason. I suppose we should address the issues in front of our group."

"Yes, of course," Baltr said with a nod.

Both men stood, markedly slower than they normally would. Dalton slicked back his mid-length, dark brown hair and placed a tin miner's helmet on his head. They approached the center of the cave.

"Attention, everyone! Dalton is going to address the group! Gather 'round!" Baltr's shouts echoed all about the cave and several heads of tired miners popped up under the thin veil of blue light in response.

Dalton rolled his eyes at the unnecessary and loud announcement. He heard some murmurs and groaning, but eventually, the workers gathered and then made a circle around their two leaders.

"It has been brought to my attention that we have run out of glowing bulb markers to leave behind for the next team to find and rescue us," said Dalton. He paused for a moment to gauge the reaction. No one appeared surprised. Or was it that they were too exhausted to care? "To counteract this, as we continue to search for alternate exits, we will leave behind less important pieces of equipment and articles of clothing."

Groans and grumblings sounded off throughout the cave.

"Silence!" Baltr boomed. There was a sudden hush about the group.

"Erm, thank you, Baltr…" Dalton said with reddened cheeks. He cleared his throat and returned his focus to the miners. "I'm sure you can all agree that this place is a death trap; not just because of the fragile walls, but the predators that lurk within, too. So then, I have decided that we need to keep moving. We can't risk sitting around and waiting for long."

Louder and angrier grumbling erupted in the circle before giving way to *clangs* and *clunks*: Frustrated men threw their equipment down with what little energy remained in their arms. Baltr opened his mouth and inhaled, but a mere glance at Dalton's iron-willed expression stilled his tongue. After the crowd settled down, the leader continued.

"I understand your concerns, but-"

"We cannot afford to venture any further into this horrible place!" one voice from the crowd shouted.

"What about the new precious metal we discovered? Surely, we can obtain more and sell it for a higher price? We still have the village to think about!" another called out.

"We're starving. We must start hunting all wildlife we encounter!" The group cheered.

"Agreed," Dalton chimed in, and the crowd simmered. "Before, I forbade everyone from attacking the wildlife because we knew so little about it. After all, our weapons proved useless against the Night-crawler and that got some of our men killed... but it has become clear that we are no longer here to find precious metals. Our priority is to *survive*, now."

"But the Miner's Guild said-"

"Balls to the Miner's Guild!" Dalton bellowed back. "It's their fault we're in this situation in the first place."

The crowd fell silent. Dalton could see some heads nodding. A smattering of relief came to him.

"But we need more..."

"Yes... more..."

Some murmurs came from the crowd. Dalton's ears twitched. Could these have been the mad ramblings that Baltr had been referring to? He remained silent, hoping they would give themselves away. However, after some uncomfortable moments, he could feel the stares from his men. They were ready to be dismissed and no one had stepped forward.

"I'll give you all some time to rest and gather your important belongings. Then, we'll be moving on. The next animal we see, we'll hunt as a group. I know this has been a difficult experience for you all, but there is a light at the end of the tunnel. Whether we find an alternate exit, or the next team finds us, we *will* make our escape. Until then, we carry on and focus on our survival. That's all for now," Dalton said.

Baltr nudged him as the miners began to disperse.

"Sir..." he insisted.

"Ah, right..." Dalton muttered before clearing his throat. "Oh, and one more thing. If any of you feel that you are not of sound mind, or are experiencing anything odd, please see Baltr over here," he said and then patted his second-in-command on the shoulder. *"Or* you could grow a pair and not waste our time. The choice is yours!"

He began to laugh and some of the group joined in, but most others paid no attention and continued to walk away.

"Well… I see we're in high spirits…" he trailed off.

Baltr flashed an icy glare. "This is not a joking matter. Something is *wrong,* here."

He began to walk away.

"You're right…" Dalton said. Baltr stopped and turned back to stare at him, wide-eyed.

"Something ain't right about this place. I know it's ancient, but the shafts are so poorly built; it's as if they *wanted* a collapse to happen. And that's not all. There's a spirit about these mines. Something within it calls to me, and I'm worried that if I follow where it wants me to go…"

"You too, eh? It seems many are succumbing to madness. But unlike you, most of us have been in a mine pit for days at a time before. This is nothing new. Why is everyone going stir-crazy?" Baltr asked.

"I believe there is a connection to the madness and these particular mines. I don't think it's only because we are trapped. With each passing night, I've had these dreams, y'see…" Dalton said.

"What kind of dreams?"

"At first, I couldn't remember what they'd been about after waking up. But lately, it has become clearer," he said with tired eyes. "Much like Ollie and the other men who are going mad, there is a common theme: Something about a 'Dark Savior', and how I must 'have more.' Could that mean more gold?"

Baltr was silent for a few moments. "You know this means that-"

"I know exactly what it means," Dalton interrupted with sudden urgency. "If I start acting strange, you take a pickaxe and plunge it straight into my skull. Understood?"

"P-please be serious, sir…"

"I *am* serious. If I'm taken by the madness, I might lead you all to your deaths. When I was out at war, it was the ultimate shame to let a soldier of lower rank die on your watch. The same applies here. I'd rather be dead than get you lot killed. If it comes to that, you'll need to take over as leader," Dalton said with a nod. "Understood?"

With more determination in his voice, Baltr said, "I understand."

"Good," Dalton replied. He turned and walked toward his belongings. Baltr followed close behind.

"What if there was a way to fight the madness?" he asked. "Surely, there must be a way to save you and the others."

"No, I don't think so. I think we are dealing with forces far beyond ourselves," Dalton said without looking back.

"How can you say that? I've heard many a tale of your heroics during the War of the Bird; how you're supposed to be Faiwell's unbeatable champion! Yet, a few dreams have you ready to give up hope? You have been fearless while leading us through the treacherous mines! Don't surrender just yet! We can make it through this!" Baltr said with clenched fists.

Dalton looked down and took a long breath. "Y'see, in my dreams… it's always there… a dark figure off in the distance, getting closer every time my mind drifts off. His eyes, a blinding yellow, but I can't look away. I keep getting closer… closer… I need more… to reach him…"

"You 'need more'?" Baltr asked, his posture becoming defensive.

The warrior's eyes widened.

"I need more food, ye knob!" a passerby called out. Laughs echoed throughout the cave, and Dalton joined in on them.

"Now is not the time for jokes…" Baltr mumbled.

Dalton's laughs settled down.

"I thought it was in good taste, but perhaps that's the madness talking." He reached a hand into his old pants pocket, feeling the precious metal ore inside. "I suppose you could say I've got Gold Fever, eh?"

"'Gold Fever', sir?"

"Yeh. The Miner's Guild keeps on saying that like it's such a great thing. Well, it may get us all killed, so I say that Gold Fever should be used to describe miners who've gone mad," Dalton said with another laugh. As the chuckles tapered off, he said, "Now, if I die and you live, you have to give me credit for the 'Gold Fever' name, alright?"

Baltr looked back at his leader with concerned eyes. Dalton playfully shoved him. The stringy man cracked a smile.

"I should get to packing up my things," he said and then walked away into the dim blue light.

Dalton decided to take some time to write in his journal. He had been recording much of the strange happenings since entering the mines, but as time wore on, he treated it more like the entries could be his last words. Especially if Gold Fever would soon plunge him into the depths of lunacy.

"Ah, 'Gold Fever'… I've got to write that one down…" Dalton muttered as he pulled out a thick book.

~

ABOUT AN HOUR INTO HIS WRITING, Dalton was disturbed by a piercing scream from across the cave. He looked up, but the fading blue light did nothing to show him what had happened. He looked back down at his journal. His eyes widened to the size of gold coins and his gasp took all of his breath away. The final entry he had written said:

> **Give me more. Its shimmering beauty in the darkness of these mines fulfills my greatest desires. I must have more. It is his will… and those who do not follow must die. I will kill the non-believers.**

Dalton's hands began to shake. He concentrated hard on the dark, bolded words, but couldn't recall when he'd written such vitriolic filth. He buried his face in a palm, lurching his brain to give him an answer, when he heard another scream from across the cave.

He dropped the journal and grabbed his pickaxe. There was no time to worry about himself. Was it another wildlife attack? Or had someone else finally lost their mind?

Skreeeeeeee

The shrill cry of the beast confirmed Dalton's first instinct and worst fears. *The Nightcrawler,* he thought. He charged in the direction of the screams, his light chainmail jingling with each stride. As he ran, Dalton began thinking up exit strategies and how he could best minimize the body count. The best option, in his estimation, was not a pleasant one.

He halted behind the group of miners and looked upon the bloody scene. Before the men stood a dark green monster no less than five meters tall. Its angular head was tilted up, and the wriggling tentacles at its mouth, hiding rows of razor-sharp teeth, were tented out. Hanging out of the beast's mouth was a pair of kicking legs, and Dalton could hear the man's muffled screams from within its bulging throat. *Good God,* he thought. It was attempting to swallow him whole like a snake would its prey.

Snap

The crowd gasped as blood exploded out at them and the severed lower half of the man fell from the Nightcrawler's mouth, entrails and all. It hunched over and began feasting on the remains. Dalton shuddered at its eight glowing, blood-red eyes; some of which gazed aggressively at the crowd, while the others focused on its meal. It was biting through the bone and flesh with such ease that he knew time was short before it would finish and move on to the next victim.

Some men tended to an injured miner to the right of the monster. Next to him lay a broken pickaxe. Dalton did not doubt that the man had attempted to help his friend, but just like the other times, even iron had proven ineffective against the beast's hard skin. He could see three slash wounds across the struggling miner's midsection. They were of similar depth and severity to sword cuts he'd seen on corpses while on the battlefield. One thing Dalton had learned about the creature was how incredibly easy it was for it to kill them. Every other encounter had seen it slaying its victims with one blow. This miner had been lucky, though Dalton figured he would still die from blood loss.

Within the buzzing crowd, Dalton spotted Baltr. He dashed over to him, grabbed his shoulder, and then spun him around. The stringy man flinched and threw his hands up in defense.

"Baltr, it's only me!" he said, grabbing both shoulders now. "There is little time. You and the others must escape and continue further into the mines. It's your only hope to escape that beast."

"What about you, sir?" Baltr asked.

"I'm going to distract the monster. You lot need to leave," he said, pointing at the tunnel across the cave.

"But we can't-"

"You can, and you will. That's my final order. There is no time for you to be stubborn about this!" Dalton said while turning away.

"Everyone! Follow me! We must make our way further into the mines. Quickly, before it gets you!" he heard Baltr command from behind.

Dalton pushed through the crowd of men fleeing the opposite way. After withstanding the barrage of elbows and shoves, he stood alone before the beast. Its eyes remained on the corpse. It had already eaten the remains down to the shins, leaving very little time for him to launch an attack while it was distracted.

The monster must have had a weakness, he thought. Its thick, green skin was certainly a defense, but what about the red patches on its body? There was one on each elbow, shoulder, and knee. Could they have been like its own version of human tendons? Could the pickaxe pierce through that?

With the most vigor he had mustered in days, Dalton raised his pickaxe. The Nightcrawler paid no heed and continued to feast on its original victim. Knowing they could very well be his last moments, he let out a battle cry, so loud that it was as if the cave shook. Even he had not anticipated such a loud noise to come from himself, and that was when he realized: It wasn't just him yelling. There were many others in the cave shrieking and crying out. The reality of the situation took Dalton's attention completely. He stopped himself in mid-swing and looked out of the corner of his eye.

In the subdued light, off in the distance, he could make out a series of struggles. It was difficult to see exactly what was going on, but he could perceive men being tackled to the ground, pickaxes being swung, punches being thrown, items from sacks being taken, and men crawling away in desperation.

Fear grew in Dalton's mind that Gold Fever had taken more of his men.

"This is the will of the Savior, my friends!" a voice shouted.

"What are you doing? Listen to me! I'm your leader! Get off!" Baltr cried out.

"The Dark Savior will help us!"

"Give me more! I must have more!"

"For the will of our Savior!"

Positive chants quickly turned to angry and threatening talk.

"If yer not with us, then yer a non-believer!"

"Kill the non-believers!"

"Fools! History frowns upon you!"

"You do not deserve to be free!"

"You do not deserve to *live*!"

Dalton's fears had been confirmed. Yet, there was nothing he could do about them now. He had to focus on giving those remaining a fighting chance to survive. It was his duty.

He once again raised the pickaxe and turned his sights to the Nightcrawler. His mind, however, was clouded with the dread of his inevitable death.

"This hardly seems a fair fight," he said and cracked a smile up at the monster. It paid no attention to him. "I don't wanna deny you a fine meal like myself, but… as you can see, my team *really* falls apart without me." He let out a chuckle and pointed behind himself. "Surely, you have a weakness to even the odds. Is it the tentacles? Those red marks on your body? Or are those just some bad rashes?"

After a few awkward moments, Dalton brought down the pickaxe with everything he had, aiming for the red patch upon the Nightcrawler's knee. His swing had just the right amount of wind resistance to make it feel unstoppable.

Upon contact, a loud *crack* echoed throughout the cave, even louder than the chaos around him. His stomach sinking, Dalton knew it wasn't the sound of piercing flesh, but of iron breaking. He froze, looking down at the broken axe head on the ground for what felt like an eternity, but it had truly only been a split-second.

After a brief pause in eating, the Nightcrawler howled and pulled its right arm back, ready to strike. With lightning-fast movement, the beast swung its claws at Dalton's face.

Dalton's warrior instincts kicked in. He bent backward and saw the glimmers of its claws flash by his face. As he fell to the rocky ground, an odd sensation overcame him: his hair flowing in the wind. It was refreshing, but as soon as he heard the loud, skidding *clanks* of his helmet behind, he understood just how close he had come to death.

The beast looked down at Dalton and tilted its long, angular head. With a loud bellow, its mouth tentacles fluttered and the smell of warm human decay blasted his face. It held its left arm up, ready to strike a piercing blow. The claws came down and Dalton's instincts kicked in once more. He rolled out of the way and chunks of rock peppered his face as he did.

He jumped up and noticed the Nightcrawler was still hunched over, its claws firmly lodged in the ground. His first thought was that they were stuck, but there were no signs of struggle. It seemed the monster was surprised that its attacks had been dodged. Dalton was shocked, too. He had witnessed its ferocious speed before and never would have dreamed he was capable of avoiding those attacks.

"Guess all that combat training came in handy, eh?" he said to the creature as it turned slowly to face him.

There wasn't much to be boastful about, however. Dalton looked down to see that he was holding a broken stick. Blood streamed down from his forehead and cheeks, reminders of just how fragile he was compared to the monster now stalking toward him.

"I could use a sword right about now..." he muttered.

Just then, Dalton's vision blurred. The world around him spun and his head became light. His legs buckled and he fell to the ground, temporarily paralyzed. While contemplating the possibility that Gold Fever had overtaken him, he heard a deranged voice:

"There will be *no* resistance in the way of our Dark Savior when he returns!"

It took a moment for Dalton's dazed mind, but he soon realized that a Gold Fever-infected miner had struck him on the head from behind. He tried to figure out who it was, to reason with him, but the man had too much blood on his face to be sure. Dalton looked straight into his eyes, which he could swear had turned yellow. The attacker's gray cheekbones protruded outwards, as if malnourished. He no longer looked human. Now, he reminded him of a demon.

With a great, crooked, smile, the miner plopped down on a dazed Dalton. He then grabbed his wrists. The warrior could do nothing but stare back into his piercing yellow eyes.

"Where is it? Where have you hidden it? I must have it! I must have it all! We must have it!" the crazed man bellowed. Dalton did nothing but stare back at him, confused.

After a brief pause, the man narrowed his eyes and asked, "Do you know about the will of our Savior?"

"Eh?" was all Dalton could ask.

"He is the one who will save us. It will be glorious when our Dark Savior returns!" the miner continued as his smile grew and his eyes widened.

"Get off me, you fool! Can't you see that it's going to get us?" Dalton shouted. He turned his head to see the beast closing in.

The miner's head tilted, and in a hushed tone he asked, "So… you're a non-believer?"

His face faded from deranged happiness and turned to bitter anger.

"You would denounce the one who will purge our evil ways? Who would save you from self-destruction? He, who would liberate us all from ourselves? You do not yield to him?" The words echoed through Dalton's head. None of it made sense to him; though strangely, his confusion comforted him.

"Then, I shall do the only reasonable thing! If you cannot understand, then you are beyond saving! Those who do not stand with us will not be allowed to stand at all!"

The crazed man wrapped his cold hands around Dalton's throat and throttled it. He could feel the breath ripping out of his lungs. Gurgling noises arose that he never expected to hear come from his own mouth.

As Dalton's vision blurred, the miner continued, "Yes! After we purge those like you from the land, we shall usher in a new era of prosperity under our great Savior…"

Dalton knew that he had only a few seconds of consciousness left. He took that time to flail his arms around as the darkness started to take him. The pathetic nature of his 'attack' brought a smirk to his face. His chest ready to burst, he resigned to listen to the miner's last words, hoping that somehow, they would bring him comfort.

"Do not fret! Your death is a building block of our revolution. After which the Dark Savior will ensure safety, security, and happiness for all-"

The miner was cut off by a back-handed swing from the Nightcrawler. Dalton watched with wide eyes as the miner's body soared to nearly the other side of the cave, exploding like a bloody and bony display of fireworks as it did. Some of the blood had splattered on Dalton, but his rushed, relieved breaths took top priority over wiping it off.

His relief was short-lived, however. The beast loomed, its tentacles wriggling and its blood-red eyes all focused on him. Though he could barely move thanks to the earlier exchange, Dalton couldn't help but smile.

"Ah, you saved me… could it be that you are simply misunderstood?" he asked and then chuckled. The beast let out a light hiss. "I didn't think so… an equal opportunity killer. I like that."

The monster stood straight and raised its right arm. After some near-misses, this was the end, Dalton thought. He took those brief final moments to wonder if the next team would be able to save the other, non-infected men. The beast began to bring down its claw with immense speed. Dalton snorted and closed his eyes; not wanting to watch his own death play out. At least this way, he wouldn't have to continue through the cursed mines of Mt. Couture.

CHAPTER 2
JOEL AND ALDOUS

Old man Aldous paced back and forth to the tune of rumbling thunder and pounding rain atop his cozy hut. The crackling fireplace whisked back and forth as his movements turned frantic, wafting a warm, pleasant, and earthy smell over to Joel, who lay in bed across the room. He peeked over the covers and leaned in to try and make sense of his rambling.

"Is it my place to be meddling now?" he mumbled. "No, no, no… they have made their choice. I'll let it all play out. Besides, the Mountain King will stop them…"

He turned to face the dimming fireplace, and there was a long silence. The faint light showed how ragged his blue tunic was becoming, but most of all reflected the concern on his pale face.

"Ah, but someone needs to warn him of their arrival." Aldous let out a long sigh. "I have to go… there might be terrible consequences if I don't interfere."

The fire continued to dim as Aldous' sky-blue eyes stared intently. He stroked his short, gray beard and resumed pacing back and forth.

Then, there was a loud *boom* that shook the tiny hut to its very core. Joel couldn't help but shift in his bed. Aldous turned to face him.

"Don't worry, Joel; only thundery noises and such," he said with a half-hearted smile. "Now, where's my walky-do?"

The old man rolled up his sleeves and walked to the corner of the hut to grab a tall walking stick that looked to be carved from oak. He then strolled over to the bed where Joel lay, thumping the stick on the floor with every other step.

"The time has come, my friend… I had hoped we could stay out of this, but I've got… a bad feeling, or some such thing?"

Joel remained silent.

"Even if the chances of disaster are nearly zero, I still feel that we can prevent needless death by intervening," Aldous said, smirking. "With gentle nudges and suggestions, of course."

The young man gave Aldous a pat on the back to reassure him.

"I appreciate the vote of confidence." He chuckled and then continued, "But your time may come, too. If you don't hear from me by tomorrow morning, you'll need to accompany the second group to Mt. Couture."

Joel nodded, which fluffed his brown hair enough that it was sticking out in all directions.

"Ah, and I almost forgot…" Aldous knelt and rummaged beneath Joel's bed for a short time before retrieving a sheathed sword. "Could I borrow your bladey-do for my trip? I doubt I'll be needing it, but one never can be too sure."

With a snort, he pushed the sheath into Aldous' chest. He had no intention of using a sword anytime soon. Aldous smiled and then strapped the sheath to his hip.

"Thank you. And remember this," he began, sharpening his expression. "We tread on thin ice with our interference. These miners don't have the first clue of what they're stepping into, and it is our duty, first and foremost, to ensure that it stays that way."

Joel crossed his arms and crinkled his nose.

"I don't like it, either," Aldous said with a shrug. "But those are the rules. You must only act as a passive guide to them, and if they are unwilling to listen, then their fates are their own. The less they know, the better. Exposing the truth to them could bring about dire consequences…"

Concern swept over Joel's boyish face. He had never seen Aldous so nervous before.

"Don't worry. If all goes well tonight, you may not need to go or worry about giving away too much. But just in case…" Aldous trailed off with a grandfatherly smile. "Get some rest. With any luck, I'll see you in the morning. Oh yes, I'm sure I'll be back. Almost sure of it!"

Joel waved goodbye and rolled over to get back to sleep. Aldous made his way to the front door, where he began talking to himself again.

"Now, how do I get there, again? Was it… there?" he asked aloud.

Joel turned back over and looked up from his bed. The old man continued to stand in front of the door, talking to himself, until finally, he seemed to have an epiphany.

"That's definitely where it is! Surely! Certainly!" he said while opening the front door. Rain relentlessly struck the ground outside, and a cold draft flooded the hut.

Aldous took one step outside and landed in a puddle of muddy water. It splashed all over the pant legs under his tunic. He looked down and groaned while Joel chuckled through his nose.

"This trip is off to a bad start! I knew I should have worn my booty-majiggers!" he shouted before slamming the door shut.

Just after, the windows lit up a bright yellow, and a sharp stroke of thunder rocked the hut. Joel hopped up and opened the old wooden door to check on his friend. No one was there. He stared out into the dark, rainy night for a moment before shutting the door and going back to sleep.

CHAPTER 3
THE B-TEAM

The second group of miners walked in line along a damp dirt path that was wedged between withered, towering trees. The line was two or three people wide, with some men wheeling carts to be used later in the journey. Most miners held their equipment in a backpack or at the hip.

Trailing at the back of the pack was the quiet young man, Joel. His oversized miner's helmet bounced as he walked, loosening more and more with each step. A hexagonal medallion bounced at his chest to the beat of his strides. It was a shade of dull, darkened blue, and contained mysterious engravings on the front and back of it.

After adjusting his helmet, Joel buried his face in the map he was holding. He could hear chatter up ahead but paid it little mind. Now was the time to focus on his surroundings. His concentration abruptly snapped as he crashed into a stone wall and then fell to the muddy ground. He attempted to wipe the mud off his old, gray tunic but only succeeded in spreading it further to the dark sleeves of his undershirt.

At the clearing of a throat, he looked up to see he hadn't crashed into a stone wall, but a top-heavy, red-haired, giant of a man. He was looking down on him with a snarl. The miners up ahead had also stopped, probably at the team leader's discretion, he thought.

"Oi! Watch where yer goin'!" the man said. His voice was raspy, but it didn't hold quite the deep, intimidating tone that Joel had expected from a large fellow. He covered his mouth and some snorting chuckles escaped his nose. "Oh? Is somethin' funny?"

Joel returned to his feet, tipped his miner's helmet back in response, and then looked back down at his map. He raised an eyebrow as a big, swollen hand swatted the map downward. It had been the big man, whose face was beginning to turn red. He nudged one of the miners lined up beside him multiple times.

"Oi, Henic! Can ya believe this waif? *He* bumps into *me* and then acts like *I'm* tha one bein' rude! I oughta knock him 'round for a wee bit. That'll show him!" the big man bellowed with a scoff.

Henic, a balding man with built arms and legs to offset a round gut, glanced at Joel and sighed.

"Go easy on him, Alistair. Don't you know who he is? That's Joel, y'see-"

Alistair threw his hands up. "Oooooo! *Joel*, eh? Well, I suppose that changes everything, then! I guess ya think yer a hotshot and that ya can just barge into anyone ya want with no consequences, *eh Joel*?"

Joel looked up with blinking brown eyes to meet Alistair's glare. He tipped his helmet to him once again, but before he could look back at his map, Alistair pushed it down.

"I can't believe this guy! Yer tryin' ta tell me that *you* bump into *me*, and ya expect *me* to apologize for it?" Alistair asked. Henic nudged him, but he continued on.

"That IS what yer tryin' ta tell me with yer silence, ISN'T IT?" he said while spitting from the intensity of his words.

Alistair's heavily accented shouts echoed around the decaying trees. Joel could see that some of the miners were beginning to look back at the commotion. Hoping to disarm his anger, he simply smiled back, but Alistair's round face was beet-red by now.

"Answer tha question, boy!"

Joel tilted his head.

"Answer tha question, Joel!"

Henic nudged him a little harder, but he continued to be ignored.

"ANSWER THA QUESTION!"

Joel put his map away and started moving his hands in specific formations. Alistair growled like a feral beast.

"SPEAK TO ME!" he shouted at the top of his lungs and then picked Joel up by the collar. There were grumblings in the background from the other miners. Joel's cheeks turned red from embarrassment.

"Alistair! Stop it already!" Henic said as he grabbed his shoulder and tugged. "I've been trying to tell you. That fellow, Joel… he's a mute. Doesn't talk."

"Oh… oh… so, those hand signals…" Alistair trailed off as he let go of his collar.

"Joel trying to communicate, probably. I don' know him too well, but he's my neighbor back in the village, so I'd appreciate ye not bringing any harm to him," Henic said, looking over his shoulder at the stares of the other miners. "*Or* unnecessary attention on me."

Alistair turned flush-faced.

"Erm…" He rubbed the back of his curly-haired head. "I meant ya no harm, boy. Just don't be bumpin' into me again, ya got that?"

Joel nodded and then got back to his map.

About an hour later, the group stopped again for breakfast. At the front of the pack, a man named Faramond ate a small biscuit. It was a cloudy day; one not many would enjoy, but he tried to let his mind wander in the clouds, anyway. It was better than thinking about how he'd been chosen to lead a band of misfits instead of the first team. Faramond had been part of the Miner's Guild for most of his adult life. What did *Dalton*, a warrior, have that he did not? Thinking that it might rain again soon, he brought up the hood on his cloak to cover his ginger-brown hair.

Faramond had his back turned to the group as he ate, but could feel a presence behind him. He turned to see a young woman looking back up at him. Without pause, she flipped her golden blonde hair back and started talking.

"So, I have a status report on that commotion from earlier…" she trailed off.

"I don't recall asking for a status report," Faramond said, wiping the biscuit crumbs from his mustache.

"As your second-in-command, I must investigate the happenings of our team, *sir*."

Sensing the twinge of sarcasm in her voice, Faramond paused and considered reprimanding her, but then he looked her up and down. She was wearing a light red dress that was modified to go down just past her knees, stylish walking boots that only the rich could afford back in Faiwell, and a large leather belt that accentuated a shapely figure. He had an undeniable attraction to the blonde beauty, and it was one of many reasons that he would rarely speak ill to her.

"And? What did you find?" he asked.

"The commotion was between that big oaf, Alistair, and a strange young man, Joel. An argument… about something pointless, I'm sure. Too bad it didn't come to blows. That would have been entertaining!" she said with a grin. Faramond rolled his eyes.

"Some tenderness wouldn't kill you, Edith."

"They are not like you or I, Fara," she started. He hated that nickname, but that sharp face and those soft lips distracted him, allowing her to continue. "Half of these men are useless; dregs of society. They accompany us only because we needed as many workers as possible."

"Well, the Miner's Guild placed us on this team with these people…" Faramond trailed off.

"And?"

"Can't you see? We were deemed unfit for the first team, too. Clearly, the folks in charge see us the same way as *you* see *them*," he said, pointing over her shoulder at the workers. "We're on the B-Team, Edith. Let's not be arrogant."

Edith smirked. "Oh, Fara! That's what I like about you," she said, putting her cold hand on his forearm. "So modest…" She moved her face closer to his. He could feel her hand moving further down his body until she suddenly stopped.

Inches from his face, she whispered, "But deep down, you know the truth, even if you're afraid to say it out loud: We are simply better than these people…"

She closed her eyes and moved in for a kiss. Faramond put his finger in front of her lips. Their merest touch sent ripples up his arm. Edith's piercing green eyes opened, demanding an explanation.

"Not here. Not in front of the others…" he whispered. She frowned back at him and pouted, playfully. "Perhaps we'll find privacy in the mines, though."

"We'd better…" Edith said with a giggle.

"Could you inform the 'dregs of society' that we are soon to resume our journey?" he quipped.

"Of course. I'll be right back," she said in an overly pleasant tone.

～

Joel studied his map while Alistair's ravenous chomping of food provided background noise. It sounded like the miners ahead were stirring, too, but he pushed it out of his mind; hoping for a little more time to focus on the map's details before resuming the journey.

"You, there," a sharp, feminine voice called. Joel looked up to find a blonde beauty pointing at him. He recognized her as the second-in-command of the expedition, Edith. "Get your nose out of that map. You're here to mine, not read. Understand?"

Edith turned to head back up the line, but she came to an abrupt stop after a few steps. She did not turn back to face him.

"I said, '*Do you understand*'?" Her tone was striking and authoritative. She finally turned her head and shot an icy glare his way. Joel looked back at her and blinked. Obviously, another misunderstanding was afoot. She would mistake his inability to talk for disrespect, just like Alistair had.

"Oi, miss?" Alistair said. She grumpily looked over at the big man, but her expression softened almost immediately. Now, there were hints of judgment and amusement mixed into her gaze.

Even Joel, who did not like to judge appearances, could understand why: He wore a light gray worker's tunic that looked brand new, but it was a size too small for his large upper body. His brown boots and dark pants were standard attire for expeditions, but again, they were clean, marking his inexperience in the mines. His big, fuzzy head was made to look even bigger by a clean-shaven, chubby face.

"What do you want, big-head?" she shot back.

"'Big-head'? Why you little-" Alistair started, but Henic grabbed his shoulder before he could say any more. The big man looked back to see him shaking his head. He sighed and seemed to recompose himself. "There's no need for the insult, miss. I was tryin' to inform ya that the lad is a mute. I tried everythin' to get him talkin', but nothin' works. All he cares about is his stupid lil' map!"

Edith scoffed. "That makes him a liability, then. The mines of Mt. Couture are dangerous… it would be a shame if a rock fell and bashed his skull, wouldn't it? He wouldn't even be able to cry out for help."

A wide smile came across her face. Alistair cocked his head.

"Uhh…" he stammered.

"'Uhhh, me have big empty head! Can no speak words!'" Her tone was biting and mocking all at once.

Alistair clenched his fists and growled at her like an attack dog.

"Save your anger for the rocks, oaf. That's all you're good for," she said before taking a pleasant tone. "See to it that you are set ready to depart in a few moments…"

After Edith had taken some steps up the line, Alistair decided to complain aloud.

"Why is everyone so RUDE around here?"

"You know who that is, don't you?" Henic asked.

"No, but let me guess: You know, don't ya?"

"Uh-huh."

"Well, why don't ya explain ta me why she's a mean, nasty, busybody, then?" he asked while digging his hands into an animal fur that rested over his hips.

"She is Edith Danvers, daughter of the Mining Guild president," Henic said.

"Wha-what's she doin' on this journey, then? Shouldn't she be back in the village, livin' an easy life?"

"I don' have all the answers, but you would be wise to sit there and take any abuse she sends yer way. Edith knows she can get away with it, but you'll be ruined if she says anything bad about you to her father," said Henic.

"Aye… a good point. Thanks for havin' mah back, there," the big man said, looking down. "I just immigrated to Faiwell, ya see. I don't wanna be givin' anyone the wrong impression."

"Exactly. Keep your head down, get to minin', and hope we find some gold in there," Henic said while pointing. "Stay out of trouble and all will be well."

"Well, I ain't off to a good start keepin' mah head down, with all these conflicts!" Alistair said with a chuckle. "Isn't that right, lad?" He looked back at Joel, who returned a brief nod before looking back down at his map.

"Aghh! Hopeless!" Alistair cried.

~

MIDWAY through the pack of trekking miners, a blond young man traced the scars on his cheeks. With each step taken, dust rained down from his filthy worker's tunic, and some found its way into his boots. He crinkled his nose and considered stopping to empty the boots, but that would mean breaking rank and falling behind. Washing his clothes before the trip had seemed pointless to him, until now. By nightfall, he would be covered in soot, anyway. *The joys of mining*, he thought with a scowl. It was all so tiresome.

"Hey, Wolfy." He felt a jab at his shoulder, then turned and cocked his arm back to punch whoever had been foolish enough to bother him while in such a foul mood. He lowered his fist when locking eyes with Edith.

"Ye know that I hate when ye call me that. Call me 'Wolfgang'," he said.

"Aw, but I like 'Wolfy'…" she said, masterfully mixing poutiness and playfulness in her tone.

He sighed. "I'd guess ye came to talk 'cause ye want something."

"Is that all I am to you? Someone who wants things from you?"

"Yes."

Edith giggled. "You know me all too well."

"So? What is it, then?" Wolfgang demanded.

"At the back of the line, there's this quiet fellow. He kept looking at his stupid map, and wouldn't respect me when I gave him orders. He practically ignored me." She huffed, blowing some strands of her golden blonde hair up.

"Ye want me to rough 'im up a little, is what yer saying?" Wolfgang asked, his mischievous eyes brightening.

"I want you to rough him up *a lot*, my dear Wolfy. Take as many liberties as you like," Edith said as she put a hand on his cheek. He grabbed and caressed her delicate hand with his own, sandpaper-like hands.

"Oh, and one more thing…" she said while withdrawing her hand and walking faster. "Wait until the next time we stop, and make sure Faramond doesn't see. We wouldn't want you getting in trouble, now, would we?"

Wolfgang called up to her, "One of these days, yer gonna have to do somethin' for me!"

"Oh, I will, don't you worry…" Edith replied and then winked back at him.

"That'll be the day, *Wolfy*," a giant miner next to him said. His brisk chuckle rustled a bushy, blond beard and long, wavy hair. Contrary to his laughs, though, was a stone-faced expression that seemed nearly incapable of changing.

Wolfgang shot him a glare and punched him in the gut with lightning-like speed. The giant doubled over, but he continued to walk alongside him with no sign of retaliation.

"Shut up, Angus. Know yer place."

Angus coughed for a few moments and then choked out, "Right… my apologies…"

The B-Team of miners continued down the dirt path, and the trees grew larger and more barren with every stretch of distance covered. They felt endless, and it seemed as if even the most experienced map maker could get lost in them if they ventured too deep. It wasn't long before the group started to see giant Xs carved into tree trunks on the path, oftentimes with a circle around it.

It seemed as if the path was a loop of the same thing, over and over. They had been on the same road for six hours, and worrisome grumbling began to break out amongst the miners. Their current path cut through the Dead Woods, which were known to become highly dangerous at night. Had they underestimated the length of time it would take to reach the mountain? As if an answer to their prayers, the end of the woods and the beginning of the rolling hills came into view at the edge of the horizon.

Upon reaching the end of the woods, the miners stopped for a lunch break. Everyone scattered to their own spots, but most gathered near a calm stream just off the beaten path.

Wolfgang walked down the creak while looking around. Angus accompanied him, and a short yet wide miner named Bronrar stumbled behind them.

"Ack! This guy blends in too well with the crowd," said Bronrar, who scratched the dark scruff on his face with a nervous twitch.

"Yeh, how are we supposed to find him, anyhow? What Edith told us sounds like it could be any one of these people…" Angus said.

"Nonsense! We can find him. We just have'ta look out for a fella reading a map. Shouldn't be that hard," Wolfgang reassured his crew. There was a blood-thirsty look in his eyes.

The group of thugs walked along the trees until they noticed a large, redheaded man munching on an apple all alone.

"Ye, there!" Wolfgang said. The big man looked up. "There's a fella we're lookin' for. Have ye seen-"

"Well, yer askin' the wrong guy. I barely know anyone around here!" he interrupted with a hearty chuckle.

"Well, the guy is real quiet, you see. Doesn't like to listen. Seems to really like his map. Does that sound familiar?" Angus pressed.

The big redhead raised an eyebrow and then stood.

"Oh, yer talkin' about Joel, then. He's an odd one fer sure!" he said, pointing behind himself with a thumb. "What's yer business with him, anywa-"

Wolfgang smirked as they passed him without another word. He had no interest in befriending such an oaf.

"So rude..." came the mumble from behind. Wolfgang stifled a laugh.

~

JOEL HAD TAKEN out the map again while resting under a tree. He took a moment to rub his eyes, which had grown tired from drawing and looking at drawings the whole day, thus far.

"Now, what do we have here?"

He looked up to find mischievous eyes staring him down, and quickly recognized him as one of Faiwell's well-known troublemakers, Wolfgang. As soon as his mind registered who it was, Wolfgang swiped the map from his grip.

Joel rose and lunged out, but found himself restrained by a giant of a man whose rigid face reminded him of stone.

"What's wrong? Ye don't mind if I look at it, do ye?" Wolfgang jeered. Joel continued to struggle, but it was no use. The giant was well over twice his size.

Wolfgang looked down and studied the map until a raspy voice called out to him.

"Oi! What's that map say, anyway? I've been curious 'bout what has the lad so interested," Alistair said.

The blond brute looked up from the map with a grimace, but answered anyway, "It's a map of the Faiwell territory."

"That's all?"

"Yeh... and it's all wrong!" Wolfgang said with a derisive laugh. He then crumpled up the paper and tossed it over his shoulder before returning his vile gaze to Joel. "Did ye draw this? Ye've ruined a perfectly good map by drawing things that aren't supposed to be there. What a fool ye are!"

Joel continued to struggle. His cheeks turned red as he looked down at the crumpled-up map. All of his work had been ruined.

"Eh? Ye wanna do something about it?" Wolfgang asked with a smile. "Go ahead and let the lil' rat go, Angus."

Angus obeyed his command. Joel stumbled at first, but ever determined, went straight toward the map. Before he could reach it, however, he saw a dark boot stomp on it. It was Wolfgang, and he finished by rubbing it out in the dirt.

"Oh, that's just rude…" Alistair said under his breath.

"Let this be a lesson to ye," Wolfgang said as he threw a booming right hook that connected with Joel's cheek. It caught him by surprise and he stumbled backward. With some effort and awareness, he managed to keep his footing.

"Oi! Whad'ya think yer doin'? That's so… *rude*!" Alistair bellowed, now marching toward Wolfgang. Angus blocked his path. "Move it, meat-stain!"

"Go on. Try it," Angus replied with a smirk. He brought both fists up near his chin.

Though Alistair was a large man, Joel could see that even he couldn't match Angus' size. The man was built like a brick wall and had to be at least two meters tall, he thought.

As the thoughts occurred to him, Joel felt a deflating reality hit in the form of Wolfgang's fist to his stomach. He stumbled back and the offensive flurry continued with a few glancing blows to the cheek and jaw. Finally, he backed into a tree, sagging down and then looking up at his attacker. His face bloodied and his miner's helmet knocked to the ground, Joel's light brown hair flowed in the breeze.

"That's it! You waifs have taken this too far!" Alistair cried as he lunged out and threw a haymaker at Angus' jaw.

The heavy punch connected, but it had little effect, as Angus had turned his cheek in time to avoid a major impact. In response, the giant grabbed Alistair's hairy arm and put it in a lock. The big redhead cried out in pain as he was taken to the ground with a thud. Angus applied pressure to his back and arm simultaneously, so Alistair could do little more than lay face-down in the dirt.

Wolfgang looked down at Joel, now grinning. He raised an eyebrow and reached out, grasping the dark blue medallion that hung around his neck.

"And what is this ye've got here?" he asked while rubbing the metal hexagon with his thumb.

"This looks valuable," Wolfgang continued, bringing the medallion closer to his face. "Yer not holdin' out on the village, are ye? How about I take that off yer hands…"

He lifted the chain around his neck, as if about to yank it off. Wolfgang was free to beat him up and even destroy his maps, but that medallion was something Joel absolutely *had to* protect. The mute slapped his hand away with a speed and precision that saw the blond brute rubbing his hand with bewildered eyes.

The blond brute walked over to a stubby miner, who Joel hadn't noticed until just now. He let out a nervous stutter as Wolfgang swiped a pickaxe from his hand.

"Whoa! That's going too far, Wolfgang! Give that back to me-"

"Be quiet and watch, Bronrar. This is what happens to lowlifes who don't respect their superiors," he said with a crazed smile. Joel remained still and looked up at his attacker. "I hear ye don't respect authority. That all ye care about is sticking yer nose in that *stupid* map. Ye think yer too good to talk to us, do ye?"

There was a brief period of silence.

"That's what I thought. Ye don't respect me, do ye? What good are ye, anyway? Ye don't talk, ye don't listen, ye don't fight back... ye can't even get a map right!" he said, and yet there was still no response.

Bronrar cleared his throat. "Wolfgang, I think we should-"

Wolfgang put his free hand up. Bronrar became silent. He looked at the ground with uncomfortable eyes.

"I think ye should be put out of yer misery like the frightened little critter ye are..." he said and then raised the pickaxe. Joel remained still.

"Oi! Run away, lad!" Alistair squeaked out before Angus applied more pressure to his already strained arm. He gasped out in pain.

"What's this, now?" a voice called out from behind the scene.

Joel looked past Wolfgang to see a cloaked figure with a hand on his sword's hilt. The man pulled down his hood to reveal himself: It was their leader, Faramond. Wolfgang frowned.

"It looks like you're about to attack one of your fellow miners. Do you have a good reason?" Faramond asked in a curious tone.

"Well, I-"

"Surely, you're not as dimwitted as you look, Wolfgang. I'm certain you didn't think you could get away with murder because you're out in the wilderness... then again, the wilderness *is* where a snake belongs: A slimy snake that would squeeze the life out of others for fun."

Wolfgang's mouth fidgeted, but no words came out.

"You're only an immature grunt. Exactly why you're not leading this expedition. You will forever be held back by your delinquency. But you're not a murderer, are you? That would take *some* courage, at least," Faramond said. Even from Joel's perspective, his words had pierced like the sharpest of arrows.

The blond brute scowled back, then his expression slowly morphed into a sinister smile.

"We were havin' a *slight* disagreement over here, sir," he said with a shrug. Everyone breathed a sigh of relief. In the moment Faramond took his hand off the sword hilt, however, Wolfgang swung the pickaxe horizontally with the speed of a predator pouncing on his prey. All gasped when the axe head found its target, but not Joel. He had been the first to notice that the pickaxe struck the side of the tree trunk, mere inches from his neck.

"But as ye can see, cooler heads prevailed," Wolfgang said with a chuckle.

He motioned to his entourage, and they began to walk away, but Faramond sidestepped and blocked their path. "Just know that the only reason you're not being kicked out of this group is because we are far from the village, and I wish to keep everyone safe. Even a *cretin* like you."

Wolfgang laughed as he walked by him.

"However," he continued, gripping the sword hilt at his hip once more. "If I catch you doing anything like this again, *I'll take care of you myself.*"

The entourage paused briefly, and Wolfgang let out a long, exasperated laugh that seemed to stun even his cohorts, but then they continued out of the woods. After a momentary silence, Alistair spoke up.

"Phew! That was close! How did ya know we were in trouble, sir?" he asked while rubbing his arm.

Faramond smiled back at him and closed his eyes.

"Alistair, was it?" he asked.

"Yes, sir."

"Well, Alistair, I think you may be the loudest worker I've ever had on a team. I could hear you all the way upstream," he said with a chuckle.

"Oh…"

"That, and anytime Wolfgang and his cronies go missing, I know that trouble is afoot."

Faramond looked over at Joel and said, "Be sure to avoid Wolfgang, if possible. If you won't fight back, he'll keep coming for you. I've seen him do it to others, and I cannot have my eyes on you all the time. Understood?"

Joel picked up his helmet and nodded back in return. He made some hand signals toward Faramond. The leader smiled and slicked back his short hair.

"You're welcome," said Faramond. He turned to walk away, but after only a few paces, he stopped and looked back at the duo. "Oh, and one more thing: Don't stray too far into these woods. It becomes dangerous off the beaten path, even in daylight. We call it the 'Dead Woods' for a reason."

"Thanks fer yer concern, sir, but we'll be fine! Don't ya worry 'bout us!" Alistair reassured his leader as Joel walked by and retrieved the crumpled map. He flattened it out, held it up, and then smiled at the big man. "I hope that map was worth gettin' yer face pounded in! Yer not lookin' so good, lad, and that ain't no lie comin' from my ugly mug!"

An inaudible chuckle escaped Joel's mouth, and then he made some hand signals. He'd been trying to thank him for coming to his aid, but the mixture of bewilderment and frustration in Alistair's expression told the whole story. Instead, he tipped his miner's helmet and made his way for the stream up ahead, where he could wash his face.

CHAPTER 4
WIZARD

Further up the stream, a young man with blond, slicked-back hair stared at the reflection of his clean-shaven face in the water. He wore a dark green-patterned tunic with light brown pants and a nice pair of black boots. Conrad had spent most of his life in a financial setting. His parents owned a bank in Faiwell, where he had worked since he was a teen. He had become skilled at handling money and was primed to take over the business, but then the shortage of valuable metals began.

In truth, Conrad was excited to go out and try something different. Despite his training as a banker, he was well-versed in other areas: He had learned swordplay through various fencing exploits but had no use for it because now was a time of relative peace. History was his favorite subject, and he had put much time into learning legends from around the land, but few people in Faiwell appreciated such things. As a settlement forged in its precious metals, material wealth was the top priority of its citizens.

At the very least, Conrad thought that he could become skilled at mining. He had learned much in the months leading up to the expedition, but his lack of experience had landed him on the B-Team. He continued to think about where this journey would take him, but his train of thought was interrupted by a grating noise.

Shing

Shing

Shing

His shoulders tensing up at the vile sound, Conrad looked around for the source. On the other side of the path from him, he spotted a young woman with her back to a tree. She was sharpening her sword. With his curiosity piqued, he walked across the path to speak with her.

"I believe that's the wrong tool for this trip," he said in a jovial tone while eyeing her sword. The woman didn't look up and continued to sharpen.

"Depends who you ask," she said.

"I assume you've brought this sword to defend yourself from the rumored dangers of Mt. Couture?"

"It is not a mere sword, but a claymore."

The woman looked up at Conrad. She had a red crescent-shaped tattoo around her right eye, and it distracted him; he wanted to know what it stood for. Her long, dark hair was in a ponytail, and it complimented the soft features of her face. A pair of defensive, if experienced, dark brown eyes stared a hole through him.

"If you are aware of Mt. Couture's dangers, then why don't *you* carry a weapon?" she asked.

"I studied the art of fencing back at home..." he began while pointing behind with his thumb. "My rapier is back there with my belongings."

"A little piece of advice: The dangers of the mines aren't the only reason you'll be needing a sword, friend. Keep it with you at all times." She motioned with her head to the left. Conrad looked that way to see Wolfgang and Angus terrorizing another miner further upstream. This was not the first warning he'd received of the two troublemakers.

"I agree that you should always be armed, even when it seems like you aren't," he said before lifting a pant leg to reveal the grip of a dagger that was sheathed in his boot. Now, she was smiling. "But would you raise your sword against a comrade?"

"Claymore," she corrected. "And I don't consider scum like them my 'comrades'."

"Interesting..." he began before fixing his gaze on her great and shiny blade. "I've never seen a claymore up close before, but yours..."

She finally stopped sharpening the blade. "What about it?"

"It appears to be oversized."

"Indeed, it is. Two or three-fold the size of a normal claymore, I'd say. My blade cuts with enough force to end the fight in one swing, every time."

"I suppose we're at odds, then," he replied. She raised an eyebrow. "You see, I've been trained to favor quick, stabbing attacks with the rapier's superior reach. Once my opponent has been cut or stabbed, I only need to wait for their reactions to slow from their blood loss. Or I could simply play defense and let them bleed out. With your oversized blade, I feel your movements would be too slow to counter me."

Her eyes twitched. "You doubt my abilities?"

Sensing her growing unease, Conrad attempted to explain, "I meant no offens-"

"Let me show you something," the woman said before rising.

It was then that Conrad realized her imposing figure. She stood nearly a head taller than himself and wore a dark, leather-like torso armor that appeared tough, but flexible. It stretched out into a majestic mid-length skirt. In addition, she wore metal shoulder protectors and several leather belts where her weapons would normally be attached. Without a doubt, she had come prepared for a battle. He took particular notice of how compact and solid her legs appeared. It was as if they were tall, sturdy trees propping her up.

She turned to face the tree trunk she'd been sitting against and raised her claymore, two-handed. Then, she whirled the sword horizontally with a brief battle cry and struck the barren tree. It cut nearly a quarter of the way into the trunk.

"So? What did you think of my speed?" the woman asked before pulling her blade out of the tree. She turned back to face Conrad with a confident snort.

"At a glance? Nothing compared to the speed of my rapier."

She scoffed. "My claymore could slice your little sword in two. I'll take my power over your speed."

"You mean 'rapier'?" he asked with a smirk. She tried and failed to choke back laughter.

"What is your name?" she asked.

"I'm Conrad," he said. "And you?"

"Lucia."

"A beautiful name! It's a pleasure to meet you." He stuck out his hand. She grabbed and shook it firmly.

"I have to ask…" she started. "Did my claymore truly interest you so much that you would come and talk to a stranger about it?"

He raised his index finger and said, "Actually, the sound of you sharpening the blade is what drew me over. It was grating to my ears. I figured striking up a conversation would get you to stop, and it appears my plan succeeded." They both laughed.

As their chuckles tapered off, Conrad continued, "I think you should consider a lighter sword, though."

"Why are you so concerned about the speed of my attacks?" Lucia asked with crossed arms.

"The beginning of your earlier attack was near-perfect. You have great explosive strength in your legs, that much is clear..." he began, mimicking her prior sword swing in slow motion. "But after you swung the claymore into that tree, I could see that your arms lagged behind your legs, so the attack was slower than it should have been. That blade is too heavy. Even if you got your hands on a normal-sized claymore, it would make a great difference."

Lucia sighed. "I admit, it's a problem sometimes, the speed of this blade..."

Conrad nodded with a smile.

"But I'm not ready to give up using this beauty," Lucia said, hoisting the blade up and gazing upon it, almost lovingly. "While your analysis is correct in some ways, it fails to capture the most important element of all in a battle: fear. Opponents who know that they're in for a deep cut or bludgeoning will be twitchy; slower to react. Where I come from, the intimidation factor has won me many fights. The creatures of Mt. Couture and the scum we call allies may not have learned to fear me yet, but they will, with time."

"Fair enough," Conrad replied, nodding. "It seems you have some experience on the battlefield. Let's talk strategy."

They sat by the tree and continued their chat.

Alistair feasted on his lunch alone until a rustling off in the distance stilled his heavy chomps. The disturbance seemed to come from deeper in the woods. He looked around but didn't see anything, so he got back to eating. Moments later, there was more rustling, and this time, it seemed closer.

"Who's there?" he called out with bravado on his tongue. No response was returned.

The big man grumbled and then returned to his food. It wasn't long before he heard the sound of a twig snapping, even closer than the rustling he had heard before. He looked around, frantically. Another ambush by Wolfgang and his goons, perhaps?

"Awright, whoever's out there, I'm comin' ta find ya, now!" Alistair hopped up and ventured further into the woods.

~

"I *TOLD* you not to get caught, you dolt," Edith snapped at Wolfgang. He struck a defensive pose in return.

"And I told *ye* that Faramond came outta nowhere. We were in the woods. There was no reason to think-"

She cut him off with a scoff. "Implying that you have the ability to think! What a laugh!"

"It really wasn't his fault, though…" Bronrar said in a near-whisper.

"Did I ask for your opinion?" she growled back. He looked away. Edith took a deep breath and closed her eyes in an attempt to regain her composure. After a long pause, she asked, "So, is it true that he didn't fight back? Even when you were about to kill him?"

"He did nothing. I could have plunged that pickaxe into his neck and he would have never even raised a hand to defend himself," Wolfgang said.

A vile smile slowly took shape on Edith's sharp face.

"So, he's like a wounded animal, then. Utterly worthless. We should put him out of his misery," she said. There was a hint of controlled excitement in her voice.

"What is the benefit of killing a comrade on this trip?" Angus asked.

"It's simple. These mines are more dangerous than anything we've ever encountered. Believe me. We need workers who we can trust to have our backs in difficult times. We cannot count on the weak to do anything of worth," she replied.

Wolfgang and Angus nodded, while Bronrar grumbled to himself and continued looking away.

"And there is more to this expedition than meets the eye," she continued, her voice lowering to a whisper. "I have inside information about these mines that no one else is supposed to know, understand? Let's just say that what we'll find in Mt. Couture is even more valuable than gold." Her smile turned to a crooked grin.

"So, we take care of some knobs and get paid more for it?" Wolfgang said. "I like that, but Faramond has his eyes on me after that incident in the woods. How am I supposed to pick off the weak ones while under his watchful gaze?"

"You leave that to me. I have my ways..." Edith said, her green eyes glinting.

~

BACK IN THE WOODS, Alistair had ventured in deeper to investigate the noises. He was ready to give up, when, out of the corner of his eye, he spotted a figure hiding behind a tree. He could see the head poking out to look at him. The big man couldn't make out their face due to his poor vision, but with an old pointed hat and a blue robe of some kind, Alistair concluded that it had to be *a Wizard*. He became giddy with excitement.

"Oi! I've always wanted ta meet a Wizard! Come on out! Don't be shy, now!" he said.

The Wizard continued to poke his face out from behind a tree, but he did not attempt to completely reveal himself.

"Ohh, don't be bashful!" Still no response. The Wizard looked on, tilting his head at Alistair. "Awright, I'll come to you, then!"

After advancing a few steps in his direction, the Wizard disappeared from his hiding spot. Dead leaves rustled from behind the tree.

"No! Wait! I just wanted ta say hellooo!" Alistair cried as his walk turned into a run.

By the time he reached the tree, there was no trace of the Wizard. He continued to wander through the maze of dead trees in the hopes that he would encounter him again.

~

BACK ON THE path outside of the woods, Conrad and Lucia continued to discuss battle strategies while getting to know one another.

"A slash from my claymore doesn't only cut. It crushes, it severs... even with armor on, my opponent stands no chance," Lucia said.

"Ah, but what if the opponent dodges? You'll be left wide open," Conrad countered

"Don't be so sure of that. Footwork is my specialty," she replied.

"I think this comes down to tactics vs. brute force. I tend to lean toward the former," he said with a shrug.

"That's just it. Even though my claymore is meant for brute force, you have to be tactical, or you'll get caught... it hasn't failed me so far."

"This is why I'm glad to have met you, Lucia. I like to get different perspectives, but they have to come from a respectable source. We may not be at war, but if we were, I'd want you on my side," Conrad said, to which she smiled. "Think about it. My quick stabs could weaken the opponent via blood loss, and then they would be too tired to dodge one of your mighty claymore swings."

"Perhaps we'll have the chance to fight together at some point on this trip..." she trailed off, darting her eyes toward Wolfgang and his crew. "Whether it's against the dangers of the mines, or our supposed comrades."

"If it comes to that, I've got your back," he said.

"And I have yours..." she responded, half-heartedly. "There is something you should know about Mt. Couture and this trip, Conrad."

"Oh?"

"Maybe you'll have no reason to believe me, but there is-"

"Alright, everyone! Break's over! Get moving, or we'll leave without you!" Edith called out. Lucia's eyes sharpened to meet her disinterested expression.

"Never mind, I'll tell you later. You should gather your belongings," Lucia said.

"Right..."

After grabbing his things, Conrad joined Lucia in line. Since they were breaking rank by standing together, they took spots near the back of the line. Faramond was not a strict leader so far as Conrad knew, but it was a precaution worth taking.

As they chatted some more, Conrad took notice of a young man behind him. His boyish cheeks flushed red with worry, and he kept looking over his shoulder.

"Is something wrong?" Conrad asked. The young man remained silent. "Not the talkative type, are you?"

"I already like him better than most of the others, then," Lucia said.

Conrad gave a token chuckle, then flashed some hand signals at the quiet fellow. He gasped and then signed back to him.

"Ah, I see," the strategist said while nodding.

"What's that the two of you are doing?" Lucia asked.

"USL: Universal sign language," Conrad said while fixing a curious glance on the quiet young man. "It would seem this fellow is either deaf or mute."

"What are you discussing with him, then?"

"I asked him what was wrong. He said that his friend hasn't returned from the woods," Conrad replied, a coating of concern lining his voice. He pointed to a small cluster of trees near the stream. "Apparently, he left his belongings over there."

"The Dead Woods can be dangerous, even during the daytime. His friend might be dead…" she said, solemnly. The three of them looked into the thick of the woods. A fog seemed to be spreading from there.

Up ahead, the miners stirred, and grumbling broke out over the shifting of equipment and packs. They were about to depart. The quiet young man had his back turned to the group, staring into the fast-accumulating fog.

Conrad placed a hand on his shoulder. "It's dangerous to go deep in there. I can tell you're thinking about it…"

The miners ahead of them started to move. Lucia looked back and motioned them to get moving. The quiet man, however, took a few steps toward the woods.

"Wait!" Conrad pleaded.

In response, he looked back and flashed a series of hand signals. Then, he took off his medallion necklace and tossed it to him. Conrad caught it with both hands as the mysterious young man wandered off into the woods. After examining the medallion for a few moments, Conrad's face lit up with wonder. The group of miners had gotten farther ahead.

"What did he say?" Lucia asked. She then squinted at the medallion and continued, "And what is that he gave you? It's beautiful…"

"He said that if he doesn't return from the woods, to make sure I take this with me to Mt. Couture…" he replied, his eyes remaining fixed on the medallion. "I'm unsure what this is, exactly, but it appears to be a type of metal… one I've never seen. Most mysterious of all, the engravings on it look to be in the *ancient language*."

"*The* ancient language?"

"Yes, that one," he said, feeling the hexagonal shape out with his thumb. "What a fascinating fellow, and we only just met him, too… I would like to know more about this, wouldn't you?"

"I know what you're thinking, and I say this to you now with confidence: Don't do it. Going into those woods with that thick fog is suicide," Lucia said in a stern tone.

"Even still, I feel that I must go. Perhaps you could provide some protection with your unbeatable claymore?" he said while smirking.

Lucia shook her head. "You want to risk our lives for someone we just met? We have to be smarter than that. I cannot follow you in there, for I must make it to Mt. Couture alive."

"I understand," he said with a nod and then placed the medallion in his pocket. "We should be fine, anyway. You leave with the group, and we'll catch up with you later."

Conrad dashed for the misty woods with his rapier drawn.

~

DEEP IN THE WOODS, Alistair had run out of breath. He stopped his jog and then looked around while panting and wiping the sweat from his wide brow. There was no sign of the Wizard, but even worse, no sign of where he was or where he had come from. Everything looked the same.

"Aye… that pesky… Wizard!" he complained aloud before panting some more. "Which direction… did I come from… again?"

Adding to his anxiety was a heavy fog that seemed to thicken by the second. Alistair took one more look behind himself and squinted hard. The Wizard had reappeared out in the open.

"Oi! There ya are! Can ya lead me back to tha trail, mista Wizard?" he asked while approaching him with a smile. He couldn't make out a face, but his outline was certainly visible 10 paces ahead. "An odd fog we've got here, eh? Is this the work of yer magic?"

The Wizard remained silent.

"Why do ya keep ignorin' me? It's rude, ya know!" Alistair shouted. Yet, his blood never truly came to a boil. He couldn't shake the ominous feeling in his gut. The Wizard still turned away and huddled over in response to his half-hearted outburst.

"Oh… uh… sorry," Alistair muttered. "Sometimes, I can get a *wee bit* carried away. I see now that yer only a little shy, is all."

He was within arm's reach of the Wizard, now. The fog was now as thick and disorienting as smoke from a raging fire. He could barely make it out, but the Wizard was hunched over and shaking. Feeling guilty, Alistair reached out to comfort him.

It took a few seconds of a sure hand on his shoulder, but the Wizard eventually stopped shaking.

"Ya see that? There's nothin' ta be afraid of. Now, whad'ya say we get out of these woo-"

The Wizard turned around to face Alistair, and that's when he realized it wasn't a Wizard at all. This creature; this pale imitation; had light blue and wrinkly skin with a white, scraggly beard that looked like an old bird's nest. He appeared much like a man who had frozen to death. Yet, nothing could prepare Alistair for the horror that was this creature's eyes. They were deep, dark, black, and without pupils. Soulless, callous, and gluttonous in their soul-eating ability, there was nothing save for darkness; pure instinct.

Alistair dropped to his knees. His ears rang unbearably, and the creature looked down at him while drooling. The woods had become dark and cold, and he could feel nothing but the sensation of falling. He'd been rendered unable to move or speak. He couldn't even breathe, let alone understand what was happening.

The creature put its frigid hand on his face. Again, Alistair could do nothing. The falling sensation worsened and he became light-headed. He saw only the creature's ice-blue palm but could feel its horrible eyes penetrating his soul.

That was it, his soul! It had to have been trying to steal it, he thought. However, the reality quickly sank in that there was nothing he could do but accept and let it happen. The darkness began to close in around him.

Then, out of the corner of his eye and outside the range of the closing darkness, he spotted Joel, of all people. He couldn't tell if he was seeing things, but it comforted him nonetheless to see a familiar face. The darkness began to spread out in response.

He wasn't the only one to notice Joel. The creature took its hand off of Alistair's face and it let out a piercing shriek, like a high-pitched snake hiss. Joel pulled out his pickaxe, yet the fake Wizard paid no heed.

It lunged out, but Joel rolled to his left and out of the way with surprising speed. It hissed again and then disappeared into the thick fog. Alistair wanted to thank Joel, but he was still unable to speak. He could feel his health improving, though. He'd be sure to give the lad a thunderous pat on the back for his efforts once he made a full reco-

Alistair's eyes widened. The creature had snuck up behind Joel. It closed in with inaudible steps. He watched helplessly, trying to formulate words; to warn him; but nothing would come out. Of all the times he couldn't flap his gums, *it had to be now*, he thought.

The creature jumped out of the fog and thrust its palm into the back of Joel's head. However, the attack only knocked off his helmet. The creature tilted its head as Joel fell from the surprise impact. He rolled over on the ground to look up at the monstrosity before him.

It hissed some more and opened its inhuman mouth twice as wide as any man could. Inside was a dark void, much like its eyes. Like Alistair before him, Joel became paralyzed and could only watch on, helpless.

Alistair summoned all of his willpower in trying to move, but he was only able to wriggle his fingers and toes. He had nearly given up hope for the mute when suddenly, the creature's control over him ceased. It let out a pained hiss and Alistair looked up to see a dagger stuck in its shoulder. Dark blood spurted from the wound.

"I told you it would be dangerous," a man with slicked back, blond hair said, smiling down at Joel.

The creature pulled the dagger out of its shoulder, lunged out at its new foe, and attempted to use his own weapon against him. The challenger took a sideways stance with his rapier, and in one graceful motion, stabbed the horrible thing in its heart. The fake Wizard stopped dead in its tracks. It spit out dark blood and stared back with cold, black eyes. He ripped the blade from its chest, which sent it barreling to the ground.

He approached Alistair first and gave him a hand in getting to his feet.

"What *was* that thing?" Alistair asked.

"I believe they call it a False Wizard," he said while putting Joel's arm around his shoulder to hoist him up. "As the name implies, they imitate Wizards and try to steal unsuspecting victim's souls by luring them deep into the woods. What you need to remember is that most *true* Wizards prefer not to reveal their sorcerous ways, unless you are a personal acquaintance."

"Aye, I've learned me lesson fer sure. Thanks for savin' us, mister…"

"I'm Conrad. I presume you're the friend this quiet fellow was worried about? He refused to go along with the group until your safe return, so I followed him here to make sure everything was alright," he replied.

Alistair paused for a few seconds, looking down. A heavy guilt swept over him. "Aye… he's a friend. The name's Alistair. Nice to meet ya."

"The pleasure is all mine. We can talk some more when we get out of here. We must be quick. The group left us behind, and this fog is getting worse," said Conrad.

"I've been lost in here fer a while. That False Wizard conjured up the pesky fog, methinks. Funny, I thought it would've gone away after it died, the wretched beast!" the big man said with a chuckle.

Conrad's eyes widened. He let Joel slump down from his shoulder and drew his rapier again, frantically. As he turned in the thick fog, his eyes met the False Wizard's soulless stare. It was very much alive and tackled him to the ground, but the strategist managed to block its hands with the rapier as he fell.

The creature screeched while on top of him. Conrad closed his eyes and looked away, struggling to get the monster off.

Alistair, feeling much better, seized the opportunity while the False Wizard was wrestling with Conrad on the ground. He charged over like a raging bull and punted the creature in its stomach with all of his might. It flew several paces back, and Alistair thought that he might have even heard a few ribs breaking. However, moments later, he was shocked to see it rising once more, none the worse for wear.

"How are we supposed ta defeat this pesky creature?" he asked.

Splat

Suddenly, the False Wizard's head was soaring through the air. Alistair looked on in wonder as it arced downward, the dark blood tricking from where its neck should have been. It was as if it were falling in slow motion. As soon as its head hit the ground, the fog began to dissipate, and a tall figure appeared in the form of a well-armored woman. She yanked her claymore from one of the dead trees before wiping it off with a rag.

"That's claymore, one; rapier, zero," she said with a triumphant laugh.

"Ah, you came after all," Conrad said with a nod. "And it's a good thing, too. I had forgotten False Wizards don't have hearts. That's why they eat souls."

Joel arose and picked up his helmet. He strode over to the armored woman and gave her a big hug. She looked surprised and embarrassed all the same. Given their statures, it almost looked like a boy hugging his mother, and out of courtesy for her help, Alistair did his best to stave off laughter. Joel flashed some signs after releasing her. She looked to Conrad for translation.

"He thanked you for saving us."

She blushed, slightly. "Oh, um… you're welcome."

"Aye! There can be no doubt ya arrived just in time, lass! Thank ya!" Alistair chimed in.

"I can't thank you. It would make me look bad," Conrad joked.

"Let's save the pleasantries for later, boys. We must get back to the group before we're completely left behind," she said.

Joel put his hand up, grabbing everyone's attention. He flashed some hand signals to Conrad, who cocked his head in response.

"He says that he knows how to get us back to the path, and to follow him."

The group swiftly retrieved their items and followed Joel out of the woods.

CHAPTER 5
THE MOUTH OF HELL

The trip out of the woods felt far shorter than the trip in. Proper introductions of the new acquaintances while running had ensured that all of them were panting by the time they reemerged onto the path, but it had served well as a distraction while Joel navigated the treachery of the Dead Woods and its fog. However, now it seemed that their team was out of sight. Everyone looked at each other with panic in their eyes.

"It should be alright as long as we follow the trail," Conrad said.

"Still, unless any of you know the route to Mt. Couture's mines, we cannot be sure if they will veer off-road at some point. We need to catch up. Are you boys up for a jog?" Lucia asked.

"Aye..." Alistair choked out; the only one still panting from the jog out of the woods. "But I need... ta rest for a moment!"

"Fine, but only for a moment. You have troubled us enough today," she replied with crossed arms.

"Why were you so deep in the woods, anyway?" Conrad asked.

"I've always wanted... ta meet a Wizard... he kept runnin' away... so I thought he was shy... but now I see... he was lurin' me in, the pesky beast!" Alistair said with a breathy chuckle.

Lucia scoffed. "How many times were we warned to stay out of the woods? Do you have a listening problem?"

"Oi! Ya don't have'ta be rude about it! Me hearing's not what it used to be!" he said.

Conrad cocked his head and asked, "How old are you?"

"24 years young! Why do ya ask?"

Joel let out a few snorting chuckles and Conrad joined in with him. He had made it sound like he was an old man with deteriorating ears.

"More to the point," Lucia said, pointing at the big man with authority. "I can't keep risking my hide to fix your poor decisions. Smarten up."

"Yer bein' too harsh on me, lass! It's not very lady-like, I'll tell ya that much!" Alistair retorted.

"And it's not very manly to be felled by a wrinkly old imitation of a Wizard, is it?"

Alistair grimaced, and then bellowed, "You doubt me? Do ya wanna test me strength? Because I'm more than happy to-"

Joel jumped between them and put his hands up. He fought off more laughter as they continued to mutter obscenities under their breaths. What a funny bunch, he thought. They'd make nice companions for the trip. However, he knew that time was short, and motioned toward the hilly path ahead.

"He's right. We need to get moving," said Conrad.

All nodded in agreement and Alistair gathered his belongings from the edge of the woods. Before they left, Conrad approached Joel and took the medallion out of his pocket.

"I believe this is yours," he said, handing it over. As Joel hung the medallion back around his neck, Conrad said, "I have some questions for you, but let's save them for when we catch up with the group, agreed?"

Joel nodded while biting his tongue. He wasn't supposed to speak with anyone about the medallion, let alone *entrust it* to anyone. He would need to be smarter, from here on. Even if Conrad was trustworthy, there were some burdens he was not meant to carry or know about.

With that thought, the group began their jog on the path. Lucia led the pack with long, brisk strides. Following close behind her was Conrad, with shorter, faster strides. A few paces back was Joel, who jogged without focus; his mind was elsewhere. Bringing up the rear was Alistair, who, as the journey went on, lagged more and more behind the others. As the hills became more plentiful, the big man started to pant and wheeze. Joel slowed his pace to match, but Alistair took notice of his pity.

"Don't be… waitin' up fer… me, lad! I'll catch up… don't worry!"
he said while shooing him away.

Although it had at first been refreshing to see a new, open landscape, it didn't take long for Joel to tire of the endless hills and generic
plains off in the distance. At least it would be easy to memorize for
whenever he next got a chance to draw more maps. As the group
jogged up a new hill, the creek to their left veered off and out of sight.

This hill was a long, tiring battle against their legs, but upon
reaching the top, Lucia called out, "I see the group!"

She picked up her pace as the hill sloped downward, much to Alistair's audible dismay. Joel smiled back at him and chuckled. After one
more burst of speed, they caught up with the group, which was
heading up another hill with a rocky terrain. Nobody seemed to notice
their arrival as they slipped right into the back of the line. They all
breathed a big sigh of relief.

"Let's not… do that again…" Conrad said, wiping sweat from his
brow.

"Aye…" was all Alistair could muster.

The B-Team continued along, incident-free for a little while. The
terrain became more mountainous by the stride, as they reached higher
elevations and rockier climates. The air grew colder, the grass became
deader, and the rocks turned darker. No wildlife, save for the False
Wizard, had been seen for hours.

As they walked through the rocky terrain, the group began to see
more markings, which always had similar messages. They were signs
telling travelers to turn away, the most common of which was an
engraved 'X'; sometimes with a circle around it.

Eventually, they reached a gigantic plateau that was split in two.
There was a path that came between two rock faces where the plateau
was divided. Joel could hear some grumbling from miners ahead that
they were entering *Allie's Pass*. As far as he'd been told in the past, it
was the last major landmark before Mt. Couture. Some ways into the
pass, the group slowed to a crawl.

"Another break? When we're this close?" Lucia asked aloud.

"No," said Conrad. He pointed ahead at some miners huddled
together, facing one of the rock walls. "Everyone is looking at the rock
face. More engravings, perhaps?"

They trudged along until finally, they saw what had everyone's
attention on the rock wall to their right: drawings. Conrad and Joel
stopped to inspect. Alistair and Lucia kept walking.

Lucia looked back and asked, "What is it, Conrad?"

"These engravings… I believe they were done by *the Ancient Ones*," he said while tracing the carvings with a finger. Conrad looked at Joel, who had begun writing notes in a book.

"Your medallion has similar engravings to these," Conrad began while pointing at the rock wall. "Can it be that you understand what this says?"

Joel stopped writing and looked over at his new acquaintance. How much could he afford to reveal? If Aldous were around, he'd tell him to avoid an inquisitive fellow like Conrad altogether, but he had saved him back in the Dead Woods. Little details could be revealed here and there, he thought.

The mute nodded and Conrad's eyes widened. Joel adjusted his miner's helmet and got back to taking notes, hoping that would be the end of the conversation. Lucia and Alistair walked back over to them.

"You don't want to fall behind *again*, do you?" Lucia asked as she playfully shoved Conrad. He didn't respond. "Conrad?"

"Tell me… what do you think *that* means?" the strategist finally responded and then pointed at a drawing on the rock wall.

Both Lucia and Alistair studied it. Several figures, men and women, were gathered around piles of dark, bar-shaped materials that sparkled like gold. The people were bowing and praying before the material. In the background of the engravings, a shadowy figure loomed over them all. It had glowing, yellow eyes.

"It looks like people and gold," said Lucia. She squinted. "But the gold is discolored and looks too dark. Perhaps the color faded over time?"

"Methinks it's a message about the evils of money n' greed. Those folks in that thar picture are worshippin' tha gold like a God. And look at that evil-lookin' knob in the back! Creepy… maybe it represents tha banks controllin' our money… and our lives!" Alistair concluded with a proud smile.

Conrad shot him a pointed smile and said, "Did you know that I was a banker back in the village, Alistair?"

The big man blushed. "Oh… sorry, lad."

"What interests me is the fact that the 'gold' is discolored, but the sparkles and people are all the right color. Why would time only affect that one color and nothing else?" he asked. No one replied, so he returned his gaze to the mute. "Joel, if you can understand what these markings mean, will you tell us?"

Joel sighed. Now, he was going to have to disappoint them. He looked up from his book before flashing some hand signals. Conrad frowned.

"What is it?" Lucia asked.

"He says that he's not supposed to tell anyone."

"Oi, Joel! C'mon, now! We're just curious, is all!" Alistair said and patted him on the back, roughly. Joel smiled but also shook his head. His helmet nearly fell off.

"Tell us this much… do these engravings depict gold?" Lucia asked.

Joel took in a deep breath. Aldous would be furious to know he'd revealed this much already. But why not? Didn't they have a right to know the truth? To have a fighting chance? They had given him a fighting chance against the False Wizard, after all. He flashed more signs to Conrad.

"No…" Conrad translated.

"It seems like he said more than just 'no'. What else did he say?" Lucia asked.

"I'm not sure I fully understand," Conrad replied. He made some hand signals back at Joel. Some gestures were sent in return.

"He said it's called 'black gold'. I've never heard of it. Have either of you?"

The others shook their heads.

"He also said that it may seem valuable, but we'd be better off not finding any."

"Eh? That doesn't make any sense! Are ya sure yer translating right?" Alistair asked.

"I double-checked."

"Maybe there is a poisonous property to it. Something that can hurt us?" Lucia said.

Conrad paused for a moment and then signed to Joel. The mute hesitated for some time. He had already told them so much. While there were good reasons for keeping everyone in the dark about what lay in Mt. Couture, he felt that it was reasonable to warn them of the dangers. In response, he sent several hand signals back.

"Well?" Alistair demanded.

"He says that black gold will poison our minds…" Conrad trailed off.

Lucia turned toward the group ahead. They had left them behind once again but were within a quick jog's distance.

"I'm sure he is warning us not to become greedy," she said while beginning to walk away. "But it can't be helped. Wherever there are riches, greed will follow. We've got to meet up with the first team and save our village. That is the priority."

The others began to walk down the path again, while Joel finished writing in his book. He hoped that they would heed his warning, but feared the worst.

"If this black gold stuff is so valuable, why have none of us heard of it, eh?" Alistair asked.

"A fair question," Conrad replied while rubbing his eyes. "Perhaps it was hidden around these parts by someone long ago; someone who wanted to hide their fortune."

"Oi! Like a buried treasure? How excitin'!"

Conrad snorted. "I'm curious how Joel would know all of that by only looking at some engravings. In all of my historical studies, not once have I ever heard of black gold."

"Well, maybe yer not as great in that subject as ya think!" Alistair said while giving him a playful slap on the back.

"Maybe…"

Joel looked at him with a knowing smile. Maybe Conrad would be able to put two and two together, he thought. Maybe there was hope. They all increased their walking pace to catch up with the rest of the group.

The rock walls featured many more engravings as they continued, but most of them were repeats of the Xs with circles drawn around them. One engraving, however, caught Joel's eye: An otherworldly beast drawn on the wall. Tentacles on its mouth, a long, angular face, many blood-red eyes, and sharp claws at its three-pronged hands and feet. The creature was depicted dismembering people in a bloody scene. Joel stopped to draw it for a moment and then scrambled to catch up with the others after having fallen far enough behind.

Alistair tapped Lucia on the shoulder.

"Remember how you were goin' on 'bout how I need to listen better? Well, these here rock walls are tellin' me to turn 'round and leave this place. Whad'ya say to that, missy?" he asked.

"If you want to go home empty-handed, feel free. But the way I see it, Faiwell won't survive without our help. Even if that were not the case, I would still be here. There is someone I need to meet up with from the first team," she replied with a shrug.

Soon, the messages on the rock walls ceased, and the walls themselves became so tall that the tops of them couldn't easily be seen. The group continued as it grew darker. After about an hour more, they finally exited Allie's Pass and made a bending left turn on the path. Rumblings from the miners ahead informed Joel and the others that they had reached Mt. Couture's base. The massive mountain loomed over them and the wind howled like an animal defending its nest. After a long curve around the base, which almost felt like a trench or ravine, they reached the first team's camp. Faramond declared it was time to stop and rest again. Ahead, a dark tunnel beckoned them.

There were several tents and fire pits scattered around the area near the entrance, but no sign of life aside from that. Some miners raised concerns, but Faramond managed to assure them that they were probably still mining inside the mountain.

"We should be going in there now. There is no time to waste..." Lucia muttered with a frown.

"This could be the last time that we taste fresh air for a while. I suggest we enjoy it," Conrad said while plopping down against the beginnings of the mountainside. She looked down at the strategist and breathed a loud sigh before sitting next to him.

Conrad smiled and nudged her with an elbow. Her eyes darted over to him.

"Is something else on your mind?" he asked.

"Not at all."

He took a few nibbles of his white bread.

"I remember you were going to tell me something about the mines earlier, weren't you?" he asked. Alistair looked over at them with curious eyes. "Something important about this trip, wasn't it?"

Lucia stretched her arms and yawned.

"Well? Are ya holdin' out on us, lass?" Alistair asked.

"You wouldn't believe me even if I told you. All I'm going to say is: Be ready for anything in those mines," she said.

The group remained silent. There was a great sense of foreboding in Joel's mind. Here they were, about to enter one of the world's most dangerous places. He hoped the others would heed his warning, but his expectations were low. His train of thought was snapped by Edith barking orders at a miner up ahead. She focused her sights on him and the others, next, and approached them.

Her eyes widened and she gasped before saying, "Oh... you lot are still here? I thought we left you behind at the Dead Woods."

Lucia stared a hole through Edith. Her hand clenched the claymore scabbard. Edith, however, focused on Joel and his book. The mute looked up at her and then down at the book multiple times to see if she would say anything, but silence had overcome her.

"Are ya serious? You left us to perish back there on purpose? What is wrong with you? Why are ya so RUDE?" Alistair bellowed. He stood and faced down Edith, but the fire in his eyes was put out by Edith's ice-cold glare, and he backed down.

She snarled back at him. "What *is* your point, meathead? If you're too weak or too dumb to even survive the trip, then we don't need *or* want you here. You can die, for all I care."

"Tough talk coming from someone who's been coddled all her life," Lucia said with a smirk. Her tightening grip around the claymore scabbard betrayed the cool demeanor she was attempting to portray, however. "I'd like to see you survive out here by yourself. I think that would be entertaining."

Edith frowned back and said, "Watch yourself, behemoth. Don't forget who is in charge of whom. I can end your mining career in a split second. Remember that."

Lucia began to stand, but Conrad grabbed her shoulder. She stopped and looked back at him with a grimace. He shook his head. "Now is not the time."

The blonde beauty scoffed. "That's right. Sit back down. Know your place. The lot of you are outcasts around here. Your opinions mean nothing."

While sitting, Lucia muttered, "We'll see how it all plays out in the mines…"

Edith walked away. "Indeed, we shall…"

After some brief grumbling, Joel and the others began eating a modest dinner. With no animals around to hunt, they stuck to bread, fruits, and vegetables.

With his mouth still full of food, Alistair groaned. "Gwheat! Vhat foul hlash ish back again!"

All in the group turned while frowning to see Edith standing over them with hands at her hips.

"*You*," she said, pointing at Joel. He cocked his head. "Come with me."

"Oi! Why should he? Why should any of us trust ya?" Alistair asked.

"Unlike the rest of you misfits, Joel can be of at least *some* use to us," Edith said.

"Do tell," said Conrad.

Edith sighed dramatically.

"There is a sign at the entrance of the mines. It's in a different language," she said while looking at Joel. "I saw you writing a similar language in that book of yours. We need you to translate."

"I don't suppose you'd mind if we came along? I'm interested in what Joel's translation will be," Conrad said.

Although she glared back at him, Edith said, "Very well. Outcasts have to stick together, I suppose."

Lucia scoffed as she stood and loomed over Edith.

"Problem?" Edith asked with a wooden smile.

"I'm just imagining what it would look like if you were skewered on my blade," she replied with a smile of her own.

Edith turned while flipping her golden blonde hair and began to walk ahead. The rest of the group followed. Midway up, Alistair tapped Joel and Conrad on their shoulders.

Between muffled laughs, he whispered, "Wow, they hate each other's guts, don't they? *Women*, am I right?"

"Something tells me there's more to it than that; something Lucia isn't telling us," Conrad whispered back.

Joel rubbed his chin. Could it be that Lucia knew more about the mountain than she'd been letting on? If so, he needed to speak with her alone, and soon. However, there was the issue of her not being able to understand his sign language.

Before he could process anything more, Alistair tripped and fell to the hard, rocky ground with a thud. Everyone stopped as the big man looked up to see Wolfgang cackling along with his goons.

Alistair hopped to his feet, face beet-red, and shouted, "Have ya no decency? I've had it up ta here with you! I'm gonna bash in yer skul-"

"You clumsy oaf!" Edith screeched to a chorus of gasps from the nearby miners. "Don't blame others for your bad footwork. Get moving."

Alistair grumbled, but he eventually turned away. The group began walking again, and Joel could have sworn he saw a smirk hidden behind Edith's golden, flowing locks.

Soon, they arrived at the front of the line, where Faramond was sitting and eating an apple. Behind him, wind blew noisily into a large, dark hole; like the gaping mouth of a giant monster howling at all who neared. Most mine shafts in the Faiwell territory were only wide enough to fit a few people side-by-side, but this one was at least 20 meters tall and wide, by Joel's estimation. A rocky path led to the inside where it was eventually swallowed up by darkness. Next to the entrance was an old, weathered sign.

"Ah, there you are, Joel. And you brought a little group with you, I see?" Faramond asked.

"Yes, sir. We were interested in Joel's translation, if it's all the same to you," Conrad said.

"I don't see why not..." Faramond began, then looked over at Joel, who had already begun studying the sign. "So, then, can you tell us what it says?"

He nodded, this time catching his helmet before it could fall off. Then, Joel jotted down the translation in his book. Everyone nearby looked down to read what it said:

The Mouth of Hell
(Beware the Beast)

"Not terribly inviting..." Faramond trailed off.

"'Beware the beast', it says... but Joel translates the ancient tongue, so the warning would have to be many millennia old, wouldn't it? Perhaps this beast has perished since then?" Conrad said.

"The ancient tongue, you say?" the leader asked while rubbing his chin. "We can only hope 'the beast' is long dead, but we should prepare for the worst... this place has a reputation, after all."

"Not to mention that a wooden sign, weathered as it may be, is not meant to last for millennia. It could be a recent warning left by someone who happens to speak the ancient language," said Lucia.

"Yes. Just in case, we must gather the best fighters of our group to protect the workers," he said, nodding at her. "Speaking of which... if I didn't know any better, I'd say you were dressed for combat."

She smiled. "I am always ready for a fight."

"Odd, though. Faiwell is a large village, but a woman of your stature who likes to fight..." Faramond trailed off, holding his flattened hand well above his head. "Surely, you would stand out. How have I never seen you around before? Have you had formal training?"

"To make a long story short," she said, snorting, "I left Faiwell when I was younger. Not only have I been trained in swordsmanship, but I have also fought in many life-or-death battles."

"Excellent. We need warriors with real experience, and that sword looks deadly-"

"Claymore, actually," Lucia corrected.

Faramond narrowed his eyes. "Right… well, I'm sure our miners will be in good hands under your protection."

Edith scoffed in the background, but everyone ignored her.

The leader next looked at Alistair and asked, "What about you? You're the size of an ox! Any combat experience?"

Alistair scratched his nose and muttered, "Erm… not quite. I've had a few scraps in me day, I suppose… but that's all."

"I see. Well, you *look* strong, at least, so we may have some use for you."

Edith cleared her throat and said, "If we're going to put our lives in someone else's hands, shouldn't we make sure it's someone *experienced* fighting for us?"

"Our options are limited," Faramond replied with a shrug.

"But Wolfgang-"

"Cannot be trusted," he shot back. "Neither can his friend, Angus. They have combat experience, yes, but they may well stab us in the back."

Lucia crossed her arms and leaned far forward so that she loomed over the blonde beauty like an imposing cliff. "And who gave you a say in this, little girl? Why don't you man the front lines and fight with *us*?"

"Yeah!" Alistair shouted with a raised fist.

Edith darted her eyes over to Faramond, but he merely chuckled through his nose. Her glance then turned into a glare, and he took a deep breath.

"Well, Edith is here to advise me," said Faramond. "We must focus on our strengths over what is fair."

"I could be of service," Conrad said while placing a hand on the rapier hilt at his side. "I have fencing experience."

"Ah, I recognize you. You are the first son of the Mercer family, aren't you? The bankers?" Faramond asked. He nodded in return. "I appreciate the offer, but we will require different services from you. We shall need your accounting skills on hand, should we find any precious materials. You will be working closely with Edith and I on that."

"Yes, sir," he replied with a hint of disappointment.

"And how about you?" Faramond asked, turning to Joel. "You don't appear to be much of a warrior, so I suppose you will have to stick with mining, for now."

Joel flashed some hand signals back.

"Ah… I hadn't thought of that. We could certainly use a map maker as we go."

Edith snarled. "You're going to use *him*? I have it on good authority that his maps are of poor quality!"

"On *whose* authority?" Faramond asked as he shot an icy glare her way. Edith, for the first time that Joel had ever seen, fell silent and darted her eyes down. After a brief silence, he continued, "I think it's time we lay out the structure of our operation for when we enter the mines. Edith, gather everyone around for a meeting."

"Yes, sir…" she muttered.

In short order, the entire B-Team crew gathered around the mine entrance.

"Alright, everyone, listen well! We need to organize. Obviously, we are here to mine for materials, but there are other needs as well. Those of you with combat experience, see me after this meeting. We may soon enter a hostile environment…" Faramond said. There was some grumbling amongst the group. "I feel that we haven't taken the threats described to us seriously enough. I want to find gold and help Faiwell as much as the rest of you, but not at the needless expense of lives."

Chatter picked up in the crowd. Their restlessness was growing.

"If you brought any additional weapons along for the journey, you may also qualify to stand guard for us. After all positions are settled, we will explore the mines for a couple of hours. Then, we shall rest for the night."

After Faramond's brief speech, a small crowd gathered around him to discuss the matter of standing guard and protecting the miners. Edith had been put in charge of grouping together the different miners depending on what their jobs were.

Of the 73 miners on B-Team, 21 had volunteered to stand guard and claimed to either have additional weapons or fighting experience. Among the 21 were Wolfgang and his crew, but Faramond immediately shut down the idea of being protected by them, save for one exception: He appointed Bronrar as a front guard.

It was decided that 13 of the volunteers would be allowed to guard the group. Seven would lead the way, with six guarding from behind. The spare weapons of others were pooled over to the guards if they didn't wield anything better than their pickaxe. There were plenty of weapons to spare, so to Conrad's relief, neither his dagger nor rapier were taken.

Lucia and Alistair were initially dismayed to find themselves paired among the seven front guards, but they found common ground in their dislike for Bronrar, who was also appointed to the front with them.

Conrad seemed dismayed, too, and Joel could sympathize. Pretty as Edith was, working closely with her was sure to leave a bad taste in the strategist's mouth. Still, it was probably for the best. He couldn't put his finger on why, but Joel got the impression that Edith was up to something. Conrad would probably be sharp enough to catch her in any nefarious acts.

Joel was relegated to mining duty, even though Faramond had liked the idea of him navigating for the group. Edith put him down as a miner, but Joel planned to take his map-making seriously. Henic, the miner that had been walking with Alistair earlier in the day, told him to stay close, and that he would keep an eye out for him.

After a half-hour of preparing, the group was ready to enter the cave. They left much of the base camp intact, as they planned on returning to it in no more than a couple of hours. Faramond had also made it clear that there would be no mining on their first trip in. The focus was to find and meet up with the first team while scouting out the area. So, the group left the carts behind.

"Well, my friends, the sign says this is 'The Mouth of Hell'," Faramond began as he faced the crowd with a blank stare. "I suggest we tread lightly to start. Keep your eyes open, and Godspeed."

He turned and walked through the gaping hole in the mountain. The others followed behind. One by one, they were swallowed by the darkness.

CHAPTER 6
OMENS

Shortly after entering the mines, it became too dark for anyone to see. Luckily, the B-Team came well-equipped: Each miner had a flint stone, a piece of metal that they could spark, and a torch that could easily be reused if needed. It wasn't long before the tunnel walls were illuminated to reveal old, rocky passageways that looked uninviting.

Legends told that the Ancient Ones had dug the mines of Mt. Couture millennia ago with advanced technology. However, Faramond was disappointed to see that the structure of the tunnel was held up with ill-cut wood that didn't appear sturdy.

"I'm surprised termites or rot never got to the wooden structure…" Conrad remarked.

As the miners walked down the tunnel, curious noises echoed all around; the most common of which were light clicking noises in the walls. Most shrugged it off as the natural inner workings of the mountain, but others were certain they could hear distant shrieks and cries. Faramond reminded his team that the shafts back home had made similar noises, and that seemed to simmer their nerves.

After about a quarter-hour of walking, the group found themselves in a large cave. The ceiling was high enough that the light from their torches couldn't reach it.

Lucia, who led the pack, looked back at Faramond. "Sir, it looks like there's a lighting system here. To our immediate right and left."

"That's what I like to hear. Light it up," Faramond said.

She walked to the right as the miners began to fill the cave, while Alistair went off to the left. Upon lighting the torch stand, a chain reaction was set off. Glowing, blue energy passed through some lines on the wall, and it spiraled beautifully like constellations in the sky until eventually, they all combined on the ceiling high above. At the top, a blue light illuminated the entire cave. All in attendance gasped at the display.

"Incredible. I've never seen anything like it..." Conrad muttered. "The work of the Ancient Ones?"

"That must be it," Faramond said with a nod. "It would seem the legend of their advanced society was at least somewhat true."

The group remained still. In the cave, there were three paths before them. Directly across from them, there lay another tunnel. It was illuminated the most by blue light. To the left of that tunnel was another one. It was also lit up, but dimmer than the first. Finally, to the group's direct left was another path. It remained shrouded in complete darkness. Faramond brushed by the front guards to get a better view of his options. Edith remained close behind him.

He twirled his mustache in thought, when, with his keen eye, he noticed something on the path directly in front of them that looked different. They were small flowers growing out of the light soil on the ground. Though they were bright green, their glow was dim and looked to be fading. Each bulb was lined up one by one every five or six paces.

"Glowing bulbs..." he muttered.

"What was that, Fara?" Edith asked.

"Look ahead. The first group left us some glowing bulbs. That is a good sign. We know which way to go already," Faramond said.

Edith put her cold hand on Faramond's forearm and tugged.

"My eye caught something else," she said, seductively. He raised an eyebrow, but it wasn't long before a smile took shape on his face. "Look around. These walls have been mined, recently."

"Ah..." he muttered beneath a disappointed breath.

"And if you look closer, you'll notice there are some glints on the walls. They didn't mine everything in here. There is still some left for us," she said with cheer.

Faramond sighed. "I'm only glad there are *some* precious metals in here to begin with. This expedition was a true gamble, but it may pay off, after all."

"Eyes on the prize, Fara. Eyes on the prize," Edith said with a smirk.

"I get it. You want to stay here and mine before meeting up with the other group. But we need to-"

He was cut off by the blonde beauty slithering up close to him. She got on her tip-toes and whispered into his ear, "Actually... *I'm the prize.*"

Tingles sauntered down his neck, and then his spine as she nibbled on his ear. Faramond's head began swimming and his worries were whisked away.

She took a moment to stop, and then whispered, "I think you should listen to what your *prize* has to say, don't you?"

The nibbles turned to kisses on his neck. Like a snake slithering down a tree, her hands descended his torso, slowly but surely.

As he staggered, Faramond said, "W-well, I suppose we could-"

"It would be ill-advised to make anything besides finding the first group our priority, sir," Conrad interjected.

Like he had awoken from a dream, Faramond sprung himself away from Edith and then paused to catch his breath.

"R-right. As I was saying, Edith, we need to follow those markers and meet up with the first team before we get to mining," he said in an official tone. Edith rolled her eyes.

"You're in charge," she said. The blonde beauty turned away and walked back into the group of miners.

"Don't be deceived. I'm not sure what it is, but she wants to use you for something," Conrad said while looking back at her out of the corner of his eye.

"I can handle myself, thank you," Faramond said with a hint of annoyance in his tone.

"Yes, sir."

Soon after, Faramond announced to his team that they would be taking the path across the cave, straight ahead. He reminded everyone that their priority was finding the first group of miners.

AS THE GROUP MARCHED, led along by the glowing blue lines on the wall and green bulbs on the ground, Edith began to lag and ended up in the middle of the pack, where Wolfgang was. She playfully shoved him.

"Hey, Wolfy-"

She was cut off by a sudden pain in her arm. The blond brute had grabbed it and held on tight. Wincing, she looked up at him with a mixture of confusion and anger in her eyes.

"What the hell was that, back there? Why were ye *kissin'* that lowlife? Yer *my* gal," Wolfgang said in a hushed tone. He tugged harder at her arm with each word.

"It was nothing..." She winced again as his iron grip tightened further.

"What are ye playin' at, Edith? Eh? Do ye take me for a fool?"

"He is nothing to me. To get close to him, I need to work my charms on him. We talked about this already."

"Well, I don't like it. Do ye want me to kill him? 'Cause that's what I'll do if ye get too close with him," he said. Edith's eyes widened and a smile cracked on her sharp face, but only for a split-second.

"Again, I must ask: What is the benefit of killing our allies?" Angus asked.

"Shut yer mouth, Angus. Nobody will be stealing my woman. That's the benefit," Wolfgang said, finally letting go of Edith's arm.

"You truly are simple-minded. But when it's all said and done, you will understand why I had to get close," Edith said while massaging her arm.

"I have little else in this world besides mining and ye. And I don't much care for mining. If he steals ye away from me, I'll-"

Edith moved in front of Wolfgang and jumped up. He caught her by her soft bottom, and they started to kiss. The blonde beauty gazed out of the corner of her eye to see Angus and a few other miners looking anywhere but at them. *Of course,* she thought with a pleased snort, nobody would dare bat an eye for fear of Wolfgang's physicality and her authoritative power. The thought of their fear thrilled her and intensified the kissing even more. After a few moments, she hopped back down.

She readjusted her ruffled outfit, and after breathing heavier for a few moments, Edith said, "Are you still worried?"

Wolfgang had no response. He only looked back at her in apparent wonder.

"Don't forget, tonight we talk about the plan," she said before increasing her pace and weaving her way between the miners ahead. She could not risk breaking rank for long.

~

"I'm tellin' ya, lass, there ain't no way yer correct 'bout this!" Alistair said.

"And I'm telling *you* that silver became more valuable than gold!" she argued back.

Alistair chuckled. "No! Wrong! Wrong, wrong, wrong, wrong, wrong!" he sang aloud, marching to the beat of each word.

"Is that your best argument?"

"Oh, come on! Everyone knows gold is the most valuable metal! It's common knowledge!"

"Maybe where you're from. But I'm telling you, in some places, including where I spent the last five years, silver is more valuable, now," she said.

"Yer just tryin' ta *seem* well-traveled, with yer odd thoughts on matters. Well, yer not foolin' me, lady!" Alistair said, growing louder and more obnoxious with each word. "What you say is little more than hogwash!"

Lucia scoffed. "I don't know why I bother trying to convince the fool who wandered into the Dead Woods."

"Why, you…" he grumbled, drawing his newly-acquired battle axe at the hip.

She drew her great claymore in response. "You wish to challenge me?"

"You doubt me?"

"I do!"

"Will you two cut it out?" a nervous voice called out from behind them. They looked back with sharpened eyes to see Bronrar staring at them.

"No one asked you, fella!" Alistair fired back.

"There's no need to fight amongst ourselves, is all I'm sayin'. This place is supposed to be dangerous enough as it is," he said.

"That's funny, coming from one of Wolfgang's crew," Lucia said.

"I only want to coast by on this job and then get out of here in one piece. What's wrong with that?"

Alistair and Lucia looked at each other and then laughed in unison.

"I think ya came to tha wrong place if ya just wanted to coast by!" the big man said before letting out another hearty laugh.

"For once, I agree with him. You won't get anywhere coasting by. Especially here, I'm sure," Lucia added.

Bronrar became red in the cheeks and looked down as the others turned forward and resumed their argument.

He wasn't finished talking, however, and interrupted once again, "For what it's worth, by the way…" The pair looked back at him again with raised eyebrows. "Gold is certainly valued above silver. At least 'round here."

"Aha! See that? You were wrong!" Alistair said, pointing a finger just inches from her nose.

She batted his hand away and said, "You think his opinion is worth a damn?"

"But it's two votes to one! It must be true!"

"You're only saying that because he agreed with you."

Their argument continued, and Bronrar groaned.

TOWARD THE BACK of the line, Joel looked down at his book. He had already begun drawing a map of the path they were on. Sometimes, he would fall behind and bump into some rear guards, to their annoyance, but he persisted with his drawings of the layout. He had even marked points in the previous cave where the lighting mechanism could be activated.

He was drawing a few more details on the map when the group came to a stop. Joel bumped into a miner in front of him. The man stumbled forward and looked back with fiery eyes.

"What is wrong with y-" He cut himself off. "Oh, it's only you, Joel… sorry, somethin' about these mines has me on edge. I ain't sure what it is."

Joel nodded and flashed some hand signals to apologize, though the miner likely didn't understand. The man standing before him was his neighbor back in Faiwell, Henic Foreman. It was nice to see a familiar face again, even if it was a scruffy one that he didn't know too well.

Henic had always been hard at work on his farm in daylight and drank most of his nights away. Aldous and Joel found it best to avoid people back at home, even their neighbors. Though, Aldous and Henic had chatted quite a few times in the past year or so, as Joel recalled.

"What's that you've got there?" he asked as the group got to walking once more.

Joel held up the paper, and Henic squinted.

"Ah! It's a map," he concluded with excitement on his tongue. "Come to think of it, I don' understand why we didn't have someone scout the mines first, and then make one of these. This place is supposed ta be dangerous, after all."

Joel shrugged. Not much about the trip's planning made sense to him.

The group eventually stopped at the center of a smaller cave. The paths branched off two ways: One continued straight, while the other was to their left. Many miners were forced to light their torches again, as the blue lighting from the previous cave had faded along the tunnel.

After a short time, they continued straight, and at his feet, Joel noticed a consistent pattern of glowing bulbs. It meant that Faramond was staying true to his goal of finding the first team, he thought. Yet, he wondered how long that focus would last as his gaze wandered about the cave. Along the walls and ceiling was a substance that, contrary to its sparkling, remained dark. *Black gold*, Joel thought, a lump coming to his throat. Even he had to admit that it was a beautiful sight to behold; like looking at the stars on a clear night.

Up ahead, Faramond called out, "As you can see, there is plenty to mine in here. Rest assured; we'll return to this spot after we find the first team!"

There was grumbling amongst the miners, and Joel's stomach turned. The clicking noises from earlier returned, although they were faint echoes compared to what he had heard in the first tunnel.

Midway through the cave, Henic nudged Joel. He had gotten back to drawing out the map as a distraction from his nerves.

"Look at all them sparkles, Joel. Temptin' to jump out and grab some, eh?" he asked.

Joel looked up from the map and into Henic's eyes with intensity. He firmly shook his head no.

"Oh… not one for material things, are we?" he asked with a nervous laugh.

Joel patted him lightly on the back and forced a smile. Then, he got back to work on his map.

After a short walk, the workers entered a new tunnel. The pathway became narrow, and the ceiling shrunk, too. Soon, the taller miners found themselves having to crouch to continue.

"Mind your heads, everyone," Faramond's voice echoed down the passage.

The darkness and confined space made it feel like something could pop out and attack at any moment, but nothing did. There was only ever silence and dark, except by their feet, where the glowing bulbs continued to guide them. Then, the tunnel began to open up again, though not quite into a cave. In this new area, the group came to another abrupt stop. Joel inaudibly groaned. Too short to see past the other miners, he could only wonder what the holdup was.

It was Lucia who had caused the halt. She and Alistair shared the same look of concern. Before them was a fork in the road. One continued straight, and the other was a hard left. Both paths were laced with glowing bulbs. Faramond emerged from the crowd to face his guards.

"What's the hold-up?" he asked.

"There are two paths… both of them have markers left by the first team," said Lucia.

Faramond chuckled. "I knew that our journey was faring *too* well." He looked left and then straight while shifting his feet in the dirt. Edith appeared behind him and he looked to her for council. "What do you think?"

"We've been going straight for so long, Fara. I feel it is time for a change. Let's take the left path," she said with a playful tug at his arm.

"Very well. Let's continue to the left!" he called out to the crew.

While turning for the leftward tunnel, someone bumped into Alistair, causing him to stumble forward. Lucia chuckled to see Bronrar clumsily shuffling about from the collision.

"You! Watch where yer goin'! I don't trust you. I'll give ya a beatin' if I have'ta!" the big man said with a shaking fist.

"Oh… sorry…" Bronrar mumbled while looking down.

Lucia approached Alistair and whispered, "He's a clumsy fellow, isn't he? Doesn't appear to fit in with Wolfgang and the large one."

Alistair nodded and said, "Aye, I was thinkin' the same thing. He ain't much ta be afraid of!"

"Yes… he fits in more with you, I suppose." She laughed and then walked ahead of him.

Alistair groaned. "So rude…"

As the group entered the left tunnel, a thick, musty smell filled the air, but there were no hints as to the cause. Only darkness and the dim glow of the bulbs on the ground continued to guide them. Every once in a while, the light clicking noises returned, and they had Lucia on edge. She kept a hand at her claymore's hilt, ready to cut down any wildlife that might attack.

However, it wasn't long before she and the other front guards came to yet another abrupt stop.

"That's not good..." Bronrar trailed off.

Faramond appeared from behind and joined the others to see what had caused the stoppage: Before them stood many large boulders taking up the pathway. Some remnants of the wooden supports could also be seen, but they were broken into many pieces. The tunnel was filled to the ceiling with debris.

"This explains why the bulbs lead two different ways," Faramond said. "Well, then, we carry on down the other path. Everyone, reverse direction!"

With that order, the rear guards became the front and vice-versa. Faramond, Edith, and Conrad cut through the crowd to be near the front, but otherwise, everyone remained in their usual position, albeit reversed.

Upon exiting the collapsed tunnel, the group took an immediate left and followed the other bulbs on the ground. The musk about the air had faded, but it was replaced by a harsh smell that became stronger the further they ventured.

"Smells like death..." Lucia said.

"You ain't kiddin'! Smells worse than rotten goat cheese!" Alistair complained.

She rolled her eyes and said, "No, I mean it *truly* smells like death in here. Something, or someone, has been killed in this tunnel, recently."

Bronrar sighed. "Great..."

"Oh, grow a pair, ya ninny! I for one am ready ta fight any beast that dares attack me crew!" Alistair said.

"Just be ready..." Lucia said.

Ahead, she heard the panicked words of other miners.

"Over here!"

"Look at this!"

"Oh, lord..."

～

FARAMOND PUSHED through the crowd and walked over to the commotion. The front guards had discovered a corpse lying against the left wall.

Though it had decomposed slightly, there was clear evidence of wildlife having picked at the body: There were cuts, stabs, and even burns. The man's frozen expression was horrifying: His eyes were rolled back and the widest grin Faramond had ever seen was spread across his face.

Upon closer inspection, Faramond's eyes widened. The sharp face, light scruff, short blond hair, and a small gold pendant around his neck were artifacts that he recognized.

"Ollie…"

"*That's* Ollie?" Edith asked.

"No doubt about it. He has seen better days to be sure, but I recognize him. I've been working with Ollie for years in the mines. What could have happened, here?" Faramond asked, choking up. It was partially out of sadness, but the smell up close was almost unbearable.

CHATTER BEGAN to ensue amongst the miners. Joel, Henic, and Conrad had a good view of the corpse. Henic nodded at the strategist and cleared his throat.

"I remember seein' you a few times at the Mercer bank as a worker. What was yer name, again?" he asked. "I'm Henic, by the way."

"Ah, I remember you," he replied with a nod. "You own a farm back in Faiwell, isn't that right?"

Henic nodded while looking down. "Yeh, that's right…"

"I'm Conrad. It's nice to meet you, officially," he said. Sensing an awkwardness in Henic's posture, he searched for a new topic before smiling at the mute. "Is Joel a friend of yours? I met him on the way over here."

"Well, we've been neighbors fer a few years, now, but I only just started speakin' with him while on this trip. We both prefer keepin' to ourselves, methinks," Henic replied before casting eyes on Ollie's corpse. "What do ye think could have done this?"

"It's hard to say. We've been told about the dangerous wildlife around the mountain, so it's not unreasonable to think that an animal could have done this… but what concerns me is the look on Ollie's face," Conrad said.

Henic eyed the body with a shudder. "It *is* disturbing to see that someone was so joyful just before their death."

"Did you know Ollie well?"

"Can't say I did. He seemed to always be out on mining expeditions, while I've spent most of my time workin' out in the fields, y'see."

"Ollie would come into my parents' bank once in a while..." Conrad said while looking back at the pale corpse. "And not once did I ever see him smile. He was the most straitlaced man I've ever met." The nervousness in his tone grew with each word. "Never mind that, as you pointed out, it is odd to see a dead man smiling so profoundly. It was out of character for him to be smiling in such a manner, to begin with. Something tells me there is more to his death than meets the eye."

Joel's expression became lively, and he nodded.

"You agree, Joel? Did you know Ollie?" Conrad asked.

He shook his head and then flashed some hand signals back at Conrad.

"Black gold?" Conrad said.

"Eh? What's 'black gold'?" Henic asked.

"Remember those engravings on the rock wall in Allie's Pass?" he replied.

"Hm... I think so," Henic said while scratching his chin.

"One of the engravings depicted a group of people worshipping a dark, yet shiny material. Joel claims that it's called black gold, and that we can find it in this very mountain. In fact, I think we may have walked past some of it in a previous cave."

Henic raised an eyebrow and said, "Not to say I don't trust the lad, but why do ye think he would be an expert in such a thing? He's not a miner by profession."

"A fair point, but Joel here knows the ancient language. I believe those engravings were made by the Ancient Ones, so there is a possible connection," he said before frowning at Joel. "But as you said, he tends to keep to himself. He wouldn't tell me much about black gold, or the meaning behind the engravings. All I could get out of him is that it would 'poison our minds'."

Joel signed some more to them. Conrad's eyes widened, and he broke out in a light sweat.

Henic asked, "What's wrong?"

"He says... Ollie has black gold."

"So? Is the black gold poisonous, then?" he said with a hint of disbelief in his voice.

"I'm not sure. When I think of gold 'poisoning the mind', it makes me think of greed, not true poisoning. Wouldn't you agree?" Conrad asked. Henic nodded in return.

There was a brief silence.

"We must confront this head-on, I think. If Ollie does indeed have black gold in his possession, we should examine it up close and personal," Conrad said as he started toward the corpse. However, he felt a tug at his shoulder. He turned to meet an intense gaze from Joel, and it took him aback. "Please, don't worry."

Joel dropped his huge backpack and pulled out a pair of gloves. Conrad bit down on the nail of his thumb, deep in thought. Did this mean that black gold truly *was* poisonous? Whatever the case, he decided to follow Joel's advice and put the gloves on before making his way to the front of the line.

Conrad found Faramond and Edith huddled around Ollie; not touching, but visually inspecting the body.

"Sir, if I may?" Conrad asked.

"Who gave *you* the authority to examine this corpse?" Edith snapped back at him.

Faramond didn't look back, but added, "She has a point. Methinks this should be handled by someone else."

"I don't wish to examine the body, sir," he said.

"So, then? What is it you want with Ollie?" Faramond asked with defensiveness in his voice growing.

"I believe that if we search Ollie's belongings, we could find a possible reason for his death," Conrad said.

Faramond turned and focused on him with curious eyes.

"A bold claim. What could he possibly have that would have caused *this*?" he said before pointing to Ollie's distorted face.

"Black gold, sir."

Edith's eyes widened, but she quickly returned to her usual piercing glare. It had happened fast, but Conrad had noticed, and his confidence in Joel's claims strengthened.

"What is 'black gold', exactly?" Faramond asked.

"Please, sir... will you trust me on this? I will show you everything."

"Very well..."

The strategist pushed the body up slightly and unstrapped Ollie's backpack. He then rummaged through it as the others huddled over him, watching his every move.

"The bag's heavy. It must be in here…" he muttered.

Conrad retrieved a chunk of metal ore the size of his hand. It sparkled, yet its subdued, dark hue brought to mind a night sky. Even in the dimly lit tunnel, it shined for all to see. Faramond and Edith looked on in wonder.

"This is it… black gold," Conrad said, holding it out in front of them.

"It's the material from the cave walls, earlier," Edith said.

"How would it have killed Ollie?" Faramond asked. His eyes were fixed upon the ore as if it were a prize to be won.

"As I have been told, black gold corrupts people and poisons their minds. I believe that wildlife in the mines did the actual killing, but his weakened state of mind allowed it," he said.

"So, if it does that, why are you holding it? You seem fine to me," Edith replied.

"These gloves have provided me with protection," said Conrad, clapping one hand off the enchanting ore. "It would be unwise to touch it directly-"

"I have to disagree!" Edith cheerfully said as she swept the black gold from Conrad's hand.

"No!" he cried, but it was already too late.

Edith held the black gold out in front of the two men, and they both stared at her. Nothing had changed.

"See that? I'm fine." She chuckled. "Have a look for yourself, Fara."

Edith tossed the dark rock over to Faramond, who caught it with both hands. He looked deep into the material as if a moth to the flame. A bead of sweat streamed down Conrad's forehead. The leader looked at it for what felt like an eternity, in his mind.

"She's right. I feel fine. Where did you get the idea that a precious metal could hurt us just by touching it?" he asked.

In confusion, Conrad looked back at Joel. Upon returning his eyes forward, he found Faramond, frowning. The strategist breathed a loud sigh.

"It seems I was mistaken, sir. My apologies," Conrad said.

"If nothing else, you made a nice find. This metal truly is beautiful," Faramond said, placing a sure hand on his shoulder and smiling.

"It is. I think it would fetch a hefty price among traders from other lands, wouldn't you say?" Edith asked.

"Agreed. I must have more of this… black gold," Faramond said while gazing upon the ore, lovingly. Then, he abruptly looked back up. "I mean, *we* must get more black gold to aid Faiwell, of course."

Conrad returned to Joel and Henic. Edith and Faramond continued to talk joyfully amongst themselves in front of Ollie's corpse.

"Well?" Henic asked.

"As Joel said, Ollie had black gold on his person," he replied while taking the gloves off and handing them back to the mute. "But both Edith and Faramond held it in their hands, and no harm came to them."

"Then, Joel was wrong? It's alright to touch?"

"Well, perhaps…" he trailed off and then looked back at Faramond and Edith. "They both seem enamored with it. Almost as if they treasure it more than regular gold already. The truth is, they have no idea what its value is… but even now, they are sitting there, looking at it as if it's a one-of-a-kind art piece. Otherwise, I saw nothing wrong with it."

Joel only frowned.

Ahead, Faramond stood from Ollie's corpse and turned to face the crowd.

"Alright, everyone! As you may have seen, one of our fellow miners, Ollie, has died in the mines. Out of respect for the dead, we will bring him back outside the mountain and bury him."

Conrad noticed that next to Faramond, like a parasite to its host, Edith was in his ear. She was frowning and appeared to be pleading her case for something, but he couldn't hear what. He suspected that she was trying to convince him to stay and mine for materials.

Faramond brushed her off and darted a judgmental eye her way, to Conrad's relief.

"I know that many of you are anxious to catch up with the first team of miners, but I feel it's more important to honor the fallen. I also consider Ollie's death to be a warning; or an omen, if you will. We shall sleep outside the mines tonight."

Faint grumbling echoed off the tunnel walls, but no one dared complain directly. Edith was visibly angry. She grabbed his arm and whispered some more into his ear, but he shook his head and shrugged her off. Conrad smiled. He had worried that Edith would control his every action by leveraging her beauty, but it appeared that Faramond was having none of it.

No one volunteered to help carry Ollie's corpse outside, so Faramond picked miners at random out of the group. Alistair was one of the unlucky few to be chosen. As the group reversed direction and began to make their exit from the mines, the big man loudly complained.

"Ack! He smells like me mum's cookin', and that ain't a good thing!"

"Why is he so happy to die? That makes me nervous!"

"Why did I get picked fer this? Do ya think Faramond has it out for me?"

At the front of the pack, Conrad caught up to Lucia and tapped her on the shoulder.

"Oh, there you are. Couldn't stand any more time with the scum?" she asked, glaring back at Edith.

"She's up to something. It's difficult to tell if Edith is motivated by simple greed, or if there is a larger scheme at work here, but she is clearly trying to manipulate Faramond," he replied. "Luckily, he has been resistant to her charms, thus far."

"You and I have much to talk about," Lucia said.

"Agreed. I'll tell you about what happened with Ollie, but I also wish to know what you've been wanting to tell me about the mines. It has been on your mind from the beginning, hasn't it?" Conrad asked.

"Yes, I will tell you everything. I think you've now seen enough to believe me… but let's wait until later when no one is listening," she said. Conrad nodded.

❧

JOEL AND HENIC continued strolling together. Joel had been adding finer details to his map when he noticed Henic watching out of the corner of his eye. He squinted briefly, then widened his eyes, as if in shock.

"Can I see that, lad?" he asked.

Joel smiled. He could feel the genuine interest irradiating from him as he handed it over. The farmer squinted while practically burying his nose in the paper.

"Hm, is this accurate? Yer map is confusing…" Henic said. Joel only nodded in return. "But methinks it's harder to tackle a map when you have more to consider than just width and height. Ye've gotta think about the depth of the mountain, too, right?"

Joel nodded even faster, then pointed to a position on the map.

Henic tilted his head for a moment before gasping. "Our current location?"

The mute smiled and patted him on the arm. With some guidance, anyone could understand his maps, he thought.

"Aldous always told me ye had hidden talents. I admit that I can't truly read yer map, but mayhap that's because it's too much fer my pea-brain." He handed the paper back to Joel and then chuckled.

"Now, forgive me for prying, but I noticed the welts on yer face," Henic said, putting a hand on his shoulder. "Someone's been giving ye a hard time, eh?"

Joel opened his mouth, but as usual, no words came out. He didn't want to nod, for fear of dragging Henic into his problems. Alistair had already suffered for his interference in Wolfgang's business. What could he do to convey that he was alright, and not to worry?

"Say no more," he continued, waving a hand. *Oh no*, Joel thought. He was about to offer his protection, wasn't he? And all because he had refused to defend himself, earlier. "Now, I ain't gonna stick my neck out for ye-"

With a stumble in his step, Joel nearly crashed to the ground, but found his footing just in time and let out a snorting chuckle. He had almost forgotten that Henic didn't like to get into other people's business. Joel had been the same way; at least up until this expedition.

"Ye alright, lad?" he asked, patting him on the back. "Anyhow, I don't wanna see ye get hurt anymore, so try and blend in with the crowd. If anyone threatens ye, just give 'em what they want and move on, alright? That has always worked for me, and ain't no marks on my face!"

Henic laughed, and with some uneasy and inaudible laughs of his own, Joel gave him an assured nod. In truth, he wasn't sure that Wolfgang and his cronies would leave him alone, even if he did give in to their demands; especially if black gold was to be added to the mix. He felt a pit take hold of his stomach.

After nearly a half-hour of walking, the group reached the cave that was filled with black gold again. The twinkles caught everyone's eye as they walked through, but they continued on, obeying the commands of their careful leader. The light clicking sounds returned, although they felt a little closer than before, to Joel's ears.

A short time later, they reached the first cave that had been lit up. They found that the light had faded, however, so their torches remained out. In the darkness, the miners were stirred by a faint cry from far away, but it was distinct from the noises they had heard earlier. As they walked through the cave, the cry grew to a screech. Whatever it was, it was getting closer.

"Everyone! Something is coming. For our safety, increase your pace!" Faramond commanded.

The miners did as they were told and turned their stroll into a speedy walk. Soon, they were out of the large cave, but the shrieking continued to feel closer and closer, echoing throughout the tunnel as a haunting reminder of impending doom. It was a transcendent noise, like nothing they'd heard from an animal or man before. Down the long stretch to the Mouth of Hell, without any instruction, the group's stroll turned into a jog.

Skreeeeee

The jog turned to a run, until finally, a faint light could be seen at the end. It had fallen dark out while they were in the mines, but even moonlight made the tunnel seem like an eternal darkness. As the group exited the mine entrance, one last cry could be heard coming from behind them, and it was closer than ever before.

Skreeeeeeeeee

However, whatever had made the noises stopped as soon as all of the miners were outside. After that, there was nothing but the chirping of crickets and the sound of miners grumbling. Tents were set up, and small fires were lit all around. Few miners went straight to bed, as there was much to talk about that night.

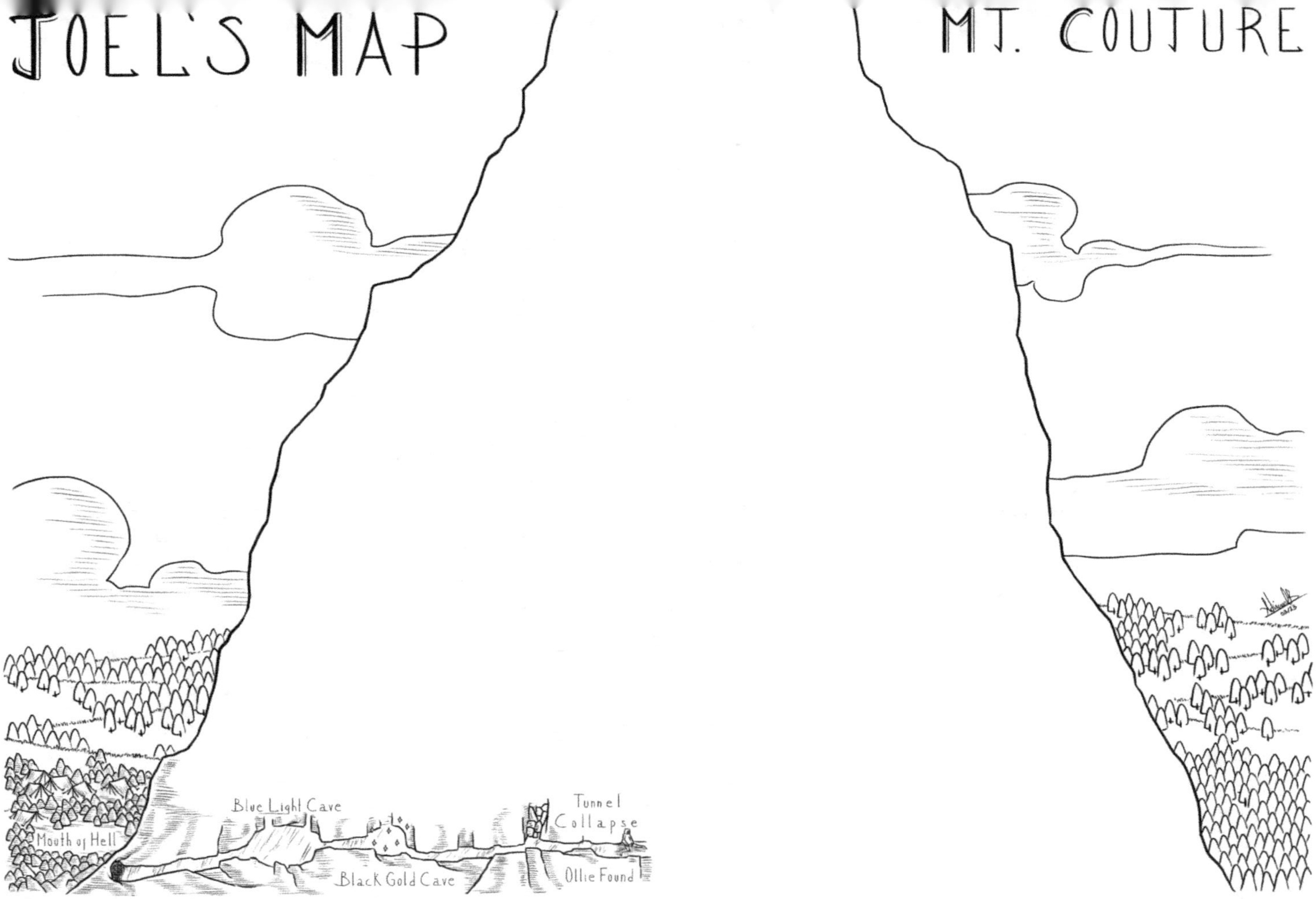

JOEL'S MAP
MT. COUTURE
Mouth of Hell
Blue Light Cave
Black Gold Cave
Tunnel Collapse
Ollie Found

CHAPTER 7
A QUIET NIGHT

Two days before the B-Team had set off for Mt. Couture, Lucia had gone to the Faiwell village market so she could buy some food for the upcoming journey. She found that, since running away at the young age of 14, not much had changed; except that she now had money to spend. Over the years, Lucia had become a successful and sought-after mercenary on the other side of the world.

Upon hearing the news that Faiwell was under financial strain, she had felt a duty to return and help her people. Moreover, she was anxious to find her former mentor, Dalton Rayleigh. They hadn't parted on good terms, and she wished to make amends.

However, with her return to Faiwell, she found out that Dalton had already left for Mt. Couture, along with a group of miners he was leading. Remembering the mantra that had always been repeated around her: 'Stay away from the mines of Mt. Couture,' Lucia asked the Miner's Guild to let her join the next team of miners so that she might fight off the dangers alongside her teacher. They accepted her with open arms, despite a lack of knowledge or experience in mining.

At the market, Lucia walked down an aisle, when out of nowhere, a blonde woman in a fancy red dress wedged herself between her and the apple she had been reaching out for. Not appreciating the rudeness, she shoved the woman to the ground. Edith looked up at her with flared-out cheeks.

"How about you watch where you're going, simpleton? Maybe I

should teach you a lesson-" She stammered after reaching her feet, having to crane her neck to meet Lucia's eyes.

Lucia tilted her head down and smiled. "Oh? And what lesson could you teach me, I wonder?"

"Just watch where you're going, next time..." she trailed off, unsteady in her tone. "Hold on..." Edith said, looking her up and down. "Aren't you Lucia de Vesci?"

"That's right," Lucia said with crossed arms.

"Well, it's nice to see you aren't a sad, pathetic little girl anymore. Perhaps you could be of use to us on the next mining expedition... although you seem to have turned into a clumsy oaf, so maybe not!" Edith said with a crass chuckle.

Lucia's parents had died when she was young. Without a parental figure to look up to or provide her with a consistent meal, she had grown up appearing and acting younger than she truly was. Edith and her entourage were a couple of years older and had been sure to make her life difficult at every possible turn. Standing up to Edith had been Lucia's motivation for taking up swordplay under Dalton's tutelage, back then.

The bitter memories came flooding back, and she grabbed a gasping Edith by the collar, lifting her off the ground with little effort.

Face-to-face, she said, "I suggest you go about your business. What was it you that you do, again? Besides living like a spoiled princess?"

Before Edith could respond, Lucia threw her to the ground. There was a crowd growing around them now, and Edith was huffing and puffing, as if about to throw a tantrum. She jumped to her feet, her normally fair face beet-red.

"Why you brute! *Do you know who I am*? I could ruin your life at any time if I wished to!" she shouted while pointing at Lucia with conviction.

The mercenary leaned in and grinned. "Go ahead and try. I'm signed up for the next mining expedition to Mt. Couture. They practically begged me to join. Let's see how much your word is worth. Go on... cry to your father. See if he cares."

Edith's face somehow turned even redder, but then she looked around at the crowd of villagers and took a deep breath.

"You're not worth it, anyway. Just watch your back on the mining expedition. You never know what could happen out there..." Edith ominously trailed off before slithering away in the other direction.

Lucia's line of work overseas had included many threats similar to the one Edith had just made. Whether it was meant to be taken seriously or not, she decided that buying food could wait until tomorrow.

By cutting through the alleyways, Lucia tailed an unaware Edith as she traversed the main roads. She had a hunch that the blonde beauty was on her way to the Miner's Guild to visit her father.

They eventually arrived at a looming stone building that was several floors tall. There were a few statues of men outside its walls and a nice fountain. Only the best for the mining big-wigs, Lucia thought. The building stood proudly in front of the water mill, where miners would crush down ore deposits into valuable metals.

Edith entered the building and Lucia waited a short while before following her in. Upon entering, it was clear that most of the Miner's Guild was closed for the night. No fireplaces were going, a shroud of darkness covered the function hall, and no people sat at the tables, either. It was a lucky break, as typically miners would spend the night drinking and telling stories to one another; or so Lucia recalled.

Although over 100 had signed up for the journey to Mt. Couture, it was far from all of the miners that Faiwell had to offer. Despite the shortages, Lucia had heard through the grapevine that most of the miners were deployed to the surrounding mountain range. The goal was to gather as much precious material as possible from their current digging sites.

Using the stroke of good luck to her advantage, she crept up the first set of stairs to her left. On the second floor, Lucia could make out a room off in the distance that had the door shut, but there was light coming from under it. She snuck down the hall and peered through a small hole in the wooden door.

Inside the room, sitting in front of a fireplace and enjoying some wine were Edith and her father, Drake. He had slicked-back blond hair, with the same piercing green eyes as his daughter. Although he was 47 years old, he was blessed with a youthful face that could have fooled Lucia into believing he was in his 30s. He wore a fancy red and white tunic that was fit for a prince, and in Faiwell, that's exactly how he was treated.

Lucia had been told the story of Drake Danvers many times as a lesson for how hard work would pay off. Drake had been born into a working-class family of miners. He had dedicated his life to mining from a young age, and by his 20s, he was leading expeditions. On what became his final expedition, a tunnel collapse had killed half of his team, but he had managed to find a way out while saving some of his crew and bringing back all of the ore that they had obtained. For his bravery in the face of disaster and continuing his duty in that difficult situation, he had been honored across the village; a popularity that had catapulted him into the presidency of the Miner's Guild.

Under Drake, the Guild saw a golden age of trade with other settlements and nations, and there was prosperity all across Faiwell. That was until the shortages of precious metals had become apparent. It had been Drake's suggestion to make an expedition to Mt. Couture as a possible solution to the issue.

"But father…" Edith trailed off, snapping Lucia out of her train of thought. She couldn't help but roll her eyes at the whining.

"I'll hear none of it, young lady. She stays on the second team," he said with authority.

"She disrespected me, though!"

"That's the end of it, Edith. She will remain on the second team."

Lucia smiled. Even if Edith was a wicked woman, her father at least seemed principled.

Drake sipped his wine. "Besides, if you hate her so much, why don't you simply *kill her*?" Lucia's eyes widened. Edith remained silent. "What? You don't have the courage to take a life?"

"No… I can do it."

"What was that?" he asked, leaning in.

"I can do it," Edith said in a more confident tone.

"That's right. Don't forget how instrumental you are in this plan. You can't start hesitating now."

"But what about the first team of miners?"

Drake scoffed. "I'd wager those men were honored to be chosen as the first to enter Mt. Couture… but what everyone forgets is that the front lines are unfortunate souls who are all but guaranteed to die. They are little more than scapegoats, so you can see first-hand what dangers lie within the mines and use that to navigate safely."

He paused for a moment to sip his wine and then stared into the fireplace.

"A difficult time is coming, Edith. One where you must make sacrifices for our greater goals. You do understand that, don't you?"

"Yes, father," Edith replied while looking down.

"Do not fret, my dear…" Drake said before leaning over to stroke her golden blonde hair. Lucia raised an eyebrow as Edith balled her hands into fists and began trembling.

"The strong will survive. The weak will die. We are strong. We are survivors," he concluded before abruptly dropping her beautiful hair strands from his grip. She let out a quiet breath and her shaking ceased. "If there are any salvageable survivors from the first team, feel free to bring them along with you, but if they are injured, finish them off. They will only slow you down on your journey."

Lucia gritted her teeth. Not only was Drake's friendly persona as president a guise, but Dalton and his team were intentionally being thrown into the lion's den for the convenience of these fiends. But why? Was it to keep more of the spoils for themselves?

"I understand. This is for the greater good. I'll make sure the weak ones are picked off in the dark while hanging onto any of the easier miners to control. Wolfgang and his crew will be easy to use," Edith said as she took a sip of her wine.

"Good. Faramond is one of our best, so he should be adequate for keeping you safe. More importantly, though, you should be able to manipulate him to our needs. He's had an eye on you for a couple of years, I'd say," Drake said.

"Right. I think that I can work my charms on him. I daresay he's already smitten, the fool," she said with a devilish smile.

Lucia felt sick to her stomach. Edith had always been cruel to her when they were younger, but to hear her and Drake speak of killing their own people so casually brought to mind her worst targets as a mercenary.

"Now, remember, this plan hinges on you getting that *special ore* we talked about. It could help us change the landscape of not only Faiwell but the entire world," he said while spreading his arms in a grand gesture. "Your first objective is simple: Obtain the new metal by any means necessary and bring as much of it back with you as possible."

"Of course, father. We've been over this," Edith said in an annoyed tone.

"And do not forget about the most important part of the plan. You must reach the *Gold Pit*. Be assured that you will likely have to sacrifice much of your crew to get there. But stay strong. Their lives pale in comparison to what awaits you in *the pit*. There, you will be able to-"

"Yes, yes, I know what to do, father," Edith interrupted with a scoff.

"Really?" he asked, grabbing a lock of her hair once more. Edith fell silent and looked away. "Why is it that you struggle to remember the incantation, then?"

"I-I only made one mista-"

"A mistake that will cost you dearly in the mines," Drake said, tugging lightly on her hair. Edith winced. "So, we will go over the plan again..." he trailed off, yanking on her hair. "And again..." He pulled her hair once more. "And again!"

Even Lucia flinched when she heard a loud *rip* just before Edith's yelp drowned it out. She could spare her no sympathy, but at least Edith's wicked ways were beginning to make sense: They had been passed down to her by her father.

Drake let the stray blonde hairs fall from his hand as Edith took a rickety gulp of her wine.

"Repetition," he said. "We will continue to go over the plans until they are engraved in your mind. Understood?"

"Yes, father. I will sacrifice the miners to-"

Lucia grew tired of listening to the scum and left the hallway in a rush. She slipped out of the Miner's Guild headquarters and quietly into the night, wondering if anyone would believe what she had just witnessed.

~

"Wow! That Edith and her pappy... so rude!" Alistair said over the crackles of the campfire, which had been set up a short way from the entrance to the mines.

"That's one way of putting it," Lucia said and then looked around the fire at Joel, Conrad, and Henic. "But do you all see, now? The first group, and even *this group*, are all expendable. This whole trip is for Drake and Edith's benefit, not Faiwell's." Her voice flared up in anger as she spoke. She clenched her fists and they shook. "And how could they do this to Dalton, a war hero? I have to find him... I have to hope he's not dead in there."

Conrad put a hand on her shoulder.

"Dalton is thought to be the most capable fighter in Faiwell. If anyone from that group is alright, I'm sure it's him," he said with a reassuring smile. Lucia only stared back into the flame.

As silence overcame the group, Joel and Conrad began exchanging hand signals.

"Wish I knew what they were sayin'," Henic said.

"Aye, you don' know the half of it!" Alistair chimed in.

Conrad received some more hand signals before explaining, "Joel says that Drake and Edith want the black gold. He's told me a few times now that it's a bad idea to take any for ourselves." He looked back at Joel and frowned. "But I witnessed for myself: The black gold did not affect Faramond or Edith when they touched it."

"What I don' understand is: What's so bad about it, anyway? It may be valuable and there looks ta be plenty of it in tha mines! Why not use it ta save the village?" Alistair asked.

"It's not clear to me, yet. But I do know this: Among Ollie's possessions at his time of death, we found black gold ore," Conrad said, and once again cast his gaze on Joel. "I wish you would explain everything to us…"

Joel squirmed internally. He had already revealed more than he was supposed to. He and Aldous had originally agreed to try passively guiding the miners away from black gold without them knowing, but that had gone completely out the window. He was skirting on the edge, now. Revealing any more would expressly betray his duty, the scope of which was much larger than any of their lives, his own included.

"I don' get how a piece of metal can kill ya unless it's a sword or somethin'…" Alistair trailed off.

Joel scribbled into his notebook and handed it over to Alistair.

"Ah… so yer finally goin' ta explain it then, laddie?" he asked with excitement in his voice.

Upon reading the notes, however, Alistair frowned. It read:

Black Gold will poison your mind.

"Erm… ya already said that! But thanks fer tryin', I suppose?" he said with a crooked smile while handing the book back. "What we wanna know is: *How* will it poison our minds?"

Joel gritted his teeth. He couldn't give an honest answer.

After taking a swig from his flask, Henic said, "Yer all concerned about this black gold, but if what this young lady here says is true, we should be more worried about Edith and her father."

Conrad nodded. "It's clear that she is trying to manipulate Faramond, but what is her end goal? Even without controlling him, I'm sure he would try and bring back as much black gold as possible to save the village. And what of the Gold Pit that her father mentioned? I had always thought it was little more than a bedtime story of buried treasure. But they seem to think it's real. There must be more to their plans. I will continue to keep a close eye on her, tomorrow."

The group fell silent, and they watched the magic of their fire dancing in the wind to pass the time, instead.

~

FURTHER UP THE PATH, Wolfgang and his crew had set up a large tent. They had all gathered inside and were waiting for Edith to come in and discuss the plan moving forward.

Bronrar scratched the back of his head and said, "I don' understand what we're here for. Isn't the plan to get as much valuable material as possible? What's so hard about that?"

Wolfgang rolled his eyes and said, "Ye dolt! There's *much more* to it than that."

Angus added, "If we do a little more than grab gold, we stand to gain a lot of power in Faiwell. Think about yer future, my friend."

"That's right," Wolfgang said as he put a hand on Bronrar's shoulder. The nervous miner's stomach sank. "The way I see it, there are two ways yer future can go… one: Ye enjoy a nice, easy life ruling over the plebs after doing a few dirty deeds fer the greater good. Two: Ye go ass up in yer grave because ye weren't smart enough to see a good deal even when it smacked ye right in the face!"

He then lightly slapped Bronrar on the cheek a couple of times.

"There is no need for that. He will stick to the plan. We have always stuck together, haven't we?" Angus asked Bronrar while smiling as much as his stone face would allow him to.

"Right…" he trailed off, looking away. Everything about his current situation made him nervous.

A few moments later, Edith entered the tent with a stride in her step.

"Alright, boys," she said, clapping her hands together. "Tomorrow is a big day that will shape not only our future, but Faiwell's, too. Let's discuss the plan."

~

BACK AT THE FIRE PIT, Conrad looked at Wolfgang's tent with unease in his eyes. Edith had walked past them to reach the tent, and it had put everyone on edge after hearing Lucia's story.

"They have been in that tent for a while, now," said Conrad.

"What if they're…" Alistair trailed off before breaking out into laughter. "*Doin' tha deed?*"

Everyone at the campfire groaned.

"What? I'm just wonderin'!" Alistair said before taking a gulp from Henic's flask. His cheeks had turned a rosy red. "Speakin' of which, would any of ya ever wanna lay with that foul lass, Edith?"

Henic narrowed his eyes and ripped the flask away from him. "That's it! Yer cut off for the night!"

"Well?" Alistair asked with a noisy hiccup while looking around the fire. "I'm waitin' fer an answer!"

Joel shook his head and flashed some hand signals to Conrad.

"He says that he's got a girl, but she's not around right now," the strategist said.

"Tha hell does that even mean?" Alistair asked as laughter overcame him once more. "Look, laddie, ya don't have'ta be ashamed. You can tell us if ya got nobody! I'm a *very* popular bachelor me'self, and I still wouldn't lay with a *rude* woman like that!"

"Implying that she would lay with you…" Lucia muttered before scoffing. Everyone else at the fire laughed.

"Oh, shut it! Ya haven't answered tha question! Would you? Or wouldn't you?" Alistair replied while grinning at her.

Lucia crossed her arms and turned up her nose. "A stupid question."

The group looked intently at her and after a brief time, her eyes widened. "The answer is obviously no."

Everyone looked at Conrad, next.

"No. Too evil for me," he said, holding out his hands and shaking them.

There was a long silence at the fire.

"I would… if I weren't married to me wonderful wife, anyhow," Henic said. Everyone stared back at him. "And I ain't ashamed to admit it! She's gorgeous!"

He laughed and took another swig from his flask.

"Finally! Some honesty 'round here!" Alistair laughed along with him.

Lucia flashed him a judgmental eye and said, "Aren't you about twice her age, though? You dirty old man…"

Henic burped and then looked at Joel.

"Joel! Have you been tellin' folk my age? Now everyone thinks I'm an old fart. You rascal!" Joel held out a hand in defense and shook his head. The group erupted in laughter again. "But then... how'd you know my age? It must've been Aldous, the bastard!" He chuckled.

"Who is Aldous?" Conrad asked.

Henic rested his cheek on a hand. His eyes were becoming droopy. "Well, all I know is that he and Joel live together. I suppose he's his grandfather? Mayhap an older uncle? Such a nice fellow, Aldous..."

Joel signed over to Conrad.

"Ah, so he is your caretaker? Interesting. Why couldn't he make it on this trip? Too old?"

The mute replied with more hand signals.

"He left to help the first group last night? Aren't you worried about him?" Conrad asked.

Joel shook his head and signed some more.

"He said that you'd get along with him, Alistair," Conrad said, looking at the big man with raised eyebrows.

"Is that so?" he mused. "I wouldn't get yer hopes up, lad! I don't like many people!"

"There's that charm of yours at work," Lucia said with a roll of her eyes.

Alistair stood and kicked up some dirt. "Does yer rudeness know no bounds? We can settle this right here and now, if ya want!"

Lucia hopped up and brought a hand to her claymore's hilt. "I have cut down many amateurs like you in the past!"

Henic groaned and then said, "Can you lot keep it down? I'm startin' to get a headache..."

"Yes, I think it's time for you to get some sleep, Henic," Conrad said while smiling. He looked at the two ready combatants and continued, "And I think that goes for all of us, agreed?"

A collective sigh was let out, and the tension faded. They put out the fire and made their way to the tents that had been laid out earlier. In short order, Joel lay cozily in his makeshift bed. He had the nagging feeling that he was forgetting something as he drifted off to sleep.

～

In Wolfgang's tent, Edith had just finished laying out her plan.

"Whoa, I did *not* sign up for this. It's out of the question," Bronrar said as he held out his hands and shook them.

"You don't have a choice, fool," Edith said with crossed arms. "Be thankful that you're friends with Angus, or we wouldn't have included you."

"Think about it. This is our chance to live a life of luxury, and all we have to do are a few dirty deeds. I say it's worth it. Come now, have I ever led you astray?" Angus asked.

"I suppose not, but I know it ain't right…" Bronrar said.

"Yer not seein' the big picture. Not only is this for the greater good, but it leads to us gettin' everything beyond our wildest dreams… ye better not ruin that for me," Wolfgang said while holding up a fist.

"That's right. 'The greater good.' We will be heroes for saving our village, and *you* will be handsomely rewarded for your part in it all," Edith added as she pointed her index finger into his chest.

Bronrar breathed a deep sigh and argued no further. Edith then turned her attention to Angus.

"And you…" she said. The giant cocked his head. "I have a special task in mind for you. We shall talk about it more tomorrow."

Wolfgang and his crew returned confused expressions.

"Talk to me about what? Why can't you tell us all?" Angus asked.

"Look, I have special duties for each of you. I will explain more tomorrow, but-" She cut herself off to peek out of the tent opening. *Perfect timing,* she thought with a smile before returning inside. "Faramond is coming up the path. I'm going to continue getting close with him, so he'll be easy to manipulate."

"I don't like this, Edith… yer supposed to be with me," Wolfgang said.

"And I already told you, I *am* with you, Wolfy. But we need him to be compliant with our plans. Got to make some sacrifices," she said, now halfway out of the tent. "Now, I must depart… just make sure you stick to the plan tomorrow."

Edith trotted up the path and tapped Faramond on the shoulder after catching up with him. He glanced back while continuing to walk toward his tent, near the mine entrance.

"How did the burial go?" she asked.

"As well as it could have," he said in a solemn tone.

"You seem bothered. Is there anything I can do?"

"I think it's something I have to sleep off," Faramond replied.

"How about I sleep it off with you?" she asked, coyly.

The leader raised an eyebrow and cracked a smile before quickly returning to a melancholy demeanor. "I don't know if that's appropriate right now…"

"Come now, Fara. You promised we would get some alone time, remember?"

"Well, alright." He was smiling now.

At the top of the path, they entered Faramond's tent. As he started to get undressed, Edith looked around and noticed something missing.

"What did you do with the black gold from earlier?" she asked.

"'Black gold'? Ah, so you are adopting Conrad's name for it, then?"

"Well, the name fits," Edith said.

"I buried it with Ollie," Faramond said.

Edith's eyes widened, but she quickly forced them into becoming tranquil. "You know, we need as much black gold as possible to save the village. We can't go wasting it like that."

"There seems to be plenty of it in the mines. I'm not worried, Edith, and you shouldn't be either."

"I'd worry less if you let us start mining it first thing tomorrow," she said.

"I don't know about that... we should focus on finding the first group," Faramond said, looking down. *There it was*, Edith thought. She could see in his eyes and tone that he was already having doubts. All he needed was a little push, and she'd have him in her grasp.

Edith jumped and knocked Faramond to his makeshift bedding. She straddled him and looked straight into his eyes with a knowing smile.

"Let me convince you," she whispered, and they began to kiss.

LATE IN THE NIGHT, Edith awoke next to Faramond under his covers. He had an arm draped over her body, which she slowly but surely shimmied her way under. He eventually let go and rolled over the other way. She used the opportunity to get out of bed and get dressed.

Edith grabbed the spade that the leader had used to bury Ollie earlier and took it outside the tent with her. As she had expected, everyone was asleep, so sneaking down the trail to Ollie's shallow grave was quick and easy.

She pouted. "Making me do all the dirty work..."

The blonde beauty began to dig away at Ollie's grave, growing more and more frustrated with each shovelful of dirt.

"Why did this idiot need to be buried, anyway?" she grumbled and took another shovelful of dirt out. "When I take over, I'll make it a rule: You must leave behind the dregs who can't handle themselves."

As Ollie's gray corpse became visible, Edith muttered, "Looking mighty ugly, Ollie…"

She noticed the black gold ore had been placed deliberately in his folded hands by Faramond. Not much of a memento, she thought with a snicker.

"I'll take that off your hands, you ugly pile of-" Edith got out before yanking on the black gold to find Ollie's hands resisting.

Edith pulled harder and harder, working up a sweat and grunting in frustration, until finally, with a loud *snap*, she flew back onto her bottom. She looked down and gasped to see that Ollie's wretched hands still clung to the black gold and had detached from his arms. She dropped Ollie's cold, lifeless hands and then covered her mouth in shock. Could the black gold have been so powerful that even the dead wanted to keep it?

With a deep breath, Edith retrieved the spade. She wedged it between Ollie's hands and the black gold, pulling back with all her might. After a brief struggle, she finally separated the disembodied hands from her prize.

The blonde beauty then snorted and punted the detached hands back into Ollie's grave.

"Good riddance…" she said while throwing dirt back on his body.

After packing the soil in and attempting to make it look similar to before, Edith turned back, black gold in hand, to make her way up the path. On that quiet night, her plan would be put into action.

CHAPTER 8
GIVING IN

Edith awoke in Faramond's tent. She was once again in his arms, while he was wide awake, looking at her with warm eyes.

"Did you sleep well?" he asked.

"Like a baby," she replied while eyeing his backpack with a smile. "How did you sleep?"

"I had this strange nightmare… but it's all so hazy, now. I can't remember a thing about it," Faramond said while shrugging.

Edith's smile grew wider.

After getting dressed, they exited the tent together. Faramond ordered Edith to assemble the miners for a quick briefing of the schedule for the day. She gathered them around the entrance to the tunnel in her usual grumpy way.

"Alright, everyone. The agenda has not changed. Our priority is to find the first group and to be safe while doing so," Faramond said. Edith eyed him with heaps of disappointment. Had her plan not worked? "I want to explore the same path we were heading down before discovering Ollie, rest his soul."

Edith stared a hole through Faramond, and she could see that he had taken notice out of the corner of his eye.

"Oh, and this time, we shall take the carts into the mines, so if you notice any valuable materials around, feel free to start picking them up. We won't be mining until we've found the other team, however. We need to ensure their safety, first."

The blonde beauty frowned. She could feel that he was teetering on the edge of choosing to mine over searching out the first team, but he'd need another push, she thought.

"Today may be difficult for us all. So, I suggest you all eat a hearty breakfast if you haven't already, and enjoy the fresh air for the last time in a while!" he said.

~

THE NEXT HALF hour of preparation consisted of the miners cleaning up their tents, gathering equipment, and eating. Joel, meanwhile, got his map and quill pen ready for the upcoming trip into the mines. Moreover, he was preparing himself for difficult times. A conflict was on the horizon, but he needed to stay strong; if not for all of the miners, then at least for his new friends.

Eventually, the miners formed rank like the day before. Alistair, Lucia, and Bronrar were among the front guards to protect from any potential dangers; while Faramond, Edith, and Conrad were just behind them in the pack. In the middle, Angus and Wolfgang walked along to the discomfort of the other miners, while Joel and Henic were toward the back, in front of the rear guards.

With little fanfare, the B-Team entered the Mouth of Hell, plunging themselves into the darkness once more. Like last time, it became too dark for anyone to see, so torches were lit. Joel heard the same clicking noise echo in the tunnel, as it had yesterday, but it was nearly drowned out by the squeaking wheels of the carts and chattering miners.

Then, the workers came again to the first large cave. Lucia and Alistair respectively lit the mechanisms on each side, and the result was just as beautiful as the last time: Intricate blue wirings danced along the walls to the top of the cave before casting one brilliant blue light down upon them.

"It's even more amazin' the second time around, ain't it?" Henic asked Joel. The mute smiled in return. "Now, remember what we talked about, yesterday…"

Joel cocked his head.

"We've gotta try and blend in with the crowd. Don't wanna be drawin' attention to ourselves, y'know? Especially if that Edith is up to anything nefarious. If we keep our heads down and work hard, she and her cronies won't target us. I'm sure of it."

That was one approach to the situation Joel couldn't take. A refusal to mine the black gold would surely make him stand out like a sore thumb, and with the knowledge that Edith was planning on sacrificing other miners to meet her own ends, opposing her was now more important than ever.

~

AT THE FRONT of the pack, Alistair and Lucia were in the midst of another argument.

"Yer gonna tell me that yer primitive sword is better than me beautiful battle axe?" Alistair asked.

"Claymore," Lucia said. "Why do you have an attachment to something you only obtained yesterday?"

"Well… I like it! That's good 'nuff fer me!" he replied. Lucia laughed derisively. "Oooo, ya think yer *so* superior with yer big, fancy sword, do ya?"

"Claymore," Lucia said.

"If we come across any trouble in these mines, I'll show ya what a *real* weapon is, lass!" Alistair boasted while pounding his barreled chest a couple of times.

Bronrar groaned in the background. Both looked back at him with curious eyes.

"You seem quieter and less of a bother than yesterday. Something must be wrong," Lucia said.

"Naw, it's just… I hate being shouldered with terrible burdens. I wish to get through life worry-free. Is that too much to ask?" Bronrar said.

"Oi, it's only a mining expedition! Hardly a terrible burden, even if this place is supposed ta be dangerous!" Alistair replied with narrow eyes.

"You don't understand…"

"Oh, will you shut yer yap, already? Save the moping and brooding fer someone who'll appreciate it, like the lass," Alistair said while pointing at Lucia with a chuckle. She rolled her eyes in response.

"Just make sure you're ready for anythin'," Bronrar said.

Lucia's gaze cut through the pack to pick up on Wolfgang and Angus. They both appeared to be minding their own business. "Is it something to do with those unruly friends of yours?"

Bronrar remained silent. It was all the answer she needed.

~

As the group marched into the tunnel across the cave, Edith grasped Faramond's arm and leaned her head up against his shoulder.

"I understand why you want to find the first team so badly, Fara… but think about it. They are led by the greatest warrior in Faiwell. I'm sure all is well with them."

"You *did* see Ollie, didn't you?" Faramond asked, raising an eyebrow. "It should have been me leading that first expedition. Dalton has little experience in mining. I would have kept Ollie safe…"

"True. We both deserve better than this team of misfits, but we must make do with what we have. Why not prove everyone wrong by taking back the most spoils? You deserve it," she countered.

"Yeah, I do-" He hushed himself and became red-cheeked for a moment. A sly smile came to Edith's face.

After a quarter-hour of traversing the tunnel, they entered the second cave. Despite a lack of light source, the area was illuminated partially by the black gold sparkling all around on the walls and atop the ceiling. Miners gasped and spoke in hushed excitement at the sight.

"Look how beautiful it all is, Fara. How many times are we going to pass by without taking what could save us all?" asked Edith.

"As many times as it takes…" Faramond paused. "Before we find the first team."

"But why? Dalton had his chance, even though you deserved it more; and he *still* failed Ollie," she said.

"That's true."

"You have held the black gold in your hands before; seen it up close; felt it. You cannot deny that its value will be immense once it circulates," Edith continued.

"True."

"It is our best hope to save Faiwell."

"Also, true…" he replied with more hesitation before massaging his forehead.

Conrad stepped forward to meet their strides and said, "Remember that we have a duty to the other miners. Don't let a personal gripe with the Mining Guild's decision cloud your judgment."

Faramond rubbed his eyes and said, "Right… right…"

Edith frowned at Conrad. *That damned know-it-all*, she thought. Of course he'd be trying to meddle. He smirked at her.

"We have a *duty* to our village, too. We have a *duty* to protect our own team, do we not?" she said, smashing a fist into her open palm with conviction. Faramond tilted his head. His eyes demanded clarification. "You saw what happened to Ollie. Why are we going this way? Why not stop and plan out a better route? And in the meantime, we can get some mining done."

Faramond lurched his head and breathed out a heavy sigh.

"Fine. You win, Edith," he said. The concern on Conrad's face brought a deep joy to Edith that she decided to tuck away. Appearances needed to be kept up, after all.

The leader halted his group.

"Attention, everyone! There has been a change of plan," his voice echoed throughout the cave. Chatter broke out amongst the team.

"It has occurred to me that we have yet to do any mining. This beautiful material you see sparkling on the walls is what we call 'black gold'. I believe it to be a highly valuable metal that will help save our great village."

The chatter reached a fever pitch of excitement.

"So, for now, my friends, let's get to mining!" he called out to cheers from the group.

Wolfgang and Angus pushed through the others and strode over to the nearest cave wall. They got right to swinging with their pickaxes, and many of the other miners weren't far behind. It was mere moments before the clanking of metal striking rock echoed all around the cave. Torch stands were set up at each spot for a better view.

As the pack of miners all went to their own sections of the cave, it became clear to Edith that a small group had stayed behind: Joel, Alistair, Conrad, Lucia, and Henic remained. She nudged Faramond and then pointed at them with demanding eyes.

"Well? Shouldn't you get to mining?" Edith asked.

Conrad looked at Faramond and gestured his arms outward. "Sir, please understand. I believe we should take a closer look at the effects of black gold. Ollie-"

"Was killed by something in these mines, we know that much," Faramond interrupted. "But not by black gold. I have been around it and even buried Ollie with it. It has brought me no harm."

"You heard the man. Now, get to mining," Edith said while smugly smiling.

The group collectively turned their gazes to Faramond, but he only pointed to a nearby cave wall that was vacant.

"You've got work to do."

~

THERE WAS a solemn air about the group as they walked over to the cave wall. A torch stand had been set up nearby, illuminating the already sparkly black gold ore even more. Joel squirmed in his boots. He had earlier compared the cursed metal ores to a clear night sky with twinkling stars, but now he saw them as stray embers on an unsuspecting night: The harbinger of a deadly inferno that would engulf them all. Somehow, some way, he had to convince the others to stay away from it.

Joel flashed hand signals and Conrad translated, "He says that we can still follow Faramond's orders without directly touching the black gold. Chip away at it, but never touch it directly, and certainly don't pick any up."

"I dunno…" Henic muttered, looking around. "Won't that draw attention to us?"

"It almost certainly will, but think about what we know: Ollie died with black gold in his possession. Edith has some nefarious plan in mind that involves the very same ore. And Joel says that it will poison our minds. Until we are sure that it is harmless, I say we heed the warnings we've been given," said Conrad.

The mute smiled at his assessment. It had at least bought some time.

All in the group nodded, some with hesitance in their eyes, and then they began swinging at the rocky walls with their pickaxes.

Cries of delight from the miners echoed all around. Many had successfully mined their first black gold ores. To Joel's ears, they may as well have been cries of agony. He noted that some had managed to mine both gold and silver ores, but as time went on, it became clear that the workers valued black gold the most. Some were even leaving silver on the ground to make more room for black gold in their bags.

Faramond got in on the action with Edith's encouragement. With each piece of ore obtained, he would stare intently into its brilliant, sparkling form. He'd be one of the earlier victims if something didn't change soon, Joel thought. He also noticed that Edith hadn't mined a single ore. She appeared to be overseeing the operation in Faramond's stead.

Adding further to his stress, Joel could see that Wolfgang and

Angus were beginning to antagonize other miners. Bronrar tagged along, but he did little besides stand around. Wolfgang took stray ores away from other hard-working men while they weren't looking, and on one occasion, where he'd been caught, Angus had intimidated their victim into looking the other way.

Joel eyed the piles of black gold ore at his feet as Wolfgang and crew approached. His stomach sank.

"See? I told ye he was an idiot!" Wolfgang laughed aloud with Angus before shoving Joel from behind. Having expected some physicality, the mute caught himself on the wall instead of falling face-first into it. Lucia dropped her pickaxe and drew her blade in response.

"There is plenty of room to mine around the cave walls. Leave us," she said.

He scoffed. "I couldn't help but notice that none of ye are even pickin' up yer ores. What's the point of mining if yer not gonna collect yer reward?"

"Maybe we don't *want* the black gold. Did ya ever think of that? Noooo, because yer an inconsiderate knob!" Alistair roared.

Wolfgang laughed some more until he began to cough.

"The most beautiful rock I ever did see..." he trailed off while looking down at the dark, sparkling material at his feet. "And ye lot are too *stupid* to even pick it up."

"How about you let us take that ore off yer hands? Then, we will be on our way," Angus said.

There was a brief silence among the group. Bronrar continued to watch from further back, twiddling his thumbs.

Conrad grimaced. "Fine. Take it."

Gleefully, Wolfgang and Angus collected the piles of ore at their feet and placed them into sacks. As they took Henic's black gold output, Wolfgang wrapped an arm around his shoulder, causing him to flinch.

"Just like back in the village, eh old fella?" he asked.

"Y-yes..." Henic looked down.

"Now, don' go thinkin' ye've finished payin' yer debt, alright?" Wolfgang's arm tightened around Henic's shoulder and Joel raised an eyebrow. What were they talking about?

As Angus had promised, after grabbing everything, the men went about their way. Bronrar followed close behind, but then he stopped in front of them.

"At first, I was cautious 'round the black gold since Ollie had it when he died," Bronrar said.

"Good," Conrad replied with a hint of doubt in his voice.

"But I wanted to let you all know that I've picked up a few pieces myself, and I'm fine. You shouldn't have let them take the ore. It's gonna be valuable back in the village."

Conrad remained silent. Bronrar gave them a nod and walked to where Wolfgang and Angus were stealing more black gold from unsuspecting miners.

The others got back to work striking the cave walls. They had made a dent in the black gold deposits, but there was still plenty left.

After a brief period of the group clanking their pickaxes against rock, Henic threw his tool down. The others stopped swinging and looked at him.

"I'm sorry, my friends, but I can take this no longer!" he said before bending over to pick up a piece of black gold ore. Joel rushed over to stop him, but it was too late. Henic held the chunk of rock close to his face and examined it with a child-like curiosity in his eyes. There was a sense of dread about the air as everyone watched on in silence.

"Well? Do you feel any different?" Conrad asked.

"No. I feel fine. It *is* beautiful, so I understand why someone might be greedy for it. But I think anyone with a sense of will knows not to let material possessions take over their life," he said.

Joel attempted to swipe the black gold from Henic's grasp, but he moved his hand away to avoid. The mute inaudibly groaned.

"Really, I'm alright. Yer bein' superstitious, Joel," he said with a grimace.

"Yer tryin' ta tell me that I've been givin' away somethin' that won't do me any harm?" Alistair asked.

"Not only that, but it's supposed to be valuable, too," Lucia said.

Panic began to overtake Joel. His earlier success in getting them to listen had only been false hope. As always, the allure of the black gold reigned supreme over his pleas; over reason. Yet, he had to try. He couldn't simply stand there and let them be swallowed up by dark- ness. He quickly signed over to Conrad in a last-ditch effort to convince the group.

"He's trying to assure us that the black gold will bring us harm…" the strategist trailed off before frowning back at Joel. "But nothing observably bad has come from it, up to this point. If I'm going to continue believing you, I need to understand how you know of its insidious nature."

Joel clenched his fists. How much more could he reveal? Saying too much might be catastrophic. He had to be careful. The mute made hand signals as fast as he could.

"He claims to have witnessed black gold's poisoning of the mind before," said Conrad.

"If that's the case, then why have none of us ever heard about it? Who is it that was hurt by *mere treasures*?" Lucia asked.

More hand signals were made, and Conrad translated, "He says that he's not supposed to tell anyone…"

"Not good 'nuff, lad," Alistair said in a disappointed tone. He bent over to pick up a piece of ore. Joel reached out and opened his mouth, but no words came out. Only light gasps, as if the life were being choked out of him.

Like Henic before him, there was a foreboding silence, but nothing happened. Alistair burst out laughing. "I'm fine! We've been worried 'bout nothin'!"

Next, Lucia picked up a piece. She examined it closely and a smile came to her face.

"Well?" Conrad asked.

"It's beautiful. Like no other metal I've ever seen," she said.

"But is it affecting your mind?" he said.

"No."

Joel shook his head at the response and flashed more hand signals.

"You're asking me to put very much faith in your word alone. And the truth is, we only met yesterday. Why is that? Why have I never seen you around Faiwell?" Conrad asked.

Joel gritted his teeth. One by one, he was losing them. However, it was too dangerous to reveal everything. He had already told them far more than he was supposed to. The mute signed some more, but Conrad only frowned in return.

"That's not a good enough answer, I'm afraid. If you want me to take your word at face value, I'll need to you to stop being cryptic and explain yourself."

He hung his head as Conrad bent over to pick up his piece of ore. Like the others before him, he looked closely at what he had grabbed. A beautifully sparkling dark metal laid out in his hands, like a clear night sky.

"I think, for now, it should be alright to keep mining this material. As a precaution, I'll only hold on to one or two pieces of ore myself."

"A precaution?" Alistair said before chuckling. "What is there to worry about? You've seen fer yerself! It's harmless!"

"Something about Ollie's death still bothers me," Conrad said. "And we cannot ignore that Edith's plans involve the black gold."

"Suit yourself," Lucia said as she got back to swinging her pickaxe at the wall. The rest of the workers fell in line and they ignored Joel's silent pleas.

Bit by bit, they gathered the black gold ores and stored them in their bags. Joel could only watch on, helpless to stop them. Aldous had warned him to take a passive hand with this group; to guide them from afar, but he had come to like these people in his short time knowing them. It made it all the more painful to witness the beginnings of their inevitable corruption. He eyed Conrad, the only one to let most of his black gold output lay on the ground. If he could convince anyone, it would be him, Joel thought.

ON THE OTHER side of the cave, Faramond stood before one of the branching tunnels. He looked up the path, where there were chunks of black gold up and down its walls. A ravenous smile filled his face as he turned to face Edith.

Before he could say anything, Edith asked, "So, you wish to go down that new path?"

"I do."

"Why?"

"Look how much black gold lines the walls," he said with a grand gesture to the tunnel. "I think if we follow the tunnel, it will lead us to a treasure trove."

"Don't you think we should finish up in here?"

"We can split up, then. More for me. I need more of this beautiful material," Faramond said.

Edith raised an eyebrow, but only for a brief moment. A smile grew on her face as the leader marched to the middle of the cave. The more he wanted to search for black gold, the more likely he was to find the Gold Pit, she thought.

"Everyone! Gather 'round! I am going to address the plan moving forward," Faramond called out.

After some grumbling, the miners slowly but surely made their way to the middle. He pointed toward the black gold-filled path on his right and said, "Down this tunnel is more black gold. I believe it will lead us to an even larger cave that is filled with it."

There was excitement among the crew, but none of their smiles could compare to Faramond's.

"With that said, we need some miners to stay here and finish working on this cave. So, we will split up into two teams. One team will come with me to explore the tunnel, while the rest will stay here under Edith's command."

After some deliberation, it was decided that a group of 30 would travel with Faramond through the tunnel, while the rest would remain. Rather than wait for volunteers, the leader picked his own team. Among the chosen were Joel, Alistair, and Henic.

∽

FARAMOND WASTED no time leading his new team into the tunnel. Alistair and Henic stuck together, leaving Joel further behind on his own. As they accumulated more black gold, he could feel their distrust for him growing.

Joel was drawing on his map to mark new locations, but out of the corner of his eye, he could see Alistair nudging Henic. He whispered, "Do ya think this whole time he wanted the black gold fer himself?"

Because it was Alistair's loud and raspy voice, Joel had heard every word. He buried his face further in the map, pretending not to notice.

"I don't know…" Henic trailed off as he peered back at Joel. "But here's what I *do* know. He has always been a mysterious fellow. I'm not sayin' we shouldn't trust him, but…"

Alistair, for once, remained quiet. *Unbelievable*, Joel thought. He felt helpless under the immense weight of the black gold's influence. What else could he do besides suffer in silence?

CHAPTER 9
KNOCKERS

Faramond's group of 30 traversed the tunnel path while gazing along the walls in wonder at the twinkling black gold. Some workers had suggested they start mining, but Faramond forbade it. He brought to light concerns that mining in the more confined tunnels might cause an accidental breakage. He insisted that soon, they would come upon a cave filled with more of the precious metal than ever before.

Toward the middle of the pack, Joel could hear Alistair and Henic arguing.

"I'm tellin' ya, there's somethin' in these tunnels besides us! Can't ya hear tha noises?" Alistair said.

"Yer goin' stir-crazy, big fella. There's nothin' else in here," Henic said with a laugh.

Alistair snorted and shot back, "And *I'm* supposed ta be the one with poor hearin'!"

Joel focused his ears. The chatter of the miners and their noisy footsteps faded into the background. At first, he thought that Henic was correct: He heard nothing. Then, a new sound became apparent. Every once in a while, a clicking noise would enter his ears; similar to the ones he had heard near the Mouth of Hell, but fainter. It was like two rocks colliding underwater.

As he felt a wave of suspicion wash over him, the mute moved closer to the left wall. The clicking noises became louder and more frequent. Joel's eyes widened and he began to increase his pace. He wished to inform Alistair and Henic, but their newfound distrust for him was a problem. Instead, he had his sights set on Faramond.

By the time Joel reached the front of the pack, Faramond and the rest of the group had stopped. All had directed their torchlights at a ladder up ahead. It poked through a small hole in the ceiling. Without a word, Faramond held a hand up, signaling the others to remain in place, and then he climbed the ladder. Only his head fit through the hole.

"Peculiar…" Faramond muttered while climbing back down. At the bottom, he turned to face the group and said, "The hole is too small for any of us to fit through, and it's too dark to see anything up there. Let us continue."

Joel raised a hand to get his attention, but he had already spun around and resumed his march up the path. Several miners pushed and shoved past the mute, and he let out an inaudible sigh. Before he knew it, he was walking in step with Alistair and Henic once more.

"What's tha point of havin' a ladder that leads ta nowhere?" Alistair asked aloud.

Henic chuckled and said, "It must belong to the knockers."

"What are 'knockers'?" Alistair asked while raising an eyebrow.

"You don't know much about mining, do you?" Henic said in an amused tone. The big man frowned, but he offered no retort. "It's an old legend. As the tale goes, knockers are little creatures who inhabit the mines, knockin' on the walls to play tricks on unsuspecting workers. The problem is, all of that knockin' can lead to a tunnel collapse, the little buggers!"

Alistair's jaw dropped. "You mean-"

"I know what yer thinking," he interrupted. "But I'm tellin' you, they ain't real. They're a myth made up to explain why tunnel collapses happen. That's all."

"But back there, I heard knockin' noises!" Alistair said. Henic only laughed in response.

Joel fidgeted his mouth as he walked along. What bothered him more than the possibility of little tricksters in the mines was how Alistair and Henic were acting around him. His denouncement of the black gold had given way to a reaction he hadn't anticipated: Instead of being angry or distrustful of him, the others seemed to not be taking him seriously. It was as if he were a child among adults who cared little for his thoughts. He may as well have been invisible. It didn't help that they couldn't understand his sign language. Somehow, he had to get a word in with Faramond.

As the group proceeded, Joel noticed some more troubling developments: The clicking noises grew louder, and once in a while, he'd see pebbles falling from the ceiling. Now, he *had* to say something. He pushed past the herd of miners, to the front where Faramond was marching. The mute tapped him on the shoulder. He peered back and frowned.

"Ah, it's you. What do you need?" Faramond asked with uncharacteristic shortness.

Joel raised an eyebrow and flashed hand signals back at him.

"I'm perfectly fine. It is you that I worry about. Conrad was *convinced* that black gold had poisoned Ollie's mind, and I believe it was you who told him that," he said in a stern tone.

Joel nodded in return. His helmet loosened, and as he went to fix it, he felt a pebble bounce off his head. He looked up to see fine dust falling from the ceiling. *Something's wrong*, he thought.

"Look at me," Faramond said, firmly placing a hand on his shoulder. Joel jerked his head down and left to meet his fiery eyes. "There is nothing wrong with black gold. It's going to save Faiwell. I need you to understand that."

Joel signed back, and Faramond frowned.

"If you're going to be a problem, I will have no choice but to take you off this team and send you home."

Joel thought back to when Faramond had said he wouldn't even leave *Wolfgang* on his own. He sharpened his eyes and made more hand signals.

"My mind has not been poisoned," he replied and then cocked his head. "You're mistaken. I am only trying to weed out the troublemakers… what is it you wanted to speak with me about?"

He sighed before signing back to him. Faramond raised an eyebrow.

"I haven't heard any peculiar noises, no. Perhaps your paranoia isn't limited to black gol-" Faramond cut himself off. Up ahead, there was another ladder that reached the roof of the tunnel.

The group approached the ladder before Faramond stopped them once more. In the ceiling was another tiny hole, but noises were coming from it: The same *clicking* that Joel and Alistair had heard before, louder than ever.

~

Back in the cave, Lucia and Conrad mined the black gold ore at a steady pace while constantly looking over their shoulders to keep tabs on Wolfgang and his goons. They had recently migrated to the other side of the cave to bother some other miners for ore, to their relief.

Conrad took a hefty swing with his pickaxe before stopping to wipe the sweat from his brow. He eyed the piles of black gold at his feet, and then the sack of ore sitting beside Lucia. He had kept his word and only held onto a couple of pieces for himself. As tempting as it was to take more, too many questions about the ore were tugging at the back of his mind.

"Are you feeling alright?" he asked.

The mercenary took another hack at the cave wall before she stopped and glanced back at him with a smirk. "You've already asked me that. Twice, now."

"We have to be vigilant. Just in case…"

"You have placed very much faith in Joel's word, yet you hardly even know him," Lucia said.

"True, but I have a bad feeling. He is obviously keeping something important from us, but I don't think him a liar, either," Conrad replied.

"At the very least, he is wrong about black gold. Look at how much I've gathered," she said, gesturing to her half-filled bag. "Yet, I am just fine."

As she resumed striking the wall with her pickaxe, Conrad found himself deep in thought. There was something that he was forgetting; something that *she* was forgetting. His eyes widened.

"Weren't you worried about Dalton?"

Lucia raised her pickaxe for the next strike, but she froze. She remained silent for a few moments as if comprehending something.

"How could I have forgotten?"

"I'd say you have a distraction." Conrad eyed her sack of black gold ore.

"But I feel fine."

"I worry that this material has an addictive quality. I've only held onto a couple of pieces, and I have to admit that there is a temptation to take more," he said with a blank stare. "But it feels more like a reflex; something that I cannot help. It's as if I'm starving and have only been given crumbs when a full meal sits before me."

"What are you trying to say? That the black gold has cast a spell over us?" Lucia asked, her tone growing defensive. "You want more because it will make you wealthy, Conrad. That is human nature; your instincts urging you to act. You might want to listen."

"I'll hold off, for now," said Conrad. He wondered how much longer he could.

~

BACK IN THE TUNNEL, Faramond climbed the ladder and poked his head through the small hole in the roof. Joel passed him a torch, and upon shimmying his arm up into the space, the light revealed a tiny, rocky hall that stretched off into infinite darkness, but no one was there. After a few moments of looking into the abyss, he passed the torch back to Joel and began to climb down.

Suddenly, the ladder shook, and Faramond, in a panic, hugged his body around it. There was a deafening crash from down the tunnel: The ceiling and walls had collapsed, and given way to falling rocks and boulders. They were followed closely by an eruption of dust that permeated throughout the path. Faramond remained frozen on the ladder as panicked screams and rocks slamming together echoed off the walls. It was over in only a few seconds, but to him, it felt like an eternity; a disaster in slow-motion.

Faramond had little time to comprehend the implications, as when he looked up, a little creature peered down from the hole above. While nearly at the bottom of the ladder, he froze again and stared at the oddity before him.

Looking back at him was a creature no larger than a toddler, with warped, pink skin, a large nose, and bushy gray hair. It wore what appeared to be a small tunic, but from a distance, Faramond could have mistaken it for a brown rag. Its large feet were rotten, and its face was covered in warts. The little one cocked its head to the left, then to the right, but didn't make a sound.

Finally, Faramond broke the silence and said, "Hello there, little fellow. Is it you we've been hearing this whole time?"

The little one smiled back, revealing row upon row of razor-sharp teeth. Faramond's eyes widened as the creature let out a high-pitched shriek and leaped from the hole. It landed with a *thud* on the leader's face, knocking him off the bottom of the ladder and onto the ground.

It latched onto Faramond's face and clawed away at it with surprisingly sharp nails. He called out for help, but instead of a response, he heard more shrieking and the panicked cries of his team. *They were under attack.*

~

WITH THE LITTLE cretins swarming around him and the other miners, Joel rushed to his struggling leader's aid and ripped the pest off of him.

Faramond's pale face had been bloodied by scratches, but they were only superficial. He turned over to see that the little monster was rummaging through his pack.

"You! Get away from there!" he cried, but it was too late. The creature got its hands on some black gold and scurried off into the darkness.

With panic in his eyes, Faramond turned and called out to the group, "Everyone! This way! We must catch and kill this monster!"

He ran, full speed ahead, deeper into the tunnel. Joel, sensing more danger in his leader's future, gave chase. What remained of the rest of the group ran along with them.

"Oi! Tha hell is goin' on?" Alistair complained between breaths. Joel breathed a sigh of relief to hear the big man's bombastic voice and fell back to his pace.

"I don' know… Couldn't get a good look… at what happened," Henic said as he panted from the full-on sprint.

"And what about… behind us? The tunnel appears… to have collapsed… and we're not even gonna… check on it? What if someone… got hurt?" Alistair asked.

As they ran by another hole in the ceiling, the trio looked up to see even more small creatures coming out.

"Oh, for the love of-" Henic complained.

Alistair laughed and said, "Ya see that? I was right! Those are knockers, aren't they?"

"It can't be…"

Soon, many knockers penetrated the running group and began to attack. Several men tripped and fell, squirming and screaming on their way down. Alistair kicked one away, while Henic brushed another off of his pant leg. His eyes widened to see that it had bitten a sizeable hole out of the fabric.

"We've gotta get away from these things!" Henic shouted as he increased his pace to get past the other miners.

Joel wasn't sure what worried him more: The knockers, or the fact that Alistair and Henic were *still* ignoring him.

After running for some time, the tunnel began to open up into a cave, just as Faramond had predicted. The glimmer of black gold greeted their eyes from all around the walls and even on the ceiling. The knocker who had stolen the ore ran brazenly into the cave through a field of mushrooms. Joel's eyes widened and he put his head down while increasing his pace. Faramond pressed on with determined strides despite his loud panting.

However, before he could close in on the thief, Joel tackled him to the ground. Faramond looked up to see the knocker disappearing into the darkness ahead.

The leader attempted to claw his way up and back to his feet but to no avail. Joel put full weight on his back, rendering him nearly immobile. Other miners passed by along with the mischievous little creatures laughing with delight while attacking them.

"You fool!" Faramond cried with desperation on his tongue. "It's getting away! It has my black gold! It's mine! I must have it!"

Joel shook his head and pushed down harder as Faramond wriggled around like a struggling worm.

"Why you little… how are you able to keep me down?" he asked.

"What do ya think yer doin', attackin' our leader? Yer bein' rude!" Alistair's angry voice echoed. Joel let out an inaudible gasp as he was picked up and then tossed to the ground like a hunk of meat. He looked up to see both the big man and Henic staring back at him with disapproving eyes.

Faramond hopped to his feet and held a fist up in Joel's direction. "You see that? It got away! With *my* treasure! I've had enough! You're off the team!"

Joel felt a frog in his throat. He couldn't help but take in the chaos of the situation. A tunnel collapse had likely trapped them, they were being attacked by little monsters, the entire group had split up in the darkness of the cave, and now he was off the team. He looked over to Henic for support.

"Sorry Joel, but he has a point. Did we not agree to keep our heads down and stick to our work? But here you are, causin' trouble. At the very least, ye've got some explainin' to d-"

An explosion boomed up ahead, and the cries of men and shrieks of knockers alike echoed off the cave walls as their silhouettes soared through the air. Joel and the others shielded their eyes as the cave rumbled. Some rocks fell from the ceiling before another explosion went off, further away. After removing his arm from his eyes, Joel could see that Faramond had broken out into a sweat.

"What in the world is going on?" he asked.

Joel stood and flashed some hand signals.

"Explosive mushrooms…"

"What's that all about?" Alistair asked.

Henic looked back at Joel and said, "He just saved us."

As if coming out of a trance, Faramond shook his head and rubbed his eyes. "Yes, it would seem he has… excuse me for a moment."

The leader walked ahead. He tip-toed around the mushrooms and slowly disappeared into the darkness. Soon, from the dark, he called out:

"Attention, everyone! There are explosive mushrooms in this cave! Tread lightly! Any contact could cause another explosion. I am going to light my torch. Make your way toward me!"

Joel, Henic, and Alistair found their way to Faramond, guided by his flame. Other miners appeared at the cave's center and formed a circle around their leader. When it was all said and done, 17 miners remained.

"That's all?" Alistair asked.

"Not good…" Henic muttered.

Faramond said, "It should be clear to us all by now how dangerous these mines are. And we're not even deep into the mountain, yet."

"We need to get out of here!" one miner said.

"Those little monsters! They have a taste for human flesh!" another cried out.

"Indeed," Faramond said with a nod. "We need to get away from here as soon as possible. I am going to take a small team back to the tunnel and see if there are any survivors. The rest of you, be on your toes and wait here. If we are not back within a reasonable time, then you should start searching for an exit on your own."

～

IN THE CAVE where Edith's team was mining, three men had died. One miner had been sent along with Wolfgang to investigate the path that Faramond and his team had taken. The blond brute had returned with the solemn news that the tunnel had collapsed; and that a stray rock had fallen and bashed the man's skull. Next, a series

105

of violent vibrations had caused rocks from the ceiling to fall. Two miners perished in the commotion, both from deadly blunt force to the head.

Conrad cast a suspicious eye on Wolfgang and his crew, who were near the dead miners. Wolfgang and Angus continued along like nothing had happened, while Bronrar meandered in the background with his head hanging.

"Alright, everyone! We were told that these mines were dangerous and now we see why. We can mourn their deaths later tonight. Back to work!" Edith commanded.

With another swing of his pickaxe, Conrad whispered to Lucia, "I think we should try to speak with Bronrar alone. He must be feeling guilty about his friends' actions."

Lucia scoffed. "We all know that those scum are responsible for the deaths that have happened so far. But Edith will cover for them. Bronrar seems the cowardly type. I doubt he'll be of much use."

"I see some good in him," Conrad said as he stopped to take off his helmet and wipe the sweat from his forehead. "It's only a matter of speaking to him alone…"

"You'll have to wait until we get moving again," she said. "And I worry that may not be any time soon. The cave-in may well have trapped Faramond and his group."

"Indeed," Conrad said as he got back to swinging his pickaxe. "We have to hope that those alternate paths from earlier caves connect with the tunnel they went through."

With unrest growing in her voice, Lucia said, "We can't stay here much longer, either way. Dalton may be Faiwell's best warrior, but he can't be trapped in here with a team for several days and be expected to live. There are water and food supplies to consider."

As he continued to chisel away at the rock, Conrad looked at Lucia out of the corner of his eye and asked, "How do you suggest we get moving, then?"

"We force our way through."

"Nonsense."

"I mean it," Lucia said, turning to him. "You were right. I became distracted by all the black gold, but now my head is clear. This place is dangerous. We have to save the first team."

"Edith commands too much power right now. Faramond put her in charge, and if we go against her… we will have to contend with nearly 40 other miners, some of them armed," he replied.

"Do you truly believe that everyone is falling for that farce of a leader's words? I see right through them," the mercenary said.

Conrad sighed. "That's only because of what you overheard between her and her father. Many others can acknowledge that Edith is not a pleasant woman, but they also know she is the daughter of the Guild president. There is no question of who's in charge, here."

"Then, we make a run for it," Lucia said. Conrad widened his eyes. "I can take no more of this waiting around, and I don't care if she is in charge. I will cut her down if I must."

She threw down her pickaxe. Conrad remained silent.

"The only question is…" she trailed off and then looked at him with piercing brown eyes. "Do you have the guts to join me?"

Conrad had stopped swinging his pickaxe. Looking at her shaking fists, there was no doubt in his mind that she was prepared to battle.

"I'd be willing to fight alongside you, Lucia…" he trailed off as a smile grew on her face. "*But* I want to wait a little longer before we resort to that."

She snorted and then frowned. "Fine. I'll give it a little longer, but then I'm going. With or without you."

Conrad couldn't help but smile in return. If black gold *had* poisoned her mind, he was convinced that she had shaken it off for the time being.

~

BACK IN THE explosive mushroom-filled cave, Faramond took eight miners, including Joel and Henic, to investigate the tunnel collapse. They left a group of nine at the cave's center, their weapons drawn and at the ready.

"Awright, laddies!" Alistair's bombastic voice echoed from behind. "If any of ya see those little buggers approachin', don' hesitate ta swing away! Don' forget what they did ta the others!"

Joel let out a snorting chuckle as he heard the groans of the other miners left behind. Alistair's bluster was best enjoyed from afar, he thought.

As they neared the tunnel where the knockers had attacked, Henic approached Joel on his right. "I don' know why you've been so secretive, Joel, but I do know that yer heart's in the right place. Our leader may well have died, if not for you. So, I apologize fer misjudgin' you. I don't know what came over me."

Joel smiled back and put a hand on his shoulder. He gave him a brief nod, happy that whatever hold the black gold had on him earlier was lessened, for now.

Further ahead, Faramond lifted his torch, which exposed the tunnel they were traveling toward. A light dust still floated about, lingering like a bad odor.

"Everyone, stay close and be ready," he said while drawing a tastefully crafted broadsword that gleamed in the light of the torches and black gold sparkles.

As the team walked down the tunnel, the clicking noises returned. Distant screeching filled the tunnel with fear and despair, as with each step, the noises drew closer.

Suddenly, Faramond dashed ahead at full speed. Joel and the other miners stumbled at first, but soon after followed his pace. They soon found their leader huddled over a body, checking its vital signs.

"Dead," he said; his voice cracked with nervousness.

Henic directed his torch toward the body to see the ghastly expression of a dead man. His eyes were wide with fear, and his mouth was agape; the corpse had gashes and slices all about him. Most noteworthy were the bite marks on his neck, where blood leaked down and reached his shirt.

"So, it's true. This is the work of knockers, ain't it? The little ghouls that trap people in the mines and feast on flesh?" Henic asked.

"I thought those were silly myths from the old ages," one miner chimed in.

"But we saw for ourselves! They're real!" another said.

"There is no point in arguing," Faramond said. Everyone fell silent. "Let's check the tunnel for any more survivors, and survey the damage of the collapse. We must be quick. One thing I'm sure of is that those little creatures caused the cave-in. They could do it again, and trap us in here."

He continued down the tunnel, and the others followed. Joel strode up to his leader and flashed some hand signals.

Faramond nodded and said, "Yes, I hear them, too. They'll be coming for us, soon. Be ready for a fight."

~

IN THE CIRCLE OF NINE, the shrieking and clicking noises grew louder. High-pitched laughter taunted them from afar. The miners had grown fidgety and wary at the noises, often swinging their weapons at nothing in the dark.

"Hold steady, lads! They'll come ta us, in time. And then, I'll crush 'em!" Alistair said. The circle of men collectively groaned. "Oh, come on! If yer gonna have'ta fight, at least it's these wee, pathetic creatures and not some big monster, eh?"

Alistair chuckled, but no one laughed along with him.

Out of the corner of his eye, he spotted a figure no more than five paces away. He moved his torch in that direction, but nothing was there. He narrowed his eyes and continued to focus.

"They're close…" he muttered.

The group of miners remained silent, with their weapons held out in front of them. One miner, to Alistair's left, nervously moved his torch back and forth. Then, there was a piercing shriek, and Alistair turned in time to see a small, bearded creature flying toward the miner. Its mouth was open, with rows of sharp teeth ready to clamp down on its prey. The miner could only let out a gasp before the knocker latched onto his face and bit down. He screamed out in pain and tried with all his might to pull the monster off, but its jaw held tight.

The rest of the workers rushed to the man's aid. They all attempted to pull the creature off, but their efforts were in vain: It had sunk its wretched claws and teeth into its victim's face. Alistair, fearing that time was short, knew what to do.

"Step aside!" he said, raising his mighty battle axe. The other miners called for him to halt and stood in his way, but he pushed past them.

Like a knife slicing through hot bread, the battle axe came down smoothly. The axe head plunged into the knocker's tiny skull, chopping down to its upper torso. Blood splattered as it shrieked aloud and wriggled in pain.

Finally, the creature let go of its victim and fell to the ground, lifeless. The miner placed hands on his face and felt the blood soak. After moments of heavy breathing, he calmed down.

"I'm… I'm alright?" he asked aloud.

"Hoo boy! Am I glad ta see that I didn't hack off yer face, laddie! That was me first time swingin' a battle axe!" he shouted before bursting into laughter and slapping him on the back. The other miners looked at each other, wide-eyed.

The shrieks and clicking became more numerous and sounded closer.

"On yer guard, everyone! There be even more lil' goblins ta kill!" said Alistair. Despite the dangers, he struggled to remember the last time he'd been this excited.

~

BACK IN THE TUNNEL, Faramond's group came across a grisly scene: Limbs of miners left behind on the ground and blood pooling around them. A foul stench filled the air, which made Henic dry heave.

"Good lord! These creatures are more violent than I ever could have imagined!" he said while shielding his nose from the smell.

As they approached the ladder of the initial attack, Faramond readied his sword. There were high-pitched mumblings in the darkness, and blood was dripping down the ladder.

Then, a tiny figure darted out of the void and toward the ladder. It was a knocker, and it had a disembodied human hand in its mouth. Faramond gave chase, but it was already halfway up the ladder by the time he reached it. In desperation, he swung his sword upward and struck one of the steps, but missed the knocker. The little monster scurried up into the hole and let out a high-pitched giggle after it was enveloped in darkness.

"Damn it all! Are there truly no survivors?" he asked aloud.

The group made their way toward the musty smell of the cave-in and saw even more carnage laid out before them. In addition to broken supports and giant boulders, the bodies of several men could be seen crushed underneath the collapse; with limbs, fingers, and equipment sticking out.

After standing for a few moments in silence, Faramond said, "It would seem that in my steadfast approach to gathering more black gold, I lost sight of why I was the team leader in the first place." He got down on one knee and bowed his head before choking out, "Forgive me for not keeping you safe…"

The group continued to stand in silence as their leader knelt. The only thing that could be heard was the sound of light clicking off in the distance. Joel glanced over his shoulder to see nothing but the darkness of the mines beckoning him. Yet, he knew that they couldn't stay still for long. In here, they were sitting ducks. He walked over to his leader and tapped him on the shoulder. He looked back up at him with tears in his eyes, but quickly wiped them away before anyone else could notice.

"Yes, we should go," he said while standing. He brushed past the others. "Let's find a way out of here."

Down the tunnel and from out in the cave, the high-pitched wails of knockers and the shouting of several men erupted. Panic filled Faramond's eyes.

"There will be no more deaths under my watch! Let's go!" he said before sprinting up the path. The group followed suit with their available weapons drawn.

~

IN THE MUSHROOM-FILLED CAVE, Alistair looked out into the darkness. A few other knockers had jumped out at his allies and were successfully thwarted, but none had jumped for him.

"Come out and fight me, ya ninnies!" he shouted while waving his axe around. "Oooo, what's wrong? Am I not tasty 'nuff for ya?"

Alistair laughed as he pulled up a pant leg and stuck his big, hairy leg out.

"See? Got a nice, fat leg for ya!" he said before whispering to the miner on his right, "Little do they know, I'm all muscle."

He laughed some more and continued to nudge the miner, who narrowed his eyes and looked away.

In a split second, he turned his head to see one of the vicious little monsters lunging out at him from the darkness. Its shriek pierced his ears like an arrow through flesh, but he remained undeterred and swung his mighty battle axe from right to left, hacking the knocker to bits. A welt of dark blood splattered on the ground like paint thrown at a canvas.

Alistair heaved the axe handle onto his shoulder and said, "Oi! Did ya see that? There's nothin' left of im'!"

He had little time to brag, however, as over a dozen knockers suddenly appeared out of the dark. They surrounded the group and began to close in, their pale pink faces grinning with delight.

The big redhead stared down a couple of knockers who were licking their lips. He held his battle axe in position with the anticipation that they would jump out at him like the others had done. However, before they could attack, a torch appeared behind one of the little cretins. The monster turned around in time to see the torch jammed in its face.

Fire enveloped the knocker as it ran around in circles, a trail of smoke acting as its tail. The knocker next to it turned to see Faramond, who had already begun to swing his shining broadsword. In one fell swoop, the cretin's head was lopped clean off.

The other creatures noticed their fallen comrades, and in their confusion, the miners went on the attack. One impaled a distracted knocker in its stomach with his pickaxe, and another nearly split his target in two from a sword slash.

In a panic, the little monsters screeched and began to scurry away to the opposite side of the cave.

"After 'em!" Alistair bellowed.

"Wait!" Faramond said. The miners all stopped in their tracks. "We have lost enough men for one day. These creatures probably know the mines well. We, on the other hand, do not. For this reason, I shall lead the way, but slowly. That way, I can keep an eye out for mushrooms."

Alistair joined back up with Joel and Henic as the miners marched through the cave, cautiously, behind their fearless leader. There was an odd mixture of unease and optimism in the air.

CHAPTER 10
MUTINY

In the black gold-laden cave, business continued as usual. Wolfgang and Angus terrorized other miners for their ore while Edith looked the other way. Bronrar sulked behind his violent companions as they made their way back to Lucia and Conrad, wringing their hands.

"How 'bout you hand over the black gold like before, and we leave you be?" Angus asked.

"Not this time," Lucia said. She threw down her pickaxe and placed a hand on her claymore's hilt. "This place is beginning to stress me out. All I need is one excuse to draw this blade..."

Angus' expression remained as stone as a statue.

"I don't think ye understand. Maybe ye came to yer senses and understood that the black gold is valuable..." Wolfgang trailed off as he looked at Lucia's sack of ores. "But ye already permitted us to take any further ore that ye mined, remember? It's ours, now."

"The hell it is!" Lucia shot back.

"There is still plenty of ore to be mined in this cave," Conrad said. Wolfgang didn't respond; he only stared back at him with malicious eyes.

Conrad looked past the troublemakers and at Bronrar, who was fidgeting his feet. The nervous miner's eyes darted downward when their gazes met. Wolfgang took aggressive steps forward, and Conrad refocused himself.

"As I said, gentlemen…" he trailed off before wrapping a hand around his rapier's grip. "There is plenty of ore left to go around."

Wolfgang chuckled as he took another step closer. He was only a few paces away, now.

"But if you refuse to leave us," Conrad said as he drew the rapier from his hip. "We'll fight you for it."

"That's right," Lucia said. She brought out her weapon, too.

Wolfgang continued to walk until Conrad's rapier was at his throat. Finally, he stopped. The tip of the blade lightly poked his neck, and Conrad looked into his eyes. He was surprised to see not fear, but *excitement*.

The blond brute howled with laughter. It went on for a few moments too long. His laughs echoed off the cave walls and began to draw attention from other miners. Even Edith looked over her shoulder, despite Conrad's full confidence that she'd been trying to keep her gaze away from them.

After finally settling down, Wolfgang said, "Ye think ye can defeat me, pretty boy?"

Conrad pushed the tip of his blade a little harder into his neck. He didn't even flinch.

"Let me tell ye somethin'…" he said while grabbing the rapier by the middle of the blade. Conrad's eyes widened as blood trickled down from Wolfgang's rugged hand. "I've seen and done things that ye could never imagine. Yer threats are *empty*, but mine ain't."

A bead of sweat dropped to Conrad's cheek. He looked over Wolfgang's face, covered in battle scars. Never before had he met someone who so readily embraced death. Truly, he was dealing with a madman.

"So, hand over yer black gold. Or I'll kill ye, *and* yer gal," he said and then smiled at Lucia.

"I've heard enough!" Lucia shouted as she swung her claymore in an arced motion toward Angus. He narrowly avoided her blade by stepping back. Even still, his stone-faced expression remained and he held a pickaxe out in a defensive position.

"Wait!" Conrad cried before they could truly start fighting. He withdrew his rapier from Wolfgang's throat. The blond brute grinned.

"What are you doing?" Lucia asked with a snarl.

"I'll hand over my black gold ore peacefully…" he said, looking at Bronrar with a smile. "But only if Bronrar takes it."

Wolfgang raised an eyebrow and looked back at his teammate. Bronrar cocked his head and his mouth hung open.

"Ye realize that he'll hand it over to me anyway, don't ye?" Wolfgang asked and began to laugh once again.

"I don't care about that. All that I require is that *he* takes it," Conrad replied before looking over at Lucia. She scowled back at him. "Also, she gets to keep her black gold."

Wolfgang sighed and then said, "Fine. But I want no arguments from now on. Ye give me yer black gold every time we come 'round, no questions asked."

"Oh, and one more thing. I require Bronrar to be *alone* while collecting the ore. You lot need to leave," Conrad said.

"How do we know you won't try to hide any pieces of ore from us when he's the only one here collecting?" Angus asked as he lowered his pickaxe.

"Nothing prohibits you from watching from afar. I won't make any strange movements, either. I'll just continue to mine. I simply don't trust any of you to pick up the ore peacefully. Bronrar over here seems to be the least dangerous of your group," he replied while fixing his gaze on the nervous miner once again.

Wolfgang grunted. "It's an odd request, but if yer handin' it over peacefully, I don't care how we get the ore." He looked over his shoulder and bared his teeth. "Bronrar! Drag yer sorry arse over here and get to work!"

"Right…" he mumbled while walking over. He approached the first pieces of black gold at Conrad's feet, and the others walked away, as agreed.

After the troublemakers had gone out of ear's reach, Lucia narrowed her eyes at Conrad. "What the hell was that, back there? You let them walk all over you when we had the weapons and training to take them down!"

Conrad smiled as he continued to mine. Without looking back at her, he said, "At least now, we can speak with Bronrar."

Lucia's eyes widened and her anger dissipated. "Oh, I see… that was clever of you."

"And what do you wish to speak with me about?" Bronrar asked. He picked pieces of ore up from the ground and began placing them into a sack. His eyes never met Conrad's or Lucia's. Instead, his gaze stayed on the black gold.

"It's simple, really," Conrad said as he took another large swing with his pickaxe at the wall. "Those two miners who died from falling rocks… was it actually Wolfgang who killed them?"

There was a long silence before the strategist looked at Bronrar out of the corner of his eye: His mouth fidgeted, but no words came out. A sweat came to his brow. He took his helmet off and slicked his dark hair back.

"Well?" Lucia asked.

"I can't say… there was a big commotion, and-"

"We're talking about innocent lives taken. Did he? Or didn't he? It's a simple question," Conrad said in a stern tone.

"I-I… uhh…"

"It's not too late for you to do the right thing. If Wolfgang murdered someone, you must tell us. Or tell us he is innocent to put our minds at ease," said Conrad.

"Even you have to admit, he has been close to three separate deaths in one day. It doesn't *look* good," Lucia said.

Bronrar let out a long sigh. "*Of course* it was him."

Conrad and Lucia turned to face one another, each with the same concerned expression.

"That man is a monster. I worry that he's poisonin' my friend Angus' mind. It's the whole reason I went on this trip, y'see," he said.

"And that miner who died in the tunnel with him?" Conrad asked.

"I don' know, but what I *do* know is that he paid the death no mind. It didn't affect him at all."

"Edith and Wolfgang are planning something, aren't they?" Lucia asked.

"Yeh. They want to pick off the weak miners and keep more black gold fer themselves," Bronrar said as he began to wrap up the sack. His job was finished. "Angus and me want nothin' to do with it, though. We got mixed up with the wrong people, and now there's nothin' we can do about it. Edith has Faramond wrapped around her finger, so we can't appeal to him. We're trapped under Edith and Wolfgang for this whole expedition."

"Don't be so sure," Conrad whispered. "Faramond hates Wolfgang. We could still tell-"

"Naw, you don't understand," Bronrar interrupted. "If Wolfgang or Edith find out that Faramond knows any of this, Angus and me will be killed."

"That sounds about right for Edith. She has little regard for human life or loose ends," Lucia said, crossing her arms. "But you should consider the possibility that she may kill *you*, even if you do as you're told."

"Please, I only ask that you give me some time to work this out. I think I can get Wolfgang to expose himself as the murderer he is in front of Faramond. He is growin' more and more reckless by the moment," Bronrar said as he began to walk off with the sack of black gold.

"That's *if* Faramond returns…" Conrad muttered.

IN THE MUSHROOM CAVE, the group of 17 cautiously walked across the landscape. Joel had gotten back to drawing his map, although he had little light to see the area around him; most of the torches were pointed downward to make sure they avoided explosive mushrooms.

After walking for a short time, they reached a new tunnel. Joel guessed that it was almost directly across from the one they had originally come out of. At a crawl's pace, they traversed the new path. Even as the environment became rockier and without a mushroom in sight, the group continued to tread lightly for a while before changing their pace to a normal one.

While making a bending turn to their left, the clicking noises from earlier returned.

"Bah! Those little monsters are back at it!" Henic said.

"The question is, how did they get back in the walls and ceiling? There are no holes or ladders, this time," Faramond said.

Joel scanned the walls and then noticed something peculiar. He tapped Alistair on the shoulder and motioned to follow him over to the rock wall on their right.

"What's that? Ya find somethin', lad?" he asked. Faramond looked back and halted the group as Joel walked over and pointed out a small hole in the wall.

All of the miners gathered around the hole. The familiar clicking noises and screeches could be heard, but they were off in the distance. Faramond bent down to inspect. After a few moments of silence, he stood and turned to face the group.

"I believe with a few solid swings; we could break through. The wall is thin."

"Would it be wise to follow the little monsters, sir?" Henic asked. Faramond looked down and let out a heavy breath through his nose.

"Fair point," he replied. "The issue here is *not* getting revenge for our fallen, but escaping with our lives. The question is: Which path will bring us to where we need to go?"

Joel approached Faramond and opened up his map. Though incomplete, the map showed that their location was above one of the previous caves: the first one with the lightning mechanism. If the path continued downward as it seemed to be doing, it would lead them back to that familiar cave.

"Let us hope that you are better with maps than you are with precious metals," said Faramond.

Joel let out a discouraged snort, but on the bright side, Faramond was at least starting to listen to him again. If he was correct on this call, perhaps he could regain his trust. His eyes wandered to Alistair and Henic, who had begun walking down the path behind Faramond. They would be good indicators of how much recent events had swayed their trust in him, he thought. The mute walked up to the two men and gave Alistair a pat on the back.

"Oh, there ya are, lad!" he said in a cheerful tone. "Was startin' ta think ya got left behind."

Joel smiled. It was as if there had never been distrust, to begin with. At the very least, he was satisfied not to be completely disregarded, as before.

"Ya know, just 'cause you were wrong about black gold doesn't mean we hate ya," the big man said. Joel's smile fell to a frown.

"Yeh, we're only sorry that yer missin' out," Henic added. "It truly is beautiful, and look at us! We're fine."

Joel shook his head.

"How can ya not see it, lad? It might just be the prettiest metal in all the land, and it's gonna fetch us a high price when we get home! Yer tellin' us to avoid it, but I say we gotta have *more*!" Alistair said before taking a piece of ore out of his pocket. "Here, take it."

The big man held the black gold out in his palm. Henic's jaw dropped.

"Why would ye wanna give it away? There is plenty for him to take elsewhere."

"The lad has saved me arse twice on this trip already! It's the least I can do… only the one piece, though," Alistair said.

Joel looked at the black gold with wonder. Even he, who vehemently hated it, could not deny its beauty. It was such a contradiction, to see a dark material so shiny and brilliant. It was like a series of guiding lights in the darkness; a sign of hope in a hopeless situation. It was so beautiful that he had to have it, he thought.

Slowly, he reached his hand out to the beckoning black gold. Yes, one piece should be fine, he thought. It wasn't only his hand moving slowly, however. Time itself seemed to slow all around him. The noise of footsteps and chatter ceased. He could see nothing save the precious gem before him; all else had turned to black. A great wind in the tunnel howled and passed through his body. It penetrated his soul, but he didn't care.

His hand stopped above Alistair's palm, ready to take the ore. The howling wind turned into a series of familiar blood-curdling screams, which gave him pause. His eyes showed panic and he looked up at Alistair, who returned a raised eyebrow and cocked head. The big man's lips moved, but no sound came out. Joel looked back down at his prize, only to see that Alistair had closed his hand and yanked it away. The screams ceased.

In an instant, everything came back to normal: Joel could see and hear all around himself once more.

"On second thought, methinks I'll be keepin' this fer myself..." Alistair said with a hint of nervousness in his voice.

Joel breathed a sigh of relief.

"You should try to collect some black gold for yerself, Joel," Henic said. "Your protest of it is silly. It'll make you a target to Wolfgang, and maybe some of the others. We've all collected the ores, and we're fine. Yer mind's playin' tricks on you, m'boy."

Joel shook his head and readjusted his mining helmet. Alistair and Henic looked at each other with concerned expressions before the big man shrugged.

"More for us, then!"

∼

BACK IN THE FIRST CAVE, Lucia grew restless. She swung her pickaxe harder with each strike. The loud *clunks* irritated her further; a reminder that every passing moment was another that her former mentor could be suffering.

Finally, she dropped her pickaxe and said, "I have waited for long enough. I'm going to find Dalton."

She began to walk away, not expecting Conrad to follow, but she was surprised to hear his tepid footsteps behind her.

"Wait!" he whispered harshly. She paused and glared back at him over her shoulder. "Consider the consequences, first. Faramond and his group may return. As a matter of fact, shouldn't we try to find him and our friends before anything else?"

"Sorry, but I have known Dalton for longer, and I owe him too much. I won't sit back and let him rot in a place like this," she said.

"But he could be fine-"

"He could be, but I'm not leaving it to chance. They have been here a long time. Their supplies must be dwindling. I'll go alone if I must," Lucia said before resuming her angry march toward Edith.

"Very well…" Conrad muttered.

Lucia snorted like a bull ready to charge when she reached Edith. The blonde beauty looked up at her with dull, bored eyes, and asked, "What do *you* want?"

"We have been ignoring our original objective for long enough," she said with impatience on her tongue. "I would like to venture out into the tunnels to find the first team."

"If a whole team is trapped in here, what makes you think that one person could make a difference?" Edith flipped her golden hair back and let out a crass chuckle. "No, we shall wait here until Faramond returns, just as he ordered."

Lucia frowned and said, "You obviously don't care about the other team or myself. Why not let me go?"

"I said no," she replied. "And that's my final word on the matter."

The mercenary stomped by Edith and said, "I'm going. That's *my* final word on the matter."

She strode toward the tunnel they had all entered yesterday, knowing that it was her best lead to Dalton's location. If she explored the tunnel beyond where they had found Ollie's corpse, she was sure to find the first team.

While walking, she could hear the chatter of other miners. A part of Lucia hoped some would follow her, but none did. Not even Conrad was by her side. Perhaps she was committing a blunder? There was likely a good reason that the first team hadn't returned, after all. Lucia shook the self-doubt out of her mind. She had to find Dalton and fight by his side if need be. She had to make amends.

Then, out of the corner of her eye, Lucia saw a glimmer; not of the black gold, but of a weapon. Her years of battle instincts kicked in and she rolled to her right on the ground, after which she heard a loud *clang* behind her.

Down on one knee, she looked up to see a grinning Wolfgang raise his pickaxe for a second strike. The blond brute laughed hysterically as he ran toward her and started a downward swing of his tool. In response, Lucia planted a hand on the ground and twisted sideways as she threw a kick that connected with his gut like a battering ram on a door.

Wolfgang gasped and stumbled backward, but remained on his feet. Lucia stood and drew out her claymore while he panted and held onto his stomach.

"You've been asking for this," she said, inching closer with her blade held outward in both hands.

He laughed once more. "Ye've more to worry about than me…"

Lucia darted her eyes to the left to see Angus looming over her with his pickaxe ready to strike. Before she could turn to face him, the giant brought down his axe with ferocious speed. She attempted to move her claymore into blocking position, but she had been caught unprepared with a heavy weapon and was certain that it wouldn't make it in time to block.

In the split-second she had given up hope, however, Lucia noticed Angus' swing had gone off course, and by flexing her upper body to the right, was able to narrowly avoid a hit. She cartwheeled after the dodge and then spun to face the giant, who winced in pain.

It was only then that she noticed Conrad had intervened: His rapier was sticking into Angus' right leg. Conrad pulled the blade out and said, "Leave now; while you're still being shown mercy."

Angus brought a hand to the fresh wound, and blood seeped through his fingers. He turned his gaze to Bronrar, who only looked away in response. With a grimace, he looked to Wolfgang, who smiled back at him. There was bloodlust written all over his face.

In that instant, Wolfgang leaped out at Lucia, pickaxe raised over his head. She swiftly curved her blade in an arced motion as he brought his axe down. Using the explosive power in her legs, she turned and swung the claymore. It cut through the wooden base, and the axe head fell to the ground with a loud *clang*.

Without hesitation, Lucia brought the mighty claymore overhead for a decisive downward slash. Wolfgang's jaw hung open and his eyes widened. *There's the look,* she thought; the familiar expression of fear. It was a paralyzing fear of what her giant claymore would do to his fleshy, mortal body when inevitable contact was made. It had won her many battles in recent years.

She brought the blade down with as much force as she could muster, but in the moments before it reached its target, Lucia was surprised to see Wolfgang licking his lips and grinning.

He rolled on the ground to his left, and the claymore *clanked* loudly off the rock. Lucia used the momentum from her heavy swing bouncing up to bring it back into attacking position. She pursued him with long strides as he scrambled. Soon, he turned over onto his bottom and looked up at her with a smile. She had the tip of the blade near his face.

"Well… what are ye waitin' for?" Wolfgang asked. His expression hadn't changed, and it gave Lucia pause. How could he have been unafraid? Even the bravest of her opponents in the past had flinched before the last blow.

The mercenary raised her great claymore once again, but then she heard a voice call out, "What do you think you're doing?"

Lucia lowered her blade and darted her eyes to the right to see a cross-armed Edith standing beside Angus. She then quickly returned her gaze to Wolfgang and pointed the claymore at him. Even a moment of not paying attention to him was dangerous, she thought.

"First, you disobeyed my direct orders, and now you are picking fights with the other miners?" Edith asked. Her loud voice echoed off of the cave walls.

A small group of miners had already been watching the conflict, but it appeared that Edith now had everyone's attention.

"And *you*," she said, pointing at Conrad and gesturing with the other hand toward Angus. "I saw it all. You wounded this man, simply for attempting to protect his friend."

Bronrar scoffed in the background. The other miners gathered around the scene and chatter began to pick up.

"Why are they makin' trouble when we've got all this precious metal here fer everyone?" one asked.

"That lot are outcasts fer sure," another said.

"There's no place fer that kind of horseplay in the mines!" a worker complained.

Lucia withdrew her claymore; it had only just occurred to her how incriminated she appeared with a blade pointed at a defenseless man.

"If I had a *real* weapon, ye'd be dead right now…" Wolfgang muttered as he hopped to his feet. The same sinister smile remained on his face.

"They're a dangerous lot!" one miner called out.

"They should be kicked outta here!" another said.

Edith's smile turned to a devilish grin. Conrad looked over to Bronrar, but the nervous miner avoided eye contact. *Of course* he'd be useless in this situation, Lucia thought.

Just when all looked dire, however, one miner said, "I saw the whole thing!" The attention of all turned to a scruffy, dark-haired man. "And I'll tell ya right now, that feller over there attacked the young lady first!"

He pointed at Wolfgang. The blond brute's smile turned to a frown. Lucia nodded. The small group of miners who'd been watching her leave earlier had seen everything. Edith and her goons would soon be exposed, she thought. Arguments started breaking out amongst the miners.

❧

Faramond's group continued down the tunnel path. The clicking noises had quieted, and the shrieking had stopped. There was a collective sense of ease about the miners, aside from Joel, who feared that the black gold had overtaken his friends' minds. If even the brutality of Mt. Couture couldn't snap them out of their trance, then what could?

However, the group acted normally for the time being: Faramond returned to his more cautious ways, Alistair continued to speak louder than necessary, and Henic went back to keeping his head down. Even still, the mute knew that their earlier shift in behavior had only been a precursor of the horrors to come, and he felt powerless to stop it. If only Aldous were there, he thought.

To distract himself, Joel buried his nose back in his map. The way he had drawn it out, he believed that they were close to reaching the lit-up cave from earlier. There was some guesswork involved, however. Most maps only took into account length and width, but in Mt. Couture, Joel was forced to think of depth, too. Different paths could be at different heights, widths, and depths, and might greatly affect the direction they were traveling. It was difficult to translate such things to paper.

Yet still, after a short time at the group's brisk pace, they found themselves back in the lit-up cave. The blue lights were dimming, but the area contained all of the artifacts that the group remembered. Faramond stared blankly at Joel in silence for a few moments before a smile came to his face.

"It seems that I owe you an apology," he said, shifting his gaze to the tunnel on their immediate left. "Although you are misguided with regards to the black gold, your heart is in the right place. I would be honored if you stayed with us and continued work on your map of the mountain."

Joel nodded back with a rigid expression. Faramond's taste for the black gold still worried him. He looked around to see the other miners' smiling faces. They were happy with him now, but it wouldn't last, he thought.

"There is little time to waste, gentlemen," Faramond said as he walked ahead to the front of the tunnel. "Let's get back to our team and regroup!"

The miners let out a small cheer as they traveled along the tunnel's fading light.

IN THE CAVE AHEAD, the situation had spiraled out of control, and a mutiny was about to break out. Several miners appeared ready to come to blows. On one side were Edith and her followers who had been swayed by a mixture of fear and Faramond's orders. On the other side were Conrad, Lucia, and the group of miners who had witnessed the truth. Although they were outnumbered, they could still make a splash.

"I'll give you lot one more chance to side with the *right* people," Edith said with a frown.

The other miners crossed their arms in response, and Conrad said, "We have mined plenty of black gold. Shouldn't we get back to looking for the first team? Our brethren may be dying in here."

"Yeah!" some miners shouted.

"We stay here. Faramond's orders," Edith said with shortness in her tone.

"Do you care that the tunnel collapse happened? And that Faramond and his group haven't returned since then?" Lucia asked.

"It hasn't been long. Give him time," Edith replied. The impatience in her voice grew with each word.

An eruption of grumbling came from the miners. Wolfgang and Angus had retreated behind their new leader. The giant wrapped his leg tightly with a cloth to stop the bleeding from his stab wound.

The miners became rowdier, but the tides were turning. Edith began to sweat profusely as some men switched to Conrad and Lucia's side.

"It would seem your fear-based tactics could only work for so long," Conrad said with a smirk.

Edith became red in the face and said, "If you side with them, you side against your leader. It makes you a traitor to Faiwell. And traitors will be dealt with!"

The blonde beauty turned back to the remaining miners and motioned them forward. Lucia held out her claymore in a readied position with a grin.

"When we break through, I get the first hit on Edith," she said.

Conrad fought back some laughs. Still wanting to be diplomatic, he kept the rapier sheathed at his side.

"There's no need to-"

"These people would rather fumble about in the mines than save our precious village. Think of your families... your friends!" Edith called out as the miners on her side advanced.

Both sides readied their weapons and pickaxes. They were only a few paces from each other, and there was a feeling in the air that even the slightest hint of aggression would signal the beginnings of a bloody battle.

"And if they don't want to save our village, our family, our friends... then, they don't deserve to *live*!" Edith cried as Wolfgang barged through to the front of his group. He had obtained another pickaxe in the confusion.

"Any one of ye, come at me if ye've got the guts!" the blond brute said with a confident smile.

Lucia inched her way toward him with the claymore held outward. Several of the other miners followed suit. Conrad's mind scrambled for something; anything to avoid this fight. It wouldn't help anyone to kill each other, he thought.

"That won't be necessary!"

Edith and her group turned around to see Faramond and his men lumbering toward them. Conrad looked on in wonder as many of the miners' anger and aggression turned to smiles and visible relief. Their true leader had such an effect on their morale that they were immediately able to put aside their differences.

As he walked up to his second-in-command, Faramond tilted his head and said, "It would seem you let things get out of hand." Edith darted her eyes to the floor and her mouth quivered. "But I have no right to judge. For you see, things got out of hand for us, too."

The miners began to notice the missing men from Faramond's group. Mild panic set in for some of the men, who couldn't find their friends. To explain it all, he decided to hold a briefing right there and then.

He first explained the vile nature of knockers, how they had caused the tunnel collapse, and advised all who heard light clicking noises and screeches in the walls to report it immediately. He then detailed the explosive mushrooms and informed his crew to be on the lookout for anything on the ground from now on.

Next, he explained how Joel had saved the group with his hunch on the explosive mushrooms, and general knowledge of the tunnel layouts. He commanded his crew to assist the mute in any way possible while working on his map of the mines.

Afterward, Edith told the tale of how the collapse in the tunnel had killed a man, while quakes from the explosive mushrooms had caused large rocks to fall from the ceiling and crushed two others to death. Conrad wanted to contest that it had actually been Wolfgang committing murder, but he kept his word to Bronrar and held his tongue. Lucia did the same, although the strategist suspected it was for reasons of her own: She had a score to settle with him.

After the briefing, Faramond declared it to be a lunch break and said they would discuss what to do after everyone had eaten. Although the recent deaths had made everyone uneasy, there was a sense of hopefulness in the air. Their leader had returned, and no further violence ensued when the situation easily could have been plunged into chaos.

However, the tears at the seams were beginning to show, from Conrad's perspective. He believed it was only a matter of time before Edith, Wolfgang, or the feuding miners tore down the order that their revered leader temporarily brought; unless he could fully expose Wolfgang and Edith for their vile deeds. In the back of his mind were thoughts about what Joel had told him about black gold. Was their attachment to it natural? Or a sign of trouble to come? One thing he knew for sure was that if something didn't change, disaster was set to strike again, and soon.

CHAPTER 11
DRATAGON

As the miners ate lunch, Joel, Alistair, and Henic took the time to catch up with Lucia and Conrad. There was a new understanding among the group: Mt. Couture was living up to its infamous reputation. In one disastrous hour, the B-Team had gone from 73 to 57 miners, and as Faramond had pointed out, they hadn't gotten very far into the mines.

"Explosive mushrooms…" Lucia trailed off, crinkling her nose. The others looked at her, inquisitively. "When I worked as a mercenary in Luneria, I had many encounters with criminals who operated out of the wild jungles of Maug. They stayed there because the explosive mushrooms native to the land provided a natural defense from authorities. Going there was considered suicide unless you were familiar with the layout. That was one of my toughest missions, come to think of it…" She looked up to see everyone leaning in with interest.

"I won't be going into detail," she said. The group let out a collective sigh. "But the point is that I was led to believe those mushrooms were unique to the Maug Jungles. What are they doing in a place like this?"

"Perhaps they have always grown here, too; and few people knew of it because of how dangerous the mines are," Conrad said before taking a bite out of his peach. "But I agree that it is peculiar. I can't think of many mushrooms that would grow in dug-up mines."

"Alright, alright! But what about tha knockers? Now we know they're real!" Alistair said with a child-like grin and shaking fists.

"You act as if that were a good thing…" Henic groaned.

Joel made hand signals in front of the group. Lucia looked at Conrad with sharpened eyes.

"Let me guess: He said that black gold is what we have to worry about?"

"More or less…" Conrad muttered with a half-hearted smile.

Lucia walked over to Joel and put a hand on his shoulder. She directed him to the right until his gaze met Wolfgang and his crew, who sat across the cave, eating.

"See them?" she asked, the sternness in her voice growing. Joel nodded. "They are the ones we truly need to worry about. Stop troubling your mind over pieces of metal and realize this: Those people over there are trying to *kill us*."

"Let 'em try!" Alistair cried while spewing crumbs from his mouth. "They can taste a piece of me axe!"

"I heard that you fought well against the knockers," Conrad said.

Lucia scoffed. "Fighting toddler-sized creatures is one thing. We'll see how you do against men who've had combat experience." Alistair grumbled, but before he could respond, she continued, "Yet, it looks like you may get your wish. At the next sign of a commotion or chaos, Wolfgang will try to kill again. I'm certain of it."

The group remained silent and got back to eating.

~

IN THE MIDDLE of the cave, Faramond and Edith butted heads over what course of action they should take next.

"I understand that you wish to save the others, Fara, but it has been *days* since they got here, and all we've found from their group is a corpse," she said.

"Exactly why we must act quickly," he replied with crossed arms. "This place seems to become more dangerous the deeper we delve into it. I can only imagine what *they've* encountered…"

The blonde beauty frowned and said, "You claim to have our group's safety as a top priority, but is that actually true? You could be leading us into a death trap."

With a raised eyebrow, Faramond said, "We all knew what we were getting into when we agreed to this trip. Don't try to place that blame on me. Everyone here *volunteered*, Edith. We will continue further into the mines in search of the first team. End of discussion."

Edith let out an exasperated sigh and stalked off toward Wolfgang and his crew. Faramond watched as she smiled at Wolfgang and playfully tugged on his arm. After some conversation he couldn't hear, she burst out with a happy laugh and put her hand on his cheek, caressing it. Wolfgang put his hand over hers and held on tight. She was flirting with him, he thought. Faramond's stomach felt like a sinking ship as he turned away in anger.

～

BACK ON THE other side of the cave, Conrad and Joel had walked away from the rest of the group briefly to discuss something: The unique medallion around the mute's neck.

"You entrusted me with this medallion yesterday; when you ventured into the Dead Woods," Conrad said while pointing at Joel's chest, where it hung. "I've never seen anything quite like it before, and the engravings on it appear to be in the ancient language."

Joel nodded in return.

"What do the engravings say?"

Shifting his eyes around, as if searching for his thoughts, Joel eventually made a couple of hand signals in response.

"'Greed'?"

Another nod.

"But why did you give it to me? What is its purpose?" Conrad asked.

The mute signed back and Conrad felt disappointment overtake him.

"We may need it later? Could you give me a little more to go on? I'm only trying to understand what you're thinking."

Joel shrugged and Conrad sighed. Whatever secrets he was keeping must have been iron-clad, he thought. It made him want to know the answers all the more. They walked back to the others, who were still eating.

Lucia whispered to Conrad, "Well? Did you get anything out of him?"

"Not much…" he muttered.

"Alright, everyone! Gather around!" They turned to see Faramond beckoning the team to the cave's center.

In short order, the other 56 miners gathered around their leader in a circle. Conrad noted that Edith chose not to join him in the middle, and stayed with Wolfgang and his crew instead. Could her earlier failure at leading the team have soured their relationship?

"We have obtained enough black gold ore to start. Excellent job, everyone!" he said. The miners chimed in with cheers. "With that said, we have the first team to consider as well. We have a duty to help them if they're in trouble…"

Chatter amongst the group picked up. It was a mixed reaction: Some sounded like they were in high spirits, while others grumbled angrily.

"For this reason, I have decided that we will resume our search for the first team," Faramond said. More chatter came from the crowd, and it turned into a mostly negative reaction. "After we sort everyone's earnings, we will return to the base camp outside and store them. Then, we shall venture back in to search for the others."

"We can't leave the black gold out of our sight! What if someone steals it?" one miner shouted.

"Yeah!" some collective shouts echoed around the cave.

"A fair point," Faramond said, crossing his arms. "In that case, we must appoint some of the most trustworthy of our group to guard everyone's earnings."

The groans and complaints calmed, but there was still unease in the air. The unpopularity of Faramond's decision was obvious; nearly everyone's spirit seemed to dampen.

"We will discuss this matter further upon returning to base camp," he said and then picked up his large sack of black gold. "Now then, gather your belongings and valuables so we can get to counting."

The grumbling continued, but the miners listened and grabbed their things, regardless. Faramond enlisted the expertise of Conrad to count and divide up the black gold ore. As was standard of the Miner's Guild, 60% of whatever was recovered from an expedition went to the guild, while the rest was for the workers to keep.

In their home country of Federland, each settlement was not required to pay the governing body unless in a time of war. Instead, the government was made up of one representative for each settlement who made important decisions regarding the safety of the country. The only other elected official of the land was the Grand Chancellor, who oversaw all decisions made and led an army if the situation called for it. All of these officials, regardless of who they were or how much power they commanded, were required to have served at least two years in the Federland army. The requirements for Grand Chancellor were even stricter, as only those who had reached and held the rank of General for at least five years were eligible.

The hands-off approach of the Federland government, while allowing settlements to do as they pleased, also meant they were on their own when it came to solving internal problems. There was no rescue coming for Faiwell if the shortage of precious metals were to cause a famine. That was one reason why the Village Elders had been quick to accept Drake Danvers' proposal of the Mt. Couture expedition.

With the help of Conrad, it didn't take long to divide up the Mining Guild's profits, which were stored in the large carts for men to push. It wasn't as simple as dividing up the black gold, either. They had to estimate its value compared to other materials like gold, silver, and copper; which had also been mined off the walls; albeit less frequently. Conrad, Faramond, and Edith eventually agreed that black gold would be even more valuable than gold.

After settling the Mining Guild's profits, workers gathered their remaining ore, stored it in brown sacks, and lugged it over their shoulders. They began to form rank, as had been established earlier in the day: Lucia, Alistair, Bronrar, and a couple of others guarded the front, while Faramond, Edith, and Conrad remained just behind them in line. Toward the end were Joel and Henic, who were now protected by fewer rear guards than before.

FARAMOND WAS PLEASANTLY surprised that not one incident occurred in the half hour it had taken them to reach the Mouth of Hell. He did, however, take the time to reflect and consider his options moving forward. The leader was beginning to wonder if he should take a small team back with him to recover and bury the fallen when he felt the nudge of an elbow.

Warm feelings blanketed him as he looked to see it had been Edith. However, his hopefulness morphed into dread upon realizing that she was looking straight ahead and didn't pay him any mind. She was still angry with him, but he was sure it would fade over time.

Within the hour, everyone had their correct shares stored with their belongings at the base camp. The tricky part was deciding who would guard it, so Faramond called yet another meeting.

"I thank you all for your patience. Now, on the matter of who will stand guard of our findings..." he trailed off while looking through the crowd.

Several volunteers stepped up, to Faramond's lack of surprise. He realized that his decision to stop mining and look for the first team had little popularity. He could hardly blame them, having gotten a taste of the precious black gold for himself.

Among the first volunteers to stay behind was Wolfgang, who smiled at his leader and said, "With my combat experience, I'd be a trusty and fearsome guard of the treasures, sir."

Faramond raised an eyebrow and then scowled. "No, Wolfgang. You've proven that you need supervision, so you shall along with me into the mines."

Wolfgang grimaced before smiling again and bowing his head.

"Conrad!" Faramond called out. The strategist's eyes widened. "I am appointing you as temporary leader of this base camp. Earlier, when that fight was about to break out, I noticed your call for cooler heads to prevail. You are trustworthy and good with money. As I understand it, you also have combat experience. You will make for a fine leader."

Angus scoffed, but he didn't speak up.

When it was all said and done, Faramond had assigned 15 miners total to stay back and watch the black gold ore. Among the 15 were Conrad and Henic, while the additional 41 were to accompany him back into the mines.

FURTHER BACK IN the base camp, Conrad approached Lucia. She was staring off into the clouds, which had finally begun to part. The sun peeked through enough to shine down, and the crescent around her right eye gleamed in its light. She turned to face him.

"Problem?" she asked in a grumpy tone.

"I-erm..." he muttered. "I was curious about that crescent moon tattoo around your eye. What is its meaning?"

"You may just be the most inquisitive man I've ever met," Lucia said with a chuckle, but then her face turned to stone. "I wonder if someday, that curiosity will come back to bite you."

He rubbed the back of his head. "If you'd prefer not to talk about it-"

"No, I want to tell you," she replied. "Do you know how the country of Luneria got its name?"

"Nightfall happens earlier and more frequently there than in any other place in the world, correct?" Conrad said.

"*Of course* you would know," Lucia said while rolling her eyes. "In Luneria, if you are a foreigner who wishes to make good money, your best chances lie in working directly for the king. As it turned out, he needed mercenaries to hunt down and protect him from the blood-thirsty rebels of the south. You see, his rule was questioned and challenged by these people. Some even infiltrated his personal guard in attempts to assassinate him."

"I can imagine such experiences would leave him paranoid."

"That's an understatement," she replied with a laugh. "Mercenaries must first prove their loyalty to the crown through a series of trials, the final one being a ceremony where you bear the mark of the moon."

"Ah, so you passed the trials and were forced into it, then," Conrad said.

"Not exactly." Lucia wagged her index finger. "I was a weak little girl at age 14. Dalton taught me the basics of swordplay and much of my technique, but I lacked the strength to follow through. I failed the trials an uncountable number of times, but I never gave up. That would have meant returning home, and back then, I was determined to become my own woman."

Conrad raised an eyebrow and said, "If that's the case, how did you end up obtaining the mark of the moon?"

"Eventually, the king approached me and said I should give up. He had no use for weak hired hands, after all," she said, looking down. "But I refused. Instead, I begged for him to bless me with the mark. I told him that I would do anything…"

"And?"

"And he agreed, but only on one condition. You see, the mark of the moon normally doesn't *have* to be tattooed on your face like this," Lucia said, tracing its outline with her finger. "Most people choose to have the tattoo placed on a part of their body that can be hidden by clothing. Bearing the mark makes you a target of the rebels and crime lords in Luneria, after all. Since the good king questioned my strength, but not my loyalty; he reasoned that if I could survive with the mark on my face for everyone to see, it would mean I was strong enough."

"Fascinating..."

"Within an hour of leaving the castle after my ceremony, I was attacked in plain daylight out in the streets. And it was far from the last time I would be attacked. I quickly learned how weak I was, but the truth is..." she trailed off as a smile grew on her face. "It was the key to making me stronger. I had help along the way, too, but wearing this mark of the moon for all to see was where it all began."

"Impressive. You must have been looking over your shoulder at all times to survive something like that," Conrad said.

"Yes, it was tough at first. There were a few times where I nearly died, but after a year or two, I started to turn the tables on my attackers, and I eventually became one of the king's top mercenaries," Lucia said. "Care to guess how I accomplished that?"

The strategist smirked. "The claymore?"

"In a manner of speaking, yes," she replied with a snort. "My first kill as a mercenary was the beheading of an infamous rebel. It only happened because he underestimated me. From that battle, I learned a valuable lesson: No matter how great of a warrior you might be, you can always lose; even to an amateur. One slip-up is all it takes."

"Hence, your preference to strike fear into an opponent."

"Precisely. Since I became blessed with unnatural height and a reputation for beheading rebels over the years, my targets began to fear me. I added the oversized claymore to my repertoire to further sway opponents into making mistakes or simply turning themselves over peacefully. I'd say that more than half of my rewards collected were from rebels who surrendered without even raising their sword at me."

She breathed a sigh and stared blankly ahead. Conrad cleared his throat. "But Wolfgang is different."

"You read my mind," Lucia said with a furrowed brow. "Even the wildest of my opponents, the ravenous rebels of Maug, showed fear when I cornered them with the claymore; but not Wolfgang. I don't think he's afraid to die."

"Which is why you need a lighter weapon. He kept on dodging your heavy swings. A more traditional blade would have tagged him."

"Don't forget that I had him beaten, and it was only Edith's interference that stopped me from striking the final blow," she replied, pointing at him. "And while I do appreciate your assistance with Angus, you cannot leave it to chance when it comes to fighting a killer. You should have stabbed him in the chest instead of the leg."

"It got the job done," he said.

"Next time, it might not. When someone acts like they want to kill you, believe them. Show them no mercy," Lucia replied.

Conrad turned to see Wolfgang and his crew, chatting by his big tent. "You're the one who will have to worry about them."

"True, but it's still a philosophy that you should consider. I noticed that some of the men you'll be leading were on *Edith's side*, back in the cave. Just be careful…"

"You as well. I only wish I could go in there with you. Wolfgang will surely try to kill again when under a veil of darkness."

"You have better things to do, anyway," Lucia said, putting hands to her hips. "I'm sure you'd make a better second-in-command to Faramond than Edith… and if you do well out here, that may come to pass."

"Even still…" Conrad muttered. "We promised to look out for one another. With the speed of my rapier and the killing power of your claymore, we could thwart Wolfgang and Angus."

"Yes, I think our combined strategies would complement each other well. It's a shame we won't get to test that out anytime soon," Lucia said before shrugging. "But if all else fails, I can use Alistair as a meat-shield."

They both burst out laughing.

"Be sure to keep an eye on Joel, too. I think he knows far more than he's been letting on," Conrad added. "He could be helpful."

"Well, his advice about the black gold was wrong, but he seems to have a talent for map-making," Lucia replied. "I'll be sure to indulge him… to the best of my abilities. I don't know USL."

"Thank you. Good luck in there."

"And to you as well," the mercenary said before striding over toward Faramond's group.

NEAR THE ENTRANCE to the mines, Henic and Alistair were having a chat of their own.

"I hate to ask too much of you, but you seem like you've got a knack for swingin' an axe…" Henic said. Alistair smiled from cheek to cheek. His chest swelled with pride that he could be thought of as a warrior, even with such little battle experience. "But could you keep an eye on Joel? Keep 'im safe? The lad's drawin' too much attention to himself by speaking out against the black gold, and that makes him a prime target for Wolfgang."

"Say no more!" Alistair replied heartily. Some other miners were startled by the noise, but they soon went back to their business while grumbling. "With me trusty battle axe, I'll cut down anyone or anythin' that dares to lay a finger on the lad!"

"I appreciate it," Henic said as he slapped him on the shoulder. "And while yer at it, see if you can get it through his thick skull that black gold is gonna make him filthy rich!"

The two men laughed in unison.

Faramond's group lined up similarly to before, albeit with less manpower. Alistair and Lucia served as front guards once again, now with only two others up front with them. Faramond and Edith were right behind them to see what was going on. Toward the middle of the pack were Wolfgang and Angus, with Joel not being too far behind them. Trailing Joel was Bronrar, who had been moved to rear guard duty along with three other men. There were 42 in total, which felt sufficient to Alistair's eyes, even if a bit less secure. After all, it had only taken nine of them to fight off the knockers when they had been prepared to fight.

"Alright, everyone!" Faramond called out. "We shall return by nightfall, with or without the first team. If we are not back by then, something may have gone wrong...."

"And in that case, I would ask that some of you come in to help us, but it is *not* a requirement," the leader said to the gasps of a few others in the crowd. "It may well be wiser to turn tail and go home with your share of the spoils. But as your leader, I simply *ask* that you come to our aid, should we need it. I would do the same for you all."

All around remained quiet for some time before he broke the silence and continued, "With that said, I'm hopeful that we'll find the first team and return with more help than ever; which means more black gold, my friends. Farewell!"

Alistair and the other front guards marched once more into the Mouth of Hell. The other miners followed along, as they always did, into the darkness.

For the fifth time, the group heard light clicking noises as they walked through the first tunnel. Alistair growled while gripping the handle of his battle axe.

"Those lil' buggers are *still* in the walls?" he asked before raising his fist. "Come out and fight me, ya cowards!"

"Quit embarrassing yourself," Lucia said.

"What?" the big man asked while shrugging. "There's plenty more of 'em, lass. Trust me. We're eventually gonna have'ta fight 'em!"

"Haven't you noticed that they stay away from some parts of the mines?" she replied. Alistair tilted his head. She was right. "It probably means that they are hiding from something much worse…"

"Well, it ain't hard to be prey when yer a wee 'lil rodent! What hunts them, I wonder?" he asked aloud in feigned curiosity. "Oh! Maybe it's the next step up: a badger!" He burst out laughing.

Lucia rolled her eyes. "Just be ready. Between the killers in our midst and the dangers of Mt. Couture, something bad is going to happen… I can feel it."

BEHIND ALISTAIR AND LUCIA, Faramond was doing his best to appeal to Edith.

"You must realize that as a leader, I have many difficult decisions to make," he said. She darted her eyes away from him and pouted. "We did some mining and obtained our prize: the black gold. Now, it is time to help our friends."

Edith frowned. "And yet, you know that in your heart, it is not enough to save the village."

"It's a start."

"You're missing the bigger picture," the blonde beauty said while crossing her arms. "You prioritize 50 people over *thousands*."

"Just because we're not mining *now*, doesn't mean we'll never mine at all," Faramond said.

"It seems like you don't value my opinion as your second-in-command, so why not appoint someone else?" Edith asked with a snarl. She slowed her walk and began falling behind.

"I do value your opinion," he said. Edith smiled and tried her hardest not to laugh. It was all too easy. She sped back up to match Faramond's pace again. "Please, go along with it for a little while longer. If we don't find the first team today… we can get back to mining tomorrow; and for the entire day."

Edith let out an exasperated sigh and said, "Fine. You win, Fara."

Once again, she found it hard not to burst out in laughter. Without Conrad there to challenge her, Faramond was eating out of the palm of her hand.

The group continued through the tunnel, and once again reached the cave where the lighting system resided. This time, they opted not to light the torches, for they knew exactly where to go. They walked straight for another half hour through the cave filled with black gold and continued forward at the fork in the path, until reaching the point where they had found Ollie the day before. The glowing bulbs continued ahead as far as the eye could see in the darkness. The smell of rotting flesh once again permeated the air, which filled the group with buckets of unease.

"Oi! Joel! Where are ya?" Alistair called back to the group. "Quiet lil' bugger… I'm supposed ta be keepin' an eye on ya! Come up here!"

"Excuse me!" Edith interjected like a scolding mother. "But there will be *no* falling out of rank on this journey. Joel needs to stay where he is."

"What does it matter if the lad is up front with us?" Alistair asked.

"This is why we don't pay you to think, big-head," she replied. Alistair groaned. "Front guards are supposed to protect the entire group. I won't have you getting distracted to protect one person. The rear guards will look after him."

Alistair cast his gaze at Faramond. There was hope in his eyes, but Edith was confident that she had guilt-tripped Faramond into agreeing with her every word, as long as it was within reason.

"Edith is correct. He'll need to stay back there, where he was assigned," he replied

Lucia looked back and scowled at the blonde beauty, but offered no words. Alistair's big mouth may as well have painted a bright target on the quiet boy's back, Edith thought with a grin. She wondered if he would cry aloud when Wolfgang finally got him. Or would he suffer in silence?

∽

NEAR THE BACK of the line, Joel was attempting to brush past the other miners to see what Alistair had been calling out to him for. However, he found himself blocked by Wolfgang and Angus, who continued to move to each side that Joel tried to slip past them. The blond brute looked back and smiled devilishly.

"Where do ye think yer goin'?" he asked. Joel sharpened his eyes and pointed ahead.

"So, yer tryin' to break rank?" Wolfgang asked. Joel nodded. "Ye truly are one of the most useless people I've ever met, boy. First, ye get a simple map wrong, then ye won't fight back when yer life is on the line, next ye don't even grab the black gold that was sittin' right at yer feet, and now yer tryin' to break rank? The simplest rule we have..."

Joel's face turned red as the two men laughed.

"The Miner's Guild must truly be desperate to take a scrub like him," Angus chimed in. Joel noticed that he continued to limp from the stab wound Conrad had inflicted on him. He pointed at the bloody fabric wrapped around his leg and smirked.

"Hm? So, you think it funny that I was stabbed?" Angus asked, still monotone; but now he was grimacing. He rubbed his leg tenderly. "Your friend did this to me... he is lucky to have stayed behind, or I would have snapped him in two while we were in here."

"Not that he'll live much longer, anyway," Wolfgang said as a sick smile grew on his face. He chuckled but held back full laughter. Joel could feel the madness bubbling at the surface, ready to burst out of him. At any moment, he might lash out. "Ye and yer friends are as good as dead. I'll see to it personally."

He shoved Joel, and the mute found himself toward the back of the line once again. His head sank in disappointment. It felt lonely near the back without Henic there, even if he didn't understand Universal Sign Language.

"Don't bother tryin' to get by those two..." Joel heard a voice murmur from behind. He looked back to see Bronrar staring at him through the dimming light of his torch. "Once Wolfgang has his mind set on somethin', it happens. Believe me."

Although it was a long shot, Joel attempted some hand signals before Bronrar, hoping he would understand. The nervous miner's face lit up when he saw them, but then swiftly turned to a frown.

"I am *not* a slug-head!" he replied. Joel raised an eyebrow and shook his head.

"Oh, my apologies. I learned USL years ago. Seems I've forgotten more of it than I realized. Could you give me a refresher?" Bronrar asked. Joel shook his head again.

"Ah, right... you don't talk..." Bronrar trailed off. An inaudible sigh escaped the mute's lips. "Erm, anyway, steer clear of Wolfgang. Angus ain't a bad guy once you get to know him, though."

Next, Joel mimed a shoulder tackling motion and pointed at Wolfgang and Angus. Bronrar's eyes widened.

"Are you mad? No way can we barge through 'em..."

Joel frowned. Yet, as they continued, it seemed that changes in the landscape would give him hope to escape Wolfgang's clutches. The path was widening.

Soon, the tunnel became a cave; by far the largest one they'd been in so far. There were no dark, sparkling metals like in the previous cave, but there was a dim light shining down from the ceiling, which hinted at how truly massive the area was. Joel estimated that the roof might be up in the clouds and that the other side of the cave would have been at least a quarter of Faiwell's total length, end-to-end.

Although light shined through a hole in the ceiling, much of the cave remained shrouded in darkness. Some oddly shaped rock spikes hung from the roof, but otherwise, it appeared barren. Joel's gaze waded through the crowd. Up ahead, it seemed that the glowing bulbs had come to an end.

"Let's continue forward, to that light in the center," Faramond said. "Be on the lookout for mushrooms or anything that seems out of the ordinary."

Most of the group nodded at Faramond's command and continued forward, but Joel had other plans. He looked back at Bronrar and mimed himself sneaking, before pointing at Wolfgang and Angus. It was plausible this time, as the cave was vast. There was no way that they could block him.

Bronrar shook his head and said, "No, stay back here... I'm tellin' you, Wolfgang is actin' crazier than usual... he may *kill you* if you disobey him..."

Joel ignored his advice and increased his pace. He took an arced path along the left of the group, hoping to sneak by slowly but surely. As the miners approached the light at the center, Joel was about level with where Wolfgang and Angus were, albeit far to their left. Suddenly, Wolfgang's eyes darted in his direction.

"Ye little weasel! I caught ye!" the blond brute shouted out as he lunged at and tackled Joel to the ground.

Wolfgang straddled Joel and began pounding him over the head as he laughed aloud. The mute did his best to block, but he returned no attacks of his own. Out of the corner of his eye, he could see nearby miners watching. None were willing to cross the crazed man.

"When are ye gonna defend yerself, boy?" Wolfgang shouted while taking another swing at his bloodied face. "If ye can't stop little ol' me, then how are ye gonna survive anything else in here?" he asked, then took another clubbing swing. "Ye've disrespected me for the last time! I'm gonna put ye out of yer misery!"

Joel tightened his fists, but he did not raise them. He needed to survive, for only he knew of the black gold's vile purpose. Yet, he couldn't bring himself to fight back against his attacker. The thought made him sick to his stomach. All he could do was wait and hope for a rescue.

～

WOLFGANG'S OUTBURST had echoed throughout the cave and caught the attention of everyone in the group. Lucia and Alistair had nearly reached the center when they heard the commotion and rushed back to investigate. Although he had recognized Wolfgang's voice, Faramond ignored it and continued into the center.

He looked up to see the blue sky shining through the hole in the roof. He then surveyed the landscape. To his immediate left, far off, he could barely make out a new tunnel opening. No bulbs led in that direction, however. The leader searched around at all other angles, but nothing else save dark, rocky terrain revealed itself to him.

Faramond closed his eyes and focused his ears. Outside of the commotion, which was starting to become a hindrance, he was almost certain that some other noise was being drowned out. That was when he heard it again:

Rrrirp

Rrrirp

Rrrirp

He cocked his head. "What was that?"

The noises grew louder. It was like a cat purring and a bird chirping: High pitched, yet soft all at once. An odd contradiction, he thought. Could it have been birds outside the hole in the ceiling? The noise seemed too close for that. He scanned the roof and found nothing but the oddly shaped, sharp rocks. Everything about the area seemed typical for a cave, in fact, but something nagged Faramond that he couldn't quite put his finger on.

～

Wolfgang wound up for his greatest clubbing blow yet, when, from his right, Alistair pounced and punted him off. Wolfgang could only stay doubled over, clutching his stomach as he gasped for air.

"Hah! Let that be a lesson to ya!" Alistair bellowed as he knelt to see that behind the blood and welts, Joel's face looked back up at him, smiling. *The lad's mad,* he thought, opening his mouth; but before he could say anything, Joel motioned to his side. The big man looked up to see a limping Angus charging at him.

"You again? How's about ya taste a piece of me trusty axe!" he said while detaching the weapon from his side. He was too slow, however, as Angus planted a gnarly shoulder tackle into his chest before he could ready it.

Alistair tumbled over and began to gasp for air himself.

"Yer fortunate that I have a leg injury. I am only at half-strength," Angus said. Alistair looked up at him with bloodshot eyes, coughing. "How did you like my grappling hold, yesterday? How about I apply it once more?"

Lucia was next to join the fray, and though Angus had noticed her lengthy strides and turned to intercept her; she was already in the process of throwing a kick while at top speed. He could only watch as her boot landed with a *thud*, right where Conrad had wounded him on his leg. The giant stumbled back while grasping his leg and wincing. He fell to a knee and looked up at Lucia with narrowed eyes.

"That was a cheap shot..." he muttered.

"So was your attack on the big mouth," Lucia said while pointing a thumb back at Alistair. The big man wanted to retort, but he was too busy catching his breath.

Wolfgang jumped to his feet and said, "Ye bitch! I'll take care of ye in short order, this time!"

He unstrapped his pickaxe and unhinged laughter escaped his lips. However, as his crazed cackles bounced off the cave walls, Alistair heard something odd.

Rrrirp

He could see that Lucia was looking around, now. She had to have heard it, too, but there wasn't time to pay it any mind, as now Wolfgang was charging straight at her. She unsheathed her claymore and readied it the best she could, but just as suddenly as he had gotten going, Wolfgang stumbled and fell flat on his face. Alistair looked across from him with wide eyes to see that Joel had tripped him up. Between his wheezing, he began to laugh.

"Nice one," Lucia said as Wolfgang dislodged his bloody face from the unforgiving cave rocks and glared at Joel. She pointed the tip of her blade into the blond brute's neck, and he froze in place.

"Ye lot… I'm gonna kill ye all!" he cried.

Rrrirp

"Quiet! All of you!" Faramond called out from the cave's center.

Rrrirp

"Does anyone else hear that noise?" he asked. No one had a response for him.

A sense of unease enveloped the miners, except for Alistair, who was relieved that he hadn't been the only one to hear that odd noise. Yet, it bothered him all the same. It was all-encompassing but quiet. He couldn't figure out what direction it was coming from.

Then, while looking into the crowd of miners, he saw one of the men ascending rapidly; like he was flying away. The worker let out a panicked cry before disappearing into the unforgiving darkness.

"What the hell was that?" someone said

"Where did he go?" asked another.

❦

THE MEN BEGAN TO FRENZY, but Faramond froze into position and remained quiet; contemplative. Had something picked the worker up and flown away? A bat? A bird? None of it made sense. He looked down at the illuminated patch of ground while thinking, and that's when he noticed: A large, circular shadow was shrinking beneath him. With lightning-fast reflexes, Faramond dove ahead toward his group and heard a thundering *thud* behind him.

He looked up to see Edith staring at something, her mouth agape. Faramond stood and then turned to face his attacker. Before him was a giant, winged creature. It stood nearly as tall as a house, even while hunched over. The beast's large, squished-in nose, pointy ears, light brown fur, and narrow grayed-out eyes reminded Faramond of a bat. On the other hand, its long, spikey tail, massive claws at the end of its great wingspan, and jagged-toothed jaw reminded him of a dragon.

"A *dratagon*…" Faramond muttered with fright as the creature let out a piercing roar that managed to sound both low and high-pitched all at once.

Flapping noises echoed all around the cave. Faramond looked

above to see that *the rock spikes were moving*. They had been dratagons resting on the ceiling the entire time.

He shuddered as the beast before him inhaled through its gaping nostrils. In a panic, he rushed Edith from the side.

"Watch out!" Faramond cried as the dratagon breathed out two great fireballs from its nose. The leader felt the flames' heat graze his legs as he tackled Edith to the ground. He cradled her in his arms for protection from the fall.

"Are you alright?" he whispered, looking back to see that his legs had avoided contact with the fire.

"W-we've got to get out of here," she said with quivering lips.

The massive creature flew away upon missing its attack, but Faramond knew there was more to come. He could hear them flapping and shrieking above, and it sounded like there were many of them.

"Everyone! We're in the den of dratagons! We must hurry to the exit! Over here!" He pointed at the new tunnel on his right.

The panicked miners dashed for their leader, who himself started running for the tunnel. Edith followed close behind and held his hand tight. The shrieks and flapping grew louder and more plentiful with each stride taken by the group. Faramond looked back as he ran to see the winged monsters swooping down to pick off his men one by one. He halted and then struck a spark on his flint to light his torch ablaze. Next, he drew out his broadsword.

Edith ran past him and slowed down when she lost her grip on his hand. She looked back; her piercing green eyes demanding an explanation.

"Go on without me! I must help them!" he said. She nodded and continued at her fast pace ahead.

Faramond absorbed the chaos erupting around him. Before this expedition, he had prided himself on being the safest leader of the Miner's Guild. Now, he had seen over a dozen men die on his watch. *No more*, he thought, tightening the grip on his blade. If the safety of his remaining team meant that he had to die fighting the dratagons, then so be it.

CHAPTER 12
MASSACRE IN THE DARK

As the dratagon attack had begun, Wolfgang and Angus abandoned their skirmish and slipped into the crowd of frenzying miners. Alistair, Joel, and Lucia had been left in confusion.

"Oi! Tha hell is goin' on?" Alistair said.

"Dratagons… they are a cross-breed of dragons and bats," Lucia said before she looked up at the ceiling. "Back when wars were breaking out left and right, Federland would use them to raid enemy bases at night. They were effective, from what I've been told, but I thought they went extinct after the army stopped using them. We need to get moving."

She began jogging toward the tunnel that Faramond had pointed to. Alistair and Joel followed close behind.

"Well, why would we… stop usin' such powerful beasts?" Alistair asked between panting.

"They were too volatile. A bat can be tamed, but a dragon cannot. During the night, dratagons would often attack their caretakers as they slept. I suppose too much of its dragon nature shined through."

As they ran, Joel looked back and noticed that Bronrar was being swarmed by multiple dratagons. He remembered that the nervous miner had tried to give him helpful advice earlier, so he changed course and ran toward him without the others noticing.

When he reached the swarming dratagons, Joel lit his torch. The brightness of the flame distracted the monsters long enough for

Bronrar to scurry away. They must not have been completely blind like bats, he thought. The light may have confused them if anything. Joel then threw the torch as far as he could toward the opposite end of the cave. The dratagons took the bait and flew in the direction of the light source, to his relief.

Joel ran at full speed, eventually catching up with Bronrar and nudging him. He then pointed to the cave wall, where they could stop the winged beasts from swooping down on them by cutting off their angle. From there, they could comb the cave wall safely until they reached the tunnel.

"What? No! We've gotta get to the tunnel!" Bronrar said in a panicked tone.

Joel grunted in frustration and began to push him; steering him toward the cave wall as they ran.

"H-hey! Stop! How are you able to push me so easily?" he cried. Joel ignored his pleas.

Silhouettes of miners struggling against the swooping dratagons caught Joel's eye, but he dared not stop to observe. Pickaxes *clanging* and harrowing cries echoed among the dreaded flapping of massive wings and the beasts' odd calls to one another. He chanced a look back to find Faramond fighting off a dratagon with his shining broadsword close to the cave's center. Some others appeared to be successfully warding off the fell beasts with their pickaxes, and it gave him hope that they might escape with few casualties.

Close to the cave wall, Joel noticed that a dratagon was sweeping down on them. He tackled Bronrar and they came to a skidding halt, right up against the rocky wall. He heard a great *whoosh* overhead, followed soon by a screech that made his ears ring.

"You saved us..." Bronrar mumbled as he sat up, but Joel knew there was no time for pats on the back. Both of them stood and began to creep along the wall. Behind them, Joel heard a loud thud: One of the beasts had landed.

Thud

Thud

Thud

It was hopping toward them. Joel increased his pace without looking back but not too fast. He didn't want to alert any more dratagons frenzying in the cave. Bronrar, on the other hand, plodded along and began to pant. The mute looked back and put an index finger up to his lips. He gulped in some air and then fell silent.

To the duo's horror, they heard another loud *thud*, but this time, ahead of them on their path to the tunnel. Another dratagon had landed and began to screech wildly. Joel's eyes widened. The beast was winding up to swing its club-like tail. He pulled down on Bronrar's shoulder to make him duck. When they hit the ground, he heard a loud *whoosh* overhead and then a smashing impact at the cave wall. They both looked up to see small rocks sprinkled out onto them harmlessly, but there was little time to admire such a sight, as the dratagon behind them launched its attack next.

The beast jumped high up and landed so that it was looming over them. They crawled away, but the dratagon began to hop on one leg. It was trying to impale them with its spare claw, Joel thought. The pair rolled, in different directions, out of the way at the first strike; but it jumped a second time to bring down its claw again. This time, the two miners rolled together and the claw missed again.

Bronrar, from a knee, plunged his pickaxe into the monster's great foot as it loomed over them. It shrieked aloud and hopped backward in retreat. Joel and Bronrar returned to their feet.

"Now, he *has* to hop on one foot, eh?" Bronrar said with a snort. Joel smiled back at him, but the dratagon wouldn't be held off for long, and the beast that remained in front of them still had to be dealt with.

Joel did his best to mime the actions of lightning a torch; knowing that Bronrar struggled with USL.

"Oh, that's right. You used a torch to distract them before, didn't you?" he asked. Joel nodded emphatically. The dratagon in front of them was closing in with each hop.

Bronrar pulled out the old torch that was strapped to his belt and began to strike his flint rock with a small piece of iron. He attempted a few times, but was only able to get a couple of sparks; no flame came to his torch.

"Damn it… of all the times…" he mumbled while looking up and gasping at the sight of the dratagon winding up with its tail.

Joel pulled Bronrar back from behind as the clubbed tail flung in an arced motion. A spike on the tail hit the torch, breaking it in half. The tail finished by slamming into the cave wall, as it had earlier. A storm of small rocks flew at Joel and Bronrar, and they shielded their faces.

"Now what?" Bronrar asked as Joel looked behind them. The other dratagon had recovered and approached once more. Both were within striking distance and had the duo backed against the wall. Joel's mind raced, but it gave him no answers. The only thought coming to him was that he couldn't let it end here.

The winged beast to their left sucked in the air around its giant nostrils and leaned back. Joel knew that the monster was preparing to shoot fireballs at them. However, as it was bending back, he noticed Alistair standing behind the dratagon, his mighty battle axe raised high.

As the beast leaned forward to shoot fire from its nose, Alistair brought down his axe like a guillotine and chopped its tail off in one swift motion. The dratagon howled and in its distracted pain, shot the fireballs out of its nose, but not in the direction of Joel and Bronrar. Instead, the fire flew overhead and hit the dratagon that was hopping on one leg, behind them. The second beast was lit ablaze and screeched out in a wretched pain. It jumped and flew off erratically, trying to extinguish itself, before finally giving into the flames and crashing to the ground off in the distance.

"Ya see that, lass? Me battle axe is unbeatable!" Alistair said as the beast behind him began to turn itself around. Joel held a hand out, trying to warn him, but he seemed too pleased with himself to notice.

"Not bad…" Lucia trailed off as the dratagon loomed behind him and opened its mouth to reveal large, jagged teeth. It lowered its head, about to take a bite out of the big man.

The mercenary lunged out past a gasping Alistair and plunged her claymore into the beast's open mouth. The blade shot out the other side of its skull, leaving an eruption of blood in its wake. She ripped her blade out of its head and then it collapsed, lifeless, on top of Alistair.

"But next time, aim for the head," Lucia said with a smile.

Struggle as he might, Alistair couldn't move underneath the corpse of the dratagon, so Lucia bent over and grasped its body. Before attempting to lift, however, she looked over at a stunned Joel and Bronrar.

"A little help over here?" she asked with narrow eyes.

"Oh… right…" Bronrar muttered as he bounced off the cave wall and made his way over to the dead monster. Joel nodded and followed close behind.

Even with their combined strength, the massive beast was only lifted a few inches off the ground, but it was enough leeway for Alistair to shimmy his way out. The big man hopped to his feet and remained in high spirits.

"Now tha only question is: Do we run away like cowards, or do we kill tha rest of these wretched beasts and become legends of Faiwell?" he asked with palpable excitement and a shaking fist.

"Stop trying to act tough," Lucia said before sheathing her great claymore. "We've got to catch up with the group."

Joel and Bronrar nodded at her assessment. Alistair groaned.

As the group approached the tunnel entrance, they came upon a corpse lying by the wall and had to run around it. It was a grisly scene; the man had been picked to pieces, presumably by the dratagons. Some limbs were missing, and the rotting flesh appeared to be melting off his bones. Although his face had been badly damaged, Joel was sure he could see remnants of a smile.

"Good lord…" Bronrar muttered between breaths. "To think they did… so much damage… to him in so little time. We're lucky to be alive…"

"No," Lucia said with a look back as she continued her strides. "That body has been rotting for days. He was from the first team…"

She grimaced before putting her head down and running faster. She must have been worried about Dalton, Joel thought. He could hardly blame her. All signs thus far had pointed to the first group meeting with an unfortunate fate. Had Aldous been too late to help them? Or had he succumbed to the terrors of the mines, too?

Finally, they reached the tunnel and made a hard left to enter. The path was spacious, yet it lacked the wooden supports from earlier tunnels, giving it a natural feeling; as if it had been broken down over time by the elements. Only a few strides in, blood-curdling screams echoed from a leftward bend up ahead. This time, they were the screams of men, and they were followed soon after by a continuous shriek that grew closer and closer.

Lucia held her torch up high, and then she gasped. Joel looked past her to see, like a blazing comet, a dratagon flying at them, on fire. It screeched once more, now mere meters away and on a collision course with the group.

"Everyone! Get down!" Lucia cried. The group plopped face-down onto the floor all at once. Joel heard a loud *whoosh* pass overhead, and soon after came a skidding crash. He looked up and over his shoulder to see the fiery monster on the ground, twitching. The foul smell and sizzling of its cooked skin told him that it would be dead in mere moments.

"Hah! That's another one on fire! That'll show 'em, the stupid beasts!" Alistair said with cheer as he rose.

Joel stood and tapped the big man's shoulder. Alistair gazed back at him with confusion in his eyes as the mute tried miming what he wanted to say. Then, Alistair looked down to see that a pant leg had caught on fire.

"Ack! Me pants! Me precious pants!" he cried.

Bronrar pulled an old rag out of his pocket and ran over to pat the fire down.

"Ouch, ooooch! Yowch!" he whined as Bronrar put out the last of the flames.

"Oof! That was a close one! Luckily, the fire only singed me leg hairs!" Alistair said with a hearty laugh before giving Bronrar a hard slap on the back. He then looked down at his pant leg. "Aw! Me beautiful pant leg… it's ruined!"

"Erm… right…" said Bronrar with narrow eyes.

As the group continued along the large left bend of the tunnel, more cries of men could be heard up ahead. Lucia, Alistair, and Bronrar drew their weapons. Joel remained behind them, hard at work on his map once again. He had a lot of catching up to do, even if he wasn't completely out of danger.

With the combined light of Lucia and Alistair's torches, the group could make out the figures of several men gathered up ahead. They increased their pace as the yelling and chatter grew louder.

Then, something caught Joel's eye, on the left wall: A man was sitting and slumped over, making unintelligible noises. The mute veered from his group once again without them noticing and approached the man.

To Joel's horror, the miner was leaking buckets of blood out of his neck. His skin had turned pale, and he could see the pure despair on his face. He held the wound near his jugular tightly, but the blood was coming out too fast, and it was only a matter of time, Joel thought. The mute got down on one knee and put a hand on his shoulder, so he wouldn't be alone while embracing death.

The miner opened his mouth to speak, but blood gurgled out of it. Joel waved his hand frantically, hoping that he would save what little remaining strength he had, but the man persisted.

Eventually, the miner choked out, *"Wolfgang…"* before slumping over and letting go of his wound. Joel paused to think of the implications and then closed the deceased miner's eyes. It was the least he could do.

~

FURTHER AHEAD, Bronrar, Alistair, and Lucia approached the group of miners, who were attacking each other. Bronrar could see swings of weapons in the dim light of the torches, but it was near-impossible to make out who was fighting who. They were behind too many others to see. As they grew closer, he could make out the silhouette of a man stabbing another with a pickaxe. The victim cried out and fell to the ground.

Finally breaking through the crowd, the group got close enough to see Wolfgang and Angus blocking their way. Wolfgang pulled his pickaxe out of the lifeless body's spine. He then bent over and picked up a short sword, which gleamed in the light of Lucia's torch. Grunting at the reflection, the blond brute cast vile eyes on the new arrivals with a grin. Angus stood beside him with crossed arms.

"Now, then… how 'bout we have ourselves a little test?" Wolfgang asked, looking down at his newly acquired sword. Somehow, his grin grew even wider, and Bronrar's stomach sank. "Who has the guts to try and pass us?"

"The hell're ye playin' at, Wolfgang?" one miner asked.

"It's simple," Angus replied as he cracked his massive knuckles. "In these mines, there are many dangers. The dratagons, for example. We need to know that you can be relied upon when such dangers arise. Thus, a test: If you are strong enough, we let you live. If you are a weak link, then you die."

The giant began striding toward the trembling men. Wolfgang walked alongside him.

"Ah, and he forgot to mention…" Wolfgang said with a chuckle. "The test is mandatory!"

His walk turned into a run and he lunged out at a miner who had raised his pickaxe in defense. However, the short sword slipped between his attempted block and plunged into the shocked worker's midsection. Bronrar and the others watched on in horror as Wolfgang's victim doubled over. The blond brute ripped his blade from the miner's stomach as he gasped and fell to the ground.

"Enough of this!" a nearby miner called out. "There's more of us than them! I don' know 'bout any of ye, but I ain't dyin' in this hellhole!"

The worker turned and suddenly found himself facing down a charging Angus. He threw a right hook upward at the giant, but the punch was ducked, and as the miner followed through on his swing, Angus pivoted behind him and wrapped a massive arm around his neck. He gasped for air and flailed his arms as Angus increased the pressure of his bicep and lifted him from the ground. Soon, the gasps turned to wheezing, and then came the gurgling. His face turned a deep, dark red, and then suddenly, Angus jerked his arm violently. A loud *crack* echoed around the tunnel, and the struggle immediately ended. He dropped him to the ground like a hunk of spoiled meat.

Another miner came at Angus from behind with a spiked mace in hand. However, Wolfgang intervened with a vicious slash that cut all the way through his arm and to the bone. It had been such a clean downward thrust that the resulting explosion of blood hadn't even touched his blade. The man cried out in surprise and pain alike as the arm dangled and the mace fell to the ground.

"Ah, this should be a fine weapon," Angus said as he picked up the mace and Wolfgang stabbed his sword into the neck of the doubled-over worker, silencing his cries.

"Everyone! Attack the bastards at once!" an enraged miner said.

One man jumped out of the pack and swung his pickaxe at Angus horizontally. However, the giant halted the attack by holding out his mace to the left with his long arms; stopping the pickaxe at its wooden base. He then pulled back hard on his weapon, which caught the axe head and ripped it from the gasping miner's hands.

The worker attempted to retreat, but Angus swung the mace at his head with the speed and ferocity of an angry bear. A loud *clang* echoed in the tunnel. Although the tin mining helmet had protected the top of his head to some extent, his face hadn't been so lucky. At least half of the club had struck him in the left cheek, and the spikes had pierced through. The worker stumbled back as teeth and blood flew out of his mouth like shooting stars in the night sky. Dazed, he fell to the ground as another miner hopped over him and charged. He leaped forward with his sword overhead.

Angus lunged his mace out in a straight, stabbing motion. The miner had already committed to his attack and crashed straight into the spiked club. It dug well into his stomach and stopped him in his tracks. The giant violently ripped his weapon out of the miner, who let out a weak cry and fell to the bloodstained floor, disemboweled. Angus then walked over to the man whom he'd clubbed in the face, earlier. He remained on the ground, convulsing in a bloody heap, and his helmet had fallen off. Angus, without hesitation, lifted his great boot and brought it down to squash his head like a rotted pumpkin.

Bronrar looked on in horror as his friend continued with the vulgar display of power with little regard. *This ain't Angus*, he thought. *It couldn't be.*

On Wolfgang's side of the tunnel, he contended with two other miners. He swung his sword wildly at one of them, and the man blocked the slash attempt with a blade of his own. However, Wolfgang was dual-wielding: The blond brute cackled while arcing his pickaxe around to hit the unsuspecting worker in his spine as his sword was being parried.

The man let out a bloody scream as Wolfgang sang, "Less of ye means *more for me!*"

Behind him, a miner jumped out with a dagger in hand. Wolfgang turned with apparent killing intent, but the pickaxe got stuck in the other worker's back. He quickly let go of the tool to respond, but by then, it was too late. The miner landed a slice on his right arm while he was pivoting out of the way.

Wolfgang felt the injured arm and gazed at the blood as it trickled off of his hand. He howled aloud in laughter, and the others could do little but stare back at him with confused expressions.

"About time one of ye grew a spine!" he said, looking at the miners who had remained behind. Bronrar gulped, hoping he hadn't noticed him. The miner who had landed the cut turned to face him again.

"Stay back, y-ye madman!" he said while holding out his knife. Wolfgang cocked his head.

"Oh… so yer not much of a fighter, eh?" he asked, and then ripped the pickaxe out of his previous victim's body. "Ye know what that means?"

"It means ye were *lucky!*" he shouted while throwing his pickaxe. The axe head plunged into the gasping worker's chest and sent him barreling to the ground, where he fidgeted, wheezed, and gurgled up blood from his mouth. Wolfgang walked up to him and pulled the axe head out with a villainous grin to finish him off.

His wild gaze turned to the surviving miners, and Bronrar ducked his head. Only four others remained nearby besides himself: Lucia, Alistair, and two others who had been too scared to approach the murderous duo. With so few remaining, Bronrar was sure that he'd be noticed soon, and the thought sent him spiraling into a pit of despair.

However, his worries proved to be unfounded, for the moment: Wolfgang was looking *past him*, not *at him*.

"Faramond?" the blond brute muttered with a hint of worry in his tone.

Bronrar turned to see a figure approaching in the darkness. Relief came to his mind. Faramond would bring an end to all of the senseless killing, and then Wolfgang's crimes would be exposed, he thought. However, only moments later, a sinking feeling returned to his stomach: It was Joel, not Faramond, walking toward them.

Wolfgang's hysteric laughter bounced off the tunnel walls. "Perfect timing! Nearly all of the idiots I want dead have gathered in one spot!"

Angus looked at Bronrar and said, "There you are... where have you been?"

Bronrar struggled to find words as he looked back at his lifelong friend. "Y-you murdered 'em..."

"That *was* the plan," he retorted with hands at his hips. "'A few dirty deeds', remember?"

"It ain't worth it, Angus! Can't you see that?" Bronrar asked. Angus frowned in return.

"Don't bother with the fat man, Angus," Wolfgang said as he rubbed the blood off his new sword. "He's no different than the others... only prey."

He licked his chops while staring Bronrar down. Angus held out a free hand between them.

"There is no need to jump to conclusions. Bronrar will come around," he said, and then looked back at his friend. "Won't you?"

Wolfgang scoffed. "He don't have the stones to do what we do, my friend!" He then pointed at Joel in the crowd and continued, "I bet ye wouldn't even be able to handle *that waif*." He burst out laughing once again. "Ye make a great pair, ye do!"

Bronrar felt a fire in his gut. He snorted and said, "I'll have you know this feller saved me back in the cave!" He looked at Angus with sharp eyes. "And where were *you* instead of helpin' yer friend? You were off killin' innocent workers!"

Angus raised his hands and shook them in defense. "Please, Bronrar, be reasonable..."

"I *am* bein' reasonable! You two are the ones who ain't..."

"I told ye he was worthless, Angus! Garbage!" Wolfgang said and then pointed at Bronrar with his sword. "I said this would happen from the beginnin', but ye just *had* to have yer *useless* friend be a part of this!"

Angus didn't speak, but he shot Wolfgang an icy glare. Coming from Angus' normally stone face, Bronrar knew that a nerve had been struck. However, the blond brute only shrugged back in return.

"We can discuss this later," Angus said, waving Bronrar over. "Come here, my friend. We have a score to settle with those three."

Bronrar looked back at Joel, Alistair, and Lucia with hesitation. They had helped him escape from the perilous dratagon-infested cave. He couldn't possibly betray them. On the other side of that coin was his lifelong friend Angus, however. He couldn't go against him, either. As he pondered the consequences of his potential decision, he felt a meaty hand grab his shoulder.

"Don' worry, lad. Stay back here an' let the warriors battle it out, as it was meant ta be!" Alistair said.

Lucia scoffed. "Implying that you're a warrior..."

"Oh, shaddup! We're supposed ta be on the same side, remember?" the big man bellowed back.

"I suppose..." she replied, drawing on her great claymore. Alistair also drew his battle axe, and then they approached the two killers.

Lucia walked up to Alistair and whispered, "Are you sure you can handle this?" He looked back at her with a grimace. "They seem to have a bit of skill, and this time they have *real* weapons. I will only be able to focus on one at a time..."

Alistair opened his mouth and took in a long breath, seeming ready to give her an earful, but then he let out a long, calm exhale. He only nodded in response before they advanced toward their opponents. They left Joel, Bronrar, and the other two surviving miners behind to watch.

"He's *yer* friend, Angus, so do whatever ye want," Wolfgang said as he pointed his sword at Lucia. "But the bitch is *mine*."

Angus smiled in return. Alistair approached, holding his battle axe out in front of him. The giant mimicked his stance with the blood-soaked mace. As Alistair came within range, Angus lightly swung his club and tapped the axe blade. The big redhead shook the mace off by pulling his weapon back. Much of the same jockeying for position continued as they inched closer to one another. Angus had the arm reach advantage, but Alistair's axe had a greater reach than the mace.

After walking to the other side of the tunnel, Lucia held her claymore up defensively while Wolfgang remained still, staring back at her. He appeared loose and uncaring. Her first thoughts were to get a good swing of the claymore in and break whatever stance he might choose. The problem, however, was that she wasn't sure how fast Wolfgang could swing the short sword, especially because it was dark. Still, she was tempted to take a full swing with her great blade; just to see if she could frighten him into making a mistake. *Tactics vs brute force*: She thought back to the first conversation she had with Conrad, and it made her smile.

"What are ye smilin' for?" Wolfgang asked as he playfully sliced the air with his blade. "Are ye lookin' forward to death's sweet embrace?"

"*Your death*, perhaps," she said. "Come at me!"

He obliged and jumped out at her. He attempted a diagonal slash to her right, but with the great length of her claymore, she was able to parry the attempt. The sword bounced off with a loud *clang*, but the blond brute wasn't finished. He whirled the blade above his head and attempted a diagonal slash from the other side, instead. Once again, Lucia was able to block due to his exaggerated swing, and the sword bounced off.

Wolfgang used the momentum of the bounce to pull his sword back quickly to his left side, primed to make a stab. He lunged out with a thrust attempt at her stomach, but it was yet another move that Lucia had already prepared for. She flexed her torso to the left and angled her sword downward until she felt it connect with Wolfgang's stabbing blade. While dodging, she forcefully pushed down on her claymore, directing the short sword toward nothing but the air. In that moment, Wolfgang was thrown off-balance; and as he stumbled, Lucia wound up and chopped down with her great blade.

In response, Wolfgang contorted his lunging body to the left, barrel rolling as the blade came down. However, thanks to the claymore's length, it managed to slice his right leg while he crashed to the ground.

Sensing he was weakened, Lucia dashed over and swung her blade down for a decisive blow, but the blond brute rolled around like a monkey and dodged. He hopped to his feet and stared her down as she turned to face him. Now, he was smirking.

Behind Wolfgang, the two frightened miners made a run for it by his right side. He darted his eyes toward the running men and let out an explosive laugh. Predictably, he gave chase to the escapees, but Lucia had other ideas. She swung her blade horizontally at Wolfgang, who ducked the slash and crawled briefly on all fours before picking up speed and passing her.

"Damn it!" she cried while straining her arms to steady the blade. The blond brute had bolted past her and now stalked his newest prey.

He caught up with the back miner and swung the short sword at his calf. It was a direct hit, and the man screamed as blood spurted and his leg contorted, sending him skidding to the ground. While the wounded miner fell face-first, Wolfgang dragged his blade across the spine and up to his head to finish him off.

The other miner continued to flee, so Wolfgang chased him down. He tackled him from behind and cackled without any sense of control until they both fell. The escapee struggled to free himself; scratching, clawing, flailing at the ground, but it was no use: Wolfgang had a knee on his lower back.

"No! No! No!" Wolfgang said playfully as he pounded on the defenseless miner. "Yer supposed to fight, ye coward!" he called out while bringing his sword back to make the final stab. He plunged the blade into the miner's back, and he let out a brief whimper before going limp.

Wolfgang stood and made his way back over to a disgusted Lucia. In the dim light, she could make out spatters of his victims' blood on his cheeks. The man who stood before her was an efficient, unapologetic killer.

"Now, where were we?" he asked, dusting himself off.

～

ACROSS FROM THE SPEEDY DUEL, Alistair and Angus continued their standoff. The giant had attempted to bait Alistair into attacking a few times, but he wasn't biting.

"Have you no confidence in your axe?" he said while gently swinging his mace in front of him.

"Aye, I do! I'm just waitin' fer the right moment ta cut ya down, is all!" Alistair replied as he swatted the mace away.

Angus crossed his feet over several times, moving in an arc to Alistair's right. The big redhead followed along, axe out in front, continuing to face him. He then noticed the damp, reddened cloth around Angus' leg. It gave him an idea.

Alistair pulled his axe back, ready for a big swing downward. Then, he jerked his arm forward briefly before stopping the motion immediately. His feign was enough to get Angus on his heels, and more importantly, to put most of his weight on the injured leg. The giant winced and then reached down to grab his wound.

"Gotcha!" Alistair cried as he charged in for his real attack. However, as he began to bring his axe down, he realized that Angus had been faking, too. The axe came down at half-force, and as the metal of the axe head *clanked* off rock, the giant swung his club at Alistair's head.

Thanks to his half-hearted axe swing, Alistair had the energy and time to react and duck under the devastating swing of the mace. He responded by whirling his battle axe upward, coming mere inches from a backpedaling Angus' face.

Just as suddenly as the action had begun, the big men halted and resumed their standoff.

"Oi! Next time I'll take yer face clean off!" Alistair taunted.

"Maybe..." Angus said, whisking his club around, to which some blood from his victims sprinkled off. "Or maybe I'll bash your brains in."

～

Wolfgang stared down Lucia, still as the darkness around them. She continued to hold her claymore up and outward in a defensive stance; a true obstacle for him, she thought. His short sword had the speed, but not the range to land a solid hit on her.

After a few moments, Wolfgang smiled and flipped the short sword to his right hand.

"Did ye know I'm both right *and* left-handed?" he asked while swinging the blade freely through the air.

"Fascinating," Lucia said with an eye roll.

At a moment's notice, the blond brute charged and lunged out in a stabbing motion. Lucia was surprised to see him attempt the same move that had failed him only moments ago, but to her, it meant an easy block. Just the same as before, she flexed her upper body to the left and directed Wolfgang's sword downward with her heavy blade.

However, instead of stumbling, Wolfgang continued unhindered and swung the sword with his right arm in an arced motion. The follow-through of the attack landed with a resounding *clank* on Lucia's right shoulder armor, just as she was counterattacking. The groan of crumpling metal filled her ears, and for the first time that battle, she was worried. The blunt force of the blow was enough to send her claymore off-course on its slash; and the blade came up short of Wolfgang, striking the ground with little power to it.

Wolfgang laughed aloud after the exchange and said, "It didn't take me long to figure out yer feeble technique, did it?" He turned and pointed his sword at her claymore. "Yer too slow with that hunk o' metal. Ye'll never land a meaningful hit on me!"

Lucia attempted to lift the claymore, and her eyes widened as she came to realize the damage had been done: Her arm shook like a jitterbug as she raised the blade, and the pain immediately swelled up in her right shoulder. The armor had partially crumbled into her shoulder, and blood was already leaking out. She quickly switched hands.

"Oh?" Wolfgang said with a raised eyebrow. "Are ye both left and right-handed, too?"

"Damn..." Lucia muttered.

Lucia fixed her position and held the claymore with two hands once more, but she knew that it was all for show and so did her opponent. Her attacks would no longer have speed or power behind them, and wielding the oversized blade with one hand was out of the question.

As Wolfgang approached, he said, "I told ye what would happen if I had a *real* weapon, didn't I? I told ye that I'd kill ye, and I'm a man of my word."

Like a pouncing lion, Wolfgang closed in on Lucia and took a two-handed swing at her blade. She raised her blade to make the block, but in doing so, her shoulder buckled under the sudden strain. The claymore soared through the air and landed by the tunnel wall with a series of *clanks* and *clunks*.

Wolfgang raised his sword and slashed downward at her. Lucia rolled to her left and planted her left hand on the ground. She then attempted a similar kick to the one that had felled him earlier in the day. Wolfgang sidestepped. He raised his blade once more, targeting her outstretched leg. The mercenary resorted to her only option and kicked with the same leg, connecting with his shin.

The attack was strong enough to send Wolfgang stumbling backward, but the downside was that it had also hurt Lucia's shin. She desperately clawed backward and turned around to reach out for her claymore, but then felt a sharp pain in her hand. Wolfgang's big, black boot was rubbing it out against the rocky ground. Lucia gasped as she watched him drag the claymore and knock it further away with his blade. Her hand, shin, and shoulder all felt like they were on fire.

He pointed the blade at her head. "Ye at least put up a fight. I like that, but I already said I was gonna kill ye, so ye gotta go."

Wolfgang raised his short sword like an executioner. Lucia turned her head and closed her eyes. There was little left that she could do.

Just when all seemed lost, an unbearable screech erupted from down the tunnel, and then the sounds of panicked men followed. Wolfgang looked back and Lucia turned her gaze up to see light sources headed their way.

"Everyone! Hurry! They're right behind us!" Faramond called out. It seemed that he and the surviving miners were fleeing the dratagons hot on their trail. Their voices and struggles echoed down the tunnel path.

While he was distracted, Lucia ripped her hand from Wolfgang's boot and hopped to her feet. She gained some distance from him, and in the dim light of the remaining torches, she could see him frowning. He lowered his sword.

"Bah! That damned Faramond! It seems he's brought some dratagons with him! Looks like we'll need to settle this later, eh?" he said and then looked over at his giant accomplice, who was still standing off with Alistair. "Angus! Time to go!"

Wolfgang and Angus joined together and then fled the scene. Lucia ran over and retrieved her claymore before saying, "We must hurry off, too!"

The group began to jog up the long tunnel path. The loud struggle continued behind them, but they put their heads down and pressed on. After a short time, Lucia saw a faint blue light ahead, where many silhouettes wandered. With the end in sight, they increased their jog to a full-on sprint.

Upon reaching the end of the tunnel, they found themselves in a new corridor with several miners sitting and standing around. Edith, Wolfgang, and Angus glared in their direction but did nothing else. The area was illuminated by a dim blue light, fading in and out, slowly but surely. It was an incredible sight to behold, as it was coming not from a torch or even a device of the Ancient Ones, but from the rocks on the walls. Lucia had never seen such a thing before, even in her many travels as a mercenary.

The new tunnel went in a few directions. To the group's left, there was a cave-in. The same musty smell filled the air, and a mixture of snapped support beams, rocks, boulders, and dust littered the ground. Some miners could be heard grumbling that it was the same tunnel collapse they had encountered yesterday. To the right, another tunnel seemed to lead down a path where the blue light became stronger. Along that portion of the tunnel, there seemed to be an entire system of paths that crossed over each other. However, the miners were staring at and chattering about the tunnel in front of them. It was dark, yet gleaming with densely packed black gold; more than any of the tunnels or caves before it.

CHAPTER 13
TROUBLE BREWING

Conrad sat by the mountainside and looked up at the clouds with a frown. They appeared to be gathering and darkening into a storm. Not that there was much for the group of 15 to do besides guard everyone's spoils, but he had even less interest in spending the day inside a tent.

Henic had been appointed Conrad's unofficial second-in-command while Faramond and Edith were away, as the strategist trusted him the most out of his group. There were some familiar faces among the men from his days working at the bank, but it was strictly on a customer basis. He had at least spoken to and journeyed with Henic; and most importantly, he knew of Edith's insidious plans. The others were unknown quantities, and Lucia's final words before entering the mines still haunted him: Some of these men had sided with Edith back when the mutiny nearly broke out.

He looked at a group sitting down the path. In the middle was a short, big-nosed man. He had surrounded himself with four other miners; the large, muscle-bound types. Laughter erupted from the group of five as Henic sat next to his new leader.

"They're a chatty lot, ain't they?" Henic asked, interrupting his train of thought.

"Yes, I suppose they all know each other…"

"Yeh. That group has been together fer years," Henic said.

Conrad scratched his nose before asking, "You know them?"

"In a manner of speaking..." Henic muttered, looking down. "They're known as 'The hooligans' among most miners. Wolfgang used to be their leader, but now it's that big-nosed feller over there, Brice."

"'Hooligans'... sounds like we don't have good things to look forward to from that group, then?" the strategist asked.

"Yeh, and their trouble-making ain't limited to the mines, either. Plenty o' mischief-making has been done by them around Faiwell. They've been quiet on this trip so far. Hopefully, it stays that way," Henic said while looking shiftily around the base camp. Conrad could almost swear that he was trying to avoid eye contact with that group. Aside from the hooligans, most other miners stayed in packs of two or more. "How 'bout you? Do you know any of these people?"

"Only as customers at my parents' bank," Conrad said. He nodded in the direction of an old man with a long, gray beard sitting across from them on the path. "That older fellow is Cyriack. He grinds up the ore back at the Miner's Guild. He's been doing that for years, as far as I know. I'm surprised to see him on this trip."

Henic nodded. "Methinks the older generation feels a strong attachment to the village. He's doing his duty."

Conrad crossed his arms and said, "Agreed. He seems like someone who is putting the good of Faiwell over his own well-being. Perhaps someone we can trust." He then pointed to the miner sitting next to him. He was another older man who had a salt-and-pepper mustache to decorate an otherwise uninviting expression. "And that's Peter. He was a former customer at the bank."

"Former? So, he took all of his money and kept it somewhere else?" Henic asked.

"Precisely. Peter is the type of man who can find problems with anything. He grew suspicious of my parents and thought that they were stealing his precious gold because they 'looked at him funny' one day," Conrad replied.

"Ah, so he's a real knobber, eh?"

"That's one way of putting it."

Henic pointed Conrad in the direction of another man further down the path. "How 'bout him? Do you know that fella?"

He was another old man, with long, gray hair, a stubby frame, and a great smile on his face. His disposition seemed rather cheerful as he chatted with some other miners.

"He looks familiar," Conrad said.

"That's Solomon. He fought in the War of the Bird and lost most of his friends, but he's one of the nicest fellas I ever did meet," Henic said, a smile coming to his face. "He *does* tend to prattle on, though. Methinks it's to help him forget the horrors of war."

"The War of the Bird, you say?" Conrad asked. Concern swept over his face. "Few aside from Dalton came out of that one unscathed… or so I've been told."

"It's not the injuries, but what it does to yer mind. Trust me on that one," Henic said in a somber tone.

"Did you fight in that war, Henic?"

"I was kept in reserve," he replied. "I'm truly a lucky soul to have missed out on the fighting. Just when I got the call to battle, the treaty was signed to end it all."

"I'd dare say that I'm even more fortunate. We've not had a war since then…" Conrad said and then drew his rapier to wave it gently through the air. "I learned to use this blade out of curiosity, but I'm not especially looking to take another man's life with it."

"Aye." Henic kept cautious eyes on the blade. "It's not a burden that you want on yer conscience," he said before looking far down the path at another group of miners shooing away a tall, gangly man with ginger hair. "What about that feller down there? Do you know him?"

Conrad chuckled and put his rapier away. "I'm sure *everyone* knows William at this point. He would come into the bank as I was trying to close up, and talk to me for hours."

"Hah! That's right! Nobody can out-talk ole' William! If anyone ever needed a wife, it was that lonely guy!" Henic said and then howled with laughter.

As if he had heard the pair talking about him, William hiked up the slope toward them, his eyes wide with curiosity and excitement. Conrad and Henic looked at each other and chuckled.

"Ooooo, hellooo!" William said, stopping before the duo. "I do so very much appreciate that yer our leader, Conrad. Oh yes, I do!"

Holding back more laughter, Conrad said, "And to have as much cheer as yours within our little group makes me glad, William."

"Now, I apologize if I'm talkin' too much, but I think there's a storm comin'! We gotta prepare for that…" William said, his demeanor souring a bit.

"What's to prepare for? We can simply take cover in the tents, can't we?" Henic asked.

"Oh, yes, we can! But the problem, y'see, is who's gonna watch the spoils while we're all taking shelter from the rain?" he asked, loudly. Conrad noticed some sharp eyes pointed at them, now. "Y'see, I don' want anyone's black gold to get stolen… oh dear no, that would be just awful!"

"A fair point…" Conrad trailed off, looking around to see more miners peering their way. "However, I think we should handle this discreetly, wouldn't you agree?"

"Oh, yes! Yes, indeed! I've spoken too much, haven't I? My apologies! I can be too anxious for my own good, sometimes!"

Conrad could see that Brice was now making his way up the path with such vigor that his dark hair constantly peeked out from beneath his bobbing miner's helmet. He stopped in front of them and fixed on them a blank stare.

After an awkward silence, William said, "Oooo! Hellooo thar, Brice! What brings you to my neck of the woods?" He chuckled. No one else laughed with him.

"Just wanna see what the lot of ye are talkin' about," he replied, eyeing Conrad. "I heard talk about who's gonna be watchin' the spoils. Figured I should hear what ye have to say, eh?"

"Right…" Conrad said with a sidelong glance at the gangly man. "William here was just saying that a storm is coming," he continued while pointing at the darkening sky. "Which means most of us will wish to take cover in our tents. With that said, someone will need to stand guard. My first thought was to have us take shifts-"

"And how do ye suppose we can trust *anyone* alone with the treasures?" Brice asked, his big nose twitching in annoyance.

Henic cleared his throat with a marked nervousness and said, "F-Faramond appointed the 15 of us as the most trusted of B-Team. We've no reason to believe-"

"Well, well! The farm boy speaks up at last!" Brice interrupted. "Don't fool yerself into thinking ye have any authority here."

The farmer growled and clenched his fists. "You little-"

Brice wagged his finger and said, "Don't forget about our lil' agreement. Speak outta line against me again, old man, and there'll be trouble! Understand?"

Henic sighed and then looked down. "Yes…"

"Anyhow, Faramond's judgment is questionable," Brice said before looking over his shoulder. "Seems like there are some suspicious characters in the group, eh?" He tilted his head toward Peter.

"Why would you suspect Peter of anything?" Conrad asked.

"He's always accusing people of things. Ye know what I think? I think he does that so nobody will suspect *him* of wrongdoing. I don' trust the wretch," he replied.

"Come on, now!" William said loudly while patting Brice on the shoulder. "Peter's a good man! He wouldn't steal a thing!"

Predictably, and to Conrad's chagrin, Peter stomped up the path next. William's bombastic nature could rival Alistair's at the worst of times, he thought.

"Who said I'd be stealin' anythin'?" cried Peter as he neared them. He removed his miner's helmet to reveal a balding brown head of hair. Although growing older, Peter was still an imposing figure; standing nearly as tall as William, but with more muscle on his frame.

"I said so, what of it?" Brice replied with a snarl. Peter fixed his angry gaze on him.

"Why, you little rat! Ya know what happens to rodents? They get stomped on!" Peter said through gritted teeth.

"Try it, old man," Brice said. He looked past him and then nodded at his crew. They began trekking up the path in his direction.

"There is no need to fight," Conrad said as he put his hands up. "Remember that we all have spoils to take home, and it is a home that we are trying to save."

The hooligans arrived, and one of them pushed Peter from behind. The grumpy man turned around and faced the others down, now red in the face.

"I ain't the one to be pushin'!" he said before pointing at Brice. "This lil' rat here is the one tryin' to start trouble. Like he always does."

Brice smiled and said, "I'm not starting anythin', old man. Those days are behind me…"

"It sure seems like trouble's brewin'…" Henic muttered. Conrad noticed that beads of sweat were forming on his brow. What was it about Brice that had him so nervous?

A few other miners joined the group to see what was going on. The chatter and arguments began to pick up, but most of it was between Brice and Peter.

"Ye ain't trustworthy. I don' trust ye watching my spoils," Brice said.

"I'm not the one that these here folks have'ta worry 'bout! Everyone knows that you and the hooligans are trouble-makers!" Peter shouted with a stomp of his boot. "I say Faramond's choice to leave you here was a poor one!"

"And how about you? Faking an injury so you didn't have to fight in The War of the Bird?" Brice asked aloud. Gasps came from the crowd and Peter seemed to have lost all breath, his face redder than ever.

Peter remained quiet for a moment. "I'll have ya know that I had a terrible foot injury, and that was why I couldn't fight!"

"Yer full of-"

"That's enough, everyone!" Conrad called out. "If, and only if, it is raining heavily outside, we will all take shelter inside the mine entrance. This way, it acts as a cover to the rain, and no one will have to worry about their valuables being stolen."

The crowd simmered and then William clapped his hands together. "Oh my, that is a lovely idea! This is why Faramond made you leader, Conrad!"

"Thanks..." the strategist replied. William had unknowingly started the whole argument, but at least it was over with. Better to settle it now than in the middle of a storm, he thought.

The group seemed satisfied and began to disperse until a voice spoke out, "What of the creature that dwells in the mines?"

Conrad looked back to see that old man Cyriack had been the source.

All in the group halted and then turned to face him. He continued, "We all heard the same terrible howls last night, did we not? And that sign... it says, 'Beware the Beast'. It may be dangerous to stay in there."

"Either way, the mines are a dangerous place. The noises probably came from those lil' knockers," Henic said.

"No. The cries were different, an' we only heard 'em near the entrance," Cyriack countered.

"We're dealing in too many hypotheticals," Conrad said. Most of the group cocked their heads in response. "Too many 'what-ifs'," he clarified. Everyone nodded. "Let us adapt as we go: If it rains, we take shelter. If that shelter is dangerous, then we stay in the tents and assign groups at a time to stand watch. Does that sound fair?"

"Only if I get to watch over the rat..." Peter trailed off. He stared a hole through Brice, who paid him no heed and walked away.

"Until those times come, I say we stop worrying and arguing amongst ourselves. Everyone may go back to whatever it is they'd like to do," Conrad said with a reassuring nod. Most of the miners left, but William stayed behind, smiling down at both him and Henic.

"Erm… that includes you as well, William," Conrad said with a crooked smile.

"Oh, but I was over here talkin' to you already!" he replied with a nervous laugh as Henic held out his hand.

"Rain…" he muttered.

It didn't take long for the spaced-out drops to become a heavy rain complete with booming thunder.

"Everyone! The rain is picking up! Into the mines!" Conrad cried while pointing to the tunnel entrance.

He and the other miners ran into the Mouth of Hell to take shelter. Inside, the strategist looked around to see many concerned faces, Henic included.

"Why is everyone so somber?" he whispered to his second-in-command.

Henic frowned. "I'm nervous about me black gold shares… wouldn't want anythin' happenin' to 'em in this storm…"

Conrad's eyes widened, but he quickly readjusted himself to show no concern. "You have nothing to fear, my friend," he replied before clapping him on the shoulder. "You and I both know that everyone's stash is safe."

Henic remained silent and continued to look out into the rain with longing eyes. Then, He gasped and pointed out to the base camp. "Look! Out in the rain! Who goes there?"

Conrad squinted to see a figure standing by one of the tents. He walked toward the tunnel entrance where cool drips of water plopped on his head. He was trying to get a better view, but the dark of night approaching and rain made it difficult to make out who it was.

"He better stay away from me black gold, or I'll…" Henic said, clenching his fists.

"Worry not. I'll go out to see who it is. A misunderstanding, I'm sure," Conrad replied.

He turned to see that the others had taken notice of the man standing by the tent. There was an eerie mood about the cave; none of the miners appeared to be angry or scared, but there was a certain blankness to their eyes. Like a pack of wolves staring down potential prey, it felt to Conrad like they could lash out at any moment.

"Alright, everyone!" he said. His calm, yet firm voice echoed throughout the tunnel. "One of our friends didn't get the message, it seems." He chuckled, but none of the others laughed along. "I'll go to bring him in. Ease your minds… everything is fine."

None of them responded and the palpable tension in the air remained. The last thing Conrad wanted was to let the situation get out of hand, so he ran out into the rain toward the man standing in front of the tent.

"Excuse me," Conrad said as he approached the mystery man. He was peering into the tent, head-first. There was no response. He tapped him on his back and repeated, "Excuse me!" The man flinched and dragged his head out of the tent. His long, gray hair splashed about in the downpour. It was Solomon.

"Oi! It's only you, sir?" he said and then huddled over with a relieved breath. "T'was nervous that some wild animal was attackin' me!" Solomon nudged his head in the direction of the cave. "And I don't mean them wild animals over thar!" He howled aloud with laughter and slapped Conrad on the back.

"Right…"

Suddenly, the memories of Solomon came flooding back to Conrad. He was a frequent customer at his parents' bank, and he enjoyed snappy jokes and long conversations. Unfortunately, he was also poor at handling his money, which was part of the reason he'd come into the bank so often. Still, he had always seemed a genuinely nice man.

"What are you doing out here, Solomon? We agreed to take shelter in the mine entrance if it rained," Conrad said.

"Ah… right…" Solomon said as he rubbed the back of his neck. "I was a wee bit nervous about me spoils, is all. Wanted ta check up on it before goin' into the mines. Make sure everythin' was in order! You know how it is!"

"I understand, but…" Conrad flashed Solomon a stern eye. "Isn't this Brice's tent?"

Solomon looked back a few times before laughing again. "Oh, my! Sorry lad, I truly thought this was me own tent! An honest mistake… like marryin' me first wife!" He chuckled some more.

Unamused, but also wanting to avoid confrontation, Conrad said, "All is forgiven, Solomon. Let's get out of this rain."

The two men returned to the tunnel, where the mood seemed to have calmed among the others. Conrad breathed a sigh of relief as he returned to his spot along the rocky wall, where Henic sat.

"Feeling more at ease?" he asked.

"I suppose…" Henic replied and then crossed his arms. "I don' see why we can't stay in our tents to watch over our spoils, though."

"In that case, we wouldn't be able to watch over the other miners' tents. This is the easiest way to stay dry while keeping watch over our valuables," Conrad said, gazing into the infinite darkness of the mines ahead. "For now, anyway."

"That was *my* tent ye were tryin' to loot, ye crazy old man!" a voice across the tunnel shouted. It was Brice. He and his crew had surrounded Solomon and were pushing him around.

"Now, now fellas! It was a mistake, honest!" Solomon pleaded as they continued to shove him.

"I don't trust ye. Yer always flappin' yer gums; all happy and such," Brice said as he pushed Solomon from behind. "No one's touchin' my black gold. If anythin', I deserve more!"

Conrad eyed the commotion and called out, "Hey!" The rough-housing ceased, and the men looked at him, some cocking their heads. "That's enough. He said it was an honest mistake."

"Bones to that!" Brice replied, clenching his fists. "I don' trust him…"

Peter cackled from further down the tunnel. "What a laugh! *You* don't trust someone? Yer the least trustworthy of us all!"

"Quiet, old man," Brice said.

"That's enough out of *everyone*," Conrad said, his tone sharp as a blade. "The point is, we're all in here, now. No one can get at anyone's treasures from here."

The workers began to calm down and Solomon separated himself from Brice and the hooligans. There was silence about the tunnel for some time, and it had Conrad in a curious mood. He could see from Henic's face that something was still bothering him.

"Anything I can do to ease your mind?" the strategist asked with a smile.

"I'll be stayin' on edge as long as I'm so far from me spoils," he said. Conrad held his breath. He had noticed a change in how everyone was behaving. Was the black gold poisoning their minds?

"Y'see, me wife is sick back at home…" Henic trailed off. Conrad let out a relieved breath. "And so, my boy has been minding the crops and livestock while I'm gone. It has been a difficult year for the village… do ye know what happens to us farmers when a place like Faiwell falls on hard times?"

Conrad rubbed his chin. "I'm not sure."

"People start to blame us."

"What for?"

"You may already know this, but there ain't enough farmland in Faiwell to sustain everyone. My crops and livestock are meant to complement the food and supplies that we trade for. I can't provide for everyone," Henic said.

"Ah, so people become jealous that you have immediate access to food, and they don't," said Conrad.

"Aye," the farmer replied with a slow nod. "Me father warned me that this day might come, back when I was younger. He told me to put my head down and keep to my work instead of gettin' involved in other folks' business. He said that when hard times come around, the mob comes for farmers, first."

"We have more in common than you might think," Conrad said. "My parents have been forced to hire security, lately. Some unruly people have tried robbing us. I think it was out of desperation."

"The problem is, I can't afford security," Henic replied, his fist shaking. "Months ago, I started findin' uprooted crops on my land. Some of my livestock began to disappear. Ole' Farmer Russell smartened me up to the culprits: Wolfgang and his crew. He suggested that I cut a deal with them, so they'd leave me alone. He said that it had worked for him!"

"Why not alert the authorities? They were trespassing, after all."

"Farmer Russell already tried that, but to no avail. Somehow, that knob Wolfgang is exempt from the law of the Village Elders," Henic replied, sulking. "I gave in. Offered to give him food and supplies in exchange for sparing my farmland and livestock from his grubby hands. There was no choice…"

"And I'm sure that Wolfgang went back on the deal?" Conrad asked.

"Not exactly," Henic said, holding up an index finger. "He kept up his end of the bargain, but then he started demanding more from me. I had to work harder than ever, but somehow, I managed to fulfill my promise, and the farm was spared. Then, last month, things got worse. My farm was attacked yet again, but not by Wolfgang and his cronies."

"The hooligans," Conrad said, darting his eyes to a point further down the tunnel, where they sat.

"Indeed. With two groups extorting me for my supplies, I had to put my boy and my wife to work in the fields. That was a grueling month for us all… and what's worse is that those damned hooligans left one of their members behind to keep on collecting. Since my wife is sick, my son has had to do everything by himself while I'm gone."

"What a cruel situation to find yourself in," he replied.

"Then, surely you can understand why the black gold is so important. It's the key to *everything*! If we enrich the village, then eyes will be taken off of my farm and my family can live in peace," Henic said with hope in his voice. "And with the riches I've gathered today, I can live a comfortable life; one where I don' have to worry about bad crops or jealous men who seek to destroy all I've worked for. I *must have more* of the black gold… to make my dream life a reality…"

Conrad's eyes widened.

"Somethin' wrong?" Henic asked. His voice grew defensive.

The strategist cleared his throat. "No, it's nothing…"

As justified as Henic was for wanting to bring treasures home, Conrad couldn't help but notice that his troubles were creating a fixation on the black gold. His fear of losing everything he'd worked for drove a desire for more; and that same anxiety had come into play earlier, when his team had nearly been worked up into a frenzy over Solomon standing near a tent out in the rain. None of them seemed to care about the other precious metals obtained. They had only ever mentioned worrying about their black gold. Was the belief in black gold's value that strong? Or was something insidious at play with the mysterious, sparkling metal? He could only be certain of one thing: Trouble was brewing.

CHAPTER 14
ALTERNATE PATHS

Faramond panted as he stood before his remaining men to address them. He looked around to see considerably fewer workers than before, and some were injured to make matters even worse. By his tally, a mere 26 miners remained after the attacks. *16 men, devoured by dratagons*, he thought with a shudder. However, there was no time to panic. Faramond had an important decision to make: He could attempt to escape through the cave of the dratagons, delve deeper into the mines by traversing the gleaming blue path, or they could explore the black gold-filled tunnel before him.

Although Faramond was still against mining in tunnels, the allure of the black gold was undeniable. He suspected that it would lead to a cave filled with even more of the precious metal, like the last time he had taken a team out to explore. However, also like last time, he worried that they would find the knockers lurking about; or something worse.

Another factor on the leader's mind was time. In his estimation, nightfall would come soon, and his crew was growing more restless by the moment. He wished to continue in his search for the first team but also realized that he had promised safety to his workers. With night approaching, he did not wish to cross through the dratagon cave again when they'd be more awake and alert than ever.

"We need to salvage this trip," Edith whispered in his ear. His neck hairs stood on end.

"First of all," Faramond replied, grasping her cold hand. "Are you alright?"

"I'm fine, Fara," she said. "The important thing is the other workers. They are restless."

"Well, over a dozen of us were slaughtered by those cursed creatures. It's a normal reaction…"

"We need to assure them that it wasn't for nothing," Edith said as she nodded at the black gold-filled tunnel. "We could mine some black gold into the night, then in the morning, trek carefully through the dratagon cave back to safety."

"But the first team-"

"You saw the dead bodies, didn't you? Those weren't our workers. The wildlife in this mountain probably got to them all," said the blonde beauty.

"Perhaps you're right," Faramond said, crossing his arms. "I'll need to think about it. Let us rest for now."

Edith's face turned grave. "Make the right call. We're counting on you…" She turned away and walked to Wolfgang and Angus. Faramond felt his stomach churn.

∼

LUCIA TENDED to her injured shoulder from the battle against Wolfgang. The metal shoulder plate had crumbled from the force of the blow and penetrated skin. She knew that it needed to be removed so that she might clean the wound, but even touching it was unbearably painful.

"Can you remove it?" she asked Alistair while sitting down.

The big man raised an eyebrow and then focused on the plate. Blood was flowing out of it from the inside.

"Alright, lass," he said, grabbing a piece of the plate with his hand.

He bent over, ready to pull, but paused for a moment. She looked up at him and smirked.

"I know it's going to hurt. Just get it over with…"

"Well, I've been thinkin'…" he trailed off with a cocky smile coming to his round face. "Ya took damage from yer fight and I didn't! That proves once and for all that me battle axe is better than yer weak lil' sword!"

"For the last time, it's a claymo-"

Without warning, Alistair ripped the metal shard out of her wound.

Lucia gasped at the sudden pain and then gripped her shoulder, now burning hot and wet. The blood from her crumpled shoulder armor splashed onto Alistair's hand. He immediately dropped it and wiggled his hand to get it off.

"I need something to wrap it," Lucia choked out, taken aback at the pain. She had felt worse before, but not *much* worse.

"Sorry, I got nothin' for that!" Alistair said as he wiped the remaining blood on his pant leg.

"I got somethin'," said Bronrar. He pulled an old rag from his pocket.

Lucia eyed him with suspicion. She then turned to Joel, who nodded in approval. There wasn't much other choice, so she accepted the rag and began to wrap it around her shoulder. Even when tied up, it didn't take long for the makeshift bandage to turn red.

"That don't look so good…" Bronrar said.

"It'll have to do, for now. Thank you," Lucia said before breathing a sigh of relief.

Bronrar smiled and nodded.

"Now what?" Alistair asked.

"There's not much we can do besides wait for Faramond's orders," Lucia said, eyeing her leader. He was huddled in a corner of the tunnel, alone. "And it had better be the *correct* orders, or I won't be following him."

"What do ya mean by that?"

"I'm going to search for the first team… whether Faramond supports that or not. I'll go off on my own if I must," she said.

"But ya saw how deadly them dratagons were!" the big man said with a huff. "There ain't no way they could'a survived here fer *days*."

"You overestimate the dratagons' bloodlust. They were untamable and deadly to their masters back in the days of war, but now? Humans are not their prey. How could they be in a place like this?" Lucia said.

Joel raised his hand and then wrote something down on part of his notebook. He held the words out for all to see:

Wolfgang's Crew — 11 confirmed kills
Missing Workers — 16

"Yer sayin' that Wolfgang and Angus were deadlier back there than those winged beasts?" Bronrar asked with disbelief on his tongue.

"The numbers speak for themselves," Lucia said.

"I expected as much from Wolfgang, but Angus... I've never seen 'im act this way before..." Bronrar trailed off.

"Well, maybe ya didn't know yer pal as well as ya thought, lad!" Alistair said.

"He's done bad things, but we've been friends through thick an' thin. I cannot abandon him."

"Loyalty is an admirable quality, but eventually, you reach the point of stupidity," Lucia said with a finger pointed at him. "Your friend hasn't simply 'done bad things'. Innocent people were slaughtered by him."

"Aye. Gonna have ta agree with the lass on this one. We should tell Faramond what *really* happened in the tunnel," Alistair added.

"Please. Give me more time..." Bronrar muttered, looking down.

Joel wrote in his notebook once more.

Don't tell Faramond yet. Will lead to bloodshed.

Lucia shook her head. "You think that if we confront Wolfgang, he won't go down without a fight, correct?" Joel nodded. "If that's the case, at least we'll outnumber him, as opposed to him picking us off one by one."

"I beg you. Give me 'til tonight. If I cannot get Angus to snap out of it by then, I'll offer no resistance toward you lot tellin' Faramond the truth," Bronrar said.

"Fine... nightfall should be in but a few hours, anyway," Lucia said. She crossed her arms, but winced at the searing pain in her injured shoulder, frustrating her all the more. Even now, it felt like the tip of a blade was stuck in the wound and being twisted. "But then, I'll tell Faramond the truth of who has been killing his men."

～

FURTHER DOWN THE TUNNEL, Edith spoke in whispers with Wolfgang and Angus. They were all sitting together with their backs against the rocky wall, its blue light slowly fading in and out.

"Excellent work back there," Edith muttered as she smiled and placed her icy hand on Wolfgang's cheek.

"This is just the beginnin'..." Wolfgang said, placing a hand on her leg. It rode up higher and higher until she slapped it away and off of her exposed thigh.

"Now is not the time, Wolfy," she said in a playful tone. "We must only make Faramond jealous. I can't have him believing that he has no chance with me."

"And why not? Yer *my* gal," Wolfgang replied and then pounded his fist onto the ground. "I should be able to do as I please with ye. If he's got a problem…" he trailed off while glaring at Faramond. "Then let 'im come and settle it with me."

"She has already explained this, Wolfgang," Angus chimed in. "Edith must maintain the illusion that she wants to be with Faramond. That way, we can manipulate him."

"Oh yeah, and what about ye? Yer friend sure is gettin' cozy with the lowlifes over there," Wolfgang shot back. He nudged his head toward Joel and the others.

"He will come around. Give him time," the giant said.

"He has a point, Angus," Edith said. "Get it sorted with Bronrar, or we'll have no choice but to cut off a loose end."

"Bronrar won't rat on us if that's what yer worried about," he replied. "Anyway, it's more important to focus on Faramond right now."

"I don' prefer all this sneakin' around. We should kill him and take charge of the group ourselves," Wolfgang said, his fists shaking with excitement.

"We can't do that; not right now. The workers are still on his side, and if we were to try and take the leadership role by force, it wouldn't go well for us. However…" Edith trailed off as a grin came to her sharp face. "If it were to look like an accident…"

"Give me the word, and I'll take care of him," Wolfgang said.

"We must wait for the right moment. For now, steer clear of confrontation with Faramond, understood?" Edith asked in a stern tone. Wolfgang nodded. "Good, now leave us," she said, shooing him away like a bothersome fly.

Wolfgang's eye twitched. "What do ye have to say to him that ye can't say to *me*?"

"It is in regards to Bronrar. There is something private that I need to ask Angus about him," Edith said.

With a groan, he got to his feet and began stomping away from them. "Make it quick, will ye?"

The blond brute looked back to see that Edith and Angus were already whispering to each other with smiles on their faces. He took the opportunity to bandage up all of the cuts he had received earlier.

~

AFTER A SHORT TIME, Faramond walked to the middle of the tunnel and said, "Everyone, gather 'round! Let's discuss the next course of action."

The survivors of the group walked to their leader and appeared more disgruntled than ever before; a fact not lost on Faramond. Edith strolled up next to him and gave the leader a playful nudge. He could only smile half-heartedly in return.

"I know we have already faced many a hardship on this journey. But we next face a difficult decision." Faramond paused to see many frowning faces in the crowd. "And so, this time, I consult you. I have asked so much of you already. Our next move should be a group decision."

Chatter picked up amongst the miners.

"There's a lotta black gold over thar…" one muttered.

"Yes! More for us! That will be our reward for this wretched trip!" cried another.

"So, we put it to a vote. Since night is approaching, going through the dratagon cave once again would be a costly mistake. That leaves us with three options, for now…" Faramond said, holding up three fingers. "One: We wait here until we believe that the next day has dawned. Then, we travel through the dratagon cave to eventually reach the exit. Two: We explore the glowing blue tunnel system up ahead. Three: We explore the black gold-filled tunnels."

The crowd continued to grumble as Faramond walked to the other side of the path. "Those of you who wish to wait here until morning, stand here." None besides Bronrar made their way to the spot.

Faramond then walked to a point further up the tunnel and said, "If you wish to explore the glowing blue tunnel, stand here." Joel and Lucia were the only ones to fill the spot.

Finally, he walked to the other side of the tunnel. "And if you wish to explore the black gold-filled path…" he trailed off as the remaining 22 miners rushed over to him. "Well, then… I suppose that settles things…"

~

JOEL AND LUCIA GROANED. The mercenary shot an icy glare at Alistair, who shrugged back at her.

"What? Tha first team might be where the black gold is! Ya ever think of that? We can find riches *and* yer *precious* Dalton!" He taunted her with puckered lips and smooching noises.

"As always, you misread the situation, oaf," Lucia said with a grimace.

Alistair chuckled and said, "Whatever ya say! If he's half tha warrior everyone claims, I'm sure he'll be fine!"

"Say what you will, but if we venture into those tunnels and find no sign of the first team, I'm turning back," she replied.

Joel nodded at the assertion. Alistair raised an eyebrow.

"Oi! Come on, lad! Mere metal ain't gonna hurt us!" he said while slapping a meaty hand on his shoulder. "Tha only way that can happen is if someone forges it into a weapon."

"Right you may be, but I agree we should stay out of that tunnel. Last time we followed black gold, the knockers attacked…" Bronrar said.

"'We'? 'WE'?" Alistair shouted, spit flying from his mouth. "Last I recall, ya weren't with us when the knockers attacked! I can handle those lil' buggers with me trusty axe!"

"Best not be too arrogant," Lucia said with a smile as she gripped her wrapped-up shoulder. "That's when they get you."

From the middle of the group, Faramond said, "Everyone, gather your belongings and drink some water if you have any. We venture into the black gold-filled tunnel in but a few moments!"

Due to a heavy loss of manpower, Faramond and Edith had to do some restructuring of the lineup. Lucia and Alistair remained front guards, but Bronrar joined them. The rear guards were only comprised of two others, and Joel was placed behind Wolfgang and Angus, all alone. Faramond and Edith remained just behind the front guards, as usual.

Alistair and Lucia tried to argue that Joel should be with them and not Wolfgang, but when Faramond pressed them on why, they were unable to give a straight answer without going back on their promise to Bronrar. Thus, they held their tongues in regards to Wolfgang and Angus' murderous acts; albeit with difficulty that was plain for Joel to see.

⁓

Before the group got moving, a conflict broke out. Faramond had noticed that Wolfgang and Angus were sporting new weapons, and confronted them.

"Gentlemen… where and when did you obtain these weapons?" he asked, placing a hand on his sword's hilt.

Wolfgang smirked. "What business is it of yers?"

"I am your *leader*. Where did you get the weapons?" he repeated.

The blond brute drew his short sword, stained and scented in dry blood, and began to swing it around playfully.

"Ye see, *sir*…" Wolfgang said as Edith shot him a scornful look. "These weapons belonged to the unfortunate souls killed by the dratagons. We used 'em to defend ourselves."

"Is that right?" Faramond asked while drawing his sword. "Why is it, then, that I wonder…" he trailed off, looking between Wolfgang and Angus with suspicious eyes, "If I'd find any burn marks on the dead men in that tunnel?"

Wolfgang's smirk turned into a full-on grin. It was near-impossible to hold back his laughter. "What is it that yer tryin' to say, sir?"

"You told the group that we would explore the tunnel over there," Edith interjected, grabbing Faramond's shoulder. She then pointed toward the beckoning black gold-covered walls ahead. "Morale is already low… don't go back on your word."

Faramond looked back and grunted. "Very well. We will not search the bodies in the previous tunnel. It's dangerous, anyway," he said while re-sheathing his sword. Wolfgang continued to grin, harder than ever. "However, I cannot be restful knowing that you've got weapons. Hand them over."

"Ye want me to continue travelin' through these dangerous passages, unarmed? That ain't fair!" Wolfgang said, whipping his sword up and into a defensive position. "If ye want it, why don't ye take it from me?"

He could feel Edith's gaze burning through him but ignored the sensation. This was a fight that rivaled his lust for the black gold. Faramond took a step forward, his hand on the hilt of his broadsword, when Angus got between them.

He dropped his mace and said, "Yer our leader, and I trust that you will keep us safe. I hope that in time, you will come to trust us."

"What are ye doin', Angus? We need these to defend ourselves!" Wolfgang said.

"Now is not the time for in-fighting. Hand over the weapon. There may come a time when he needs us, and then, he will return our weapons," the giant said with a nod.

Wolfgang's anger sunk to disappointment. He sighed loudly and let his short sword fall to the ground.

A short time later, Faramond gathered his remaining team in front of the black gold-filled tunnel and addressed them again.

"Alright, everyone! Just the same as before, we must be on the lookout for explosive mushrooms, and listen closely for the knockers. In addition, be mindful of your surroundings. We now have dratagons to worry about, and who knows what else," Faramond said. There were looks of concern across the group.

"But otherwise, I believe this path will lead to a cave filled to the brim with black gold. Please, do not attempt to mine anything in the tunnels. Wait until it opens up into a cave."

The group formed rank and began to walk into the tunnel, which sparkled in the darkness surrounding them. Wolfgang nudged Angus and then motioned back with his head. Behind them, Joel was huddled over his map and shaking as he walked.

"Let's put him out of his misery, soon," he whispered. Angus only nodded.

"More for us!" some miners chanted up ahead.

"More for *me*…" Wolfgang muttered.

CHAPTER 15
TELL ME

Lucia, Alistair, and Bronrar led the way with their torches and looked carefully at the ground for explosive mushrooms. The black gold glimmered down from the walls and ceiling, beckoning them as they walked.

"We shoulda stayed in that other tunnel until mornin'…" Bronrar said with a groan.

"I don't see how that would help us. We need to find the first team, and we cannot be sure if the dratagons would attack us in there, too. If we can get some black gold on the way to helping our friends, even better," Lucia said.

Bronrar sighed. "I have a bad feelin' about this tunnel, is all…"

Alistair slapped him on the shoulder and said, "Ah! Quit worryin' so much! We're all gonna get more riches from comin' down here! What's so bad about that?"

The nervous miner offered no response. He instead looked back to where Wolfgang and Angus were walking. The giant nodded at him. Wolfgang, on the other hand, scowled. Bronrar darted his eyes down and faced forward once more.

~

FURTHER BACK, Wolfgang was growling in Bronrar's direction. He nudged Angus.

"Ye need to take care of that guy. If ye won't, then *I will*."

"Relax," Angus replied, placing a head-sized hand on his shoulder. "Think of how much black gold lays ahead."

"We won't be gettin' anything with these rats hoverin' around, knowing what we've done. They don't understand the cause. They don't understand his will…"

Angus raised an eyebrow, but he returned to his usual stone expression almost immediately after. "I believe Bronrar is keeping them from saying anything. He can still be used to our advantage, for now."

Wolfgang smiled. "Ye got a good point, there. Still, I gotta start pickin' these rats off, one by one…" he muttered before directing a toxic glare at Joel. "Startin' with this pushover. He should be easy to make it look like an accident." Joel looked up from his map and frowned at the duo. "Finally, ye do somethin' wise!" Wolfgang chuckled. "Ye best be keepin' yer eyes on me… yer my first target."

Angus cocked his head to see that Joel was locking eyes with Wolfgang, and in his eyes was not fear, but defiance. He was gripping the pickaxe at his side. Perhaps the quiet one was braver than he'd been given credit for, Angus thought. However, moments later, the mute slipped back behind the two rear guards, who looked confused.

"What do ya think yer doin'?" one asked. Joel smiled back in return and offered no response.

"Hold up, ain't this feller the quiet one?" the other rear guard asked.

"Ah, right. He must not understand. Best let 'em be," the guard said with a half-hearted smile. "Ya keep a lookout for us back thar, ya hear?" Joel smiled and returned to writing on his map.

"An odd feller fer sure…" the other rear guard murmured. Angus kept eyes on him for a few moments more before turning back to face Wolfgang, who was now gritting his teeth.

"It seems he won't tolerate us as a distraction," the giant mused. "I find it odd that you would be the most concerned with him, anyhow. He's the only one who *doesn't* speak; clearly a halfwit."

"There's somethin' about him that I don' like…" Wolfgang said. "It could be his cowardice, or mayhap he thinks he's better than us. All I know is that he stood there, watchin' as I killed those other pathetic men. But at least they had the guts to face me…"

"His non-violence is what bothers you? You let the strangest things get to you… a quiet boy who we can easily dispatch of, a woman sleeping with another man to make us all rich…" Angus trailed off. He noticed the frown on Wolfgang's face. "I mean it. After we're through here, we'll be able to get any woman we want, not only in the village but in the entire country. So what if she lays with another man?"

Wolfgang tightened his fist and slammed it into Angus' wound. The giant stumbled and gasped at the sharp pain spiking up his leg.

"Ye best be knowin' yer place, Angus," he said. Angus' strides slowed and his limp became more pronounced. "Edith's *my gal*, and that's the end of it. She wasn't meant to be with a waif like Faramond."

"If you insist…" Angus said. A smirk came to his normally grim face.

Up ahead, Alistair, Lucia, and Bronrar stopped. The tunnel had given way to a vast cave. Greeting them, like an old friend, were twinkles of the black gold; it filled its ceiling and lined the walls. Excitement amongst the workers picked up.

"Finally! More for me!" a voice called out.

"Beautiful! Glorious!" another said.

Faramond cut through to the front of the group and surveyed the area, holding his torch up. The black gold glimmered off of his flame, but even with increased visibility, there was no end to the cave in sight. The landscape was barren, with no signs of life.

"I know you're all anxious to get some mining in, so I'll make this brief: You have free rein to mine as much as you like in here, but be safe. Keep an eye out for knockers and explosive mushrooms." He emphasized by crashing a fist into his palm.

"I can see here that some black gold has been mined, recently. After we are satisfied with our spoils, we shall resume our search for the first team," Faramond said, his spirits as high as the cave ceiling. No one objected.

With haste, the workers went to their respective parts of the cave and began mining. As before, torch stands were set up and then lit to give them a better view. In short order, clanging and clanking echoed around the cave, followed shortly by cries of joy.

JOEL WANDERED through the darkness in search of his new friends. He could hear clanking and elated cheers, but to his ears, they may as well have been screams of bloody murder. He had all but given up on changing the minds of complete strangers, though. Now, all that mattered was convincing Alistair, Lucia, and Bronrar to abandon the black gold. From the center of the cave, he was unable to see them, so he began to wander along the walls. He passed by man after man on the left side but didn't encounter his group, so he crossed to the right side and walked along that wall.

The next miners that Joel noticed were Wolfgang and Angus. The wise option would be to take the long way around them, he thought. However, the mute felt a stubborn fire in his gut; one he'd not felt in a long time. Wolfgang had called him a coward on more than one occasion. But Joel was not afraid of any man on this trip, and he aimed to show it now.

As Joel got closer, Wolfgang took several hard swings at the wall with his pickaxe. The sweat that flew off of his forehead gleamed under the sparkling black gold, and he was taking heavy breaths. Despite his apparent distraction, Joel kept his eyes on him while beginning to walk behind Wolfgang. At that moment, the blond brute pivoted and swung the pickaxe while turning toward him.

"Gotcha!" he cried before immediately following up with, "Huh?"

Wolfgang fell off-balance and stumbled as his pickaxe flew through nothing but air. Catching himself before falling, he looked to his left to see that Joel had jumped back to avoid the swing. The mute adjusted his miner's helmet and then snorted.

"Ye should watch where yer goin'," Wolfgang said. He turned and got back to mining as if he hadn't just tried to commit murder.

Joel walked past the two men with haste after the incident. Some strides away, he heard Angus say, "A fast little bugger, isn't he?"

Wolfgang's scoff echoed off the walls. "He got lucky, is all. Next time, he's a dead man."

Finally, after scaling the right side of the cave wall most of the way around, he came across Bronrar, Lucia, and Alistair swinging their pickaxes. Lucia had to swing with one arm because of her injured shoulder, however, so she had less results than the others. Alistair was the first to notice his arrival.

"Ah! There ya are, lad!" he called out with a grin plastered on his round face. "Ya sure do get lost a lot for a feller who likes maps, eh?"

An inaudible chuckle escaped Joel's lips. He had a point, actually.

"Well, then? What are ya waitin' for? Get ta minin'! Yer already *way* behind us in riches! I don' wanna have'ta keep lendin' ya money when we get back to the village!" Alistair laughed and gave him a hard slap on the back.

Joel shook his head, but took out his pickaxe and began to swing at the cave wall anyway. He was doing what he had done before: Mining the black gold ore, but not taking any for himself. Bronrar was the first to notice Joel's stubborn behavior.

"You're still not taking any for yourself? You're missin' out! This stuff will make you rich."

"He's right, lad," Alistair said. "I know ya got it stuck in yer noggin that black gold is bad, but ya gotta admit…" he trailed off and then looked lovingly at the shiny ore by Joel's feet. "It's beautiful, ain't it?"

"More importantly, we have seen no evidence that it's as harmful as you claim," Lucia added. She held out a piece of ore in her hand and looked at it lovingly.

Joel didn't have a response. They wouldn't be able to understand his sign language; not that it mattered. He couldn't reveal any more than he already had. Not without betraying his duty. Somehow, he needed to gain their trust.

The situation worsened as time went on and the black gold piled up by his feet. Now, his friends were beginning to desire what he was refusing to take.

"All I'm sayin' is if you don' want it… why can't we have it?" Bronrar asked as he approached the mute. Joel held up his pickaxe defensively. The nervous miner put his hands up and shook them.

"Oi! He's right! Quit bein' selfish, lad! There's no reason ta drag us down with ya!" Alistair chimed in.

His stomach sinking and a lump in his throat, Joel held firm. They were getting worse. The transformation of their minds was beginning, and he was helpless to do anything but watch it unfold. How easy it would be to just give in, to join them! To live in ignorant bliss and simplistic hatred for whoever was deemed an 'enemy'. To live only in the pursuit of what made him feel good: black gold. Tempting as it sounded on the surface, Joel knew it could only lead to ruin.

"He is quite stubborn," Lucia said as footsteps thumped behind her. "But I'd take 'stubborn' over 'murderer' any day!" She and the others turned to face Wolfgang, who smiled back at them, licking his lips like a fox in a chicken coop.

"I see ye lot have got a good amount of ore this time around," Wolfgang said. "Yer puttin' a lot of it to waste, though. How 'bout I take it off yer hands?"

Lucia remained silent and held her pickaxe out toward him.

He scoffed. "I ain't here for *yer* treasures. I'll take those later; after I finish ye off!" Wolfgang said, then pointed at the black gold by Joel's feet. "I'm only here for this *good for nothin's* ore."

"Joke's on you, ya scruffy lookin' knob!" Alistair said with a derisive laugh. "He won't hand it over ta anyone! Not even us-"

Joel handed Wolfgang a sack and stepped away from the black gold on the ground.

"Th-this must be some kinda joke!" Alistair said, wide-eyed.

Wolfgang howled aloud with laughter as he picked up the ore and placed it in the sack. After turning to leave, he said, "Maybe ye should pick yer friends better. This rat can't do anythin' right! And he ain't even good to his friends!"

Joel grimaced and then pointed over Wolfgang's shoulder, telling him to leave. For once, he listened and walked back to where Angus was still mining.

Alistair gritted his teeth and his chest welled up. "Ya wouldn't give us, yer friends, anythin'… but ya give that pig of a man *everythin'*?" The big man threw his pickaxe down. "Th-that's just…"

"Rude," Lucia said.

"Erm… yeh!" said Alistair.

"If anyone deserves it the least, it's Wolfgang," Bronrar added while scratching his nose.

Joel looked down and sighed. They weren't thinking clearly, but then, that was expected. The question on his mind was: How could he take their minds off of the black gold?

"I think it's time we explore elsewhere in this cave, wouldn't you say Alistair and Bronrar?" Lucia asked.

"Right…" said Bronrar.

"You forgot Joel, ya idiot!" Alistair said. Lucia sharpened her eyes at him. "Oh… right…"

The three ventured further into the cave as Joel stood alone in the darkness, contemplating his next move.

~

THE TRIO eventually reached a new spot in the back-right corner of the cave. There was another tunnel entrance to their left. Alistair peered into the passage; squinting in the dimming light of his torch to try and get a good view.

"Well, would ya look at that? Another tunnel! I wonder if *Dalton* is in there!" Alistair said while grinning at Lucia. Instead of a retort, she remained silent as the group began to swing their pickaxes once again.

"Something wrong?" Bronrar asked her.

"I have this uneasy feeling…" Lucia trailed off. "Every time I start mining, I forget about the true objective at hand. Why is that?"

"You *did* say that you were going to go off on your own if we didn't find the first team in here…" Bronrar said.

"Could it be that the black gold distracts us? Makes us greedier?" Lucia asked.

"Aw, don' tell me yer buyin' that load of lamb!" Alistair jumped in with a chuckle. "It's a bunch of rocks, lass. They ain't doin' anythin' to us!"

She snorted. It was a sign of the end times if Alistair of all people was the one talking sense. "Perhaps I'm imagining things." In her peripheral vision, she noticed Joel approaching. "And yet… he continues to stay with us; to encourage us not to take the ore…"

Alistair and Bronrar looked over their shoulders to see Joel mining close by. He tipped his helmet and waved to the group. They waved back, half-heartedly. The mute wasn't the only one who'd been following them, however. Angus approached, his monstrous silhouette sticking out like a sore thumb; even in the darkness.

Lucia dropped her pickaxe and drew upon her claymore. She held it one-handed, outward, and in Angus' direction. "What do you want?"

"I wish to speak with Bronrar and nothin' more," he replied. He looked over Lucia's shoulder and smiled at his friend. There was noticeable discomfort in Bronrar's expression.

"Ya don' have'ta do anythin'. We'll protect ya, fella. Besides, we got a whole bunch'a treasure ta protect, too!" Alistair said in an apparent attempt to whisper that had come out loud.

"Please, Bronrar, I only wish to explain myself. As you can see, I am unarmed," Angus pleaded. The nervous miner rubbed his chin.

Lucia stepped forward, the tip of her blade mere inches from Angus' torso. "Leave here at once, or I'll-"

"You won't be doing much in your current condition," he interrupted. "Please, believe me. I'm not here to fight. I only wish to make amends with my friend."

"Very well," Bronrar said.

Lucia looked over her shoulder and raised an eyebrow. "Are you sure?"

"He is unarmed," Bronrar said while readying his pickaxe. "So, I at least stand a chance fighting back if I need to. We won't go far, just in case," he replied while pointing Angus to a spot from the left of the new tunnel. With that, they strode away.

"I don' like this…" Alistair muttered.

"Agreed," Lucia said, her eyes wandering over to Joel. The mute continued to chip away at the wall, not taking any of the black gold ore at his feet. The shadowy, yet sparkling form of the ore beckoned her from the rocky floor. How could he turn his nose up to such brilliance; such majesty? With an extra stride in her step, she walked in his direction.

"Where ya goin'?" Alistair asked.

"To find answers," she replied without looking back.

Upon reaching Joel, she cleared her throat. The mute looked up from his previous axe swing and smiled at her. Lucia bent over and picked up a piece of the ore at Joel's feet. She held it out in her hand and gazed upon it with wanting, sparkling eyes.

"The most beautiful metal I've ever seen…" she trailed off before looking back up at him. "And you hate it. You say it will poison our minds, but what evidence have you to offer?"

Joel crossed his arms and looked down for a moment. He then reached into his gigantic bag for a pen and notebook. After a few moments of jotting something down, he raised it up for her to see. Lucia squinted at first, but soon they were wide and she nearly gasped.

Have you forgotten about Dalton?

"That's right!" she said as a shiver ran down her spine. "I thought that perhaps the black gold distracts us; makes us greedier. Is that what you meant?"

Joel nodded and then wrote some more in his notebook. He held it up once again to communicate:

Yes, but that is only the first stage. It begins to consume your every thought until it's one of the only things left in your mind. Only the most important things to you can break the spell.

"But how do you know this? How can I know for sure?" she asked.

The mute once again wrote in his notebook. He held it up after a brief period of scribbling.

Pay attention to the others. They will grow more desperate for black gold as they gather more of it. Eventually, they will become so consumed by it that they'll begin to worship the ---- ------ black gold to the point of insanity.

Lucia crinkled her nose and said, "What is this you've crossed out? I think it says d-dark… bah, I can't read it! What are you hiding?"

Joel gave no response and instead pointed back at 'black gold' in his notebook. However, Lucia didn't believe that it had been a spelling mistake. She was sure that he was still withholding information.

"This is why I have trouble trusting in your word, Joel. I am a mercenary by trade. My work is *not* to take people's word at face value. Tell me *everything*," she demanded.

Joel darted his eyes away and returned his notebook to the backpack. Lucia sighed. She walked back over to Alistair, who was still mining. However, instead of stopping to mine with him, she continued past; intending to make a right around the bend of the new tunnel.

"Where do ya think yer goin', lass?" Alistair called out. She stopped, but kept her back turned to him. "We're supposed ta stay with the group, remember?"

"I know…" Lucia trailed off, resuming her strides for the tunnel.

"What did he *say*?" the big man asked.

"Nothing helpful," she said, looking over her shoulder. In the growing darkness, Alistair had become but a faint, if large, figure to her. "But I now realize that there's no more time to waste."

"Bah!" she heard Alistair cry from behind. Shortly after, in the tunnel, she heard his plodding footsteps approaching. The mercenary narrowed her eyes and snorted. He was like a needy puppy dog, she thought.

Across the cave, it hadn't taken Bronrar long to start laying into Angus for his murderous ways.

"Yer a killer, Angus! Yer as bad as Wolfgang is!" he said.

"You must realize that I had little choice in the matter," Angus said while putting his massive hands up and bobbing them. "You know how it is with him: Kill or be killed."

"And yet here I am, alive and kickin'."

"You were lucky to get out when you did, and you received protection from that group of outcasts. Had I known that was an option, I'd have been right there with you…"

"It's indefensible. You killed innocent people," Bronrar shot back.

"I know…" Angus replied, hanging his head. "I am in league with the wrong people. You escaped such a fate, and I am happy for you. But me? I have little choice. Wolfgang will kill me and make it look like an accident. Faramond doesn't like me, so I doubt he will care."

"I wanted to believe that you were bein' controlled by those two monsters, Angus. I truly did…" Bronrar said. "But then I saw how casual you were about killin' them miners. They didn't deserve it."

"I don't think you grasp the situation entirely, my friend," Angus said.

"How's about you tell me everythin', then."

Angus sighed. "The truth is that Wolfgang has slowly been losin' his mind." He took off his miner's helmet and slicked back his blond hair. "He's been threatenin' myself and Edith more and more. He also wants to kill you, but of course, I won't let that happen."

"But you murdered people, too. Ya can't just take that back!" Bronrar said.

"He said to help him back there or I was a dead man," Angus said.

"I ain't buyin' that explanation," he replied through grit teeth. He could feel Angus trying to smooth-talk back into his good graces. "Edith told us last night that we would need to kill others as part of her big plan, and you were fine with it."

"You don't understand how deep this goes," Angus said, shaking his head. "Edith has lost control of Wolfgang. He will no longer listen to her… the original plan was to pick off weaker miners, true, but *his plan* is to kill as many as he can get away with. No one is safe, and now she fears him…"

"Edith is a foul woman on a power trip. Yer makin' her sound help-less," Bronrar said.

"I never said she was nice, now did I? All I'm sayin' is that there is someone far worse in this group, and if we're not careful, he will kill us all," Angus said before looking over his shoulder. Wolfgang was approaching. "Will you speak with me later? I believe we can stop Wolfgang, but we must come up with a plan…"

Bronrar nodded and then got back to mining where he stood. He looked to his right and realized that Alistair and Lucia were gone. He only spotted Joel, staring back at him with his usual friendly expression.

～

NEAR THE CENTER of the cave, Angus met with Wolfgang. The blond brute frowned up at him.

"What were ye talkin' about with the rat over there?" he asked and then cracked his knuckles. "Are ye thinkin' of betrayin' me, too?"

"No, the opposite," Angus said, forcing as much of a smirk as his stone face would allow. "We've reached an understanding. I will speak with him in more detail later, but you must give him some time before he joins up with us again."

"I don' know… it'll probably be easier to kill 'im." Wolfgang took a step forward, but Angus put a hand to his chest, stopping him.

"Please. I ask that you trust me on this one…" he said. Wolfgang looked at him with cold, reptilian eyes. He was like a snake coiling, ready to strike. "As a show of good faith, I'll give you a large sum of my black gold."

"Now yer talkin'," he said and then turned around. Angus followed Wolfgang back to their previous mining spot. His smile returned, larger than ever.

CHAPTER 16
RIGGITS

On his way back to Joel, just past the tunnel, Bronrar tripped and stumbled over something on the ground.

"The hell?" He looked down to find Alistair's battle axe. He picked it up and whisked it through the air. "Where did those two go, anyway?"

Joel approached and then pointed at the tunnel. He stared at the battle axe Bronrar had just grabbed.

"Why would they go in there alone? That's dangerous..." he replied. Joel pointed at Alistair's axe, and then himself. "Ye want this, do you?" The mute nodded.

"Welp, I have no use for it, so here ye go," he said. Joel took the axe and started jogging toward the tunnel. "Wait! Where are ye goin'?"

No response was returned as the darkness enveloped him.

IN THE TUNNEL, Lucia and Alistair hung upside down and slowly rose closer and closer to the ceiling. They had become ensnared at their ankles by something similar to a rope, except it was slimy like a tongue. Lucia had tried to cut them free, but she forgot about her injured shoulder and dropped the claymore from the resulting jolt of pain.

"So, what? You're the loudest man I ever met and *now* you decide to be quiet? Call for help!" Lucia said.

"Oh, shut yer mouth! I'm gettin' to it! I'm just a wee bit nervous, is all!" Alistair said as he flexed and flailed his upper body so that he could see above him. It was still difficult to make out exactly what was pulling them up, but he could swear that it had *teeth*.

"HELP! Please! I don' wanna die!" he cried out and then widened his eyes to see Joel standing below him, axe in hand. "Oh… well, that was fast!"

The mute pulled the axe backward, as if ready to throw it.

"Whoa! Whoa! Hold on thar, laddie!" he said. Joel halted. "Nothin' personal, but have ya ever swung one of them axes around before?"

"That never stopped you," Lucia chimed in. Alistair groaned.

Joel smiled back and nodded. He pulled the axe back once again as Alistair inched his way higher.

"Steady, now!" the big man said. Joel threw the axe and Alistair closed his eyes.

The grip of the rope-like substance loosened. He then fell to the sticky ground with a great thud and heard a desperate shriek from above. As he was on his hands and knees, Joel used his back as a boost, leaped into the air, and sliced the rope-like material around Lucia's ankles. She, too, came crashing to the floor but used her uninjured shoulder to take the blow. Again, something shrieked aloud from the ceiling.

The mercenary stood and nodded at Joel before grabbing her claymore and torch off the ground. She lit the torch and directed it up at the ceiling. Slimy, pale-green pods with sharp teeth hung upside down, their long tongues dangling lifelessly.

"Tha hell are those things?" Alistair asked.

"I'm unsure," Lucia said as she wiped the sweat from her forehead. "But I think we should alert Faramond to the existence of these creatures."

The group nodded in unison and began making their way back to the cave. As they walked, Lucia looked at Joel with a smile.

"For someone who dislikes violence, you are quite accurate with the axe," she said. "More so than the oaf. Perhaps you should keep it for yourself."

She nudged a grumbling Alistair. Joel shook his head before handing the battle axe back to him.

~

BACK IN THE CAVE, Faramond's calm pace of mining for black gold had increased to a furious tempo. Like a dog who hadn't eaten for days, he craved it more and more, letting his instincts take over as black gold filled the brown sack on the ground. The first team no longer mattered to him.

He gasped and snapped out of his trance. *Of course the first team mattered*, he thought. Faramond dropped his pickaxe and took off his miner's helmet. He looked over his shoulder to see Edith still watching him.

"I like a hard-working man," she said, playfully.

Faramond sighed. "Tell me honestly, Edith. Do you have feelings for me? Do you think we could be together?"

Edith placed a hand on her chest as if taken aback. "Fara… I was only waiting for you to ask."

"That's what I had hoped, but something is bothering me," he replied. Edith cocked her head. "Wolfgang… what is your relationship with him?"

The blonde beauty chuckled and said, "He and I used to be entangled, but he is such an abusive man." She looked over her shoulder with nervous eyes.

"I don't like to admit this, but I'm scared of him," she continued, her tone becoming sad. "I know he still wants me, but the truth is that I wish to be with you. I'm too frightened to tell him that, though. I feel safe when I'm with you, Fara. It's as if I can tell you anything."

"I already felt disdain for that snake of a man, but now, to hear that he's frightening you into staying with him…" Faramond trailed off, the rage in his voice growing with each word. "I'll *kill him* if he lays a finger on you again. The black gold is wasted on him, anyway. It would be more for us."

Edith gasped. "Faramond…"

His eyes widened and then he buried his forehead in his palm. "I'm sorry. I don't know why I said that."

"I appreciate your vigor, but I wish to see no more bloodshed in these mines," Edith said. Faramond looked up. He could have sworn her voice was wavering; as if she was about to laugh. But then he saw her wandering green eyes. *She's scared*, he thought. "However, the next time he tries to force me into anything… if you could use your authority over him…"

"Say no more. I will do my best not to harm the man, and I would prefer to use my authority as leader over him, anyway," Faramond said with cheer. "I love you, Edith. I would do anything for you."

Eyes wide and head tilted, Edith choked out, "I-I... love-"

"Sir! There's somethin' in tha tunnel up ahead that ya need ta see!" Alistair bellowed. His voice seemed to shake the cave.

Faramond let out an annoyed sigh. "What is it?"

"You'll have to see for yourself, sir. He's right, it's important," Lucia said. Joel nodded in addition.

"Very well. Lead the way."

As they walked toward the tunnel, Faramond asked, "What is it you wish to show me? I have more black gold to mine, so it had better be important."

"A creature of some kind, sir," Lucia said, looking back at him. "We traveled into a new tunnel system, and the wildlife was on the ceiling. I'll show you when we get there."

"Breaking protocol once again..." Edith said with a smirk. "We were all supposed to stay in this cave and get mining done. Venturing off alone is dangerous. It seems you have a listening problem, so perhaps I should stay and watch over you lot from now on."

"Oh, come on! We ain't a bunch'a children! We can take care of ourselves!" Alistair argued.

"Still, she's right," Faramond said. "You disobeyed direct orders. How many times will I allow you to get away with that, I wonder?" he asked in a cross tone. The group remained silent until they reached the new tunnel.

As they walked in, Bronrar followed along. Soon, their hard steps on the rock floor turned into light splashes. Faramond directed a torch toward his feet to see that there was an odd slime stuck to his boots. It was a dark red color that blended in well with the ground.

"Interesting..." Faramond muttered as they continued to walk. Within a few moments, Lucia and Alistair stopped.

The mercenary directed her torch up at the ceiling and Faramond followed suit. Pod-like creatures hung upside down, and from their open mouths dripped the same sticky liquid they had been stepping in.

"Just as I thought," Faramond said with a smile. "The slimy substance from earlier makes sense, now."

"Well? What is it?" Alistair asked.

"Your inexperience in the mines is showing, oaf," Edith said as she looked up at the pod. The creature's cut-off tongue dangled from its mouth, and it remained lifeless. "These are riggits, I believe. This is what their young look like. Isn't that right, Fara?"

"Correct," Faramond replied with a smile back at her. She had such wisdom despite her lack of experience, he thought. "Riggits were sometimes encountered in the mines just outside of Faiwell, too. Since you three hadn't been on previous expeditions, it makes sense that you wouldn't know about them. But most importantly, the riggits need a body of water nearby to live. Once they grow out of their pods, they become able to walk on land, but they are still primarily creatures of water. Considering how deep we are into the mines; I think this means we've found an alternate exit."

"Let's not be hasty," Edith said, her tone grave. "Dealing with riggits in high numbers is dangerous, especially with our team being so short on manpower. And God help us if we come across a king or queen…"

"Indeed," Faramond replied with a nod. "With that said, it's worth the risk of venturing out carefully. Especially if that's what the first team did."

"B-but there ain't no sign of the first team," Bronrar said.

"Who invited you here?" Edith shot back and narrowed her eyes at him.

"My apologies ma'am…" he mumbled. "I was curious what you lot were up to, is all."

"It's alright, Bronrar," said Faramond. "You were going to see this tunnel sooner or later, anyhow."

Edith frowned. "No Fara, you can't mean…"

"Yes, we need to explore this as an option. It could be our only way out of here," he said, raising an index finger. "And just think: With an alternate entrance and exit, it will become that much easier to transport the black gold. We can still salvage this expedition."

"We're better off waiting until tomorrow morning when the dratagons sleep. Dealing with the riggit pods is one thing, but fully grown? We can't handle many with our depleted numbers, and you know as well as I do that when their population goes unchecked, they become overwhelming," Edith said.

"I agree with you," Faramond said as he put a hand on her shoulder. "Which is why, if or when we see a group of riggits, we'll turn back: That's a promise. I believe it to be an option worth exploring."

The blonde beauty sighed and offered no further argument. The group exited the tunnel, and Faramond and Edith returned to the center of the cave.

"Everyone! Gather 'round!" he called out. The clanking of axes against rock began to cease. "I have interesting developments to share! Developments that I believe will satisfy all in the group!" The miners slowly made a circle around him and Edith.

"In a tunnel up ahead, we have discovered some riggit pods," Faramond said, pointing a torch to his front. "As many of you will know, riggits dwell near a water source. This leads me to believe that we will find an alternate exit to the mines if we follow the tunnel."

"But riggits are dangerous!" one miner said.

"How many of them are there?" asked another.

"We should stay here and continue to mine!" someone shouted to a few cheers.

"Frightening as it may be, we must not let our judgment be clouded. We must find an easy exit for the black gold. How can we be expected to carry it through the dratagon cave?" Faramond said. The miners quieted down.

~

ALISTAIR WHISPERED TO LUCIA, "Didn't he say it was ta find tha first team? What's he gettin' at?"

Lucia crossed her arms and fidgeted her mouth. "Perhaps it's to convince the miners that he has their best interests at heart. Or was he trying to convince *us*?"

"Soon, we will venture down the tunnel path. I will give you some time to prepare," Faramond said.

In short order, the group gathered in front of the new tunnel, falling into their usual rank. While traversing the path, their footsteps splashed in the odd slime once more. Alistair could hear some interesting tidbits from the miners behind him. They muttered that it was a slime excreted from the riggit pod's tongue. The more slime produced, the stickier their tongues got; and typically, the more victims they were able to ensnare. The more they ate, the faster they would reach their next form.

Up front, Alistair, Bronrar, and Lucia held their torches high. After the first two that had ensnared them earlier, they walked by a few more dangling tongues no more than ten paces further into the tunnel. The front guards were thorough about instructing where to avoid the pesky creatures, however, and no one was trapped. After walking in a straight line for some time, the path began to spiral downward and to the left. It felt unnatural to Alistair; almost like a spiraling staircase in a castle. As they twisted and turned, the path steeply declined.

"Watch your step, everyone," Faramond said.

After the initial twist, the path became straight again, but it continued to drop. At this point in the tunnel, a clear environmental change was taking place. It began to feel more organic: A mild pink color coated the rock and support beams, and instead of occasional puddles of slime, it became a constant. The riggit pods overhead were now prominent: There was a tongue hanging from the ceiling every five paces.

Feeling more confident in himself than ever, Alistair increased his pace on the steadily declining terrain.

Lucia whispered to him, "What are you doing?"

"Ah, don' worry! I can handle a couple of unmoving pods!" he replied with a chuckle.

As if the tunnel were responding to him, Alistair's boot caught a pointed piece of terrain that sent him tumbling to the ground. He happened to fall right in front of a hill, and so he rolled down uncontrollably, flailing his arms and panicking for a short time before landing at the bottom with a great *thud*. Next came the loud clanking of his axe rolling away from him.

"Can't he do *anything* quietly?" Bronrar's harsh whisper echoed. Alistair's ears pricked up. He wanted to yell back up at him, but that'd be proving his point, he thought with a groan.

"Everyone, we are now going down a hill. Mind your step," Faramond said in a hushed tone.

The big man got to his feet and felt himself all over. He let out a sigh of relief to not feel any pain from the fall, but he had lost his torch and axe. He could see the dimming torch to his right, but the battle axe had fallen and careened to his front and into the darkness. First, he grabbed his torch, noting that the flame had mostly been extinguished from the slime on the ground. Some embers remained, however, so he could make out minor details around him.

Alistair walked forward and surveyed the ground until he finally saw a gleam in his dimmed light. His battle axe was up ahead, covered in the same slime that had enveloped him. An odd warming sensation enveloped him like a blanket, but he paid it no mind, as the axe was what he was most worried about.

The big redhead bent over to retrieve his prized weapon, and as he looked up, he saw something odd: a deformity in the landscape. It appeared to be a boulder, but he couldn't be sure without the bright light of his torch, so he approached it. With each step, the puddles of sticky residue grew louder and louder, but Alistair didn't care. Curiosity had overtaken him.

Getting within arm's reach of the boulder, Alistair widened his eyes. It wasn't a boulder at all. It was moving ever so slightly with each breath. The dim light of his torch revealed a large, scaly creature that was sleeping. It lay curled up, like a dog taking a nap, and its short snout occasionally blew the remaining embers off of Alistair's torch. It had large, webbed feet with hooked claws at the end of each toe, but the most notable feature was what it lacked: This odd creature had no eyes to speak of; not even eyelids. Its scales appeared crusty and old, as if the animal was ancient and had never once seen the light of day. Finally, Alistair could make out what appeared to be a tail at its back. It reminded him of a turtle's tail, but longer.

Never one to keep thoughts to himself, Alistair said, "Tha hell is tha-" before a hand covered his mouth from behind and his words muffled. The big man looked back to see Lucia frowning at him.

"Don't you ever shut up?" she asked in a low, yet stern tone. She then removed her hand from his mouth.

Alistair attempted to quiet himself and said, "What? I was only wonderin' what that odd beast was..."

"It's a riggit," Bronrar whispered. "It looks a wee bit different than what I've seen, but I'm certain it's one of 'em."

Faramond appeared out of the darkness and inspected for himself. "We may have been fortunate," he whispered to the group. "Riggits are heavy sleepers."

He nudged his head forward and then began walking at the group's front. The miners followed their leader into the darkness, now able to make out several of the large riggits sleeping on the ground. Alistair grimaced and rubbed his arms. The warm sensation was starting to *burn*.

"Oi, tha slime is gettin' all spicy-like on me arms..." he said as quietly as he possibly could, and nudged Bronrar.

"The older a riggit gets, the more irritatin' their slime is. We need'a wash it off with some water," Bronrar said. He pulled a canteen from his pack. Before he could pour the water, however, he bumped into Faramond, who had stopped dead in his tracks.

Unbridled fear was painted on the leader's face. Alistair looked ahead to see two possible things that could have worried him: One was the ladder leading up to a hole in the ceiling. It was a sign that knockers could be nearby, and the last thing they needed was another tunnel collapse. However, the other, more noticeable detail was a giant riggit sleeping up ahead. Not only was its sheer size enough to take up most of the tunnel itself, but it also had a large horn on its snout.

"A q-queen riggit..." Bronrar murmured.

"Of all places..." Faramond said as he turned to face his crew. "We must turn back at once. A queen riggit is upon us. Most of you know what that means."

"Enlighten us," Lucia whispered.

"In a single cry, the queen commands the whole pod of riggits. All of those beasts we passed earlier... if we awaken the queen, we'll have to deal with her *and* the pod. It is no longer worth the risk," he replied, walking past her. He froze in place, however, when some high-pitched giggles echoed around the tunnel.

Faramond turned and looked up to see a few knockers peering down the hole from the ladder. One wore an oversized, horn-plated helmet, while the other two had wild, gray beards. They held rocks in their little hands.

"Everyone! Run back to the cave, now!" Faramond cried as the knockers began throwing stones at the queen riggit.

AT THE BACK of the pack, Joel could understand little besides his leader telling them to flee, so he listened. Suddenly, the back had become the front, and he was leading the team to their escape. A great roar from behind shook him to his very core, and the tunnel rumbled like a giant stomach. Dust and wood shavings from the supports fell, striking fear into his heart that a collapse was imminent. Yet, like the weakening beams and rocks around him, Joel managed to hang on and press forward. He could hear splashes from hurried strides through the vile riggit liquid behind him, but it sounded like someone was catching up. Could it have been one of the riggits, giving chase?

He looked back just in time to see Wolfgang kicking his legs out from under him. Joel tumbled to the ground and winced in pain as he rolled in the slime and was trampled on by several miners. He thought it would never end until he felt something pick him up by the waistband of his pants. A riggit? No! Alistair had grabbed him with his mighty strength as he ran.

"Ya gotta watch out, lad! That queen riggit is tryin' ta eat us!" he said as Joel dropped down and began to run alongside him.

A monstrous roar shook the tunnel once again, but then came weaker cries. The smaller riggits must have been awakened, Joel thought with a shudder. Many of them sounded close, but could not be seen in the darkness. He looked back to see Faramond running behind him, his broadsword drawn. Further back, he could see the massive silhouette of the queen riggit clawing her way through the narrowing and straining tunnel. Up ahead, he saw the slimy hill from earlier. Some of the men were struggling to make it up.

Alistair had begun to run in place on the sharp, slippery incline, so Joel got behind him and pushed. They made their way up the hill at a snail's pace as others passed them. Near the top finally, Alistair looked back and his eyes became inhumanly wide with fright. Joel gazed over his shoulder and gasped to see the queen's giant mouth, open and ready to swallow him in one bite. A giant tongue flung out and wrapped around his waist. It began to pull back on him. Joel's heart raced as Alistair grabbed hold of him. He pulled with grit teeth and desperate grunts from near the top of the hill, but both he and Joel were slowly being dragged down by the queen. Joel looked back once more to see a gaping mouth with slime dripping from every row of sharp teeth that it bared.

Lucia slid down the incline, and with one arm, brought down her claymore onto the queen's tongue. She gasped as her blade bounced back and she fell off-balance.

"Impossible..." she muttered as Faramond jumped in to confront the beast. Instead of slashing with his broadsword, he pushed his torch into the monster's tongue. The queen riggit let out a pained roar and released Joel from her grip.

"They don't like fire," Faramond said as he motioned Joel and the others to follow him up the hill.

The queen clawed her way up in pursuit, but as the hill turned to a flat surface, she was no longer able to fit between the ceiling and floor. In one last attempt to get them, the queen took a deep breath and shot out a burst of the slimy liquid from her mouth. The fleeing miners had already gained some distance, but the vile fluid still reached the back of the group. Joel could hear a searing noise, like a flame hitting the water. He looked to his right and noticed Alistair dropping to the ground, crying out in pain.

Alistair grabbed his left leg and rolled on the ground. "Oooo, me leg! It's on fire! The worst pain I've ever felt! Since me mum last gave me a whoopin'!"

Bronrar sprang into action with his canteen in hand. He ran to where Joel stood over the big man and dumped his remaining water supply all over him. Alistair's eyes widened and he let out a relieved sigh.

As he ran by, Faramond smacked Alistair on the shoulder and called out, "No time to sit around! Get moving!"

The big redhead chuckled and got to his feet. He then ran alongside Bronrar. "I owe ya a great debt, lad!"

"Think nothin'… of it! I've been in… the same situation," Bronrar said between breaths.

Joel smiled. Bronrar was coming around to doing the right thing more often. He was happy that he'd gone back to rescue him back when the dratagons attacked.

However, the group was not out of danger, as the remaining riggits had been awakened by the queen's roar. The old, scaly beasts scurried with surprising quickness toward unsuspecting miners who ran by. Some spewed the sticky liquid at them, while others attacked more directly, like cats chasing a rodent. The most common issue was running into the dangling tongues of the pods, however. In their panic, some miners hadn't noticed or remembered the pod locations and became ensnared by the ceiling-dwelling creatures.

Joel heard the cries of multiple men up ahead. He swiped a torch from a panting Alistair and lit it with a quick strike of his flint rock. As he ran by the dangling men, he touched the riggit pod tongues with his lit torch. The creatures screeched and the men shouted as they fell. Just as Joel was feeling good about helping his fellow miners, he tripped over something and crashed to the sticky ground. He looked up while shaking the cobwebs out to see that it had been a riggit's tail. The beast was chewing on a bloody corpse. Each *crunch* of its victim's bones sent shivers rippling through his body.

The others had run past Joel, and he had lost his torch upon falling. The riggit turned, blood dripping from its snout, and let out a roar. The horrid noise made Joel's ears ring and disoriented him. His head felt as light as a feather. When he came to his senses, he found himself staring at the bloodthirsty riggit, face-to-face. The beast wrapped its tongue around Joel's ankle and began to drag him in. Try as he might, the mute couldn't reach the dimming torch on the ground.

As panic began to overcome him, Joel felt the tongue release its grip and the creature wailed. He watched as it scurried off into the darkness of the tunnel, its long, scaly back ablaze. The mute looked up to see Faramond standing before him, torch in hand.

"Quickly! We have to get out of here!" he said before turning to run off.

Joel picked himself up and followed the light of Faramond's torch. As he made his way through the tunnel, he passed a couple of dead men. The remaining riggits were feasting on them. A few had also been taken by the pods on the ceiling. The dangling men were covered in a slime that slowly digested them, and the pod's teeth had already sunk into them. Their intestines hung down from the ceiling like decorations at a lavish party. Joel shuddered to think that he had almost shared the same fate, and at that moment, he was thankful to have Faramond as his leader.

CHAPTER 17
THE CALL

Conrad looked outside the Mouth of Hell as the rain began to wind down. It had been a quiet couple of hours. To his surprise, most of the other miners kept to themselves, save for William, who couldn't help but talk to everyone. Most had turned him away, but Conrad felt the need to engage him; whether it was his tendency to treat him as a customer or his natural curiosity, he wasn't sure.

Although things were looking up, Conrad could sense a coming conflict from the rain ending. Black gold was still a sensitive subject for the group, and so he decided to address everyone on the matter before they even had a chance to become worried. He stood in the middle of the tunnel and cleared his throat.

"Well then, it looks like the rain is beginning to fade," he said. All faces in the tunnel brightened. "I propose we go back to business as usual. Let's stand outside and guard our treasures once again."

"An' make sure ye stay away from me stash this time," Brice said. He and the hooligans glared at Solomon.

"T'was an honest mistake!" Solomon said with a nervous chuckle.

"A conflict is on the horizon, methinks," Henic whispered to Conrad while nudging him in the direction of Brice and his cronies. He only nodded in response.

As the rain turned into a drizzle, the strategist led his small group back out to the base camp. William pranced along the puddles joyfully to the annoyance of those around him, while many of the older men took slow, plodding strides behind. Everyone returned to their usual spots; to guard their stashes of the black gold. The lone exception was William, which didn't escape the notice of Conrad. Feeling curious, he walked over to the gangly man.

"You don't have any treasures to guard?" Conrad asked.

"Oh no, no, no. Wolfgang took it from me," he replied with cheer.

"You don't seem disappointed…"

"Well, I'm just glad to be out and about! There's nothin' better than freedom, sir!" William said as he looked up at the gray clouds. "No treasure is as valuable as that. He can take all he wants…"

"I see…" Conrad muttered.

"Something wrong, sir?" William asked.

"Ah, it's nothing," he replied with a shrug. "I was only wondering if there was a different reason for your lack of treasure. We'll see to it that Wolfgang returns them when he and the others return."

William only smiled in response. Conrad noted that it was darkening outside. He began to worry about whether Faramond and his team were coming back at all. It was another possibility he would need to plan for.

Further up the path, Conrad joined Henic. He was staring, arms crossed, at Cyriack. The old man was pacing back and forth in front of the Mouth of Hell, mumbling to himself. On occasion, he would stop to inspect the inside of the tunnel.

He nudged the strategist. "Did ye notice ol' Cyriack over there? Just standin' in front of the tunnel, talkin' to himself? Odd, wouldn't you say?"

Conrad studied the old man for a short while and decided that Henic had a point. He began making his way to the mine entrance when Henic grabbed his shoulder. "Where are ye goin'?"

"To understand what he's up to, of course," Conrad said with a smile back at him.

"Should we really get involved? There can be nothin' but trouble afoot when a man like that is actin' so curious. It's odd enough that he would leave his black gold unattended, but now he's actin' like he's lost his mind completely…"

"I understand that you don't like sticking your nose into other people's business, but for now, it is our duty to see what's wrong," he replied.

"I don't mean to speak outta line, but I say it's best to let him be. If we ask him what's wrong, we're askin' for trouble. Faramond will be back soon, anyhow. Nightfall approaches," said Henic.

"That's the best-case scenario," Conrad argued. "I'd rather prepare for the worst. If Cyriack has legitimate concerns, and Faramond doesn't end up returning, then I must settle the matter quickly."

"But what about your black gold stash? You really wish to take your eyes off of it?"

"Not to worry," the strategist replied with a nod. "I didn't take many spoils from the mines, anyway."

He frowned while turning to the tunnel entrance. His suspicions about the effects of black gold continued to grow. Even Henic was feeling the effects, he thought. Could Cyriack be trying to avoid it? Conrad was looking for a sign: Something to confirm or deny his suspicions.

"Is something wrong, Cyriack?" Conrad asked while tapping him on the shoulder. He turned around, startled, but his frightened expression calmed almost immediately.

"Ah, it's only you, lad," he said before turning back to the tunnel. "Ye ever get a bad feelin' about these mines?"

"All the time," Conrad said.

"Ye may think I'm imaginin' things, but I believe there's an evil presence about this place," Cyriack said and then paused as if listening for a noise. "Somethin' ain't right."

"You seem to be focusing on the tunnel. Are you worried about Faramond and his company?" Conrad asked.

"No... I refer to someone over there..." Cyriack pointed in the direction of the base camp. "I know it sounds odd, but I'm a spiritually in-tune feller, ye see. I know when there are magical folk about."

"You refer to a Wizard?"

"When we first arrived at the mountain, I thought fer sure I felt the presence of one. But now? I only feel an *evil presence*; one filled with malicious intent. But he's hidin' it well, now. I can't tell who it is," the old man said.

Conrad massaged his forehead for a moment and then asked, "So, a Dark Wizard of some kind?"

"Hard ta say."

"Could it be that you feel the dark presence in a *material*, not a person?"

Raising an eyebrow, Cyriack said, "I cannot recall anythin' of the sort happenin', but if it were a cursed object, I don't see why not."

"If I brought something over to you, do you think you could feel its presence? If it has any at all, that is?" Conrad asked.

Cyriack nodded, so Conrad turned and trekked back down the path to Henic. He intended to conduct a test; one that could satisfy his questions about the black gold. Although it was a long shot, his curiosity had gotten the best of him once more. Even if Cyriack was a crazy old man, it was worth a try.

Upon arriving, Henic approached him. "So, what did the old fella say? Has he gone crazy?"

"I'll explain, but first, could I borrow a piece of your black gold?"

"W-what for?" Henic asked. He stepped back and turned sideways, as if to protect his stash.

Conrad put his hands up and shook them. "Relax. Cyriack claims he can feel a dark presence amongst our group. I believe it could be the black gold."

"Oh, Conrad… not you, too," he said, relaxing his posture. "Why is everyone questionin' this wonderful treasure? It'll make us all rich! Is that so bad? I need it for me family… me farm…"

"Please," he pleaded, holding out a hand. "Only for a moment and only one piece. I'll give it right back. That's a promise."

Henic reached into his pocket and grabbed a chunk of ore. He held it out in his hand, ready to drop it into Conrad's grasp. His hand shook and the piece of ore teetered in his palm until he finally closed it into a fist.

"Wait, don' you have yer own black gold? Use yer own!" Henic snapped back.

Conrad widened his eyes. It was the first time he'd heard him so angry.

"Right… my apologies…" he said, turning to his tent.

He heard Henic mutter from behind, "Nothin' personal…"

The strategist entered his tent and grabbed one of his few black gold ores, along with some generic items: A spade, a pickaxe, and a silver ore that he had mined. He had decided that instead of being unsure, he would test Cyriack's abilities with ordinary items. If he claimed the spade to be a dark presence, for example, then he would know him to either be lying or a madman.

Conrad exited the tent and walked straight up to Cyriack, who once again had his back turned to the group and was looking into the tunnel.

"Sorry for the wait. I have gathered some items that I suspect may be cursed. I was hoping you could tell me which ones are and which ones aren't," Conrad said.

The old man nodded as he laid the items out on the ground. Cyriack first picked up the pickaxe and examined it. It wasn't long before he put it down and stated, "Nothin' peculiar 'bout this one. It's a normal pickaxe."

Next, Cyriack examined the silver ore. Shortly after, he placed it back on the ground and shook his head. Then came the spade. The old man examined it for a bit longer. Conrad cocked his head. Could it truly have been cursed?

"Ye haven't used this spade much, I see."

"Erm…" Conrad muttered, darting his eyes away. "No, I haven't. As a matter of fact, I bought it for this trip."

Cyriack chuckled. "No need ta be ashamed of yer inexperience, boy," he said and then placed the spade back on the ground. Next, he picked up the black gold ore.

As the magnificent sparkles of the ore reflected in his eyes, he stared back into the rock as if it were the love of his life.

"Now, this…" he trailed off. Conrad leaned in. He could feel his suspicions being confirmed. "It's the most wonderful thing I may have ever seen…"

He frowned. His reactions were the same as everyone else's. He put hands to hips and then eyed the old man with suspicion.

"Do you feel a dark presence in it?"

Cyriack didn't respond immediately. Instead, he held the ore in both hands and stared down at it in wonder. His eyes stretched wider with each twinkle it gave off, and his breaths labored more with every second that passed. Conrad could see that a burden had come upon him. He was sweating, now.

"I… I don' know…" Cyriack mumbled.

"You don't know?"

"I've never felt anythin' like this. Not in me entire life. I've felt good, and I've felt evil, but this… what the hell *is* this?" he asked as his hands began to shake. Conrad raised an eyebrow. He leaned in, his expression alone demanding an explanation.

"At first, it felt great to hold, but when you asked if I felt nothin', I concentrated a wee bit more… and then… darkness…"

"So, we are to assume that's bad?" Conrad asked.

"I don' know. It's never happened before. It seems ta me like an absence of a feelin'. That's the only way I can describe it. I have'ta admit, it's frightenin'. If it weren't worth so much, I'd never touch it again," he said, dropping the ore onto the ground.

Conrad gathered the items and said, "Thank you. Sorry if I disturbed you. Perhaps we can speak more at length about this evil presence you've felt, later." Cyriack nodded and then turned back around to face the tunnel.

As the strategist walked toward his tent, he pondered about Cyriack's reaction to the black gold. Rather than obtain the answers he was looking for, he got more questions. Excluding the possibility that Cyriack was deranged and making things up, his observation was that every time he tried to figure out whether the black gold was good or bad, the answer was always gray.

The only one who had claimed black gold to be bad, Joel, either refused to prove it or could not. Meanwhile, the others were generally quite happy with its beauty and value. Cyriack was the first to have a neutral, if startled, opinion.

Conrad walked by Henic and entered his tent to return the materials. As he exited, the farmer stood before him and bowed his head.

"I wanted to apologize for my rudeness, back there..." Henic said with a half-hearted smile. "I'm worried about the fortune, is all. There are some shifty characters about this group, but you ain't one of 'em, so I was wrong not to trust ye."

Although Conrad paused for a moment, he held no grudge against Henic for his behavior. Instead, he was more interested in testing theories about the black gold.

"It's alright, but from now on, I need you to trust me. Can you do that?" he asked.

"Of course, of course!" Henic replied with a nod.

"Good," Conrad said, holding out his hand. "Now then, hand me a piece of black gold."

Henic paused, mid-nod. He looked down, and a frown came to his face. Now twitching, he reached a hand into his pocket and retrieved the ore. He held it out, and his hand shook feverishly. Within moments, his fingers began to close around the black gold piece.

"Henic..." Conrad said in a stern tone.

He looked back up as beads of sweat formed on his brow. "W-why did you need it again, sir?"

"To prove a point," Conrad said, then motioned his hand to give him the material.

"A-and you'll give it right back?"

"Yes."

Finally, he turned his palm over and the black gold piece plopped onto Conrad's hand. Henic let out a deep breath, as if he'd dropped a heavy bale of hay. After a few more breaths, he seemed at ease.

"You see? That wasn't so bad, was it?" Conrad asked.

"No, but..." Henic trailed off as he stared intently at his hand. "When can I get it back?"

"Right now," the strategist replied as he handed the ore piece back. "Now, hand it back to me again."

"What?" Henic burst out. He closed his fingers around the precious metal. "What are ye playing at?"

"This is an exercise in control," Conrad said. "I have accepted that you wish to hold onto your black gold, but that doesn't mean I'll let it control you. I suspect it is poisoning your mind."

"Nonsense! I'm fine."

"And yet, you wish not to hand it back over to me?" Conrad asked.

Henic paused, looking up, as if in deep thought. "I'm only makin' sure it stays in safe hands, is all."

"You said that you trusted me only moments ago. I just handed that piece of ore back to you. Why would I take it now?"

As his posture became less defensive, Henic held his hand out once again, black gold in his palm. "Point taken," he said, dropping the ore back into his hand.

"Good," Conrad said as he dropped the black gold back into Henic's hands once more. "We'll continue this way until you are comfortable."

"Do you truly believe my mind's been poisoned?"

"Perhaps, but even if you don't believe that, go along with it for now. It's not as if we have anything better to do at the moment," Conrad said. Henic nodded and reluctantly placed the black gold back in his hand.

AFTER AN HOUR PASSED, Henic showed signs of comfort in handing his black gold to Conrad. The strategist had become convinced more than ever that the ores were affecting the miners. If it were simple greed, why wouldn't people try to hide that? Every time Henic had snapped at him and refused to hand the ore over, he had been transparent in how protective he was of the precious metal. Most greedy individuals that Conrad had known in his lifetime were better at hiding it.

Upon reaching this conclusion, however, Conrad realized something else: The sun was setting. Soon, darkness overtook the base camp. He gazed at Henic, who shared the same look of concern.

"Nightfall is upon us, and the group ain't back..." Henic said as he handed him the black gold ore once again. "What should we do?"

Conrad sighed, placed the black gold in Henic's hand, and then closed his fingers around the ore for him.

"I think that our exercise was a success," Conrad said with a smile that soon fell to a firm frown. "As for it being nightfall, I know what I want to do, but I don't believe it will be a popular decision."

"You can't mean venturing in there tonight, can you?" Henic asked.

"Indeed," Conrad said, crossing his arms. "Faramond would do the same for us. Besides, we should think of our friends. They may need our help."

"True, but..." Henic trailed off, looking back at his stash of black gold. Conrad raised an eyebrow. Had the past hour been for nothing? "Bah! I cannot in good conscience leave them, either," he said. Conrad breathed a sigh of relief.

"I'm glad you're with me, but the others, I'm not so sure of..."

"Stubborn they may be, but why not appeal to their wallets?" the farmer asked.

"You mean lure them back in with the promise of more black gold?"

"Yes, sir," Henic said, eyeing his stash. "I don' think many of 'em will want to risk losin' their spoils, but with the promise of adding to it..."

"A brilliant idea!" Conrad said, clapping him on the shoulder. "Shall we address the group, then?"

The duo walked to the center of the base camp. A few fires had been set up: Brice and his crew sat around one of them, laughing and telling stories. The other fire had a few of the quieter miners sitting at it; and finally, Peter, Solomon, and William sat at another. He noted that Cyriack had not moved from his spot in front of the mine entrance. It was something he chose not to focus on, however. The more pressing matter was Faramond and his team.

"Attention, everyone!" Conrad called out. The faces by the fires looked up, and Cyriack looked back from the tunnel entrance. "I would like to call a meeting. It won't take long."

When everyone arrived at the center of base camp, complaints rained down on Conrad nearly as much as the previous downpour had.

"This better not be what I think it's about!" one miner said.

"I ain't goin' back in that hellhole!" Peter chimed in.

"It's safer out here…" another said.

"We're stayin'!" Brice added, and his crew nodded along behind him.

This was the reaction that Conrad had expected, so he felt lucky to have been given the earlier suggestion by Henic.

"I understand all of your concerns," he said. "But hear me out, first. Perhaps we can make the prospect of returning inside worth your while. I'm sure many of you would like to return with even more black gold, no?" The groaning and complaining quieted down.

"Those of you who venture back into the mines with Henic and I will be handsomely rewarded. I'll see to it personally that you get extra time to mine the black gold. We all know that there is much of it left in the caves."

That promise alone was all it took. Even Brice, who was known for his stubbornness as much as his troublemaking ways, agreed to the deal: The team would search for Faramond and his crew, while also stopping to obtain more black gold ore along the way. Conrad knew it would slow them down, but he also knew there was strength in numbers. He and Henic braving the mines alone would not be enough, especially with knockers lurking about.

Quickly, the group gathered their things and prepared for their journey back into the mines. There was some grumbling about leaving their black gold behind unattended, but the prospect of filling up another empty cart excited the miners. Aside from that, few others ever visited Mt. Couture, so the odds of their belongings being stolen were low.

As they entered the Mouth of Hell, Cyriack approached Conrad.

"Sir, could I have a word?"

"Of course," Conrad said. The two men increased their pace until they were out of ear's reach from the front of the pack.

"The evil presence that I mentioned before… it has followed us into the mines," the old man whispered.

Conrad shot Cyriack a sidelong glance. Black gold had not been brought in with them as far as he knew. Was the evil presence truly one from their group? Or had the old man gone mad?

"You're certain that it's one among us?" he asked.

"Yes, sir."

"How do you know it's not me?" Conrad asked. Cyriack cocked his head.

"I have a good feelin' about ye, is all… ye don' believe me, do ye?" he replied, darting his eyes to the ground.

"It's not that-"

Click

Conrad looked at the ceiling. He raised his torch, expecting to see some knockers or a small hole. However, nothing was there.

Clack

Click

"Sir?" Cyriack asked.

"Don't you hear that?" Conrad asked.

"Indeed, I do. Ain't that the sound of the knockers?" the old man said.

"Yes. According to Faramond, anyhow."

Cyriack let out a small breath. "Odd…" Conrad eyed him for further explanation. "It's odd because, around these here parts, I get a *good* feelin'. But the knockers ain't supposed ta be good."

Click

Clack

The two men continued to look up as they walked, but soon, the noises faded. Conrad was becoming suspicious of Cyriack's 'sixth sense'; or at least beginning to wonder if he was unable to tell what was good and what was bad with it.

"How about now? Do you feel anything?" he asked.

"The good feeling has faded," Cyriack said. He rubbed his forehead and strained his eyes. "Up ahead…" Cyriack pointed a jittery finger into the foreboding darkness. "W-we must t-turn back…"

The old man stopped. Conrad looked back at him to see that he had turned pale, and sweat dribbled down his cheek.

"What for?" Conrad asked.

"Somethin' bad… somethin' *deadly* is up ahead," Cyriack replied, now backpedaling. Without realizing it, he bumped into Henic.

"Oi! What's the big idea?" Henic complained.

"I'm sure it's nothing," Conrad put a hand on Cyriack's shoulder to calm him down, but the old man tensed up instead.

Brice cut through to the front of the group and said, "What's the hold-up, eh? I got black gold ta mine!"

Conrad nodded. "Just hold on a momen-"

Skreeee

"What the bloody hell was that?" Henic asked aloud.

Conrad thought back to the night before. He remembered that same call from the depths of the mines as they'd been exiting. The shriek sounded otherworldly, like nothing close to any animal growl or howl he'd ever heard. It was the beginning of nightfall, the same as yesterday when they'd heard it last.

Skreeeee

The screeches from down the tunnel grew closer to the group.

"There is little time," Conrad said as he turned to face his men. "This is obviously a creature of the mountain, whatever it is. We can choose to either face it or flee. Let's decide, swiftly."

Skreeeeeeee

"I ain't stayin'!" Cyriack said. He began jogging back toward the entrance.

The other miners stood for a moment in apparent shock, but it wasn't long before they followed suit. Brice and his crew left immediately, while Peter was next to shuffle off, more likely to keep an eye on the hooligans than anything else. Solomon was next to leave, but to Conrad and Henic's surprise, William stood among them when all was said and done.

"Well then, what shall we do?" William asked in a cheerful tone.

Skreeeeeee

"You aren't worried about the noise?" Conrad asked.

"Oh no, not at all! There are noises all around us, all the time! Besides, what if it were but a friendly creature?" William said.

"It doesn't sound friendly…" Henic muttered.

SKREEEEEEEEEEEE

Conrad could feel panic setting in his gut. He was confident in his swordsmanship and believed that the three of them could take on one creature, whatever it may be. Why then couldn't he shake the feeling that Cyriack had been correct? Why did it feel like death itself was coming for them?

"We must return to the outside. I have a bad feeling," Conrad said, turning to leave. He could hear something heavy moving down the tunnel from them. It sounded like an animal's claws scratching against rock.

The three men ran back toward the mine entrance. Along the way, they encountered the same clicking as before.

"Odd to hear... the knockers in... this one spot," Henic said between breaths as he jogged. "They followed us around... last time..."

"Oho! Best not to disturb those vile creatures, then!" William chimed in.

Eventually, the trio made it out of the mines to see the others waiting for them. After resting for a moment, Conrad addressed the group.

"As this is the second night in a row that we've encountered a loud creature of some kind, I think it's safe to say we have a nocturnal predator that roams the mines. Luckily, it never seems to pursue its prey outside the mountain. We should be safe for now," Conrad said as he noticed the uncomfortable expressions around him. "With that said, there is still Faramond's team to consider-"

"I ain't goin' back in there!" Peter called out. Other miners shouted out in unison to let Conrad know they agreed.

"The old man's got the right idea," Brice chimed in, crossing his arms. "It ain't safe in there. Everything's tryin' to kill us in those mines. It's Faramond's own fault fer goin' back in, especially at night!"

"Think about this: Would Faramond leave *you* behind in there?" Conrad asked.

"No, but then again, I ain't stupid enough to go back in there! Especially when I got all the riches I'll ever need!" Brice said with a smirk. He motioned over to his crew and began to walk away. "I've had enough of this place. Time to leave."

"You would leave this place at night? Through the Dead Woods? Yer as foolish as I thought! It's suicide!" Peter said.

"I'll take my chances. Feel free to stay here and die, ye old fool!" Brice called back. He stopped in his tracks when he noticed Henic standing in front of him.

"Now Brice, don' be makin' any rash decisions. We must stay together. It's our best chance for survival," Henic said.

"Step aside, farm boy. Don't think yer in any spot to be givin' me orders," Brice said before pointing at Conrad. "The same goes fer you, too. Faramond is my leader, and as far as I'm concerned, he's dead. We're on our own, now."

Henic's fists began to shake. "Y-you ignorant child! Faramond put Conrad in charge for a reason! He's best equipped to lead us until he returns!"

Brice scoffed and said, "Faramond is dead. When was the last time he failed to keep a promise? He promised he would be back by nightfall, and yet there's no sign of him. An outsider like ye wouldn't understand." He then paused for a moment and laughed. "Besides, ye should be the first of us hurrying back with the black gold. I notice ye've been workin' that sickly wife and raggedy son of yers to the bone, lately. Mayhap they could use a break!"

Henic's eye twitched and he gritted his teeth. "Why, you little–"

"Enough!" Conrad called out. The others looked his way. "Faramond indeed put me in charge of this group, but he also stated that anyone who wants to leave by nighttime will be allowed to do so. I shall respect his wishes." Grumbling began to pick up. "Those of you who wish to leave along with Brice, do so now. Those who are staying, I thank you. We can discuss the plan moving forward once the others leave."

Silence fell over the workers. Brice and the hooligans obviously planned to depart, but the others didn't seem so sure.

"I've faced worse than this mountain before, yes I did!" Solomon said as he walked to Conrad's side.

"This place ain't worth the trouble!" another miner called out, siding with Brice.

"Cowards! The lot of you!" Peter said, joining Conrad. "As if I'd travel willingly with a rat!" he added for good measure.

Ultimately, besides Brice and his four cronies, two other miners offered to go along with them. The rest wished to stay at the base camp. After about a quarter-hour of gathering their belongings and packing up their tents, the group began trekking down the path that led to Allie's pass.

However, Conrad's keen eye noticed the rapidly changing weather. Seemingly out of nowhere, the clouds gathered around in the clear night sky and rain began to pick up once more. It was not just rain, but intense winds that knocked the men back at first. Thunder began to clap and lightning flashed, all before anyone could leave.

As Brice and his group walked down the path, a bolt of lightning struck a dying tree in front of them, setting it ablaze. Conrad, who had led the remainder of his team back to the Mouth of Hell for shelter from the storm, smirked while watching them scramble back up the path.

When they reached base camp, he waved them over with a knowing smile. The men sulked as they made their way into the tunnel entrance. Their mood had dampened even more than their clothing and supplies.

"Ah, wonderful! My friends have returned! Oh, it is so good indeed to see you're all in good health. The weather truly took a turn for the worse," William said.

"We ain't yer friends!" Brice shot back. The water was dripping off of his giant nose, a fact that made it difficult for Conrad to hold back his laughter, but somehow, he persisted with a straight face.

Instead of rubbing their faces in their failure to leave, he decided to keep his message hopeful. "It would seem fate has brought us back together. Welcome back, gentlemen."

There was no response. Instead, the men sat against the wall to dry off and warm up. Cyriack continued to keep his distance from the group, Peter kept a suspicious eye on Brice and the hooligans, and William proceeded to converse with those who clearly didn't want to speak. Conrad and Henic started to plan out their next move, in the meantime.

The clicking sounds could still be heard down the tunnel shaft, but it seemed far off. However, most importantly, the shrieking and calls of the creature from earlier had ceased. It led Conrad to wonder: Where had the monster gone? He hoped they'd heard the last from it.

CHAPTER 18
DALTON'S JOURNAL

After returning to the black gold-filled cave, Joel found the survivors of the riggit attack off in the distance, toward the middle. They were gathered in a circle around Faramond and Edith. Joel noticed Alistair and Lucia's heads poking out of the crowd and went to stand by them.

"Ah, there ya are, lad," Alistair said as he slapped Joel on the back. "Ya had me worried thar fer a moment. Been lookin' around for ya!"

Joel smiled at him.

"We can't catch a break, can we?" Bronrar asked aloud.

"We were told the mines were dangerous, weren't we? The most concerning thing to me is that between the dratagons, riggits, and those two," Lucia said, nudging her head toward Wolfgang and Angus. "Their death count is the highest."

"Erm, right..." Bronrar trailed off. He looked down and his chest welled up. Joel could tell that he wanted to say something more, but he decided not to force the issue.

"Alright, looks like this is everyone," Faramond said with a frown. "By my count, there are now 21 among us. Five men lost their lives in those tunnels..."

The leader let out a stuttering sigh. He opened his mouth, but no words came out due to the apparent frog in his throat.

"Our numbers have been cut in half, then," Wolfgang chimed in.

The hysteria shined through in his voice. "Some leader ye are. I thought yer main goal was ta keep us all safe."

"Watch your tongue," Faramond said with sharpened eyes. Wolfgang looked ready to fight, but Angus put a hand on his shoulder. The blond brute chuckled.

"Yes, sir…"

Faramond's eyes darted around the cave. Wolfgang's blatant attempt to shame and distract him had worked. He couldn't seem to find the strength to continue speaking. Edith tugged at his arm.

"Erm, anyhow…" he muttered.

Joel could feel how much the loss of his men was impacting him. He couldn't have known that more than half of those deaths had been instigated through Wolfgang and Angus' hands, and not his own mistakes as leader.

"We cannot stand around here much longer. It isn't safe," Edith said in his place as she nudged him once more.

"Right…" Faramond said before taking a deep breath. "We shall gather the spoils and make our way through the other tunnel that we saw earlier: The one that was glowing blue. We'll depart shortly. Be swift!"

The miners walked to their respective spots in the cave and packed up. Naturally, Joel had no black gold to take, but Bronrar was surprised when Lucia decided to leave her black gold behind as well.

"Yer throwing a fortune away!" he cried.

Alistair scoffed. "The lass is convinced that tha black gold is gonna git her mind scrambled and *as usual*, she is wrong…" He paused and flashed Joel a half-hearted smile. "No offense, 'course." Joel rolled his eyes.

"I said nothing of the sort," Lucia replied with a snort. "I only said that it distracted me. There are more important things to worry about."

"Oooo, That's right, I fergot about yer lover, Dalton! I'm sure he'll be fine-"

"For the last time, he was my mentor," Lucia snapped back with a growl. "It's not like that."

"Erm, speakin' of misunderstandings…" Bronrar trailed off. The others looked at him with curious eyes. "There's somethin' I think you all should know. I don' know if you'll believe it, and I'm not even sure *I* believe it, but…"

"Well? Spit it out, ya mumblin' munchkin!" Alistair said. He then laughed at his description.

"It's about what Angus told me..."

Everyone else let out a collective groan.

"Didn't ya learn yer lesson, earlier? The man's a cold-blooded murderer! Don' listen ta him!" Alistair said.

"It's not often I agree with the oaf," Lucia began.

"Hey!" Alistair whined.

"But he is correct. Angus, Wolfgang, and Edith are all killers. You're not like them, and it would be wise for you to avoid contact. Their words will only serve to twist and confuse you," she said.

"Hear me out," Bronrar said as Alistair and Lucia scoffed. Joel leaned in with interest. "Angus claims that Edith has lost control of Wolfgang. He aims to kill us all... and Edith has proposed we work together to stop him." The group groaned once more, this time with more emphasis.

"Look," Lucia said, placing a hand on his shoulder. "I heard for myself. Edith and her father Drake want half of the miners to die on this expedition. And so far, half of *our group* is dead. Do you think that's a coincidence? Anyone who allies with her is *evil*."

"I don' know nothin' about Drake, but I'll tell you this: That killin' spree from earlier was all Wolfgang's idea. Angus wanted nothin' to do with it," Bronrar said.

"Oh, boo hoo! Angus is tha largest of us all! He should be able ta handle a knob like Wolfgang!" Alistair said.

"You underestimate Wolfgang's skill in combat. With weapons, he could kill Angus," Bronrar replied.

"I agree with that much, having fought him myself," Lucia chimed in while clenching her fists. "He fights with great intensity and speed."

"More importantly, Angus takes the brunt of his abuse," Bronrar said. The others raised their eyebrows. "Edith fears Wolfgang more as he becomes harder to control, so she stays by Faramond's side. Angus has nowhere to run. He either submits to Wolfgang's decisions, or he'll become a victim."

"I find that hard to believe," Lucia said as she touched her shoulder wound. Blood stained her fingertips, drawing a frown out of the mercenary.

"Even if you don't believe him, I can tell that he and Edith truly fear Wolfgang. I was told of a plan to expose him for his murderous ways without creating further conflict. They would like us to help them," Bronrar said.

"There ain't a chance in hell that I help those waifs!" Alistair said, pounding his chest proudly like a gorilla.

Joel wrote in his book. He held the words up for his friends to see:

Edith probably can't be trusted, but mayhap we should hear her plan out. Wolfgang is the most dangerous of us all. We should focus on him before Edith. She uses people to get things done. Wolfgang kills on his own, regardless.

"I'll have no part in Edith's plans," Lucia said.

Alistair, on the other hand, scratched his chin and looked up in thought. "Well, Joel has a good point…"

Before the group could discuss it at length, Faramond called out, "Alright, everyone! Time to leave!"

They formed rank once more and traversed the tunnel from whence they came. The group of 21 eventually reached the same clearing from which they had multiple options. They opted to go left, toward the glimmering blue light.

The blue light was similar to those powered by the Ancient One's technology back in the first cave. The difference was that it kept fading in and out, like a flickering ember in the wind. On the right, they carried on past a system of tunnels, several in a row. They appeared to weave in and out from each other, but there was never even a discussion of taking such a confusing route. For now, it made more sense to continue toward the light source.

Soon after, the group found themselves in a new cave. It contained a few of the blue rocks, but the main source came from a tunnel up ahead. After a brief look around and finding little of interest, they continued on.

In the new tunnel, many of the miners found that they could see well enough and extinguished their torches to save resources. Although the flickering blue light provided less visibility than being outside during the day, it was paradise to the workers, who had become used to complete darkness in their short stay at Mt. Couture.

After walking up an incline, the miners reached a new cave, and it was easy to conclude that it was the source of blue light. The previous tunnels had a few odd rocks giving off the glow, but in this cave, the majority of rocks were emitting light. The cave itself was around the same size as where the group had been attacked by dratagons; and although it was somewhat illuminated, Joel could not see entirely to the other side.

However, what was obvious from the moment that they stepped

into the cave was that it had at one point been populated by miners. Several materials such as pickaxes, spades, and even mine carts were laid out and abandoned.

After halting the group and surveying the area for a moment, Faramond said, "Good news! The first team has been here. Let's search the cave for now, and perhaps take a rest."

The miners split up to explore. Most were drawn toward the abandoned mine carts to see if they had any additional black gold within them. Joel, on the other hand, made a direct left to look for anything interesting along the rocky walls.

The first thing he found made his stomach drop: dry blood. He also came across discarded and broken pickaxes as he walked, but little else of interest. As he considered having a look around elsewhere, Joel noticed out of the corner of his eye something peculiar; something he'd not seen anywhere other than in his own hands since entering the mines: a book.

Joel crouched and retrieved the book. It was a journal. He opened it up to the first page to see inscribed:

The Journal of Dalton Rayleigh: A Recounting of the Mt. Couture Expedition

That's a mouthful, he thought.

"It would appear that there is much to explore in this cave. I'm officially calling a break for now. We shall travel no further until I give the word!" Faramond called out.

Joel put his back up against the wall and sat. He was happy to be right next to a glimmering rock. It made the text easy to read. The journal said:

Day One, Dawn

Although I volunteered to help Faiwell in their time of need, I was shocked to find out that the Miner's Guild chose me to lead the first team on an expedition to Mt. Couture. I thought they were going to reject me! I only signed up to impress Village Elder Ward's granddaughter… ah, I've forgotten her name, but she would have been a fine lay, indeed! Instead, I'm traveling with a group of men to what I'm told is one of the most dangerous places in the world. That's what I get for trying to show off, I suppose.

Perhaps they chose me because of my experiences during the War of the Bird, but even early on in this trip, I feel out of my depth. I know little of mining and I'm supposed to lead these men? They seem like a good bunch, though. Mayhap I'll learn a thing or two on this trip. That said, if I do survive this expedition, that Village Elder's granddaughter had better still be available!

Day One, Midday

We made our journey through the Dead Woods with few incidents. Some of the workers complained that they were seeing things in between the trees. One even claimed to see a Wizard, but luckily these men are easy to keep in line. Ollie is my second-in-command, and though I mistook him for a stick in the mud at first glance, he has been invaluable as my council in leading the team.

I have stopped us by Gen Creek to rest and eat lunch. It's nice, but too close to the Dead Woods to truly enjoy. I'll keep this entry brief because the closer we get to nightfall, the more dangerous this area becomes, and so I must be quick. Next to come is the journey through Allie's Pass.

Day One, Dusk

The journey through Allie's Pass was successful. There were many odd markings along the way, carved into the walls. Ollie told me that 'The Ancient Ones' probably made the engravings and that we should try to figure out what they mean. I told him that I don't give a damn what some primitive folk have to say! We've got a schedule to keep, after all.

We have established a camp outside the entrance to the mines at the base of the mountain. I believe we will venture into the mines tonight to have a look around. The workers seem to be in good spirits. We were told the journey would be perilous, and it was not. Many seem to believe that the mountain will not be as dangerous as the others say, too. I'm not so sure. In my experience, life is a bloody struggle, and then you die. The only question is: What will our struggle be in these mines?

There is a sign outside the mine entrance, but none of us can read what it says. Ollie claims it's in the ancient language. I see no reason to read a sign that obviously gives the name of this mountain. It probably says, 'Mt. Couture', or whatever those ancient folk called it back then. Seems unimportant to me.

Day One, Nightfall

I am unsure whether to be elated or horrified. The first thing of note is that the inside of these mines are like a maze. The first cave, right away, gives us three choices of tunnels to venture into. Even stranger, there is a device that allows us to light up the cave entirely. Presumably, it was built by the Ancient Ones, so Ollie was sure to make me eat my words about them being primitive.

It truly is amazing, but upon lighting the area, we were even more surprised to find a new, sparkling substance all around the walls. It's a beautiful paradox, really: It shines and sparkles in the darkness all on its own, yet the material itself is the darkest of blacks. I've never seen anything like it, and apparently, neither have the other workers.

I gave the order to start mining so we could see exactly what the material was, and as the men mined, I would hear happy cries from them. I'm only an outsider to them, but do they always become so excited when mining a material? It's not terribly professional.

Upon mining the ore myself, however, I began to understand its brilliance. It will surely fetch a high price when trading. Not only will this save the village, it will make us rich!

My first thought was that I had to have more, but before I could do anything else, I heard it: A piercing shriek that came from the deepest depths of hell. The next cry I heard was not of a creature, but of a man. I rushed to the worker's aid to find a monstrosity that I cannot fully describe by word, but I will do my best. It had dark green and slimy-looking skin, many blood-red eyes upon its oddly angled face, and long claws, each as sharp as or sharper than a sword.

When I arrived, it was already too late to help the worker. He had been torn to shreds, and the beast was feasting on him with rows of teeth beneath the nightmarish tentacles on its face. My first instinct was to draw my blade and slay the creature, but the sword broke over its hardened skin. Other men had come to help me, and had they not done so, I would be dead.

After breaking my sword over its back, the monster turned around with God-like speed and slaughtered the man next to me. There was nothing I could do against this thing. I called for a retreat, but even worse, the men were hesitant to leave their treasures behind! The greedy fools! Even Ollie refused to leave at first, but I think watching their fellow worker be devoured by the creature changed their minds.

We rushed back to the base camp. The monster never gave chase to us. I decided that we should try to rest for the night and then decide whether to reenter the mines in the morning.

In summary, there are valuable treasures within the mines, but also there lurks a horrid creature that seems unstoppable, at least for now.

Day Two, Dawn

I thought it would be difficult to rally the men into returning to the mines, but I was surprised to find that it took very little convincing. They were all excited at the prospect of mining that beautiful metal once again. Such an odd bunch, they are. Although I'm excited to mine the ore again, I don't wish to encounter that monster, either. I'm already without a weapon and two of my men because of it.

Ollie is eager to get back in the mines, so I'll keep this entry brief. I'm just happy that monster didn't pursue us any further. That said, if we encounter it again, we may need to consider leaving the mountain altogether. Is it worth losing more men over?

Day Two, Midday

It's a relief for me to say that we did not encounter the monster this time, at least so far. However, there is nothing left of the miners it attacked last night. No remains, no equipment, not even blood. Truly horrifying.

I forgot to mention in the last entry that we've been hearing a clicking noise in the walls of the tunnels. The miners tell me that it's the work of knockers, which I corrected them on. Knockers are baseless folklore, after all! Even still, I wonder what the noises could be.

We have resumed mining in the cave where we were first attacked. Most of the men have been preoccupied with the unique ore on the cave walls, but some, including myself, are on guard for the beast to return.

With that said, I would like to get some mining done soon. Don't want to be left out of the spoils!

Day Two, Dusk

Ollie is acting strange. He has become paranoid that other miners are trying to steal his treasures. I have tried reassuring him that there is more than enough for everyone, but he has become distant.

On the bright side, I managed to mine more precious metal for myself. Even on day two, nobody knows what to call it. I wonder if the folks back in the village will know what it is. We're all confident that it will fetch a high price, regardless. It surely is a wonderful thing. It's almost as if I'd be sad to part with it…

Day Two, Nightfall

Ollie has disappeared without a trace. His precious metals are also missing. The group has agreed that we should search the tunnels for him. It came down to a close vote in the end, however. Do these men not care for their own? They seem to care more about the treasures.

While searching for him, I will drop glowing bulbs for the next team to find us, should we get lost.

Will update if or when we find Ollie.

Entry Nine

I have lost track of time inside these mines. I can't be sure if it's nightfall or the next day, yet. What I do know is that we've been searching for some time now and there is still no sign of Ollie.

We did however enter a cave filled with dratagons. Dratagons! Of all the places these wretched creatures resided, it had to be here! Luckily, we were able to flee before riling them up too much.

Continuing the search for Ollie. Will update with anything new soon.

Entry 10

On our way back from the dratagon cave, we were attacked by that vile creature from yesterday. It claimed another of our comrade's lives. It seems to hunt slowly but attack quickly. I can't understand its pattern, or even begin to comprehend what this thing is, but I do believe that it's a nocturnal hunter. It would explain why we made it this long without encountering the beast a second time. Since I don't know its true name, I'll call it 'Nightcrawler', for now.

While fleeing from the Nightcrawler, there was a tunnel collapse that killed some of our men, and in the chaos, we lost half of our equipment. Now we are trapped in an unfamiliar area. The trip has been a disaster, but thankfully, most of our treasures were recovered.

We still haven't found Ollie, so I've appointed Franko as my temporary second-in-command. He seems to be a helpful fellow.

Entry 11

The group is exhausted, so we've decided to rest. I am unsure if it is day or night. Keeping this short since I'm tired and my head feels like it is spinning. Something about these mines is wearing me down more than normal.

Entry 12

Had a strange dream as I slept. It's hazy, but I know that I didn't like it. I fear these mines are starting to take a toll on my mind. I am beginning to hear voices, and all I can think about in this dire situation is treasure. What is wrong with me? We resume the search for Ollie soon.

Entry 13

We came upon a cave filled with more of the sparkling metal. Most of the men wished to stop, but I told them that we needed to find Ollie before we did more mining. Although even I had at first wanted to stop. There was some resistance, but a fellow named Baltr shut them up and they listened to him.

He's a tall, gangly thing, but has a backbone. I like his style, even if he does overdo it sometimes.

Franko pointed me in the direction of another tunnel. We'll explore that route, next.

Entry 14

The tunnel was filled to the brim with riggits. I have never encountered one before today, but I'm told that these were different from what the miners were used to. The queen attacked and killed Franko, so there goes another second-in-command. They seem to be dropping like flies.

I have appointed Baltr as the new second-in-command. He seems good at keeping the workers under control.

Aside from Franko, we suffered two other deaths at the hands of the riggits. It would seem that between the Nightcrawler, dratagons, riggits, and tunnel collapses, this place is trying to kill us. I have given up trying to find Ollie. Now, I'm only trying to find an alternate exit.

Entry 15

Whoever built this place deserves my boot up their ass! After much searching, we came upon a new set of caves that felt promising. We were then led into a labyrinth filled with traps. We walked around in circles for some time with no success.

During this time, more of our men disappeared. How is this possible? Wouldn't we eventually find them if we were walking in circles? None of it makes sense.

The men are exhausted, so we are retracing our steps. Many of them wish for no more than to rest and watch over their treasures. I must admit, I feel the same, even if I'm supposed to be their leader.

Entry 16

We have been sitting in the same cave for some time, now. I had another dream, this time far more vivid. It was about a 'Dark Savior' of some kind. Truly the strangest of things, so imagine my surprise when Baltr tells me that Ollie was muttering something similar before he disappeared.

*My thought is that something in the mines is making us all crazy. I'm coming up with the name for it now, so someone else doesn't come up with something uninteresting: **Gold Fever**. To whomever is so fortunate, or unfortunate, to find this log, be sure to give me credit for the name, or I'll haunt you 'till the day you die! That's a promise.*

On the subject of Gold Fever, It seems to affect people at different speeds. I can feel my mind starting to go, but Baltr still appears to be alright. Many of the other workers are acting odd. For them and myself, it is only a matter of time.

The only thing that can be done is to sacrifice myself when the time comes. Mayhap when the Nightcrawler strikes next, or some other danger comes up. Is pain better than the grave? I think not. I would die an honorable death before suffering any further in this horrid place.

Even still, what would happen to my treasures when I'm gone? It seems to be such a waste. I shouldn't waste my life and leave it. If anything, I should have more.

Give me more. Its shimmering beauty in the darkness of these mines fulfills my greatest desires. I must have more. It is his will… and those who do not follow must die. I will kill the non-believers.

Joel closed the book with wide, frightened eyes. He understood the implications of Dalton's final log. He and his team were succumbing to the effects of black gold. Because Dalton had lost track of time on the voyage, the mute couldn't be sure of how much longer they had before the effects took hold over their minds, but at the very least, he knew they were in trouble if they were still alive.

He rushed over to Faramond, who was trying to settle a dispute over the carts left by the first team. While reading, Joel had overheard the commotion: Wolfgang had attempted to lay claim on all black gold left within the carts, and naturally, the other miners complained that it wasn't only his, but all of theirs.

"Be reasonable, Wolfgang," Faramond pleaded. "There is more than enough for us all, and besides, you cannot carry all of that on your own."

"Mind yer own business! This is mine, all mine!" Wolfgang said.

"It *is* my business," Faramond said, the sternness in his tone growing. He put a hand on the hilt of his sword. Wolfgang chuckled in return.

"I've been playin' nice with ye up until now…" he said, now standing face-to-face with the leader. "But if ye come between me an' my treasure, the choice is clear."

"Is that a challenge?" Faramond asked while drawing his sword.

"Yer the one challengin' me."

"No, I'm giving you an order. Stand down, now," he said.

Wolfgang turned to face the carts filled with black gold. He made a fist, and it began to tense up and shake. The blond brute pulled out his pickaxe.

"Wolfgang, no!" Edith cried.

"Shut yer mouth, Edith!" Wolfgang replied. He looked at her over Faramond's shoulder. "I'll deal with ye when I'm finished with *him*."

"You'll do no such thing, snake! Edith is with *me*, now," Faramond said, inching closer with his blade at the ready. Wolfgang howled with laughter, and Edith turned her head from him in apparent shame. His laughs changed into growls and his face turned red.

"Ye think ye can just take my gal from me like that?" he asked.

"Not only is she mine, but now too, is the treasure! Hand it over!" Faramond shot back. The blond brute cocked his head.

"Yers?" Wolfgang asked as he took another step closer. "Ye think it's *yers*?" Chatter began to pick up amongst the other miners.

Faramond sighed and then said, "I… I meant that I was taking it back for the rest of us…"

Joel jumped in between the conflict and tugged on Faramond's sleeve. He looked back at him with fiery eyes.

"What is it? I'm dealing with something important right now," he said in a short tone. He tried to show him the journal, but Faramond wouldn't take his eyes off Wolfgang. "I don't have time for this. Talk to me later, after I've dealt with this scum!"

Wolfgang cackled once more and said, "Yer overconfident in yer abilities! Just 'cause ye trained with Dalton fer a while? We all know yer skills are below standard with the sword! That's why ye stopped trainin' with 'im! That's why ye became a miner!"

Faramond remained silent.

"And some leader ye are! Lettin' half yer men die horrible deaths in this place. The least ye can do is give me as much black gold as I want fer puttin' up with ye this long!"

"Enough!" Faramond shouted. There was doubt in his eyes.

"Don't listen to him, Fara," Edith said and then put a hand on his shoulder. "I saw for myself: You single-handedly fought off dratagons while *he* ran off like a coward. You can beat him."

"Why ye traitorous bitch! Ye dare speak against me like that? After all I've done for ye?" Wolfgang shouted; his face beet-red now. With deliriously wide eyes and veins popping out of his forehead, it felt to Joel like he might lash out at any moment.

With no time to waste, Joel turned to find someone else who might listen. He spotted Lucia, Alistair, and Bronrar sitting in a different corner of the cave. He rushed over to them with the journal in hand.

"What's that ya got thar?" Alistair asked as he arrived. Joel held up the book in front of Lucia's face.

"Dalton's journal?" she read aloud as hope filled her voice. "May I read this?"

Joel nodded, emphatically.

"I think he *wants* us to read it," Bronrar said.

The trio sat in silence as they scanned through the entries. Lucia was holding the book, and so she was in charge of turning the pages. However, Alistair was unhappy with the speed at which she turned them.

"Slow it down, lass! Quit skimmin' an' read the whole thing!" he said.

"Not my fault you can't read," she said.

"I can so read! Me mum taught me how!" Alistair argued.

"Her page-turning seems fine to me," Bronrar said.

"Oh, shut it! You two are always gangin' up on me! Ain't that right, Joel?" Alistair said as he looked at his mute friend with hopeful eyes. Joel chuckled, but then became straight-faced and pointed back at the journal.

"Oh, right…" Alistair mumbled.

A few moments later, Lucia closed the book. Alistair wasn't finished reading, so he swiped the book from her and began to read the remaining entries.

"'Gold Fever'…" Lucia trailed off.

"We've heard about this before… is it the black gold that's doing it?" Bronrar asked. Joel nodded excitedly. They were finally beginning to believe.

Alistair burst out laughing and the others looked at him with confusion in their eyes. "This Dalton feller is funny! 'The granddaughter better be available', he says!" the big man choked out before another laugh.

"That's it?" Lucia said, narrowing her eyes. "That's how far you got?"

"Don' even start! Some folk prefer ta *enjoy* what they read! So, I take me time," Alistair said. Lucia rolled her eyes.

"What about this 'Nightcrawler' creature that he spoke of? I don' remember seein' anythin' like that," Bronrar said.

"That much is out of our control," Lucia said as she stood. "What we *can* control is whether our group succumbs to Gold Fever or not. We have to warn Faramond… and I have to hope that Dalton overcame it, somehow."

Joel made hand signals, which Bronrar took notice of.

"Erm… I believe Joel is sayin' that Dalton can still be saved," Bronrar said.

"How?" she asked, placing a hand on his shoulder. "Please, tell me." The mute made more hand signals toward Bronrar, who tilted his head and fidgeted his mouth in response.

"I-I don' understand. Sorry, my USL ain't what it used to be…" he said.

Joel sighed and then snatched Dalton's journal from Alistair.

"Hey! I was readin' that!"

The mute wrote in the book and then held it up for the others to see:

If he isn't already too far gone, only his strongest emotions can snap him out of it. If we are quick, there is a chance we could save him. It's different for everyone. It depends on the amount of exposure and their willpower.

Lucia looked up with hope in her eyes. She said, "We must be quick, then. Let's tell Faramond."

Joel handed the book back to Lucia and the group jogged over to Faramond, who was still arguing with Wolfgang. It seemed as if they were ready to come to blows when Lucia butted in.

"Sir!" she called out.

Faramond didn't look back, but said, "I'm busy, here. Can it wait?"

"No, this is urgent. I assure you this is something you *need* to see," Lucia said while handing him the journal.

He finally took his focus off of Wolfgang and glanced at the cover of the book. The leader gasped before sheathing his blade and then started walking to a nearby cave wall.

"So, ye don't wanna fight?" Wolfgang asked with a scoff. "I knew ye were a coward!"

"We'll settle the matter later," Faramond said, half-heartedly. "However, that treasure is *not* all yours." The leader reached the cave wall and slumped down. He opened the book and began to read the entries aloud. Edith stood by him, listening.

After a short time, Faramond put the journal down, and Joel and the others walked over to see his reaction. There was a grave look on his face; as if he'd seen a ghost. A dark thought occurred to Joel: Those journal entries may very well have been Dalton's final thoughts. In some ways, perhaps Faramond *had* seen a ghost. The leader began to play with his mustache.

"The black gold…" he trailed off, looking up at Joel. "Is it the cause of Gold Fever? What Dalton described sounds exactly like what you've been trying to warn me about."

Joel nodded and then adjusted his mining helmet.

"But how did you know?"

Joel signed to the leader. He frowned in return.

"You can't tell me? This is no time for mucking about. Tell me. Now. That's an order," Faramond said. His eyes were twitching now.

"Aye, I think it's 'bout time ya told us the full story, lad. If we're gonna give up the stuff that would make us rich, at least give us a reason!" Alistair said.

Perhaps telling them a bit more would be helpful, Joel thought. But he had an important duty to uphold. He had to be careful with how much he revealed. The mute hesitantly began to make hand signals, but then, a horrifying shriek echoed from outside the cave, startling him and the others.

Skreeeeee

"W-what was that?" Bronrar asked aloud.

"Dalton described a monster we have not yet encountered in those entries… the Nightcrawler," Faramond said.

"How can we be sure?" Lucia asked.

"There is no way to be certain, but is it worth risking? Everything in these mines seems to bring death upon us," Faramond said as he forced his eyes shut and let out a stressed exhale. "What a disaster this expedition has been. Losing half of my crew, and now the only thing that can save the village would poison our minds, too!" He pounded his fist into the ground.

Skreeeeeee

"Oi! There ain't no time ta be feelin' sorry fer yerself, sir!" Alistair said as he picked a wide-eyed Faramond up off the ground. "We gotta get outta here if what I'm hearin' is true. I… uh… haven't gotten to tha part about tha monster…"

"You're right," Faramond said with a nod. "Everyone! Gather 'round! I need you all to listen carefully…"

The workers assembled, aside from Wolfgang, who stood by the mine carts to guard his new treasure.

Skreeeeeeee

The beast drew near.

CHAPTER 19
RISING SUSPICIONS

Unlike the first time they had entered the refuge of the mines, Brice and his crew brought their black gold along into the tunnel. It made Conrad uneasy, as his growing suspicion of the material had him believing Joel more and more that it was poisoning their minds.

Although Brice wasn't a nice fellow to begin with, Conrad had observed how his behavior worsened as time went on, especially when the black gold was with him. He and his crew had grown increasingly antagonistic toward Peter and Solomon. It never took much for Peter to clash with them, but the hooligans hadn't forgiven Solomon for eyeing their treasures, earlier.

"Oi! What're ye lookin' at?" Brice asked, angrily. "Ye best not be eyein' our spoils, or ye'll end up like yer friends from the war!"

Solomon's cheerful disposition fell somber.

"Watch your tongue, Brice," Conrad said in a stern tone. "I have been fair with you so far, but if you keep pushing it, you and your crew will have nowhere to go but out in the pouring rain or deeper into the mines. And I don't think you'll prefer either of those options."

Conrad stood, and so too did a frowning Henic.

"Hah! Ye think ye can force me to do anythin'? Ol' farmer boy will crumble before me, just like back at home! And yer not my *real* leader. Me boys over here will back me up!" Brice said. The hooligans stood behind him with crossed arms.

"In case you hadn't noticed, your poor behavior hasn't made you any friends," Conrad said with a smirk. The hooligans looked around to see many cross faces in the tunnel. "By my count, that's 10 against five. By all means, feel free to try me."

Brice and the hooligans fell silent and sat with their backs against the wall. Conrad breathed a sigh of relief, and out of the corner of his eye, he could see Henic wiping sweat from his brow. Hopefully, this trip would prove to him that Brice was toothless when it all came down to it.

"I say we send 'em deep into the mines, anyway! What do we need you plebs for? Yer not good for anythin' but trouble!" Peter said. A couple of miners nodded along.

"Shut yer mouth, old man!" Brice snapped back.

"All of you should shut up!" Solomon burst out, his voice cracking. All in the tunnel turned to face him. Conrad hadn't heard him take anything but a friendly tone since the start of the expedition.

Solomon curled into a ball and lay against the tunnel wall. He pulled out a piece of black gold ore and looked upon it with wavering eyes as he rocked back and forth. In silence, he continued in this way for some time as all in the tunnel stared at him. Occasionally, he rubbed his forehead, as if trying to comfort his mind in some way.

"Should we go talk to him?" Conrad whispered to Henic.

"I feel we should leave him alone, for now," he replied. The strategist snorted. Henic still had a penchant for staying out of other people's business. As one of the group leaders, he would eventually need to get more involved.

That was a conversation for later, though. For now, Conrad's focus shifted to Cyriack, who was sitting further into the tunnel, once again away from the group.

Conrad walked up to the old man and sat next to him. Cyriack paid him little mind. He seemed preoccupied by something else.

"Still worried about that 'evil presence'?" Conrad asked.

"I understand if ye don't believe me, but it's here, lad. Believe me, someone here is not who they claim. They're tryin' to hide their presence, but I can feel 'em, and they're bad. Real bad..." Cyriack said.

"So, you're convinced it's a Dark Wizard?"

"I believe so."

Conrad had written off Cyriack's claims as the ramblings of a crazed old man. Yet, he had also been able to correctly pinpoint strange properties of the black gold and had known that the other objects were ordinary. The timing of the storm also seemed odd; as if someone had wanted it to stop Brice and the others from leaving. The strategist had heard stories of Wizards able to conjure up storms before, but he'd never taken them as anything more than folklore.

"Why don't we try a test?" Conrad asked.

"A test, ye say? What sorta test?" Cyriack replied.

"We have nothing better to do, so why don't we bring each member of the team over to you, one by one? Then, you'll be able to see which of us it is for certain."

The old man frowned and said, "I ain't too sure about this… tryin' to reveal an evil power may get us killed."

"A fair point, but if they are evil, would they not try to kill us anyway?"

"I suppose…" Cyriack muttered. Conrad could feel his fright growing with each word.

"I won't force you into anything you do not wish to do," he reassured him.

Cyriack nodded. "I think yer right, though. A confrontation with this nefarious person is inevitable."

The pair walked back to where everyone else was sitting.

"What were the two of ye schemin' about over there?" Brice asked. His big nose got right up in Conrad's face.

"Funny you should ask," Conrad said with sharp eyes and a smile. "You see, I have a theory, and I wish to test it. But I require *everyone's* cooperation."

"What?" Brice asked with a shrug. "I'll be cooperative if the demands are reasonable."

"Cyriack over here is in tune with magical beings, it would seem. He has sensed an evil presence among our group, and although I had my suspicions that it was something else before, the recent storms have told me otherwise," Conrad said. The group began to mumble amongst themselves. Everyone seemed confused. "What I'm saying is that I believe there are forces at work that don't want us to leave this mountain. When Brice and his crew tried to leave, something stopped them. That storm came out of nowhere."

"And yer tryin' to tell me that some evil magician conjured up the storm?" Peter called out grumpily. "I find it hard to believe, not only that a Wizard wouldn't want us to leave this wretched place, but that they'd have the power to call upon such a fierce storm! I've seen a couple o' Wizards in my day, and rarely did they perform more than parlor tricks!"

"It *is* possible for a Wizard to conjure a storm of such force. A Conjuring type that has practiced magic for hundreds, if not thousands of years fer sure, but I've seen such things; I promise you that much!" Cyriack replied.

"There is no need to argue, gentlemen," Conrad said as he held his hands out. "The rain is beginning to calm and the skies grow clearer. Let's try to leave, soon. If the storm picks back up, we can take that as a sign."

The explanation seemed to please most within the group, but to Conrad's surprise, William stepped forward.

"Pardon me, sir?" he asked. "You say that an evil magic force is responsible for this, correct?"

"That's right," Conrad said, searching the gangly man's eyes for answers. He stayed as cheerful as ever.

"I see. In that case… what if the evil mage changes their plans because of what you said? If they have the power to conjure a storm, I worry that a direct conflict with them would be bad for us all. Ooooo yes, indeed," William said.

"A fine point," he replied. "The way I see it, though, we don't have enough information. To what lengths is this Dark Wizard willing to go? Are they truly malevolent? Is it a Dark Wizard at all? Could there be more than one force at work, here? We don't know, but at least this is a way of finding out."

"Ah! You're a smart fellow," said William. He patted Conrad on the shoulder. "I'm glad to have you as leader!"

"Erm… thank you…" Conrad said. Sometimes, William was a little *too* over the top, he thought. As he walked back to the wall where Henic sat, he could see from his expression alone that he was about to question him.

"What's the meanin' of all this? Things were just settlin' down. Why rile everyone up?"

There it was again, Conrad thought. If Henic had it his way, he and everyone else would simply keep to themselves while hoping for Faramond's return. Yet, it was feeling more and more like Faramond and the group weren't coming back tonight, and problems were already beginning to crop up.

"We must be proactive, my friend. I can see problems coming for us on the horizon; can't you? I say we get ahead of them."

"You don't truly believe Cyriack, do you? He's always been a superstitious old coot, hasn't he?" Henic said.

"He was able to identify black gold as an object with a strange energy. I believe him when he says there is evil magic among us. Besides, we have little else to do," Conrad said in a playful tone.

"Still suspicious of the black gold, eh? I feel yer worryin' too much, or mayhap yer a wee bit bored for yer own good. Why rock the boat when the worst we've had to deal with so far is a measly storm?" he asked with a chuckle.

Conrad offered no response. As he had it figured, Henic wasn't ready to snap out of whatever hold the black gold had over his mind. In the case of Lucia, bringing up someone important to her, Dalton, had helped snap her out of the trance. However, Henic's family was exactly why he'd fixated on the black gold as the cure to all of his problems. He would need to find an alternate method to end the farmer's lust for black gold, but he wasn't quite sure what that entailed, yet.

On the other side of the tunnel, Conrad noticed Solomon shaking and huddled over. Ever since Brice had taunted him about his departed friends, he'd been that way. He held onto a piece of black gold ore with both hands. The strategist got up to speak with him, but he felt a tug at his shoulder. He looked back to see Henic shaking his head. He sighed. Perhaps it was best to leave him be, for now.

AFTER ABOUT AN HOUR PASSED, the rain had turned to a drizzle. Brice and his goons were the first to stand and announce that they were leaving. As the hooligans packed up their things and walked outside, Brice looked back to see Conrad and Cyriack following them.

"And what do ye think yer doin'?" he asked.

"Do you not remember? I am testing to see whether the earlier storm was purely a coincidence, or if someone doesn't want us to leave. Cyriack here is joining us for the short trip," Conrad replied.

Brice snickered and said, "Fine, just make sure ye steer clear of my treasure and leave us be when yer done with the stupid test."

Conrad shrugged and continued to follow the group. Cyriack stayed close behind. As they walked down the slope, black clouds swiftly gathered overhead once again and the wind picked up.

"I-I'm sure it's nothin'," Brice said, looking up. "Keep going!"

A gale of wind hit the group next, and it knocked Brice over. He hopped to his feet, now red in the face, but continued to press on as the wind howled. The rain picked up until it felt like daggers were hitting them in the face, and then the thunder and lightning returned.

Unlike last time, however, there wasn't only one lightning strike. Several bolts shot to the ground near the struggling group, lighting up all of the base camp in brief flashes.

"We must retreat to the mines! Don't be foolish!" Conrad called out. His voice felt insignificant in the commotion of the storm.

"Nonsense! We can make it!" Brice shouted back as a lightning bolt hit the ground right in front of him. He fell to his bottom and stared at the charred ground before him while taking stuttered breaths. He groaned while standing, and then signaled his men to turn around. They all made a sprint toward the mines as the torrential downpour raged on.

Upon returning to the Mouth of Hell, Conrad slicked his soaked hair back and observed that the entire group was in a state of shock.

"Well, gentlemen… it seems that… my prediction came true…" Conrad said, panting from his sprint up the hill. The group remained silent. "Now, it's time for phase two of my test. My guess is that a Dark Wizard of some kind is conjuring up these storms; and that Cyriack over here senses his presence."

"This is nonsense!" Brice cried as he threw his wet belongings to the ground. "It could still be a coincidence."

"Care to try a third time, then? With how dangerous this mountain is supposed to be, is it terribly unbelievable that a Dark Wizard would reside here?" Conrad asked. Brice sighed and offered no further resistance.

"Alright, let's suppose yer right about the storms bein' conjured. How do we figure out who's doin' that?" Henic asked.

"Simple. We use Cyriack. He has agreed to feel the magic presence in us all. I've asked him to do it one person at a time. This way, we can confirm if someone is magically inclined," said Conrad.

"What rubbish!" Brice said. "How do we know he ain't makin' all this up?" Some others in the tunnel nodded along.

"He predicted that someone was conjuring the storms, did he not?" Conrad asked as he pointed at the downpour outside. "It's not as if we have much else to do, anyhow. If you would like to wait for the storm to die down once again, we can, but I see it as little more than a waste of time at this point. Those lightning bolts were *aimed*."

Conrad smashed a fist into his palm to imitate the thunderclaps outside, and all fell silent. He took the quiet from the others as an invitation to proceed.

"Alright, everyone, let's line up to be examined by Cyriack. I am happy to go first-"

"Hold on!" Peter jumped in with a grumpy snarl. "Let's suppose there is a Dark Wizard among us. How do we know that ol' Cyriack over here ain't the Dark Wizard himself?"

"A fair question, but I doubt it. He was the one who made it known to me in the first place. Why raise suspicion of himself when no one suspected a thing to begin with?" Conrad said and then crossed his arms. "I'll answer it for you all: power. If he were lying, it would be to manipulate us. That is why I brought him outside with me when we followed Brice. A lightning bolt nearly hit him, and I witnessed him performing no incantations."

Conrad scanned the cave. Everyone seemed as satisfied as he could have hoped with his reasoning. Of course, Brice and Peter would be problems, but he figured that being examined by Cyriack first would be a show of good faith.

"As I said earlier, I'll go first," the strategist said as he looked over at Cyriack. "What do I need to do?"

"Hold out yer arm an' be still. This won't take long," he replied.

Conrad held out his arm and Cyriack immediately grabbed it. An odd sensation overtook him: It was as if he were there, but not of present mind; like an out-of-body experience. His head felt as light as a feather, and his eyes became droopy. His senses dulled to such a point that he could no longer feel Cyriack's grip. The tinny smell of the damp tunnel stood out to him, and it was starting to feel overwhelming. Then, just as suddenly as it had begun, the sensation ended. He shook the cobwebs out and rubbed his eyes before seeing that the old man had released his arm.

"Yer certainly not an evil presence. Mayhap a wee bit too curious, however," Cyriack said and smiled back at him.

"Well, isn't that lovely to hear," Conrad replied, letting out a long exhale. He looked back at the remaining members of the group. "Who's next?"

Henic took tepid steps forward.

"I'd rather get it over with," he said while walking up to the old man. He stuck his arm out like Conrad before him, and Cyriack grabbed it.

There was a longer pause than when Conrad's arm had been held.

The farmer broke out into a sweat and began breathing heavily. Cyriack's eyes flicked and then strained a few times before he finally let go.

Henic said, "Well? Why did it take so long? Am I an evil Wizard without even knowing?" He let out a nervous laugh.

"No, lad, I do not detect evil magic within you, but..." Cyriack trailed off as he motioned Conrad over. He then lowered his voice and said, "I feel the same presence within him as I felt when concentrating on the black gold, earlier."

"W-what is *that* supposed to mean?" Henic asked with wide eyes.

"You may recall that earlier in the day, I had Cyriack feel the presence of a few items. Black gold was among the items, and when concentrating, he could feel nothing but darkness," Conrad said.

"Yer tryin' to say I'm evil, and so is the black gold?" Henic said, his tone shifting from nervousness to anger.

"No," Cyriack said. Henic appeared to calm down, but his eyes demanded an explanation. "When I say 'darkness', it ain't the same as 'evil'. Evil is right up in yer face. When I feel darkness, it's like standin' in those mines without a torch. It feels empty, but somethin' is ready to jump out at ya."

"This seems like hogwash to me," Henic replied. He turned toward his leader with a suspicious eye. "Conrad, you've had a bias against the black gold fer some time, now..."

"Are you implying that I would make all of this up?"

"Take it however ye will," Cyriack jumped in. "But I can see how much it has worn on ye. Yer not a Dark Wizard, but I'd be mighty careful around the black gold if I were you."

Henic remained quiet as he turned around to walk back. Conrad was unsure if Cyriack had scared him straight or simply angered him. He began to worry that this test would do little more than cause fragmentation within the group.

The next miner to step up was one of Brice's goons. He was a big man with long, wavy hair and a permanently arrogant smirk in his expression, but Conrad couldn't remember his name for the life of him. He held out his arm and Cyriack took hold. This time, he held on for the longest yet, and after letting go, said, "Not the evil source I've been feelin', but you too should be wary of the black gold."

The big man shrugged before walking back to his group. Next up was Peter, who scowled while holding his arm out.

"This is a big ol' crock of..." he trailed off before mumbling and grumbling obscenities under his breath. Cyriack grabbed his arm, but didn't hold it for as long as the others'.

"I sense much anger in you, Peter."

"What? I thought you were lookin' fer an evil magic presence?"

Cyriack chuckled and then said, "I'm only jokin', ye grumpy bastard! Everythin' is fine, aside from yer poor attitude!"

Peter scowled before walking back to his spot on the tunnel wall and slumping down. A few other miners were examined by Cyriack, but little of note happened aside from him mentioning that he felt the black gold's presence within them.

Then, Solomon approached the old man. He shook and slumped over as he walked. Conrad had noted the change in his behavior ever since Brice taunted him about his fallen comrades in war. Although usually cheerful and ready for any activity, Solomon had a meager, weak feeling to his step: It looked as if every stride was an effort.

~

SOLOMON STUCK out his arm for Cyriack to hold, but he didn't look him in the eye. As the old man grabbed his arm, he could hear under Solomon's breath, "More…"

As soon as he made contact with Solomon's skin, Cyriack was transported to a different world. 'Cold' was the only way to describe it; cold and dark. He couldn't see anyone aside from himself and Solomon. His hairs stood on end and goose bumps filled his body, as if chilled water had gone down his spine. Beginning to feel uncomfortable, Cyriack removed his grip, or at least he thought he had, but upon looking down he realized that his hand had refused to obey.

Panic began to set in as the cold, quiet, and dark started to turn noisy. It began as a slight ringing in his ear, but it quickly turned unbearable. He wanted to cry out, but couldn't, and he wished to leave, but he was unable to move. All he could do was feel a horrible presence pierce through his ears, and look on as Solomon's face began to turn up toward him.

It was then that Cyriack realized it wasn't Solomon; not at all. It was a pale imitation of a man who had deteriorated beyond the point of repair. His face began to deform like soup mixing in a bowl and what remained of his eyes glowed a bright yellow. The ringing intensified and his other senses numbed as the monster before him looked into his eyes with its nightmare-inducing gaze. Cyriack wanted to cry out in a vain attempt to get help, but his voice would not obey. He was completely at this monster's mercy.

"You want more, don't you? You're a good man, aren't you? Follow the Dark Savior. Follow his will!" the monster hissed. Cyriack's eyes widened. He couldn't respond. "Kill them… kill the non-believers!"

The old man could only watch as a dark matter dripped onto his arm and began to take hold of him. He could feel his mind slipping as his vision began to turn yellow. The buzzing was all he could hear, and the darkness was all he could feel.

~

CONRAD and the others watched on in bewilderment. It had been some time since Cyriack took hold of Solomon's arm, and from the beginning, the two men had been in a trance. Solomon had mumbled from time to time, but Cyriack remained silent. Out of curiosity, Conrad approached the old man.

"What is it? What do you see?" Conrad asked as he grabbed his shoulder and turned him around. The strategist gasped to see Cyriack's eyes rolled back and his mouth agape. He was drooling. "Snap out of it!" Conrad shook him to no avail.

"What's goin' on?" Brice asked aloud in a panicked tone.

"Come to your senses!" Conrad cried out before tugging at his arm. He was amazed to find that it wouldn't budge, and neither would Solomon. "I don't understand…" he mumbled before finally coming up with a solution. He wound up and then slapped Cyriack across the face.

Finally, the old man released his grip and exhaled loudly as he tumbled to the ground and fell into a coughing fit. Solomon, on the other hand, let out frantic breaths until he was wheezing. "Bah! Stay away from me and my treasures! Leave me alone!" He took a piece of black gold ore out of his pocket and cradled it like a baby in his arms.

The group huddled around the men until Cyriack finally regained his wits. Solomon scuttled away toward the tunnel entrance.

"The rain's almost stopped," he said. "I ain't stayin' in here any longer. I'm guardin' me treasures…"

Conrad decided to ignore him for the moment and cast his gaze back on Cyriack. "What happened?"

"My treasures… are they safe?" Cyriack asked, his right eye twitching. Conrad cocked his head. He opened his mouth but found himself at a loss for words. The old man stood and then brushed past him. "I need more…"

Cyriack too wandered out into the drizzle of the night.

"The hell is goin' on?" Henic asked aloud. "Did he find the Dark Wizard or not?"

"I think if he did, we would have been attacked or witnessed some magic just now," the strategist replied. "No… I think those two witnessed something different. I need to find out what."

"Haven't ye done enough already?" asked Brice. Conrad looked at him with a raised eyebrow. "Ye wanted to mess about with forces ye don't understand, and now look what happened! Their minds are scrambled! I'll tell ye right now, I ain't havin' that happen to me!"

Peter scowled from across the tunnel. "Sounds like the talk of a guilty man to me! Yer probably the one scramblin' their minds!"

"What are ye on about, ye crazy old man?"

"Just admit it, ye big-nosed rat!"

"Enough!" Conrad shouted. The miners gave him their undivided attention. "As you all can see, the rain is beginning to slow. I suggest we spend the rest of the night in our tents. I'll investigate what's going on with those two in the meantime."

The group seemed to agree. Everyone exited the mines once more and walked to their tents at the base camp. Before Conrad could reach Cyriack's tent, however, Henic stopped him.

"Ye think that situation back there was because of the black gold, don't ye?" he asked.

"That's right, I do," Conrad said.

"I dunno if it's a good idea for you to disturb ol' man Cyriack…"

The strategist sighed. "Henic, I understand why you prefer to keep to yourself; why you'd rather mind your own business… but can't you see? Something isn't right."

"Well, it may sort itself out." He put his hands in his pockets and shifted his eyes around.

"There are times when that doesn't work. Think of how you put your head down and kept to your farm without bothering or wronging anyone, over the years. Yet, when Faiwell began to struggle, some people *still* found an excuse to blame you, didn't they?" Conrad asked. Henic frowned, but he acknowledged the truth with a nod. "Sometimes, sitting back and letting things play out is the worst decision you can make. You risk the possibility of acting too late to fix your problem."

Henic grimaced. "Are ye tryin' to say that the attacks on my farm were *my fault?*"

"No," he replied, holding up a finger. "I'm saying that we find ourselves in a peculiar place, in a peculiar situation. If we don't confront the problem, it may become too much for us to overcome."

"The black gold?"

"Right," he replied with a nod. "Whatever is going on, I don't like it. It needs to be addressed. Now, if you'll excuse me-"

"Would it be alright if I came along? If it truly is as bad as you say, I wish to hear all the evidence myself," Henic said.

"Of course. Follow me," Conrad replied with a smile.

The duo entered Cyriack's tent to see the old man huddled up with his black gold ores. Conrad crossed his arms and Henic tilted his head.

"What is the meaning of this, Cyriack?" the strategist asked. There was no response.

"What did you see when you held Solomon's arm?" Henic chimed in.

"Dark… Savior…" Cyriack mumbled as he clutched a black gold ore. "Need more."

"More black gold?" Conrad asked.

Cyriack lifted his head slowly. Conrad saw a yellow glint in his eyes as he lunged out like a wild animal. "YES!"

Before he could get to anyone, however, Henic trapped the old man in a headlock and took him to the ground. Cyriack hissed as he pulled at Henic's grip, but it was no use. He then resorted to flailing his arms and wriggling around like a worm. Yet still, Henic held strong.

"Yer goin' against his will… you wanna do *good things*, don't ye?" Cyriack choked out. In short order, the old man slumped and finally simmered.

Henic released him, and Conrad drew his rapier in case he got out of line again.

"My apologies… I… I need some rest… is all… please…" he said.

"Very well," said Conrad as he sheathed his blade. "But I will need to speak to you about this in the morning. Get some rest."

As the two men were leaving Cyriack's tent, Conrad glanced over his shoulder to see that he had gotten back to holding his precious black gold. He was cradling it as if it were his child.

"The hell was that all about?" Henic asked.

"Joel tried to warn us," Conrad said.

"But how can a piece of metal make a man act like *that*?"

"I don't know, but how much more proof do we need? Black gold *is* poisoning our minds. We just witnessed a man go from not caring about it to thinking it's the most important thing in the whole world," Conrad said.

"And did ye notice?" Henic asked. Conrad cocked his head. "His eyes were yellow, I swear it. Did ye see it?"

Conrad looked up, in thought. "Yes, now that you mention it…" The duo began walking toward their tents. "I think it'll be best to sleep on it for tonight and see how things are in the morning."

"Now, there's an idea I can get behind, sir," Henic said. They both laughed.

"Oh, and Henic?" Conrad said as he turned back to meet his eyes. "Get rid of your black gold. You don't want to end up like Cyriack."

"R-right…"

Conrad could tell it was an insincere promise, so he had a change of plan before going to sleep.

"Attention, everyone!" he called out. Many groggy heads stuck out of their tents. "I would like to have one more meeting before we all go to sleep."

The strategist waited in the middle of the base camp as men slowly but surely made their way into a circle around him. He noticed that Cyriack and Solomon did not obey the order. Were they too far gone?

"You all may have noticed the odd behavior of Cyriack and Solomon earlier," Conrad began.

"Damn right! They've turned into right knobs, they have!" Peter said to the laughter of a few others.

"True as that may be, I wanted to share what I believe the cause is," Conrad said. "Earlier, I had Cyriack feel the presence of several objects to see if that was the evil he was feeling among our group. He didn't find the evil in those objects, but he *did* find a dark presence within a piece of black gold ore."

Conrad paused to hear if there was any anger from within the crowd. To his surprise, no one seemed to have a problem.

"I believe that black gold poisons the mind. Not in the typical way that gold might poison our minds with greed, but something that truly changes us, and takes us over. I believe that is the behavior Cyriack and Solomon are displaying right now: The black gold is getting to them."

"What rubbish!" Brice cried.

"Yeah!" a few voices from the crowd said in unison.

"They're a couple o' crazy ol' coots! They were bound to crack, some time. Who wants to bet Peter goes next?" Brice said to a few laughs.

"Ye little runt! Yer goin' to be next... *to die!*" Peter shouted.

It was as Conrad had feared. It had taken much evidence for him to believe that black gold was poisoning their minds, and even then, there was no way to confirm completely. Of course no one was going to believe him. Especially not over a material that they thought would save Faiwell and make them rich.

"Believe what you wish," Conrad said, his spirits dimming. "But I'll say it, anyway: Dump your black gold and keep away from it. Keep your sanity."

He hung his head and walked over to his tent. The circle of miners eventually followed suit. The rain had stopped, and the night was silent. As Conrad lay in his makeshift bed, he couldn't help but wonder about so many things: Where were Faramond and the others? Who was the evil magic presence? Was the black gold going to destroy the group from within? He hoped that he would wake up to a better situation the next morning.

CHAPTER 20
A RED NIGHT

Shrieks bounced off the cave walls as the workers looked at each other in concern. There could be no mistaking it: A monster was coming. Faramond had explained to them what Dalton detailed in his journal entries, but there was more resistance to the idea of running than he had anticipated. Many of the workers were tired and wary of their treasures. They refused to move, even for their leader.

Faramond wondered if it was 'Gold Fever', as Dalton had described it, but he knew little on the matter aside from it driving the men mad. By his count, only Wolfgang had lost his mind; and yet it could be argued he never had a full grasp of it in the first place. He thought of the cheek-to-cheek grin on Ollie's gray face when they had discovered his corpse. Would that be the entire group's true fate? Had all of the first group wandered off on their own as Ollie had, leaving themselves to be finished off by the cursed mines?

Skreeeee

There was little time left to think. It was the time to act, Faramond thought. If the group wouldn't listen to him because of Gold Fever, then perhaps he could appeal to their newfound greed.

"Attention, everyone!" he called out as the miners looked back at him with uncaring eyes. "Those of you willing to follow me will be rewarded with the black gold I have gathered so far. But only if you come with me immediately!"

"Don' listen to him!" Wolfgang shouted. "He's tryin' to trick ye all, so he can take yer treasures fer himself!"

"I'm trying to help you all! Can't you see? Come be safe with me *and* you will be handsomely rewarded!" Faramond said.

The workers began to grumble. Some appeared interested in going, while others prattled on about wanting to stay and rest with a watchful eye on their spoils. Joel, Lucia, Alistair, Bronrar, and Edith all came to Faramond's side.

Skreeeeeee

"We are out of time! Everyone, follow me!" he said before turning and running toward a new tunnel.

As he ran, Faramond could hear a growing number of strides behind him. Occasionally, he would also hear strange babel from his workers.

"Must have more…"

"For our Savior!"

"Give me more!"

He also heard the grinding of a mine cart's wheels, which meant that even Wolfgang had come to his senses and followed him. For better or worse, it seemed that everyone was coming along. Faramond knew in his heart that difficult times were coming if Dalton was to be believed, but at least he wouldn't allow more of his men to perish.

The group dashed into the new tunnel and heard the shrieks of the beast become faint. Slowly but surely, their sprint turned into a jog, and then a walk. Soon, the screeches came to an end, and Faramond breathed a great sigh of relief.

"My hero," Edith whispered into his ear.

"Let's not get too excited, my dear. There are other problems to deal with when we stop," Faramond replied.

"Leave Wolfgang to me," she said.

"Absolutely not. He has terrorized you for long enough."

"Please, let me do this. I don't wish to see conflict come about in the group. Especially when the workers have started to rebel…" Edith trailed off. Faramond frowned.

"Very well, but I'll be watching. If he so much as touches a hair on your head, I will be there to respond," he said.

"Fair enough. I shall speak with him when we stop next," Edith said as she began to drop further back in the line of miners. Faramond raised an eyebrow, but quickly returned focus on the path ahead. For all he knew, there could be explosive mushrooms lying on the ground, or knockers lurking about.

~

AT THE BACK of the line, Angus and Wolfgang were pushing the mine cart. They gazed at Edith, who slithered between the miners before she was next in line ahead of them.

"Angus, could I have a word?" she asked without looking back.

"What're ye sayin' to him that ye can't say to *me*?" Wolfgang snapped back.

"Nothing. I have little to say to you right now," Edith said as she motioned Angus over with a head tilt.

"Answer me this, then..." Wolfgang said. The blonde beauty groaned. "Why would ye leave me fer a scrub like Faramond, eh? After all I did fer ye? We were supposed to get rich and be together forever..."

"You did that to yourself. Perhaps you should have treated me better," she said before huddling over and shivering.

"I think it would be best if I went up to speak with her," Angus said to a frowning Wolfgang. "To at least calm her down. If we wish for more black gold, we don't need her causin' any commotions. We have already drawn too much attention to ourselves."

Wolfgang let out a defeated sigh and said, "Fine... but we better get more black gold outa this." Angus left him to push the cart on his own, which took considerably more effort, but the blond brute was strong enough to do it. As Angus approached Edith, Wolfgang called up, "Will ye at least talk to me when we stop? Please..."

"We'll see..." she muttered.

Angus approached her from the side and wrapped his massive arm around her comparatively tiny shoulders. Wolfgang frowned. *That damned Edith*, he thought. She was playing mind games again, and yet he didn't care. In fact, she didn't matter in the grand scheme of things. She was only a channel for his greatest desire. If she continued to get in the way, he'd have to kill her.

Wolfgang's eyes widened at the thought. He had never come close to thoughts of killing Edith before, despite her manipulative ways. He loved her, and yet he now loved other things more. If she did not follow the Dark Savior's will, she would need to be dealt with. Yet, in his heart of hearts, he hoped it wouldn't come to that. He hoped that he could make her see his side of things.

His train of thought was interrupted by an oddity in the tunnel: To his left was a rock that leaned up against the wall. Truly something that stood out, as aside from tunnel collapses, he had not seen any loose rocks on the ground. He remembered thinking of how 'clean' the mines looked despite their age and the apparent poor craftsmanship of the shafts. Could it have been a secret passage? Perhaps it would be worth checking out, he thought.

He changed his mind as Angus returned to the cart and Edith increased her pace up through the crowd. The giant began to push the cart alongside him once more, lessening the burden on his aching body, though not on his troubled mind.

"Well? What did she say?" Wolfgang asked.

"She spoke mostly of Faramond's plans," Angus said with a nod. "She is trying to help us. I believe that she still cares for you."

"Then, why not talk to me?" he asked while slamming his fist into the cart frame.

"I think that she fears you, although I'm unsure. I needed to calm her down for a moment before she could even speak with me," Angus said before placing a massive hand on Wolfgang's shoulder. "However, she also told me that she would like to speak with you when we stop."

Wolfgang's eyes lit up and a smile came to his face. "Now, about Faramond's plans…"

∾

Lucia noticed Edith pass by her for a second time. She shot her an icy glare, but the blonde beauty didn't seem to notice.

"She's up to something…"

"Don't forget that she's tryin' to help Angus escape from Wolfgang," Bronrar chimed in. She glared back at him, to which he looked away, red-cheeked. "That's all I'm sayin'…"

"You cannot trust a snake. I say we treat all three of them as enemies, even if they truly are fighting with each other," said Lucia.

Joel made hand signals to Bronrar, who attempted to translate. "Erm… I think what Joel's tryin' to say is that we should hear Edith out. Wolfgang's gotta be addressed, or he'll try to kill us again."

"I beg to differ," Lucia replied, rubbing her injured shoulder. "I've been through situations like this before. Edith cannot be trusted, even if Wolfgang is a greater threat."

"Oh, quit yer whinin'! Just hear what she has ta say. Ya might be pleasantly surprised!" Alistair said.

Before an argument could break out, there were grumblings up ahead that the group had reached a new cave. This one was only about half the size of the previous, and it was dimmer. The terrain was also the most uneven so far, with rocks sticking out of the ground and many incomplete digging sites decorating the area.

Faramond stopped the group toward the center, as was typical, and announced, "This is where we shall rest for the night. As promised, for coming along with me, I will divide my black gold up for you all. I'll call you over when I'm done separating the treasures accordingly."

Many of the miners sounded happy at the announcement and let out some cheers. After a few moments, the workers walked to their own spots in the cave. Lucia and the others sat against a wall that was next to what appeared to be a tunnel. However, for the first time, this tunnel was blocked off by an odd stone door. It had markings on it that appeared to be in the ancient language. The others looked to Joel for translation, so he wrote it down in his notes for them to read:

Exit Only

Alistair frowned and said, "Tha hell is with this place, anyway? None of it makes sense!"

"The poorly-designed corridors, only one entrance and exit, the many hazards… it's a death trap," Lucia added.

"W-we *will* make it out, won't we?" Bronrar asked.

"We can survive if we steer clear of your former friends," said Lucia as she stretched her arms out. "They are nothing but trouble."

"Can't we simply hear what they have to say?"

"*You* can hear them out. I won't be listening," she replied. Bronrar sighed.

As time passed, Alistair and Joel decided to play a game of slaps to keep themselves busy. The attacker would hold out two of his hands, palms facing up, while the defender would place their hands palms down, on top. The attacker would then try to slap the defender's hands. If they missed, the roles would be reversed. Despite its simplicity, Joel had never played the game before.

"Ya don't know what slaps is, lad?" Alistair asked loudly, clapping him on the back like thunder might in the sky. "Don' worry, I'll go easy on ya!"

However, Alistair was surprised to find that no matter how many times he tried to get the slap on the mute, he missed. The big man hit nothing but air every single time. Meanwhile, Joel only made half-hearted attempts every time it was his turn to try and slap.

"Wait! Yer the one goin' easy on me!" Alistair complained as Joel missed again, clumsily. The big redhead then attempted to land a surprise slap, but he still missed the mark. He instead flung forward from the force of missing so badly. "Gah! Yer good at this…"

Lucia scoffed and said, "Your reactions are simply too slow. Let me show you how it's done."

She sat next to Joel, who turned and put his hands on top of hers. The mercenary closed her eyes and began to focus. She visualized the motion of what she wanted to do: A quick slip of the hands, with little elevation as she turned them over to slap Joel's. She felt confident in her reaction speed.

The mercenary opened her eyes with a sudden intensity and then flipped her hands over and brought them down with all the force she had. *Got him*, she thought.

"Wha?" Lucia gasped as she felt the air dance between her fingers. Amid her miss, she bent over awkwardly from the momentum. Lucia then felt her shoulder flair up, as if she'd pushed it into fire. "Gah! My shoulder… forgot… it's injured…"

She rolled onto the ground, back-first, and stared at the ceiling.

The others laughed. Although initially annoyed, Lucia began laughing herself as she grasped the injury. However, her laughs ceased when the fresh blood seeped between her fingers. It still wasn't healing quickly enough. Another confrontation with Wolfgang or Angus didn't bode well.

"Now, don't be tryin' ta use yer shoulder as an excuse!" Alistair said.

"Oh, shut it!" Lucia shot back before sitting back up and returning her gaze to Joel. "I must compliment you on your hand speed. It wasn't just my injury; my eyes didn't completely follow you. If you were to train yourself to use a weapon…" she trailed off as Joel shook his head. "I understand that you don't wish to hurt anyone, but you must consider the possibility that you'll have to choose between your own life and someone else's while in these mines."

Joel opened his mouth, as if to respond, but then Bronrar jumped in. "How 'bout I try?"

Alistair and Lucia looked at each other, wide-eyed.

"If neither of us could get 'im, what makes ya think *you* stand a chance?" the big man asked.

Bronrar held up a finger and wagged it. "I have a secret technique for this game. Watch and learn."

He placed his palms upward, underneath Joel's hands. However, instead of going for a fast approach, he remained silent and motionless. The mute tilted his head, and Lucia did the same when she noticed that Bronrar was tickling his palms. Suddenly, Bronrar moved his hands in a swift motion. Joel tried to pull his own hands away, but the distraction had worked. A light slapping noise sounded off as the mute jerked his hands away.

"Huh… still barely managed to get you," Bronrar said with a shrug.

"Yer a fast lil' bugger, ain't ya, Joel?" Alistair said with a chuckle. He turned to Bronrar and grabbed one of his hands. "Now, show me this 'secret technique'…"

However, before he could show him anything, Faramond called out, "Alright, everyone! I have divided up the treasures accordingly. Come and form a line so I can give you your share."

The miners all around the cave began to converge toward the center where Faramond had laid everything out. Alistair and Bronrar stood with the apparent intention of doing the same.

"Where do you two think you're going?" Lucia asked. They turned and shared the same confused expressions. "How can you continue to lust for black gold when Dalton's journal proves what Joel has been trying to tell us all along?"

"About that…" Bronrar said.

"We haven't seen enough evidence!" Alistair blurted out.

"Erm, yes, what he said."

"What more evidence do you need? Dalton documented that the black gold was changing the way he thought!" she replied.

"Could be a coincidence," Alistair said with a shrug. "He never said that it was the black gold. He only says the *mines* were makin' him crazy and such!"

Joel and Lucia looked at each other with frowns as the two men made their way into the line. There was no arguing with them.

～

AT THE FRONT of the line, Faramond handed out his black gold shares to the miners. Most men were either silently intense or elated in their reactions, but the leader himself was in low spirits. Not only was he beginning to lose the loyalty of his team, but he was also handing them what could very well have caused their personality change to begin with.

"I'm proud of you," Edith whispered in his ear. Tingles shot down his spine. He looked back at her with a mixture of excitement and confusion. "If you hadn't come up with this idea, I don't know that some of these men would have followed you…"

Faramond chuckled. "I'm not sure they'll follow me anymore after thi-" He was cut off by Edith laying a kiss on him, and it didn't take long for him to start enjoying it. They were interrupted by the clearing of a throat. Faramond gazed at Angus, whose grim face brought him crashing back down to reality. Wolfgang stood behind him, and it was easy to see that he was livid: He was baring his teeth at him like a feral beast.

"Our black gold, sir, if you please," Angus said.

"Right, of course," Faramond said. He gave the giant his promised share. Wolfgang approached next and held out his hands.

"Thank ye, sir…" Wolfgang said through gritting teeth as he was handed the black gold ore. His wild eyes wandered over to Edith, and Faramond's heart skipped a beat. In those eyes, staring intently at the blonde beauty, he could have sworn that he'd seen a glint of yellow. Was he simply imagining it? "I thought we were supposed to talk."

"I think it would be best if you left her alone," Faramond said.

"Mind yer own business! Everythin' was great between us until *ye* came into the picture!" Wolfgang shot back.

"Edith is with *me*, now," said Faramond as he lowered his hand to the hilt of his sword. "Take the black gold and be on your way."

Wolfgang looked at Faramond's hand and burst out laughing. He then returned his venomous gaze to Edith, who now had turned her back to him. "Ye want me to kill him, don't ye? That can be the only reason yer actin' this *stupid*!"

He took a step toward her. That was all that Faramond needed to see. He drew his sword and then jumped between them.

"This is your last chance to stand down. Any more moves like that one, and I'll kill you where you stand," Faramond said.

Wolfgang scoffed and replied, "No wonder ye confiscated my weapon. Ye can't take me in a fair fight, and ye know it, too!" He then turned back to Angus and said, "Let's go. At least we got more treasures…"

Faramond breathed a sigh of relief and sheathed his sword. He then turned to face Edith and asked, "Are you alright?"

Edith, who had ceased her shivering, turned around and said meekly, "Will you stay with me tonight?"

"Of course," Faramond said. It felt good to be her protector.

In short order, all of the miners who wanted their share of the black gold had gone through the line and retrieved it. Faramond noted that Joel and Lucia hadn't taken any, and he felt it was the smartest decision. Although Dalton's journal entries hadn't specified that black gold had been the cause of Gold Fever, everything else pointed to it. Faramond himself had experienced a shift in priorities up until he realized that his workers were in danger. Since that time, he'd been able to keep a clear head, but even still, he could feel something clawing away at the back of his mind. Something didn't feel right.

His train of thought was interrupted by a tug of his hand. He looked back to see Edith staring at him lustfully. That's *the look*, he thought.

"I'm tired, Fara. Do you think we can find somewhere private to spend the night?" she asked, letting out a yawn.

"Mayhap one of the incomplete digging sites could give us some alone time," he replied with a smile.

"I thought you might say that. Look at that spot over there. It's perfect, isn't it?" she asked, then pointed to an area of the cave that was obscured by rocks. It was to the left of where they had entered, earlier.

"Yes, I think that will do," said Faramond. They walked together toward the rocks and held hands.

~

MEANWHILE, Alistair and Bronrar sat with Lucia and Joel once more, trying to figure out what to do next.

"So, she told ya to go see Angus, then?" Alistair asked.

"Well… she nodded her head toward him… erm, I think?" said Bronrar. "I don' know what she expects, though. Wolfgang hasn't left Angus' side for a while."

"It could have been nothing. In fact, I bet there's no plan at all. Edith cannot be trusted," Lucia said.

"There's only one way to be sure," Bronrar replied, standing. "I'll go check with Angus myself."

"With the way Wolfgang's been acting lately? Even *that* may set him off. Don't put your life in danger needlessly," she said.

"She's got a point, lad! Maybe we should wait fer her to come to us," Alistair said.

"Angus won't let anythin' happen to me," Bronrar argued.

"You misplace your faith. Don't forget what he was capable of, earlier. The dratagons killed less than he did. You shouldn't trust a murderer," Lucia said. Joel nodded.

"He's been my best friend since we were children. And you lot? I haven't really known you for more than a day. I'm goin' to speak with him. If you still wanna be part of the plan, I'll check in with you later," Bronrar said before walking off into the darkness of the cave.

"Good news, Alistair," Lucia said. The big man raised an eyebrow. "I think we found someone on this trip who's dumber than you."

"Oooo, very funny!" Alistair said with crossed arms.

ON THE OTHER side of the cave, Edith and Faramond went behind the rocks in the ground and set up a bedding area. No one was around besides the two of them; and with the rocks standing high and wide, it was like their own private room.

As soon as Faramond finished with the bedding, Edith tackled him to the ground and they began kissing. He knew this had been her plan all along, but even still, he separated himself and asked, "I thought you were tired, dear?"

Edith straddled him and said, "I've had a stressful day, Fara. It's time to work it off."

She then got to kissing Faramond's neck, and now light-headed with pleasure, his hands began moving of their own accord. He flung off the straps of her dress and then grabbed the back of her blouse, ready to rip it off. However, Edith grabbed his wrists, stopping him. His thoughtless bliss grinding to a halt, he looked up at her in confusion.

"Wait… you go on top…" Edith said. She then took the blouse off herself.

Faramond's eyes lit up and he smiled from ear to ear. Such beauty, he thought. How could he say no to *that*? "Anything for you, Edith."

~

ON THE OTHER side of the cave, Bronrar approached Angus and Wolfgang, who each sat and leaned against the cart of black gold. They stood as he got closer.

"Well, well… I knew ye were daft, but this is a whole new level of stupid!" Wolfgang said with a chuckle. "Ye know I wanna kill ye, right? What the hell do ye want?"

"Er… well…" Bronrar trailed off.

"Get to the point!" Wolfgang said. Bronrar flinched and Angus could have sworn that his eyes had turned yellow, if only for a moment.

"I-I wanted a word with Angus."

"Well? Go on and say what yer gonna say!"

"I meant alone…"

Angus started for Bronrar, but Wolfgang put a hand up to his chest and stopped him.

"Hold up… I've had enough of ye lot sneakin' around and having yer private conversations!" Wolfgang shouted. Bronrar quivered in his boots. "Say what ye were gonna say in front of me… or I'll kill ye."

"Now, now," Angus said, placing a firm hand on his shoulder. "Don't forget that Bronrar was thinkin' of joining back up with us. Isn't that right?" He smiled at his friend.

"Well…" Bronrar trailed off.

"He ain't reliable, Angus! It's time we tied up a loose end. I'll take care of the fat arse, and then we'll be done with it." Wolfgang reached for his pickaxe.

Angus blocked his path to Bronrar. "There is no need to harm him."

"I'm gonna give ye a few moments to think about what yer doin', Angus," Wolfgang replied while pointing the pickaxe at him. "Yer in the way. Ye know what that means? Ye don't follow his will, and if ye don't follow his will, yer a non-believer… and if yer a non-believer…"

"I can always come back some other time," Bronrar said as he turned to leave. He scurried away as Angus continued to block the blond brute's path.

"The non-believers must die, and that includes him!" Wolfgang shouted as his eyes yellowed once more. "Are ye a non-believer?"

"Of course not," Angus said.

"Then, come with me. Let's take care of these pests once and for all," Wolfgang said as he brushed past. Angus followed close behind.

~

FURTHER AROUND THE bend of the cave, Bronrar reached his new friends. His face was flushed and beads of sweat were coming down his forehead.

"I take it things didn't go well?" Lucia asked with a smile.

"Er… about that…"

They all looked past him to see Wolfgang storming in their direction with Angus in tow.

"Get ready, everyone. Looks like Bronrar dragged them over here," Lucia said while hopping to her feet. Joel and Alistair also readied themselves.

"S-sorry…" Bronrar mumbled as the two men stopped in front of them.

"What do you sorry sacks want?" Alistair asked.

"I'm sick of ye lot conspirin' against me! With yer secret meetings and yer little groups! All of ye are non-believers!" Wolfgang shouted.

Joel and Alistair looked at each other in confusion.

"Especially *you*," Wolfgang said, pointing his pickaxe at Joel. "Yer a good fer nothin' who thinks he's good for things! What do ye even *do* for this team? Ye've given nothing! Yer only a hindrance to our Savior, and those like you will be the first to go!"

Joel's eyes widened as Wolfgang approached him with a pickaxe in hand. The others jumped between them with weapons drawn and Angus put a hand on his shoulder.

Wolfgang darted his eyes back at the giant. He was like a wild, hungry beast, ready to pounce; but before he could do anything, Angus whispered something in his ear and he froze in place.

He looked back with a terrible glare and said, "Show me."

The pair walked away just as quickly as they had shown up, and the others could only watch on with wide eyes and cocked heads.

"Tha hell was that all about?" Alistair asked aloud.

Joel squinted as Angus and Wolfgang disappeared into the darkness. They were traveling in the same direction that Edith and Faramond had gone after giving away the remaining ore. The mute's stomach sank.

~

MEANWHILE, Wolfgang glared at Angus as they walked.

"Where are they?" he asked.

"Be patient, and I'll show you where I saw 'em go," Angus replied.

"I'll kill him… I'll kill him for the Savior…" said Wolfgang as a deranged smile came to his face. Angus observed that his eyes were a solid yellow. No longer did the striking change only come in flashes or glints.

Wolfgang cocked his head. He had taken notice of his staring. "What's wrong? Ye don't follow his will? Ye do wanna live, don't ye? Don't ye care about yer fellow man? If ye did, ye'd be doin' everythin' to bring *him* back," he said, wrapping a hand around Angus' neck and squeezing. The giant coughed and gagged while struggling to breathe, but did not retaliate. "But yer not doin' anything! None of ye are! None of ye are worthy to meet our great Savior!"

"You misunderstand…" Angus choked out. Wolfgang leaned in. "I come to you with a mission from the Dark Savior, y'see…"

"A mission?" Wolfgang asked, letting go of his throat. They abruptly stopped, and Angus coughed for a few moments to catch his breath.

"Yes… a mission. The question is: Do you possess the bravery to accept it?" asked the giant.

～

BEHIND THE ROCKS, Edith and Faramond let out satisfied breaths in unison. The leader looked down on her and smiled. Though she'd often caused him headaches on the expedition, her heart was in the right place, he thought. Besides, on nights like tonight, she more than made up for any trouble she had caused. He was happy to have her around, and now he wanted to express it.

"I love you."

Edith's eyes widened and Faramond snorted. How cute, he thought. Even when taken completely off guard, she maintained a natural beauty that few possessed. However, as time passed, his stomach began to sink. She simply stared back at him with those piercing green eyes. It was as if she was looking through him; unsure of how to respond.

"You *do* feel the same way, don't you?" he asked. Edith continued to stare straight back up at him. Now, it was his heart sinking, not his stomach.

"I…" she trailed off. The leader, still on top of her, tilted his head and crossed his arms.

"Say it…"

"I-" Edith gasped as a familiar noise rang in Faramond's ears: A sound he had heard many times since entering these horrid mines. The sound of a blade piercing flesh.

Searing, red-hot pain flared in the side of Faramond's neck and his mouth fell agape as he attempted to cough, only to find himself choking: Choking on blood; choking on metal. With a shaky hand, he patted down the right side of his neck and felt the head of a pickaxe. He could feel the blood spurting out of the wound like a leaking bucket trying desperately to hold water. It couldn't be true! It was only his imagination or a minor wound, he thought. With vision blurring, Faramond brought his hand before his face to see it covered in dark red. *It was real*, he thought.

His surprise quickly turned to panic as he reached his rickety hand out to Edith for support. He could not speak, he could not shout, he could not cry. He could only choke and reach out to his last lease on life.

Even if he was about to die, Faramond could take comfort that the love of his life was there, smiling back up at him. Such a beautiful smile, he thought. *But wait*, he thought. Now wasn't the time to smile. What was there to be happy about? He, the love of her life, her protector, was about to die. And why wouldn't she take his hand? Why didn't she rush to comfort him in his final moments?

As his vision grew dark, the last thing he could see was Edith's grinning face. It was not a smile of happiness, but one with ill will behind it. As comfort left him and despair took hold, all Faramond could think about was why. *Why was she smiling?*

Faramond let out his last gurgle of blood and fell face-first onto Edith's bare chest. She frowned in disgust. He just *had* to get all of that blood on her. What a nuisance, she thought.

"Thank you for your services, *sir*," she remarked before tipping him over and off of her body.

She looked up to see Wolfgang standing over them, breathing heavily. A delirious smile came to his face, and then he said, "My mission is complete."

"Well done, Wolfy," Edith said as she stood and covered herself with the makeshift sheets. Faramond's blood began seeping through them. "Our Dark Savior will be pleased with your work."

"Y-ye follow his will, too?" Wolfgang asked with puppy-like eyes and hopefulness in his tone. "I was worried I'd have'ta purge ye like the others, but to hear that ye too are a part of his plan…"

Edith approached him and pressed her body up against his in a long, warm embrace. She whispered in his ear, "Your mission is only half-done." The blonde beauty began to kiss him on his neck as he listened and she said, "This will be even more difficult than your first task, but our Dark Savior has chosen you, and that is his will, so it must be done."

"Yes… it shall…" he replied, militantly.

"Good, now the first thing you need to do is take Faramond's sword…"

~

ON THE OTHER side of the cave, Joel, Alistair, Lucia, and Bronrar leaned up against the rocky wall and tried to figure out what had happened.

"Angus didn't seem to have a plan after all. Wolfgang wouldn't let us talk alone, and now he thinks we're plannin' somethin' against him," Bronrar said.

"I tried to tell you: Your friend has been corrupted by Edith," Lucia said.

"You weren't there… you wouldn't understand! It wasn't his fault!"

"None of it makes sense! Wolfgang and Angus didn't even go back ta guardin' their mine cart of treasures!" Alistair said.

Joel found himself wondering about the same thing. He could accept that Wolfgang would be suspicious of forces conspiring against him, but why would they abandon the mine cart that they so desperately wished to protect? Whatever Angus had whispered to Wolfgang changed everything, but he couldn't be sure what was said. There was another element to the whole situation that Joel couldn't put his finger on, and it made his stomach churn.

As Joel continued to think, a blood-curdling scream echoed around the cave. It was the cry of a woman.

"That's gotta be Edith!" Bronrar cried as he ran toward the source of the noise. The others followed close behind.

While running to the commotion, more screams and cries could be heard, and Joel noticed other miners close behind them, as well. As they neared the rocks in the ground where Edith was, Joel noticed a figure in the distance running toward the tunnel that they had come from.

Eventually, they reached the area to see an undressed Edith wrapped up in bloodstained sheets. She was shivering and crying.

"W-Wolfgang… he k-killed Fara…" she mumbled between sobs. All in attendance gasped and spoke in hush tones. Everyone made their way around the rocks to find Faramond lying in a pool of blood. There was a pickaxe in the side of his neck and terror was all that remained in his dead eyes.

"Damn it…" Lucia trailed off with clenched fists.

Joel's mind raced at the implications. Wolfgang had truly come unhinged to attack and kill his own leader. Had it been Gold Fever? Or had it merely been a continuation of his murderous ways?

For now, though, Joel chose to focus on the sadness in his heart. Faramond had been a good leader and an honorable man. One of his last actions had been saving him from the jaws of a riggit, and who could forget how he had bravely fended off the dratagons when they attacked? He wanted nothing more than to protect his team, and yet he had been killed by a man with the opposite intentions.

The miners began to question Edith, who had trouble responding and seemed shaken up, so Angus stepped in.

"I didn't see anythin' happen, but I was with Wolfgang earlier, and he did say that he wished death upon Faramond. He has become less stable in the mind, lately. I do not know where he ran off to, so we should be on high alert."

"H-he killed… him… without hesitation…" Edith trailed off as she looked down at the bloody sheets hugging her body. "Please excuse me… I must dress myself."

She retreated to where her clothes lay, behind the rocks.

"This is bad," said Lucia. Sweat began to drip down her forehead.

"No doubt! That knob Wolfgang won't hesitate ta kill nobody! Now who will protect us from 'im?" Alistair said.

Lucia scoffed. "No, that's not what I mean. Are you not seeing the bigger picture? Edith is going to use this as an opportunity to become the new leader of our team."

"What? After all that's happened, *that's* what yer worried about?" Bronrar asked with a raised eyebrow.

"Think about it. She was second-in-command, and now our leader is dead. It stands to reason that she would take his place. This was her plan *all along*," Lucia said, grinding her teeth. "I'm certain that the first thing she will do is attempt to take leadership."

Joel was taken aback. Given the cutthroat nature of Edith and her father, it was plausible that she would plan Faramond's death. But why? What was the final goal? There had to be more to it than just thinning out the number of miners. He then remembered Lucia's story from the night before. *The Gold Pit,* he thought, wide-eyed. Drake had mentioned it in his plans: That was the final goal. Many incorrect legends had been passed down over the years about the Gold Pit, however. The question was: Had Edith and Drake planned this entire expedition based on those myths? Or had they somehow uncovered Mt. Couture's true secret? Joel shuddered at the thought.

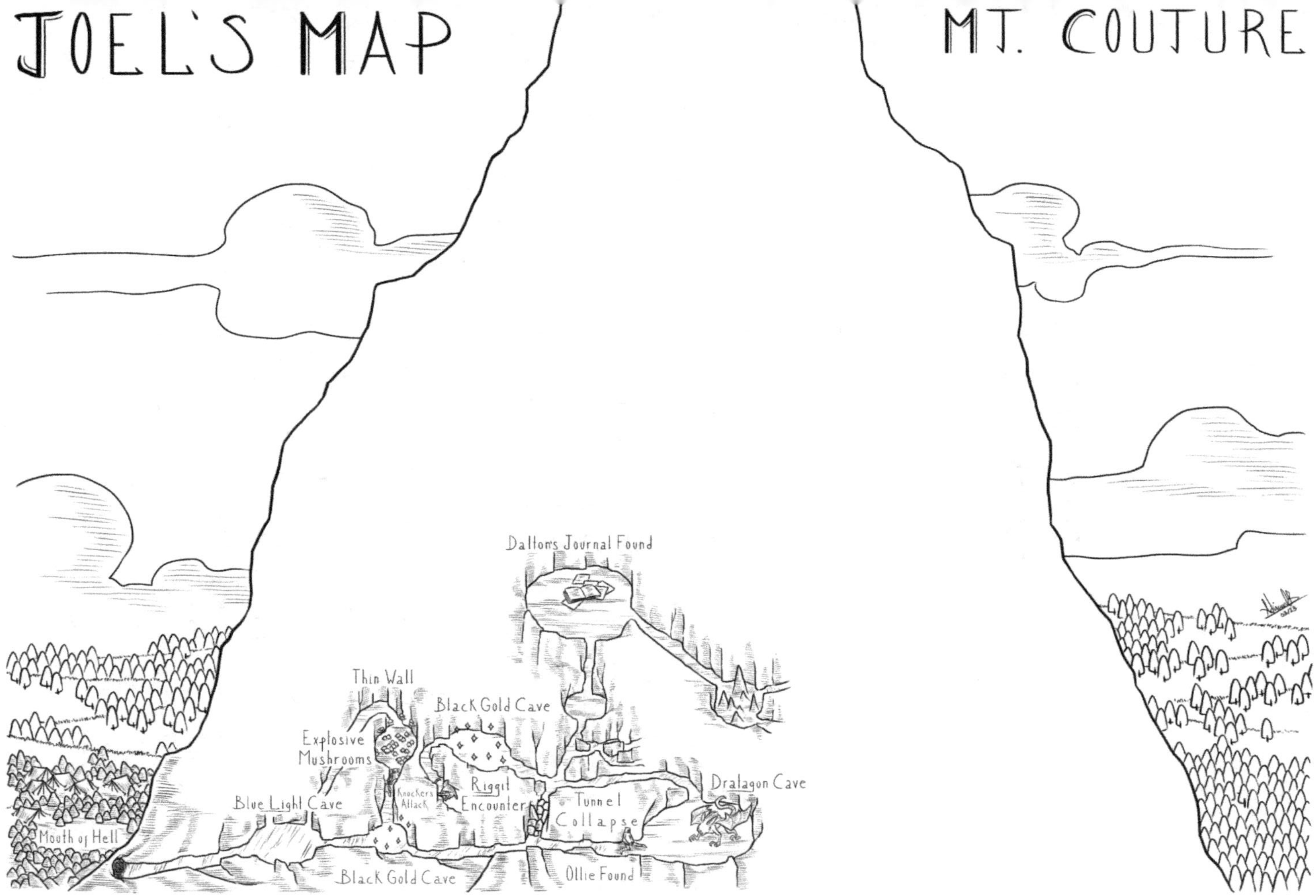

JOEL'S MAP

MT. COUTURE

Dalton's Journal Found

Dralagon Cave

Thin Wall

Black Gold Cave

Explosive Mushrooms

Mockers Attack

Rugat Encounter

Tunnel Collapse

Ollie Found

Blue Light Cave

Black Gold Cave

Mouth of Hell

CHAPTER 21
LABYRINTH

While most were focused on the gruesome murder of Faramond, Joel wandered off toward the tunnel where the group had previously come from. He was certain that Wolfgang had escaped through there.

Joel's eyes widened as he noticed his torch reflecting a different color off the ground: it was blood. Perhaps Faramond's blood from the treacherous attack? It was fresh, so regardless of its origin, he knew it was evidence that someone had been there recently. The mute walked up the path and scanned the ground for anything new. After a few moments, he came upon more drops of blood. It, too, was fresh, and that was all that he needed to see.

Yet, who would he report the news to? Logic followed that Edith would become leader since she was second-in-command, but she seemed too shaken up by the incident to hear the news. Instead, Joel decided he would tell his friends of the findings.

He sprinted over to where the group had gathered and found his friends by spotting Alistair's red, thumb-like head, which popped out of the crowd. He tapped the big man on the shoulder, and he turned around, a big frown on his face.

"What tha hell do-" He paused, and his frown bent up into a smile. "Oh, it's only you, lad! What is it?"

Joel pointed to the tunnel where he had found the blood. Alistair raised an eyebrow.

"What about the tunnel? We can't be leavin' just yet! We gotta figure out where Wolfgang went ta, that lil' rat!"

Joel rolled his eyes and then mimed the act of Wolfgang killing Faramond. He stabbed an invisible knife into his stomach, stuck his tongue out, and then pointed to the tunnel again.

"Well, of course we'll die if we don' get outta here. Tell me somethin' I don' know!" said Alistair. Joel let out an inaudible sigh.

"I think he's tryin' to tell us that's where Wolfgang went to," Bronrar said. Joel nodded emphatically. "We should tell Edith-"

"Not a chance," Lucia interrupted. "Even if I'm wrong, and she played no part in Faramond's death, she is not of sound mind at the moment. I say we investigate on our own."

The group was quiet for a moment, but they seemed to agree. They followed Joel back to the tunnel and walked up its path. Joel searched the ground for blood drops until finally he found it and shined his torch upon it for others to see.

"Blood! But whose?" Alistair asked.

"It's fresh," Lucia said, kneeling to inspect it. "Whether it's Faramond's or Wolfgang's, this tells us where he went to."

"Well, that's a good thing, ain't it?" asked Bronrar. Joel shook his head, and the nervous miner frowned.

"Now he can surprise us with an attack at any time, and our numbers are dwindling..." Lucia said.

Skreeee

The group turned and looked at each other, but didn't speak. All eyes reflected fright.

Skreeeee

"Methinks we won't need ta be worryin' about Wolfgang, now..." Alistair muttered.

"I-it's that monster Dalton described in his journal, ain't it?" Bronrar asked, his lips quivering.

"I think so," said Lucia.

"Good! I hope it eats that knob!" Alistair said.

"I think we should worry more about ourselves, right now," Lucia said.

Skreeeeee

The noise grew closer. Bronrar shifted around where he stood. He began to shake in his boots before saying, "W-we should warn the others..."

Alistair looked over his shoulder and said, "I think they know, lad." He then pointed to the growing crowd behind them.

Out of the group emerged Angus, who approached Bronrar.

"These noises…" he said with crossed arms. "The creature has followed us here. Perhaps instead of running, we should attempt to kill it."

"Dalton's notes said that it was invulnerable to even his blade," Bronrar said, looking up at him with doubtful eyes. "How could we hope to defeat it?"

"You underestimate me," Angus replied, clenching his massive fist and holding it up in the darkness. "With a well-organized strike, *none* are invulnerable."

"Go on and rush to your death then, big man," Lucia said as the beast screeched again off in the distance. It was the loudest yet. "I for one will be leaving. If Dalton couldn't defeat this monster, none of us can."

"That's alright, you're all but useless with that injury of yours. Feel free to leave any time. The true warriors will stay and fight," Angus said with a smirk.

"Why, you-"

Skreeeeeeeeeee

"There ain't no time for arguin'! We stayin' ta fight? Or are we leavin'? I say we fight!" Alistair shouted.

"We will stay and confront the monster," Edith said from behind the crowd. Everyone turned to see her in more disarray than they were used to. Perhaps because of the blood on her chest, the dress' bust cut far lower than usual, and her hair was in dire need of brushing. Yet, she wore the same piercing stare as always. "We cannot keep running away, and in either case, we must hunt down Wolfgang and bring him to justice. As far as I can tell, he went where that monster's screeches are coming from."

"If he went toward the Nightcrawler, wouldn't it have simply killed him?" Bronrar asked.

"We haven't heard any human commotion. No screams or battle cries. He must be alive," Edith said. The sharpness in her voice began to return. "And if any of you are too cowardly to help us catch the murderer, then you are a traitor."

"Who made you leader of the group?" Lucia shot back.

"Since I was second-in-command to Faramond, his death makes me the leader," said Edith. A crooked smile came to her face. "Do you have a problem with that?"

"Of course I do. You schemed your way to the top, and you proved earlier today your incompetence in leading a group. I say we vote for a new leader," she said.

The group remained silent. Joel began to understand the situation: Edith had garnered so much sympathy from being at the scene of her lover's murder that no one dared question her. It was hard to fall out of line, too, because the second-in-command taking charge in a leader's absence was the standard. In the group's collective mind, Edith had been handpicked by Faramond himself. To question that decision would be to dishonor his memory.

"It seems you have been overruled," Edith said with a smile from ear to ear. "Satisfied?"

"For now..." Lucia said as she started cutting through the group. As the mercenary walked, she grabbed Joel by the wrist. "Come with me. It won't be safe up front." He nodded in return.

As they walked to get Alistair and Bronrar's attention, Edith darted past them and to the front. She then announced, "Angus will be the new second-in-command. You all would do well to listen to him closely."

Skreeeeeeeeeeeee

The miners grumbled nervously and some men were shaking.

"It won't be long before the Nightcrawler arrives. When the time comes, we shall all attack it at once. Understood?" Angus said aloud.

As the giant was giving out orders, Lucia snuck up behind Alistair and Bronrar and tapped them on their backs. Alistair looked back with a snarl and said, "WHAT DO YA WAN-"

Lucia slapped his mouth shut with a free hand before he could blurt out any more, and his words became muffled. Bronrar looked back and chuckled. Angus continued to bark orders up front.

"Listen closely. The two of you need to follow us to the back. It's our greatest chance for survival," she whispered while gently letting go of Alistair's mouth.

"And go against orders?" Bronrar replied with a furrowed brow. "Yer always tryin' to go against orders. Why not listen?"

"Haven't you been paying attention? Edith is trying to kill us off."

"I ain't a coward, so I ain't runnin'!" Alistair attempted to whisper, but it came out too loud and drew the attention of a few nearby miners.

"You oaf… this is no time to be stubborn…" Lucia muttered. Joel gestured for them to come along, too.

"You go along with her, lad," Alistair said as he gave him a playful slap on the shoulder. "I know ya ain't one fer fightin'."

Joel sighed and then looked at Bronrar, who also shook his head. "I'm stayin' up here with Angus. I know he'll have my back."

"I was correct about the so-called 'plan' earlier, was I not?" Lucia asked as her hushed voice grew more strained. "You'll regret not listening to me this time." She turned and made her way to the back of the group. Joel looked back at the two men for a moment, but both gestured for him to go with Lucia, so he followed her.

"We'll need to be ready to make a run for it," the mercenary muttered as she walked. A lump came to Joel's throat. He worried for Alistair and Bronrar's safety.

~

Up ahead, Edith stood behind Angus and a row of other workers who awaited the Nightcrawler. However, after several moments, the creature's cries ceased and little could be heard besides men grumbling to themselves.

"Has it turned around?" Edith asked.

"I'm unsure. Haven't heard much of anythin' since the last screech," Angus said with a look back at her. "Shall we consider advancing to confront it head-on?"

As he spoke the words, a harsh noise bounced around the tunnel: claws scratching against rocks rapidly. The miners shuddered as they heard another piercing shriek, seemingly right in front of them.

"The beast is here!" Angus shouted out as everyone readied themselves. The clawing of the rocks ended, and silence fell upon the tunnel once more.

~

"Well? Where is it?" Alistair asked, eyeing Bronrar.

The nervous miner frowned. How was he supposed to know? He gave a token look around the dark tunnel. The blue lights, fading in and out, were more frustrating than helpful. He couldn't see a thing besides rocks and the darkness, despite there being a light source.

Then, in the brief moment that the blue rocks glimmered, something caught his eye.

He searched the area again, and sure enough, something stood out once more. Then, he finally locked eyes on it. He didn't speak. He only looked up, his mouth agape.

"Tha hell're ya doin', munchkin? Do ya see it?" Alistair asked.

Bronrar pointed at the ceiling of the tunnel. Alistair looked, and staring back at him were several red, glowing eyes reflecting in the blue glimmers. Each eye seemed to carry with it an intense desire to kill, and each one struck terror into Bronrar's heart as they darted around in different directions.

"Up above!" Alistair cried. The other miners stirred and pointed their torches at the ceiling. The beast screeched once more and Bronrar fell to a knee, clutching his unbearably ringing ears.

THE NIGHTCRAWLER LANDED with a great *thud*. The tunnel shook and the torches flickered at the might of its weight. In the shadows of the fading blue light, a creature towered over them despite its hunched posture, and its dark green hide and enormous claws became apparent. Angus felt a tingle run down his spine, not just at the horrid stench of decay that had overtaken him, but its source: The wriggling tentacles at the monster's mouth, making a vile, wet noise; like worms being squished together in the mud. Behind those tentacles were many rows of sharp, jagged teeth.

Suddenly, the Nightcrawler lunged out of the darkness and tackled a worker who had been standing next to Angus. He didn't even have enough time to scream before the monster was ripping him to shreds on the ground. It let out an otherworldly cry as bloody organs flew into the crowd. Angus turned to face the attacker, feasting on the man's flesh. Edith hid behind him.

"Attack!" Angus shouted. He and the others closed in on the Night-crawler and swung their weapons. Many *clangs* rang hollow around the tunnel, and it confused the giant. It hadn't been the sound of blades piercing flesh, but instead, metal striking metal.

Angus was horrified to find that even with over a dozen strikes at once, the Nightcrawler was unfazed. Instead, the beast turned and lunged out at another worker in response to the attack. Like the miner before, it pinned the poor soul to the ground and began to feast on his flesh, but this time, its victim was conscious while it happened. His cries quickly turned to silence and the monster's tentacles fluttered about as it ate. The other workers could do little aside from stare.

"There must be somethin' we can do!" Alistair called out as he marched up to the creature. It paid him no heed.

He raised his battle axe, and along with him, other miners brought up their weapons for another strike. However, before he could bring his mighty axe down, Lucia tackled him from behind. The other men followed through with their attack, and once again loud *clanging* noises echoed off the tunnel walls.

The Nightcrawler screeched and then turned with lightning-like speed to strike the worker who had been next to Alistair. Blood painted the walls, the ground, and worker tunics alike as the blow sent the man flying back into the crowd. He was dead before landing.

It lumbered to its latest victim, parting the group. No one dared to move a muscle, and it paid them no mind while walking past. It howled once more before lunging over to feast on the corpse. Its many red eyes were looking around manically, in different directions, as it ate. Alistair looked up at Lucia and gave her a quick nod before standing.

Angus now better understood what he was dealing with. The Nightcrawler had casually killed three of his men, but not in the way he had been expecting. A creature that could strike so quickly should have been able to take all of them out in no time, he thought. However, its behavior couldn't have been more opposite: Despite striking quickly, it took its time feasting upon prey, and only once at a time. While eating, it would only attack when provoked by another attack.

"We have to leave," Angus whispered to Edith. She frowned back at him.

"And what about your grand plan? I thought you could kill this beast," Edith hissed.

"The creature is beyond anything I've ever seen. Our weapons are useless against it. Shall we go back to where we first found Dalton's journal? Or explore further into this cave?" he asked.

"We have no choice but to venture further into the mines. If we go back, we'll be trapped between the riggits, dratagons, and..." Edith trailed off, looking at the Nightcrawler in disgust as it continued to eat its bloody meal. *"That thing."*

"Very well," Angus said as he gestured toward the cave behind them. "Shall we?"

"Everyone, listen well!" Edith called out as the horrified men glanced at her. The beast was still feasting on its prey and the sound of crunching bones seemed to distract the workers. "We need to venture further into the mines. Follow Angus and I!"

Edith walked through the crowd, and back into the cave. Angus followed, and so did the others. The Nightcrawler paid no attention and continued its feast.

~

AS THE GROUP crossed the cave, Joel noted how few of them remained. There were only 16 left by his count, and the number was dropping fast. As the thought occurred to him, he noticed that Edith was leading the group toward the 'exit only' door. He increased his pace in the hopes of catching up with and explaining things to her.

"I noticed a passage, earlier," Edith muttered to Angus. "It has a door of all things, but I figure the workers can open it with enough manpower." Joel tapped her on the shoulder. The blonde beauty looked back with a scowl. "What do *you* want? I'm busy."

Joel tried his best to mime a door being locked, but it was no good. Edith stared right through him with dull, green eyes.

"You heard her, runt. Get back in line," said Angus. Joel sighed. He fell back into the pack behind them, knowing full well that the direction they were going was pointless. Eventually, the group came to a stop at the door.

"Well?" Edith asked as she put hands to her hips. "Open it!" Several men, including Angus, attempted to push the door, but to no avail. They next tried to lift from underneath, but there was no opening to slip their fingers under.

Lucia walked up to Edith and chuckled. The blonde beauty shot her a cold glare and asked, "What's so funny? You should be there helping them."

"See those markings on the door?" Lucia asked. Edith squinted. "Joel translated that for us, earlier. It says 'exit only'."

"That worthless little… why didn't he tell me?" she muttered, wringing her hands and eyeing Joel with contempt. He snorted in response. "Alright, everyone!" she called out. "I have been informed that the door is an exit only. Which means that there must be an entrance around here, somewhere."

Everyone regrouped, and Edith led her team once more. They

combed around the circular shape of the cave, and it wasn't long before they stumbled on a new tunnel entrance. However, this passage was no longer lit up with the glowing blue rocks.

"Torches out!" Angus said.

The tunnel narrowed and lowered and Joel felt himself shrink. If the Nightcrawler attacked them in here, they would stand no chance. Most of the other miners seemed too preoccupied with their abandoned spoils to worry, though.

"What about me black gold?" one worker complained.

"Yes… it's mine… why should I leave it here?" another asked.

"I deserve it…"

"The non-believers will perish," someone whispered, although it was the quietest complaint of them all.

Joel's shoulders came up to his ears. The Nightcrawler was now the least of his worries. Gold Fever was overtaking the others at an alarming rate. It wouldn't be long before they turned violent, he thought. He stayed close to Alistair, Bronrar, and Lucia; and they, too, began whispering among themselves.

"So? Do you believe me now?" Lucia said, nudging Bronrar. "She aims to kill us. I wouldn't be surprised if she was behind Faramond's death."

"How could you accuse someone of such a thing without proof?" Bronrar asked.

"Think about it. Would it truly shock you to discover she was murderous? Edith was manipulating Faramond the whole time," she said.

"Oi! Methinks we got more ta worry about than her. What about that monster back there?" said Alistair.

Joel tapped the big man on the shoulder and mimed himself eating, then moving slowly. Alistair cocked his head.

"I think he means that the Nightcrawler seems to only care about eatin' one meal at a time. Them three poor souls will buy us some time," Bronrar said. Joel nodded.

"That creature could have killed us all, easily," Lucia added as she gripped her injured shoulder. "It is *choosing* to kill us only one at a time."

"If you've got it all figured out, lass, then tell me this much: Why are three men dead instead of one then, huh?" Alistair asked.

Lucia looked up and stroked her chin. "After the first victim, it only attacked when provoked… whenever we tried to interrupt its meal."

"I've never heard of no animal that behaves in such a way," Bronrar said.

"We should be thankful that it *does* behave that way, though," Lucia said, staring ahead blankly into the darkness. "And we should hope that this path leads to an exit."

After walking a short distance, Edith and Angus stopped the group. Everyone held up their torches to look around at the area they were in: At first glance, it appeared to be a boxed-in cave, but there was an entrance to another tunnel no less than 10 paces ahead, and the ceiling seemed high. It also seemed as if the group were standing on top of a slope, and there was a vast emptiness in front of them. The walls before them were clearly lower than the slope that they were standing on. Lucia looked to her right for a few moments before nudging Alistair.

"Have a look at this," she said, pointing to a couple of devices. They were similar to what they had encountered in the first cave, but this time there were two spots each to light up. "You know what to do."

Alistair nodded and brought his torch over to the devices on the left. At nearly the same time, they both lit the devices up and a dashing blue light began streaking along the walls.

Everyone gasped as the lines traveled all around the room and then eventually to the ceiling. However, it didn't stop there: After lighting up the ceiling, it was revealed that the walls in front of them were far shorter than the height of the roof, and the light on the ceiling traveled far across to reveal that the group had reached a giant labyrinth within an even larger cave. With the entire cave illuminated, Joel could see the end of the maze where yet another tunnel waited for them. While looking, his eyes caught some movement in the labyrinth. His stomach sank and he prayed that he'd only imagined it.

The group plodded down the slope under the bright blue light and stood by the entrance to the labyrinth, its dry stone walls now seeming much taller. Few had anything to say, and Edith and Angus were whispering among themselves as they looked around. Joel noticed some lettering etched into the stone next to the entrance.

"It would seem we have little choice but to enter the labyrinth," Edith said as she turned to face everyone. "That blue light is on a timer as you may remember, so we must be quick. Stay close, and keep your eyes focused."

"The spaces will be tight when we enter, so if you see somethin' that needs attackin', mind yer swing!" Angus added.

"Fer our Savior… we must find more…" a voice murmured within the group. No one called attention to it.

Alistair tapped Joel on the shoulder as the group entered the maze.

"Oi, lad…" he said, pointing at the etched lettering in the stone. "That's tha ancient language, ain't it?" Joel nodded. "What does it say?"

Joel pulled out his ink pen and paper and began to write in his book. He then held the book up for him to see:

THE TEST

After taking some time to read it, Alistair said, "Aye… I had a feelin' that our journey wasn't gonna get any easier…"

Joel looked up at the blue-streaked ceiling as he walked into the maze with Alistair by his side. He agreed with his assessment. More difficult trials were to come.

CHAPTER 22
THE TEST

The group of 16 trudged down the maze path in rows of two. Joel walked next to Alistair, while Lucia and Bronrar walked next to each other in front of them. The mute took in the tall stone walls, filled with engravings and smattered with dust. There was even more dust on the ground, and it was apparent that all of these walls had been carved and laid out by a talented architect.

It wasn't long before the group had a decision to make on their direction: Left, right, or straight. The left turn presented an immediate right if they took that path. As for the right path, it continued straight for some time. However, what truly caught the collective eye of the group was the straight-ahead route. There, many sparkles beckoned them, and they all knew what that meant: more black gold.

"We'll continue straight. I see something up ahead," Edith said.

After a short walk, they stopped at a dead-end that was shaped like a room. It was square but lacked a roof. Many in the group cheered while Joel groaned. The room was filled to the brim with black gold ore, and they didn't even need to mine it! It was sitting there, waiting for them on the ground. The last thing the others needed was more black gold right now.

"I heard complaints from some of you that we left our treasures behind," Edith said as she turned to face the group. "But as you can see, there is more than enough for us to take!"

Most of the miners gladly walked over to the piles and began to fill their pockets with the shiny material. Joel and the others stayed behind, however, and Edith and Angus didn't pick any up, either.

"You see? She is trying to poison our minds. Why else wouldn't she take any for herself?" Lucia whispered to the others.

"Aye! Methinks she's every bit tha snake you've been sayin' she is," Alistair said.

Bronrar frowned. "But Angus-"

"Is a traitor, too. You need to accept that, Bronrar," she replied, putting a hand on his shoulder. He shook her hand off.

"You don' know Angus like I do. I've known him my whole life. He wouldn't steer me wrong."

"Think about it, lad. First, he kills a bunch o' innocent men, and then he ends up in a position of power after Faramond is killed under mysterious circumstances. Methinks they've planned it out this way from the beginin'," Alistair said.

"That…" Lucia began, widening her eyes. "Was a good analysis of what happened. Faramond's death was such an obvious power grab that *even you* could figure it out…"

"Why is it that everythin' ya say makes me wanna chop ya down with me axe?" Alistair asked as he puffed up his chest and stuck his nose in her face. "The only reason I haven't so far is because yer injured! Wouldn't be sportin' of me. But after all of this is through and you've healed, all bets are off. Yer rude!"

"We'll see about-"

"Will you lot shut up and take your share of black gold? We are on a strict time limit," Edith interrupted.

"We don't want it," Lucia snapped back. "And why aren't *you* taking any?"

"I'm confident that we will get our shares back from the previous cave. And as group leader, it is important that my hands remain free and lightweight for now," Edith said, a smirk coming to her sharp face. "I wouldn't expect *grunts* to understand, of course."

"I'll be needin' to be at my fastest as well," Angus added. "Should we face any more creatures within this wretched place, you'll be thankful I had my hands free."

"You two don't think we're falling for this act, do you?" Lucia asked with a scoff. "I know that you have lusted for power, and now you have it. A shame you're leading such a small group as a consequence of your wicked actions." Edith's eye twitched and her face reddened for but a moment. After a deep breath, she regained her composure.

"Believe what you wish. The fact of the matter is that I'm your leader now, and so is he," Edith said, pointing a thumb back at Angus. "You would do well to listen."

Joel frowned at the confrontation. Edith hadn't even tried to deny any of Lucia's claims. Although she hadn't confirmed anything, either.

After the miners finished lining their pockets with treasures, the group turned around and returned to the intersection where they had previously gone straight. Edith decided to turn right, but something inscribed on the wall grabbed Joel's attention. He tugged at Alistair's shirt and pointed to the engravings as they walked by them.

"Oi? What does it say?" Alistair asked. Joel scribbled into his book and held it up for the big redhead to see:

Black Gold This Way

"So, yer sayin' that it ain't the right way ta go?" he asked. Joel nodded. "Well, what are ya waitin' for? We gotta turn ourselves around!" Alistair grabbed Joel by the arm and started plowing through the people ahead of him.

Upon reaching the front of the pack, Alistair cleared his throat before he announced, "We've gotta turn around!"

Edith glanced back at him and said, "Quiet, oaf. We'll go whatever way I desire."

"Ack! So rude!" he said with a clenched fist. "But no matter! Ya need ta understand. Joel says that we gotta turn around."

"You heard the lady," Angus boomed back. "Fall back in line, or there *will* be trouble."

Alistair's stout chest deflated and he slumped while falling back to his spot in line. Joel followed close behind. There was no point in trying to reason with Edith on his own.

"What was that all about?" Lucia asked.

"Joel says this ain't the right way. There was some ancient text on the wall," said Alistair.

"What did it say?"

"We're headin' fer more black gold..." the big man trailed off.

"Must... have... more..." someone muttered up ahead. There was no way to tell who it had been.

"The last thing we need is *more* of that filth," said Lucia.

Nevertheless, the group continued through the maze before they came to their first true dead-end. However, there was another path that could be taken, so Edith led the group down that way, instead. She then took a right, and that led them to another sparkling room. More black gold filled the area, and like before, the ore sat on the ground.

"I told ya!" Alistair called from behind. Edith grimaced.

The group turned around, and after snaking through the corridors, they found themselves at the same intersection from earlier; at the beginning of the maze.

"Look at that! We wasted a bunch o' time 'cause ya didn't listen!" Alistair called out. The miners began to grumble. The group had come to a stop, even though there was only one way they hadn't tried, yet.

Angus leaned over and whispered into Edith's ear. She frowned and shook her head. They exchanged more words, becoming harsher whispers by the second before Edith finally let out a sigh. Joel could have sworn that she was now grinning. She licked her lips and then stood on tip-toes to say something else into his ear. Angus only narrowed his eyes at whatever she had said.

"Alright, then!" Edith called out. The miners ceased their grumbles. "It would seem the quiet one's knowledge of the ancient language can come in handy. Come up here at once."

Joel and Alistair cut through the crowd, and when they reached the front, Edith held up a hand in front of Alistair's face.

"Not you, oaf. I only asked for *him*." She pointed at Joel with the other hand.

"Hah! As if I'd let me pal over here stay alone with the likes of *you*! I trust ya about as far as I can throw *his* fat arse!" Alistair replied while pointing at Angus, who raised an eyebrow in response.

"I think you misunderstand…" Edith said, her face reddening with each word. "That was an *order*, not a suggestion. I knew you were daft, but this is incredible. You can't even listen to orders!" She threw her hands up. "If you can't even figure that out, what *are* you good for?"

"Well… I…" Alistair began.

"Grunt work, and nothing else," Edith interrupted as she pointed over his shoulder. "Back of the line. Now."

Joel nodded at Alistair to assure him that he'd be alright. The big man offered no further argument than a groan before returning to the back of the line.

Angus looked down at Joel with his usual stone face. "Well? Lead the way, little one," he said, gesturing a hand outward.

Joel looked at the wall before him and read the inscribed ancient text. He looked back and pointed to the corridor they hadn't been down yet.

Edith scoffed while crossing her arms. "That much was obvious!"

After walking down the path for a brief period, Joel stopped. There was a turn that the group could take to their left, but they also had the choice to continue straight. He read the ancient text on the wall and then took the left. After a similar period of walking, the group had no choice but to take another left. At the end of this corridor was a choice: Joel could go left or right. He chose to go right.

The group next walked to the end of the corridor until they had to take a right, and then another immediate right after that. Despite the constant change in direction, the walls didn't constrain them any less, and little changed aside from the lettering of the inscribed text.

Joel next took a left, and there was another immediate left that could be taken, but he led the group straight down the corridor instead. After walking for a length, Joel had no choice but to take a right. Suddenly, the maze began to feel different.

Before them were signs of life: Mining equipment and blood on the walls. The group stopped to inspect the items and there was a cautious excitement in the air. Joel, on the other hand, wasn't feeling as optimistic due to the blood on the wall. The movement that had caught his eye when he first gazed upon the labyrinth from high up hadn't been his imagination, after all. The mute tugged at Angus' shirt and then pointed to the blood.

Angus ran a finger across the streaks of red. None of it got on his finger. "It is new, but not *that* new. I'd reckon it has been here for a day or two."

"What are we waiting for?" Lucia asked aloud with palpable excitement. "The first team could be in this very maze!"

Edith rolled her eyes. She motioned Joel to proceed. The mute obeyed and walked down the path.

At the end of this corridor, Joel took a left, and after walking for a bit longer, took another mandatory left. The next corridor was long: At least a hundred meters, if not more, and it was riddled with more mining equipment. As the group walked through the equipment, Joel observed that much of it was broken and that there were chunks of the wall taken out from apparent pickaxe swings. Had they truly grown so desperate?

After many twists and turns, Joel found himself staring down another long path, and his eyes wavered as it seemed to lengthen before him. He had grown wary, wondering if the text on the walls had been misleading on purpose. After all, it was a maze, and mazes were meant to entrap. Yet, he pushed forward and didn't make a fuss about his worries. Everyone was counting on him. Still, it wasn't long before some of the miners began grumbling about their predicament.

"Where tha hell is he takin' us?" one asked.

"I think we're lost..." said another.

Midway down, Joel took a left into a new corridor. After walking on the new path for a short while, the group reached a new intersection. With little hesitation, Joel continued straight. At the end of that path, there were two choices: left or right. The mute looked upon the walls for guidance and went right after some deliberation. However, after traversing that corridor for a few moments, he came to a stop. There was a new path to his right, and along that wall was a new inscribed text that Joel focused on for some time.

"What's the hold-up?" Edith asked, twirling her messy golden hair. "Don't tell me you've gotten us lost?"

Joel turned and shook his head. He then pulled out his book and began to write. After a few moments of scribbling, he held the book up for Edith and Angus to see:

The text says that the path to our right leads to more black gold. It says that we will need as much black gold as possible for 'the test'.

Edith raised an eyebrow and said, "We already have plenty."

Joel got back to writing in his notebook.

I believe we should all carry black gold to the next test, so we don't have to backtrack through the maze. Some of the text says that we are close to the test. We should not have to hold on to it for long.

She sighed. "Very well. Lead the way, quiet one."

Joel took the right into a new corridor and after following the path and taking a left, led the group to another chamber of black gold.

"What's this? Even more!" a miner cried out, happily.

"This is surely a blessin'!"

"Let the lil' one lead us to even more!"

"Yes! More!"

Joel could do little but groan. Even though he hated to carry it, there was little choice. The text hadn't led him astray so far, and the last thing he wanted to do was backtrack through a labyrinth.

Lucia, Alistair, and Bronrar all approached Joel and asked for an explanation. He showed them what he had shown Edith.

"Well, if it's only for a while..." Bronrar trailed off. "B-but I don't wanna end up like Wolfgang."

"Wolfgang lost his mind long before Gold Fever set in," Lucia said before she stared down the piles of black gold. The workers, Angus, and even Edith took a share. "Still... I hope we don't have to hold it for too long."

"I ain't worried! I have a will of iron!" Alistair chimed in.

"A fine way of saying, 'stubborn like a donkey'," Lucia replied with a chuckle.

"Yer just jealous that the black gold won' affect me. That's alright, lass," Alistair said as he put a hand on her shoulder. He hadn't realized it was the shoulder that was injured. She winced in pain, but the big man ignored it. "I'll be sure ta slap ya to yer senses if ya succumb ta Gold Fever!"

"You idiot..." she muttered while shaking him off and then walking over to a pile. The others followed close behind and began to collect the ore and hold it in any way possible.

Joel stood behind his friends and looked upon the horrid metal with dread. He approached, but with every step he took, that familiar howling wind returned. It seemed that no one could hear it aside from him.

He bent down and with his hand shaking, approached the spectacular rock. His ears began to ring and he wanted to turn back, but he knew that would be looked down upon within the group. Mere inches from it, the howling wind turned to screams that penetrated his mind. It was unbearable; so much that he wanted to scream himself, but he couldn't; he had to pick up the ore. A single inch from touching the rock, the banshee screamed louder than ever. His whole body trembled, and he closed his eyes.

"Hello?" a far-off voice echoed as the mute shook his head and regained his wits. "Is anyone out there?" Although it was a shout, the voice felt weak.

Everyone in the group froze. Had they finally found the first team after all of this time?

"We're here!" Lucia shouted with child-like excitement. "This is the B-Team! We're coming to find you!"

"Please... hurry!" the frail voice called back.

Lucia turned to everyone in the group and said, "What are we waiting for? Let's go find him. I believe the voice was coming from south of this location."

"Hold on a moment," Angus said, his stone face hitting like a skull-splitting reality check. "Do you not find it odd that only one voice called out? How do we know this isn't a part of 'the test'?"

"Maybe he was left behind! Who cares! We can figure that out when we find him," Lucia said.

"Feel free to try and find him in this maze on *your own*," said Edith with a catty smile. "Now that we have collected enough black gold, Joel over here will be leading us to the test." She nodded toward the mute. Lucia looked his way, too. There were lofty expectations in her eyes.

Joel had a tough decision in front of him: Either disobey Edith and test how far Angus' murderous tendencies would go, or go against Lucia, one of his few friends throughout the entire ordeal. The more he thought about it, however, the more he realized that he had leverage. Without him, no one would know where they were going, and time within the labyrinth was at a premium. Navigating a maze in complete darkness would be a nightmare, after all. With that in mind, Joel walked up to Lucia and stood beside her.

"What do you think you're doing?" Edith asked in a cross tone.

"I think it's clear what he's doing. I'm not asking for much; only that we do our duty and find the first team, as Faramond had intended," said Lucia.

"You dare to use his name in your favor?" Edith asked, aghast.

"I am only stating the facts. Joel is coming with me, and he is your only hope of navigating this maze."

"I'm goin' with 'em, too!" Alistair added, standing by their side. The trio next looked at Bronrar.

"I-I…" the nervous miner muttered. He cast eyes on Angus, who gave him a light shake of the head. "I… think we should stay on course."

"Are you serious? You would betray your brethren? Your friends?" Lucia asked. Bronrar could not look her in the eye. The miners began to grumble. "If you follow me, I promise to give all the black gold I've obtained to you after the test!"

More miners came to Lucia, Joel, and Alistair's side. Edith let out a deep sigh.

"Very well. Since you are taking us hostage… lead the way," she said with contempt.

Lucia then turned and shouted, "We're coming to find you! Call out!"

After a brief pause, the voice replied, "I'm here!"

However, to everyone's surprise, a different voice also called out to them, "Here!"

"Multiple voices?" Lucia asked aloud before looking back at Edith and Angus. "See? The group is here! We have found them!" She jogged back into the corridor. "Everyone! Follow me!"

Lucia dashed down the path and made a right. The others followed, but all aside from Joel had trouble keeping up with her great speed. At the end of the path, she could go either left or right. In this case, she chose left, and after a brief sprint, she took another left.

"Hold on…" Alistair said between his huffs and puffs as he ran. "She's retracin'… our steps! Why?"

"I believe she is… tryin' to find… a new way south," Bronrar said, sucking in even more air than Alistair. His stout frame and short legs were built well for mining, but not for running.

"Don't be tryin'… ta act all nice, now! Ya need to choose… a side, laddie! It's us, or… yer pal, Angus!"

Bronrar remained silent as the group made their first right heading southward, which led to a left-hand turn. However, this brought them to a dead-end. Lucia turned everyone around and led them back up the path to take a right. She continued straight across the intersection and then made a right once more. That led the group to yet another dead-end.

"Damn!" Lucia shouted.

"Hello?" a weak voice called back from the east. It was closer than ever before.

"We are close! Hang on!" she shouted back.

Joel held up a finger and motioned for Lucia to follow him. He had an idea of how to reach the voice, based on some of the patterns present within the maze. The mute dashed past everyone and made his way back to where they had been prior to the intersection.

Eventually, they found themselves in the same long corridor where they had taken a right to get the black gold, but this time, Joel continued to run straight. He eventually reached a path where there was a mandatory left, followed by a mandatory right.

"Call out!" Lucia cried.

"I'm here!" a voice cracked from the south. It seemed as if they were directly above whoever it was.

Joel sprinted down the corridor and took the next right. After a few moments of running, he took a mandatory right and then an immediate left. More mining equipment lay ahead, but the mute decided not to pay it any mind and jumped over it, instead.

"I'm here…" a frail voice said as Joel halted and looked down the corridor to his right. On the short path sat a man, huddled over with his back against the wall. He looked frail and sickly, but a smile spread across his face at the sight of the B-Team. He had long, scraggly, and blond hair; and his face was covered in soot, no doubt from the cave-in described in Dalton's journal.

~

"Ah… there you are," Lucia said cheerfully between breaths. "Where is the… rest of your team?"

The man cocked his head and said, "Say… what is that you've got, there?"

"Oh, this?" Lucia asked as she held up her black gold. "It is-"

"GIVE IT TO ME!" the man shouted as he lunged out and grabbed hold of her wrists. "I DESERVE IT! IT'S MINE!"

He tried to shake the black gold from Lucia's hands, but she held firm. She looked down at him to find a pair of yellow eyes piercing her soul.

Due to her shoulder injury, Lucia had to use her left hand alone to fend him off, but because of what appeared to be malnutrition, the man was frail, and she was able to shove him to the ground.

Lucia turned back to the group and said, "He has Gold Fever!"

Hobbled footsteps sounded off behind her, and she turned to face the crazed man charging at her with a pickaxe. He brought the axe head down, but Lucia sidestepped and let the metal strike the ground, throwing him off-balance.

While he stumbled, she grabbed his head and pushed it down while bringing her knee up for a powerful blow to his face. A wave of blood came gushing out of his nose as he stumbled back and fell onto his bottom.

"Snap out of it!" she cried, but to her dismay, the man began to laugh as he held his face. Soon, it turned into an uncontrollable cackle. He stood while gripping the pickaxe so tightly that his hand began to bleed. Lucia backed up and the group followed suit, behind her. They turned and ran, and then took a right into the new corridor.

"Ye won't be leavin' with what's rightfully mine!" the man cried as he hobbled after them. He was far too slow to catch them, but nervous jitters coursed through Lucia's striding legs, anyhow. Never had she been so mindlessly attacked before, not even by Wolfgang or the rebels of Luneria.

~

EDITH AND ANGUS found themselves at the front of the group once again, and as they ran, to their horror, they saw two more men step out from corridors on their left and right.

"Do ye follow the will of the Savior?" a worker asked. His skin had turned gray, and his eyes were a more intense yellow than they'd ever seen. They were glowing.

"Yes! Let us pass!" Edith pleaded as she stopped in her tracks.

The other Gold Fever-infected man tilted his head and said, "I don' care if they do follow his will!" He lunged out at Angus. "I need more!"

Angus drew his mace, which he had re-obtained in the chaos of Faramond's death, and clubbed the man in the head before he could reach him. He fell to the ground and blood pooled around him as his body twitched. A mixture of his skull fragments and blood had splattered on the tall stone wall and slowly dripped down.

~

"KEEP MOVING!" Angus called back as he and Edith ran forward. The others followed, but they were harassed by the other Gold Fever-infected man. Luckily, he was sluggish and weak, so the worst he could do was disrupt them by grabbing hold of their arms. Joel pushed his way through the chaos, knowing that he was the only one who could accurately lead them out of this death trap.

He finally made it to the front as the group zigzagged into a new corridor. Out of the corner of his eye, Joel spotted more men coming from paths on his left and right, but he continued straight and did his best to ignore them.

"For the will of the Savior!"

"Give me yer gold!"

"This is fer a better world!" he heard voices call out.

As he read the inscribed text on the wall, Joel took the second left corridor, which was a long, straight pathway; the longest straightaway they'd come across so far. It was at least a few hundred meters, and Joel's legs were beginning to burn, but he pressed through it.

After what felt like an eternity of sprinting, Joel reached a new chamber. He could tell by looking around that this was where 'the test' would occur. Soon after, others entered behind him.

"Never make me… run like that… again, lad," Alistair choked out between hoarse breaths.

"Everyone was infected… with Gold Fever…" Bronrar trailed off with a shiver. "Is this our fate… as well?"

Joel looked around the room and realized that Lucia was missing. She had been as fast as him at running. There was no reason for her to be so far behind unless one of the infected miners had gotten to her.

Edith looked around the chamber briefly and said, "So, what is this test, Joel? What does the text say?" She pointed to a wall with slots on it and various ancient texts inscribed above.

Joel held up a finger and then dashed for the exit.

"Where tha hell're ya goin' lad?" he heard Alistair ask. There was no time to explain.

The mute ran down the corridor and scanned for clues of what could have happened to Lucia. About halfway down, he noticed drops of blood on the floor. It practically glowed thanks to the blue light above. Perhaps it had come from her injured shoulder, he thought. The trail of blood led to Joel's right, so he dashed down that corridor in search of his friend.

BACK IN THE TEST ROOM, Alistair finally realized what was wrong. "Oh, I understand, now! The lass is missin'! He went ta go find her!"

"We can live without the ox-woman, but we need Joel to read the directions for whatever this test is," Edith said.

"Say no more! I'll find 'em both and ensure they return safely!" Alistair said with a potent mixture of confidence and pride.

"I'm not so sure ye should go alone…" said Angus.

"Fine, then! I'll take Bronrar!"

"W-wha? Me? But why me?" he asked.

"Yer not a coward, are ya? Come help yer friends out," Alistair said. Bronrar looked down and wrung his hands. "Fine! I'll go me'self!"

Angus looked at Edith, who shrugged. She said, "If he dies, he dies."

Alistair narrowed his eyes and muttered, "So rude..." before he dashed back into the corridor himself. He had little strategy going into the maze and decided on a whim to take his second right down the path.

～

MEANWHILE, Joel crept through the maze while keeping an eye on the blood trail. It had nearly run dry, and he was confident that he wouldn't be able to see it if not for the blue light cast above him. To his left was a corridor, and as he looked up, he caught a man lunging out at him out of the corner of his eye.

The man grabbed him by the neck and slammed his head into the wall behind him. His vision blurred, and the hollow bounces of his mining helmet off the wall and the ground seemed insignificant compared to the piercing, yellow eyes of his attacker. The man's skin had turned wrinkly and gray, and his face was covered in soot.

"Give me more..." he muttered while wringing Joel's neck up against the wall. The mute sagged down until he was sitting. He offered no resistance. "More..."

～

AT THE CORRIDOR'S END, Alistair took a left. It led to a longer path where he saw Lucia being dragged away by two men. One of them held his hand over her mouth, and the other dragged her by the injured shoulder: She was helpless. It was a long way down the corridor, so Alistair knew he had to act quickly.

The big man charged down the path like a raging bull with huffs and puffs. He saw Lucia struggling to the best of her ability, but the two of them combined had her overpowered. As they began to turn a corner, Alistair finally caught up to them and laid a vicious shoulder tackle on the man to his right. That sent the infected worker flying, and the other man who held Lucia stumbled back.

That was all the opportunity that the mercenary needed, as she drew her claymore with her left hand and plunged the blade into her captor's chest. The man let out a surprised cough as he tumbled to the ground. The other infected miner stood and growled, but before he could do any more, Lucia swung her great blade and struck his neck. Blood splattered on the walls, and the man could only cling to his throat as he faded from existence and crashed to the floor.

As she sheathed her blade, Lucia looked at Alistair and nodded. "Thank you."

"Well, it ain't no trouble, lass," he said, crossing his arms. "But I came here lookin' fer both you *and* Joel."

"There is no time to waste, then. This part of the maze is crawling with Gold Fever-infected," she said as they both began to jog down a new path.

❧

JOEL SAT with his back against the wall as the miner continued to choke him out. His vision faded and he began to hallucinate from the lack of air going his head, but even still, he refused to defend himself He wouldn't do it, even if it meant dying unceremoniously and letting everyone down.

He looked up at his attacker, and he was surprised to see that the man's face had turned into a woman's. She wore a great grin that stretched unnaturally long across her face, and those familiar yellow eyes sent shivers down his spine. She had black, wily hair and gray skin; except around her eyelids, which had turned black and seemed to sink into her face. Blood began to trickle down her crooked nose. It was *her* again, he thought. Anyone but *her*.

The woman shrieked in his face like a wild bat fleeing from its cave and there was a fiery rage in her eyes that was all too familiar to him, yet horrifying all the same. Joel ignored his instinct to fight back as she cackled and twisted her neck like a snake that coiled around a tree. He could feel his life slipping away. *Never*. He would never attack her, he thought.

The woman's face came close to his as the darkness took him. They were nose to nose. She began to say something; something that he knew would be familiar if he could hear it, but his ears rang like a million bells and death was moments away. However, at that moment, Alistair knocked her in the back of her head with the butt of his battle axe.

That was when Joel realized it wasn't *her* at all, but another Gold Fever-infected miner. The man tumbled over as the mute had a coughing fit and regained his breath. Alistair held out his hand and

Joel could see that Lucia stood behind him with a relieved smile on her face.

"Consider us even, laddie!" the big redhead said as Joel took his hand and was picked up as if he were light as a feather. "Now, then, can ya lead us back ta that test room?"

After catching his breath, Joel ran north and then took a right down a new corridor. He then took a left and they found themselves on the long path from before, which was a straight shot to the test room. They jogged up to the room, keeping keen eyes out for more Gold Fever-infected workers lurking about along the way.

"Phew! That was close!" Alistair said before slapping both Joel and Lucia on their backs and laughing. They both frowned in return, but Joel eventually shifted to a smile. Alistair had saved him in much the same way he'd saved the big man back in the Dead Woods.

"Enough patting yourselves on the back. Remember that we are on a strict time limit in here," Edith said with crossed arms and a tapping foot. "Joel, can you read this text or not?"

The mute walked up to the wall where the text was inscribed. Before him stood a great stone door that was covered by an iron cage. It contained an entry for people to walk through, a slot in the wall, and all of the inscribed text. There was a lot to translate, so he got to writing it in his notebook right away.

Test One

Those who are infected shall not pass this mighty stone door. You have lined your pockets greedily with black gold, and now it is time to test your resolve. Enter the cage and place black gold ore into the slot on the wall until the door opens for you. The slot can accept anywhere between one and 10 pieces at random, so you must be vigilant in your willingness to give it up.

When the door opens, only one may pass through at a time, and for anyone else, they will have to sacrifice their black gold as well. Show that you do not bow to the dark one, and the first steps shall be taken to your survival.

Joel finished writing and handed the book over to Edith, who studied the words carefully. She then read it out loud to the group. In particular, most of the miners groaned at the prospect of giving up their black gold.

"Leave me black gold? Again?" one miner said.

"I should have more!" another added.

"I don' like this..."

"Your options are to either surrender your black gold or be trapped in this miserable place like those other men. Do you wish to end up like them?" Edith asked. There were no further complaints. "That's what I thought. I will start us off."

The blonde beauty walked up to the cage and entered. The slot in the wall was little more than a hole, and it seemed infinitely deep. She placed a piece of her ore into the slot, and then nothing happened. Edith placed another in, and the gate began to open. She looked up with curious eyes as the door rose and she could see the other side. Edith sighed, and Joel cocked his head. What had she seen? However, before he could inspect for himself, she stepped through to the other side, and a mechanism activated that caused the door to slam shut. It hit the ground with a harsh *thud* that shook the ground, and Angus approached the cage, next.

"Nobody better try anythin' funny with this door. The shutting mechanism is too fast to react to," he said before stepping into the cage.

He placed five pieces of black gold ore in the slot before the gate opened. Angus walked through quickly and joined Edith on the other side as the door slammed shut once again.

The process continued with several other miners hesitantly putting their black gold into the slots and reaching the other side. Eight had passed the test thus far, and Bronrar was next. As he approached the cage, he paused at the sound of Lucia's voice.

"We have a slight problem, here..." she muttered. Bronrar turned and had another miner go in front of him.

"What's the issue?" he asked and then joined the inner circle of Alistair, Joel, and Lucia.

"Turns out Joel never grabbed no black gold," Alistair said with a frown. "And the lass over here got hers taken away when she was attacked by the Gold Fever-infected miners."

Bronrar crossed his arms and said, "Why not just go back for more?"

"Do you truly believe that Edith will wait around for us?" Lucia asked. "And besides that, there are too many infected walking around that maze. It's dangerous to go alone."

"Mayhap we can pool our unused black gold ore together and see if that gets everyone across," Alistair said.

"I don' know if I like that idea..." Bronrar said.

"Tha hell is wrong with ya, lately?" Alistair asked before grabbing him by the shoulders and shaking him. "First ya don' come with me ta help 'em, and now yer refusin' to help again?"

Bronrar brushed Alistair's big hands off and took a few steps back. He looked down and clenched his fists.

"Why you little..." Lucia muttered before pausing and letting out a smooth exhale. "We have helped you a number of times and never asked for anything in return. You know that the black gold is bad for you. Why do you wish to keep it for yourself?"

"W-well, Angus told me-"

"Stop listenin' ta that meat-stain! The man's a murderer!" Alistair shot back.

"Wolfgang forced him into it! How many times do you need to be told that?" Bronrar asked.

"Your friendship with him is blinding you," Lucia said with a scoff. "So, go ahead and join him on the other side."

Bronrar put up no further arguments. He took his black gold ore, entered the cage, and placed four pieces into the slot. He took everything with him to the other side before the gate slammed shut behind him.

"Well, now what?" Alistair asked aloud. He looked at Joel, who pointed at the cage, encouraging him to go. "Aw, naw laddie, I ain't leavin' ya behind after all the troubles we've gone through!"

"I can't... do it!" a voice called out from the cage. One of the miners exited and curled up in a ball against the wall to the right. "I can't hand it over..."

"Do you think he'll give us some, then?" Lucia asked with a snort as some other miners went over to calm him down. The man lashed out at them and began to swing his pickaxe around. The men left him alone. "Then again, he may turn violent..."

The miner sat back against the wall and curled into a ball as he muttered to himself. Gold Fever had taken him.

"I gots an idea," Alistair said with a smile from ear to ear.

"Uh-oh," Lucia said as she and Joel looked at each other, blankly.

"What? It's a good idea! Just hear me out..." Alistair began as he held up his index finger. "We know that tha gate closes behind us goin' through, right?" Joel and Lucia nodded back at him. "Well, what if I carry ya both through at the same time? Tha mechanism won't be able ta tell the difference!"

"No way am I trusting you to hold on to me, let alone both of us," Lucia said and then crossed her arms. Joel shrugged and nodded. He agreed with Alistair's idea. They both looked over at the mercenary, who turned her head. "You'll have to go without me."

Joel and Alistair looked at each other as Lucia pouted. The big man went behind her and pushed from the back, while Joel pulled her left arm. Her reaction went from gasping, to growling, to sighing in defeat.

"Fine…" she said.

As the last miner passed through the gate, Alistair, Joel, and Lucia piled into the cage. There wasn't much room, as they were shoulder-to-shoulder. The big redhead began to place his black gold into the slot. After putting a whopping nine pieces in, the gate finally opened.

"Awright, then, are we ready?" Alistair asked as Joel hopped onto the right side of his back and grabbed hold of his shoulder. The sudden load caused the big man's legs to stiffen, but he soon regained balance and seemed to be fine. "Yer turn, lass."

Lucia hopped onto the left side of Alistair's back and grabbed hold of his shoulder like Joel had. This time, his legs buckled from the load and he began to lower himself. "Oh my, heavier than ya look, aren't ya?" Lucia's face turned red. "But don' worry, even the two of ya combined ain't as hefty as me mum!" He laughed aloud.

Both Lucia and Joel raised eyebrows and flashed each other bemused looks, but there was no time to make snide remarks. Alistair charged at full speed through the gate. He tripped over an oddly-shaped rock as he ran and the trio came crashing to the ground, but they had made it. Joel shuddered as he heard the gate thunder down behind him.

"I can't believe that worked!" Lucia said excitedly as she stood.

"Of course it worked! I'm as strong as an ox, after all…" Alistair said, thumping his chest. However, his eyes widened and his mouth hung open as he looked around. "Hold up… this is…"

"Another labyrinth…" Edith said with a groan.

Joel was unsurprised, as his view from before they had entered the maze seemed to show a greater distance to the finish than they had traveled. With one miner succumbing to Gold Fever and inner turmoil taking over the group, he had to wonder if things were only going to get worse, and what new tests lie ahead.

Even still, he was happy to have made some good friends who were unwilling to leave him behind. He would stay strong and help lead them to the end or die trying.

CHAPTER 23
DIMMING HOPES

Joel and the group found themselves facing a new section of the labyrinth, and right at the start was a path that led to a sparkling room. The mute winced at the sight. It seemed they could never escape the black gold's pull.

"Someone is missing. There should be 16 of us, but I count 15," Edith said. One of the miners approached her.

"I didn't know the lad well, but we tried gettin' him ta go, and he refused to give up his shares. He even attacked us when we got too close," the worker explained.

"What a bother..." Edith said. She cuffed her hands around her mouth and shouted, "Hey! You over there! There is more black gold on this side! Give up your share and come join us!" There was nothing but silence in response.

After waiting a short time, she muttered, "Contemptible fool..."

"More importantly, we have another section of labyrinth before us," Angus said with a frown. "I had hoped that test would be our final obstacle..."

"First thing's first..." one miner said as he stepped up to Lucia. "The lady over here promised us her remainin' black gold if we followed her."

"Ah, that's right!" Edith said, a hint of excitement creeping into her voice. "Well, then? Hand over your remaining spoils." She grinned at the mercenary.

Lucia put up her hands and said, "I'm sorry... the Gold Fever-infected miners... they took it all from me."

"How many times are we gonna fall fer these tricks?" one of the miners asked.

"It ain't fair! I deserve more!" said another.

Edith jumped in between them. "Now, now gentlemen. *She* may have lied to you, but *I* will not." The miners fell silent, their yellowing eyes demanding an explanation. "Up ahead, you'll notice there are sparkles. More black gold for you to take."

The workers' silence shifted to happy chatter. Bronrar stood next to Angus and looked up at him. "Do we really need any more?"

"Of course, my friend. Don't forget, this ore will make us rich beyond our wildest dreams," he replied.

"But it could be dangerous..." Bronrar said.

"The reward greatly outweighs the risk. Think about it: You can live a relaxing life and never have to worry about anything else. Isn't that what you always wanted?" asked Angus. Bronrar offered no retort.

Joel tapped Alistair on the back and pointed at the corridor to their right. Alistair cleared his throat and announced, "Oi! Joel says we gotta go this way! I ain't gonna take any more black gold unless we have'ta fer another test!"

The mute nodded and flashed a triumphant smile. Earlier, the situation with his friends had looked grim, but his resilience in the face of the black gold's allure had truly paid off; at least in the cases of Alistair and Lucia. He would still need to work on Bronrar.

"Very well," Edith said, to which Alistair tilted his head. "You lot have caused nothing but trouble for us, so far. Go whichever way you please." She walked forward and the other miners followed her.

Bronrar stayed behind. "Please, come along with us. We'll need you..."

"Like we needed *you*, earlier?" Lucia asked, practically spitting fire. He flinched in response.

"Bronrar, are you coming?" Angus called back.

"Best of luck to you," said the mercenary. Bronrar turned and jogged to catch up with the group.

"Good riddance to 'em!" Alistair shouted before turning to Joel. "So then, lad, you were sayin' we gotta go to the right?"

Joel nodded and led the way to the corridor with an immediate right, then a left, and another right again. It was clear early on that this part of the labyrinth would be more complicated, but as long as he read the text on the walls, he was sure to find his way. Edith, on the other hand, didn't stand a chance.

❧

EDITH LED her group to the black gold chamber. Many of the miners jumped for joy and began to line their pockets once more, while Bronrar timidly bent over to grab some. He looked back up at Angus.

"Aren't you going to take any?"

"Not needed. I have an entire cart of black gold waiting for me in the previous cave," Angus said.

Bronrar nodded. He knew that he shouldn't take any more, but for some reason, he still wished to. It was like wanting too much food. At times, even when he knew he shouldn't have any more, he had continued eating for the sheer pleasure of it. With black gold, he could get all the pleasures he ever wanted, and no one would complain because he could afford it. A good, easy life was within his grasp, he thought while picking up another ore piece.

The miners grabbed as much black gold as they could while Edith and Angus watched on from behind. After some vigorous collecting, they could take no more, as their pockets had been filled and their hands were full.

"Well then, it would seem you all are satisfied, correct?" Edith asked to some cheers from the miners. "Good. Always remember that I keep my promises. Now, let us get through this maze."

Upon exiting the chamber, Edith took her first right down a new corridor, followed by another right. She stopped and then read some ancient text on the wall.

A devious smile came to her face as she whispered to Angus, "We no longer need the quiet one." Angus cocked his head. She pointed at an arrow inscribed on the wall: It was pointing down the path. "We can use the arrows as a guide."

❧

JOEL, Lucia, and Alistair continued to twist and turn through the maze with confident strides.

"I'd wager Edith and her goons are lost, by now." Lucia giggled as Joel took them to the left.

297

"Oh yeah, I'm sure we'll be hearin' 'em cry out fer help, soon!" Alistair laughed along as the mute steered them down a right-hand corridor. He then took another right, followed by an immediate left.

Joel estimated that they were a little over three-quarters of the way to the exit, and he wasn't sure how much longer the blue light above would hold. He looked up to see it gleaming but could have sworn it had dimmed, somewhat. He went to adjust his oversized miner's helmet, only to find his bouncy brown hair. He had been attacked so quickly and ruthlessly by the Gold Fever-infected miner that he hardly even noticed it falling off his head. In reality, it had probably saved his skull from being cracked against the wall. From here on, he would have to be more careful.

The next corridor led to a new room, and as he approached, Joel's mind began to wander. Was it a new test? Had they finally reached the end? Or was it something else entirely? When they entered, something caught Joel's eye, and he stopped the duo behind him.

He pointed at the floor. Lucia looked over his shoulder and gasped when she saw that mushrooms sprouted up from the ground.

"They really are just like the explosive mushrooms that I encountered in Luneria…" she said, her brown eyes wide.

"What's so amazin' 'bout that, anyway? You can find roses in a bunch'a different places, so why does *this* bother ya?" Alistair asked, his eyes darting back and forth across the ground for the pesky mushrooms.

"Because explosive mushrooms are only known to grow in the jungles of Maug. To find them here, inside of a mountain…" Lucia trailed off.

However, she didn't have long to admire them, as a noticeable drop in visibility occurred. The trio looked up to see the blue lights dimmer than ever. It reminded Joel of dusk, but with a blue tint.

"Gah! The lights are already goin' out on us?" Alistair asked with panic in his voice.

"We should hurry. Navigating this maze in the dark would be a nightmare… but let's look closely for explosive mushrooms, too. I have seen what they can do when set off, and it is quite gruesome," Lucia said. Joel nodded in return and the trio carefully tip-toed through the room.

After they took two more rights and two lefts, they found themselves staring down a long corridor. That should cover most of, if not all of the remaining labyrinth, Joel thought.

~

EDITH and her group had followed the arrows on the walls until they reached a new room. She began to step into it, but Angus caught her with his mighty strength, picked her up, and then placed her behind himself.

"What do you think you're doing?" Edith asked in a cross tone.

"Look," Angus said. He pointed further into the room. There lay a corpse, and it was riddled with darts. "It would seem those 'arrows' you were following led us to a trap room where darts shoot out."

Edith crinkled her nose and then looked at the wall to her right. After a few moments, she tugged at the giant's shirt. "Look at this."

Inscribed on the wall was a diagram of the room and its stone tiles.

"Ah, it seems to me that the creators of this maze had need to go through it themselves. This may tell us which stone tiles we can step on, and which ones are traps," said Angus.

On the diagram, some tiles were colored red, while the others were the same color as the stone itself.

"So then, it's reasonable to think the red tiles will set off the trap, is it not?" Edith asked.

"I agree," Angus said as he looked back at the group of miners, who grew restless. "The trouble will be memorizing the pattern, especially for some of *them*."

"If they die, they die," Edith whispered before she turned to face the group. "Alright, everyone! This room is booby-trapped. If you step on the wrong stone tile, it sets the trap off. You will study the diagram well if you don't want to end up like this poor soul." She shuffled sideways to reveal the dart-riddled corpse lying on the ground.

"Can we not turn around and find another way?" one miner asked.

"Yeh, if I die, who'll look over me black gold?" another protested to some sarcastic laughter.

"I know that this path will lead us out of here," Edith said with crossed arms. "In fact, I believe this is another test. The lettering around this diagram is similar to what we saw earlier."

Angus raised an eyebrow at that assertion. He knew it was a lie, but was shocked to see that the others *believed* her. Had the black gold led to such an easy deception? The giant looked over at Bronrar, who seemed nervous, as usual. *He* wouldn't believe her; not yet, he thought.

~

BRONRAR FELT a big hand slap him on the shoulder, disturbing him from a worried train of thought. Angus smiled back down at him.

"One frightening task that will lead to a lifetime of wealth and joy."

"R-right..." Bronrar muttered.

"Relax. Have I ever steered you wrong?" Angus asked.

Bronrar wanted to say yes, and that the reason he was even on the expedition was because he had chased after him to make sure he would be alright; but instead, the usual came out of his mouth:

"No..."

After studying the diagram on the wall for a few moments, Angus led the way. "Follow my steps closely, and you will survive."

The giant stepped onto the first stone tile slowly but surely, and no traps were set off. He walked straight for a couple of steps, stopped, and then turned left; zigzagging to nearly the quarter point of the room. Edith followed close behind him, and others within the group started to follow along as well.

Bronrar broke into a nervous sweat as he walked behind one of the other miners, who seemed to not have a care in the world. He could swear that he even heard him lightly whistling. It made no sense to him how the man could be so lax when one false step would kill him.

About halfway through the room, Angus took a right and walked across several tiles before he turned left and made way for the exit. He then came to an abrupt stop and closed his eyes, as if to visualize the correct pattern.

"You don't remember?" Edith asked, playfully. "Don't worry, *Angy*. I'll lead the way. I have a great memory."

"And how do you propose we do that?" Angus asked as he looked back at her, stone-faced. "If you step on any of these tiles to get around me, the trap will be set off."

"Simple. Pick me up and place me in front of you," Edith said.

Angus blushed as he put his hands around her waist and lifted. Edith smiled down at him as he lifted her through the air and placed her one tile ahead.

"You know, I like a strong man..." she trailed off with welcoming eyes.

"Let's focus on the task at hand," Angus said. Edith gave a playful pout, but she didn't press any further.

"Follow me, closely." She began to walk in her own formation across the stone tiles.

After an elaborate walk through the room, Edith finally made it to the end and said, "See that? Not so ba-"

Skreeee

The miner ahead of Bronrar tripped and fell at the Nightcrawler's cry, and as he picked himself up, Bronrar heard a peculiar noise:

Whoosh

A dart struck the recovering man in his neck.

Blood spurted out onto Bronrar, and he froze in horror at both the sight and feeling of it. Three more darts came flying out: One missed the miner, but two more struck him in the leg and midsection. The miner had no time to cry out in pain; he could only grunt as he fell to the floor by Bronrar's feet.

Whoosh

Bronrar now knew what the noise meant, but he had no time to react. Instead, he felt a force tug his arm and pull him away. The wind from the darts tickled his arm and face, and even in that split-second, he realized how close he had come to death. As he landed in front of the corpse of the unfortunate miner from earlier, Bronrar refocused himself and looked up to see Angus standing over him.

"Y-you saved me..." he choked out.

"Like I said. I wouldn't steer you wrong," Angus replied, cracking a smirk at him. He looked back at the other miners. "Alright, everyone! Be mindful of yer steps from here on. You don't wanna end up like *him*." He pointed at the corpse.

Soon after, everyone else made it through the dart room unscathed. Bronrar was still overcome with shock at what had happened, but he snapped out of it with a reminder of what had started it all:

Skreeeeee

"Th-that monster! It's coming for us!" he cried, the lump in his throat nearly drowning out his words.

"Relax," Edith replied with an eye roll.

"Why should I relax in a situation like this? We all saw what that creature could do!"

"I'll tell you why: Those men who were too greedy to give up some of their ore will distract the beast. It appears to take its time eating... and we can use that time to our advantage," Edith explained, a sharp smile coming to her. The rest of the group remained silent. "Stay close to me, follow my orders, and you will make it out of here."

~

JOEL, Alistair, and Lucia finished their trek down the long corridor and took a mandatory right. They had encountered little in the way of hazards up to that point, and Lucia was confident that they were about to reach the final test without any problems. The only issues on her mind were how much light they had left, and how the Nightcrawler's cries had grown closer to them. Facing the Nightcrawler was practically suicide, to begin with, but fighting it in the middle of a pitch-black labyrinth was out of the question. None of them would survive.

The mute took a left onto a path that led them into a new chamber. Upon entering, they spotted two additional entrances on the left. Edith and her group could still reach this room if they hadn't already.

To the right, there stood a great stone door and a lengthy text inscribed next to it. An odd, rusty statue also stood beside the door. Its face was a haunting mix of dread and desperation, and its main body, adorned in dress, was fitted with handles at the front. It almost looked like a pair of latches that could be opened. Joel wasted little time in approaching the ancient text to translate.

As he wrote, Lucia scanned the area. In the southwest corner of the room, a glimmer caught her eye. She darted over and knelt to find a pickaxe.

"The first team made it this far, at least," she said with little enthusiasm. It was hard for her to get excited about team one's survival prospects when every time they found something good, there were many more bad signs; such as the Gold Fever-infected men earlier in the maze.

"That's *if* it ain't one from Edith's group," Alistair added.

"Oh, I'm not concerned about them," Lucia replied with a smile. "I'm sure they are quite lost by now."

"Are ya certain? She seemed so sure of herself…"

"Her newfound power as leader has gone to her head. I'll give you an example," Lucia said, raising her index finger. "Before, Edith obviously hated Joel. Yet, she was wise enough to realize that he was useful for translating ancient text and mapmaking. But now? She doesn't care about any of that. She will happily wander aimlessly in the maze, leading her team to their doom. All because she is drunk on her own power."

They remained silent for a few moments before Joel turned around, translation in hand, and approached them. He held the book up for the pair to read:

Final Test: Blood Sacrifice

Friendships and teams can be powerful assets, but they can also be explosive when put under strain. This test will see which of you have formed bonds, which of you have a killer instinct, or which of you refuse to make sacrifices. The statue next to the door is called an iron maiden. It is a torture device with spikes under the lid that pierce the skin when shut on a person. Their blood then runs to the bottom and pools in a tank below. The only way this door will open is if enough blood fills the tank.

One sacrifice will be enough to fill the tank and open the door. However, you may want to reevaluate your decisions before doing so, as it is something you will live with for the rest of your life. Your freedom lies on the other side of this door.

"This can't be right... how would the first team have made it? Wouldn't the door still be open?" Lucia asked aloud.

"Have ya been skimmin' again? There ain't no way yer already done readin'!" Alistair complained. The blue lights above dimmed once more. It was like the beginning of a warm summer night in the cave.

"We don't have time, so I'll explain," Lucia said as she looked up at the ceiling and took in a gulp. "That statue over there is called an 'iron maiden'. A person can go inside it and there are spikes that will impale them. The blood then drips below into a tank. According to what Joel translated, we have to sacrifice someone to make the door open."

"What? But there's gotta be some other way!" Alistair said.

Joel mimed projection from his voice. Lucia flashed Alistair an amused smile at first, but then she realized what he was suggesting: He wanted to regroup with Edith and the others.

"Why should we team up with them again? She will lead us to our deaths," Lucia replied.

"Yeh, and besides, she can't help us with this problem! I bet she'd wanna sacrifice *us* to tha statue!" Alistair added.

The mute wrote in his book and after a few moments, held it up for them to see:

With all of us combined, maybe we can lift the door, so no one has to be sacrificed.

Lucia's nose twitched. "I suppose, but..."

"We may not have a choice. The lights are dimmin', and that monster ain't far off!" Alistair pointed out.

Lucia then snapped her fingers and said, "I've got an idea!" Joel and Alistair looked back with hopeful eyes. "I thought the test description was odd, and then I realized… 'Explosive under strain'? It was trying to give us a hint. We can use the explosive mushrooms to blow a hole in the wall and get out of here."

"But we can't use 'em, lass! They'll blow up in our faces!" Alistair said.

"Is that so? Because when I was a mercenary of the Maug Jungles, we used them as weapons all the time," Lucia said with a smile. "The key is to only hold them by the stem. You see, it is the mushroom *head* that explodes on contact. The stem can be touched at any time."

Joel and Alistair exchanged excited glances, and then the trio rushed back into the corridor behind, to retrace their steps and find the room with explosive mushrooms.

After some twists and turns through the darkening maze, Joel, Lucia, and Alistair reached the room filled with explosive mushrooms once more.

Lucia knelt next to a patch of mushrooms and carefully placed her fingers around the stem of one. Joel watched on with a nervous curiosity. Was she about to blow up? Yet, no harm came to her as she plucked one from the ground. Then, with another hand, she did the same and pulled up another explosive mushroom.

"These should do…" she said.

Skreeeeee

"Let us be quick!" Lucia said. They headed back toward the final test at a brisk pace.

～

MEANWHILE, Edith and her group were going in circles. Despite Angus' pleas, the blonde beauty had been insistent that she was going the right way. Of course, Angus thought, circles in a labyrinth meant an eventual dead-end.

"I tell you now, we are certainly going the wrong way…" he whispered as they continued.

Without looking back, Edith said, "No, Angy, I have a good feeling about this way." The giant groaned. She had already come up with a pet name for him. The turns down each corridor became tighter and tighter. He looked up in concern at the dimmed blue light.

Skreeeeeeeeeeee

The group stopped as soon as the otherworldly cry reached their ill-prepared ears, but this time, it was accompanied by the sounds of screaming men. Their blood-curdling cries chilled even Angus' bones, but just as quickly as they had started, the noises abruptly ended.

Angus leaned over and whispered into Edith's ear once more. "Please… we don't have much time."

"It's a good thing I'm leading us to the exit, then," Edith said. The giant sulked. She couldn't be reasoned with.

Then, when they were further into the labyrinth, Edith came to a sudden stop. She looked up at Angus and whispered, "Wait a moment, we *are* going the wrong way. What was I thinking?" He only shrugged in return.

"Now the men will think that I led them astray. I'll need you to take the blame on this one. But don't worry, I'll make it worth your while, later…" she said, caressing his chest as she walked by. She cleared her throat in front of the group. Angus remained silent. "Alright, everyone, I'm sorry to say that Angus took us in the wrong direction, but don't worry, I shall lead us out."

The workers groaned. The black gold had made them more prone to restlessness, and they had certainly grown weary of the maze. Bronrar was making the largest fuss, which was unlike him, Angus thought. If even he was speaking out, then the situation among the rest of the crew must have been dire.

～

Lucia, Alistair, and Joel returned to the final test room, but before they could get to blowing up the wall before them, the mute jumped in front and protested.

"What's the problem, lad? Ya wanna stay in this dump? Or do ya wanna leave?" Alistair asked.

Joel wrote in his book and held the text up for them to see:

We shouldn't leave the other group behind. The Nightcrawler will kill them. Can one of you shout out to give them directions?

"You *must* be joking!" Lucia said, her face twitching with rage. "We are finally safe without Edith dragging us down, and you wish to bring her back into the fold?"

"Can't we just leave 'em behind after escapin' this wretched maze?" Alistair asked.

Lucia sighed. She turned, chest puffed out, and then shouted, "Edith! Are you close? We're at the final test!"

"We aren't far off! Keep calling out with your husky voice! I'll follow it!" Edith replied, her voice ringing hollow off the walls between them.

"I swear, if this trip doesn't end with my sword in her gut…" Lucia muttered through grit teeth. Alistair and Joel were holding her back by the arms. She cleared her throat and then called out, "Alright, just try not to get lost again!"

Joel and Alistair looked at each other and chuckled in unison.

As Lucia continued to give condescending directions, Edith's voice got closer and they could hear the jingling of the group's equipment. However, the lights above dimmed even more. Alistair and Joel were forced to bring out their torches and waited by the entrance for them.

SKREEEEEEEEEE

Though it couldn't be seen yet, the Nightcrawler sounded closer than ever. If it managed to reach them in the darkness of the labyrinth, they'd be like lambs waiting for their slaughter. Lucia and Edith shouting back and forth to one another had almost certainly attracted the beast, Joel thought. Still, helping them was the right thing to do. Regardless of Edith and Angus' wicked deeds, the other miners were innocent.

Then, Edith and her group finally came into view at the end of the corridor. Their torchlights bobbed up and down and approached quickly. It had become too dark to even see their faces from afar.

"Took ya long enough!" Alistair yelled down the path.

While awaiting their arrival, something caught Joel's eye. Something *red*. Many red things, in fact. He looked up, only to see the last remnants of the blue light on the ceiling. Further down, he caught the red again. *On top of the walls*, he thought with a shudder. Eight glowing, red eyes dashed across a large section of the maze. He nudged Alistair, who ignored him at first. His nudges soon turned to shoves.

"Oi! What's tha probl-"

The torchlights, now halfway down the corridor, stuttered as the ground rumbled and Joel heard a great *thud*.

SKREEEEEEEEEEEE

Of course, Joel thought. The Nightcrawler had been skipping sections of the maze by climbing atop its walls. With those sharp claws at its disposal, even something so smooth, vertical, and tough could be scaled; and once on top, it could easily see their torchlights.

"It's the Nightcrawler! Run! Run for your lives!" Edith cried as she and Angus dashed for the final test room.

"We're not gonna make it…" Lucia muttered. Joel and Alistair turned to see that she was now facing the wall next to the iron maiden.

The mercenary wound up and threw one of her explosive mushrooms at the wall.

Alistair gasped as the shroom flew at its target. "Oi! Tha hell are ya do-"

A great explosion erupted and a potent combination of yellow, orange, and red blinded Joel's eyes. He shielded his face as the heat struck him, but he knew there was no time to flinch. Amid the bouncing rocks and searing debris, he could hear the speedy claws of the Nightcrawler scratching the ground nearby. He unshielded his eyes and the white in his vision faded to see that the mushroom had punched a hole in the wall, no less than three meters wide. Joel and Alistair looked at each other in breathless amazement.

"Come, now! Move!" Lucia said while hopping through the newly made hole in the wall.

～

LUCIA FOUND herself in a small clearing. There was a new tunnel merely 50 paces ahead. She peeked her head back through the hole to see Alistair and Joel approaching. Edith and her crew weren't far behind.

"Hurry! This way!" she said, stepping to the side and waving the others through.

The first to hop through the hole were Joel and Alistair. Edith and Angus followed close behind, and then the rest of their group. Lucia stayed behind them all with a purpose. She had a plan: To use her last explosive mushroom on the Nightcrawler. She fiddled with the stem in her fingers as sweat came to her brow. If this didn't work, she would be skewered alive.

As the beast galloped into the final test room, it ground to a halt and she froze as its massive claws dragged against the rock. Now, Lucia was staring into its soulless eyes, and its mouth tentacles fluttered as it snorted at her. She felt its putrid breath hit her face, and the smell of rotted flesh overcame her senses.

The Nightcrawler tilted its head, as if confused, and that was her signal to run. She turned and dashed for the new tunnel ahead. A few strides away from her destination, she heard a great crash behind, and the mercenary looked over her shoulder to see that the monster had burst through a section of the wall next to the hole she had made; as if to show her that not even thick and sturdy stone could stop it.

SKREEEEEEEEEEE

It howled before beginning its charge. Lucia made it a short way into the tunnel before stopping and turning. She and the Nightcrawler locked eyes once more, and she couldn't believe how far it had gotten in just a few strides. It was by far the fastest creature she had ever encountered. It would only be another second or two before it reached her and ripped her to bits. *But that couldn't happen*, Lucia thought while readying her remaining explosive mushroom and backing into the tunnel some more.

As the beast entered the tunnel, Lucia threw the mushroom and hit it with a mighty explosion that rocked the passage like an earthquake had hit. The Nightcrawler let out an otherworldly cry as the flames engulfed it and rocks from the wreckage collapsed onto its body. The piling of rocks quickly turned into a cave-in, and Lucia ran back to the onlooking group as the last of the debris fell.

All in the group observed the wreckage. It had become clear they were in an all-or-nothing situation. If this wasn't the way out, then they were trapped for good. Lucia still held out hope, however. They hadn't found enough of the first team to assume they'd all succumbed to the same fate as those Gold Fever-infected men near the halfway point of the maze. There was still a chance that they could find Dalton and escape this wretched mountain together.

CHAPTER 24
RIVER

After the dust settled from the cave-in, Edith and Angus approached Joel, Lucia, and Alistair for an explanation of what they had been up to as their group wandered the maze. At first, Edith attempted to blame them for the Nightcrawler's appearance, but she immediately backed down after pushback from the trio. Then, they detailed the final test of the maze: The blood sacrifice. Edith yawned and waved them off before leaving for a spot further into the tunnel. It didn't matter that they had been expected to complete a bloody trial if they had avoided it, anyhow.

A familiar musty smell filled the air as Edith pressed her back up against the wall and closed her eyes. Angus sat next to her.

She smiled, one eye open and looking at him. "I wonder… do those fools realize that if they hadn't gotten around it with the explosive mushrooms, we'd have sacrificed them to the iron maiden ourselves?"

"Ah, but the Nightcrawler would have surely taken another of our group by the time we shoved them in that torture device," he replied, raising a finger.

"A worthy sacrifice to rid ourselves of those rodents, Angy."

Silence overcame them. Angus wasn't sure what bothered him more: The speed at which she would sacrifice one of her loyal followers to destroy an enemy, or her repeated use of that vile pet name.

"What is our next move?" he asked.

"I think now is as good a time as any to rest," Edith said as she started to nod off. Other miners put their backs to the walls and rested, too.

~

Near the wreckage of the tunnel collapse, Joel was distracted by a weak sound. He could swear that he heard running water. It seemed to be coming from further down the tunnel.

"That damned Edith," Lucia muttered with a frown. "She didn't even bother to thank us for rescuing her."

Alistair scoffed. "We didn't do it for her, lass! We did it fer the rest of tha crew! She and that big ol' meat-stain Angus can be supper fer that Nightcrawler, fer all I care!"

"Well said," she replied. Joel nodded and smiled. Those had been his thoughts on the matter, too.

"Do ya think tha mushroom finished that beast off?" Alistair asked, eyeing the cave-in.

"I'll put it to you this way: If that didn't finish it off, I have no idea what will," Lucia said, plopping to the ground and resting her back against the tunnel wall. A single pebble fell from the wreckage to the ground and she jerked her head over to it, her eyes suddenly wide. After focusing on the pile of rocks and boulders for a little longer, she closed her eyes and let out a long, relaxed breath through her nose.

Joel sat next to the others and retrieved his book. He hadn't been able to draw any maps in the chaos of navigating the labyrinth. The mute was anxious to get back to work on it, but he couldn't be sure exactly how to scale the map after the maze. It was like a missing puzzle piece. Joel placed the book in his pack and sealed it tight. He hoped to do a better job on it later.

As he was putting the map away, something caught his eye by the wreckage; something that didn't quite look right. He went over to inspect and his eyes widened when he realized what it was. Joel walked over to his dozing friends and woke them up.

"Bleh! What is it, lad? I'm tryin' ta sleep, here!" Alistair said. Lucia appeared groggy and said nothing. Joel motioned them to come over to the wreckage. The trio went to the collapse and Alistair groaned.

"What am I supposed ta be seein', here? It's just a bunch o' rocks!"

"He's right, Joel. There's nothing here-" Lucia cut herself off. Suddenly, her dreamy state vanished and she was alert. "It can't be…"

"What? What is it?" Alistair asked.

"The Nightcrawler…" she muttered, pointing at the many blood-red eyes in a sea of brown rock. They stared back at them with killing intent.

"But, how?" Alistair said as some rocks began to shake. "Can that thing *move* under all them rocks?"

"We have to leave…" Lucia trailed off as she turned and began jogging. "We have to leave!" she yelled while running past Edith and Angus.

"Why?" Edith asked in a groggy state.

Skreeeeeeeee

"It's alive?" the blonde beauty asked aloud with a gasp.

Joel and Alistair followed close behind Lucia, and they tapped the resting miners along the way to warn them. Soon, everyone was running down the tunnel, and a faint blue light faded in and out from afar.

SKREEEEEEEEEE

Rock loudly clanked off of rock from behind them, and the tunnel rumbled in response. Joel's shoulders shot up to his ears as he heard the potent claws of the Nightcrawler scratching against the ground.

"The beast is free!" Angus cried.

Joel's ears next picked up on a noise he had heard earlier: Running water; and it grew louder the further into the tunnel they ran. The glowing blue rocks sparingly appeared around them again and brought some light to the path.

Then, just as suddenly as they had needed to run, the group came to a stop. Before them was a small ledge, and moving parallel to their path was an underground river. A shade of blue faded in and out from the underwater rocks, and it shined all the way up to the surface and even the ceiling to provide a good view of their surroundings. Joel could see that there was a continuation of their path across the river, but it was at least a five-meter swim to the other side, and the rapids looked strong.

"Can w-we make it across?" Bronrar asked.

"I don't believe so. The current is too strong. We may have to ride it downstream, wherever that may lead," Angus replied.

"It's for the better, anyway. A stream may well lead us to an alternate entrance and exit. The water has to go somewhere," Edith said.

"But what if I lose me black gold?" a miner complained.

"Yeh, I thought we'd be able to get back ta minin' by now..." another said.

Skreeeeeeeee

The Nightcrawler's cry silenced further complaints.

Edith turned to address the rest of the group. "Life or death, gentlemen. The choice is yours."

"B-but I ain't so good at swimmin'..." Bronrar mumbled.

With a growl, Edith lunged forward and shoved him into the river. He landed with a great splash that soaked several of the miners on the ledge.

"Oof! It's cold!" Bronrar said after resurfacing. The current carried him down and around the bend.

Angus frowned at the blonde beauty. She shrugged and flashed him a playful smile. "He needed a push. It looks safe enough. Let's go, Angy!"

The leaders hopped in and like Bronrar before them, were carried downstream and out of sight. Next to jump in were Joel, Lucia, and Alistair. They heard splashes from the other miners behind them as they were swept down the beautiful current of glimmering blue. As they let the river take them, the cries of the Nightcrawler quieted down.

"Ya don' think it'll follow us into tha water, do ya?" Alistair asked.

"We have to hope not-" Lucia gasped and started fidgeting in the water. "What was that?" Panic was in her voice.

"What's what?" Alistair asked.

"Something brushed against me in the water," she said, waving her arms around underwater. After many attempts to no avail, her eyes widened and she pointed next to the mute. "Joel... next to you..."

He looked down to see a long, pale creature with an angular face and bright red ears swimming next to him. It looked like a giant salamander with a worm's body; or to the untrained eye, a dragon as depicted in mythical times.

His heart beat furiously through his chest at first, but it didn't take long for him to realize this creature was docile. With some caution, Joel petted it, and it wriggled around joyfully with each stroke. Although it was underwater, it felt slimy to him.

Alistair swam over to Joel and petted the creature. He let out a hearty chuckle. "It's harmless! We finally found a friendly creature in this wretched place!"

"I don't believe my eyes..." a voice muttered. Joel and the others looked up to see that they had caught up with Bronrar in the stream. "That there is an olm."

"An olm? Never heard of it," Lucia said.

"Not surprisin'. They are rare creatures, only found in caves. We come across 'em in the old minin' sites, sometimes. 'Cept I've never seen one so big before; that's gotta be at least three meters long," Bronrar said as he petted the docile creature. It wriggled around in joy once again.

"I wonder…" Alistair trailed off as he grabbed hold of the olm and straddled it with his legs. "Aye! We can ride 'em! This is great!"

Joel chuckled as he grabbed hold of the creature. He instead elected to ride it from the side. Other miners' voices echoed with joy as more olms were discovered swimming among them.

~

FURTHER DOWNSTREAM, Edith and Angus also encountered an olm.

"Yuck!" she whined, pushing the creature toward Angus. "It's slimy. How could anyone enjoy the company of such a beast?"

"Just be glad to encounter somethin' friendly. So far, this is the first creature that hasn't tried to kill us in these mines," Angus said.

"We can't count on that, Angy. It may still be deadly," Edith whispered before leaning in closer to him. "The only one you can trust in these mines is me, and I can be *quite* friendly."

She then nibbled on his ear playfully and it sent chills down his spine, but he did his best to ignore the sensation.

"Though rare, we've come across them before in some old digging sites back home. They are called olms," Angus said while grabbing ahold of one. "These ones are much bigger and stronger, though."

Edith remained silent, only returning a sly smile and sharp eyes. Somehow, she had him more on edge than any of the monsters they'd encountered thus far in Mt. Couture.

~

MEANWHILE, Bronrar had tried warming up to Joel, Alistair, and Lucia; but had received a cold reception.

"Yer pal Angus is up there. Why don't ya go have a chat with him, instead?" Alistair asked in a harsh tone.

"That's true. You should go up there and talk to him. He 'never steers you wrong', after all," Lucia added.

Joel didn't say anything, as was characteristic, but Bronrar still felt ganged up on.

"I don' think you lot appreciate the tough situation I'm in. I'm fond of you, but I've known Angus my whole life," said Bronrar.

"Did Angus force you to keep your black gold when you could have used it to help us?" Lucia asked.

"It's a necessary evil. The only way I'll get to live a comfortable life after this whole mess," he replied while petting a nearby olm as a nervous tick. "Surely you understand…"

"No, I don't," Lucia said with a frown. "You have seen what it does to people, and after we helped you back there against the dratagons, I thought you would return the favor. And where was your 'lifelong friend' while you were being attacked, by the way? He was off hacking innocent men to bits!"

"Wolfgang made him-"

"Give it up, laddie!" Alistair interrupted as he splashed water into his face. "Yer gonna twist it around so he's a good guy no matter what, but we know otherwise."

Bronrar said little else. He looked over at Joel, who appeared somber but offered no compromise. The nervous miner sighed before swimming ahead to Angus and Edith at the front of the pack.

THE RAPIDS WERE a perfect ride for the miners. It was a strong current, but not strong enough to make swimming a problem, and it was smooth, too. No one had hit rocks while being swept away. To make matters even better, it was a beautiful sight with the glowing blue rocks in the water and overhead. The light bounced off the pale scales of the olms and crystal-clear water fresh from the mountaintop. It was the first peaceful moment that the group had experienced in some time.

After a while, the stream began to narrow and make a turn toward the east. There were more slopes as well, but it remained a comfortable ride for the miners and olms that accompanied them. Even Edith, who had turned her nose up to the olms before, gave in and decided to hang on to one so that she might rest her arms and legs.

Within an hour, the river began to widen. Not only that, but they could see what looked to be an underground lake up ahead. The stream calmed as the river turned into a body of water, and the olms turned around to swim upstream in response.

The lake stretched at least a kilometer from end to end, and although there were pieces of land on each side, the raised rocks made it impossible to reach. From their current perspective, it looked like there was a beach at the other end of the lake, so that's where Edith directed everyone to swim.

"This water must be going somewhere..." Edith said between breaths as she swam for the shore.

"Perhaps there is an exit underwater. I'll check," Angus said as he took a deep breath and dove down.

While submerged, he could see that the lake went quite deep thanks to the clear water and glimmering blue light from the rocks of the floor. To his left, there were nothing but rocks that made up the shoreline of the lake, but on the right, he was positive that he could see something different. A hole or passage, perhaps. With some excitement, he surfaced to report back to Edith.

"Over there," he said, pointing to the raised shoreline on the right. "Underneath all of that rock, there is a passage. It is a hole no less than 30 meters, I'd say. But it's about halfway across the lake. I shall take a better look when we get closer."

"Excellent. Maybe we have found a way out of this place," Edith replied with glee. "And perhaps an easy entrance to return and get more black gold..."

About halfway across the lake, Angus and Edith stopped.

"It was around here." He pointed to the shoreline on their right. "I'll go under once again to check." He took a deep breath and went down.

This time, Angus had a much better view, and as he had suspected, the hole was an underwater tunnel. He was aware that a body of water called Frez Pond resided next to Mt. Couture. Could this cavern have been its water source?

However, something else caught his eye as he peered into the depths. It had initially blended in well with the rocks below, but at the right view and at the right time of the blue rocks fading in, he could see it was no mere rock.

Angus surfaced and grabbed Edith by the arm. Then, he began paddling toward the shore ahead with the blonde beauty in tow.

"What are you doing?" she asked, trying to wriggle her arm out of his powerful grip.

"We must be swift," he said.

"What did you see?"

"I believe this cavern is home to a *king riggit*," Angus said. Edith gasped and ceased her struggles.

~

FURTHER BACK, Joel and Lucia observed Alistair's strange swimming form as he started to lag. They gave each other knowing looks and chuckled as the big man struggled to keep up.

"Erm, what *is* that swimming technique?" Lucia asked.

"It's called the 'doggy paddle', a real man's swim!" he replied.

Lucia burst out laughing and said, "I think you'll notice everyone is leaving you behind. Try something else."

"Bah! I'm fine. I'll catch up!" said the big man. Joel and Lucia slowed their swim anyway to stay back with him.

Lucia's lighthearted mood quickly turned sour when she looked forward. "Angus and Edith are moving fast; almost like they are panicking… what's going on?"

"I'm sure it's… important, lass," Alistair said between breaths. "Go on… without me… I'll catch up!"

Joel took a deep breath and went underwater to have a look around. He saw nothing but empty space and rock on his left. It was remarkable to him how clear the water was. However, when he looked to his right, he saw something moving; something big. It was a crusty brown color, with old-looking scales and a flattened face that lacked eyes. There were great horns on its head to distinguish itself from the other riggits, and even from afar, Joel could tell that it was considerably larger than the queen had been. The monster swam slowly toward them, its massive turtle-like tail making a visible current behind it.

After resurfacing, Joel turned to face Lucia with panic written all over his face. He pointed to the shoreline on the left, where they could take refuge.

"But that shoreline is too high. There is no way we can reach it," Lucia replied before shaking her head. "What did you see, anyway?"

She dove under, and after a short time, came back up with a furrowed brow.

"Alright, I see your point. We should head for the shoreline. It's our best chance." After making a few swimming strokes to the left, however, she stopped. "We have to warn the others; to give them a fighting chance."

Joel nodded in agreement.

"What's goin' on?" Alistair asked.

"Everyone!" she called out. Alistair groaned and Joel chuckled. He was getting a little taste of what it was like to be ignored. Many of the miners ahead looked back. "I believe there is a king riggit in this lake. It is bigger than the others and heading for us right now. Hurry to the shore!"

There was a brief pause as the miners looked underwater for themselves, but it didn't take long for panic to set in. The men began to splash violently in their attempts to quicken their pace as Lucia, Alistair, and Joel swam in the direction of the left shoreline.

$$\sim$$

"IDIOTS!" Edith shouted back to her men. "Splashing will attract the beast!"

"I don' wanna die… I don' wanna die!" Bronrar chanted to himself as he brushed past a couple of miners. In his estimation, this was the fastest he had ever moved.

Only 100 meters away from the shore, some miners began to breathe a sigh of relief.

"We're gonna make it…" one said, breathlessly.

"No monster's gonna get me!" said another.

"I gotta survive so I can make use of me black gol-"

Something dragged him underwater before he could finish professing his love of the sparkling ore. The men around him stopped briefly, but then returned to paddling ahead, and much faster. Another unfortunate man next to Bronrar got tugged down as he swam. The nervous miner knew that a king riggit could find anyone's exact location thanks to the vibrations of their panicked strokes in the water.

Unlike the other riggits, the king had multiple tongues at his disposal. Bronrar pictured the miners being dragged into the deep, their chests nearly bursting from panic and a lack of air. He just knew that they would be sucked violently into the monster's great mouth and chewed to bits. His stomach twisted and turned, but somehow his water strokes remained smooth.

Bronrar looked back as the blood of the riggit's victims surfaced.

"Oh, God…" he muttered.

"Everyone! Paddle slowly in the water. It will make you harder to find! Remember that riggits are blind!" Angus called out.

The men slowed down and pushed themselves along gently in response. Multiple geysers spurted amid the lake as tongues burst out and then quickly retracted back in when they missed. Bronrar shuddered. He was guessing, now, and with so many tongues at his disposal, he didn't like the odds of survival. To distract himself, he peered over his shoulder once more to see that Alistair, Lucia, and Joel had reached some rocks at the left side of the lake. Though they weren't able to reach the top of the shoreline, he still envied them for managing to escape the water. He looked back forward to see that he was nearing a shore, himself. Yet, with a king riggit on his tail, it felt impossibly far.

Bronrar whimpered as tongues flung out of the water ahead of him. One had come out right next to a miner in front of him, but the man continued his steady strokes as if nothing had happened. It was his best chance for survival, after all.

Then, the nervous miner did a double-take as the great shadow of the beast shrunk beneath the miner up ahead. Bubbles rose to the surface, surrounding him like a swarm of bees.

"Look out!" Bronrar cried, but it was too late. The king riggit shot out of the water like a catapult projectile and flailed his massive body as he fell. This monster dwarfed the queen riggit that they had encountered before him. Including the tail, he had to be close to twice her size, by Bronrar's estimation; and the riggits of Mt. Couture were already larger than the ones from the mines back home. The beast's scales were old and weathered; like that of a creature from ancient times.

Bronrar could only watch in horror as the king landed on the poor man in front of him. It all happened so fast that he couldn't have known what had hit him. The sheer force of the splash sent Bronrar spiraling backward and underwater. An odd concoction of unbridled fear and foolish hopefulness kept him motionless upon resurfacing. Mayhap the beast would be satisfied with his latest meal and leave, he thought.

"Get back to swimmin', Bronrar!" Angus called back to him. He snapped out of his stupor and shifted his attention forward. Angus and Edith were far ahead of him, near the shoreline. "That man is dead! Squished! You have to continue on!"

Bronrar swam once more, but he quivered with each stroke. He passed through the warm, thick blood of the man who had been in front of him only moments ago as it bubbled up. That was it, he thought. That was what awaited him.

~

ON THE LEFT side of the lake, Alistair grimaced as he sat on the rocks, just above the surface of the water. Joel and Lucia were trying to reach the top of the shoreline behind him, but it was too high and had no place to grasp with their hands or push with their feet. It was almost like a sheer cliff.

The big man had a crazy idea, and he knew the others would hate him for it, but he had to do something. He hated being powerless to help, even if Bronrar hadn't helped them earlier.

"Oi! King riggit!" he cried. Lucia and Joel stopped making noise behind him and he almost laughed. He was sure that they were cross with him, now. "You ain't so tough! COME GIT SOME!" Alistair jumped off the rocks and landed belly-first in the water. A great splash erupted.

"Ooooo 'Tha king,' he calls himself, eh?" Alistair asked as he splashed his arms, noisily. "Well, ya ain't much of a king until ya bested me in combat ya ugly, poopy-lookin', salamander-copyin', waify-lookin', knobby-cockin', foul-smellin' newt!"

"What the hell are you doing?" Lucia asked with disgust in her tone.

"I gots ta do *somethin'*, lass! Sorry! You two should get outta here! I'll distract him!" Alistair replied.

"Fool! That fell beast will eat you in one bite!" Lucia shouted. Alistair continued to splash around.

Joel and Lucia looked up with terror in their eyes. Alistair gazed over his shoulder and gasped. A wave in the water saw Bronrar bobbing up, and then it began charging in their direction, fast. The mercenary bent over and extended a hand out to him from the rocks.

"You need to get up here… now!" she said.

"But I gotta help the others," Alistair replied.

"You already have. He is coming this way. There is little time, so hurry up and take my hand," Lucia said as she grabbed him by the forearm and pulled with all of her apparent might. The big man knew that he'd be difficult to lift, but to make matters worse, Lucia's shoulder wound reopened as she pulled. She winced and grunted while closing her eyes, but she didn't let go or even loosen her grip. Joel jumped in to help, and then they were able to pull Alistair up to the rocks.

The trio looked on as the wave of the king riggit grew larger and closer. He rose from the depths more and more; until his old, flaky scales became visible below the surface, and his horns poked above water like shark fins. The king's speed picked up and the waves raised until he was frighteningly close; seconds away from his prey.

"Now what?" Lucia asked aloud.

"Now, you take my hand," a voice replied from above. The trio turned and then looked up to see an arm extended over the edge of the cliff. Joel gave Lucia a pat on the back, and Alistair nodded upward to tell her to go first.

She reached out and allowed the hand to grab her by the left forearm. With some effort from both sides, Lucia was pulled up and over the shoreline. The arm reached back out. Alistair pushed Joel into it and before the mute could make an argument, he was lifted by the mysterious hand from above. The big man chuckled. Joel was so small and easy to lift, he thought.

The arm then reached over for Alistair. The big redhead looked back to see that the king riggit was so close that a light mist from his cresting waves wet his face. He hopped up and grabbed hold of the arm, which went limp from the sudden load at first, but then, slowly and surely, Alistair was lifted up and over the cliff.

The group heard a great *thud* down below, and rocks and water alike soared through the air, landing with loud *plops* in the lake. Alistair looked over the ledge to see the king riggit flailing underwater and against the rocks. After turning around, he dove back into the depths without a trace.

He turned and smiled. "Whew! That was close! How did those fellas get up here so fas-"

Alistair cut himself off. He had thought that the group got to shore and made their way around the shoreline in time to save them; but across the lake, he could see that they had only just gotten out of the water. Who had saved them?

The big man looked over his saviors. They were all dressed similarly to himself, but the one closest by stood out the most: He had a short, scruffy beard with mid-length, dark hair. His light chainmail fit perfectly around a muscular warrior's build.

"Dalton!" Lucia cried as she hopped off the floor and gave the man a big hug.

"Erm… yes, that is my name, miss… and you are?" he asked with confusion in his eyes.

"Don't play dumb!" she said before shoving him. The hug had left his clothes drenched. Alistair and Joel looked at each other and chuckled.

"Oi! The lass has talked ya up mighty fine throughout our journey… and yer tellin' me that ya don't even know her?" Alistair asked. Dalton looked back at Lucia and only shrugged in response. The big man pointed and laughed at her. "I knew it! Yer just an admirer! Do ya have a crush on 'im, lass?"

"It's not my fault the fool forgot about his own apprentice," Lucia shot back with crossed arms. She jerked her head quickly so that the drops of water flung off her ponytail and struck him in the eyes.

Dalton rubbed his eyes and then squinted at her. "Lucia?"

"About time you came to your senses…"

"Whoa, when did you get so tall?" He held his hand flat and placed it atop her head, then hovered it over himself, a couple of inches beyond his own height. Lucia's face turned red. "And… that crescent marking on your face… it's so… stupid!" He broke out into laughter.

Alistair joined in on the laugh and said, "It is, ain't it?"

"Please, tell me it isn't permanent!" he choked out.

Lucia groaned. "It is…"

Dalton suddenly calmed himself, which caught Alistair off-guard. He continued to laugh through dead silence, but quickly shut himself up out of embarrassment.

"Well, then, that reminds me: I still ain't happy with you for running away. Do you know how far and wide I searched for you?" Dalton said in a stern tone.

"Yes, well… I needed to be on my own; to find strength in independence," she replied, looking down. "I managed to find my way, but over time, I also came to value companionship… there wasn't much of that where I've been these past five years. So, I wanted to find you and make amends. I'm sorry for making you worry."

"It does seem like you have grown up a lot. Maybe it was good for you," Dalton said as he shifted from his angry tone in a near-instant. He looked to the left, where the rest of the group was on their way around the bend of the inclining shoreline. "I count 11, total… only 11 of you survived? And I thought we had it bad."

"It's a long story, but we 11 aren't the only survivors. We left an additional 15 men outside the mines to stand guard of the treasures," said Lucia.

"You don't mean the shiny black treasure, do you?" he replied.

"I'm afraid so. We didn't discover your journal until after separating from them. We know about Gold Fever now, but even so, some of the men refuse to part with their black gold."

"Ah, so 'black gold' is what we're calling it, then?"

"Aye! See that fella over there? He came up with the name," Alistair said while pointing to Joel. Dalton turned his gaze to the mute.

"Oh, hi Joel," he said. Joel waved back.

"Wha? You two know each other?" Alistair asked.

"Somethin' like that. I know his caretaker, Aldous, a little better, but Joel's a nice enough fellow. He likes to keep to himself, but I got him to speak with me a few times," Dalton said.

"*He speaks?*" Alistair and Lucia asked in unison.

Dalton put his hands up and said, "Sorry, sorry! I meant in sign language. I learned it while I was with the army, and speaking with Joel through USL has helped keep me sharp."

"Ah, well, it will be nice to have someone who can translate what he's saying once again," Lucia said.

"So, he has provided you with some useful information, I take it?"

"More than you realize. He was the one to warn us of the black gold and its effects. We didn't listen to him at first, but over time, it started to control us. Some of our men went mad. I only hope that didn't happen to Conrad's group…" Lucia said, looking down.

"Conrad? Is that your leader?" Dalton asked.

"No. Faramond was our leader. He appointed Conrad as leader of the group that remained outside of the mines. He is wise and capable, so I'm sure he didn't succumb to Gold Fever. It is the others who worry me…" said Lucia.

"Hold up. You say Faramond 'was' the leader? What happened?" The warrior leaned in.

"Killed by a madman named Wolfgang," Alistair said while shaking his round head.

"Damn… how can that be? Faramond should have been able to crush Wolfgang using what I taught him," Dalton said with growing anger in each word.

"It is not so simple. We believe he was attacked unprovoked and when he wasn't looking," Lucia said.

"Fine, we can talk more about that later. For now, who's in command of your group?" he asked.

"Edith," said Lucia.

"Edith Danvers?"

"Yes."

"Ugh… this is bad…" Dalton muttered.

"So, ya know about all the schemin' and bad happenin's that she's up to?" Alistair asked.

"No, that's not it," Dalton said with a shudder. "Y'see, a couple of weeks before this trip, I *might* have slept with her, and it didn't end well…"

"Ew!" Lucia cried, her face turning red once more. "You slept with that *pig*? How could you?"

"Now, I agree that she says many unpleasant things, but… just look at her. Can you blame me?" Dalton asked with a shrug.

"Not at all, mate!" Alistair let out a hearty laugh and slapped him on the shoulder. "An' I bet it was a great lay, too!"

"Indeed, it was, my friend! Aside from all of the foul things she said afterward, it was worth it!" Dalton said, chuckling along.

"I see that not much has changed since I left you. Your judgment in women is *still* horrible," Lucia said while sticking a finger onto the tip of his nose and rubbing it in. Dalton frowned, but he put up no fight. "Edith and her father cooked up the plan to send us all here. They wanted us to collect as much black gold as possible, knowing its ill effects. And worst of all, they *planned* for half of us to die on this expedition. I am unsure of their true goal, but I get the feeling that we've yet to fully uncover how insidious it really is."

"You'll have to give me more details, later," Dalton said as he pointed to an approaching Edith. The rest of the miners followed close behind her.

"Well, well, if it isn't the famous Dalton Rayleigh!" Edith called out as she got closer. Water dripped from her long, blonde locks, and it weighed her dress down so much that it flopped with each step she took. "I was beginning to wonder if you and your group had survived."

"Greetings, Edith. I am glad to see you in good health. You and your company should follow me back to our current refuge. It lies in a cave up ahead that should prove safe for now," Dalton said when she and the group arrived.

Only faint stains of Faramond's blood remained on her chest, though that wasn't the real reason Alistair was looking her over. The dress now hugged each well-portioned curve perfectly, and Dalton was staring, too.

"Lead the way," the blonde beauty said with a sly smile.

Dalton turned and led the group up a new path. The glowing blue rocks continued to light the way, and Alistair was thankful for it. The water had dampened everyone's torches, and it would be some time before they were usable again.

As they walked, Alistair noticed several dead riggits lying out on the rocky ground. Most of their bodies were charred black, but patches of their old scales could still be seen in some spots.

"We have been resting at this cave up ahead for some time, now. The only issue was that some riggits called it home. But we took care of 'em swiftly, and since then, we haven't had any problems. Unfortunately, there is no way to be sure if it's day or night, 'round here. I don't suppose any of you would know?" Dalton asked.

"I believe that it's nighttime," Lucia said. "If what your journal says is true and the Nightcrawler is a nocturnal hunter… that should be the dead giveaway. It chased us into the river, and that's how we ended up here."

"Good to know. We should avoid venturing out for a while, then," Dalton said.

AFTER A SHORT TIME WALKING, the group reached a new cave that was populated by other miners. In a way, it was refreshing to see some new faces. Dalton's group was greater in number than Edith's. Including Dalton himself, the group had 25 survivors, although it was obvious right away that not all of them were well. Some men were curled up into a ball and mumbled to themselves. Others had sustained injuries and were patched up with scavenged materials like old rags or torn clothing.

As they entered the cave, Dalton called out, "Alright, everyone! We have found the second team!"

"Where's the rest of 'em?" one miner asked aloud.

"This is the best they could send?" another said.

"Did they find a way outta this place?" one joked.

"Now, now…" Dalton said while bobbing an outstretched hand.

"No wonder they're on the B-Team!" a man said to some laughter.

"They'll just weigh us down!" said another.

"Quiet!" a voice boomed from a dark corner of the cave. He was a tall, stringy man, whose miner's apron was torn at the abdomen. Underneath, makeshift bandages were wrapped around his stomach and covered in dry blood. He limped to the center and said, "Show some respect. At least they came this far to help us!"

"Ah, you're awake," Dalton said before he turned to the group of 11 and pointed back. "This here is my second-in-command, Baltr. As you can see, he specializes in crowd control."

"A pleasure to see you all alive and well," Baltr said before falling into a coughing fit. He gripped his midsection and seemed to wince with each cough, but it did not deter him from approaching Edith and taking one of her hands. "Lady Edith, I cannot conceive of why you are in a wretched place such as this, except that you hold the same love of the workers as your father does." He planted a delicate kiss on her hand.

"Oh, my," Edith said with delight. Dalton and Lucia collectively rolled their eyes. "You are quite the charmer, Burter."

"Baltr," Dalton said. His cheeks flared out and he slapped a hand over his mouth. Lucia narrowed her eyes at him. He was obviously about to laugh. *Same old Dalton,* she thought.

"Right…" Edith said with an obvious lack of care. "How did you get such a terrible injury, Baltr?"

"I was attacked by the Nightcrawler," he said with a prideful smile.

"That's not the whole story," Dalton interjected. Baltr frowned in return. "Y'see, Baltr over here is as stubborn as a mule. I told him to take the team and go while the Nightcrawler attacked me, but he came back and saved my sorry ass!" He howled with laughter and some of the men joined in with him, but then his demeanor quickly turned serious. "If it hadn't been for his bravery, I wouldn't be here right now. But he certainly paid a price for that." He pointed to the wound.

"I see. Well, I must agree, Baltr. It was quite brave of you to save your leader like that," Edith said, now eyeing Dalton. "Speaking of which, could we have a private meeting, Dalton? Between us leaders?"

"Of course," he replied while nudging his head to a corner of the cave where no one else was sitting. "The rest of you, feel free to settle down and get some rest."

The two leaders began walking toward the corner that he'd pointed out. As Dalton strolled past Lucia, he muttered, "We'll talk later." She nodded in return.

Everyone from the B-Team split up to go rest in all corners of the cave. Some men started to speak as if they'd known each other before the trip, while others went straight to sleep or kept to themselves as they admired their black gold treasures.

Joel, Alistair, and Lucia settled at an unpopulated wall of the cave. It didn't take long for Alistair and Joel to fall asleep, but Lucia wanted to stay up so she could speak with Dalton. She looked at the leaders across the cave with concern. His leering eyes for the blonde beauty hadn't escaped her notice. Would Edith try to manipulate him as she had done to Faramond?

After what felt like an eternity, Dalton and Edith ended their meeting. Edith walked over to Angus, who rested near the cave entrance, while Dalton approached Lucia. He plopped down next to her with a smile.

"So?" she asked.

"So, what?"

"What did you talk about with her?"

"In no uncertain terms, she expressed her desire to lead the entire group. While I'd have the *honor* of being her second-in-command," Dalton said with some muffled laughs.

"You didn't agree to that, did you?" Lucia replied with wide eyes.

"Of course not. I told her that she could keep leading her group if she wanted to, but I'm gonna continue to lead my men," Dalton said with a reassuring nod. "She told me to think it over, anyway."

"The three of us will join up with your group, then," Lucia said before nudging her head at Alistair and Joel; who continued to snooze.

"She's that bad, is she?" Dalton asked.

"You have no idea."

"Enlighten me."

"Faramond was a good leader to us. He cared about keeping us safe, and above all else, finding the first group," Lucia said as Dalton nodded along. "But over time, Edith manipulated him into spending more time mining. There were a few times when I think Gold Fever took its effects on him, but he fought it. Even still, his judgment was clouded by his love for her. Members of our group only died after she began to influence his decisions."

"I see. And how did he die?" Dalton asked.

"The circumstances are still not entirely clear to me, but my understanding is that Wolfgang murdered him while he and Edith were sleeping together," Lucia said.

"Out of jealousy, then?" Dalton asked.

"Perhaps. I'm not convinced that Edith didn't set it all up as a power grab."

Dalton sighed. He folded his hands and said, "Alright... now, what were you going to tell me about Edith and Drake's plans?"

CHAPTER 25
A RED DAWN

At the many cries of human plight
He arrives in the darkness, ready to fight
To right the wrongs of mankind's gall
To make us equal, once and for all
Save the world by getting more
Of that precious dark and sparkling ore
A radical change to man's behavior
You follow now, the will of the Savior

Henic awoke in a cold sweat. The dream had been so vivid that he could swear it had been real. The chanting hordes mesmerized and scared him all the same, but most memorable of all was the shadowy figure who had commanded him from the background. It had yellow eyes that pierced his soul, and a voice that felt like a whisper and a shout all at once. With each word spoken, he could feel another layer of sanity being pealed painstakingly from his mind.

As he strained to push the horrid dream out of his memory, Henic realized that it was light outside. Finally, the never-ending night had turned to day, he thought. He breathed a sigh of relief and stood to get dressed.

He exited the tent to find Conrad nearby; poking and prodding a fire carefully with a stick as he ate breakfast. The strategist looked over his shoulder at him and smiled.

"Ah, there you are. I'm glad *someone's* awake," Conrad said. Henic looked around to see that they were the only two up. He sat by the fire to join him for some food. "You still look tired… trouble sleeping?"

"Too many nightmares," Henic said.

"I can't blame you. There have been many strange happenings since we got here," Conrad said before taking a bite of his biscuit. "Even still, we have a difficult task ahead: Convincing the others to join us in search of Faramond's group." Henic remained silent. "That is, of course, if you are willing to come along?"

"I'll follow your lead, whatever your decision is," Henic said.

"But do you agree with my decision?" Conrad asked.

"I'm not sure…" Henic trailed off as he got his breakfast ready. "On the one hand, I know that Faramond would do the same fer us," he said between bites. "But on the other hand, those mines have swallowed up not one, but two groups. Should we not take that as a sign?"

"A fair point, and yet there is little we can do out here. Some dark force is conjuring up a storm every time we try to leave," Conrad replied.

"You ain't wrong," Henic said. "By the way, you hear anythin' from Cyriack or Solomon after the incident last night?"

"Not a word. I hope that some sleep will have done wonders for their sanity. Cyriack was never the same after feeling out Solomon's presence," said Conrad.

"Time will tell," Henic said. "I think it best to leave 'em be until they come back to us on their own."

As the pair quietly continued to eat, other miners came out of their tents. Brice and his crew were sure to be noisy and fussy as they set up their fire. William came out and made the rounds to say hello to everyone, as was customary of him. Peter also came out in his usual grumpy fashion and glared at anyone who dared look his way or try to speak with him. Eventually, all miners besides Solomon and Cyriack were outside and eating breakfast.

"It *had* to be those two who didn't come out, eh?" Henic asked with a nervous chuckle.

"We cannot let them wallow in their tents forever," Conrad said, crossing his arms. "Let's set a time limit: We will check on them if they're not out after everyone is finished eating."

"I don' like this…" said Henic.

∼

329

AFTER ABOUT A HALF HOUR, everyone had finished breakfast and the crowd grew restless. Brice and his crew wanted to try and leave the base camp again, but Conrad insisted that they stop trying. An attempt to flee would only cause another storm, and he didn't want to venture back into the tunnel unless the team was committed to finding Faramond's group.

"Well, I suppose we can't put this off any longer," Conrad said while standing. Henic stood along with him. "Ah! You wish to join me?"

"After yesterday's incident? Not at all. I'd rather not trouble men who are *lookin' fer trouble* if ye get my meaning…" Henic trailed off. Conrad's spirits dampened. "But you had a good point, yesterday. If I'm gonna be one of this group's leaders, I must trouble myself with the business of the others from time to time. Besides, we agreed to watch out fer each other."

"And I appreciate that," Conrad replied as he began the trek to Cyriack's tent. Henic followed close behind. Once they reached the tent, he stopped and then cleared his throat.

"Cyriack, are you awake? Morning is upon us, and I need to address the group," he said. There was no response. "Cyriack? Can you hear me?" he asked, and still, he did not reply. "I'm coming in."

They entered to find no one occupying the tent. The bedding was disheveled, but otherwise, nothing seemed out of the ordinary.

"How odd," Henic said, looking around. "Where could he have gone off to?"

"I can't imagine very far. He left all of his belongings. Even the black gold!" Conrad replied while pointing to the stash of ore. "That's not good… could he have gone back into the mines while we all slept?"

"I don' know, but before we think about that, I say we check on Solomon to make sure it ain't *both* who've disappeared," Henic said.

"A good idea," Conrad said.

The pair exited and then strode toward Solomon's tent. Outside, Conrad stopped once more.

"Solomon, this is Conrad. Are you awake? It's morning," he said, to no response. Henic shook his head. "Solomon? Can you hear me?" Conrad asked again. Silence. "Alright, I'm coming in."

Inside, the duo got answers, but not pleasant ones. Laying out on the bed like a motionless marionette was Solomon. He was covered in dry blood and had a smile from cheek to cheek plastered on his face. It was eerily similar to how they had found Ollie the other day, except these fatal injuries had clearly come from a weapon. Puncture wounds in the chest and neck were apparent.

To make matters worse, Cyriack sat in the corner of the tent, slumped over. He, too, was covered in blood that had dried. There were several stab wounds on his chest. He did not wear the same expression of deluded happiness as Solomon, but instead one of horror: His eyes bulged out and his mouth was agape.

"Oh, God…" Henic muttered. He covered his nose with his shirt collar.

"Not good," Conrad said. The putrid smell made his eyes water as they wandered around the tent.

There had to be some clue as to what had happened, he thought. However, even after combing the entire tent, he couldn't find a murder weapon or even signs of a struggle. Had the two men agreed to take their lives together? Or had they been in such a weakened state that someone had taken advantage and killed them?

Then, Conrad noticed an important clue: The black gold was missing. Solomon had come to hold it so near and dear to his heart that the only way anyone could have taken it from him was if they pried it from his cold, dead fingers.

"See that?" he asked.

"See what?" Henic replied, scratching his head.

"Perhaps I should say, 'See what's missing?'"

Henic gasped. "No black gold!"

"Indeed. That, and the presence of Cyriack's corpse, makes it all the stranger," Conrad said, crossing his arms. "We'll need to launch an investigation. Someone among us is a murderer…"

"Hold up… what if they killed each other?" Henic asked.

"A fair question, but look closely. There is no sign of a struggle. It's as if the two of them simply let it happen. Or maybe the killer placed their bodies here after slaying them."

"Alright, what next, then?"

"Next, we address the group," Conrad said as he lifted the tent flap. "Their reactions may be illuminating."

The pair approached the center of the base camp and many of the miners were already focused on Conrad before he spoke. He figured that they were anxious about the plan moving forward, and how it would affect their treasure stashes.

"Alright, everyone! Gather around!" Conrad called out. The

group made a small circle around him. "Unfortunately, I come bearing bad news. You might notice that Solomon and Cyriack are missing this morning. Upon checking their tents, we found them both dead."

"Oi! Who be the traitor?" a miner asked aloud.

"They were both crazies! Probably offed each other!" Brice called out.

"I smell a rat…" Peter muttered while glaring at Brice.

"We must leave this place!" another miner said.

"Most concerning…" William said in an uncharacteristically sad tone.

"Gentlemen! Calm yourselves!" Conrad shouted. Everyone settled down. "We must find out who's responsible for these murders-"

"Hold up! How do we know them knobs didn't kill each other?" Brice asked. "They were actin' mighty strange, last night."

"They weren't the only ones actin' strange, I'll tell ye that right now!" Peter shot back.

"Don't ye ever mind yer own business?" Brice asked in an annoyed tone.

"Not when there are rats about!" Peter replied.

"Alright, that's enough out of you both," Conrad said. They scowled at each other. "I found no evidence of a struggle, so I've ruled out the possibility of them killing each other. Instead, it would seem that someone killed both of them. We already have some evidence that could lead to finding the killer, but what we'll need to do next is search each of your tents."

"Don't ya trust us?" one miner asked.

"I ain't lettin' ye look without my supervision!" said another.

"This is stupid!" Brice said.

"Enough!" Henic cried. Everyone quieted down once more. "I don't think the lot of ye fully understand our situation. We're trapped between either staying here and returning to the mines; all thanks to the mysterious force conjurin' up storms when we try to leave. And if we're gonna be trapped here, I know that I don' want it to be with a *killer*."

"He's right. If we are trapped here, then a murderer won't help us sleep at night, I'm sure. We must find the culprit at once," Conrad said. The group remained silent. "Good. Henic and I will begin searching the tents, now."

Henic then whispered to Conrad, "Mayhap I should stay back and watch over this lot. Y'know… to make sure none of 'em try and make a move."

"A fine idea," Conrad said as he began to walk toward the hooligans' group of tents. "While you're at it, try speaking with some of them. Maybe the killer will slip up." Henic nodded, and with that, they went their separate ways.

Conrad entered the first tent of Brice's group. He looked around and found nothing suspicious or off-putting. He was on the lookout for one of three things: The murder weapon, blood, or an excess of black gold that looked to be stolen. The last of those options would be the most difficult to prove, of course, but he was willing to take his time if it meant he could expose the killer.

Although he wished to keep everyone safe, there was a genuine curiosity to Conrad's investigation. What would drive someone to betray and kill one of their own teammates? He could think of little else worse. What went through a murderer's mind? On the other hand, the dark presence felt by Cyriack yesterday might have been responsible. He did try and out that presence, after all. It may have provoked a response from whoever the Dark Wizard was. Even if that were the case, why would an all-powerful being like that use human tools to kill them? Would he not simply use magic? None of it made sense.

He found little of interest while searching through most of the hooligans' tents, but wasn't expecting to, anyway. It was Brice himself whom he had suspicions of. Conrad hadn't forgotten that Brice had threatened Solomon last night for going near his black gold. It was a logical motive, especially thanks to the irrational state the sparkling ore reduced men to.

Yet, when he entered Brice's tent, Conrad couldn't find anything out of the ordinary. Everything was in order; from his bloodless clothes to the amount of black gold in his possession checking out. However, as he was on his way out, something caught Conrad's eye: A shadow outside of the tent. Even more of a concern was that there were stains that seeped through the tent fabric.

Conrad exited and went around to see what it was. He gasped to find a bloody pickaxe leaning up against Brice's tent. It could incriminate him, but the evidence wasn't solid. Anyone could have put the murder weapon there, including someone who wanted to throw him off of their trail. Even still, he felt it important to confront Brice and see his reaction, or perhaps see how those around him acted.

The strategist swiped the pickaxe and made his way back around the tent, toward the group in the middle of base camp. Some of the miners eyed him as he walked with the bloody pickaxe, but they remained silent.

"I found *this* leaned up against the back of Brice's tent," Conrad said as he held up the bloody axe. He looked at the big-nosed miner. "Care to explain?"

The other men cast judgmental eyes on Brice, and his posture grew defensive. "What a load o' garbage! I didn't kill anyone!"

"The hell you didn't! I knew ye couldn't be trusted!" Peter said.

"Shut up, ye old fool. If I was gonna kill anyone around here, it'd be ye!"

"See? He's a cold-blooded killer!" Peter said with a sweeping hand gesture toward Conrad.

"There's just one problem with yer conclusion," Brice said with a smile. "That pickaxe ain't mine." He retrieved his own pickaxe, which was clean as could be. "The real killer must'a stashed it behind my tent to frame me!"

It was just as Conrad had feared. The situation was becoming more complicated.

"Well then, it stands to reason that the true killer would be short a pickaxe," Conrad said. The group fell silent. "To get to the bottom of this, I will require that each of you present me your pickaxe." Everyone retreated to their tents to gather pickaxes.

"Hold it!" Brice called out. "Ye've taken it upon yerselves to investigate these murders, but who says *yer* innocent?" He pointed at Conrad. "Ye and yer lil' stooge have been sittin' pretty while accusin' others, but I demand to see evidence of yer innocence!"

Although both men were taken aback by Brice's callout, Conrad quickly regained his confidence. He had nothing to hide, after all.

"Very well. We shall present our pickaxes along with everyone else," Conrad said with a smile. "Any other demands?"

Brice remained silent, so everyone dispersed to their tents. In short order, all workers returned to the middle of the base camp. Conrad looked around and saw all men, himself included, had pickaxes in their hands.

"Hm… could it be that the killer found an extra pickaxe?" he asked.

"*Hold it!*" Brice shouted. "Yer friend ain't here…"

Conrad's eyes widened. It was true. Henic was missing from the crowd. How had he not noticed? The lack of sleep, his timidity to help with the investigation, and his lust for the black gold had all been possible tells.

"Yeh! It must'a been him!" Peter said with a righteous, shaking fist held up. "He should pay for his crimes!"

The strategist held a hand out. "Let's not jump to conclusions-"

"A traitor deserves death!" one miner said.

"It ain't safe with him here!" a member of the hooligans added.

"An eye fer an eye! Kill 'im!" said another.

"Everyone! That's enough!" Conrad shouted to silence the crowd. "It's important that we don't make any snap judgments. I will check on Henic, and we shall continue from there."

Conrad marched over to Henic's tent. The possibility that his second-in-command had gone crazy and started a killing spree hung over his head like a dark cloud. Yet, it felt like a reach to him. It was out of Henic's character to stick his nose in Cyriack and Solomon's business, let alone kill them. His only possible motive would have been the black gold, which he was beginning to reject. Or had those long exercises last night been for nothing?

As the thoughts danced around in Conrad's mind, he opened Henic's tent flap without announcing himself. He found the farmer rummaging through his belongings. He looked back up at him in a panic.

"Conrad… I can explain…"

"Please, tell me you didn't kill anyone," he replied in a stern tone.

"I-I…"

"Can't find your pickaxe? Everyone else outside has one. They are already calling for your head, out there. Such a rowdy bunch… jumping to conclusions too quickly," Conrad said as he approached.

"I have no memory of doin' harm to anyone…" Henic muttered.

"And what is that supposed to mean?" Conrad asked.

"Well… I know I've had trouble with the black gold. I can never seem to let it go…"

"So? You think that drove you to murder? Why then wouldn't you remember?" he asked.

"I've been havin' these nightmares, y'see. They're so real, but I'm in this dreamy state. It's as if I'm in a trance," Henic said.

"And what happens in these dreams?"

"Chantin'… lots of chantin'. There's this dark figure, always watchin' over me… those eyes… yellow eyes. They're scary, yet alluring… I can't look away," Henic said, his eyes shifting around.

"Yellow eyes…" Conrad muttered.

"Yeh, that's right. I believe he was called 'The Savior'. His voice was but a whisper, yet deafening and almighty to my ears. Even though he frightened me, I felt the overwhelming desire to follow him and his every command," Henic said.

"So, that's why you're worried that you may have been behind the killings?" Conrad asked.

"Yes, sir."

Conrad took a moment to look around. Then, he dug through Henic's clothes and belongings, all while the farmer watched on. After an extensive search, Conrad let out a long breath through his nose. Henic was sitting, looking down in shame.

"I don't believe you've killed anyone," he said.

Henic's face lit up, but his expression quickly turned to disbelief. "What makes ye say that? Even I can't be sure if I've done somethin'…"

Conrad chuckled and said, "Not one for arguing your own case, are you? From the evidence I have found, I think that someone stole your pickaxe as you slept, and then used it." He crossed his arms and furrowed his brow. "But this is a complex situation. There is no sign of a struggle, and one of the victims is the man who pointed out the dark presence among us."

"So, what yer sayin' is that the so-called 'Dark Wizard' killed those two durrin' the night? But why would they kill Solomon?" Henic asked. "And why would an all-powerful Wizard waste his time usin' man-made tools? Couldn't he strike us all down with magic?"

"Those are good questions, which unfortunately go against your innocence," Conrad said with a snort. "Still, I think the 'Dark Wizard' scenario is more likely. It seems too coincidental that Cyriack would die the same night that he alerted us to the dark presence. That, combined with the lack of struggle, leads me to believe that magic of some kind was involved. How Solomon fits in, I am unsure, but we still have the lack of black gold as our last missing link."

"Well, ye've convinced me of my innocence. Thank you fer that!" Henic said with a laugh. "The difficult part will be convincing *them*." He nudged his head toward the outside.

"True. As a show of goodwill, you may need to turn yourself over while I continue to investigate. We'll see how they react," Conrad said as he lifted the tent flap. "Come. Let's face our team."

The pair walked to the middle of the base camp once more. All eyes were on Henic. From what Conrad could read, many in the group were hostile to the farmer's presence, or at the very least cautious.

"Well? Where's yer pickaxe?" Brice asked, putting hands to hips.

"Missing," Henic said to much grumbling among the group.

"I knew it! Ye see that! I'm innocent, ye old geezer!" Brice taunted Peter, whose expression reflected shock.

"W-well, the important thing is that we caught the *real* killer," he replied in a defensive tone.

"Hold up!" Conrad called out. All eyes turned to him. "That doesn't mean Henic is the killer."

"What a load of hogwash!" a miner cried.

"Ye had no trouble thinkin' I was guilty! Of course, yer nicer to ol' farm-boy 'cause he's yer friend!" Brice said.

"What if they're *both* responsible for the murders?" one of the men suggested.

"We ain't lettin' him off the hook! He must pay fer his crimes!" Peter said.

"Are you all done?" Conrad asked. The crowd fell silent. "It is possible that someone stole Henic's pickaxe and used it as the murder weapon," he said. Everyone else groaned. "I'm not saying he's innocent, but what I am saying is that I would like to investigate more before we jump to any conclusions."

"What more do ye need?" Brice asked.

"There is a little piece of information that I've withheld from you all until now: Solomon's black gold was stolen last night," Conrad said to a few gasps from the group. "After searching, I could find no evidence that Henic has any of it. If we find that missing black gold, I think there is a good chance we find our killer."

"That's mighty convenient! Yer just tryin' to protect yer friend!" Brice said.

"What would you have me do?" Conrad shot back. "We haven't seen all of the evidence. Until we do, I'm not ready to make a judgment."

More grumbling ensued, but it was less angry than before and eventually calmed down.

Conrad took a deep breath. He hoped that they had gotten all of their anger out. The bickering was quickly becoming tiresome. "Now then, I think we should-"

"No! We're not finished, here! I won't be satisfied until he steps down as second-in-command!" Brice said, pointing a finger of righteous indignation at Henic. The farmer's eyes widened at first, but then he sighed and looked down, dejected. "And I ain't comfortable with him lurkin' about in our circles. He should be banished back into the mines!"

"You're not being reasonable. He has not been proven guilty," said Conrad.

"Says you! Everyone else agrees!" Some of the other miners nodded.

"I find it ironic, Brice, that you would be so sure of Henic's capacity to kill another man," Conrad said, his eyes becoming razor-sharp. The big-nosed miner raised an eyebrow. "After all, you have been extorting him for his goods; forcing his sickly wife and child into field labor; bringing him to such desperation that he would visit this wretched mountain in search of treasures... *and yet you are still alive.*"

"I-I..." he trailed off, his mouth fidgeting.

"There ain't no need to make a fuss," Henic said. Everyone turned to face him. "I relinquish my title as second-in-command."

Conrad's stomach sank. *Not good,* he thought.

Brice's face lit back up and he smiled. "That's right! It is only reasonable that he would step down, considerin' the evidence! We can't forget about that!"

"But the evidence is weak," Conrad replied.

"It's quite alright," Henic said, waving him off. He looked back to the staring crowd. "I understand if the lot of you don't trust me. Even *I'm* not sure if I trust me, right now." He laughed, but no one joined in with him.

"He must be banished into the mines, now!" one of the hooligans said.

Henic shook his head. "I ain't suited to be a leader, so I have no problem steppin' down. But I'll tell ye now: I ain't goin' back into those mines alone. But since I've lost yer trust, I know I can't stay out here with you all, either. So, I think it'd be best if I stayed in me tent, fer now."

All in the group stared back at him, but nobody complained. Henic walked away. Conrad had wanted to interject but bit his tongue. Control of the team was slowly slipping away from him. He was sure, now, that someone was sabotaging them. However, he wouldn't be able to figure anything out by continuing to argue for Henic, as much as the situation bothered him.

"In the meantime, I will continue my investigation. I have more tents to search," Conrad said.

After coming up short in a few other tents, Conrad entered Peter's quarters. It was messy inside, which made the search take a little longer than the others, but eventually, he found something concerning: A bloodied shirt. It wasn't a lot of blood, but it was enough to seem like spatter from an attack. He decided it would be best to confront him directly on the issue.

"Peter!" he called out from the tent flap.

"What?" Peter asked, grumpily.

"Can I see you over here for a moment?"

Peter walked over to his tent and said, "Yes, what is it?"

"Can you explain *this*?" He held out the bloodstained shirt.

"Oh… erm…"

"Because this looks like evidence to me," Conrad said.

"I can explain. I cut my finger yesterday, alright? I used that old shirt to stop the bleedin'," Peter said in a defensive tone as he held out his hand. Conrad studied it for a moment. The scab on his finger was a dark red; almost certainly recent.

"And how do I know that you weren't cut in a confrontation with Solomon or Cyriack?" Conrad asked.

Peter let out an exasperated sigh and said, "Come, now! Ye truly think that's the only wound I woulda gotten? Solomon is a former military man; may I remind you? There ain't no way he'd go down so easily. I'd have wounds all over my body!"

"We know that Solomon was not of sound mind last night…"

"So, he'd just up and let anyone kill 'im without a fight? I'm startin' to think you need yer head examined, son!" the grumpy miner shot back.

Conrad sighed. Peter was among the most difficult to work with. He would always complain and could never seem to keep his mouth shut. Then, his eyes widened as a thought occurred to him: A blabbermouth like Peter could never keep quiet about *anything* he did; and for that reason, he now suspected him a little less.

"I'll believe your story for now," Conrad said as he lifted the tent flap. "But don't go too far. I may have more questions for you later." Peter scowled back at him.

The strategist next made his way to William's tent. It was the opposite of Peter's: Everything was neat and put together meticulously. It was almost as if no one had been staying there. Conrad felt bad going through his things. It was as if he'd ruined something perfect. However, as he rummaged through clothes, he noticed something: A pile of dark material. Conrad's eyes widened and he rushed out of the tent to call William over.

"William!"

The gangly man looked over his shoulder and smiled. "Yes, sir?"

"Could I have a word?" he asked. William nodded and then strode over. It was funny to Conrad; in nearly every way, William was the opposite of Peter. He never complained and was always cheerful. Even though he had found some evidence, his pleasant demeanor had almost disarmed him.

"Helloooo, Conrad! What seems to be the issue?" William asked in an upbeat tone.

"I've found something in your tent that is concerning…" Conrad said. William's eyebrows raised in unison. "You told me earlier that all of your black gold was stolen by Wolfgang and his crew, didn't you?"

"That's right," he said.

"Why then did I find black gold wrapped up in your clothes?"

"I'm sure there must be some mistake," William replied with a chuckle.

"No, I'm certain that I saw black gold in your clothes. Let's have a look, shall we?" Conrad said as they walked into the tent. He unwrapped the clothes to find nothing aside from some small rocks and pebbles. "What? It can't be… I was sure…"

"Ah, you've stumbled across my rock collection, I see," William said with a smile. "I must admit that it's a guilty pleasure of mine. I don't talk about it with the others because they think the whole thing is silly, but… it's a hobby, I suppose. I've been collecting 'em since I was a child."

"But I was sure of it…"

"I can see why you'd confuse 'em. Ore is kinda like rock, is it not?" William said as he put a hand on his shoulder. "Y'know, the loyalty you have fer your friend is admirable, but are you sure you aren't seeing what you want to see in order to prove his innocence?"

"What are you implying?" Conrad asked as he shook the gangly man's hand off his shoulder.

"Only that you should take a breather, and a long, hard look at things, my friend," William said, his cheerfulness unwavering. "Am I free to go, now?"

"Yes," Conrad said without a second thought. Was he truly seeing what he wanted to see? Should he have paid more attention to Henic? His gut told him no, but his eyes told him that there was little evidence against anyone else.

After he left William's tent, Conrad made his way up to Henic, who sat outside of his quarters.

"So, did you find anythin'?" Henic asked with some hope in his voice.

"Not much, I'm afraid," Conrad said. He could see the light in Henic's eyes die. "I found blood on one of Peter's shirts, but he claims it was from cutting one of his fingers. That seems to check out. Then, I thought I found some black gold in William's tent, but they turned out to be rocks that he had collected…"

"I see. It's not looking good for me, eh?" Henic asked as he scratched his head, nervously.

"The problem is how little evidence we have… and that small amount of evidence points to you," Conrad said, crossing his arms. "Even still, my gut tells me that something is off, here. Someone in our group isn't who they say they are. We must find a way to expose them."

"And how might we do that?" asked Henic.

"I think that we should-"

"Help!" a voice cried from off in the distance. From the distinct echo, Conrad could tell that it had come from the mines.

"The hell?" Henic asked aloud.

"Hellllp! Can anyone hear me?" the voice yelled. It sounded far down the tunnel.

"Someone from Faramond's group?" Conrad asked. He looked back to see that the other men had heard the voice, too.

"Help! Please!" the far-off voice pleaded.

"We should go in there and rescue them, whoever it is," Conrad said with a nod.

"I dunno…" Henic muttered. "I have a bad feelin'. What if that monster from last night is in there?"

"I will not force you into anything, of course, but I believe that 'keeping your head down' has not benefited you in any way while on this expedition. It's time to take action! Someone's life is on the line, and he is an ally. Why not lend me your sturdy hand, and prove to these men that you are as trustworthy as I know you are?" Conrad asked with a raised, excitedly shaking fist.

Henic sighed, and Conrad's fist dropped, along with his stomach.

"Sorry… I can't… I must return alive, regardless of reputation among our team. Besides, I ain't even sure I can be trusted! Yer probably better off goin' in there without me."

Whether it was fear or habit dictating Henic's behavior, Conrad knew there was no time to argue. He turned to face the team.

"Everyone! I'm going to investigate! It could be someone from Faramond's team!" Conrad said as he began to jog toward the mine entrance. Midway up, he cocked his head upon hearing labored breaths behind him. He looked back to see that Henic had tagged along. "What are you doing?"

"Ye were right, as always… this is the right thing to do… I'm no good to anyone sittin' in the tent… feelin' sorry for me'self… they probably don' trust me… without ye there, anyway…" Henic said between breaths. "Besides, ye shouldn't be… venturin' in all by yourself…"

Conrad smiled. "Fair enough."

He put his head down and increased his pace. Henic followed close behind as they entered the Mouth of Hell once more.

In the back of his mind, Conrad knew that he had acted rashly in leaving the others with no assigned leader or direction, but he wanted to get away from his current predicament. He faced a murder with little evidence, and that evidence pointed to a friend whom he strongly believed to be innocent. At the very least, a venture into the mines once more could take his mind off of the murders and allow him to refocus. The likelihood that they were off to rescue a member of Faramond's team made it more than worth the risk, anyhow.

"Helllllp!" the voice cried. It sounded familiar…

CHAPTER 26
SAND PIT

After a long night of catching up with Dalton, Lucia hadn't gotten much sleep. She had slept soundly after intense battles and slaying criminals over the years, yet to her amusement, a reunion with her mentor had seen her heart and mind racing too much to get a good night's rest.

She awoke and rubbed her eyes, groaning at the fiery pain in her shoulder. Its makeshift bandage was seeped in red. If the wound didn't close soon, she would risk an infection.

Dalton sat next to her with some fabric in hand.

"Allow me to put something better on your shoulder." She nodded and then he unraveled her makeshift wrapping. "While this material ain't the best, it will be an improvement over what you were using," Dalton said, now wrapping the new bandages around her arm. "How did you sustain this injury, anyway?"

"My armor…" Lucia trailed off, wincing in pain. "Did its job." She chuckled, and Dalton joined her in the laugh.

"I see. It sounds like you are lucky to still have your arm, then. Was it Wolfgang who tagged you?" Dalton asked.

"Yes. I thought that I had him, but his speed got the better of me," she replied.

He raised an eyebrow. "That doesn't sound right at all. With those long legs of yours and my techniques, *you* should be faster than *him*."

"Not all of your techniques are perfect, Dalton. I learned some new ones over the years…"

"Nonsense! All of my techniques are perfect," he boasted with a smile. "From the stories you told me last night, it sounds like you became too used to scaring your opponents into submission or fighting amateurs over in Lunery."

"Luneria."

"Right… anyhow, you got too soft after facing a bunch of incompetents with no formal training, and then you went up against someone who *did* know how to fight, and…" Dalton trailed off.

"Are you done with the lecture?" Lucia asked.

"Not quite," Dalton said as he swiped Lucia's blade from her hip. He stood and swung the sword around with great power. The whooshes were loud and the blade was but a glimmer in the fading blue lights of the cave.

"Hey! Give that back!" she said.

"And what is this sword? It's thrice as big as it needs to be!" he said.

"Claymore."

"Whatever you want to call it, it's all but useless against a trained opponent. I can see that it provides quite a bit of power, but…" he trailed off, taking a mammoth swing of the blade. "It is far too slow! Any swordsman worth a damn will never be hit by this thing!"

Lucia thought back to her previous battles. The claymore had worked back in the jungles of Maug because she frightened half of her opponents into turning themselves in, and as Dalton had said, they were untrained. She hadn't been able to hit even a giant man like Angus, and Wolfgang had dominated their fight after exposing her slow swings.

"I suppose…" she said as Dalton handed the claymore back to her. "What do you propose I do, then?"

Dalton looked upward and played with his beard. "Wait here. I have something for you." The warrior marched to the other side of the cave and grabbed a blade. He then brought it back to her. "This is a fine arming sword that I took from one of the Gold Fever-infected… he didn't need it, anyway."

Lucia stood and played with the sword. She nearly gasped at how fast it was dancing through the air. "It's light…"

She slashed the air one-handed some more. It had been a long time since she'd felt her blade move so quickly. It was euphoric, in a way; as if a weight had been lifted off of her shoulders.

"And it's nearly the same length as that claymore," he said.

"But it is a one-handed blade. It won't have the same power," she replied.

"You couldn't hit anyone worth a damn with that 'power'," Dalton said with a chuckle. "This sword is like the best of both worlds. You still have good range and power, but now you are quicker and more versatile, too. Best of all, you only need one arm to wield the blade… which is all you have to work with at the moment, I might add."

"But my claymore…"

"I will hold onto it for you. We may find some use for it down the line, but certainly not against any fast-moving or skilled enemies," Dalton said as he attached the great blade to his hip.

"Oi! Hows about ya show me a few of yer moves?" Alistair asked.

"I believe we'll be departing soon, but I'll tell you what, big fella: If we get out of here alive, I'll give you a free lesson," Dalton said.

"Ya mean it?" Alistair asked with clenched fists and a smile that filled his wide face.

"A lesson would be wasted on him. I'm not certain that even a whole year would improve his form," Lucia said with a chuckle. Alistair snorted in her direction, but he held his tongue.

"You took years to train properly too, if you remember," Dalton replied. Lucia remained quiet. He then cast eyes on Joel and smiled. "And what about you? Are you any good at fighting?" Joel sent back some hand signals, which made him chuckle. "I didn't ask if you *liked* fighting, but whether you were able to." Alistair and Lucia glanced at each other in confusion. "Interesting…"

"What did he say?" she asked.

"Not much," Dalton said as he rose to his feet. "I'm going to have a chat with Edith about our next course of action. You three should get some food and water in your stomachs." He began walking to Edith's corner of the cave.

～

AT THE CAVE'S CENTER, Baltr met Dalton and walked alongside him.

"I see you have taken an interest in those three over there," the stringy man said, laboring. He held a hand over his stomach wound and seemed to grit his teeth a little more with each step taken.

"Yes. Lucia was a student of mine, and she has made some interesting friends on her journey to us," Dalton said before smirking. "You haven't felt neglected, have you?"

"Very funny. I only wish to keep our eyes on the task at hand, you know," Baltr said with a frown. "We have been in this cave for some time, now. What is our next move?"

"That's what we're going to speak with Edith about. We took that extra day to rest, and I think it paid off. The men look to be higher spirits," he replied.

"As spirited as malnourished men can be..." Baltr said under his breath.

"I have a good feeling, my friend," Dalton said as he wrapped an arm around Baltr's bony shoulders. "Today's the day we escape these mines!"

As the duo approached Edith and Angus, she took notice and flashed a smile their way. Baltr smiled back and waved to her in a dreamy state, but Dalton knew better. After all he had heard from Lucia about Edith and Drake's wicked plan, he could be certain that there was only ill intent behind those pearly whites.

"Good morning, gentlemen. I trust you slept well?" Edith asked.

"About as well as one can sleep in a place like this," Dalton said.

"Have you thought about what I offered last night?" she asked with folded hands.

"What offer?" Baltr asked while tilting his head. He looked at Dalton with demanding eyes. "This is the first I'm hearing of any offer. You're supposed to tell me these things."

"Last night, she made the *generous* offer of taking over as leader while making me the second-in-command," Dalton said with a cheeky smile. Baltr raised an eyebrow. "I didn't tell you because the answer is obvious: No."

"Come now, Dalton. I think that I was being rather charitable. As daughter of the Mining Guild's president, I outrank you. I could take over *forcefully* if I weren't so nice, and I even offered you second-in-command, when Angus here is more than deserving himself," she said, pointing at the giant. He crossed his massive arms and cracked a smile.

"With all due respect, being the daughter of a president is meaningless in this place. I was appointed leader, and you only became one through *your* leader's death," he replied.

"You dare to hold Faramond's death over my head?" Edith said, her face turning red. She then took a deep breath, and her calm demeanor returned. "Why are you so adamant about leading, anyway? From what you described in your journal, it certainly seemed like you weren't fit to lead, nor did you wish to."

"Let's just say I've heard enough to know that your intentions are far from pure," Dalton replied, his face turning grim. "I cannot allow your agenda to kill any more of these workers."

"I see..." Edith trailed off, looking over her shoulder. "So, you've been talking to *her*, then?" She motioned toward Lucia on the other side of the cave. Dalton offered no response.

"That oversized ox-woman loves to tell stories, but I think you will find there is little substance to them. She has pointed an accusatory finger at me from the start of this trip, and it has done little aside from sowing distrust among allies," she said.

"I have known Lucia her whole life," Dalton said with a snicker. "She is many things, but a liar is not one of them." He narrowed his eyes at the blonde beauty. "Now, *you* on the other hand... you are known to lie."

"Ah, so the truth finally reveals itself!" Edith said. A sly smile came to her sharp face. "You cannot seriously be holding our little fling against me, can you?"

"Of course. You tricked me into thinking that you were available. You only chose to reveal your entanglement with Wolfgang after we had already laid together," Dalton said with a twinge of anger in his voice.

"You-what?" Baltr asked, incredulous. "Do you understand the ramifications of sleeping with Drake's daughter outside of marriage? He'll have your head!"

"Not likely. I'm sure he cares more about his public appearance than his daughter's innocence. Isn't that right, Edith?" he asked while trying to hold back laughter.

"That's right. My father doesn't care who I lay with. But I find it funny how you can act so pure in the face of my infidelity. May I remind you that you have earned quite the reputation among the ladies of Faiwell? I'd wager you go through women faster than practice swords!" Edith replied before letting out a vain chuckle.

"Say what you want about me, but your behavior is despicable. You choose these damned mines, of all places, to lay with Faramond... all while Wolfgang is nearby to see? No wonder he killed him!" Dalton said.

"Again, you hold Faramond's death over my head? You're a cruel man, Dalton," Edith said, now pouting.

"I think that's enough bickering," Angus interjected. His cool, deep voice caught everyone's attention. "It is obvious to me that we aren't going to agree on anything. I propose that for now, instead of fighting, we work together. When we get our bearings and find a way out of here, we can then settle things as needed."

"That seems reasonable to me," Baltr said. Dalton and Edith let out sighs and nodded in agreement.

"So then, have you lot scouted any possible ways out of here?" Edith asked.

"The path on our left leads to a tunnel that has collapsed," Dalton said, then pointed forward. "The tunnel ahead branches off into two paths: One of them leads to another collapsed tunnel, while the other leads to the river."

"So, our only choice is to go in a circle, then?" Edith said with frustration on her tongue.

"It seems that way. The good news is that this particular part of the stream is weak. The bad news is that riggit pods are hanging from the ceiling. I think that we could cross, but it will be dangerous," Dalton said while wringing his hands. "From what we scouted; it seems that on the other side of the river is a great landscape of sand."

"Sand? Inside of a mountain?" Angus asked, his coarse brow doing its best to raise.

"Yes… I still wonder if my eyes were deceiving me, but aside from that, it seemed to be a barren area. Hopefully, that means no more problems," Dalton said.

"That settles it, then. We'll cross the river and hope that this new path brings us back to a familiar spot in the mines," Edith said.

"Let us hope that we find an exit," Baltr said, his eyes sinking. "The previous area was nothing but dead-ends."

"Not so. One path leads back to the dratagon cave, and since it is presumably morning, they should be asleep by now. We could sneak past them and return to the entrance that way," Angus said.

"How do you know the layout of the mines to such a degree?" Dalton asked.

"The quiet one over there, Joel," Edith said, pointing to him across the cave. "Though a helpless little rodent most of the time, he has his uses. He drew an accurate map for us to read. If we follow it, we should have no problem getting out of here."

"Full of surprises..." Dalton muttered.

"Well then, I'll gather the men together and let everyone know what the plan is, moving forward," Edith said as she and Angus walked away. Before Dalton could even protest, she was gone.

"A true beauty, but rather pushy, wouldn't you say?" Baltr asked.

"You're one to talk," Dalton said with a roll of his eyes. "At least this will give us an opportunity to re-wrap those bandages." He pointed at the bloodstained wrappings on his torso.

"Ah... right..."

Edith walked to the center of the cave along with Angus and cleared her throat. "Alright, everyone! Listen well!" she called out. Some of the miners grumbled, half-awake, but she had gotten their attention.

"We'll be heading up this path soon," she said, pointing to the northern tunnel. "We will then cross the river and explore the sandy area." Some more grumbles ensued.

"What's goin' on?" one miner complained.

"I thought Dalton was leader?" another asked aloud.

"She's daughter to the Minin' Guild president. We gotta listen to her..."

"As long as me treasures stay protected..."

"I need more..."

"Yes! Give me more!"

Eventually, the voices fell silent, and everyone was left to their business. Joel, Lucia, and Alistair ate what little food they had left for breakfast while being gifted some water from the miners of the first team. They had gotten it from the plentiful river source. Dalton spent most of the time at work on Baltr's bandages, while Edith and Angus schemed in the corner.

AFTER A HALF HOUR HAD PASSED, the combined group of 35 converged in the center of the cave. Dalton, Edith, Baltr, and Angus all stood at the front, not wanting to concede their leading presence to one another. Joel and the others stood toward the middle of the pack, while Bronrar tried to get as close to Angus and Edith as possible near the front.

"Alright, everyone! I think it's about time we get moving!" Dalton said to some confused faces. By addressing the group only once, Edith had convinced them of her leadership, he thought with a snort. "Be on the lookout for anything strange, like riggits or dratagons."

With that, the group made their way up an inclined path. They formed rank much like the B-Team had when it was larger: In rows of three or four. The slope angled up more over time, and eventually, they reached a bend where they could either continue straight or bear to the left.

"There lies the collapsed tunnel," Dalton said to Edith as he pointed ahead.

The group hung a left and continued to march along for a quarter-hour before they finally reached the river, where they stopped. The blue glow of the rocks, fading in and out at a hypnotic rhythm, struck the riggit pods that hung on the ceiling. There were 10, all with deadly tongues hanging down and ready to ensnare prey.

"As expected, the riggits pods are still here. Everyone, mind the tongues!" Baltr called out.

Dalton was the first to step into the river. The stream was only about waist-high, and the current was weak enough that he could easily walk across. He looked back at the others and nodded before walking in a zigzagged pattern around the riggit tongues. The others soon followed behind him. In short order, the entire group made it across, incident-free. The riggit pods were helpless to do anything; for the river was too well lit if the miners stayed patient enough for the blue glow to fade in, and there simply weren't enough tongues to make them unavoidable.

"That was easier than I thought," Edith said.

"It's *never* that easy," Dalton quipped.

As the group walked into the largest cave yet, they found that the ground was filled with sand instead of rock. The blue lights from the river pass had dimmed, but they were still present on the walls, which seemed to round out into the ceiling; like a half-dome. The group could barely make out the other side of the cave, but it appeared to thin into another tunnel.

About halfway across, the miners spotted an all too familiar glimmer.

"Look at that! This cave's got the sparklin' treasure in it!" a miner called out.

"It's called 'black gold'," another from the group said.

"We should go get some while we're here."

"Yeah!" a few others cried in unison.

"No. We stay the course. Our priority is getting out of here," Dalton said to a chorus of groans.

"That's not true," Edith replied. Dalton glared at her, but she only smiled back in return. "Our priority is to save the village, as you may recall. And to do that, we need as much black gold as possible."

"Yeah!" many miners cried.

"The black gold has brought us nothing but pain and suffering so far. Look, I ain't saying that we can't come back and get some more, but we are barely surviving in here. We need to leave," Dalton said.

Some members of the group booed him. Baltr's face turned red and he looked about ready to speak up, but Dalton put a hand up to his chest, stilling his tongue.

"The majority have spoken," said Edith, her smile now a grin.

"Or perhaps only the noisy minority have spoken," Baltr replied. "I say we put it to a vote." However, many of the miners had already split up to go mine the walls on their left and right. "Damn it all..."

"Why are you trying to disrupt our exit?" Dalton asked Edith as he came to a stop.

"Why are *you* so selfish?" Edith asked, putting hands to her hips. "We've got a village to save, and all you can think about is your own cowardly hide?"

"Take that back, swine!" Lucia shouted while pushing through the crowd. "He has more bravery in his heart than you do treachery, and that's saying something!" Dalton covered his mouth with a hand, but a few laughs still spilled out.

"Why you-" Edith gritted her teeth. Her little nostrils flared out as a long breath passed through and she regained her composure. "Keep your oaf of a student under control, Dalton... and perhaps teach her some manners, while you're at it."

"More importantly..." Baltr said with a groan. "What do we do, now? Wait for everyone to mine? Continue on?"

"If you continue without us, I will report the lot of you as traitors to Faiwell," Edith said.

"There is little you can do now but sit and wait. Why not mine some fer yerselves?" Angus asked.

Lucia scoffed. "Do you truly believe we'd do something so stupid after learning about Gold Fever?"

"Nothing about that has been proven," Angus said.

"Says you, meat-stain!" Alistair interjected as Joel nodded emphatically. "We've had enough of yer lies."

The giant shrugged. "Believe what you wish. Yer the one missing out on the fortune of a lifetime."

"Then, why aren't *you* collecting any?" Dalton asked.

"I have an entire cart of it waiting for me in one of the caves. I believe this cave will lead us back to it."

"And besides that, as leaders, it is our duty to watch over the miners and supervise them; not mine alongside them. Faramond made that mistake," Edith said.

"The biggest mistake Faramond made was listening to a single word you said," Lucia chimed in.

Edith's eye twitched. "Shouldn't the grunts be mining while the *important* people speak?"

"They don't have to mine if they don't want to. Especially now that we know the risks," said Baltr.

"Very well… but just know that the Mining Guild will be hearing about your lack of cooperation when we return," Edith said, pouting.

"*To hell with* the Mining Guild!" Dalton said as he stomped his foot in the sand. "They sent us to this death trap, and when I return, they'll be answerin' to *me*, not the other way around." A sinister smile filled his face.

Edith and Angus remained silent and instead watched on as the men began to mine on both sides of the cave.

Alistair looked back at Bronrar. "Well? Ain't ya gonna join in with tha rest of 'em? Or have ya lined yer pockets enough?"

"Well, y'see…" Bronrar trailed off, looking away. "I don't have any more room to carry it. My carryin' sack is back in the cave from when we ran away from that monster."

"At least yer greed knows *some* limits, ya yellow-bellied knob!" the big redhead said.

"That ain't necessary. Can't we all get along?" Bronrar asked.

"We were gettin' on well enough until ya showed us that yer allegiance was to tha black gold… and a murderer!" Alistair said, now nose-to-nose with him.

"Is there a problem?" Angus asked, peering back at them.

"N-no… no problem…" Bronrar said. He walked closer to Angus until he was under his shadow.

"Don't let the small-minded damper your spirits," Angus said while placing a hand on his shoulder. "Just remember how close we are to livin' a life of luxury."

"Right…" Bronrar muttered, looking down.

As Dalton watched on, something caught his eye on the ceiling. Something had blotted out a glowing rock temporarily; and given the size of the blot, it was something big. He scanned the ceiling to see what it was, but it offered him no further clues.

"You see something?" Baltr asked.

"I think so, but I lost it…"

"Hostile?"

"What do *you* think?" Dalton asked with a smile.

"We can always hope…" Baltr trailed off. "What should we do?"

"We can only try to warn the others," Dalton said as a piercing scream filled the cave. He looked around frantically for the source. It had come from the right.

Dalton's eyes widened as he witnessed a giant centipede feasting on an unfortunate miner. The monstrous insect was about the length of a queen riggit, and its crusty, brown hide blended in well with the rocks. It had several long, sharp legs, and giant mandibles; one of which had pierced through the miner's stomach. He convulsed like a wriggling worm and a thick foam dripped from his mouth. *Poison,* Dalton thought with a shudder. The centipede tossed him in the air before swallowing his body whole.

"Monster! Everyone, run for it!" Dalton cried. The miners frenzied and the giant centipede scurried up the cave wall and onto the ceiling. He tracked its movement as it crawled around in search of its next target.

As the miners ran, many found themselves trapped in pits of sand. Edith cocked her head. It was almost as if their legs had been grabbed by a mysterious force. Some of them were dragged down into the pits, screaming for their lives.

"We have more to worry about than the centipede," Edith said, pointing the sand pits out to Angus. "Go now. Save them. We have need for them."

"What about you?" he asked.

"I shall protect her," Baltr said.

"Your wound does not inspire confidence. You can barely even stand up straight," Angus replied.

"Just go… I'll be fine," Edith said. The giant rushed off to the aid of his fellow miners.

∽

MEANWHILE, Lucia and Alistair had joined Dalton to track down the giant centipede, which had found its way to the other side of the cave. Joel had gone in the other direction to help the ensnared miners.

The centipede dropped to the ground, and as the sand cloud settled, it reared up and loomed over a frightened miner. The monstrous insect was about to strike him down, but it was interrupted when Dalton drew the great claymore and took a swing at one of its thin legs from behind. The leg was lopped clean off, and the beast hissed as green juices spurted out onto the sand.

"Mayhap this blade ain't so bad after all… against big monsters, at least," Dalton said.

The beast swiftly turned and stabbed downward with one of its many sharp legs. Dalton rolled out of the way, and clouds of sandy dust billowed up, obscuring his view. He had only just reached his feet when the disturbance of the sand cloud gave him advanced warning of a follow-up blow. Once again, he rolled, and more sand was kicked up, but a third attack never came. Through the light cloud, he caught wind of a large, bulky figure hacking away at another of the beast's legs with a mighty battle axe. The dust parted to reveal Alistair, who finished collapsing the leg with another swing. The centipede screeched while darting its other legs down in an attempt to stab the big man. Dalton chuckled. It almost looked as if it were dancing.

Meanwhile, Lucia dashed underneath the distracted centipede and held her newly acquired arming sword up into the monster's body as she ran, cutting deep into it. Buckets of green blood spilled out of the centipede, and it hissed as she emerged from beneath its body. With stunning speed, it turned around, reared like a halting horse, and came at her with one of its mandibles. She hopped back as the mandible poked a hole in the sizzling sand.

"See? The sword lets you capitalize on your speed!" Dalton said.

"Arming sword!" Lucia corrected as she avoided the mandible a second time.

The distraction was enough for Dalton and Alistair to hack off more legs from behind the beast, which threw it off balance and sent it crashing to the ground. Lucia closed in and stabbed the centipede in its head before it could retaliate. More green blood spurted out as it moaned and writhed in agony for a short time before going limp.

"Pretty smooth fighting, boys!" she said while sheathing her sword, now coated in a light green.

"Don't be so quick to sheath that fancy new blade of yours," Dalton said, pointing behind her. Several miners in the cave were entrapped in pits, and others were wrapped up by what appeared to be snakes from a distance.

~

JOEL APPROACHED A STRUGGLING miner who was sinking into a sand pit. The man shook uncontrollably, perhaps from fear, he thought. Regardless, he rushed forward to give him a hand. As he got closer, however, the mute realized that something was wrong. The miner was slack-jawed, and his eyes were unfocused. He was drooling.

"Hellllllp meh…" the miner spit out. Joel approached him with caution. "Hiallllp merh…"

He held his hand out, and as the miner reached to grab it, Joel pulled back. He had caught something out of the corner of his eye; something on the back of the miner's neck.

Joel walked around the man as he continued to sink, now about waist-deep in the sand pit. He gasped to see something sticking out of his neck. It was a long, brown worm. It appeared to have pierced the man's spine. He could see the outline of the worm wriggling under his skin, going up into his head. Joel shuddered; he had no idea what to do.

"Everyone! There are bot worms upon us! Some men have been latched onto! " a husky voice called out. Joel turned to see that it had been Angus. He was holding a lit torch up to another man's ankle. A long worm popped out and writhed on the ground as flames engulfed it. "Do not let them touch you! They can control your mind if they latch on close enough to yer head! You must burn them!"

Joel lit his torch. As fast as he could, he pressed the fire up to the worm, and it squealed to the flame's touch. It wriggled its way out of the miner's spine and onto the ground, shriveling up and burning to a crisp within moments. The man fell unconscious from the experience, so Joel wrapped his arms around him and lifted with all of his might to pop him out of the sand pit.

He dragged the unconscious miner across the cave in the hopes that he could get him to the group in the middle. However, dangers surrounded them as chaos ensued. Worms began to pop out of the sand and attack. With the extra weight, Joel knew that they were sitting ducks. Two worms sprouted up from the sand and blocked his path. They coiled like snakes, as if about to strike; when suddenly, they were set ablaze. Baltr had pressed his torch up to them from behind.

"Come with me, quickly!" he said while hoisting the unconscious miner onto one of his shoulders, and Joel did the same. "Oof! This man is heavy. How did you carry him so far on your own?" Joel only smiled in return. Soon after, they met back up with Dalton, Lucia, and Alistair in the middle of the cave.

"Everyone! Back to the center! We're-" Dalton became silent. The sand shifted and cracked as a large burrow plowed through the group of miners in the middle. He and the others turned to see a giant worm launching itself into the air; its body too long to comprehend, and wide enough to swallow a man whole.

"Shit…" he muttered as the monstrous worm burrowed into new sand.

The surviving miners gathered at the center of the cave before making a mad dash for the exit. Dalton led the panicked workers as the giant worm popped in and out of the sand behind them. Alistair began to lag, but Joel slowed his pace and began pushing him from the back, so he'd move faster.

"I wasn't meant… ta move… this fast!" the big man complained between breaths, but Joel continued to push with all of his might as they passed a few exhausted miners who had begun to slow down.

Joel looked over his shoulder to see a couple of unfortunate souls straggle behind. The worm shot up out of the sand, nearly reaching the half-dome ceiling, and swallowed them whole as it came back down and burrowed into the sand. There were no screams or commotion. Two men had simply ceased to exist. The mute put his head down and pushed Alistair even harder.

After full-on sprinting for some time, the miners finally reached the thin tunnel-like pass of the cave, and the worm gave up its chase. The burrow of sand revealed that it had turned around and left them at the cramped passage.

Baltr collapsed to the floor, gripping his stomach as he coughed and attempted to catch his breath. Everyone was exhausted; and after a quick count, four more had perished because of the giant insects. Up ahead, there was a great stone door and a rope mechanism attached to it. To the left and right of the door were fancy stone columns with ancient text inscribed on them.

"Could that be… the same door that wouldn't open from the other cave?" Dalton asked aloud. He attempted to open it by pulling on the rope, but struggle as he might, it didn't even budge. "Looks like we'll need a team effort."

After a brief rest, the group focused on opening the door. It seemed obvious what they had to do: Pull the door open with the rope, and then tie it around one of the columns to keep it propped up.

It took about a dozen of the strongest workers to pull the door upright, and as planned, Dalton tied the rope tightly around the right column. One by one, the remaining 31 miners passed through and found themselves in the same cave where Faramond had been murdered.

"Ah, I knew it!" Dalton said with child-like excitement. "Now, all we have to do is get Joel to guide us out of here."

"I'm afraid it's not that simple," Edith interjected.

"Oh? And why is that?" he asked.

"There's the matter of the black gold," she replied.

Dalton sighed, and so too did Joel. From here on, he knew that Edith was going to play to the weaknesses of the Gold Fever-infected men. He had to stop her from taking control of the group, somehow. Or was her grip over the others inevitable?

JOEL'S MAP

MT. COUTURE

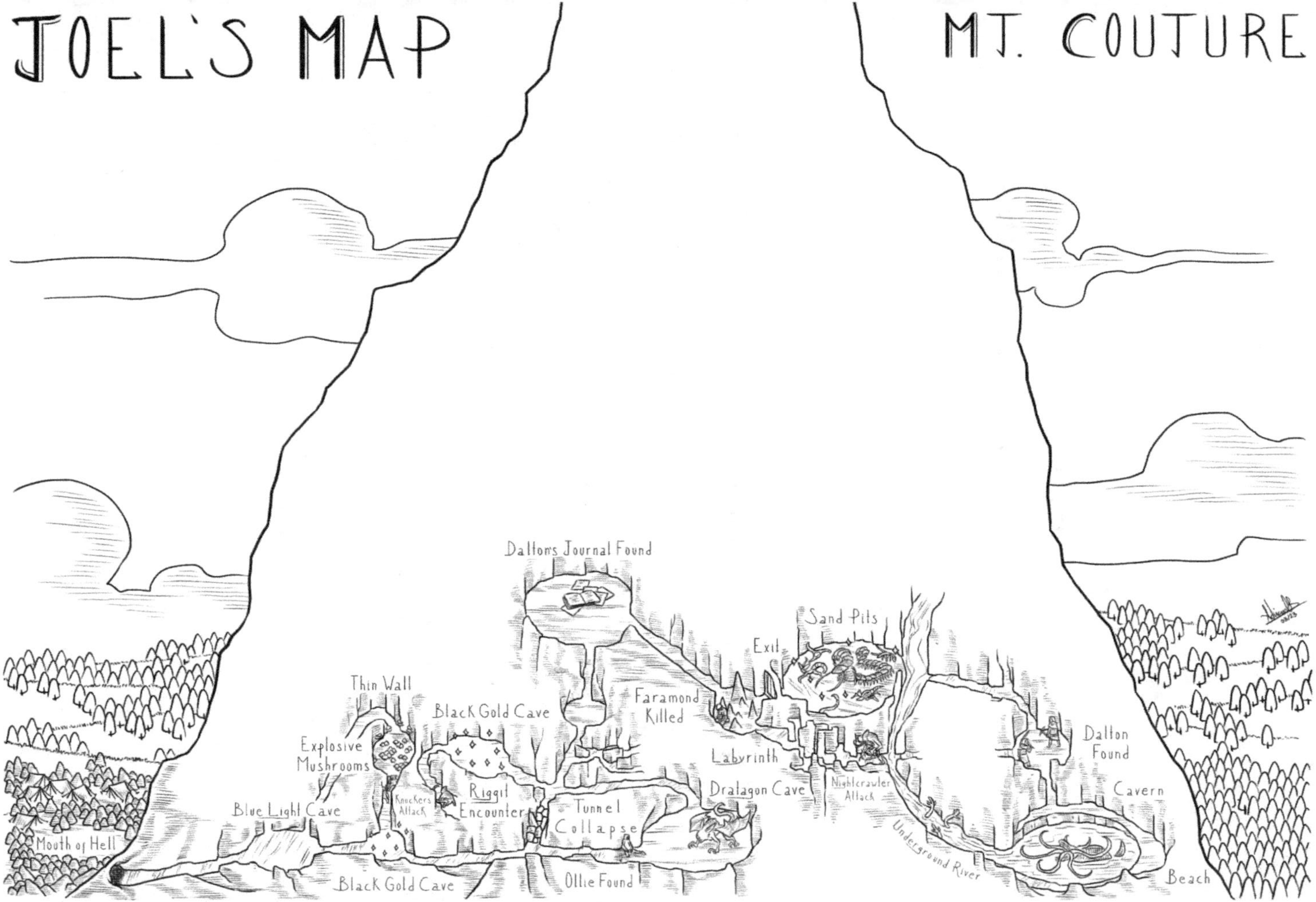

Dalton's Journal Found

Thin Wall

Explosive Mushrooms

Black Gold Cave

Faramond Killed

Blue Light Cave

Knockers Attack

Riggit Encounter

Labyrinth

Dralagon Cave

Tunnel Collapse

Mouth of Hell

Black Gold Cave

Ollie Found

Exit

Sand Pits

Nightcrawler Attack

Cavern

Dalton Found

Underground River

Beach

CHAPTER 27
WOLFGANG'S JOURNEY

On the night of Faramond's murder, a euphoria had overcome Wolfgang as Edith laid the directions out to him. *She's one of us,* he had thought. He wouldn't need to kill her after all! His smile was from ear to ear as she explained to him that there was a cave at the heart of the mountain that contained not only more black gold but an essence of the Dark Savior himself. His yellow eyes lit up with excitement as she described the Gold Pit to him. It was the best night of his life. He had killed the non-believer; the man who'd come between him and his one true love, and now he was bestowed the honor of releasing the Savior from his captivity.

"Is that understood?" Edith asked in her usual cold tone. Wolfgang nodded and turned to leave. "Oh, and Wolfy?" He turned back and looked into her piercing green eyes. "I'm afraid Faramond didn't satisfy me, so… come here…"

Wolfgang nearly howled in delight as he jumped on top of Edith, and they began to make love. Faramond's bloody corpse watched on from the rocky floor.

$$\sim$$

"Remember what you must do…" Edith said as she pushed him off of her.

"Yes… for the will of the Savior," Wolfgang said, joyously. It had been short and both had become stained in Faramond's foul blood, but it didn't matter. Never in his life had he felt so content.

Just as suddenly as he had shown up, he swiped Faramond's broadsword and then ran off. As he ran, the blond brute heard Edith do her best impression of a scream. It had only been a few moments, and he already couldn't wait to be reunited with her.

However, he had a mission to complete first, and he sprinted up the tunnel with the full intention of completing it that very night. To think, not only could he obtain even more black gold, but a chance to meet the Savior! A true honor-

Skreeeeee

The monster's screech sounded intimidating, and what was worse was that he didn't have Angus to back him up. What to do? He was trapped between a monster that may have been what Dalton had described in his journal and the people who would soon realize he had murdered their leader in cold blood. He gasped as something caught his eye on the wall to his right: The secret passage that he had discovered, earlier. It was blocked by a few well-placed rocks.

He ran to the rocks and frantically shoved them to the side.

Skreeeeeeeeee

The beast approached, but there was no time to worry. Wolfgang tossed rock after rock aside until finally, a small crawl space was revealed. He wriggled into the space like a rodent as he heard the scratches of the beast's claws against the tunnel floor nearby. He then placed some rocks up against the secret passage to camouflage his location.

Wolfgang laughed as he heard the beast's cries from down the tunnel. He scurried along the passage, barely wide enough for him to fit through, and followed it for a short time before it turned into a climb. He noticed some tiny rock stairs at his feet and cocked his head. Why would anyone craft such small stairs?

Eventually, the passage opened up into a much larger area and the incline came to an end. To his left, Wolfgang saw blue light poking through a hole in the floor. He went to inspect it and howled with laughter to find he was above the cave where Dalton's journal had been discovered. This must have been where the monster had come from, he thought. He went around the hole and found that there were two paths he could take: One to his right, which appeared more spacious, and one to his left, which seemed to shrink.

Figuring the Nightcrawler to be a large monster, Wolfgang chose the left path. This way, it would be unable to pursue him into the smaller crawlspaces. The path continued to shrink until he had to crouch to move on and to make matters more difficult, the path began a steep decline, so he was walking on his toes and crouching at the same time.

Suddenly, Wolfgang caught his foot on one of the small steps, and he tumbled down the remaining stairs until he hit a peculiar wall. It felt weak and hollow to him; something that he could chop down with relative ease. However, a great fatigue swept over the blond brute. His eyes grew heavy and his mind wandered. He couldn't wait to unleash the Savior, and yet he suddenly lacked the energy to do so. In what felt like an instant, Wolfgang's consciousness faded, his last thoughts being that he hoped he could see the Dark Savior in his dreams once more…

∼

Non-believers are everywhere
Kill them all and take your share
Man will be tamed to end the destruction
So, listen well to my instructions
Follow closely the trail of black gold
And soon you will reach the final goal
A great monolith that holds the key
To the mighty Dark Savior walking free
Kill all in your way, they are impure
You are a good man, of that I am sure

WOLFGANG AWOKE from his vivid dream, shaking with excitement. Not only had he received a direct message from the Savior, but he had also been shown where he could find the Gold Pit. *A miracle*, he thought with a hysterical cackle. A miracle had been imparted onto him.

His thoughts were interrupted, however, by the sound of high-pitched laughter. Before him were a group of tiny, bearded gnomes with sharp teeth and pinkish faces. They must have been knockers, he thought. The little creatures approached Wolfgang slowly but surely, and he drew his newly acquired broadsword in response. The knockers stopped for a moment as if to gauge his threat level, but moments later, they continued to close in.

As a scruffy knocker came within range, Wolfgang attempted a horizontal slash. He quickly realized that the space was too small for that. The blade *clanged* off the rock wall and bounced back to him. The leading knocker lunged out, teeth first. However, instead of getting to eat Wolfgang, it ate an elbow to the nose. The little creature squealed while crashing to the floor. Wolfgang then punted it back up the slope, and it crashed into the others.

Wolfgang let out a maniacal laugh as he sheathed his sword and instead drew upon the pickaxe. He began to chip away at the thin rock wall behind him, but over his shoulder, he could see that the knockers had recovered and neared him once more.

"Ye lot are gettin' on my nerves…" he muttered while continuing to swing away. It was difficult to focus on the mischievous little ones while swinging his pickaxe. He giggled nervously as sweat dripped down from his brow and into his eyes.

Eventually, another knocker leaped out, and Wolfgang was unable to react in time. It grabbed hold of his arm and then sunk its razor-sharp teeth into him. The sound of his own flesh peeling and crunching reminded him of the sound he would often hear when biting into a ripened fruit. Instead of crying out in pain, Wolfgang laughed and glared at the miserable creature with his yellow eyes. The knocker showed confusion in its glance, but it continued to gnaw on him.

With more insane howls of laughter, he slammed the knocker into the rock wall with his arm. It survived the first blow, but by the time he slammed it head-first again, the little monster released its grip and fell to the floor, lifeless. Its head was dented and blood pooled around its body as Wolfgang looked down to admire his handiwork with a smile.

"I found somethin' yer good for…" he said, staring down the next knocker in line. The little creature smiled back at him. Wolfgang swung his pickaxe in an upward, circular motion, and pierced the knocker in the stomach before it went flying in the follow-through. The little cretin hit the low ceiling of the passageway and fell to the floor along with a short rain of its blood. So damaged was the corpse that it slinked over like an accordion instead of laying out properly.

Overtaken with glee, Wolfgang wildly swung away at the knocker group in upward arcs. It was as if they'd all lined up for him.

"Everything is perfect!" he cried. "It's the perfect day to unleash the Savior on this rotten world!"

Suddenly, a sharp pain shot up his left leg, and Wolfgang looked down to see that a knocker had avoided his swings and was now gnawing on him.

"Gah! Get off me, little bugger!" Wolfgang cried as he shook his leg, frantically. While he was distracted, the other knockers swarmed him. They jumped on him and began to bite down all over his body like a colony of angry ants. Before he knew it, Wolfgang had five knockers on him at once.

In response, he grabbed one of the mischievous creatures by its head, ripped it off of him, and used its face to bash the heads of the others scattered about his body. With each collision of the head, they became dented. It only took one or two swings for the knocker in Wolfgang's hand to fall limp, and with each swing, a new knocker would fall off of him, a deformed, bloodied mess.

After he cleared all of the knockers off his body, those remaining stopped trying to swarm him. They only stared at him with hungry, primal eyes.

Wolfgang returned to his swings at the thin rock wall behind, and it wasn't long before he saw the other side. The knockers closed in slowly, but he occasionally warded them off with more vertical swings of his pickaxe in their direction. Finally, after what felt like an eternity, Wolfgang broke through the thin rock enough to climb over and out. As he climbed, he felt a tug on his leg.

"Get off me, rodent!" Wolfgang said as he felt the knocker's jaws clamp down on his leg. From his mouth came the odd mixture of a painful cry and delirious laugh. With gritted teeth, Wolfgang pushed through the pain and shook the knocker off of his leg. He tumbled to the ground on the other side.

Ignoring the blood pooling in his pant legs, Wolfgang looked around, but he was only greeted with unfamiliar darkness in a rocky tunnel. It mattered little, he thought. The path that the Savior had shown him in his dreams lay where he had just come from. But the knockers were proving to be an overwhelming force. He would need to escape from them first, and then come back later.

Wolfgang growled as a small army of knockers poured out of the hole that he had made in the wall. They ran at him with high-pitched shrieks and bared teeth. Panic set in, and the blond brute turned and sprinted down the tunnel, his bitten and bloody legs burning with each stride. After some time running, fatigue set in, and he stopped to catch his breath. He looked back and saw no knockers behind him. A weak smile came to his face. He had escaped and would return soon to-

Click

Clack

Click

Wolfgang's yellow eyes widened as he looked up. A couple of pebbles fell from the ceiling. He then noticed some holes scattered about the tunnel roof. A little pale head popped out of one. The knocker stared him down and grinned. Then, another popped out of a different hole and eyed him with malicious intent. They dropped down from the holes while shrieking with joy.

"No way…"

Drawing on a second wind, Wolfgang bolted down the tunnel once more. The *clicks, clacks,* and high-pitched laughter of the stalking knockers taunted him as he ran. He dared not look back to see how close they were.

After a short while on the run, Wolfgang found himself in familiar territory: It was the first cave that the group had encountered after entering the mines. The blond brute grinned, sure that if he made it outside, the little monsters would stop their chase; but then he felt more fatigue sweep over him. He stopped to take another breather but could hear the pitter-patter of the knockers close behind.

"Damn it all…" Wolfgang hissed. "I must get out of here. I must escape these rodents…" He gripped the hilt of his sword. "So I can meet my Savior!"

He turned and swung the broadsword with all of his might. A knocker's head flew through the air and its dark blood trickled after it like a firecracker with sparks.

Wolfgang found his swings to be slower than usual while fending off the knockers; and with each of those tired attacks, he was starting to miss more often. All he could do was push them back, but with each miss, his adversaries got a little closer.

Rather than focus on attacks, Wolfgang switched his strategy to backing up toward the tunnel on the other side of the cave. That would lead him to the mine entrance, where the knockers were unlikely to follow him.

"Ye'll never take me alive, little cretins!" Wolfgang cried as he swung his sword with little accuracy and took multiple steps back. The knockers took more steps forward and watched intently.

"Not until I've met the Savior… simpletons like ye would never understand!" he said while taking another wild swing. One of the knockers cocked its head and stopped moving. It then took a different route than the others; deciding to go around and attack from the side.

Though Wolfgang realized the attack was coming, there was little he could do. He had to focus on the greater numbers in front of him. The knocker to his side leaped out with its jaws wide open and ready to bite, but it was met by Wolfgang's fist on its nose. The little creature cried out as it dropped to the ground like a rock, but it hadn't been killed. Some of the other knockers began to adopt the same strategy.

The odd display of attack and defense continued until they reached the tunnel. Wolfgang thought to make a run for it down the path, but he had lost most of his stamina. Thanks to the thinner passageways of the tunnel, it was harder for the knockers to land a surprise attack. They began to jump at him from the front more often once again. However, just when he began to think that he was in the clear, he heard those familiar, wretched noises:

Click

Clack

Click

Pebbles fell from overhead once again, and the noises continued. Then, he heard pitter-patter behind him, but he had to keep his eyes on the knockers in front, so he didn't look back. A searing pain came to his leg and jolted up to his hunching shoulders. He snuck a downward glance to find a knocker gnawing away at the meat of his calf. With a ferocious snarl, Wolfgang bucked his leg, to which the little monster shrieked and was flung away. Then, he spun while swinging the broadsword down to slice the mischievous little creature at its chest, nearly cutting it in half. It let out its final, high-pitched cry as its dark blood painted the rocky floor.

The horde of knockers all charged Wolfgang at once. Since he knew there was no way he could cut them all down, he turned to run. However, he was jumped by more knockers that had snuck up from behind. Although he stumbled for a moment and flinched at the vile creatures that had grabbed hold of him, Wolfgang found the energy to run. He sprinted down the tunnel while trying his best to shake the knockers off of him, but it was no use. The creatures refused to let go, and the painful bites surged across his body. His head grew lighter and his breaths shorter as he ran. The blood loss was taking its toll.

Wolfgang saw a light at the end of the tunnel when something grabbed his leg and tripped him up. He crashed to the ground, along with the knockers who held on. Before he could even begin to get up, the little cretins swarmed and jumped all over him. There was little he could do besides wriggle and writhe. All at once and all over his body, bites of flesh were taken out; and rather than pain, he felt warm. It was as if his body had given up and accepted its fate. Was this how it would end? *No*, he thought. He had a duty to fulfill.

From those thoughts were born Wolfgang's final desperation; something he had never wanted to do, but there was no choice. He had to make sacrifices to complete his mission.

"Help!" he cried at the top of his lungs, gulping down the stench of rotting flesh beneath the knockers' nails and between their teeth. They began to scratch and claw at him in addition to the bites. He could sense that he didn't have long. His only hope was for someone outside to come help him.

"Hellllp! Can anyone hear me?" he called out once more. No response. "Help! Please!" he begged. Wolfgang began to hear far-off chatter, and a smile came to his bloody face. Someone had come for him, but it couldn't hurt to make it more of an urgent matter. One last time, he yelled, "Helllllp!"

Fast-moving footsteps approached from down the tunnel.

CHAPTER 28
A CHANCE MEETING

Conrad and Henic dashed down the tunnel, weapons drawn, ready to do battle with whatever they came across. Soon, a group of little cretins caught their collective eye. They frenzied around a writhing and bloody man on the unforgiving ground.

"Knockers!" cried Henic. Conrad immediately understood. Faramond had gone into explicit detail on the creatures and their vicious nature. Whoever had incurred their wrath needed immediate help.

As they reached the little monsters, Henic swung his pickaxe in an upward, arced motion. He connected with a clump of the knockers and sent them flying in a blood-soaked takeoff. Meanwhile, Conrad stabbed one in the leg with his rapier. Henic shot him a firm glare; one that took him aback.

"Those things ain't human! Ye gotta kill 'em, or they'll kill you!" he said. Conrad regained his composure and nodded. His next stab was to the head of one of the little monsters. It fell limp without any noise or commotion, but then the others took notice of the two intruders.

One leaped out at Henic, but he sidestepped the creature, and when it landed, he impaled it in the back with his pickaxe. Meanwhile, Conrad stabbed into the piles at random, slowly killing off the knockers while keeping them at bay with his superior range. As his foes fell, his view of the man on the ground became clearer, but he couldn't make out the face. The man eventually regained his strength and positioning and started throwing the knockers off of him.

Conrad's mouth fell agape upon realizing who he and Henic were rescuing: Wolfgang was bloodied and battered, but alive thanks to the interference. Soon, the knockers fell into a retreat, and Henic chased them off with his pickaxe held overhead and ready to strike.

As the farmer ran into the darkness, Conrad eyed Wolfgang, who huffed, puffed, and sniffled while struggling to sit up. His face was bloody with scratches and small bite marks, but the red made his yellow eyes stand out all the more. The strategist gripped his rapier hilt until it shook. Where were the others?

Lucia's last words to him before entering the tunnel rang in his mind: *When someone acts like they want to kill you, believe them. Show them no mercy.*

Had he just made a mistake by rescuing Wolfgang? Should he stab this monster; this sub-human; in the neck, as he had the knockers? To end the nearest and most relevant threat to him and his team? *No*, he thought. First, he needed answers.

"Goddamn cretins…" Wolfgang muttered while stumbling to his feet. His knees nearly buckled under the strain. There were holes all about his pants, and Conrad could not see a single iota of his rough, pale skin underneath. Only red. It amazed him that he was even able to stand.

"Where are the others, Wolfgang?" Conrad asked in an authoritative tone.

Click

The blond brute flinched. He looked around frantically, his mouth agape. He was panting like a dog and his eyes were wide and yellow, like egg yolks.

Clack

"Show yerselves, cowards!" he called out. Conrad took a step back and held the rapier out in his direction.

Click

Henic returned from out of the darkness and joined Conrad to witness Wolfgang yelling at nothing in complete hysteria.

"Of all the people we saved… it had to be him, eh?" Henic asked with a chuckle, but Conrad found it to be all too true. With each passing moment, he was regretting it more and more. If *this* was Wolfgang's state of mind, then what about the rest of Faramond's team?

"I don't like it either, but perhaps we can get some information out of him. With caution, of course. He doesn't seem to be of sound mind.

If he makes any moves to hurt us, then we'll have no choice but to bring him down."

Conrad motioned ahead and they took tepid steps toward Wolfgang with weapons at the ready. He shouted at the ceiling and swung his sword around at nothing but the air.

Click

Clack

"If ye won't show yerselves, then I'll expose ye myself!" Wolfgang said with a grin. He pulled out his pickaxe and began swinging away at the support beam to his left.

Throwing caution to the wind now, Conrad and Henic dashed for Wolfgang, but there wasn't enough time. The supports were even weaker than they looked, and he had already chopped one down by the time they reached him.

Henic surprised Wolfgang from behind with a bear hug. Struggle as he might, the blond brute couldn't escape his iron grip.

"Let me go, ye filthy farmin' bastard!" he cried.

Conrad pulled his rapier back and got ready to stab. But first, he wanted answers.

"Tell me what happened to Faramond and his team."

Wolfgang only laughed as he lifted his foot and then stomped down on Henic's boot. The surprise jolt of pain was all that he needed to break free, and in the process of pushing away, he turned and swung his pickaxe. The follow-through pierced Henic's stomach, and the fleshy, squishy noise was almost entirely drowned out by their surprised gasps.

Henic stood, wide-eyed and stutter-breathed, and slowly sunk to the rocky floor with his back against the wall. A tingle ran down Conrad's spine to see a streak of red following him down on the tunnel rock.

Conrad grimaced and turned to see Wolfgang gleefully swinging at a support beam across the path. He made a start for him, a fire in his gut telling him to kill, but the wooden beam snapping in half gave him pause. Pebbles and dust dropped in clumps, and they gave way to larger rocks falling from the ceiling and wall. *A cave-in*, Conrad thought. He needed to act quickly.

The strategist dragged Henic from under his shoulders as the falling rocks turned to boulders. Dust and a familiar musty smell filled the air as he coughed and closed his eyes while continuing to pull Henic with all of his might. He opened his eyes to realize that it made no difference: All light had been blotted out by the collapse; the final whimper of which occurred in the form of some bouncing rocks echoing off the walls. Conrad looked down at his second-in-command: Even in the dark, it was obvious that he bled badly from the right side of his stomach. Henic winced as he felt the wound.

After the dust settled, Conrad looked over his shoulder to see a pair of vile, yellow eyes. Wolfgang lit a torch, and the first thing that it revealed was a grin spread across his mischievous face.

Conrad lifted the rapier and pointed it in his direction. "You fool! What have you done?"

"I did what I must to release our Savior," Wolfgang said before tilting his head. "You *do* want to release him, don't you?"

"What are you talking about? Look at what you've done! Are you good for anything aside from death and destruction?" Conrad asked angrily, pointing back at Henic.

"He was in the way, and those that get in the way of his will shall perish by my hand!" Wolfgang said as he drew his sword. "And that includes ye, too…"

"You would attack the ones who came to save you? I don't understand," Conrad said. "Do you even care if you take a life? Or ruin one?" Wolfgang only chuckled in response. "Answer me!" He lunged out for a stab with the rapier. The blond brute dodged to his left while continuing to cackle.

"I'll say it again. Ye don't scare me with yer half-hearted sword stabs! When I use a weapon, I aim to kill! Ye couldn't kill a rodent with the way ye fight!" Wolfgang said as he took some steps backward. "But I'll tell ye what. This time, I'll let ye off fer savin' me from the knockers."

"Tell that to *him*." Conrad pointed at Henic, who lay on the ground, writhing and moaning in pain.

"Ol' farm-boy always did wanna keep his head down, and just like the quiet one, it's because he is weak! The weak ones will be sacrificed in the name of our Dark Savior. His days were numbered, anyway! Ye best be adjustin' yer way of thinkin', or ye'll end up just like him… or worse!" Wolfgang said before turning and running off into the darkness. Conrad took a step forward to give chase, but the coughs of Henic stilled him.

Wolfgang's laughs echoed off of the tunnel walls as he knelt to check on Henic. He was still conscious, but his eyes were only half-open and his breaths were short.

"Just had… to be him, eh?" Henic choked out between blood-riddled coughs. Conrad returned a token laugh as he examined the wound closer.

"We need to wrap this up," he said.

"Heh… what's the point? You've gotta focus on gettin' outta here. This wound will kill me," Henic said.

"You don't know that. If we stop the bleeding, there is still a chance you could make it," Conrad said before ripping off one of his sleeves. "These should help for now. If Wolfgang is still around, that means Faramond's team couldn't be far off. Perhaps they can help us." He sat Henic up, who gritted his teeth while wincing.

Conrad then wrapped his torn sleeves around Henic's torso. He felt the blood soak through them immediately, and Henic let out weak cries as he tightened them. It was little more than a temporary solution. Henic needed medical attention soon, or he wouldn't make it.

He took Henic under his shoulder and got him to his feet. His legs were wobbly, but he was able to stand with some help, at least. With one step forward, however, Henic stumbled, and Conrad had to summon all of his strength to catch him and keep him from falling.

"I hate to say it, but ye should consider leavin' me behind…" Henic choked out.

"Not a chance," Conrad said, the pressure building up in his chest. "If I hadn't been telling you to insert yourself into other people's business… if I had just stabbed Wolfgang while he wasn't looking, or while you had him restrained… then you wouldn't be-"

"There's no sense in feelin' sorry… there ain't much ye can do, and I'm only gonna slow ye down. This ain't a good place to get slowed down," he said with a few more coughs.

"I will not abandon you, and that's the end of it," Conrad said as he began to look around. It did him no good, as it was pitch-black in the tunnel thanks to the collapse. "Do you think you could hold a torch if I lit one?"

Henic nodded, and Conrad lit the torch before handing it to him. He surveyed the area to find that the collapse had taken up the height of the entire tunnel. Was there a chance that the workers outside could come to their rescue and dig them out? It didn't seem likely to Conrad, considering they hadn't even come in to help Faramond, earlier. In fact, without any sort of leadership, he worried about the outside group. Who was the dark entity? Could they escape the mountainside? Or would a mysterious storm be conjured once more?

"Oi…" Henic mumbled. "Did ye truly believe that I was innocent, out there? Or were ye only sayin' that to maintain order?"

"I believed you. There were too many other factors in play and the evidence against you was weak… it just so happened to be all we had at the time," Conrad replied. "Besides, you could hardly bring yourself to stick your nose in other people's business, let alone *kill them*."

"I see… thank you for believin' in me…" Henic trailed off as he began to slump on his feet.

"Stay with me!" Conrad said with panic in his voice. "We must find a way out of this place and get you help."

"What's the point?" Henic asked, regaining his footing. It was as if Conrad's panic had woken him up. "Every step brings me closer to my last. I would rather rest before dying than struggle."

"You embrace death too early. We can still save you," Conrad assured him. Henic shook his head.

"Could you… let me rest against the wall for a little while?" he asked. Conrad sighed. He led Henic over to the tunnel wall and leaned him up against it. "Ah… that's better…" He closed his eyes and Conrad watched on with bated breath before he heard a loud exhale through Henic's nose. He was truly only resting.

Conrad breathed a sigh of relief and took the torch from Henic. He inspected the tunnel collapse wreckage closer, and his eyes widened. Some of the rocks were *moving*. It was as if someone were trapped underneath. But how could that be possible? The strategist began to pull at and throw the manageable rocks off to the side, and eventually, a pair of arms were revealed.

All air escaped from Conrad's lungs as he stared, slack-jawed. When and how could someone have been trapped under the wreckage? Even more to his surprise was that the arms showed vigorous signs of life. They waved around as if begging for aid. He made contact with the hands to let them know that someone was there to help. However, one of the rocks that they were stuck under was a boulder.

What were the odds that someone could survive with a boulder on top of them? Despite his disbelief, Conrad began chipping away at it with his pickaxe.

With each swing, cracks in the boulder started to form. Then, those cracks turned into fissures and breaks, and the boulder crumbled. Under the rubble of the boulder, Conrad was shocked once again. He found an old man in a raggedy blue tunic, alive and well. He held his hand out, and the old man took the boost to reach his feet. Conrad cocked his head. The old man showed no sign of injury as he dusted himself off.

"H-how? How are you alive?"

"First of all, thank you for helping me outta there," the old man replied as he turned and began rummaging through the wreckage. "Second of all… ah! There's my walky-do! And the bladey-do, too!" He pulled a walking stick out of the rocks, and then a sheathed sword, which he strapped to his waist. "Erm… yes… second of all, if I told you how I'm alive right now, my dear boy, I daresay you wouldn't believe a word!" He let out a cheerful laugh.

"I wouldn't be sure of that. I've experienced many-a strange happening these past few days," Conrad said as the old man started to walk off. "Where are you going? Don't you know how dangerous this place is?" The old man stopped, but he didn't look back.

"Hold up…" Henic muttered. He struggled to get the words out. "Is that you, Aldous?"

The old man turned and squinted at the farmer.

"Henic! What are you doing here?" he asked while approaching him. "What happened to you?"

"Just a minor flesh wound!" Henic replied. He laughed, but it quickly turned into a coughing fit.

"Wait… are you the same Aldous that Joel mentioned? His caretaker?" Conrad asked.

"Why, yes. Yes, I am. Did you lot meet Joel on his journey to the mines?" Aldous asked.

"We did. He is an interesting fellow, to say the least," he replied with a smile.

"Ah, good. I trust he has been helpful? Where is the old boy, anyway? I was about to leave in search of him…" said Aldous.

"As of now, we are unsure. He accompanied a team of many others to venture further into the mines, hoping to find the first team. Henic and I, along with some other men outside, were told to stand watch of the black gold," Conrad explained.

"Black gold?" Aldous asked with a furrowed brow. "Believe me when I say you don't want to be messing about with that. In fact, it's better if you leave it here."

"Joel said the same thing, and I've suspected for some time that it was causing problems, but there is little we can do about it, now. The black gold is at the base camp outside, and now we are trapped in here," Conrad said with a frown.

"I see… that is a problem… oh yes… a big problem…" Aldous muttered as he paced back and forth. He continued in this way for some time until coming to a sudden stop, as if realizing something. "Ah! That's right! *He'll* never allow anyone to leave with it. Everything is going to be alright."

"Who won't allow us to leave with it?" Conrad asked.

"I refer, of course, to the Mountain King, m'boy!" Aldous said with a smile. Conrad raised an eyebrow. "You've never heard of him, eh? He watches over this here mining-type place."

"Could that have been the dark presence Cyriack felt? The one responsible for conjuring up those storms when we tried to leave?" Conrad asked.

"A 'dark presence', you say? No, the Mountain King is a force for good! That is why he watches over this place," Aldous said as his smile fell and his eyes sharpened. "However, I would not at all be surprised if he conjured up those storms to stop you. The black gold must *never* leave this place."

Henic coughed some more, drawing both of their eyes. Aldous walked over to him and pulled a small bottle out of the pocket of his tunic. He handed the bottle to the farmer, helping him close his shaking fingers around it.

"Drink this. You'll feel better," he said. Henic opened the bottle and drank its contents. His eyes widened as if a jolt of energy had shot through him. Henic stood without effort, eliciting a gasp from both he and Conrad.

"I'm… I'm healed?" he asked.

"I'm afraid not," Aldous said as he pointed to his wound. It still bled through the makeshift bandaging. "The drinky-do I gave you dulls the pain and energizes your body until the last breath. Unfortunately, you are still dying; it's just that your body no longer knows that."

"Oh… well, at least I feel better," Henic said.

"Indeed, but we will need to get you medical attention quickly," Aldous replied while stroking his gray beard and tapping his walking stick on the ground. "Now… how to get out of here…"

"Hold on… to dull his pain and energize him while he's on the verge of death… I have never heard of such a potent drink before. Where did you get it?" Conrad asked.

"Oh, I have my ways. I've got many do-hickeys and odds n' ends that are quite helpful," Aldous said.

"Alright, perhaps you've come across helpful potions over the years, but how was it that you were caught under the debris and uninjured? That would have killed any normal man..." Conrad said as he eyed the old man with suspicion.

"Just luck, I'm sure..." Aldous muttered, cheerfully.

"I don't believe you. Something isn't right, here. Cyriack felt a dark magic presence among us. How do I know that wasn't you? It would explain the miracles you've performed here," Conrad said as he drew his rapier.

"Oho! Let us be calm, now! I swear it; I mean you no harm," Aldous said as he held out his hands and bobbed them.

"I know Aldous, Conrad. He's a good feller," Henic interjected. "Besides, why would he save me if he had malicious intent?"

Conrad lowered his blade. "I suppose you're right, but even still; I get the feeling that we're being lied to."

"Well, I must admit that I haven't been completely honest with the two of you," Aldous said as the pair cocked their heads in unison. "But since you saved me, I feel you can be trusted with this information: I am a Wizard," he said. Henic and Conrad looked at each other and smirked. "What?" Aldous asked, snorting.

"It's just..." Henic trailed off.

"I'm not as mighty as you expected?" Aldous cut in, grumpily.

"Oh, no, no! It's not that..." Conrad said between chuckles.

"This is why I never tell anyone, y'know! People think of a Wizard as powerful; commanding; or even intimidating. They come away unimpressed when they see that I look like any other old fella," said Aldous.

"I think we can all agree that we're glad to have met a Wizard in here," Conrad said while smiling and extending a hand. "My name is Conrad. It's a pleasure to meet you."

Aldous shook his hand and said, "The pleasure's all mine, m'boy!"

"Couldn't you easily get us out of here with your magic?" Conrad asked as he withdrew his hand.

"I'm afraid it's not that simple. Magic is more complicated than most realize," Aldous said while scratching his head. "Y'see, there are many classifications. I am what you'd call an Elemental Wizard. I can only influence the things around me."

"Why not 'influence' those rocks over there, so we can leave?" Conrad asked.

"I can't."

"What? Why not? Rocks are elemental, ain't they?" Henic asked.

"It's true that an Elemental Wizard *could* possibly influence rock, but not me. There are many elements, y'see, and a Wizard must learn them to their fullest extent if he wishes to control them," Aldous explained.

"Ah, I see now. Just because you're an Elemental Wizard, doesn't mean you can control every element. You have to learn them individually, right?" Conrad asked.

"Exactly."

"What elements can you control?" Henic asked.

"I can control lightning and water... and some amount of fire," Aldous said.

"'Some amount of fire'?" Conrad asked.

"I'm in the midst of learning it. These skills take time to learn, y'see. I know the basics of fire, but mayhap in the next 50 or so years I'll become a master," he replied with a smile.

"50 years?" Henic asked, exasperated. "Don' take this personally Aldous, my friend, but I don' think ye'll be lastin' another 50 years at yer age."

Aldous snorted and said, "Wizards do not age conventionally. Did you know that I'm over 500 years old?" Conrad and Henic could only look at each other, slack-jawed. "Yep, that's right, I'm five hundred and... er... fourteen... or was it fifteen? It's all the same, after a while. You start countin' by the hundreds!"

"Can't ye blast a lightnin' bolt into here to free us, then?" Henic asked.

"Oho! A silly thought. A bolt of lightning crashing into rock is how I got stuck here in the first place!" Aldous said. Conrad and Henic stared back at him, blankly. "I can see that you are confused. You may recall that I can control thundery things and such? Well, I reckon it was a few days ago when I became one with a lightning storm and traveled along the clouds..."

"I don't understand. How could you walk on clouds?" Conrad asked.

"Quite simple, actually. I was traveling along the clouds *as a bolt of lightning that I had become one with*," he clarified.

"Wow... how can I become a Wizard?" Henic asked.

"Oho! Funny as ever, Henic!" Aldous said before clearing his throat. "Anyhow, when Elemental Wizards master an element completely, we can become one with that very thing! I traveled in the clouds as a bolt of lightning because it made for fast travel. But then, something peculiar happened… an entity caused me to strike down as the lightning bolt at the wrong location. I ended up hitting the mountainside. So, I got stuck in the ceiling of this very tunnel when I materialized once more! I had been banging against the rocks I was trapped within, hoping one of you miners would set me free. Otherwise, I was gonna be stuck in there for a *long* time!"

"So, those clicking sounds…" Conrad trailed off.

"Yes, that was me."

"Wow… I never could'a conjured up such a story, even in me wildest dreams!" Henic said while shaking his head.

"You mentioned that 'an entity' caused you to strike down at the wrong time. Any idea what that could be?" Conrad asked.

"It all happened so quickly, but I could have sworn that it was a disruptor spell. However, to disrupt an elemental magic that I had mastery over, and while I was moving as fast as lightning, no less… that would take Dark Wizardry on a level that *very few* have ever attained. But it's difficult to be sure. Before I knew what was truly going on, I was bolting down as the lightning and hit the mountain."

"It sounds to me like you encountered the same dark presence that Cyriack had felt among our group," Conrad said.

"Cyriack, you say? Ah yes, he worked at the milly-majigger back in the village. Used to crush up the ores, didn't he? Hm…" Aldous trailed off.

"Is there something else about him?" Conrad asked.

"Well, y'see… he was one of the only men in Faiwell to figure out that I was a Wizard. I kept it a secret from all others up until now, and I never admitted the truth to him. Mayhap he was in tune with magic, even if he was unable to use it for himself," Aldous said.

"So, what he said was true? A member of our group was a Dark Wizard?" Conrad asked.

"How about I take a looksey? I can feel magic presences if they are close enough. If we are near the outside of the mines, then…" the old Wizard trailed off as he closed his eyes and held out a hand.

After a few moments, Aldous began to shake. His eyes, still shut, tried to shut even more. Beads of sweat dripped down his forehead until he finally opened his eyes. They were striking; fearful. "We must find a way out of here, immediately."

"Why? Did you feel the dark presence?" Conrad asked as Aldous began to pace.

"Yes, and it's a nasty one," he replied. "The only Dark Wizard that I know to hold such malice is…" he trailed off, then looked up. "No, it couldn't be. He's gone for good!"

Conrad's curiosity grew to the heights of Mt. Couture's peak. "Who? Who are you talking about?"

"You're an inquisitive one, aren't you?" Aldous said as he let out a nervous chuckle. "They called him Wilhelm the Oppressor. He was the most powerful Dark Wizard to have ever lived; that I know of, anyhow. Over a thousand years ago, he was a high-ranking member of the Wizard's Council, but he began to exhibit, shall we say, questionable behavior? In those times, he was eventually found to be practicing dark magic; bringing death, destruction, and misery to all those who stood in his way. In particular, he developed a taste for enslaving and controlling men."

"So, what then? Did this Council of Wizards stop him?" Henic asked.

"Naturally, there was a great battle that resulted in Wilhelm's death and many other great Wizards, but it was far from the end. Y'see, a Wizard normally cannot die from natural human causes like aging, but they can die from combat or inflicted damage. Even so, Wilhelm was discovered no less than 50 years after his death to be alive and well, oppressing more innocent people," Aldous said.

"How could such a foe be defeated?" Conrad asked.

"The cycle of death and destruction continued for over a thousand more years, as it so happened! Wilhelm the Oppressor would rise up in one form or another, terrorizing another innocent nation and bending them to his will. The Wizard's Council would then declare war on, and kill him, over and over in many bloody and destructive battles… that was, until a few hundred years ago," Aldous said as a smile cracked on his wrinkled face.

"The newest leader of the Council at the time, Zequim, had sought not to kill Wilhelm, but imprison him permanently. Many great Wizards had died at the hands of those bloody battles, after all, and he wanted it to end. Tell me, have you two ever heard of The Great Chasm?" he asked. Henic and Conrad shook their heads.

"The Great Chasm is a fissure in the ground that appears bottomless. These days, I believe it lies somewhere between the Land of the Bird and Federland," the old Wizard mused. "I ain't sure, as I am aware of a territory dispute between man and the avian in that area. But y'see, we Wizards don't like to involve ourselves in such conflicts."

Conrad raised an eyebrow. "Could you perhaps be referring to Raven's Ravine? I've read up on that landmark. It was the site of the final battle in the War of the Bird."

"I am unaware of a name change, but it is possible. One disadvantage to us Wizards distancing ourselves from man's conflicts is that we are not always up to date on territories and their names!" Aldous replied, chuckling as he continued to pace. "Anyhow, the Great Chasm is an oddity in this world. It doesn't follow the rules that we all know. Falling down there is said *not* to kill you. Instead, you live on in excruciating pain, without food or water. There is a presence there that keeps you alive without these mortal needs."

"I believe it was around 300 years ago, now. Zequim and the other high-ranking Wizards fought and defeated Wilhelm once again, but this time they didn't kill him. This time, they cast him into the Great Chasm, where he would not be able to die and resurrect himself. Most importantly, however, magic is completely nullified in the chasm, so he would be powerless and unable to escape."

"Without the use of magic or being able to die, it does seem like escape would have been impossible," Conrad said.

"Indeed, which is why the strong dark presence outside troubles me. Could this be the return of the Oppressor? Or a new evil?" Aldous asked aloud as he looked toward the rubble. "Either way, I do not doubt that they are among your group. I can feel it, just outside of here."

"Do you remember what this Oppressor looked like, by chance?" Conrad asked.

"One of the many reasons he was difficult to defeat was his ability to take different forms and identities. Every time he would return from the dead, he looked different and had a new persona. He has impersonated many over the years, from king to jester, to peasant," Aldous said.

"I see... so we can only hope for the others to survive out there," Conrad said.

"Wait. If there was a Dark Wizard among us all this time, why didn't he kill us all and do what he pleased? Why the secrecy?" Henic asked.

"I am unsure, myself. As I said, it could be a new entity and not the Oppressor, but if it was him... I believe his motivation would be to hide in plain sight until recovering his powers fully. After revival from death, I've been told that it took time for him to reach full strength again. Mayhap the Great Chasm had a similar effect on him if he escaped…" Aldous said. "But enough chatting about that. We need to find a way out of here. I have an idea for how to escape if you gentlemen would care to follow along."

"Let's go," Henic said, looking at Conrad

The strategist nodded. "I am tempted to search for the others, but right now I think the priority is getting you some medical attention, Henic," Conrad said.

"If that team you mentioned has Joel by their side, they will find their way out," Aldous replied with confidence. "He is an expert mapmaker, after all."

"We witnessed that fer ourselves, now that ye mention it," Henic said with a smile. "He led us out of a maze of caves after a tunnel collapse. It was all thanks to his maps."

"Oh yes, I'm confident Joel will find his way out. It's more a question of whether the others will listen to him," Aldous said.

"I can think of at least two people in that group who will follow him," Conrad said.

"Well, I'd hope for more, but the men of Faiwell made a poor decision coming to these mines. Unfortunately, there are times where man must be taught painful lessons…" he trailed off as he began to walk. "Anyhow, my plan is to reach the upper levels of the mountain. I somewhat remember the layout of these mines from when I visited a couple hundred years ago. I should be able to get us outside, where I can control the snow to create a path for us to leave," Aldous said.

"I see," Conrad said. "Snow and ice have water in them, so it makes sense that you would be able to control those as well."

"Exactly. It will be tricky, but I'm confident that I can create a snowy passage down the mountainside," Aldous replied.

"We should be on the lookout for Wolfgang as we travel, too," Conrad said.

"Wolfgang? Who might that be?" Aldous asked.

"He did *this* to me," Henic said, pointing to his wound. "Although, you may like him. He caused the tunnel collapse that released you from yer rocky prison." He let out a laugh.

"He sounds like an unpredictable feller," Aldous said. His walking stick *thunked* on the rock with every other step he took.

"He was never a particularly good man, but I believe the black gold poisoned his mind even further. It's as if being exposed to it removed what little conscience he had before," Conrad said.

"Mhm. That is what black gold does to humans. They become single-minded in their quest for more, and eventually, they turn violent against others. The true purpose of black gold is even more insidious than that, though. So much so that I cannot discuss it with the two of you; the Council of Wizards forbids it," Aldous said as Conrad raised an eyebrow.

Disappointment overtook him. What kind of rule was that? Why couldn't he know more about the mysterious ore that had been plaguing the miners since they had found it? He began to run through ways to get Aldous talking about it again, but nothing immediately came to mind that would feel natural enough to trick a Wizard with 500 years of knowledge under his belt.

Eventually, the trio reached the first cave with the device that lit up the entire area. Henic went to light the mechanism with his torch on the left side, but Aldous held up a hand, stilling him.

"That won't be necessary. As I recall, the lighty-majigger doesn't illuminate the path we need to take," he said while pointing to the tunnel on their immediate left. It was difficult to see with only torchlight, but Conrad remembered. It had been the only tunnel *not* lit up by the mechanism, before.

"Oh… I see…" Henic muttered.

"It's a bother having such limited vision, though. Mayhap I can do something about that," Aldous said as he held his walking stick up and closed his eyes. A little ball of sparking light formed at the top of the stick and lit the area up around the old Wizard. It crackled and zapped every second or two, but remained in the shape of a ball. "Ah, that's better." Conrad and Henic looked at each other in shock.

"I thought you could only use what was around you? How did you conjure up that lightning into a ball? It's so small, too…" Conrad said.

Aldous chuckled as he looked back at the awestruck duo. "It was an odd discovery I made some time ago, but it turns out we all have a wee bit of lightning within us; so, I used some of my own," he said, but Conrad was still confused. As if the look on his face told all, Aldous continued, "You've been shocked by things besides lightning before, haven't you? By your clothes rubbing together, perhaps?"

"*That's* lightning?" Henic asked.

"Well, it's not as powerful, obviously; but yes, it is the same sort of thing. Mayhap because it's so much weaker, it could be called something else, but I don't know what I'd call it," Aldous said.

"Fascinating…" Conrad muttered. He had learned so much from Aldous in such a short time of knowing him.

"Now then, shall we get moving, gentlemen?" Aldous asked as he pointed his lit-up walking stick toward the tunnel on their left. "We've got quite a hike ahead." The old Wizard chuckled as he began to walk once more. Henic and Conrad followed close behind.

CHAPTER 29
TRAITORS

After escaping the deadly sand pits, Dalton ventured to the site of Faramond's murder, and Lucia accompanied him. He had made it known that Faramond should be brought back outside and be given a proper burial.

As the duo walked toward the cluster of rocks across the cave, they spoke of who would lead the group when all was said and done.

"We have to do something about Edith," Lucia said with a frown. "At the rate things are going, she will soon take over the group and lead us to our deaths."

"If she takes charge, then I won't be a part of it. Simple as that," Dalton said. Lucia snickered at him. "I mean it. I'm marchin' outta this hellscape as soon as we retrieve Faramond's body, and you're coming with me."

"And what of Joel and Alistair?" she asked.

"Anyone who wishes to join can come along. From what you told me about Edith and her plans, I'm sure she will try luring everyone to her side with more promises of black gold, though," Dalton said as Lucia directed him behind the rocks where Faramond had perished.

However, they were shocked to find no corpse; only a bloodied pickaxe and equally bloody sheets remained. Dalton remained silent as his heavy eyes wandered about the uneven landscape, looking for intricacies between the hypnotic blue lights, fading in and out.

"I-I don't understand…" Lucia trailed off, the horrified last expression of Faramond still fresh in her mind. "Could someone have taken his body away? Perhaps Wolfgang-"

"No, I think what's happened here is worse than that," Dalton said before sighing. "The Nightcrawler must have devoured every last morsel of his existence."

"No…" she muttered, wide-eyed. Not only had Faramond died an unceremonious death, but his body had been stripped of its right to a proper burial. "How can his soul rest, then?"

"It can't," Dalton said, focusing on the bloody pickaxe with the intensity of a hungry lion. "Wolfgang doesn't realize it yet, but he will pay a *high* price for this. He will not be thrown in jail or a dungeon. You live by the sword… you die by the sword."

"Well said." Lucia clenched her fists and smiled from ear to ear. "He won't stand a chance against you."

"Eh? Oh, no, no!" Dalton said with a chuckle. "*You* will be the one to finish him off."

"Me? But last time, I-"

"Wolfgang's a knob, and that is why he attacked Faramond when he wasn't looking! You will certainly get the better of him in sword-play," Dalton said as he poked the top of her head. "That *is* if you retained any of my training in that thick head of yours." He snickered.

"And what good did it do me when I first fought him?" she asked, rolling her eyes.

"With that oversized sword? Just surviving was impressive!"

"Claymore."

"Whatever ya wanna call it, I don't care. All I can be certain of is that I saw you out there killing a giant bug with that arming sword I lent you. Your speed and form were quite good, even with one arm. You can beat him," he said, placing a hand on her shoulder. "Besides, you can't rely on me to help you forever. Is that not the reason you ran off, to begin-"

"Dalton…"

"-with? In the end, you can have the greatest of allies, but you must be able to hold your own in battle. You should know that, having been a mercenary for some time, now."

"Erm, Dalton?"

"Ah-ah-ah," he continued, wagging a finger. "No excuses. I'm calling on you to send him to hell, where he belongs!"

"Dalton!" Lucia shouted.

"What? Can you not see that I'm in the middle of an inspiring speech?"

"My shoulder…" she said, looking down at his hand. Her injured shoulder throbbed even when grazed, let alone when under a hardened warrior's firm grip.

"Oh, erm, sorry…" he mumbled, withdrawing his hand. "Let's get back to the group, shall we?"

They began their trek back across the cave to join Joel and Alistair, who rested against a wall near the 'exit only' door.

~

"So? Where's Faramond's body?" Alistair asked.

"It's gone," Lucia said with dread on her tongue.

"Wha? What tha hell happened to it? A dead body don't just go up an' walkin' away like that, no sir!" Alistair said.

"How do you know? These mines are filled with mysterious creatures! It could be haunted by the undead, too!" Dalton said. Alistair's jaw dropped. "That's right, so keep an eye out for undead men walkin' around! I hear they go after the bigger folk, first." Laughter seeped through his trembling lips.

"At least they'll go after Angus before me, then," Alistair said.

"Quit messing around," Lucia demanded, eyeing Dalton.

"Very well… no undead, as far as I know," he replied, looking at the others with a sudden sharpness in his eyes. "I believe the Nightcrawler ate his body. It is within the creature's behavior to devour men whole, one at a time, at its own slow pace. It must have done so after you lot fled into the maze."

Joel looked down, even more saddened by Faramond's death. His fists tightened and then he began to make hand signals at Dalton. The warrior nodded a few times before signing back to him.

"It'd be nice ta know what yer sayin'!" Alistair complained.

"We have agreed that regardless of what Edith or anyone else in the group does, we are leaving this dump of a mine as soon as we're done resting," Dalton said as Joel and Lucia nodded.

"You'll get no arguments from me!" Alistair said while crossing his arms.

"It won't be as easy as leaving, though. Edith will try to make us stay," Lucia said.

"Oh yeah? And what's her scrawny arse gonna do if we don' listen?" Alistair asked with a derisive laugh.

"She will try to turn the group against us by tempting them with more black gold. Above all else, control is what she desires most," Dalton said.

Joel sighed. Conflict within the group was inevitable, he thought. The only question was whether it would come to blows. He signed over to Dalton, voicing his concerns.

"A fine point," he replied. "Edith's power-hungry ways and the black gold could prove a deadly combination for us. She may well send the whole group after us, and they'll listen, even if we *are* supposed to be allies."

Alistair smashed his fists together. "I say, 'Bring 'em on!' They can taste a big ol' piece of me trusty axe!"

Lucia groaned and narrowed eyes at him. "Don't you think anything through? No matter how skilled we might be, we would be outnumbered five-to-one."

"Bah!" The big redhead threw his hands up. "That damned black gold! Ain't there any way to reverse its effects?"

"I have no answer to that. This black gold is like a force of nature. Those who touch it are doomed to become addicted and slowly lose their minds," said Dalton. "If Edith is able to harness the Gold Fever-infected as her servants, it spells trouble for the rest of us."

"That reminds me... didn't you mention in your journal entry that the Gold Fever was overtaking you?" Lucia asked. Dalton nodded in return. "How is it that you seem perfectly fine now?"

"A good question," Baltr said as he joined the conversation from behind. "Why don't you tell them?"

Dalton rolled his eyes and said, "After much arguing with this stubborn mule..." He looked back at Baltr with a cheeky smile. "I dispensed of my black gold. You must have encountered that test in the maze, right? The one where you had to give it up?"

"Right, some of your men were left behind. They attacked us," she replied.

"We had little choice, unfortunately. They absolutely *refused* to give up their ores. Getting Dalton to give it up was difficult, but we knew the Nightcrawler was close behind, and realizing that his team was in danger snapped him out of whatever spell that cursed ore had on him," Baltr said.

"Yes, it would seem that I owe you my life two-fold, Baltr," Dalton said in a facetious tone. "So, you'll have no choice, then, but to come with us when we abandon Edith and her stupid ambitions to gather more black gold."

"Hm... is it wise to go against Lady Edith, though? That would be my only concern," Baltr said, scratching his nose.

"Balls to '*Lady Edith*'!" Dalton shot back and then threw his hands up.

"You may want to rephrase that..." Lucia muttered with narrow eyes.

Dalton let out a snorting chuckle. "Point taken." He turned his attention back to Baltr. "Now, here's *my point*: Between Edith's poor leadership, Wolfgang's murderous rampage, and that damned Night-crawler; it makes no sense for us to stay here."

Baltr let out a sigh and said, "I promised to follow you to the end, didn't I?"

"Good... now it is time to address the crowd as a whole," said Dalton. He walked out toward the center of the cave and turned to face the majority of the group, who were huddled up along the curved cave wall.

"Attention, everyone! Dalton is going to make an announcement!" Baltr boomed. The usual grumbles of the miners ensued.

"As we have witnessed over and over, these mines were not meant to be filled with roaming men in search of treasures. It is meant to be a death trap," Dalton said. To Joel's surprise, some of the workers nodded along. "For this reason, I will be leaving, along with any of you who wish to join."

"Weren't we supposed ta come back with treasures?" one miner asked

"I didn't risk my neck to come back empty-handed!" another complained.

"I ain't a coward! I won't be leavin' till I've got what's rightfully mine! More black gold!"

"Yes! We must have more!"

"More!"

"And should you choose *not* to go along with him..." Edith said as she and Angus stepped forward. The crowd simmered. "I will be staying here to lead a team that mines more of the black gold."

Dalton laughed, but it was hardly light-hearted in spirit. It was exactly as they had feared: Edith was going to try and use the Gold Fever-infected men against them.

"Oh, and in case any of you had second thoughts about following this so-called war hero out of the mines, I will be reporting back to my father who the traitors are, and who stayed to help save the village," she said, a smirk coming to her sharp face.

"Just what is that supposed ta mean?" Alistair called out.

"It's simple, oaf. If you leave before the rest of us, you are a *traitor* to Faiwell," Edith said while pounding a fist into her hand. "I'll tell my father that you deserted us, and you will *never* find work in Faiwell again."

"That's *if* you make it out of here alive," Dalton said.

"Oh, we'll make it out alive. Unlike you, Angus over here will protect the workers; isn't that right?" she asked, looking up at the giant with admiration in her eyes. He returned a firm nod.

"Is that so? Because by my count, more of your workers died in less time than mine," said Dalton with a smug smile.

"That was under Faramond's poor leadership. I worked with what I had," Edith replied.

"Hah!" Lucia's derisive laugh parted the crowd, and she stepped forward. "That's a selective memory you've got, there. Every time Faramond followed your advice, disaster came upon us! If he hadn't listened to you, more of our workers would be alive. And who knows? Maybe he would be alive too if he wasn't so smitten with you!" The crowd fell silent and Edith's face boiled red.

"Why you overgrown ox of a woman! When I return to Faiwell, my father will-"

"Will ensure that I cannot find work? Or perhaps he will get his own hands dirty and try to kill me? Neither will work, because I want no association with rats like you or your father! As a matter of fact, the first thing I'll do after escaping this place is put a blade in his throat, just as you and your lover did to Faramond," Lucia said with a grin.

Dalton tried to signal for her to stop. Her talk was beginning to scare the other miners. It didn't matter, though. Those who had Gold Fever were unlikely to listen to their pleas. Edith's promises of more black gold were all that mattered to them.

"YEAH! TELL 'EM!" Alistair called out. Joel silently cheered her on and raised a fist, but no one else joined them.

"You dare? You dare accuse me of such a heinous act? You dare threaten *my father*? What a fool you are!" Edith said before letting out a vain laugh. "Go ahead and leave, then. The other brave workers who stay behind will be heroes to the village, while you lot shall be exiled for your traitorous talk and actions!"

"Very well," Dalton said while turning to leave. "As I said, those who wish to save themselves, follow me. To the rest of you... good luck." He began to walk away.

Baltr followed his leader and whispered, "My apologies, Lady Edith," as he walked by her. She paid him no attention. Lucia was quick to follow her mentor, while Joel and Alistair began to gather their belongings.

"You oughta stay," Bronrar said as they finished packing.

"What's it to you, anyway?" Alistair asked with a snarl.

"I would hate to see you lot throw yer lives away over superstition," he replied.

"'Superstition'? Have ya gone mad, lad?"

"Do you truly believe the black gold is anythin' but helpful to our cause? Ye keep sayin' it's bad fer me, but I haven't had any problems," Bronrar argued. Joel could only let out a sigh.

"Look here, lad. I ain't got time ta argue. All I'm gonna say is that when it came ta helpin' people who saved yer ungrateful hide, ya weren't willin' ta give up yer black gold! Think about that while ya stay in this death trap with those untrustworthy maggots, Edith and Angus!" Alistair looked over at Joel and nodded. Despite conflict in the group, he was thankful that Alistair had listened to reason.

"B-but, Angus-"

"Is a murderer!" Alistair said. Joel looked at Bronrar and motioned for him to come along. The big man gasped. "You'd really trust this fella ta come with us? After he was willin' ta leave us fer dead back in that maze?" he asked. Joel nodded and smiled at the nervous miner.

"N-no... I can't..." Bronrar muttered.

"Ooooo let me guess! 'Because Angus says so', right?" Alistair said with a laugh. He turned back to Joel. "I don' know if we could trust 'im anyway, lad. Come on, let's get outta here!" He slapped Joel hard on the back as they walked off.

Joel looked back at Bronrar as he walked. Both of them seemed sad for each other, in a way. Another innocent man lost to the black gold, the mute thought to himself. Even so, he hoped that he would survive the ordeal and that they could meet again, someday. Joel was confident that Bronrar was a good man being steered in the wrong direction.

Eventually, they joined Dalton, Lucia, and Baltr across the cave. They were also surprised to find that five other workers had joined along with them. In the end, 10 miners had walked out on the group, while 21 remained to mine for more black gold.

"Good! Get outta here, ye lot of scummers!" a miner called out from behind.

"Kill the traitors!" another voice shouted.

"Buncha good-fer-nothin's!"

"I never did like 'em!"

"We need more! More black gold!"

The newly formed group of 10 hung their heads as they marched out of the cave. The miners who remained continued to jeer them, even as they entered the tunnel and left their sight.

"Whoa…" Alistair muttered, scratching his head. "I knew that Edith was a hateful bitch, but who knew our fellow workers were like that?" he asked aloud. There was no response, and as he walked, the big man's face turned a dark red under the blue lights, fading in and out.

"And fer what? Some stupid disagreement? They hate me fer not wantin' what they want? They would call me a traitor for wantin' ta leave this death trap?" he said before halting. Lucia looked back at him. "I'm gonna go back and show 'em who's boss! No one tells *me* what I am!" The big man turned and took steps back toward the cave from whence he came.

However, Lucia grabbed his shoulder, stopping him. She shook her head and motioned for him to keep going with her and the others.

"There is no use in trying to reason with them, anymore. It's the Gold Fever. Don't forget how Wolfgang turned out. Their harsh words will eventually turn to violence."

"Like I care! I'll take 'em all on!" Alistair said with a raised, shaking fist.

"But we can't bring harm to one of our own, even if their mind has become poisoned," Dalton said, looking back. Alistair turned to face him. "I, too, was suffering from the effects of Gold Fever, and was able to overcome it with some help." He nudged Baltr. "We have to believe that there is hope for them, as well."

"And what about Edith?" Lucia asked with crossed arms. "She knows exactly what she's doing, and hasn't laid a single grubby finger on the black gold herself."

"Are you suggesting we bring harm to Lady Edith?" Baltr asked, leaning in and wide-eyed.

"I would *love* to bring harm to her," she replied.

"We can worry about settling grudges later. For now, let's focus on our escape. I'm unsure of what time of day it is, but I don't want to risk missing the window for when the dratagons are asleep," Dalton said as he began to walk once more. Everyone followed in his footsteps.

Eventually, they reached the cave where Dalton's journal resided, and where the blue rocks shone brightest. Joel remembered and went off of the group's path to retrieve it in the back-right corner.

As Joel grabbed the book, he looked up to see that there was a hole in the ceiling of the cave. That must have been where the Nightcrawler had come from, he thought. He ran back over to Dalton and handed the book to him.

"Ah, this old thing!" Dalton said with both eyebrows raised. "Thank you, Joel. Hopefully, I'll live to finish my report of this hellish place." He skimmed through the pages. "So then, will you lead us back to the mine entrance? I have no idea where to go from here."

Joel nodded and made his way to the left tunnel. He then led them down a slope and passed through a small cave. The blue light of the rocks dimmed more and more as they traveled, and soon the group of 10 passed by the series of connecting tunnels and reached the intersection where the collapse had happened. As always seemed to be the case, a musty smell filled the air, but it was mixed with the faint scent of burnt rock.

"Ah, we're back at the cave-in," Dalton said while looking around. "I remember we took that tunnel over there a couple of days ago." He pointed to the right tunnel. "But in there, we were attacked by the riggits... so then, *this* tunnel is the exit?" he asked, nudging his head toward the left opening. Joel nodded with a smile, and Dalton laughed. "It was right in front of us all along!"

"There was no way you could have known that," Lucia said as she put a hand on his shoulder. "The only reason *we* even know is because we happened to come from there."

"True... so, this tunnel leads to the cave of dratagons, then?" Dalton asked. Joel nodded once again. "Alright then, everyone, listen up! These creatures have excellent hearing, and are especially sensitive to light, despite their blindness. For this reason, I will be the only torchbearer when we enter the cave. I ask that you all keep quiet. Don't say a word unless you have to."

Everyone's eyes turned to Alistair. The big man's face quickly reddened and he said, "What? I can be quiet!" No one responded and they continued to stare with great skepticism. "Ya don't believe me? I'll have ya know I'm the quietest member of me family!"

"Were you born into a family of roosters?" Lucia asked, drawing a few laughs from the others.

"See? I can be quiet..." Alistair tried to whisper, but it came out as a soft yell. The group laughed once more.

"I think it would be better if you and all the others did not utter a word while in the cave. I'll keep my big mouth shut, too," Dalton said with a smirk. "So, say what you've gotta say before we go in!" A few moments of silence went by. "Nothing? Well, I've got a lot to say. But I suppose this will do for now: Edith isn't *that* beautiful. Not enough that she can tell me what to do!" he said to some gasps in the crowd.

"What nonsense!" Baltr said with a crooked frown. "I would marry Lady Edith in a heartbeat! The only reason I didn't stay by her side was because I made you a promise."

Dalton laughed. "What? No one else? We're a buncha no-good traitors, aren't we? So, stop holdin' back! Say what you wanna say! We may never get another chance if Edith has her way!"

"You're an oaf with a big mouth..." Lucia said as she turned to Alistair, whose eyes twitched in response. "But you have an even *bigger* spirit." The big man then grinned back.

"Oh yeah? Well, yer a skilled warrior..." Alistair said as he smiled from ear to ear. Lucia raised an eyebrow. "But ya ain't as skilled as me!"

She scowled. "He said, 'Say what you want to say,' not, 'tell lies'."

"It ain't no lie, lass! I always prove me'self! We'll settle tha score when we get outta here."

"I like the sound of that."

"I don't much care fer minin'!" one of the other workers blurted out.

"I thought this expedition was stupid from tha start!" said another.

"I'm gonna be outta the job fer followin' you, Dalton! You owe me a drink!" another shouted out to several laughs.

"That cheap bastard'll give ya some water instead of a *real* drink!" a worker said to even more laughs.

"Alright, alright!" Dalton said as he held out his hands. "I told you to say what you want and now I regret it..." he trailed off. Joel was making hand signals, and they caught his eye. The warrior tilted his head. "What's that supposed to mean?"

"What did he say?" Lucia asked.

Uh-oh, Joel thought.

"Dark Savior…" Dalton muttered.

"I don't understand," she said.

"I do," Baltr chimed in. His demeanor changed to concern. "As the Gold Fever took him, Dalton had dreams of a 'Dark Savior' commanding him to collect more treasures. And he wasn't the only one to have such dreams. We had several other men mention this 'Savior' before going mad and disappearing into the mines." He turned his attention to Dalton. "What did he say about the Dark Savior?"

"He said…" Dalton hesitated as Joel silently pleaded with him not to say anything. He shook his head at the mute. "They deserve to know what they have avoided. That they made the right choice to turn down greed," he said before turning to the others.

"He told me that Edith and the others will become servants of the Dark Savior. That is the purpose of black gold: To poison our minds until we serve him," he said. Joel let out an inaudible sigh.

"Fine, but who tha hell is this Dark Savior anyway, lad? What else are ya hidin'?" Alistair asked.

Joel felt like a fool. It was exactly as Aldous had told him: If informed directly on the situation, they would want to know more and dig deeper and deeper until they got their answer; and by then, it would be too late. That was the curious nature of people, he thought. To tell them nothing at all was more powerful than any information he could give. He then remembered that by simply telling them any of these things, he was in violation of the Council of Wizards. If he managed to escape the clutches of Mt. Couture, he'd have to answer to them for sure.

Relieved that he hadn't told them *everything*, Joel decided that the best course of action was to not speak any further about what was happening, even if they were his friends. All that mattered was that they now knew the dangers of black gold.

"I don't know who the Dark Savior is, but I can tell you one thing: When you're under the influence of Gold Fever, he is *very real*," Dalton said in a grave tone. "All the more reason to never touch that black gold ever again!" he shouted to the cheers of all in the group.

"Now, let's escape this wretched place alive, shall we? Who knows, I might even buy the lot of you tosspots a pint if we make it!" he shouted to even more joyful cheers. The group marched on with hope in their hearts once more.

CHAPTER 30
A LONG CLIMB

Aldous, Conrad, and Henic trudged up an incline that felt never-ending. At first, it hadn't been bad for the trio, but over time, the burning in their legs slowed them down. After a while, they came to a fork in the road. To the left was a path that went downward, and to the right, a path that continued to ascend.

"Please tell me we're goin' left," Henic said with a huff. Aldous's nose twitched as he looked back and forth. After a lengthy silence, the farmer groaned. "Well? Where are we goin'? I'm dyin' over here, Aldous!"

"Yes, yes, I know… it's just hard to remember details from 200 years ago and such!" he replied, stroking his gray beard. "Methinks it's to the right we must go." Conrad and Henic collectively sighed.

Much to Conrad's chagrin, the path inclined even sharper in the right tunnel. The walls and ceiling seemed to close in the more they walked. It was as if they had entered the throat of some giant, rocky monster. Soon, the space became tight enough that Aldous' ball of lightning nearly touched the roof.

"Well, at least nothing has attacked us…" Conrad muttered as he took another painful step up the path.

"*Yet*," Aldous said before looking back and smiling. "The good news, my friends, is I believe this path is going to end soon."

As if in response to the old Wizard, the tunnel expanded into an open area; too small to be a cave, but too spacious to be a tunnel. A great wall of rock stood before them, and to the trio's right, they could make out a staircase from the dim lighting of Aldous' walking stick.

"The bad news is that we have more climbing to do." Aldous held up his walking stick to show that before them was not simply one wall, but many. They stacked row upon row back, each with its own stairs carved out of the rock; ascending into what seemed like an infinite darkness.

Conrad raised an eyebrow. It was almost like a vertical mine shaft or a tall building; except they were within the mountainside. Who would have carved such a structure out of the rock, and why?

"I suppose stairs are better than slopes, aren't they?" he asked aloud.

"No. Stairs are an old man's worst enemy!" Henic replied.

"Oho! How right you are! Even so, we must climb these stairs to reach an opening in the mountain where we can access the outside," Aldous said. "Keep your eyes open. There are malicious creatures that lurk about."

"You mean the knockers?" Conrad asked.

"Why yes, that's one group to watch out for! Those little buggers and their bites hurt! But when they gang up on you… they are quite deadly," he replied.

"I already had a run-in with 'em, and that's a good way to describe the lil' bastards. They killed several in my group, and they woulda killed Wolfgang too, had we not saved him…" Henic trailed off as he looked down at his makeshift bandages, seeped in red. "We shoulda let 'em eat that scum."

"Now, now…" Aldous said as he held out a hand. "It is for the best that you saved him, even if he is a vile man. It is good for the soul, my friend."

Henic grimaced. "You know how it is back in Faiwell, Aldous. They blame the farmers for their troubles first, and themselves last. Wolfgang was the worst of 'em all; the reason I preferred to keep my head down."

Conrad felt guilt strike through him like a thrusting blade. It had been he who was pushing Henic to get more involved. If not for the efforts to change his ways, would Henic have followed him into the tunnel to rescue Wolfgang? Would he be better off now? He looked down in a contemplative silence.

After some time, Aldous snorted and smiled at them. "Y'know, I've told the two of you more than any human should have knowledge of already… but I can't resist telling you one more thing: Do you know why it feels good to do nice things for people? Even when sometimes we are unsure of what we did?"

"To make ourselves feel better about any misdeeds?" Conrad suggested.

"In a way, yes. But it's even more interesting than that. Every living thing in this world is born with a soul, and they are complex. There are all kinds of workin's and thingy-majiggers to 'em that we Wizards *still* don't understand even after thousands of years of research!" he said with a loud clank of his walking stick. The buzz of the lightning ball above wavered for a moment, but soon regained its consistency. "But the one part of the soul we *do* understand is *Anima*."

"Never heard of it," Henic said before eyeing Conrad. "But you seem to know everythin'. Have you?"

"I'm afraid not. I must admit that Aldous, in this short time, has told me of many things I couldn't have even conceived of earlier today!" Conrad said with a chuckle.

"Think of Anima as a balance within your soul for all the good and bad things you have done. The more good you do, the better you feel. The worse you do, the more pain and suffering you may encounter as a result," Aldous said.

Conrad raised an eyebrow. "Hold on. There are many people out there who suffer in pain. Are you saying they deserve it because of their Anima?"

"No, not at all! Many suffer to no fault of their own. It is an unfortunate and cruel reality of the world that we live in. There will always be those who suffer as others prosper…" Aldous said as he began to pace back and forth. "But you see, Anima is more personal; more controlled. Those who consciously do good will feel good, while those who know what they're doing is wrong will feel the terrible weight of those actions."

"I see, now. It's like how a man making an honest living could very well be happier than one who backstabbed and cheated their way to the top," Conrad said.

"Exactly. And let me tell you this: A Wizard is especially at the mercy of their Anima. It determines everything, from our strength, resolve, and magic; to our knowledge, vitality, and happiness. Humans who dedicate their lives to the pursuit of knowledge and helping others may have a strong enough Anima to become a Wizard, even," he said.

"So, Wizards started off as human, but over time and by attempting to benefit mankind, rose to a new state of being?" Conrad asked.

"It is different from Wizard to Wizard, but that is how most of us came to be, yes. While Anima is a thing-a-jig that can be ignored by man at his own expense, it is *everything* to Wizards. It is a part of who we are. That is why we strive to benefit mankind, or sometimes the good deed can be something small; like helping a lost traveler," Aldous said with a warm smile.

"Alright, but what about Dark Wizards like that Wilhelm feller? How could he have become a Wizard if he was so evil?" Henic asked.

"What I described earlier was good Anima, but one can also attain *bad* Anima, and that is how Dark Wizards are made. When that point is reached, it is impossible to come back. Y'see, for magic to flow through our souls; our bodies... the Anima must be extraordinary in one way or another: Either saintly good or devilishly bad," Aldous said.

"Anything in the middle would reduce a Wizard to little more than a human. And most of us Wizards are hundreds or even thousands of years old. Without magic, we would crumble under the weight of our age. Any Dark Wizard committing to good deeds will eventually reach the Anima levels of a regular human and die. A Wizard committing bad deeds will meet the same fate, eventually."

"Whoa... this stuff is more complicated than I ever knew," Henic said.

"It's unfortunate to hear that someone too far gone in their Anima is *encouraged* to continue their evil deeds," Conrad said. "How about other magical folk like Witches and Warlocks? What is their Anima like? Or is it that people have mistaken them for Wizards?"

"Well, Witches and Warlocks *do* exist, but it is best to think of them as mages who operate outside of the Wizard's Council. Most of them use magic to their own ends, and as such, their Anima rarely grants them greatly extended life or abilities," Aldous said as he finally stopped his back-and-forth movement. "With that said, there are many different magic folks out there who use Anima in different ways. Mayhap you fellers have heard of a False Wizard before?"

"Funny you should ask. I encountered one back in the Dead Woods while we journeyed to the mountain," Conrad said. His expression fell to a frown as he remembered the horrifying abyss of its black eyes. "It tried to steal our souls."

"Yes, it needs a soul to feed on Anima. That boosts their lifespan and allows them to perform a few parlor tricks that some might call 'magic'," Aldous said with a chuckle. "Anyhow, we'd be here all day if I were to tell you how *all* of the magical folks work, so we'll leave it at this: Continue to do good deeds, my friends. It will make you feel better, and one day, if you are lucky, you shall be rewarded for it." He turned to face the first set of rock stairs. "Now, then… shall we continue?"

The trio made their way up the stairs with newfound energy. Conrad especially felt better, not only from the rest but to learn so much from Aldous. What he had been told changed nearly everything for him. In a world made up mostly of chaos, it was indeed possible to take control of your destiny, and the path was simple: Better the world and wish to understand it further. It was something he could get behind.

At the top of the stairs, the trio faced another rock wall and a set of steps to their left. They crossed a narrow path before climbing those stairs, only to face a third wall and staircase to the right after that.

"Get used to seeing this. The remainder of our journey to the outside contains many sets of stairs," Aldous said.

"Wonderful…" Henic muttered as he began to climb the third staircase.

Over and over, they did the same thing: Climb the rocky stairs and then walk over to the next set. It became much like clockwork; little more than a formality. Conrad came to miss the inclines he had decried earlier, while Henic seemed alert and on the lookout for any sort of creature who could bring them harm. It filled Conrad with relief to see that he was still full of life. After one brutal hour of stairs, it was decided that the trio would take a short break. They sat up against the rock wall and rested.

Click

Henic tilted his head up.

Clack

"Do either of you hear that?" Henic asked. "Like a clicking noise or some such thing…" he said before taking a swig of his flask. He then widened his eyes and spit the drink out. "Hold up! That's the sound of…"

Click

Clack

"Knockers," Conrad said, his tone seeped in dread.

"You two have better hearing than me, I must say. I haven't heard a thing so far, but if you are certain that knockers are about, we should get moving," Aldous said as he stood.

"Damn knockers, ruinin' mah drinkin' time..." Henic muttered.

The trio walked up a few more flights of stairs before they saw something new: Across the narrow path of the latest rock wall, a tunnel beckoned them with a steady decline into darkness.

"The knockers that we heard earlier might be coming from in there," Aldous said while squinting into the opening.

"Is it wrong that I'd rather go down there and face the knockers than climb any more of these wretched stairs?" Henic asked.

"I think I may agree with you on that one," Conrad replied with a chuckle.

"Hm... I'd say that we are past the halfway point of these staircases," said Aldous.

"Only halfway?" Henic asked while wiping the sweat from his brow.

"Ah, but I said 'past halfway' didn't I? I remember this tunnel well. Much like the two of you, I wished to take it rather than continue to climb the stairs. However, I learned a hard lesson that day: The easy path is usually the wrong one."

The trio continued past the tunnel and traveled up a new set of stairs. As they continued their slow ascent, the noises grew louder and more prominent. In addition to *clicks* and *clacks*, they sometimes heard a high-pitched laugh, a shriek, or the pitter-patter of little feet. However, it was impossible to tell where the noises were coming from due to the verticality of the shaft. Looking up revealed only rock and darkness while looking down was much the same.

"I think we're bein' followed..." Henic muttered.

"Nothing we can do but press on. Keep your eyes open for anything odd," Aldous said.

After even more flights of stairs, the group could see another oddity of the cave: A beam of light awaited them a couple of flights up. They increased their pace in excitement, and after an exhaustive run up the stairs, they came upon a hole in the shaft where the light shone through. It encompassed a small puddle on the thin path leading to the next staircase; and around that, mushrooms sprouted up from the coarse, damp soil.

"Hold up!" Henic called out. Aldous and Conrad stopped and looked back at him. "I've encountered these, too," he said and then pointed to the mushrooms. "I think these are explosive mushrooms. If we touch 'em, they'll blow us to bits!"

"Right, now I remember. That was another thing Faramond warned us about. Good eye," Conrad said.

"How odd," Aldous said while scratching his head. "I don't remember 'splodey-do's growing around these parts… certainly not this high in the mountain."

"Well, you did say it was 200 years ago when you last visited," Conrad said before taking a deep breath. "By the way, does the air feel thinner to either of you or is it only me?"

"Oho! It's a normal reaction for humans to breathe a lil' heavier up here. I'd say we're over three kilometers high by now. Be sure not to take too deep of a breath, and whatever you do, *don't* panic," Aldous said.

"This mountain sure is tall…" Henic muttered.

"The funny thing is that we aren't even halfway to the top of it yet, but luckily, we don't need to go that high. I'm not sure you humans could even breathe up there!" Aldous said with a chuckle. "Now then, shall we tread lightly, gentlemen? It would seem we have the mushrooms to deal with and some uninvited guests," he said, eyeing the path behind them. Conrad and Henic nodded and determination came to their eyes.

The trio carefully maneuvered past the puddle of explosive mushrooms and continued to make their way up the steps. After another flight, an eruption of light and fire surrounded them, and Conrad shielded his eyes as his ears rang so loudly that he worried they would bleed. Only the sound of high-pitched shrieks could bypass the ringing, but it was the narrow path at their feet and the rock wall ahead that had him worried. They shook to their very core, and another noise broke through the ringing of his ears: bouncing rocks. He unshielded his eyes and looked down to see that the ground remained intact. His gaze next turned upward to see some stray rocks hurdling at him and the others. They hopped out of the way as the rocks crashed into the path and continued their descent after bouncing off.

"The knockers are close!" Aldous shouted as his walk turned to a jog. Conrad shook the cobwebs out when he realized that he had already reached the next set of stairs.

Conrad and Henic caught up to the old Wizard and kept up with his pace. After an exhaustive run up a few more sets of stairs, another beam of light caught their collective eyes the next flight up. It came from a wall to the left.

"An exit, perhaps?" Conrad asked. He heard the pitter-patter of the knockers behind them.

"No… too soon," Aldous said.

At the top of the stairs, the beam of light blinded Conrad, and he bumped into Aldous, who had come to a sudden stop. Squinting now, he could see various puddles and explosive mushrooms laid out on the narrow path before them. There were too many, he thought. It was like a whole field that they couldn't step around.

"We've got a small problem, here…" Aldous trailed off as he pointed at the mushrooms. The scampers and scurries of the knockers echoed off the walls once more.

"I think we have *many* small problems," Henic said and then nudged his head toward the ledge of the path. One flight down, Conrad saw a couple of small, gnome-like creatures scurrying along with mischievous smiles on their pinkish faces.

"Could either of you spare me a lit torch?" Aldous asked.

"Yes, just a moment!" Conrad said as he whipped out the torch and struck his flint to make a spark. The torch came ablaze and he attempted to hand it over to him.

"No, no! Hold the torch out for me," said Aldous. Conrad did as he was told. He could hear the knockers on the stairs.

Aldous held his hand out above the flame and grunted. Conrad's eyes widened as he observed the flame transfer from his torch to the palm of the old Wizard's hand. The fire then shaped into a ball, and Aldous turned to face the explosive mushrooms.

"It would be best if the two of you stood back a bit more. All kinds of 'splosions and such are about to happen," he said with a smile. They did as they were told and watched on as he wound up and threw the fireball at the mushrooms.

The smoke trail of the flame streamed across the path as the fireball landed among the mushrooms and set off a spectacular explosion that Conrad and Henic turned away from and covered their eyes in reflex. The mighty sound made their already ringing ears ring some more, and their knees buckled under the shaking rock at their feet, bringing them to the ground. Yet still, they had the wherewithal to notice that the knockers had made it up the steps and were approaching. Aldous turned and shot a tiny bolt of lightning from his walking stick. It landed in front of the little cretins, scaring them away momentarily. It was little more than a delay tactic, as the Wizard motioned for Conrad and Henic to run with him once more.

The pair rose to their feet and followed Aldous through the now-charred path and up the next flight of stairs. However, the knockers remained close behind. They screeched and ran along with excited cries. After a few more flights of stairs, the trio came to a stop.

"I think…" Aldous muttered, panting. "We've gained some ground… on those lil' buggers."

"But for how long?" Henic asked. He was hunched over from exhaustion. His breaths were short and sounded dry.

"I'm not sure. They seem to be an energetic bunch, but at least their legs are small," Aldous said as he looked up to the next staircase. "Anyhow, we are getting close to the end of the stairs."

"That's mighty specific," Conrad said with a furrowed brow. "Does that mean the journey isn't over after the stairs?"

"Not quite, I'm afraid. But it does mean that we are near the end. There will be one more tunnel we must take. It shouldn't be too bad. Certainly easy compared to this," he said.

After what felt like an infinite number of stairs, the trio finally reached the top row. Before them was yet another rock wall, but this one didn't have stairs carved into it, signaling the end of the ascent. Tunnels flanked them on each side of the path. There was another beam of light that shone upon the ground from the ceiling. Conrad and Henic looked to Aldous for council.

"We go to the left, my friends. If memory serves, we most certainly *do not* want to face what is down the right tunnel," Aldous said.

"I don't even wanna know. Let's leave this place and be done with it!" Henic said, stepping forward. Aldous, however, blocked him. He smiled and then pointed at the explosive mushrooms, which were encased in light from the ceiling.

"Could I borrow another flame, Conrad?" he asked.

"Right." Conrad lit his torch once more. Much the same as before, Aldous held his hand over the flame and gathered it into the palm of his hand.

"We may need to make a run for it, after this," Aldous said.

"Why do you say that?" the strategist asked.

"Do you recall the sign outside of the mine entrance?" Aldous replied.

"Yes… Joel translated it for us. It said, 'Mouth of Hell: Beware the Beast'."

"Well, the aforementioned 'beast' lives down there," Aldous said and then nudged his head toward the right tunnel. "It tends to only come out at night, but if it were to be disturbed…"

"So even *you* cannot handle this beast?" Henic asked.

"Not without some water or lightning for me to use against it, no. It is quite powerful and swift, so we will need to run as fast as we can after the explosion."

Aldous wound up and threw the fireball at the mushrooms. A great explosion went off and the two men were forced to turn away from it. The ground quaked and groaned under the stress of the blast, and the heat of the inferno hit them like a slap to the face. The familiar ringing of the ears did not mask the horrifying shriek that came afterward, however.

Skreeeeeeee

"The beast has awakened! Follow me, at once!" Aldous cried. Conrad and Henic reluctantly turned around and charged through the smoke to see that Aldous awaited them by the tunnel entrance. "This way! It's the final stretch!"

Skreeeeeeeee

"That screech…" Conrad muttered between breaths as his legs tired from the inclining path.

"Ain't that the same noise we heard at the end of the first day? When we all ran outta the mines?" Henic asked.

"Indeed, and that time we all ran away while taking shelter from the rain. I'll tell you now that I don't want to meet it this time, either!" Conrad said as he increased his pace.

The trio ran for their lives, all while their legs numbed from the worsening incline. Conrad wished more than anything to stop and rest, but that horrid noise kept him from giving in:

Skreeeeeeeeeeee

Despite their best efforts to outrun it, the noise seemed to get closer and closer. Conrad felt tremors in the rock at his feet from the monster's strides behind him. They didn't have long. Just when despair started to sink in, however, he saw a light at the end of the tunnel. Desperation turned to hope, and the fatigue faded, allowing them to muscle their way to the top.

As he burst out of the tunnel, a white light enveloped Conrad. The fresh, if thin, air coursed through his nose and he had never felt so refreshed before. He smiled and snorted with excitement, only to become confused when he saw his breath in the form of a light fog.

Right, we're high up, the strategist thought as he slipped and fell in the snow at his feet. Henic did the same, but he turned it into an intentional slide. The blood from his wound trailed across the snow as he slid; a stark reminder to Conrad that his situation was still dire.

Conrad turned over and looked back to see that Aldous had stopped in front of the tunnel. He pointed his walking stick down at the snow. The wind howled and he forced his eyes shut.

SKREEEEEEEEEE

The monster appeared out of the darkness of the tunnel, charging at Aldous like a raging bull. Its massive claws scratched the rocky ground with every gallop, and its tentacles fluttered in the wind of its intense speed, exposing rows of flesh-tearing teeth. Its many solid, red eyes struck fear into Conrad's heart. He had never seen anything so horrifying in his life, and yet, he couldn't look away.

Aldous opened his eyes with a focused intensity and gripped his walking stick with both hands. He then raised it in an arced motion toward the tunnel exit. In an instant, the door-like shape of the exit was coated with ice as thick as a man was tall, and it spanned the entire height and width of the hole.

The creature stopped in its tracks right before the sheet of ice. It tilted its head and stared at Aldous, still as the night.

"D-did that stop it?" Conrad asked. His sore legs immediately seemed like less of a problem when he realized how cold it was outside. The air was also thin, just as Aldous had described. His heavy breaths made him light-headed.

"Yes… would the two of you like to see the beast?" Aldous replied. Both Conrad and Henic got up and walked over to the frozen tunnel exit. A few of the monster's eyes diverted from Aldous and focused on them.

"Ewww… so ugly…" Henic muttered.

Conrad looked the creature over. He had never seen anything quite like it. The green skin with odd red patches, the angular face with tentacles, the many red eyes, and even its bent, warped posture seemed off. Everything about the creature was *different*. It was like something out of a nightmare.

"Incredible… I've never seen or heard of anything like it," Conrad said as he held his hand out to the ice sheet. "Are there any others of its kind?"

"Not as far as I know. They didn't even bother to name it. As long as I've known it, we simply called it 'the beast'," Aldous said.

"So then, we can conclude that it is at least 200 years old," Conrad suggested as he retreated his hand from the ice wall.

"Oho! *Much* older than that. Why, I'm a spry youngster compared to the beast!"

"B-but how could that be possible? U-unless it uses magic, too?" Conrad asked as a bitterly cold gust of wind slapped him across the face. His sleeveless arms jittered, begging for a warmth that felt impossibly far away, and he was shivering, now.

"No, not magic," Aldous replied. "You two are obviously quite cold, so how's about we discuss this later?" He turned to face the monster. It had diverted all of its eyes back to him, and its thick, hunched shoulders were pulsing up and down.

"Be gone, beast!" Aldous cried while pressing his right hand against the ice. Large ice spikes shot out of the sheet and into the monster.

Aldous grimaced when the magic ice spikes shattered on impact and the beast was none the worse for wear.

"Quite durable, isn't it?" said Henic.

Skreeeeeeeeee

The creature shrieked as it pulled one of its arms back and swung its mighty claws at the thick ice sheet. The trio turned away as shavings of ice shot out at them. They turned back, and when the small cloud of shavings settled, they gasped. Three claw marks had cut through the ice in one swipe. The monster had already turned around, however, and made its way slowly down the path until it was swallowed by darkness.

"I-I can't b-believe it just let us go like that," Conrad said, his body chilled equally by both fear and cold.

"Yes, we are in quite a fortuitous situation. I observed many years ago that the beast doesn't much like the cold *or* going outside. Even though it was angered by my little attack, it would rather wait for us to return inside than come out and kill us," Aldous said. He then looked back at the freezing pair and smiled. "Now then, before we get to this business of making a path off of the mountain, it is time to get the two of you warm and comfortable. The path may take some time to make, y'see."

Conrad found a new hopefulness overcoming him. With a Wizard by their side, Henic might just make it home alive, he thought.

CHAPTER 31
DEAD-END

While traversing the long tunnel to the den of dratagons, Joel flashed back to yesterday, when they had narrowly survived the winged beasts; only to be attacked by Wolfgang and Angus. Too many innocent men had died that day, and more at the hands of those two villains than any monster the mines of Mt. Couture could throw at them. The mute was shocked about midway down the tunnel to find that the bodies of the slain remained. He had half-expected the Nightcrawler to devour their remains, just like Faramond.

"This is where it happened," Lucia said, pointing to a few of the corpses. "We were only spared because Faramond and a pursuing dratagon happened to interrupt our battles."

Dalton stopped to examine the bodies. He grimaced and turned away at first. A putrid smell came from the wounds of the deceased. After a few moments, he returned to the group with disbelief in his eyes.

"They truly killed all of these people?" Dalton asked.

"Yes," Lucia said in a solemn tone.

"What monsters! We shouldn't have left Lady Edith with that brute, then!" Baltr said.

Dalton snorted. "I'd say it's Angus who needs protection from *her*, if anything."

Lucia nodded. "She likely gave the command to kill these men."

"Anyway, are we getting close to the dratagon cave, Joel?" The mute made hand signals back to him in response. "Alright then, from what I've just been told, the cave is around the bend up ahead. So, everyone keep quiet." He looked back at Alistair.

The big man hadn't said a word since the teasing of his bombastic nature. Dalton shot him a smile and then turned forward. Joel wondered if he had been challenging Alistair to get the best results out of him. More so than his loud tendencies, it was in his nature to fight through any test head-on.

As the group of 10 made their way around the bend, Dalton came to a sudden stop. The others were unable to see why because they didn't have torches out. Only the warrior held torchlight, so as not to attract the winged monsters' attention.

However, what the majority of the group couldn't see, Dalton, Joel, and Lucia could: A dratagon stooped before them, feasting on the flesh of one of the unfortunate souls to perish the prior night. Behind it was the burnt carcass of another dratagon. It was the same one Joel and the others had to duck under last night. Dalton turned back and pressed his index finger against his lips. The group obeyed and kept quiet.

Dalton pointed his torch to the right, signaling that the tunnel wall bent around there. He walked to the wall and kept his torch pointed in that direction, and the beast continued to feast without paying him any mind. He then used his other hand to direct the group to follow behind him in a single-file manner.

One by one, at a crawl's pace, the miners walked past the dratagon while up against the tunnel wall. After exiting the tunnel and into the cave, Dalton remained and took count before proceeding onward.

Several of the group let out quiet sighs of relief and even Joel was shocked that it had gone so smoothly. Dalton peered around the cave and so did the rest of the miners. No other dratagons seemed to be lurking about, but Joel did spot those same sharp 'rocks' on the ceiling that he'd noticed yesterday. As had been predicted, the dratagons were asleep.

Dalton led the group to the center, where the light shone down from a hole in the ceiling high above. From there, the group began to follow the glowing bulbs to the exit. In short order, the miners escaped from the dratagon cave. It was a far cry from the issues they'd experienced yesterday.

"Ya see that? I CAN be quiet!" Alistair bragged once they were in the new tunnel. Other members of the group shot him a glare. "What? We're outta danger! I can talk all I want, see?"

Lucia let out an exasperated sigh and said, "Don't you *ever* shut up?"

Alistair opened his mouth for a retort, but then he and the others heard a noise:

Rrrirp

Rrrirp

Everyone in the group looked behind.

Rrrirp

Rrrirp

Rrrirp

Thud

Thud

Thud

Since they were out of the cave, other miners began to light their torches to find the source of the noises. All gasped in horror as their collective torchlights revealed the face of a dratagon, now hopping toward them.

"Run!" Dalton cried. The miners dashed away as the beast behind them shrieked. It snorted out a fireball, but the flame just missed the last worker in line, charring the rocky floor at their feet instead. The group ran at top speed until the tunnel shrank and they were confident that the dratagon had given up the chase due to its size.

Now, they were at the part of the tunnel where Ollie's corpse had been discovered. Joel decided to let Dalton know via sign language. He remembered that the warrior had agonized over his disappearance in the journal.

"Ah… so you found Ollie here…" he trailed off, almost exasperated. "And he was smiling? I don't understand."

"Indeed. This 'Gold Fever' and its effects on the mind are confusing," Baltr added. "How is it that Ollie and others ran off from the group, while others turned violent?"

"Maybe it's got somethin' ta do with their inner nature. Wolfgang's a bloody knob, so when the Gold Fever got 'im, he turned to cold-blooded murder and madness on an even greater scale," Alistair said.

"I think that I'm in agreement with the oaf, for once," Lucia said, wide-eyed.

"Ya know, just 'cause ya said somethin' nice to me once, doesn't mean ya have'ta say 10 rude things ta make up for it!" Alistair shot back. Lucia chuckled.

"What happened to Ollie's body, anyway?" Dalton asked.

"Faramond insisted that we give him a proper burial. I think that they were friends," Lucia said.

"Yeh, and he made *me* carry the smelly body!" Alistair said. Dalton darted his eyes over to the big man. "Oh, right… sorry…"

"We should continue on, then. I believe it is less than an hour's walk back to the mine exit," Dalton said. He returned to the front of the group and led them down the narrow pathway.

In short order, Dalton and his group reached the first cave, where the lighting mechanism was rigged. They entered into the final tunnel with an extra hop in their step. Everyone chattered excitedly, expecting the light at the end of the tunnel to reveal itself; but the moment never came.

Joel's stomach sank as the darkness continued to envelop them. They should have seen light by now, he thought. Had they merely lost track of time in the mines, and nightfall had already arrived? Or had something terrible happened? He grimaced as his worst fears were confirmed: Ahead of the group stood a large pile of rocks and boulders. They took up the entirety of the tunnel.

"What the hell is this?" Dalton shouted as he ran up to the tunnel collapse. "No! Not again! This Goddamn place! A deathtrap! That's what it is!" He grunted and then kicked one of the rocks.

Rather than grow angry, Joel went to investigate something that had caught his eye on the tunnel wall to his right. The other miners gathered around the wreckage and began to grumble amongst themselves.

"Now what do we do?" one miner asked aloud.

"We're gonna die in here…" moaned another.

"What about the group outside?" Lucia asked.

"What can they do? It'll take days to chip through this without water to weaken the rocks!" Baltr said.

As the others were panicking, Joel studied a streak of blood on the tunnel wall. It looked as if someone gravely injured had been up against it. Then, something on the ground nearby glimmered off of the light of his torch: a bottle. Joel immediately recognized it as one of Aldous' potions. The old Wizard had an entire collection of them back at home and tended to take one with him on trips, just in case. He couldn't be sure what exactly had happened, but Aldous had been involved in the tunnel collapse somehow, he thought. If that was the case, then he had to be in the mines somewhere; somewhere they had not yet explored.

"What's that yer lookin' at, lad?" Alistair asked. Joel held the potion bottle up for him to see. "An unmarked bottle? How odd!" he said. Joel then pointed at a distressed Dalton. "Ya got somethin' ya wanna tell 'im? Well, what're ya waitin' for? Let's go tell 'im!"

Joel and Alistair approached Dalton, who looked at them with more fire in his eyes than all of the torches in the group combined. "What is it?" Alistair swiped the bottle from Joel's hand and held it out for him to see.

"He wanted ta show you this, fer some reason…" Alistair said. Joel then made some hand signals to communicate with Dalton.

"The bottle belongs to Aldous?" he asked. His voice felt calmer with each word. "But what would he be doing here?"

Joel then led Dalton to the wall, where the blood streaked down, still fresh. The warrior looked hard at it for a few moments and then directed his torch all around as if to see if there was any more.

"Strange… so, you found the bottle over here?" he asked. Joel nodded and signed to him some more. "Finding Aldous is our only way outta here? How would he know a way out?"

It was a fair question, but one Joel couldn't answer. He had already violated the strict rules of the Wizard's Council several times on the expedition, and he worried that explaining Aldous' true abilities would break even more. However, he also realized that more than ever, it was the time for compromise. The group was nearly out of ways to leave the mines, and an explanation of Aldous' capabilities was perhaps the only way to get Dalton to go along with a search for him.

Joel signed to him once more. The warrior remained silent.

"Well? What did he say?" Alistair asked.

"Something that might save us… but I'd be going out on a real limb to believe such a story…" Dalton trailed off.

"Well, what is it? I gotta know!" Alistair begged.

"Sorry, big fella," Dalton replied with a chuckle. "But he asked that I don't repeat anything he told me." He smiled back at the mute, but then he cocked his head. "But hold on, why can't I tell them? They're going to find out anyway if what you say is true, so I might as well tell 'em now."

Joel shrugged. He thought that if he only told Dalton of Aldous' magic abilities, it would be a compromise, but in the best-case scenario, it didn't make sense to keep it a secret from the others. After all, he would need to use magic to rescue them. He sighed and then nodded at him; to give him the go-ahead in telling the group.

"Alright everyone, listen up!" Dalton called out. The frustrated workers turned to face him. "New information has come to light, which could give us some hope of escape. I have reason to believe that there is a *Wizard* in these mines." He swiped the bottle from Alistair and held it up for the others to see.

"A bottle means there's a Wizard?" one miner asked.

"Where would this Wizard be?" Baltr added.

"Seems flimsy to me," another said.

"This bottle once contained a potion and was left here. I believe that if we find the Wizard, they could help us escape," Dalton said as he looked back at Joel. He nodded in return. The group remained silent. "Now, I know it sounds a wee bit-"

"Crazy?" one of the miners interrupted.

"Stupid?" another asked to some laughs.

"Erm… yes, those things…" Dalton trailed off with narrow eyes. "But please believe me. What more do we have to lose?"

"I believe you," Lucia said as she stepped forward to join him. "And you all should, too. Don't forget that he has been looking out for us, unlike Edith."

"I *did* make a promise," Baltr said with a weak sigh. He, too, came forward.

"I ain't gonna sit 'round and rot here! I'm with ya!" Alistair said and then gave him a hard slap on the back.

One by one, the other miners joined up with Dalton. He let out a sigh of relief before looking back at Joel and whispering, "I've done my part. The rest is up to you."

Joel nodded and marched back down the tunnel. He had a good idea of which way Aldous had gone. After all, there was one tunnel the group had not yet explored, and since they had not encountered him through the various caves and tunnels passed through, he felt it likely that the old Wizard had gone down the tunnel to the left in the first cave.

In the cave with the lighting mechanism, Joel took a left and led the team toward the tunnel they had not yet explored. At the beginning of the tunnel, a loud boom struck his ears and the rock around him quaked. The mute stumbled to the floor and some pebbles and dust fell from the ceiling, but he was otherwise unharmed. He turned back to see that everyone else was also alright, despite a marked nervousness about their postures.

"Tha hell was that?" Alistair asked aloud.

"I'd say it was the explosive mushrooms, and by the sound of it, the explosion came from straight ahead," Lucia said.

"The question is, who set them off?" asked Baltr.

"I don't know, but I think we're on the right track," Dalton said and then smiled at Joel. "Shall we continue?"

The mute nodded and walked up an incline for a while until they reached a fork in the path. Joel stopped to examine the area. He had no idea which way would be best to go. He searched the ground with his torch for any further drops of blood but found nothing. Such a wound was probably patched up by now, he thought.

Dalton smiled and leaned in. "Do you know which way to go? If not, I'm a lucky guess-"

Another explosion rocked the tunnel, and the miners swayed left and right before falling and catching themselves on the walls. This time, the explosion felt as if it had come from higher up, but also directly ahead. Joel's suspicions were confirmed when he heard the clicks of rocks bouncing off of each other, again, on the path forward.

"Well, that answers that question," he said and then looked back to the others in the group. "Everyone! Be on the lookout for explosive mushrooms!"

Joel continued straight, and the incline of the path grew greater with each step. Some members of the group started to complain about a burning in their legs.

Eventually, they reached a towering vertical shaft with layered rock walls and staircases.

"Ah! Man-made stairs. It's nice to see something that is built. Haven't seen anything like that since… ugh… the labyrinth," Dalton said with disgust. "Never mind…"

The group began to walk toward the first set of stairs when a third explosion of mushrooms went off. It had come from above, but it was an oddly faint sound. However, the next noise they heard was unmistakable:

Skreeeeeee

"The Nightcrawler? But how? Isn't it daytime?" Baltr asked.

"It must have been awakened by the explosions," Dalton said.

Dalton's group of 10 had an important decision to make: Uncertainty or certain doom. The path ahead contained someone exploding the mushrooms and the Nightcrawler. Was the risk worth more deaths for something that they couldn't be sure was a Wizard? On the other hand, where else could they go if not forward? The group stopped to think the decision over.

CHAPTER 32
A MINOR INCONVENIENCE

Conrad and Henic sat in snow-made chairs around a comforting fire as wide as they were tall. Aldous had crafted a small hut made completely of snow and ice, and it did an excellent job of keeping the heat within. Even Conrad, sleeveless and freezing as he had been, barely paid the snow around him any mind.

Henic looked down at his blood-soaked mid-section and frowned. "How much longer do you think he'll be?"

"I imagine that gathering enough magic and snow to bring us down such a steep slope will take some time," Conrad replied.

"This is mad, ain't it? Wolfgang deals me a killing blow and we get rescued by a Wizard who's now tryin' to get us outta here with enough snow to fill all of Faiwell!" Henic said with a chuckle.

Conrad laughed along. "When we first began the expedition, I never once thought about Wizards, knockers, or strange creatures that could kill us instantly. We'll have some interesting stories to tell when we get home."

"About that..." Henic trailed off, his eyes once again falling to the wound in his stomach. "If I don' make it, tell my wife-" Conrad held his hand up, and he fell silent.

"No, no. None of that. You *will* make it back," he said while wringing his hands. "And Wolfgang will pay for his crimes."

"Mayhap what Aldous said about Anima was true and we make our own happiness with good deeds and living, but the other side to it is that we can't control things outside of our own power. The truth is, I was meant to die today," Henic said. "You can't break away from destiny, no matter how hard you try."

"You only say that because you think you're dying and want to make peace with it," Conrad argued.

"I *am* dyin'. The only reason it's not obvious is 'cause of the potion Aldous gave me. How long do men with holes in their stomachs last? Not long," Henic said as he touched his makeshift bandage. His fingers were drenched in red. "I know yer feelin' guilty fer encouraging me to get involved in other people's business. But this was always gonna happen, even if I continued to keep me head down. All it was gonna take was one day of sayin' the wrong thing to Wolfgang, or lookin' at him the wrong way."

"I won't let you die," Conrad said. His insistence that Henic get involved wasn't the only thing that riddled him with guilt. He had the opportunity; thrice, in fact; to strike Wolfgang down and end his murderous ways once and for all. His inaction had put Henic in this situation. "If I cannot help our team at the base camp, the least I can do is help you."

"I wonder how that lot is faring. I ain't comfortable with the idea that they are trapped down there with a killer and perhaps a Dark Wizard, too!" Henic said.

"Yes, well, we haven't had any storms, and if what Aldous said is true, that means the group hasn't tried to leave the base camp recently."

The pair remained quiet for a little while, watching the flames dance in the middle of their ice hut, and listening to the symphony of howling winds outside. Conrad, however, grew impatient. Henic appeared to have accepted his fate, but *he* could not.

"I'm going to check on Aldous," Conrad said as he stood. Henic nodded back at him and then focused his attention back on the fire.

He exited the hut and returned to the harsh cold of the mountain. To his left was the mine exit, still covered in a thick sheet of ice. The three claw marks cut clean through the sheet remained as a stark reminder of how easily the Nightcrawler could have killed them. To his right and slightly behind, there were rolling snow-covered hills and what looked to be a forest of pine trees off in the distance. The haze of the snow in the violent wind made it difficult to tell for sure. It was like a blizzard without any true snowfall. Finally, in front of him was Aldous. He stood, motionless, in front of a cliff so steep that it was more like a wall than a slope. The old Wizard had his walking stick pointed at the snowy ground with his eyes closed.

Conrad walked over to Aldous, only to realize how high up they were: He could see all the way to Faiwell and perhaps even further, if not for the clouds and mountains obscuring his view. He looked down to see the steep drop-off and felt his stomach drop along with the view. He became dizzy with a primal fear and took a step back. Yet, he couldn't help but look again.

The second time looking down, he gasped to see that they were even higher up than Grimrock Plateau, the large structure that Allie's Pass was carved into. It was an amazing sense of perspective, to see everything so vast and far away. Everything seemed small. Unfortunately, however, he couldn't see the base camp from this vantage point.

"Why, hello there, Conrad," Aldous said. He looked at him, but remained in the same position, still as a stone wall. "How can I help you?"

"Just thought I'd come to check on your progress."

"You're worried about Henic, aren't you?"

"He believes that his fate is already decided, but I still think we can save him," he replied.

"It will be a difficult task, but it is possible. If this snowy path I'm about to make works, we will need to get straight back to Faiwell. That means we will have to trek through the Dead Woods at night..." Aldous muttered.

"I know it to be a dangerous place at nightfall, but we have a Wizard on our side," Conrad said with a smile.

"Oho! Idealistic, positive, and ever curious... you remind me a bit of myself as a lad. You will soon learn to keep those expectations in check, though," Aldous said. Conrad frowned and decided to change the subject.

"So then, is that walking stick actually your staff? Wizards use staffs, don't they?"

"Some Wizards do, yes. Y'see, what we do is channel magic through what we call *artifacts*. These are objects that have held some sorta significance to us at some time of our lives," Aldous said and then looked down at his walking stick. He let out a chuckle.

"Many Wizards of the past had staffs, but that was because you don't tend to reach the level of Wizard until you are old and such. They needed those staffs to walk!" he said before laughing some more.

Conrad joined him. "As for my walky-do, it holds a special place in my heart."

"Oh? Is it different from why the other Wizards use staffs? It seems a bit shorter," Conrad said.

"Yes. In my case, it was not old age that hindered my ability to walk, but a senseless attack that crippled me. It was back when I was young and full of hope, much like you are today. My thirst for knowledge brought me to some bad places and folk who wished to do me harm simply for the way I looked and acted," Aldous said and then remained silent. The wind howled as if to replicate his memory of the dreadful attack.

"Anyhow, when I recovered from the attack, I discovered my ability to walk was hindered, and I could no longer run. At first, I hated walking and I hated my walky-do... but I then realized that it was making me miserable to feel this constant pain and hatred. In a funny way, you could say that I accidentally discovered Anima at that time. After years of hating myself and those around me, I chose to dedicate my life to learning and making the world a better place."

"And that's how you became a Wizard?" Conrad asked.

"Something like that," Aldous said with a knowing smile. "If it were *that* simple, everyone would become one. There are many things you must figure out for yourself. Most of all, everyone has their time of crisis, and when that time comes, they have two choices: Face it and then move forward, or let it influence them. I chose the former. What will your choice be, I wonder?"

"You mean to say that if Henic were to die, that would be my crisis?" Conrad asked.

"I sense a great guilt within you," Aldous said. "Have you ever felt responsible for another life before?"

"Not until I became leader of the base camp..."

"Did any of the men perish under your watch?"

"Yes... two died at the hands of an assailant sometime last night. One of them was Cyriack," he said. Aldous' eyes widened.

"I see... an underserved fate for him. I think that perhaps you are in the midst of your first great crisis."

"How so?"

"Taking responsibility for other lives is a monumental task that weighs on the soul. You have already lost two, and you may well lose a third if we're not fortunate. I can feel the guilt coursing through you.

Whatever your reasons, you should prepare yourself for the possibility of Henic's death, is all I'm saying," Aldous said.

"That sounds like giving up to me..." Conrad muttered.

"If Henic were to die, would you blame yourself?" the old Wizard asked.

"Yes. There was nothing I could do about the others, but Henic's death was preventable... it still *is* preventable. It was I who pushed him into other people's business when it was clearly not in his nature to do so," he said, his fists now shaking and his voice wavering. "He came into that tunnel with me because I guilt-tripped him into it. What's worse is that I had opportunities to kill Wolfgang beforehand. I told myself that he should be kept alive for a variety of reasons... but now, I think they were only excuses to avoid the burden of taking another life. And where did that get me? At least Wolfgang deserves death. What did Henic do to deserve this?"

"I see. It may be best for you not to think about this too much. Why not go back to the hut? You look cold," Aldous suggested. It was just then that Conrad became aware of his shivering.

"How much longer do you think it will be?" he asked.

"It's hard to say," Aldous said, closing his eyes. "I will certainly be done before nightfall. For now, though, just sit tight and get warm."

"Right... and I just now realize how rude it was of me to forget, but thank you for helping us," Conrad said with a nod.

"Oho, but of course! I'm a Wizard. It's what we do!"

Conrad made his way back to the ice hut. Inside, Henic was hunched over in his seat and his eyes were closed.

"Henic? Henic!" he cried, rushing to his side and then shaking his shoulder. Henic awoke with a start and then flashed him a grumpy look.

"What is it? I'm tryin' to nap, here..."

"Oh..." Conrad muttered before chuckling in relief. "Given your condition, I thought you were-"

"Dead?" Henic asked. The strategist remained silent. "Naw, I'm still alright. Just restin' up fer the big journey ahead. But I'll tell ye, if I'm gonna die, it'll be in a blaze of glory. Not layin' here in a hut."

"And I will be right there with you," said Conrad.

～

AFTER AN HOUR OF INTENSE CONCENTRATION, Aldous turned his gaze to the hut, and he smiled.

"Henic! Conrad! I have gathered enough magic and am about to make the path! Come out and enjoy the show, if you wish!"

The pair burst out of the hut like ravenous animals about to eat. Aldous turned and raised both arms into the air, with the walking stick in one hand. A dusting of snow swirled around him and a light gust of wind blew across the cliff.

"Erm, I don' think that's gonna be enough Aldous, my friend," Henic said.

"There," Aldous said, pointing over his shoulder. He was certain they would be amazed.

Conrad and Henic looked back to see a great tidal wave of snow traveling their way. A tremor permeated about the cliffside, and as the wall of flakes approached, it grew louder and stronger until it became like an earthquake. Soon, the snow enveloped the distant forest, and then the nearby hills.

Within a shout's distance now, Conrad and Henic's natural reaction was to turn away and shield their eyes, but then Aldous flicked his wrists and the wave of snow shot up and overhead before reaching them. The wind of such an immense event sounded even harsher than the explosive mushrooms, and it was longer lasting, Aldous thought. Still, it would be worth the brief pain in their ears. A great shadow blotted them out from the sky and the two men looked up in wonder. An immeasurably large mass of snow had gathered directly above them.

Aldous then grunted while bringing his arms down, sending the snow over the edge of the cliff. The waterfall of snow roared overhead for some time before finally, Aldous broke his concentration and stopped. He curled over and gasped for breath. Conrad and Henic made their way to the edge of the cliff. Their jaws nearly hit the ground when they saw row after row of snow-made stairs down the mountainside.

"How do you... like it?" Aldous asked between labored breaths. "I made it with snow... and ice in mind. Ice will ensure that it is sturdy, and snow will give us traction. I don't know about you two, but I don't wanna slip 'n fall off the mountain!" he said with a laugh. Conrad and Henic remained silent. They only stared back at him in apparent wonder. "Well, then... there is no time to waste. Shall we depart?"

"Right, we have little time. How are you feeling, Henic?" Conrad asked.

"I still feel alright, but the wound ain't slowin' down," he said while looking down at his stomach.

"I'll lead the way," Aldous said as he took his first step down the stairs. "See? Nice 'n sturdy."

Conrad and Henic followed the old Wizard down the first few steps until an unsettling noise stopped the trio in their tracks: A great crack of thunder pierced their ears and vibrated through their bodies before shaking the stairs at their feet.

"It couldn't be…" Aldous muttered.

Dark clouds swiftly formed above them. The rain came soon after and then followed more claps of thunder. Then, finally, bolts of lightning streaked down into the mountainside like spears breaking the surface of icy water. The trio resumed walking down the stairs, this time at a brisker pace.

"What's going on? Is this the work of the Mountain King?" Conrad asked as he fought against the high winds and rain.

"Yes, only he could conjure up a storm so quickly. But I don't understand… he knows me! We are allies; both a part of the Wizard's Council," Aldous said as another bolt of lightning streaked down, narrowly missing them and the staircase. Once again, they stopped.

"Well, whatever the hell is goin' on, I think we should go back up to the mountain 'till this passes," Henic said.

"There's no time!" Conrad replied. "It's not like he can bring the stairs down, can he?" As if to answer his question, the rain intensified and the wind doubled its speed while howling at them. Aldous flashed him a frown that told the whole story: It would be dangerous to stay on these stairs.

The trio turned around and began to run back up. They had only gone down one flight, but the return trip proved a longer and more perilous task against the raging storm. Making matters worse, the rain froze, and little balls of hail struck them often. Conrad and Henic shielded their faces to protect themselves, but Aldous was focused entirely on the sky.

Sensing a change in the thundercloud above, Aldous stopped in his tracks. His keen eye spotted the start of a lightning discharge, and so he held his walking stick up in response. As Conrad and Henic stopped behind him, the lightning bolt struck down upon them and they were enveloped in light and crackles. Aldous gritted his teeth as the walking stick glowed brightly in his hands, sparks bouncing around his body. He had been able to absorb the entire bolt, but after using up so much magic to make the snow stairs, he couldn't withstand the sudden load for long. He shot it out of his walking stick and into the sheer cliff, where it dispersed into a puff of vapor. The old Wizard let out a sigh, as if he'd just pulled a nagging splinter out of his finger.

"Hurry! Before another one comes down!" Aldous shouted, now bolting up the stairs. The two men followed close behind.

After they reached the cliff top, the trio looked back to see what seemed to be dozens of lightning bolts striking the snow stairs in succession. Never before had even Aldous seen such a thing. The heat from the lightning melted the stairs' core and caused them to become unstable, and after the last bolt, they watched in stunned silence as the snowy stairs crumbled all at once and tumbled down the mountainside.

"Why? Why would he do that? Is he trying to kill us?" Conrad asked.

"No… I think he proved with all of those lightning bolts that he could have done so if he wished to. In my current state, I couldn't have blocked all of that lightning at once," Aldous said.

"Then, why? I don' understand…" Henic trailed off. The hope had been sucked from his words.

"It would seem that the Mountain King wishes for us to enter his domain," Aldous said as he looked up to the dark clouds. The rain and wind still pelted them. "I say we wait in the ice hut for the storm to die down. It will give us time to recuperate, too."

"What's the point?" Henic asked, looking down. "I'm gonna die up here."

"Don't be so sure of that, yet. It is quite possible that the Mountain King stopped us for a reason. He may have something that could heal your injury," Aldous said, twitching his nose. "He is a Wizard, after all."

"That doesn't look like something I would do if I wanted to help…" Conrad trailed off as he looked at the wreckage of the snow stairs below.

"Yes, this is most troubling… oh, what to do, what to do?" Aldous asked aloud. After a few moments of arguing with himself, he came to a conclusion. "It may be best to think of this as a minor inconvenience."

"'Minor'? You call *this* a minor inconvenience?" Henic asked, his tired eyes twitching.

"One way or another, we will have to pass through his domain. Y'see, there *is* a secret exit to the mines on the other side of this mountain. We could go back through the mines to get there, but that would be a long and perilous journey. Passing through the Mountain King's castle would be quicker," he said.

"And less perilous?" Conrad asked with a snort.

"We can only hope. I don't see how his intentions could be bad, though. He is a Wizard, so he must commit to good deeds, or his Anima will deplete and he will die," Aldous said. He noticed the concern on both of their faces. "But enough worrying about that. Shall we rest in the ice hut?"

AFTER AN EXHAUSTIVE CLIMB up a seemingly infinite number of stairs, Joel and the miners reached the top of the vertical shaft. During the ascent, he had done his best to keep the map of the mines up to date; but it was truly a relief to stop and get his bearings. He lowered the map to see that at the middle of the top path, there was charring in the rock, highlighted by light shining down from a hole in the ceiling. Finally, they had found sources for each of the explosions that had occurred earlier. Between the char marks, there were two tunnels: One straight ahead, and one behind him.

Dalton approached the circle of light and knelt. He ran his fingers across the black residue and then looked back to his group.

"Well, it looks like we figured out where the third explosion came from, but now we have a choice. Which tunnel should we venture down?"

"Erm, sir? I think the choice is obvious…" Baltr said.

"Hm… you're right. If they went down the tunnel behind us, they wouldn't have needed to set off the explosive mushrooms, of course!" he replied with a nod.

"That's not what I meant," Baltr said as Dalton peered past him, and so too did Joel. He widened his eyes to see a horde of knockers. They stared them down from the back tunnel, their mischievous grins gleaming in the torchlight that just barely reached them.

"Who the hell are those little fellas?" Dalton asked.

"Those are tha knockers, sir! Vicious lil' bastards that'll eat ya alive if yer not careful!" said Alistair.

He raised an eyebrow. "Really? I thought they were only a myth meant to explain tunnel collapses."

"Turns out, they *are* responsible for tunnel collapses," Lucia replied. "At least, in these mines."

"Oh… I see now," Dalton muttered. The knockers inched closer to the group of 10. Joel took a step back when their true numbers were revealed out of the darkness of the tunnel. "You fought 'em before, right Alistair? Think you can take on about… erm… 30? 40?"

"I only fought a few at a time, before… there sure are a lot of 'em in here," Alistair said with a nervous chuckle.

"Might I suggest we run, then?" Baltr asked.

"Yeh, let's go!" Dalton called out as he turned to run. The others followed immediately after and they refused to look back as the screeches and scurries of the knockers behind them reached their ears.

After a sprint up the incline for some time and with distance gained on the knockers, the group saw a light at the end of the tunnel.

"We're almost outside!" Dalton shouted.

The group, however, was dismayed to find a thick sheet of ice covering the opening. Across the ice were three long claw marks that had cut all the way to the outside.

"We can still get through!" Dalton said as he looked back at his crew. Joel could hear the high-pitched giggles of the knockers down the tunnel, but they weren't within sight. "Your pickaxes! Start chipping away, if you are able! I will defend you from the back…" He drew upon the great claymore and walked past the others.

"I'll defend as well." Lucia stood beside Dalton with her arming sword at the ready.

"Now, it's time to show ya what I'm made of!" Alistair said with palpable excitement. He, too, stood beside Dalton with his battle axe drawn.

Joel, Baltr, and the others began to swing away at the thick ice. Little by little, it chipped, but not fast enough. The sheet was as thick as a man was tall and it would take time, and time was certainly not on their side. Joel looked over his shoulder to see the knockers stampeding up the tunnel with their great numbers.

"Prepare yourselves!" Dalton cried as he readied his blade.

Joel, with different thoughts in mind, stopped swinging at the ice. Instead, he lit his torch and held it up against the sheet in an attempt to weaken it. The flame was eventually extinguished, and he pointed to the spot where he had held it.

"Right! Swing there! Joel has weakened the ice in that spot!" Baltr commanded.

The miners all took their swings at the weak spot, and it did pierce into the ice further, but it was too thick to get all the way through. The torch was now dampened, so Joel couldn't immediately light it up again. The mute shifted focus to the claw marks across the ice sheet. They, too, seemed like a possible weak point; and if, as he suspected, Aldous had been the one to block this exit, he might be close. They could call out to him for help.

~

AT THE BACK of the group, Alistair, Lucia, and Dalton found themselves face-to-face with the horde of knockers. However, once within range, they did not attack. Instead, they stood, cocking their heads and staring at them with drooling mouths and the occasional high-pitched growl.

"Surprisingly patient, aren't they?" Dalton asked.

"Yeh, these lil' buggers like ta stalk their prey fer a while. Methinks it's ta get us riled," Alistair said.

"How would you know that?" Lucia asked while rolling her eyes.

"Well, it's me best guess, alright? I'm gettin' a wee bit nervous while they're starin' at me with those beady lil' eyes. They probably think I'm the fattest in tha group and wanna eat me, but they're wrong! I'm all muscle, ya knobs!" Alistair shouted at the knockers. They only giggled back in response.

"Aw, ta hell with it! I'll strike tha first blow!" the big man bellowed. He brought his axe down and into an unsuspecting knocker's head. It briefly squealed as dark blood spurted out, and then it tumbled to the floor, lifeless. Alistair pulled the axe out.

The attack set off a chain reaction: Various knockers jumped out at the trio. Dalton used the claymore's ranged abilities to his advantage and knocked his attackers back with a great low sweeping motion.

Lucia, on the other hand, made use of her newfound speed and flexibility with the arming sword and dealt with each one individually. She slashed one of the little cretins down its center as it leaped at her, halting its momentum and making it drop like a blood-soaked rock.

Less than a second later, she skewered another with a thrust and then threw the corpse off of her blade and into the tunnel wall.

Alistair took another mighty swing of his axe, this time horizontal, and splattered the poor creature up against the wall with its sheer force. Another knocker had snuck past his attack, however, and it began to gnaw at his leg.

Although panicking at first, Dalton and Lucia's skillful swordplay caught his eye. Neither had received so much as a scratch, thus far. He couldn't let the lass outdo him. She would never let him hear the end of it!

The big man let out a booming laugh and said, "Ya see that? All muscle!" He grabbed the little monster by its head and tore it off. A raging fire coursed through his leg as the teeth had torn through his flesh, but Alistair pushed through the pain for long enough to bash the knocker's face in with the butt of his axe. It hissed at him through broken teeth as he threw it into the crowd, knocking several of the others over.

"Hah! Take that, ya bottom feeders!"

Joel finally managed to break through the claw marks with his pickaxe. The ice around it collapsed and made a hole in the sheet. It wasn't nearly big enough for any of them to fit through, but what he actually had in mind was to call for help. He had originally thought for Alistair to call out with his bombastic voice, but since he was at battle with the knockers behind them, he felt Baltr would do the trick. Joel tapped him on the shoulder.

"Yes? What is it?" the stringy man asked. Joel pointed at the hole in the sheet and then cuffed his hands around his mouth to mime a shout. "You want me to call out for help?" Joel nodded enthusiastically. Finally, someone who understood his charades easily, he thought.

"I don't see how that would help…" he trailed off. A wave of disappointment overcame Joel. As if able to detect his dissatisfaction, Baltr let out a great sigh. "Fine…" He walked over to the hole in the ice sheet and cuffed his hands.

"Is anyone out there? We need help!" Baltr called out.

Joel waited with bated breath as the shrieks of the knockers and the sound blade piercing flesh haunted his ears from behind. Then, as if in answer to his prayers, Aldous, Conrad, and Henic dashed into view. They stopped before the sheet of ice, and all wore elated smiles.

"Joel is in there!" Conrad said.

"Ah, that'a boy, Joel. I knew that you would find us!" Aldous said with a nod. He then waved his walking stick at the ice wall and it instantly melted into water.

Baltr and the other miners stood silent, their mouths agape. Joel, understanding their confusion, tapped the stringy man on the shoulder and then nodded toward the exit. There was no time to gawk or even ask questions. The knockers were pressing.

"R-right..." Baltr muttered.

Upon exiting, Joel turned to see that the others had followed him out. Lucia, Dalton, and Alistair backed up slowly while continuing to fend off the little cretins.

"We've got knockers, here!" Dalton called out.

"When you reach the outside of the tunnel, stand aside. I'll handle them," Aldous said as he pressed his walking stick to the crunchy snow.

The trio of fighters did exactly as he had said after stepping out into the cold, rainy outdoors. The knockers flooded outside and gathered into one spot, surrounded by Dalton and Aldous' groups. About a dozen of the little cretins had perished in the confined tunnel, but out in the open, they would be much tougher to deal with, Joel thought.

"So many..." Dalton muttered as the creatures grinned and let out high-pitched giggles.

"Not for long!" Aldous said as he lifted his walking stick, and so too did the snow lift below the knockers' feet. The powder swirled beautifully around the creatures and formed into a ball of mixed snow and ice within seconds. Even rounder than the Nightcrawler was tall, the little limbs and heads of the knockers stuck out of their newfound entrapment and flailed about uselessly.

Aldous then whirled his walking stick around, and so too whirled the great ball of snow. He lifted the ball into the air with the motion of his walking stick, wound up, and then swung it over his shoulder to send it barreling down the mountainside. The little monsters screamed and screeched as they fell, but soon the noises ceased. Like a bad memory, they were gone.

"Good riddance!" Baltr shouted with joy. The rest of the group cheered along with him.

Dalton leaned in and whispered to Joel, "So, I suppose you were right about Aldous bein' a Wizard, eh? I can't believe he had me fooled all of this time. I wonder what other secrets the two of you are keeping…"

Joel snorted. If only he knew.

Finally, after being separated by the perils of the mines and the greed-driven Gold Fever, the original group of friends had reunited; and so too had Joel and Aldous. It was a moment of joy for all, but even still, there was a feeling of anxiousness about the air. Although they had put an end to the knocker threat, an important question remained: How would they escape Mt. Couture?

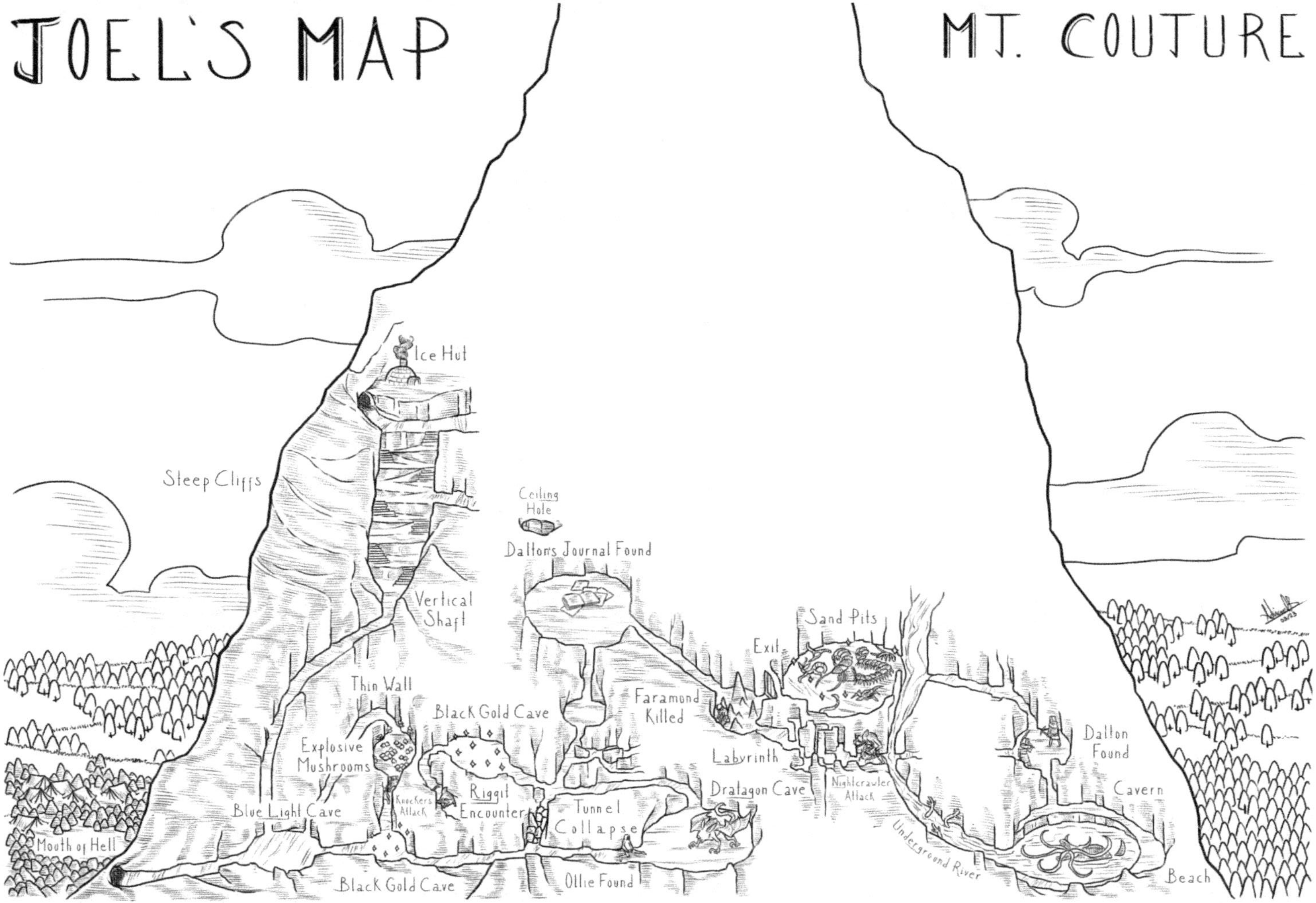

JOEL'S MAP
MT. COUTURE
Steep Cliffs
Ice Hut
Ceiling Hole
Dalton's Journal Found
Vertical Shaft
Thin Wall
Black Gold Cave
Explosive Mushrooms
Blue Light Cave
Knockers Attack
Rugall Encounter
Black Gold Cave
Mouth of Hell
Ollie Found
Tunnel Collapse
Dralagon Cave
Labyrinth
Faramond Killed
Sand Pits
Exit
Nightcrawler Attack
Dalton Found
Cavern
Underground River
Beach

CHAPTER 33
DARK SAVIOR: A BRIEF HISTORY

After their trek up the mountain, Dalton's group had been exhausted. In addition, Aldous had wanted to rest for a bit longer and let his magic recover fully. So, he created a bigger ice hut that could house them all.

"I still can't believe me eyes! A real, live Wizard!" Alistair said and then clapped his hands together. Aldous smiled back at him from across the fire at the hut's center. "Can ya do another trick fer us?"

"How about this?" Aldous asked. He snapped his fingers and little embers from the fire jumped out. The tiny flames danced around in a circle like jumping beans. The group watched on in wonder.

"Wow! Look at that!" Alistair said with a hearty laugh.

Meanwhile, Joel signed to Conrad and Henic with concern written all over his face.

"What did he say?" Henic asked.

"He said that your wound looks bad, and asked if you were alright," said Conrad.

"Good eye, lad… I need to get outta here, so I can get fixed up. But in the meantime, Aldous gave me a potion, so I *feel* fine, at least," Henic said.

Joel nodded back, but dread seeped into the back of his mind. At first glance, he had thought it to be a fatal wound for sure, but Henic hadn't seemed any worse for wear. Now, knowing that he had taken Aldous' potion, it only meant that he was on borrowed time.

Dalton then walked up to Conrad and Henic and sat next to them on one of the icy chairs that Aldous had made.

"The name's Dalton. It's nice to meet you both."

"Ah! So, that means they found the first group. I'm glad," Conrad said as he extended his hand. "I'm Conrad." They shook hands, and he smiled. "I've been meaning to ask, though: Where is Faramond?"

"He's gone. Murdered by Wolfgang," Dalton replied in a somber tone. Conrad's smile turned to a frown. "I'm sorry you had to find out this way."

"That Wolfgang... he don't appreciate life. He'll kill anyone he wants without a care in the world," Henic said.

"What about the rest of the group? Did the mines or Wolfgang claim their lives, too?" Conrad asked.

"No. After Faramond's death, Edith took over your group. When we all met up, she wanted to overthrow my leadership and combine the teams. I'm afraid she succeeded, for the most part. She lured the others in with promises of more black gold. The 10 of us were the only ones with enough sense to leave," Dalton said.

"Quite smart of you, indeed. The black gold will poison your mind until all you care about is..." Aldous trailed off, fidgeting his mouth.

"The Dark Savior?" Dalton asked with a smirk. The old Wizard's eyes grew wide. "You can't hide anything from me, Aldous. I had the dreams... I was lucky not to fall victim to Gold Fever."

"'Gold Fever'?" Aldous asked.

"Yeh, that's what we call it."

"I rather like that name. I wonder why we never thought that one up before..." Aldous muttered before turning to Joel. "By the way, m'boy... do you still have *it* with you?"

Joel held up the dark blue medallion that hung around his neck and Aldous breathed a sigh of relief.

"What is that, anyway?" Conrad asked. "Back when he ventured into the Dead Woods to find Alistair, he entrusted it to me-"

"*He-what*?" Aldous cried, his voice cracking. He sharpened his eyes, and contempt rained down on Joel.

The mute held his hands up and let out an inaudible, if nervous, laugh. It had been an admittedly poor decision to entrust the medallion to someone he'd only just met. Yet, in the end, Conrad turned out to be trustworthy, and Joel was sure to sign that argument to Aldous.

"That was reckless! Think of what a disaster it would have been if he'd lost it!"

With a sigh, Joel made hand signals back. That had been the exact reason for entrusting it to Conrad. Back then, he hadn't been sure if he would survive his trip into the Dead Woods. It had a reputation for swallowing up travelers, after all.

"It is obvious that the medallion holds quite a bit of importance to you both. Care to elaborate further?" Conrad said, eyeing the pair. "Joel didn't tell me much about it."

"It may be better if you and everyone else here didn't know…" Aldous trailed off before glancing at Joel. He nodded back in return. Despite the risks, it was time to reveal the truth to everyone. "But we are in a wee bit of a corner, now. Joel says that you can all be trusted; and from our time together, I know that Conrad and Henic are of good heart, too."

"Oh? Are ya finally gonna tell us what's goin' on?" Alistair asked with palpable excitement. He moved closer to Aldous and watched on with a smile from ear to ear. "Ya gotta explain everythin' from the beginnin', alright? Tell us a story, Wizard-man!"

"Will you keep quiet? He's *trying* to tell us," Lucia shot back. Alistair mumbled under his breath, but he didn't offer much more resistance than that.

"To fully understand what is happening and why Joel and I are here in the first place, you must first learn about the one that came to be known as 'The Dark Savior'. What I'm about to tell you has been passed down by only Wizards, and for thousands of years. You must not tell a soul what I am about to tell you," Aldous said.

"Oh, don' worry! I'm great at keepin' secrets! The best in me family!" Alistair said. Some of the group chuckled.

"Several millennia ago, mankind was primitive. The other intelligent species that you know such as the avian and marinians were in a similar situation. The world was dominated by a species that you have all come to know as 'The Ancient Ones'. Back then, they were known as *luxians*."

"Loo-Juns?" Alistair asked, his pursed lips emphasizing the pronunciation.

"Right," he replied with a nod. "The luxians advanced at an incredible rate. They were able to build and achieve wonderful things that we have not since replicated; even thousands of years later! You may have noticed some of their inventions while traversing these very mines. They had a knack for ingenuity, and with these advantages, entered a long period of peace and prosperity. With that said, not everyone can be prosperous, and the primitive species of the world suffered while the luxians lived in luxury."

"How can this be?" Conrad asked with wide eyes. "We have always been taught that the Ancient Ones were precursors to mankind. It's in the history texts; considered common knowledge…"

"I'm afraid not. The luxians and humans are quite similar in appearance and share many traits, but there are some key differences. Humans tend to be bigger, for instance. Luxians, on the other hand, developed their minds faster than humans or any other species. I'm told it was amazing, some of the things that they accomplished," Aldous said.

"I think he's callin' us stupid," said Dalton with a smirk.

"Anyhow, the luxians lived prosperously while the other, more primitive peoples lived difficult lives. It is believed that the Dark Savior arrived in response to this. It is unknown exactly *how* he arrived, though there is much speculation. Some say he was summoned by Wizards of the time who were trying to help the down-trodden folk prosper. Others believe that he was summoned by the first Dark Wizard to ever exist. Some would also say that he was born out of the pure hatred and resentment that the other species felt for the luxians…" Aldous said.

"But none of that matters, now. The point is, a powerful entity who called himself *Stalmoz* revealed himself to the world. He was human-like in shape, but enveloped in darkness like a living shadow; and he had piercing, yellow eyes," he said and then held up two fingers in front of his eyes, producing small bits of lightning to demonstrate. Alistair clapped and cheered at the performance.

"That sounds exactly like what I saw in my dreams: A dark figure with yellow eyes, ever watching," Dalton said.

"Stalmoz appeared before the humans and other species, promising that they too could prosper under him. He claimed that they would be made equals with the luxians, whom they had come to hate very much. Greed and resentment tempted many of the human tribes, and they were some of the first to accept his invitation."

"I didn't realize we were such a petty species back then," Lucia said.

"You make a fine point, young lady," Aldous said, raising a finger. "As with all things, it is never that simple. In their rise to power, the luxians used the other species to advance their civilization as quickly as possible, and humans got the worst of it. In today's world, you would call them serfs or slaves, but then imagine *all humans* doing the labor-hickeys and hardships n' such without exception. That was how things were back then. As their society became more civilized, the luxians began to reject the idea of using the other intelligent species in such a way, and decided to set them free," Aldous said.

"So, what was tha problem, then?" Alistair asked.

"The change was too sudden for mankind to properly handle. Few of them knew how to fend for themselves, and they were left with nothing but their freedom. They had no land or wealth, and many were forced into the mountains where hungry dragons awaited them; or to other lands that made life difficult. But life goes on, and the other species eventually learned to survive as the luxians continued to live much better by comparison," Aldous said.

"Generations went on, and the humans became resentful as they grew more independent and wise, yet still poor and downtrodden next to the luxians. Brutal stories were passed down, and they never forgot what was done to their forefathers. They wanted better land. They wanted *revenge*. And those were things that Stalmoz could provide."

"It doesn't sound all that different from how we treated the avian, up until recent times. They, too, wanted their own land; and to some extent, revenge," Conrad said.

"This is the law of the world: One species will always try to reign supreme over all others, and as the humans were to find out, Stalmoz was no exception to this rule. He began a campaign called 'The Trial of Lux', where human armies attempted to invade luxian territories."

The old Wizard lowered his palm to the snowy floor and closed his eyes. A mixture of flakes and ice shavings began to swirl around his arm, and out from the floor sprouted little ice sculptures of men with swords and armor. Across from them were similar, albeit smaller, folk who were clad in weapons and armor. The crowd buzzed with excitement at the display.

"Stalmoz's justification of the violent campaign was mankind's previous oppression by the luxians and the stark difference in their living conditions. His stated goal was to take these territories and combine the human and luxian populations, so they could live on as equals," said Aldous.

"Well, that don't sound so bad," Henic said.

"Mayhap if there were any truth to his claims, you would be right, but his intentions were far more sinister. The humans' first few attacks were successfully repelled thanks to the superior resources and strategies of the luxians, but eventually, the humans and their sheer numbers prevailed."

Aldous held his hand out and then made a fist. Some of the human ice sculptures shattered, but then more appeared in their place. Some luxian figures also shattered, but not as many replaced them, and he waved his hand to push them all back.

"Y'see, when a species is living well and begins to relax, their population tends to decline. On the other hand, humans were living difficult lives and tended to have more offspring. They sent wave after wave of men until finally, a luxian settlement surrendered after a year-long losing effort on Stalmoz's part," Aldous said.

"And then?" Conrad asked.

"And then, things got worse. Rather than have luxians live with humans as promised, they were put into labor camps. Stalmoz claimed it was payment for the hundreds of years of serfdom that they had put the humans through," he replied before tensing his fingers and then straightening them.

From the ground sprouted many miniature ice buildings. The display of magic created a thick fog, and when it settled, Alistair turned giddy: A small replica of a city had been created, and all from ice and snow. Aldous curled his index finger inward a few times, and the luxian ice sculptures moved into the city.

"One settlement wasn't enough for Stalmoz, of course, so the attacks continued on others. After two years and taking pieces of their land, the next target was the capital city of their people: Lux. The Council of Wizards, who preferred to stay out of non-magic-related conflicts back then, finally determined that Stalmoz's actions were causing too many deaths, and so a summit was proposed. Stalmoz and the luxian leaders would meet on the outskirts of Lux to discuss a peace treaty, while the Wizards would moderate as an unbiased third party."

"I'm sure that went well," Dalton quipped while rolling his eyes.

"On that day, the Wizards and luxians learned something quite important about Stalmoz. They all met in a tower outside of Lux and spoke in a friendly manner until the peace treaty was discussed. Stalmoz would accept nothing less than their unconditional surrender and submission. The luxian leaders didn't take kindly to such unreasonable demands and threatened him with violence. I should mention that in what seemed like an odd decision at the time, Stalmoz showed up to the summit by himself. He had no guards to protect him…"

"The leaders thought that threatening him might change his mind on the terms. It is said that in response to the threats, Stalmoz walked over to an open window with a lovely view of the city. He then held his arm out and snapped his fingers…" Aldous trailed off as he snapped his own fingers at the fire before him. Flames exploded outward and the hut was alight with a mixture of orange, red, and yellow. The group gasped and shielded their eyes, but soon after, they saw that it had only been for show and hadn't harmed anyone.

"H-he set 'em on fire?" Alistair asked while leaning forward, jaw hanging open. He then gasped to see that the little ice city and the miniature luxian sculptures had been obliterated; turned into a pile of slush.

"No… a great explosion of darkness enveloped the city, and it destroyed *everything*. Think of an explosive mushroom, but on the scale of a city, and shrouded in a crippling darkness instead of blinding light. At the mere snap of his fingers, Stalmoz had killed thousands and thousands of luxians while destroying their capital city. He then told them that he could kill them all if he wanted to. The leaders were left with two choices: Submission or annihilation," Aldous said.

"And what was their decision?" Lucia asked.

"At first, they did not answer. Understandably, they were in a state of shock at the power displayed. Stalmoz told them that they had a week to decide and then left them. However, he made a grave miscalculation. In displaying his power, he likely thought that the leaders would become demoralized and surrender immediately. Instead, destroying Lux had filled them with fighting spirit, and the terrifying display turned all Wizards to the side of luxians."

He held his palm out and then raised it. More luxian ice sculptures were created, and also sculptures of men in robes and funny hats: the Wizards. He pointed at some of the human figures, and they shattered before being sent backward on the floor.

"The ruins of Lux became a battleground between humans and luxians for another two bloody years. Eventually, the luxians defeated the humans with new advancements in battle and strategies. Having the Wizards on their side was also quite an advantage," Aldous said with a snort.

"However, Stalmoz's true plan had not yet come to fruition. Y'see, the so-called 'labor camps' were a front for the creation of his own species. He had not desired to see the supremacy of humans or any other folk aside from those like him. Since there were *none* like him, he used the enslaved luxians, injured humans, and the other intelligent species that had been captured at war, as his experiments. We believe that it was the fourth year of the war that he perfected what would come to be called the *melior*: They were similar in appearance to him while retaining some other features of their previous human, avian, or marinian life."

Within the groups of human and luxian figures, some changed to larger, more muscular sculptures. With a gesture, Aldous motioned them to another spot on his imaginary battlefield.

"If they sometimes looked human or luxian, then wouldn't he hate those creatures, too?" Conrad asked.

"No. All he cared about was that they were his own. We can only speculate the horrors that those prisoners went through during the transformative experiments, but after their creation, Stalmoz saw no more need to continue making them and enslaved the prisoners instead. The melior could reproduce, after all, and they went on to live in settlements similar to humans or luxians. The great difference, however, was that they were obedient to a fault. They obeyed his every command," said Aldous.

"If the humans were being replaced by the melior, wouldn't they have noticed?" Dalton asked.

"Indeed. About six years into the war, when the melior came to prominence and it became clear that they were higher-class citizens in Stalmoz's society, the humans diverged. Some wished to desert and betray their new lord. He noticed their wavering faith, however. Based on what he had learned from those experiments performed to create his own race, Stalmoz made something that would draw the humans back once more: black gold."

"So, the black gold was made just fer us..." Henic trailed off. "No wonder we were so easily drawn in."

"Not only humans. But I'll get back to that in a moment," Aldous said before clearing his throat. "The black gold and its alluring qualities quickly turned the human tribes into raging cults. They began referring to Stalmoz as 'The Dark Savior' from then on, as if they weren't *worthy* to speak his name. The melior and renewed energy of the humans turned the tide of the war once more."

Several of the ice sculptures on the floor shattered, but none more than the luxians. With a gesture of his hand, Aldous moved them away once more.

"Nine years into the war, Stalmoz took the rebuilt city of Lux for his own. The luxians were pushed back and forced to retreat to what is now Federland," Aldous said to some gasps from the crowd.

"Well, he had to have lost at some point, but how? If the Dark Savior could decimate a city at will, how could anyone fight back?" Conrad asked.

"I think I can answer that," Henic said. "As a farmer by trade, I understand the dynamic of power. When I have a cow or a chicken that won't listen, I don't kill 'em all. I don't destroy the barn. I make an example outta one of 'em and try to get somethin' out of the rest of 'em."

"A fine comparison," Aldous replied with a smile. "And it's true. The destruction of Lux City was little more than a fear tactic. If he went around 'splodin' cities like that all the time, he would have destroyed the very thing he wished to conquer."

"Anyhow, after fleeing their home country across the sea, the luxians and Wizards took more drastic measures. They began to ally themselves with any human tribe that had not fallen under Stalmoz's grasp, and came to terms with the avian and marinians, both of whom had either remained neutral or sided with the Savior up to that point."

Small ice statues of bird-like and reptile-like folk rose from the ground and were placed with the luxians. A few human figures joined them, too.

"I see… because the forces of Stalmoz had to cross the sea to reach them, having the marinians as allies would truly have been an advantage. They could have scouted or even destroyed enemy ships before they reached land," Conrad said.

"The avian would have had an advantage over them at sea thanks to their flight abilities, too," Dalton added.

"Correct, on both accounts! The alliances repelled the incoming humans for some time, but the melior were a different story. Since some of them had avian and marinian characteristics, they required special attention. In response, the luxians learned how to forge a new metal: They called it 'luxmortite'. It was a specialized material, harder than steel and unparalleled in its cutting ability. To this day, we still are not sure how it was crafted, but we believe it had something to do with the concentrated light sources that you encountered in the mines. Joel's medallion is made from the very same material," Aldous said, pointing to him.

"Interesting…" Conrad trailed off, rubbing his chin. "So, he keeps it around his neck because of how rare the metal is?"

"There is more to that piece of metal than you could possibly imagine on your own! But we will get to that in a moment!" Aldous said with a chuckle. "With luxmortite weapons and armor at their disposal, the luxians found it easier to repel the melior and humans. 10 years into the brutal war, the two sides found themselves at a stalemate. That is, of course, until Stalmoz employed his most insidious tactic…"

"What more could this knob do to become even worse?" Alistair asked, on the edge of his seat.

"You may recall how I mentioned that black gold doesn't only affect humans… in fact, it takes its horrid effects on other species at different paces. The Dark Savior's new tactic was to send his forces and attack as per usual, but now their ships were loaded with black gold. As some of you may know…" Aldous trailed off while eyeing Dalton. "A big part of war is looting whatever the losing side has. The luxians and their allies took the bait, and with each attack, the winners obtained more and more black gold."

"A devilish, but brilliant tactic," Dalton said.

"Indeed. And what's worse is that the black gold had an accelerated effect on the luxians. They were even quicker to crave more of it than humans and eventually pledged loyalty to the Savior; committing violent acts and such in his name. The tactic worked so well that in merely one year, the luxians were on the verge of civil war between the Gold Fever-infected and those who hadn't felt its effects. The humans and melior invaded the coast and were slowly pushing ahead. The avian and marinians tried to pick up the luxians' slack, but they simply didn't have the numbers, and they too were being swept up by Gold Fever; albeit at a slower pace."

Another set of luxian figurines popped up from the ice on the floor, but their faces were twisted. Human, avian, marinian, and melior figures alike shattered into pieces, but none more than the luxians.

"Then, how? How could the Dark Savior have been defeated?" Lucia asked.

"The luxian leaders were forced to make a difficult decision. They had two choices: Ignore the growing civil unrest and continue trying to secure their coast, or ignite a civil war and attempt to unify themselves once more," Aldous said.

"Neither of those choices are any good. How could they have won under those circumstances?" Dalton asked.

"In secret, the top luxian minds and Council of Wizards were combining their strengths to make a weapon the likes of which none had ever seen, nor been seen since. With the luxians' ingenuity and mastery of light beams and the Wizards' mighty magic, they had completed construction of it by the 12th year of the war. However, there was a catch: For this weapon to function, it required a great sacrifice," Aldous said, his eyes becoming weary.

"Y'see, this weapon fed on the power of souls to produce a beam of light with unprecedented power. However, to do what the luxians wanted to do, the Wizards estimated that it would take a sacrifice of *at least* 500,000 souls."

"No… they wouldn't…" Alistair muttered.

"You would be surprised what *anyone* would do to survive with their backs against the wall," Aldous replied as some of the melior and human ice sculptures melted rapidly on the floor. "The luxians tested the new magic-infused technology by incorporating it into some of their luxmortite weapons, and so relatively few sacrifices would need to be made. It was a great success. Even on a small scale, the weapons would poison the enemies and kill them if it was but the slightest of wounds. It was so poisonous that it could be passed on to others that the weapon had never even touched."

"So, then… they made the sacrifice?" Dalton asked.

"After testing on a small scale, the luxian leaders initiated a civil war. Not only did this lure Stalmoz into a false sense of security, but it also gave the luxians justification for sacrificing their own. From their perspective, these folk were beyond saving, and that may well have been true. Try as they might, even their brightest minds could not bring back the Gold Fever-infected from their brainwashed state."

The luxian figures with twisted faces turned to slush.

"Of course, the luxians won the civil war within a year… they had taken captive roughly a million souls; the majority of which were their own, but some were human and melior who were facing the unfortunate consequences of war."

"O-one million people? Just sacrificed, like that…" Henic trailed off.

"Yes. To obtain the power that they needed, the luxians had sacrificed so much. Half of the country had been invaded by the end of the civil war. To make matters worse, they had to commit a mass slaughter of their own people! I cannot imagine such a burden falling on my shoulders, but it was theirs and the Wizards' to bear," Aldous said.

"And did it work? The weapon?" Conrad asked.

"With the soul energy needed and after 13 years at war, the luxians and Wizards fired their weapon. Their target was the homeland of Stalmoz and the melior: The newly-named and acquired country of Stalmagna. It was said to have created a great beam of blue light so spectacular that it could be seen from other countries, but I can tell you now who certainly did *not* see it coming... Stalmoz," Aldous said to some chuckles in the hut.

However, a hush quickly came over them when the old Wizard straightened his arm out, shooting a small bolt of lightning at the melior ice sculptures. In a flash of light, they were decimated, and a small chunk of the snowy floor went along with them.

"Hah! Serves 'im right, the bastard!" Alistair said with clenched fists.

"Stalmoz had every reason to believe that he was about to win the war and attain complete dominance over the world. Half of the luxians' land had been conquered in only one year thanks to the civil war, and his melior had become so great in number that they had to relocate many human reserves to other countries: A slight which had wavered their faith in the Dark Savior, but he cared little. He had established his own country with a self-sufficient and powerful species, and he was their God..." Aldous said and then grimaced.

"When the beam of light hit Stalmagna at its center, it created a blast wave that spanned thousands of kilometers and wiped out nearly everything from villages to cities, to the few remaining humans, to melior. Whatever wasn't wiped out immediately was finished off by the accompanied poison that spread from the blast. Those who were unfortunate enough to be in the coastal areas of Stalmagna at the time died horrible deaths; ones that saw the poison eating away at their bodies and disintegrating them in the most painful way possible. Such was the power of the luxians' sacrifice and the Wizards' magic."

"Doesn't sound much like a victory to me," Dalton said.

"In a way, yes. The blast rendered Stalmagna completely uninhabitable. It created a gigantic crater at the center of the country that became a great lake of poison. Most of that land has remained poisonous, even thousands of years later. You lot know this place as 'The Wastelands', or 'The Lost Continent'," Aldous said.

"Wow, there's another piece of history I didn't know. I was always taught that the Lost Continent was a natural part of the world. But in reality, it was the result of a horrible weapon..." Conrad trailed off.

"And the carnage didn't end there," Aldous said to some shocked faces.

"But how? Surely, the war would end without a homeland or leader for the melior?" Dalton asked.

"Oho! I never said that it killed the Dark Savior, now did I?" Aldous asked with a chuckle. The group gasped in unison.

"Yer tryin' ta tell me that this beast survived a blast that wiped out his entire country *and* tha poison?" Alistair asked in disbelief.

"I'm afraid so," Aldous said in a somber tone. He created an ice sculpture of a large, demonic figure, and placed it next to the human figures. "But it did hurt him quite a bit. Y'see, Stalmoz was nearly invulnerable because he had the uncanny ability to regenerate. That's where the genius of the poison came in. Because every time he tried to regenerate, the poison would simply eat away at him to cancel that out. It ended up being that the poison kept him in a state of perpetual pain and weakness, but he was still alive."

"It's hard to believe such a monster ever existed. To think after all of that sacrifice and death, the blast *still* couldn't kill him," Baltr said.

"To make matters worse, many Wizards died as a result of the weapon going off. Their Anima shifted dramatically downward for creating such terrible death and destruction," Aldous said. He pointed at the Wizard sculptures, and most of them faded away into a snowy powder.

"Anima? What's that? How did it kill them?" Dalton asked.

"Think of it as a balance of the good and bad you've done in your life," Conrad said. Aldous nodded. "Wizards need it to outlive the normal mortal lifespan."

"With many of the Wizards dead, the luxians lost some of their most powerful allies, and regardless of what had happened in their homeland, the melior continued to press into their territory. Their numbers and resources were running out after a civil war and the deaths of millions more in such a short time. It seemed that despite striking such a decisive blow, they were still about to lose. But then, something miraculous happened…" Aldous trailed off. The hut remained silent. Everyone leaned in.

"YA GOTTA STOP KEEPIN' ME IN SUSPENSE! WHAT HAPPENED?" Alistair blurted out as some others in the hut shushed him.

"As the luxians did their best to fight off melior invading forces, Stalmoz limped out of Stalmagna and into one of the territories where he had displaced the humans earlier that year. To his horror, the humans had grown resistant to his command and the black gold was nowhere to be found. In what he believed to be his hour of victory, the Dark Savior hadn't taken care to make sure the humans were still under his influence. They had been shipped off to other countries without the material. At the time, he didn't care, because he had his own obedient folk to rule over and felt all others were comparatively weak-minded and easy to control. The humans had become an afterthought..."

"And so, the humans decided to capture and imprison their former savior. Then, it was decided that they would inform the luxians and turn him over in exchange for peace. But Stalmoz was clever and versatile. He was too weak to resist his capture, but he still had supernatural abilities at his disposal. Instead of remaining a prisoner and doubtlessly becoming enslaved by the luxians, he opted to split himself into several identities, or spawns," Aldous said. He snapped his fingers, and from the larger Dark Savior sculpture spawned seven different figures, all grotesque in their own ways.

"Quite the turn..." Conrad muttered.

"Upon splitting up, the spawns of Stalmoz fled to different parts of the world while taking unrecognizable forms. Each form seemed to have its own personality and associated abilities. The spawn of Stalmoz that wished to turn folk against one another, to dominate the world; and created the black gold to this end, was *Greed*," Aldous said, motioning forward with an index finger. A fat, grinning figure inched forward on the floor, joining with the remaining melior sculptures. Along with him, the old Wizard created some more luxians with twisted, deformed faces.

Conrad looked at Joel with a raised eyebrow, and the mute immediately remembered why: He had told him that the ancient text on his medallion said, 'Greed'.

"While most forms of Stalmoz fled and attempted to hide, Greed wished to go on the offensive. He stowed away on an unsuspecting human ship that was sailing to the luxian country, seeking to aid them. As soon as that spawn of the Dark Savior arrived, the war returned to being alive and well. Greed joined up with the invading forces and reinvigorated them with the creation of more black gold. It was also used to once again divide and incite civil conflict amongst the luxians," Aldous said.

"It never ends, does it?" Dalton asked.

"Almost there," Aldous said and then winked at the warrior. Among the human ice sculptures, three new figures emerged, each wearing extravagant crowns and capes. "By the 14th year of the war, the luxians were fading. Another civil war broke out because of the black gold, and most of the country had fallen under enemy control. However, with one species failing, another began to thrive. Three men rose to power during this time: You all will likely know them as *The Three Great Kings*. They, of course, are the ones who are said to have taken mankind out of the savagery of the mountains and led all to prosperity and wealth. The very language we speak today, *King's Tongue*, is named after them. What you may not know is that all three of them were survivors of the Dark Savior's tyranny. They declared themselves allies of the luxians and sent many brave men to aid them. Although they were more primitive in their fighting, their numbers were greater than the luxian forces. Even the meliors' numbers paled in comparison, as they had been at war for so long, and without their Dark Savior to guide them, they were dwindling."

"First, the humans helped secure victory for the luxian leaders in the civil war, and then, with the help of the remaining Wizard's Council, they led a campaign to wipe out not only the melior but the spawns of Stalmoz as well," he said. The twisted luxian sculptures shattered and then blew away as a pile of ice shavings.

"Hah! So, we humans were tha heroes in the end!" Alistair said with a grin.

"Don't be so sure of that. It was more like the three kings understood that a shift in power was happening. Years and years of war between two colossal powers had weakened them both greatly, and in overcoming the black gold, it seemed common knowledge that the era of man was beginning."

"They helped the luxians, but only with the understanding that eliminating Stalmoz and the melior was necessary for any other peoples to prosper. Thanks to their sheer numbers, the luxians would have no way to resist humans taking their country and making it theirs."

Aldous made a fist and then punched the air in the direction of the melior ice sculptures. They all shattered like glass and became one with the snowy ground. Many human figures remained, but there were now very few luxians and Wizards.

"By the 15th year of the war, the melior and Gold Fever-infected humans had been defeated in a bloody campaign that saw many more die. With the combined forces of Wizards, humans, and luxians alike, all spawns of Stalmoz had been captured, but no matter what method was attempted, they were unable to kill him. So instead, the luxians and Wizards combined forces one last time to open a portal and discover a new world."

"They named it, 'The Cold World', because being there ate away at one's soul and made them shiver. It seemed as good a place as any to lock up the spawns of Stalmoz," Aldous said as he waved a hand over the Dark Savior figures. Around them appeared little boxes made of snow, and engraved in the snow were chains holding up a lock.

"Mighty convenient that different parts of him were sealed up, too. That would make it difficult to bring him back," Dalton said.

"Indeed, but there was a catch. As the luxians and Wizards found out upon imprisoning them in the Cold World, a portal created to transport a being of Stalmoz's magnitude cannot permanently be closed. It's more like a door that has been created: It can be locked, but never closed for good. So, the Wizards and luxians sealed the spawns of Stalmoz away within monoliths," Aldous said while looking at Joel. He nodded back at him.

"At this point, there weren't many luxians left. The Three Great Kings took over and divided their country amongst themselves. They allowed the luxians to live in whichever of their settlements they liked, however. In an odd turn, they had become nomads in their own country."

"How did they die out?" Conrad asked.

"Most of them dedicated the rest of their lives to making it impossible to reach the sealed monoliths... on the off-chance that anyone would want to release the Dark Savior from his prison in the Cold World. Y'see, it was discovered that even upon sealing him away in another world, Stalmoz was so powerful that *imprints* of his influence leaked out of the monoliths."

"So, the black gold that we have encountered thus far is an imprint of Greed?" Conrad asked.

"That's exactly right. The luxians, upon discovering these influential artifacts, sought to hide the monoliths away from all other peoples of the world in the hopes that no one could be tricked into letting one of the spawns out. The mines of Mt. Couture are filled to the brim with deadly creatures, poorly built tunnels, and mazes meant to trap or kill any who dare enter. Make no mistake, this place is a death trap by design!" Aldous said.

"Well, that's just… just… *rude*!" Alistair said.

"Maybe, but think of the alternative. There is nothing that can be done about black gold leaking out of the monolith, so it was put at the heart of the mountain where it is most difficult to reach."

"*The Gold Pit…*" Lucia muttered, wide-eyed.

"Yes, it has become something of a legend, although misconstrued over the years to lead one to riches; when in truth, it holds the very essence of ruin! What's worse is that the black gold, once it takes hold of a man's mind, is always trying to get them to that monolith with the offer of *more*. Naturally, the most concentrated amounts of black gold are around the monolith, and those deep into the influence of Gold Fever will be instructed to release their Dark Savior," Aldous said.

"So, these horrid creatures are trying to work against the black gold? *They're* forces for good?" Baltr asked with skepticism on his tongue.

"Oho! I don't know if I would call 'em 'good', but they *are* natural forces that help keep folks away!" Aldous chuckled and then looked at Joel once more, smiling. "And that's where Joel and I come in. I have been assigned the role of 'Wizard Scout' by the Council. That means I live close to the monolith and monitor any activity that may threaten its safety. You lot are the reason I came here in the first place… large packs of humans mean more potential Gold Fever-infected, after all. I knew that these mines would likely swallow you up, and wished to save as many of you as possible from a gruesome fate; one way or another."

"It figures this *would* be all our fault…" Henic muttered.

"Edith and her father mentioned the Gold Pit while planning the expedition. I worry that they know about the monolith. Did they wish to release the Dark Savior? Or was it pure greed driving them and only the black gold they were after?" Lucia asked aloud.

"Are you referring to Edith and Drake Danvers, m'lady?" Aldous asked.

"I am. Before the second team left Faiwell, I overheard one of their private conversations. They discussed gathering black gold while allowing the dangerous mines to kill off others," she said. "Drake mentioned that her final goal, through many sacrifices, should be the Gold Pit."

"I see… it sounds like a classic case of greed to me, but my main concern is how they would know of black gold at all. Humanity hasn't recognized such a thing for thousands of years!" Aldous said.

"How about Joel? What is his purpose? What is the medallion for?" Conrad asked.

"Joel has been appointed 'Keeper of the Key' by the Council. That medallion around his neck is made from the same luxmortite metal invented by the luxians, but it is also infused with the magic of Wizards. It is the key to the monolith at the heart of this mountain, and can be used to open or lock the portal that holds Greed," Aldous said.

"Hold on… why have a key in the first place? Simply leave the portal locked and destroy the key," Dalton said.

"Ah, if only it were that simple," Aldous said as Joel nodded. "Y'see, the monolith holds the portal shut, and by destroying the monolith, the portal can be opened once more. The key is not required for that much. However, the key's magical properties allow it to restore the monolith and reseal the portal to the Cold World, should it ever be destroyed. That is Joel's job."

"It's no wonder Joel wouldn't reveal anything… that'd take a year to tell us in USL!" Henic said as he and others laughed.

"It seems that he has become friends with some of you. It's nice to see because otherwise, this is a lonely job. I'm not even supposed to be telling you any of this, but frankly… if Edith commands enough Gold Fever-infected at this stage, the monolith sealing Greed is in more danger than it ever has been. We must stop her and any others at all costs!" Aldous said.

"I appreciate you finally telling all. This is so much to take in, and yet… I have more questions," Conrad said as he and Lucia laughed unanimously. "You mentioned that this 'Mountain King' wouldn't let anyone leave with black gold. How does he fit into all of this?"

"Ah yes, I should have mentioned earlier that most locations of the monoliths have four protectors. There's my job: The Wizard Scout. Joel's job: Keeper of the Key. Then there are two others: The King Wizard and the Guardian," Aldous replied. "The King Wizard is of course the Mountain King, in this case. King Wizards oversee the protection of the monolith site and are among the most powerful and knowledgeable of the Wizard's Council. Being chosen for such a duty is considered a high honor, although I imagine it would become quite lonely…"

"Then, I wonder, could the 'Guardian' be the Nightcrawler? It would fit with its behavior. It tends to kill us only one at a time to chase us off, even though it could easily take many of us out at once," Dalton said.

"Oho! 'Nightcrawler' is a fine name for it! We had only called it 'the beast' up until now, but I must say, you have a real knack for inventing names, Dalton!" Aldous said in a cheerful tone. "But yes, that is the Guardian of the monolith. The luxians and Wizards of the time chose odd yet powerful creatures that were immune to aging; and trained them to guard the monoliths. I can't say for certain, but I think the Nightcrawler was discovered in the Cold World and brought over to our realm."

Joel glanced nervously at Henic, whose face had become paler and his breaths shorter as he sat and listened to Aldous' story. He made hand signals to the old Wizard.

His eyes widened and then he said, "Ah, yes! We've already spent enough time resting. Let us consider story time over, for now!"

The group stood with newfound energy. Although Aldous' story was harrowing in many ways, it had truly turned into one of humanity's finest hours. If they had helped defeat the Dark Savior back then, they could certainly do it now.

"So then, speaking of the Mountain King, it's time to pay him a visit! Mayhap he can offer us passage outta here, so Henic can receive medical treatment," Aldous said as he led the group out of the ice hut. "And if we inform him of Edith and her gang of Gold Fever-infected men, he would certainly know how to deal with them."

"I have a bad feelin' about this, Aldous. Remember the storm he conjured up? He nearly killed us..." Henic protested.

"Nonsense! He knows me... and he knows that I am a lightning Elemental. *Of course* I would catch the lightning bolt! Ohoho! It was simply his way of telling us to come to him, that's all!" Aldous said before looking down and muttering, "I hope..."

CHAPTER 34
THE MOUNTAIN KING

Aldous led the unified group of 13 up the snowy hills as the wind blew hard, burning their faces. The hills eventually gave way to a forest of pine trees. It was at least a shield to the wind, but yet another anxious moment on their long journey of traps and treachery. It felt as if something was ready to pop out and attack them at any moment, but nothing in the forest greeted them save trees and crunchy snow.

"After we pass through this forest, we should arrive at the Mountain King's castle," Aldous said as he blocked his face from a new gust of wind that had snaked through the trees.

"So, if I'm to understand, the Mountain King created a whole thunderstorm just to stop the three of you?" Dalton asked.

"Yes…" Aldous trailed off and then narrowed his eyes. "I don't understand why, but as I said before: He is an ally; one of the most knowledgeable and powerful Wizards in all the world. He must have some plan for us."

"But how well do you know him? I can't get it out of my mind: That thunderstorm could have killed us, and it's not like we had any black gold," Conrad said.

"I have known him for hundreds of years. I would go so far as to call him a mentor, even. He took me under his wing and taught me much about thundery things and such," Aldous replied.

"Methinks it'll all be fine!" Alistair chimed in, noisily. "He's a Wizard, after all! He can't be anythin' but good!"

"Do you want to tell him, or should I?" Conrad asked Henic as they both let out a chuckle.

"I should also mention, my friends, that these forests were once inhabited by mountain trolls. That was a couple hundred years ago, though, and they do tend to move around often... still, be on the look-out," Aldous said.

"Trolls? A perfect chance to try this arming sword out some more," Lucia said as she placed a hand on the hilt of her blade.

Conrad looked her way. "Ah, so I see you have switched to a more manageable blade."

"Only until my shoulder heals," she said. "Then, I will take back my claymore..."

"No, you won't..." muttered Dalton.

"Yes, I will!"

He growled. "It would be wise to listen to your mentor..."

"Former mentor," she said.

"It's obvious that an arming sword or long sword suits you better," Dalton said.

"I'll be the judge of that."

The warrior threw his hands up. "Stubborn to the last... just like your parents were..."

Lucia only rolled her eyes in response.

"What happened in the mines, anyway? How did you get such an injury?" Conrad asked.

"There was a point in the journey last night where we were chased off by dratagons, of all things," Lucia began.

"Wow, even dratagons are in these mines?" Conrad asked, leaning in and wide-eyed.

"Yes, that was our reaction, too," she said with a laugh. "But Wolfgang and Angus were even deadlier than they were. I estimate that as the chaos ensued, they killed a dozen innocent workers. They had their sights set on us, next, and I have to admit that the oaf over here did a good job holding off Angus..."

"Well, thanks fer tha *rude* compliment!" Alistair said.

"But I failed in holding off Wolfgang. He was able to get past my defenses and caught me in the shoulder. Luckily, the armor did its job, or I would have lost my arm," Lucia said.

"I see. You may be happy to find company in being attacked by

Wolfgang, then. Henic's wound is thanks to him, and after we saved his hide from a swarm of knockers, no less," Conrad said while shaking his head and looking down. "The worst part is that I had a chance to stab him in the neck while he wasn't looking, but I hadn't realized how far gone he was. I wanted to ask him about Faramond's group, first."

"One way or another, he will fall on this mountain," Lucia replied, placing a sure hand on his shoulder.

"I'm sure you're anxious for a rematch with Wolfgang. I have a feeling it will go differently, this time," Conrad said with a smile.

"And what about you? Don't you want to avenge Henic?" Lucia asked.

"There is nothing to avenge. He's getting out of here alive, after all."

"Right…" Lucia trailed off. Conrad nodded as Dalton looked back at the two with concern in his eyes.

Within a half hour, they exited the forest, and before them stood a stone castle that was covered in snow. Great pillars layered in ice propped up the grand entrance of the Mountain King's lair, and flanking it were two even greater towers. Indentations in the front of the towers held what appeared to be statues, but they were filled with too much snow to be sure. Many of the snow mounds on the ground reached halfway up the walls. Even the entrance door was almost completely obscured by a mound.

"A might bit flashy for just one man; wouldn't you say?" Baltr asked.

"I'll have you know that he created this castle all by himself. Olivier is a Conjuring Wizard, meaning he can create things with his magic. It is truly amazing because any mage could make a bunch of stone, but he had a strong enough mind to visualize the architecture. Does this not look exactly like the castle of a king?" Aldous said as if he were bragging for him.

"Ah, so his name is Olivier? Good to know, 'cause calling him 'Mountain King' all the time would surely become a bother," Dalton said.

"It would be for the best if you stuck to calling him 'Mountain King'. A Wizard of his stature demands respect. I spoke out of turn, back there…" Aldous said as they approached the great entrance. The mounds of snow blocked the gate.

Aldous pointed his walking stick at the mounds, and an explosion of white, blizzard-like conditions hit their faces for but a few moments. As the powder settled around them, revealing the full gate, all in the group buzzed with amazement. Even more curious, the gate opened all on its own as they approached; the sound of its great groans and creaks echoing from within the dark halls.

"Nice tricks, but how'd you do that bit with the door?" Conrad asked.

"That wasn't me…" Aldous muttered.

~

As THE GROUP made their way onto the castle grounds, they remained unaware of a single eyeball that floated high above, ever watchful. Its pupil dilated while focusing on Aldous, who strode through the entrance while clanking his walking stick off the stone. As the last of the miners entered, a gust of wind shut the gate behind them, and the eye disappeared.

~

THE GROUP of 13 found themselves in a corridor with lovely red and gold-colored carpet that stretched down the path. To both their left and right were gold-plated torches that had already been lit. Between each torch was a column carved intricately of stone. They held up the second and third floors above them.

"He is most likely at his throne. Straight ahead…" Aldous said, leading the way. Joel and the others followed close behind.

As they walked down the main corridor, little changed. The fancy carpet stretched on, and the lovely gold torches continued to provide light. Occasionally, they walked by stone sets of stairs that led up to the second floor, but Aldous paid them no mind. Soon, noises crept their way into the miners' ears. Every so often they would hear light footsteps or breaths, and then, they began to hear chants off in the distance: It was a brief chorus of deep voices.

Shah!

Shah!

Shah!

Joel cocked his head. How could one man make so much noise? It sounded like many people chanting at once. After a quarter hour,

Aldous stopped the group. The chanting continued, and it grew louder.

Shah!

Shah!

Shah!

"What *is* that noise?" Baltr asked aloud.

"More like *noises*," Dalton said while scanning the area. Some flames flickered behind the group. "I think we're being followed…"

"I haven't heard such noises in these halls before," Aldous said with a furrowed brow. "Then again, it has been 200 years since I last walked the grounds…"

"It sure don't sound like we're alone in here…" Henic trailed off. Joel's eyes were drawn to his wound. It looked worse than ever. The blood seeped through the bandages so much that it was beginning to drip onto his shirt and pants. A lump came to his throat. He was running out of time.

"Anyhow, I've stopped us here to show you all something. Please, follow me," the old Wizard said as he diverged to the right and between two columns. In the shadows, he stopped at a stone wall with an iron chain attached to it.

"This here is a secret passage that leads to the heart of the mountain: the Gold Pit," he said while pulling on the chain. The wall opened, much like a door. "I tell you all this now in case of emergency: If the monolith that seals Greed away is ever in danger, then this is how you get to it. Just remember that upon walking this path, you must take the first available left-hand turn… because if you don't, it will lead you to the Guardian, or, erm… the Nightcrawler, as you have come to know it. That is where its den lies."

"But how would we know that the monolith is in danger?" Conrad asked.

"The Mountain King has his ways. He would surely inform us, and who knows? He might call on us to help him protect it!"

Joel sharpened his eyes and made hand signals to him with hints of desperation.

"Yes, yes, Henic and a few others would be granted permission to leave via the secret exit, of course, but the rest of us may need to stay and fight. Desperate times call for desperate measures. It has been a long, long time since humans have strayed this far into Mt. Couture," he replied with a nod. "And besides, once entrapped by the mines, there are only three paths that can be taken to reach the heart of Mt. Couture. One is practical suicide: A trip through the Nightcrawler's den. And the other two paths require them to enter this castle. There's this secret passage here, and another way that can only be taken after passing through these corridors."

"Since Edith and Wolfgang shouldn't know about this secret passage, and the Nightcrawler would surely kill them if they dared pass through its den, the only way they could reach the Gold Pit is if they passed us in these very halls," Conrad said.

"Precisely! There was formerly a fourth way, but now there are only three. Olivier and I decided that the path on the other side of the mountain was a liability, y'see. There were many obstacle do-hickeys to get past, such as the maze built by the luxians and the riggits; but if anyone could get by those things, they'd be able to reach the monolith with little to no further resistance. So, 200 years ago, we collapsed a tunnel to seal that path off."

"It seems that we have you to blame for those blocked-off tunnels, then. The ones near the underground river?" Dalton asked.

"Indeed. My apologies, but Olivier felt that those seeking the monolith should have to go through him or the Nightcrawler, first," Aldous replied.

"I never would have imagined all of those creatures, death traps, and obstacles were built to serve a good purpose!" Dalton said and then laughed.

"And what of this secret exit? Could Edith not simply go through there to reach the Gold Pit?" Lucia asked.

"The secret exit is a mere sliver of an opening that we must shimmy through. To use it as an entrance would require her to leave these mines and travel around the mountain, which she can no longer do," said the old Wizard with an extended finger. "And to find it from the outside is nearly impossible; for it is hidden within a tiny crevice of the mountain and blends in well with the environment. Even I cannot recall where exactly it is, and that is by design!"

"Anyhow, let us get back to the path. We are about halfway to the throne room," Aldous said before returning to the fancy red carpet.

"Marry! This place is huge! An' all fer one feller!" Alistair shouted.

"I don't think only one person lives here…" Lucia trailed off as she looked around.

No one revealed themselves, but the noises remained: Cricks and creaks in the wooden supports high above; steps on stone along with something sharp dragging across its coarse surface. Joel pictured a little knocker stalking them in the shadows, wielding an oversized axe that it was ready to use on them, execution-style. Most common of all, though, were the deep-voiced chants. The further they traveled, the louder they got; and the louder they got, the longer the chants became.

Shah!

Shah!

Shah!

Shah!

Despite a creeping sense of dread and shadow enveloping them, the group continued as they marveled at what the Mountain King had created all on his own. It seemed that with every stretch of distance, the golden torches and flames became grander.

Eventually, they could see a great door waiting for them at the end of the long stretch. From that point on, the gold torches flanking them were joined by various pieces of art; from paintings to marvelous marble statues, to murals on the wall that depicted a mighty figure with bolts of lightning in his hands. Although they were collectively in awe at the pristine pieces on their way to the door, the noises all around continued to haunt them; overriding their sense of wonder. The chants became louder and more prominent than ever:

Shah!

Shah!

Shah!

Shah!

"He's a loud fella, ain't he?" Alistair asked to a few laughs from the group.

"Can't you tell that's multiple people chanting?" Lucia asked while rolling her eyes.

"Well, maybe I'll join in with 'em, then!" Alistair said in a defiant tone.

Shah!

Shah!

Shah!

Shah!

"SHAH!" Alistair cried.

"You're off-tempo, fool," Lucia said while crossing her arms and turning away in disgust.

Dalton's cheeks flared out and some muffled chuckles escaped his mouth. Joel had already become familiar with that mannerism in the short time that he'd been traveling with the warrior: He surely had something mischievous in mind.

"I wonder if they'll go along with it if *we* start the chant…"

"LET'S DO IT!" Alistair shouted as he pumped his fist with great enthusiasm.

"Shah!" Dalton and Alistair chanted.

"Shah!" More joined in.

"SHAH!" The entire group chanted.

Shah!

"It worked!" Dalton cheered as the group erupted into laughter.

"Oho! What a lively lot you are! Just don't go disrespecting the Mountain King when we meet him…" Aldous said.

The group approached a large wooden door with iron patterns bolted onto it. It was flanked by giant gold torches that had entire fires raging on them. Aldous stood, still as night, and stared at the door as the chants started up once more, thundering and deep as ever.

SHAH!

SHAH!

SHAH!

SHAH!

The chants went on as the great flames were extinguished and the mighty door creaked open on its own. As Aldous pushed with some grunts to open it fully, the chants picked up once more.

SHAH!

SHAH!

SH-

And then the chants came to an abrupt end. Nothing aside from the creaks and groans of the door could be heard. Aldous led the group into the room, filled with darkness; not a thing could be seen save for the red and gold carpet at their feet.

As they walked, more golden torches lit up on their right and left and immediately made it apparent that they were no longer in a corridor, but a large room. The group advanced in silence. Finally, a flash of light erupted in the middle of the room and all torches had flames in them.

Now alight, they could see that it was a throne room fit for a king: Beautiful marble columns held the upper floors, with large doors in the back and intricate statues windowed over them. Many treasure boxes were scattered about and overflowing with shiny gold coins and plates. A variety of weapons were laid out on the walls, all in pristine condition.

Toward the middle of the room and at the end of the red carpet stood a golden throne upon the steps. To its left and right were two chalices that were made out of luxmortite. Little lightning bolts danced around in each of the cups, crackling and zapping as the reflections of light bounced off the dark blue beautifully.

On his golden throne sat the Mountain King himself: His deep, dark eyes gazed upon the group with what could best be described as intense contempt. He had a long, white beard with a tied-up mustache that resembled bomb fuses. His hair was also white and long, and atop it was a gold-plated crown. He wore what looked to be a plain white toga from days long past. Yet, despite his apparent age, he was well-built; practically chiseled out of the same stone that held his mighty castle together.

"Whoa, look at the muscles... to be honest, I'm jealous," Dalton whispered to a few snickers.

"What I wanna know is how his skin is a light bronze when he spends all his time inside a snow-covered castle..." Henic muttered to some more giggles. Aldous shot a stern look back at the group, freezing their collective tongues.

"Who dares tread upon my hallowed grounds?" the Mountain King boomed.

"Do you not recognize your old friend? It is I, Aldous."

"Ah... Aldous..." he muttered, his expression softening and his voice calming. After a few moments, however, a frown returned to his face. "And who are these folk that you've brought along?"

"These are people from Faiwell village. They were ordered to come here and mine for precious metals, but knew not what that meant. They now understand to stay away from this mountain," Aldous said and then looked back at the group. "Isn't that right?" Everyone nodded, timidly.

"Is that so?" the Mountain King asked, tilting his head. "A few have tried passing through over the years. I have found that they always claim pure intention, but secretly harbor ill will!" he said before slamming his fist into the throne arm. The lightning bolts in the chalices erupted with activity and began bouncing around the throne and the Mountain King himself. Many in the group shielded their eyes at the violently bright display, but eventually, the sparks settled back into their original homes, and the room was calm once more.

"I have come to know some of these people over the years, and I can guarantee that there is no ill will here. Two of them even saved me, earlier today…" Aldous replied.

"Saved? By humans?" He let out a thunderous laugh. "It is *your* job to save *them*! Have you grown soft these past 200 years, old friend?"

"Perhaps that is true, but these people have done no wrong all the same and wish only to leave. Will you let them through?" Aldous asked.

"In the countless years of watching over my domain, a foolish few have challenged me in different ways. The mountain trolls tried to take my castle by force, and I struck them all down. The nomads from the north tried to raid the treasures at the heart of the mountain, and I destroyed them as well. The slavers to the far-east tried to tempt me with their beautiful women, but I crushed them all the same. I have obliterated everything from man to avian that brought danger and uncertainty to this mountain. And some of them were less deserving of death than these folk, in fact!" the Mountain King said.

"Why do they deserve to die? Olivier, they wish for nothing more than to leave and never return!" Aldous shot back, thudding his walking stick angrily off the carpet.

"Oh? You forget that I have my watchful eyes all around the mountain," Olivier said as he held out his hand, palm up. Several disembodied eyeballs materialized and hovered above, bobbing and staring at the unwelcome guests. "Those two over there…" He pointed to Conrad and Henic. "They tried to escape along with others who possessed my black gold! I conjured up a storm to stop them several times, in fact! Little thieves!"

"*Your* black gold?" Aldous asked, raising both eyebrows.

"That's right. *My* black gold!" The Mountain King's eyes flickered a piercing yellow. "So then, it begs the question… what to do with the lot of you?" The disembodied eyeballs disappeared as he held his left hand out over the chalice. The small bolts of lightning blanketed his hand and arm so naturally that they were like an article of clothing flowing in the wind. He raised that hand and looked at it.

"On the one hand, my good friend Aldous has arrived: a reunion 200 years in the making!" he said and then held his right hand out to receive lightning from the other chalice. His eyes sharpened while marveling at the dancing light. "But on the other hand, he has allied himself with thieving rats!" The Mountain King clenched both fists and the lightning bolts scattered to the floor, jumping around the panicking group in a circle several times before they came back to his hands.

"I don' like this…" Henic muttered. His eyes grew weary and his legs were shaking.

Aldous held his walking stick up in a defensive position. The Mountain King raised one of his dark eyebrows and laughed.

"You wish to challenge me? Over some humans?" he asked.

"You seem to have forgotten that helping humans is a part of who we are," Aldous said.

"No… a part of who we are is making the world a better place. That has nothing to do with humans. What a foolish thought!" Olivier replied and then chuckled once more.

"Please… reconsider letting us through. We wish you no harm! And you can check us; there is no black gold on our person!"

"You may not have it with you now, and you may leave peacefully; but humans have become such a greedy, worthless lot. They will send more back and in greater numbers! Can you not see that?"

"Ya best not be messin' about with us, mistah Wizard!" Alistair called out.

The Mountain King stood and narrowed his striking eyes as a sudden hush came over the throne room. Aldous looked back at the big man, his eyes wide with fright. Everything about his expression told Alistair to be quiet, but his mouth kept on moving.

"Not only do we have tha best warrior in all of Faiwell on our side, but we gots two geniuses, too!" He gave both Joel and Conrad slaps to the back. "We gots Aldous over here, who controls lightnin', so yer lil' parlor tricks ain't gonna work! And then, of course, we got me: The fiercest warrior you'll ever face in yer long, boring life!"

"You idiot…" Lucia muttered.

"Oh… and I suppose *she's* alright, too," Alistair said as he nudged his head toward her while grinning.

～

"Quiet!" Aldous shouted back. He looked before the Mountain King and expected great anger, but was instead greeted with an eruption of laughter.

"Aldous, I didn't realize you brought a jester along with you! He's quite funny!" Olivier said as he placed the lightning bolts back into the chalices and relaxed on his throne. Alistair exhaled deeply as if to speak once more, but Joel and the other workers restrained and covered his mouth shut. "Mayhap I should reconsider my course of action…"

"I thank you for that," Aldous said. Shocked as he was that Alistair's otherwise foolish outburst would result in good fortune, another concern swept over him: The Olivier that he knew from 200 years ago was not so cynical, paranoid, and prone to anger. He was wise, calm, and patient. What had triggered such a change? Could the black gold have truly taken him?

"I have come to a decision," the Mountain King said, now standing. "I cannot allow you to leave, but I feel that I would enjoy your company." Everyone in the group grumbled and looked at each other in confusion. "You are now my guests… *for all time*…" he trailed off into a menacing chuckle. "But don't worry, you'll be in good company!"

From behind the Mountain King's throne and beyond the pillars, figures began to move about in the shadows. The first thing that Aldous noticed were their sinister smiles, and then how *different* each of their shapes and sizes were. The first to appear were two dark-haired women who wore gold underwear and blue see-through cloth over their bodies. They walked up to the Mountain King and wrapped their arms around his.

"Those women… they look… Lunerian…" Lucia trailed off.

"They're lovely, too. This fella knows how to live!" Dalton said with a grin.

Out of the darkness of the side corridors appeared many other different folk: From trolls to men in dark cloaks, to warriors clad in chainmail armor.

Aldous felt a cold draft from above and looked up to see an avian sweep down into the throne room. He was short; about the size of a human pre-teen, and had a coat of blue and white feathers that were covered by a brown vest and white pants. His arms were a pair of wings that allowed him to fly, but Aldous knew that underneath those wings were talon-like hands that likely held small weapons. His face, while covered in a light fur, had some similarities to a human's; aside from his nose, which resembled a small beak. Instead of feet, he had large, sharp talons.

Then, from behind the throne came a knocker dressed up in a red and black tunic and silly hat with bells on the ends. It seemed to have been dressed up as a jester for Olivier's amusement. Next to appear were men in hiking clothes, and then even more men who wore fur hides all about their bodies. All told, the throne room was filled with at least 40 different folk that Aldous didn't recognize.

"What is the meaning of this?"

"I told you that you'd be in good company, did I not?" the Mountain King replied as he smiled and the women wrapped around his arms giggled.

The blood-soaked coughs of Henic drew Aldous' attention. Conrad poked through the group to his left with the farmer draped over his shoulder, barely supporting his own weight.

"We would love to be your guests, my king," Conrad said as others in the group gasped. Aldous narrowed his eyes at him.

"What are you doing?" Lucia whispered.

"What I must..." Conrad muttered back. The desperation in his voice was striking. The old Wizard eyed Henic and his heart sank. With each short breath, his face fell paler and paler. The potion's effects were wearing off.

"You see, Aldous? He understands! Staying here is a glorious, ever-lasting experience!" Olivier said.

"But please..." Conrad trailed off as he grunted and moved Henic forward as if presenting him. "Will you help our friend? He is gravely injured, you see, and I have been told much about your great power and knowledge."

The Mountain King raised an eyebrow and then leaned forward, gazing upon the wound while stroking his white beard. "There is one way to heal your friend... past this throne room and through my torture chamber-"

"'Torture chamber'?" Aldous muttered, in shock.

"-lie the *Resurrection Falls*. If he drinks the water from that pool, he will be healed..." Olivier said. Conrad's face lit up with an exasperated joy. "But of course, there are consequences for you humans! The falls have seen their effects change over the years thanks to the wonderful black gold that has taken root in the water. Your friend will be healed, but his frail human mind will be unable to handle the concentrated black gold minerals that enter his body. He will succumb to madness, and live out the rest of his days in a violent stupor."

"No..." Conrad said, looking down. Henic's whole body was trembling, now. "Is there no other way?"

"Why yes, there is. We can end your friend's suffering here and now by killing him!" Olivier's eyes flickered yellow once more and the crowd around him erupted into cheers.

"You said that we were your guests! And now you wish to kill one of us?" Aldous asked.

"Not one, but *all*, my friend! When I said you would be my guests for all time, I meant it. Everyone that you see before you once tried to challenge me in this very castle. All failed and were struck down, but they were simply misguided! It seemed a shame for that to be the end for them!"

"Don't tell me…"

"And so, I captured their souls. Then, I conjured them up once more to live alongside me!"

All within the group grimaced. Dalton grasped the hilt of the claymore at his hip and looked back at Lucia.

"Get ready for a fight…" he whispered. She only nodded in return.

"How could you do such a thing, Olivier? To kill others and take their souls is devilry of the foulest kind!" Aldous said.

"I am doing them a service! They met their fate at my hands so I could protect my black gold and the monolith, but I realized that wasn't fair! I gave them a second chance at life in my domain," the Mountain King said.

"But how? To gather their souls would require *dark magic*. The atrocities you have committed should have plummeted your Anima and killed you…"

"Surely, you must know that I am far from the first Wizard King of Mt. Couture… haven't you ever wondered why the most powerful of Wizards would eventually need to be replaced at each monolith site?" Olivier asked as he clenched a fist full of lightning in his hand and held it up. Aldous remained silent. He knew the answer.

"It is because repelling and killing those who bring danger to our world still brings our Anima down. Up here, there are no friendly interactions; no people to help. Only people to harm; to kill! Up until a couple hundred years ago, my Anima was decreasing rapidly as I defended the mountain from intruders. I felt death's grasp, and I had come to accept that…" He clenched his fist even harder and the lightning shot out of it in two directions, striking and charring the far-off columns to his left and right.

"Wouldn't the Council of Wizards have thought of a way around that?" Conrad asked.

"Nay! The so-called 'honor' of Wizard King is that I get to sit here for hundreds or even thousands of years by myself; slowly dying as I protect the monolith. In my despair, I sought comfort of any kind.

Anything that could bring me joy as I was dying. And then..." He snapped his fingers. The woman to his left walked over to one of the treasure chests and obtained a solid bar of sparkling, black metal. It was so expertly cut and clean that one could surely see their reflection in it.

"Black gold..." Aldous muttered, near-breathless.

"Beautiful, isn't it? Certainly, better than anything the humans could make," Olivier said with a smug smile. The woman handed the bar to him, and he marveled at it as if it were one of the great wonders of the world. "In my hour of despair, it was the only thing to comfort me, and then, I heard *his* voice."

"The Dark Savior?" Aldous asked. A shiver shot down his spine.

"Hmph! I am not so naïve. I spoke not to the complete Dark Savior, but to his spawn, Greed. Yet still, unlike the Council of Wizards, who left me to die a lonely death; he gave me a solution. He taught me many important lessons, but most critically, two things: One was that I could use simple dark magic on the black gold to imbue myself with a variety of possible enhancements: In this case, I chose to increase my lifespan. The second thing he taught me was how to take and store the souls of those I had killed," the Mountain King said as he held his hand out and caressed the cheek of the woman to his right.

"I then learned to conjure their bodies and combine them with their souls so that they could have a second chance in life as my guests. As I did this over and over to intruders, my Anima took a turn for the dark, but it didn't matter because the black gold increased my lifespan. Eventually, my Anima reached the same level as a Dark Wizard's, and I no longer needed the black gold to live, but I thought it a shame to let it go to waste sitting around in the mines. I have been converting them into these solid bars as of late, to admire their beauty... wouldn't you agree that they are lovely to look at?"

"You fool!" Aldous shouted. The Mountain King frowned back at him and the yellow in his eyes intensified. "You have allowed the black gold to poison your mind! And when we Wizards are supposed to be resistant to it, too!"

"You underestimate me. I am not like these weak-willed humans," he replied while pointing behind Aldous. "The Dark Savior may have helped me, but that does *not* mean I will help *him*."

"Can you not see that it has taken you? The black gold? Those are the first stages! It may be working its poison on you slower than the humans, but soon, it will overtake your mind, and when a Wizard of your power wills the release of the Dark Savior, who will stop him?" Aldous asked.

"It would seem that you need convincing," Olivier said.

He stood from his throne and handed the black gold bar to the woman next to him. He gathered the lightning out of his chalice and held the bolts in his hands. Aldous sharpened eyes at the chalices made of luxmortite. He knew that one of them was his Wizard's artifact. If he could take that away, then perhaps he might hold the Mountain King off for long enough that the others could escape.

"You may have to fight your way through some of these undead folk..." Aldous muttered back to Dalton, whose hand was still on the hilt of the claymore. "But I will do what I can to hold Olivier off. You lot can escape this place through the doors behind the throne. The secret exit isn't too far from here."

"But what about the monolith? We may need to protect it from Edith's group, or Wolfgang," Dalton whispered back.

"I was foolish to place that burden on you. If it comes to that... me, Olivier, or the Nightcrawler will take care of it. So, I mean it when I say to save yourselves... or you will be condemned to an eternity of this mad Wizard's soul slavery..."

"What are you rats scheming about over there?" the Mountain King interrupted and then stepped down from his throne. The lightning bolts in his hands grew in intensity. "You should know that whatever you have planned, there is no escape. You will soon come to see the glory of being my *guests*!"

The resurrected souls drew their weapons and began to close in. The group of 13 readied themselves for combat, aside from Joel, who gripped his carrying sack tightly at both straps; and Henic, who was only standing thanks to Conrad propping him up.

Aldous grasped the sheathed sword at his hip; the very blade he had borrowed from Joel days prior. Only his strongest magic could combat the approaching Mountain King. It was time to return the blade to its owner, he thought while looking back at Joel. He hoped that it would spur him to fight along with the others. They were going to need all the help they could get, and much, much more if they were to survive.

∿

Outside the throne room door, which was but a crack open, a pair of yellow eyes stared through to carefully survey the situation. As he saw the resurrected souls closing in on the group of 13, Wolfgang smiled and turned to face a stoic Angus, a nervous Bronrar, and 12 other men with glowing, yellow eyes.

CHAPTER 35
POWER

Back when Dalton and the other nine dissenters had left, Edith wasted little time in exacting her true plan, much of which involved waiting for Gold Fever to fulfill its true purpose. *The poor fools*, she thought while watching the yellow-eyed men admire and caress their black gold ores. If only they knew what they had gotten themselves into.

She knew that with time, it would infect the minds of the workers if they kept it on their person. Gold Fever would make the workers obedient to the one known as 'Dark Savior', and all along, she had been aware of the monolith at the heart of Mt. Couture. The black gold and Gold Fever's purpose were to lure humans to the Gold Pit so that they would unleash the spawn of the Savior known as Greed.

Edith had been told all of those things by Drake months before the expedition took place, and at first, she hadn't believed any of it. How could her father have known such things if he'd never gone to the mountain himself, after all? She had passed it off as little more than another one of his silly schemes. He was rich, corrupt, and even mistreated her on occasion, but he wasn't a *murderer*, she had thought.

However, just weeks before the trip, she had come to realize just how serious he was. Late one night, when there had been no activity in the Miner's Guild headquarters, she was summoned there by her father. She met him with a mysterious, hooded man in attendance. He wore a dark robe with several odd patterns scattered about, but it was hard to distinguish anything about who he was or what he looked like, except the fact that he was quite a tall, built man. He was even a little taller than Angus in her estimation. Drake introduced the man as a *Dark Wizard* and revealed that he was the one who had told him everything about Greed and the black gold.

The Dark Wizard repeated much of what Drake had already told Edith, but unlike her father's smooth talk, his voice had boomed like raging thunder, yet curiously, it remained low-pitched all at once. She vividly recalled how it felt like each word was a blow to her body. Everything he had said, she believed.

That night, Drake and the Dark Wizard revealed their true plan: To unleash and then take control of Greed; and then use him to produce black gold on a worldwide scale. Not only would it bestow upon them untold riches, but control of the land as they saw fit, too.

Of course, neither wished to get their hands dirty: Drake had claimed that joining on the expedition would raise suspicions among the Village Elders, and mentioned that they had been unsure about the trip to begin with. He had only lulled them into the idea with the false legend of what lay the Gold Pit. The Dark Wizard had said that guardians of the mountain would immediately identify and attack him if he got too close to the monolith that sealed Greed.

However, the Dark Wizard had promised to aid her from the shadows. He even used dark magic to ingrain a small tattoo on her wrist. It was an odd symbol, and he informed her that they could use it to communicate, but only once. When the time was right, he would contact her.

On the matter of the release and control of Greed: Edith was instructed that all she would need to do was destroy the monolith, and a portal to the creature's prison would open. She would then take control of it with an incantation that she would have to memorize. It was a form of dark magic that even a human could perform as long as it was spoken correctly. Its sole purpose, as she was told, was to gain control of the Dark Savior's split identities.

The Dark Wizard had ingrained the incantation into her mind with his bass-filled voice:

Egois sumheach voduit
Meais leatmea nunta anua
Tunun leamini thoitatum meam

She played with some strands of her hair, eyes twitching, as she recalled those nights of intense memorization. *100 times*. Each night, she had to recite the incantation 100 times straight without making a mistake, or her father ensured that there would be harsh consequences. She let out a snorting chuckle and tightened the wind of her hair as she remembered that time Drake had pulled a dagger on her and pressed it up to her neck. Another time, Edith thought while tugging on her hair strands and grinding her teeth, he had humiliated her into doing chores around the garden on her hands and knees like those filthy handmaidens.

Yet nothing, she thought with a grimace, stung quite like when he'd yank on her precious, golden blonde hair. He knew how much she valued her locks, but he'd pull on them anyway as the most common form of punishment for a mistake. How much of her beauty had he stolen from her? *Enough*, she thought, her wound-up fingers and hair strands shaking, now. Enough that he would pay-

Rip

Edith gasped out in a brief, stuttering pain as her hand fell forward. Her twitchy green eyes gazed upon those golden strands as she released them. While watching them float down to the rocky terrain, she reveled in the pain; the *mutilation*.

"Mutilation? How dramatic!" Drake would say when she had been holding back tears and pleading for him to stop.

It wasn't *her* pain and *her* mutilation that she reveled in, however.

From her early teenage years, Edith had concluded that she was different from most others. Her 'friends' would help her bully and intimidate the other girls, but they only did so out of fear. She had also been shocked to discover that most people killed small animals for food or clothing; not to watch them squirm and suffer as a form of entertainment. Yet, she couldn't help how she had felt. She hated the weak and loved to see them writhe, whether they be some pathetic little girl as Lucia had been, or a lowly, wounded animal.

Quickly, Edith understood that she would need to suppress those feelings to keep up the appearance of Drake's brilliant, noble daughter. As the years went on, she found an outlet for those repressed urges in the bedrooms of gullible young men, whom she would go on to blackmail for her benefit. Through these escapades, Edith finally understood why she enjoyed the belittling of other girls; the senseless deaths of small animals; and the complete and utter humiliation of the men she would sleep with. All were examples where she had *power*.

In more recent years, Edith had updated her strategy from simple blackmail to creating devout followers out of her admirers. Wolfgang had been her latest and greatest example. His lust for her had become so feverish that he would kill anyone in her name. Even now, under the influence of Gold Fever and at the command of the Dark Savior, she was certain that he would choose her over him. She had him in the delicate palm of her hand, and at any moment, if she so desired, she could squash him like the bug he was. *That was power*.

Faramond had been much the same. He had been willing to kill for her; to alter his plans in order to appease her. With his status as a leader in the Miner's Guild, he looked to have much promise as one of her followers, so it was a shame that he had to die. Yet, his death had been for a worthy cause. The terror and despair in his eyes as he choked on his own blood reminded her of those small animals she used to torture and kill. That, and laying with a man who had come to worship her as a Goddess, filled her with more pleasure than she'd ever felt. So much that she hadn't been able to stop herself from smiling up at him as he reached out to her in his final, desperate moments.

But even that hadn't been enough to satisfy her growing hunger for power. As if an artist putting the finishing touches to her masterpiece, she had coaxed Wolfgang into sex, and in front of the corpse of the man they'd just killed, no less. Somehow, it had made her feel even better; euphoric, even. Letting out a convincing scream to alert the others had been a difficult task while in such a happy state.

Of course, she wouldn't have had to resort to killing Faramond if it hadn't been for her father. Drake didn't believe in her abilities as a leader, commonly citing how unlikable and unskilled she was as his reasons. He had been convinced that she would die long before reaching the Gold Pit. And so, the leadership position went to Faramond, who had a reputation for keeping workers safe. Just the thought of Drake's harsh words to her on the matter filled her stomach with knots. Opposite to smitten men like Faramond and Wolfgang, who made her feel powerful; Drake had a knack for making her feel weak; pathetic; helpless. She hated every iota of those feelings.

It was out of those hated feelings that Edith had made last-second alterations to Drake and the Dark Wizard's plans. The original intent had been for Faramond to protect Edith until succumbing to Gold Fever. As it had been told to her, those deep under the influence of black gold could communicate with the Dark Savior, and he would instruct them on how to reach the Gold Pit. From there, she was to follow him to the monolith and unleash Greed.

The blonde beauty still intended to reach the heart of Mt. Couture, but at Wolfgang's direction instead. Soon, she would lead a group of black gold-influenced miners to the monolith and show her father how great a leader she was: By taking control of Greed and using him to feast upon his flesh when she returned home.

An intense pleasure came over her as she pictured *his* pain; *his* mutilation. The blood splattering, the skin tearing, her normally calm father squealing like the pig he was as he was ripped to bloody pieces. Pure ecstasy. She couldn't wait to witness it; to feel powerful in his presence for the first time. To make *him* feel weak.

Whether it was to be Wolfgang or one of the other Gold Fever-infected workers, Edith would soon be led to the monolith, and there, she would obtain unfathomable power. All she had to do was remember one simple incantation.

"Egois sumheach voduit meais leatmea nunta anua tunun leamini thoitatum meam…" she muttered. The key to her happiness.

"Are you alright?" Angus asked as Edith snapped out of her trance. She was still staring at her ripped hair strands, now coiled up on the ground. "What shall we do, now?"

"Now we put the *true plan* into action. We shall gather as much black gold as possible and gift it to the workers. After they are infected with Gold Fever, the Dark Savior will guide them to the heart of the mountain, where they can have as much black gold as they please. Meanwhile, we will destroy the monolith and gain control of Greed," she said with a reassuring smile.

"And what of Wolfgang? I thought his mission was to find the Gold Pit?" Angus asked.

"He is wild, unpredictable, and in a killing mood, so he may not achieve the goal. With that said, if he's able to find it, then it is all the better. It would only mean we reach the monolith sooner," Edith said as she caressed Angus' cheek with her cold hand. "But I'm not worried about him. He is expendable. As long as *we're* together, nothing can stop us."

Her hand started to travel down his body. Angus, to her surprise, slapped the hand away.

"Don't play that game with me, Edith. This partnership is only business. I've seen you manipulate enough men on this trip alone to know better," Angus said and then crossed his massive arms.

"Oh my… you're a tough one to crack, aren't you?" Edith said and let out a few giggles. "But you know, they *all* crack eventually."

"Soon, I will have enough money to get any woman I want, any time I wish. You, on the other hand, can already bed any man you wish. I wonder, then… what will you do once you've acquired such wealth and power?" Angus asked her.

"Oh, I have my ideas…" Edith said before a sly smile crossed her sharp face.

"Tell me the truth, Edith," Angus said. "You have betrayed your allies thus far, and plan on betraying your own father… I have no problem going along with all of that, but how do I know that I won't be stabbed in the back as well?"

"Is that why you rejected me?" Edith asked in an amused tone. Angus only stared back with his usual stone face. "You want to know the truth? Soon, you and I will have more money than God. And what will they, the unworthy have? Death, destruction, and their dear, dear Dark Savior…" she trailed off and then cocked her head. "Do you think that you are unworthy? Is that why you worry?"

"No…"

"Good, because I chose you to be part of this plan while under the impression that you were cool-headed, strong, and reliable. Stay useful to me and I'll have no reason to betray you. And besides…" Edith said and then got up close to him. She stood on her tip-toes and kissed his cheek. "I wouldn't turn on you before getting what I want out of you…" the blonde beauty began to kiss his neck and he pushed her off. She giggled while stumbling back.

"Very well, but I'll be keeping this strictly business. Shall we proceed with the plan?" Angus asked as he wiped her spit off of his neck.

"Yes, I suppose we should, *Angy.*"

The giant groaned. He would come to enjoy his pet name just like the others, she thought with a smirk. She walked to the front of the group and Angus stood close by.

"Attention, everyone!" she called out. The resting miners stood and watched on without complaint. "I promised you more black gold, didn't I? It's time to deliver on the promise!"

The crowd was alight with cheers and buzzing.

"Yeh! I want more!" one miner cried.

"The best leader we ever had; she is!" another said.

"And what if I told you that we don't have to do any mining to obtain more?" Edith said to the praise of all. "There is much left-over black gold from the traitors that left us…"

"Lotta knobs!" one miner shouted out to some laughs.

"They will know the fury of our Savior soon enough!"

"Yeh! We shoulda killed 'em while they were here! Save the village any trouble!" said a worker to cheers from all, except Bronrar, who looked away and shifted in his boots. Edith sharpened her eyes in his direction, but did not address him.

"Now, now… those fools will be taken care of when we get back. I want you lot to focus on the reward you will receive for your loyalty to our fine village," she said to more elated smiles from the workers. "Angus and I will be rounding up the abandoned black gold in this cave, and after that, we'll divvy it up equally for you all." The crowd had reached a fever pitch of excitement. "For now, just relax some more while we gather the black gold for you."

Edith and Angus began their walk toward the mine cart, to the right of the tunnel entrance. When they reached it, she peered inside to see that it was filled to the brim with not only black gold, but with extra brown carrying sacks as well.

"This is perfect!" Edith said as she grabbed a few brown sacks. "I will use these to pick up the abandoned black gold. You take the cart over to where the workers are. Don't let any of them touch it until I get back. Then, we will split it up for everyone to have." Angus nodded and pushed the cart back toward where the miners rested.

Over time, Edith gathered the abandoned bags of black gold left by Alistair, the men who had been slain by the Nightcrawler, those who had died in the labyrinth, and the men who happened to leave with Dalton. She brought them over to where Angus stood with the cart.

There was much to go through, and the miners had already begun to approach them like hungry vultures around a dead animal. One of the men came a little *too* close for Edith's liking, and Angus, sensing her discomfort like a loyal dog, blocked his way.

"Stand aside…" the worker muttered as he tried to brush past the giant, but he was pushed back.

"We still need to organize the black gold into fair shares for you lot. You must wait with everyone else," Angus said to the yellow-eyed man.

"Do you not follow our Dark Savior?" the man asked as he attempted to walk past Angus again. He was pushed back once more. "Those who do not follow his will… I shall strike them down!"

"You now have two options," Angus said as he cracked his enormous knuckles. "You can try and pass me one more time and find out what happens. Or you can wait with the rest of the group and meet the Dark Savior soon, unharmed." The man, who seemed to finally realize the great size difference between them, laughed nervously and turned back.

"I love when you threaten them, Angy," Edith said with a seductive smile.

Angus let out a great sigh. "Let's get to counting."

Discounting themselves, Edith and Angus split up the stockpile of black gold from the mine cart and left-over sacks for the remaining 19 workers. The process was tedious and the workers grew weary, but soon enough, all was sorted and ready to go.

"Alright everyone, line up! Your black gold awaits…" Edith said with a knowing smile.

Some men nearly jumped for joy as they formed a line leading up to Edith and Angus.

The line moved at a crawl's pace as each individual received a large sum of ore. Some already had enough that they weren't able to fit more into their carrying sack, so they had little choice but to leave the remaining pieces behind. Excitement built up in Edith's chest as she heard the men mumbling in line about 'following his will', 'releasing our Savior', or most commonly, the talk of 'killing non-believers'. It wouldn't be long, she thought, before one of them led her to the monolith.

After some time, Bronrar's turn came to receive his share of the black gold.

"Ah, there you are, my friend," Angus said as he began to place the ore into his bag. "I was beginning to wonder if you would be coming up here at all. But I'm glad you did… the more you obtain, the more comfortable and luxurious your future shall be."

"Right…" Bronrar trailed off before he looked at his two leaders and raised an eyebrow. "Hold on, why aren't either of you takin' any black gold for yerselves?" he asked.

"We don't need any right now," Edith said while flipping her golden hair back. "There will be plenty to take for ourselves in the Gold Pit."

"*The Gold Pit*? That old legend? I thought we were leavin' this place after gettin' our fill of the black gold…" Bronrar's tone steadily reflected nervousness.

"Edith has made a wonderful discovery: At the heart of the mountain lies the secret to the black gold's creation," Angus said as he put the last of Bronrar's black gold into the sack. "If we can create black gold for ourselves, imagine what that would mean. Not only would you be living in luxury, but all of Faiwell would be, too. No more lowlifes hangin' around and stealin', no more strugglin' in the dank mines to make a living, no more worrying about lack of funds or materials to trade, and most importantly, we will never need to come back here again."

"Aw, but I wanted to leave…" Bronrar muttered before looking over his shoulder. "Those other workers are makin' me nervous. They keep babblin' about strange things, and I even heard some talk of 'killin' non-believers'! We shouldn't spend much more time with these people, Angus."

Edith raised an eyebrow. Bronrar should have joined in with those workers by now. Why wasn't he succumbing to Gold Fever?

"They're a rowdy bunch, aren't they?" Angus said with a chuckle. "Stay close to me. I'll make sure nothing happens to you."

"Alright, but-"

"How are you able to complain when we are making you rich? So, the men are acting strange? Grow a spine and be glad that you have been included, to begin with. So far, you have done very little to aid this team," Edith snapped at him.

"Yes, ma'am…" Bronrar ducked his head and went back to his spot at the cave wall.

"Was that necessary?" Angus asked, cracking a frown.

"You tread lightly with him because he is your friend. But he would have rather gone off with those other traitors, I'd wager," Edith said and then crossed her arms. "More importantly, I worry that the black gold is not infecting his mind the same way that it is the others. If he refuses to go along with our plans, then we'll have to-"

"He will make it through this journey safely. Or you will find yourself answering to *me*," Angus interrupted.

"Oh, my…" Edith said, taken aback. "I love it when you take charge, Angy." She bit her lower lip and reached a hand out toward him, but he caught it.

"Promise me. Promise that you won't target him. I will ensure he goes along with our plans. But no harm is to come to him," he said.

"You have a real soft spot for your friend, don't you?" Edith asked as a grin came to her sharp face. "How about we make a deal, then? I shall leave him alone, and that's a promise… but *you* have to give me a chance…"

He released her hand. "There is little time for romance, wouldn't you say?"

"Of course there is. We need to wait a little while for the black gold to work its magic, after all. So, what do you say?" Edith asked as she nudged her head back to the spot where many rocks stuck out of the ground.

"Right where you slept with and aided in the murder of Faramond? A bold suggestion…" Angus said, his normally stone expression melting into a bewildered stew.

"It's the only place we can get some privacy around here… although, soon the Gold Fever will have them in such a stupor that we could do the deed right in front of them and they wouldn't blink an eye," Edith said with a snort.

"And what of Wolfgang?"

"You still worry about him? Let me tell you a little something about Wolfgang…" Edith said as she leaned in and got on her tiptoes to reach his ear. "His fate is sealed. He will either be put to death in Faiwell, or killed in these mines."

The blonde beauty then nibbled on his ear and she could see his neck hairs standing on end. She had him now.

"Very well. If I have your word that Bronrar remains safe, I suppose we do have time to kill," Angus said. Edith giggled with excitement.

They walked off to the other side of the cave, holding hands. Behind the rocks, Angus laid a set of blankets out, and as he turned around, Edith jumped up onto him. He caught her by the legs and they began to kiss. He walked over to the cave wall and pressed her back up against it. She was light as a feather while in his hands.

"So strong…" she said between kisses on his neck. "I told you before, didn't I? *Everyone cracks eventually.*"

Angus then knelt on the blanket and carefully laid Edith down. She ripped his shirt off and started to scratch at his back. Before she could go any further, however, Angus sat up. The blonde beauty only stared back. Was he truly so resistant to her charms?

"You go on top," he said.

Edith cocked her head, but she quickly understood when he refused to look her in the eye. *He's afraid,* she thought. Afraid that he would share Faramond's fate. He seemed on edge and his whole body tensed up, as if ready to attack anyone who dared ambush him.

Wanting to make him comfortable, she nodded, and then they swapped positions.

"I know why you want me on top…" Edith muttered as she unstrapped her dress and then took her blouse off. "Just know that you will come to trust me, one day."

She grabbed his hand and placed it on her bare breast. Angus smiled up at her and the tension in his body lessened. The blonde beauty smiled, too. Soon, she thought, she would obtain the ultimate power of Greed. In the meantime, though, converting Angus into yet another of her devout followers was power enough.

~

BRONRAR GROANED as he stared at the grounded rocks on the other side of the cave. He had seen Angus walking off with Edith while holding her hand, and that was all it had taken for his stomach to knot up. It was the same spot where Faramond had died under suspicious circumstances, after all. Yet, the other miners didn't seem to care. They were all too busy with their black gold or mumbling nonsense to themselves.

"Somethin' botherin' ye?" a miner to his right asked.

He nudged his head forward. "Angus and Edith walked over there a lil' while ago, and they have not returned. I worry for their safety."

"Methinks they went ta someplace private so they can focus on the illuminating words of the Dark Savior. He speaks ta all of us, friend. There ain't nothin' to be afraid of," the miner replied.

"No, no. I'm talkin' about-"

"Yer tryin' to tell me that the Dark Savior hasn't spoken to you?" the miner said, leaning in while cocking his head. The question had sounded accusatory to Bronrar's ears.

"No, it's not about that! I'm talkin' about-"

The miner grabbed him by the collar and throttled him. He brought his face to within inches of Bronrar's; eye-to-eye, and snarled at him. His eyes glowed a noticeable yellow.

"Are ye tryin' to say yer not a believer? Believers are the only decent men out there, and if you ain't a believer, then yer part of the problem."

"You don' understand…" Bronrar muttered as he slapped the man's hand away from his collar.

"There ain't much ta understand! Yer either with us, or yer against us. There is no in-between," the miner shot back and grasped his pick-axe. "So, what's it gonna be?"

"I-I am with you… we're all here to follow the will of the Savior, right?" Bronrar said before letting out a nervous laugh.

"That's more like it. Don' let me catch ye talkin' like that again," the miner said, pointing his pickaxe at him. "Now, enjoy the beauty of our Savior's voice as he speaks to us." He smiled before closing his eyes and letting the pickaxe fall.

Fear overcame all of Bronrar's senses. He began to notice more yellow eyes in the group, and all of them felt aggressive. It was as if he were a helpless rabbit trapped in a circle of wolves. What in the world was going on with the other workers? He prayed for Angus and Edith to return so that they might get moving again. Anything was better than sitting with these crazed men, he thought.

Angus lay out on the blanket, his barreled chest bobbing up and down a little less with each heavy breath. Eventually, they fell within the rhythm of the glowing blue rocks around him, fading in and out. Edith lay at his side with one of her delicate arms wrapped around him, her warmth spreading all around his body like a campfire on a cold night. Her normally demanding eyes were closed, and she was smiling. *So peaceful*, he thought. Had he truly made her feel that way? For the first time in a long while, Angus felt wanted, and it felt good.

Yet, he had to remind himself of the cold, hard reality: Edith held no loyalties and would move on to the next man whenever it best suited her. In the best-case scenario, she would leave him after gaining the riches and power that she desired. In the worst case, she might well leave him for dead in these damned mines, he thought.

He was determined not to let himself become another Faramond or Wolfgang, but some part of him hoped that he was the exception and not the rule; that Edith truly was smitten with him. If that were the case, he would be happy to make her his wife-

The giant cleared his throat, his eyes wide and cheeks red with embarrassment at such a naïve thought. Edith awoke and yawned. She looked up at him with those sharp, green eyes. A tingle ran down his spine.

"Shall we get back to the workers, then?" Angus asked, his face returning to its usual stone-like features. "Surely, the Gold Fever must be setting in by now."

"Yes, I suppose we should be getting back," Edith said as she leaned over and kissed his chest. "But let it be known that I'm not done with you, yet. After this is all over, you're all mine," she said with a chuckle and then stood to get dressed.

Angus gazed upon her and cracked a smile. Edith truly was a beauty to behold, and she made him feel wanted; valuable; powerful. It was a shame that he couldn't fully trust her. Such a shame that even now, his mind was coming up with reasons to ignore the fact that she had betrayed all men who had been smitten with her while on this expedition. In her own way, Edith was much like the black gold: Beautiful to look at, addictive to the touch, but poisonous to the mind.

As he continued to look her over, Angus caught on to something he hadn't noticed before and cocked his head. "What is that on your wrist?"

"This?" Edith asked as she held up her wrist and pointed to the tattoo. "Remember that Dark Wizard I mentioned? The night that he and my father told me of their little scheme, he used some kind of dark magic to brand me with this. He said it would allow us to communicate, but only once. I imagine he will contact me when we reach the Gold Pit."

Angus nodded and then started to get dressed. The moment of truth was nearly upon them. One way or another, he would find out soon whether Edith was truly smitten with him, or if she was merely using him as she had the others.

CHAPTER 36
EDITH'S JOURNEY

After Edith and Angus got dressed, they made their way back to the group of workers. Upon returning, they were greeted by many sets of yellow eyes and dazed scowls. Most clutched their black gold, while some others were curled up into a ball, muttering nonsensically to themselves. Bronrar was an outlier, however. He stared a hole through Angus, as if he were an angry wife ready to scold her husband for staying out too late.

"Are you having fun, Bronrar?" Angus asked with a smirk.

"Not as much fun as the two of you, I'm sure…" Bronrar said and then crossed his arms. The giant blushed. "Meanwhile, I was here bein' interrogated by ever-lovin' tosspots! They've turned into fanatics, Angus. We oughta leave here while we can… it ain't safe."

"Sorry, but that is not an option. Yet, the struggle will be worth it in the end. Stick by me. I won't let anything happen to you," he replied.

"I've heard that one before…" Bronrar muttered. Angus frowned.

"Well then, I hope you all had a good rest," Edith said in front of the crowd. Several yellow eyes merely stared back at her. She cocked her head briefly before continuing, "Are you ready to meet the Dark Savior?"

"Yes!" one miner called out.

"Finally, my great Savior will be free…" another said as tears filled his eyes.

"All for the will of the Savior!"

"The non-believers shall burn!"

"Take us to him!"

"The Savior should have spoken to some of you by now. Did he tell you how to reach him?" Edith asked.

"Eh? I ain't sure…"

"He talked ta me about gettin' more black gold…" a miner muttered.

"I dunno! Take me to 'im, now!" another shouted.

"Only those that are worthy would be told!" one worker said. "Why have you not been told, eh?"

"Yeh! Edith should know!"

"Why doesn't she know?"

"She ain't *really* one of us, is she?"

Edith gasped and took a step back as the rowdy crowd began to close in around her and Angus. All of them had weapons in hand and at the ready. How had they turned on her so quickly? Everything so far had proceeded as her father predicted, so why weren't the Gold Fever-infected being directed to the Gold Pit?

Her thoughts were interrupted when the shadow of Angus blotted her out. He had jumped in front of her and drawn a weapon as one last layer of protection. A smile came to her, despite the dire situation. She had converted him into a follower. It would be a shame if he had to die now, but if need be, he could hold them off for long enough that she might escape.

The blonde beauty shifted in her boots, ready to pivot and bolt away as she heard the moans and chants of the approaching horde. There was no avoiding it, now. She would have to-

"I know where the Savior is!"

Edith peeked past Angus to see Bronrar standing between them and the angry crowd. They were all looking at him with crooked, dumbfounded expressions. It had been enough to temporarily halt them, however, and for that, Edith and Angus breathed sighs of relief.

"H-he came to me… in a dream! And he told me of his location! Follow me, friends! For it is the will of our great Savior!" Bronrar said to an eruption of cheers.

"For the will of the Savior!" a miner said.

"Let's go!" one worker called out.

"I knew he was one of us!" said another.

Edith and Angus gazed at each other, both with disbelief in their eyes. Bronrar had been the only one to *resist* the black gold's effects, after all. Angus shrugged and Edith took a deep breath. Though it was an obvious lie, he had at least saved them for the time being.

Bronrar jumped to the head of the pack while Edith and Angus followed close behind. The rest of the Gold Fever-infected workers followed along with enthusiasm. They trekked across the cave, toward the tunnel. As they entered the passage, Angus approached the nervous miner from behind.

"What are you doing? You don't truly know where the Dark Savior lies, do you?" he asked in a hushed tone.

"'Course not. I haven't gone mad like these other men, but they believe what you say as long as they like what they hear," Bronrar whispered back.

"Oh yeah? And what happens when they realize that we *don't know*? They'll just kill us anyway, you fat fool," Edith jumped in with an angry whisper.

"I don' appreciate yer insults. Especially when I just saved yer sorry hide," Bronrar shot back. "And in case ye were wonderin', I *do* have a plan to escape these fanatics."

"And what did you come up with?" Angus asked.

"I will lead us to the dratagon cave, and then cause a commotion to awaken them. We can escape while everyone else is distracted by their attack," Bronrar said.

"Your plan is to create another enemy for us in the hopes that we miraculously survive? And then we return to the village with the pittance of black gold that we have now? We are sitting on a *fortune*, and you wish to run away? Your plan is as dim-witted as you are incompetent," Edith said and then scoffed.

"I never mentioned anythin' about bringin' *you* along, did I? Feel free to test yer luck with these madmen. I don' care what you do." He shrugged.

"Why you ungrateful little-" Edith cut herself off and then looked back with a nervous smile. They were staring at her. She had to be careful not to raise her voice too much. "Do you know how many times Wolfgang wanted to kill you? And how many times I kept you alive? You should be thanking me."

"Oh? You want 'thanks', do ya? I'll give you thanks..." Bronrar muttered while grimacing.

"There is no need for arguing. For now, they are under control, but we will eventually need to find an alternative course of action," Angus said.

"But my plan…" Bronrar trailed off, sulking.

"It was a good start, but let us finish it," Angus said as he put a hand on his shoulder. He then turned his gaze to Edith. "There must be something we're missing. Something that will allow the Dark Savior to speak with them…"

"I don't know. I followed everything my father said, and up to now, everything has come to pass. This is the first time that the black gold hasn't behaved in the way it was told to me…" Edith said.

"Hold on, you lot are manipulatin' *more* people?" Bronrar asked, his face contorting into pure repulsion. "I thought the black gold was safe to hold?" He glared back at Angus.

"Well, you're alright, aren't you?" Angus asked.

Bronrar let out a long breath. "Alright, I think I know how they can talk to the Dark Savior…"

"Oh, this should be good," Edith said before snickering.

"Dalton said in his journal that the Dark Savior spoke to him in his dreams. I thought it was nothin' but ramblin' back then, but now… it makes perfect sense, don't it? That must be how he tells folks his location, and why some of the first team up an' disappeared after goin' crazy. They must'a been tryin' to find him," he said.

"Actually… that *does* make sense," Edith said, her eyes wide.

"So, we try to get them to sleep?" Angus asked.

"It appears to be our only option, for now. It will slow our journey to the final goal, but if it gets the job done, what do I care? I can wait a little longer," she replied.

"You lot can go about with that plan. While they sleep, I'm takin' my black gold and gettin' outta here," Bronrar said.

"See? This is why you are little more than a lump. You come up with a decent plan like that and then you wish to abandon it? You have no spine. You should follow your friend's example," Edith said as she started to rub Angus' back. "I happen to know he has *plenty* of back-bone." Angus smiled back down at her.

"Can you not see she's tryin' to control you, Angus? You should come with me," Bronrar said.

"Nonsense. I know exactly what I'm doing, and I shall not be controlled. It is you who should come along with us, my friend. You could be a part of something even bigger. You would be a hero to the village," he replied. Bronrar offered no response, and the group continued down the rest of the tunnel in silence.

When they reached the cave, the group heard loud cackles coming from the other side. Edith knew exactly who it was: Wolfgang. Bronrar halted, but Angus pushed him forward.

"What are you doin'?" he asked. "He's a murderer! We should stay clear of him!"

"Wolfgang's mission was to find the Gold Pit. If he has found it, that is information we require," Angus said.

"First you tell me that yer knowingly manipulatin' the workers, and now yer gonna tell me that yer still on the same side as Wolfgang? I thought you wanted to get away from him? That he was threatenin' you?" Bronrar asked, his voice defensive.

"We must all make sacrifices to achieve the final goal," Angus said.

Edith frowned. If his objections continued for much longer, she worried that Bronrar might change Angus' mind. She snarled in the nervous miner's direction. "Are you able to do anything besides complain?"

Finally, the group reached the other side of the cave and looked up to see Wolfgang peering down at them from a hole in the ceiling. He was covered in cuts, bruises, and blood, yet there was an unmistakably sinister smile on his face.

"Ye lot must be gettin' desperate to be led by a knob like *him*!" Wolfgang said and then pointed at Bronrar, laughing some more. Bronrar blushed and grumbled, but didn't speak up.

"Were you able to find the Gold Pit, Wolfy?" Edith asked.

"I haven't gotten to it yet, but the Savior showed me the way in my dreams. Soon, he shall be free again!" he cried to the cheers of the Gold Fever-infected in the group. "I see ye got plenty of supporters. Those who follow his will. I suppose I should show ye lot the way then, eh?"

"Finally… the Savior!" one said.

"I can hardly wait!" called out another.

"I always knew Wolfgang was a good feller!"

Edith almost couldn't believe her ears. Up until now, the miners hated Wolfgang for the murder of Faramond and the theft of their treasures. Yet, now the court of public opinion ruled that none of those things mattered. All that mattered to them now was that he supported their cause. *The Gold Fever had put them into such a stupor that they were willing to ally with a murderer,* she thought while cracking a smirk. They'd be even easier to manipulate than she'd first believed.

"First, ye lot need to come up here," Wolfgang said as he pointed behind the group. "Yer gonna have to go back to the tunnel where ye came from. In there, ye'll find a secret passage on yer left. I covered it up with some rocks, but it should be obvious now that ye know what it is."

"And then?" Edith asked, crossing her arms.

"Then, ye'll follow the secret path until ye reach this here hole in the ceiling. After ye pass this hole, take the first tunnel on yer right. It'll bring ye up a tall slope. I'll be at the top, waitin' fer ye. Be quick! The Dark Savior awaits us!" Wolfgang said and then ran off as the miners cheered.

"Well? What are we waiting for? Let's go!" Edith said with authority as she turned and stormed back to the tunnel from whence they came.

~

THE GROUP TRAVELED QUICKLY down the tunnel and found the rocks blocking the secret path. With a few swings of a pickaxe, the rocks were shattered and they were able to enter one at a time. It was a narrow path and took some climbing, but eventually, the group found themselves at the hole in the ceiling where Wolfgang had been no less than a quarter-hour before.

Edith tread lightly around the hole in the floor and the others continued to follow. She took her first right as Wolfgang had commanded, and true to his word, the path turned into a steep incline. Edith and Bronrar in particular began to slow down after some time, but the Gold Fever-infected miners drove the pace. It was obvious that they had become single-minded in their desire to meet the Dark Savior.

Angus looked back at a huffing and puffing Bronrar as they continued to climb. "How are your legs feeling?"

"I ain't talkin' to you right now," Bronrar said, turning his nose up to him.

"Why not?"

"Yer in league with Wolfgang, and you also helped Edith brainwash these people… but even worse, you were fine with brainwashin' yer own friend. I thought you were lookin' out for me when you told me to keep my black gold, but I realize now what you truly wanted…"

"Well, it didn't seem to affect you, so I didn't see the harm. I do wonder why you have been resistant to its effects, though," Angus said.

"I don' know. All I know is when I start feelin' strange, hearin' voices, or have folks actin' strange around me, I get nervous. And when I get nervous, it's all I can think about…"

Angus smirked as much as his stone face would allow. "I shouldn't be surprised. You are of a stubborn sort and always have been."

"Is that all you have to say?"

"It's curious that you decided to stay with our group, rather than run off as you'd originally intended. Could it be that you were scared to enter the dratagon cave alone? No matter what you might think of me, it seems that you have come to understand the value of my protection."

"You misunderstand," he replied with a snort. "If I had run off to the dratagon cave, I have no doubt that these fanatics woulda run me down and killed me. That damned Wolfgang… he ruined my plans…"

Angus remained silent. He very much doubted that the Gold Fever-infected would have even noticed Bronrar slipping away.

Eventually, the group reached the top of the slope and found Wolfgang waiting for them at the tunnel exit. They were in a large, vertical shaft now, where rows of walkways extended up and back into an infinite darkness. Across the path was a staircase carved out of rock. Edith walked up behind the blond brute and wrapped her arms around him.

"It feels good to hold you in my arms again, Wolfy," she said. He smiled back at her. "I am pleased that you have found the way. Believe me when I say that you will be *handsomely rewarded* for your efforts."

Wolfgang leaned in for a kiss, but Edith held a finger up between their lips.

"Uh-uh, Wolfy. Business first, romance later… and I do intend for there to be *much* romance later," she said, seductively.

A surge of jealousy rushed through Angus. He knew it was a part of Edith's game, but for some reason, he couldn't help it. He calmed himself upon remembering what Edith had told him: Wolfgang was expendable and would die soon, one way or another.

"Very well…" Wolfgang said, his tone drenched in disappointment. "Not too long ago, those scoundrels that we wanted to kill passed through here. I think they were with Dalton, too."

"Yes, they split off from our group," Angus said, scratching his chin. "But why would they go this way? They claimed to be leaving the mines."

Wolfgang grinned. "That may be my fault, then. Ye see, I chopped down the supports in the tunnel that leads to the outside. Had to take care of them damn knockers…"

"*You—what?*" Edith asked, her eyes wide.

"Relax. The Savior told me many things. When we reach the Gold Pit, there is a secret exit not far from there. That's where we'll make our escape after releasing him!" Wolfgang said as he clenched a shaking fist and held it up, smiling.

"You had me worried for a moment," Edith said before sighing in relief. "So, then… lead the way."

"Alright, but ye lot had best be ready for a long climb."

After many grueling rounds of stairs, the group heard a commotion that came from above. The sound of high-pitched shrieks and footsteps thumping heavily off rock reverberated off the shaft walls.

"Seems we aren't far behind the traitors," Angus said.

"What if they're headed for the Gold Pit? We can't let them get there before us!" Edith said in a panic. "Let us be swift! Our Dark Savior depends on it!"

After more exhaustive running, the group reached the top of the shaft and found themselves with two choices: The left tunnel or the right. The noises from earlier had completely ceased.

"I think the non-believin' scoundrels went that way," Wolfgang said, pointing to the tunnel on their left. "The fools! The Gold Pit is *this* way." He pointed down the right tunnel.

With that, the group entered the passage to their right. Angus looked up as they walked, noting that there were holes in the ceiling. He readied himself for a surprise knocker attack, but it never came. Not even their *clicks* and *clacks* were present. Perhaps they had chased the traitors down the tunnel behind them, he thought.

Soon, the tunnel turned into a cave, and Wolfgang came to a sudden stop. The area was pitch black. Only torches gave them any light, and it was limited. Angus and Edith looked around as the workers behind them began to grumble.

"Quiet, fools…" Wolfgang said to them in a hushed tone. He pointed to the dark figure that lay at the cave's center, curled up into a ball, bobbing up and down from long breaths. Even in such darkness, it managed to be an even darker silhouette. "What the hell is *that?*"

"It's the Nightcrawler…" Angus muttered. "Is it necessary to go this way? Mayhap there is another way around…"

"Naw, this is the way that the Savior showed me. There is no alternative," Wolfgang said.

"Worry not," Edith said with a smile. "It appears to be asleep. And even if it awakens; as long as it isn't provoked, the beast only attacks one at a time. So, at worst, we lose one of our own and move on."

"Yer so quick to kill another of yer own? Even if they *have* gone mad…" Bronrar chimed in from behind. Edith turned and frowned at him. Angus raised an eyebrow. He could have sworn that under the dim torchlight, he had seen her shift to a devious smile.

"Sacrifices must be made fer our Savior," Wolfgang said while shrugging. He then began to walk forward again.

Edith looked at her men and then put a finger to her lips. "Everyone, keep quiet… the Nightcrawler sleeps in this cave…"

~

As they snuck around the edges of the cave, Edith let herself fall back slowly but surely, until she was behind Bronrar. *Of course* the fat lump had fallen to nearly the back of the group, she thought with a smirk.

Now was an opportune time to tie up a loose end. The blonde beauty remembered what she had promised Angus, but in the dark, she was confident that it could be made to look like an accident. She watched the Nightcrawler carefully as they continued to walk, and was ready to push Bronrar at any moment. The lies were already taking shape in her mind: 'He tripped over a rock in the darkness,' she would say. Angus had become so smitten with her that he'd probably believe it.

Edith shuddered as she saw a glowing, red eye open in the distance. Slowly, more red eyes opened up. All of them were fixed upon the group. As she had feared, the beast had too good of sense to let them slip by undetected. She raised both hands and tensed them up, ready to make the push with all of her might, but then felt someone grab her arm from behind. Edith looked back in shock to see that it was Angus' mighty grip that wrapped around her entire arm.

"What are you… doing?" she asked and tried to pull away, but as she had suspected, it was fruitless. Angus' grip was hard as iron.

"You made a promise. I kept up my end of the bargain, but it looks like you were about to go back on our deal," Angus said. Edith gazed at the beast to their left as more of its eyes opened up. It stood in its unnatural, hunched posture, and she could see its many mouth tentacles fluttering in the shadows.

"We have no choice… the beast is awake…" Edith trailed off as Angus let her go. She looked back up at him in confusion.

Angus turned to face one of the Gold Fever-infected behind him; the last in line. Suddenly, he picked the man up by his collar, and before he could so much as make a noise, the giant threw a monstrous haymaker. Angus' massive fist connected with a loud *slap* that echoed off the cave walls. Edith's eyes lit up as blood and teeth soared through the air and the man stumbled back. She reveled at the vulgar power display and bit her lower lip until blood trickled into her mouth. The blonde beauty wanted to jump up and kiss Angus right then and there, but let out a stuttered sigh and then took a deep breath, instead. *Now is not the time*, she thought.

Now, the only thing holding the dazed man up was Angus, who had grabbed him by both shoulders. With a loud grunt, he pushed him toward the Nightcrawler. The miner stumbled before falling face-first to the unforgiving ground.

The Nightcrawler let out a piercing shriek and carved its dagger-like claws against each other. The man scrambled to reach his feet, but Angus' blow had truly stunned him. With each attempt to stand, he merely fell back over and flailed on the ground some more while letting out panicked laughter.

"Fer the Dark Savior, my friends!" he cried before the beast pounced and an eruption of blood obscured him. After the sea of red splattered on the ground, the great silhouette of the Nightcrawler could be seen tearing at his limbs and eating them, slowly.

"Sacrifices must be made…" Angus muttered as he, Edith, and the group dashed for the cave exit. The blonde beauty smiled back at him as they ran.

"Almost there!" Wolfgang called back when they reached a new tunnel.

The group ran for some time and up a great incline that made even the infected miners complain aloud, but eventually, Wolfgang came to a stop. The tunnel was lit by torches that hung off the rock edges, and up ahead they could see what looked to be a false wall. To Wolfgang's right was another tunnel that glowed from the light of more torches.

Wolfgang wore a grin from ear to ear as he turned to face them. He pointed down the path to his left. "Down this tunnel lies the Gold Pit, and our Dark Savior."

Cheers erupted from the group, and without any more words, he led them down the tunnel. The passage was much like any other within the mines: Rocky with poorly built wooden supports. However, it was completely illuminated by torches on the walls to show how much damage had been done to its structure over the years.

The walk down to the Gold Pit took what felt like an eternity to Edith, who was too excited for words. As the tunnel opened up into a cave, the first things to catch her eye were legions of black gold sparkles lighting the area. She saw so well, in fact, that the silhouette of the monolith at the cave's center was apparent, and her heart fluttered like a wandering butterfly.

Flanking them upon their exit of the tunnel were torch mechanisms ready to be lit: The same technology that the Ancient Ones had set up in the first cave and the labyrinth. Wolfgang and Angus lit the torches, and then streaking blue light scattered in many lines about the walls, eventually reaching the ceiling to provide complete visibility for all. Now, they could see that the Gold Pit was large: At least the same length of the sand pit where they had been attacked by giant insects, yet also even wider and rounder. It was a near-perfect circle, and the ceiling was dome-shaped. It almost felt like they were in a building, not a cave.

The glowing blue lines along the walls and roof were truly a fascinating sight, as the energy of the Ancient Ones and the Dark Savior's black gold clashed, creating dark green beams of light that shot to the ground and scattered across the cave.

Edith took charge and led the group toward the monolith. It was a great black slab of stone that stood even taller than the dratagons had been. It was also quite thick and had writing on both its front and back.

After reaching the monolith, the Gold Fever-infected men stood in silence, their mouths agape and their yellow eyes reflecting the glowing text on the slab of stone.

"What does it say?" Angus asked as he felt the smooth surface of the monolith. "The text has been inscribed with inhuman precision; almost as if it is painted on. But I can just barely feel the engravings. Whoever did this must have been a master."

"It looks to be the ancient language," Edith replied, flipping her hair back. "But it matters little. I already know what needs to be done, and I'm sure it is little more than a fruitless warning not to unleash the Savior, anyway."

As Edith too reached out to feel the text of the monolith, a warming sensation came to her wrist. Within the second that it took for her to start feeling the smooth surface of stone, her wrist began to burn; as if she'd exposed it to the sun all day. Was the monolith *harming her*? The blonde beauty gasped and recoiled her hand.

Now, it was a searing hot pain; like a branding iron had been pressed up to her skin. She gritted her teeth and fell to a knee before letting out a weak cry. Yet, the burning sensation continued to worsen, hotter than anything she'd ever felt, and now she was in the most pain she'd ever felt. Her weak cries quickly turned to desperate screams.

"What is it?" Angus asked as he put a hand on her shoulder. Wolfgang approached and then knelt so they were face-to-face.

"Are ye alright, my love?" he asked as his yellow eyes stared past her, at Angus. For a brief moment, she wondered if he suspected anything between her and the giant, but those thoughts quickly dissipated as her wrist throbbed and blistering pain ran up her arm.

"M-my wrist! It burns! Like it's on fire!" she squealed.

"The tattoo!" Angus said as he grabbed her wrist. "That must be it!" He turned her arm over to see the odd symbol, which glowed like a poker.

"Oi! Get yer hands off my gal!" Wolfgang said as he slapped at Angus' hand. However, his grip did not falter, and the blond brute frowned.

"Make it stop! I'll do anything! Please!" Edith cried out.

Finally, a column of dark energy burst from the tattoo like a water geyser. Slowly, at least in Edith's desperate mind, the energy arced forward and began to take shape: Before them stood a man in a dark robe with odd patterns scattered about it. He wore a hood that obscured his face, save for an iron jawline that sported a goatee as black as the night.

The tattoo disappeared from Edith's wrist and her pain faded. She breathed several heavy sighs of relief as Angus wiped the tears from her cheek. Wolfgang growled in their direction.

Edith's mind was on other things, however. She stood, wide-eyed, and muttered, "The Dark Wizard…"

"Dark Wizard? What's this all about?" Wolfgang asked. He received no answer.

"I can sense that you have reached the Gold Pit. Well done…" the Dark Wizard said. His bass-filled voice penetrated her soul, just like the previous time he had spoken with her. Still, the searing pain he had just caused her lingered in her mind, overriding any fear or respect she might have felt toward him.

"Why have you chosen to contact me now?" Edith asked in a bothered tone while rubbing her wrist. Though it was no longer burning, she could still feel a phantom pain coursing through her arm; as if her very limbs were afraid to experience the sensation again. "I have done everything that you and my father laid out, and it has all gone according to plan. I don't need any help."

"You presume much when you in fact know very little, foolish child!" the Dark Wizard boomed back.

"No one talks to *my* gal like that!" Wolfgang cried as he dashed at him. A smile of ill-intent revealed itself underneath the Dark Wizard's hood.

"Wolfgang, no!" Edith cried, but he had already committed to his attack. He drew his broadsword and, in that sequence, turned it into a horizontal slash. Howling laughter accompanied the blade as it cut clean through the Dark Wizard's torso.

"Huh?" the blond brute muttered as he stumbled forward from the weight of his swing and crashed to the ground. No blood had been spilled, and the robed man remained still. It was as if he had struck nothing but the air.

The Dark Wizard let out an amused chuckle and turned to face Wolfgang, whose face was red and twitching with rage.

"Fool! We are on the same side. You couldn't hurt me if you wanted to, anyway..."

"We'll see about that..." Wolfgang said as he stood and readied himself for another attack. The Dark Wizard held out a hand.

"You don't understand. I am not truly *here* right now. What you see before you is a projection. That symbol I branded onto Edith allowed me to do this when the time was right," he said.

"Which begs the question: What do you need to speak with me about?" Edith asked, unable to mask her impatience.

"You may recall that I told you about the guardians of the mountain when we discussed this expedition. The most powerful of the lot is a Wizard known as the Mountain King. His castle is just above your current location," the Dark Wizard replied.

"What does it matter? We are already here. There is nothing any 'Mountain King' can do about it now," Edith said, crossing her arms.

"How wrong you are, child. The Mountain King is one of the most powerful Wizards in the world. His eyes are ever watchful, and even now, with the first batch of black gold ready to be taken to your father, he will not allow the miners at the base camp to leave. His power is so great that he can summon vicious thunderstorms at will!"

"I fail to see how that's my problem," Edith said and then scoffed. "I have kept up with my end. I'm about to release Greed, right here and now. If you cannot even get the easier mission done, then why are we allied with you?"

"Let me put it to you this way: If the Mountain King is not addressed, he will not allow *you* to leave, either."

"I'll have Greed on my side by then. We'll just kill him," Edith said.

"Nonsense!" the Dark Wizard boomed back. "Greed will be weakened from thousands of years of imprisonment while pumping out black gold. If he were at full strength, perhaps you could kill the Mountain King. But as of now, you would be soundly defeated."

Edith let out a great sigh of discontent and said, "Fine… what is it that we need to do, then?"

"Two things… one: The tunnel to this cave must be sealed off. As you may have noticed, another powerful guardian sleeps just one cave over, and as nightfall approaches, it will come to stop you. Believe me when I say you have no means to defend yourselves against it."

"The Nightcrawler…" Angus muttered.

"Two: Distract the Mountain King so that he will focus his watchful eyes upon something else aside from the monolith or the team at the base camp. I was able to tag another guardian of this mountain: a Wizard named Aldous. I can sense that he is leading a group through the Mountain King's castle as we speak. It would be ideal if you sent some of your men to intercept and attack them," he said.

"Oi! Why do we need to do anythin', then? *They'll* take his attention away," Wolfgang complained.

"Because Aldous is friends with the Mountain King, and I don't much expect them to fight on their own. All you truly need to do is kill a few folk up there to get the chaos going, and then you're free to leave. The castle is at the end of the tunnel where you came from and through a false wall," the Dark Wizard said.

"But we can't return if we collapse the tunnel as you suggest," Angus said.

"Indeed, but it is something you must do, or the beast will come and slaughter those who are trying to unleash Greed. There is a path through the Mountain King's throne room that leads back to this cave. You would come from the tunnel down there," the robed man said as he pointed behind the group, to a path off in the distance. "That is also where the secret exit lies. You will need to take it if you wish to escape here with your lives."

"Chaos, death, an' destruction? In the name of our Dark Savior? I like the sound of that!" Wolfgang shouted as the other Gold Fever-infected miners cheered along. Edith couldn't believe it. If what the Dark Wizard had said about the Mountain King's vast powers were true, they would be throwing their lives away. Yet, they didn't seem to mind if it was for their cause.

"Besides…" Wolfgang trailed off as a mischievous grin came to his face. "I'd love an opportunity to face those rats again. This time, I'll kill 'em all!"

"Yeh! Kill the traitors!" a miner called out.

"Kill the non-believers!"

"For the greater good!"

"For our Dark Savior!"

"It seems that you've got a lively group, here. Excellent…" the Dark Wizard said as his image began to fade before their eyes. "Did you remember the incantation, Edith?"

"Egois sumheach voduit meais leatmea nunta anua tunun leamini thoitatum meam," Edith replied, militantly.

"Well done," the Dark Wizard said, his image becoming faint. "Our Dark Savior will walk free once more, thanks to you…" He chuckled as his projection finally came to an end.

Edith wanted to laugh back at him. Little did he know that she had made some *slight* adjustments to the plan. There would be no 'freedom' for the Dark Savior. He would fall under her control, and she would use him and his black gold-producing abilities to dominate the world; but not before Drake got a full helping of what he deserved.

"Now what?" Angus asked.

"Most of us will need to travel up to the Mountain King's castle, while a small group will stay back here to release Greed," Edith said.

"Why send many when all we need to do is start a conflict?"

"We must consider the might of the Mountain King. If he truly is one of the most powerful Wizards in the world, then we shall need many men to fight him off," she replied.

Angus frowned. "So, who goes and who stays?"

"Of course, I'll need to stay here. I know the incantation, after all. The best fighters in our group, such as you and Wolfgang, should go," Edith said.

His frown bent into a grimace. He leaned over and whispered, "Shouldn't I stay here for your safety? In case the Gold Fever-infected turn on you once more?"

"Oh, you're so sweet, Angy. I didn't know you cared so much for me…" she whispered back and then nibbled on his ear.

"Quit bein' a knob, Angus! Are ye gonna fight, or are ye a coward?" Wolfgang called out.

"There *he* is, getting in our way… you know, the Dark Wizard never said *who* you had to kill up there…" Edith whispered as she pulled herself away from his ear and smiled back up at him. Angus only stared back, his mouth fidgeting. It was as if he didn't know what to say or do in response to her suggestion. Yet, she was confident that he was now one of her followers. A conflict between him and Wolfgang was inevitable.

"I volunteer to go!" Bronrar said. Angus looked back at his friend with both eyebrows raised.

The giant let out a sigh and said, "Alright, I'll go…"

WITH THE UNDERSTANDING that they were off to battle in the name of their Savior, most of the miners had been happy to volunteer for the trip to the Mountain King's castle. Edith had kept five of the black gold-infected with her to help chip away at the mighty monolith.

Wolfgang, Angus, Bronrar, and 11 other infected miners left their black gold behind and traveled up the tunnel where they had come from. As they reached the tunnel's end, Wolfgang and Angus told the others to stand back while they chopped at the support beams.

"Ye know, Angus…" Wolfgang said as he swung his pickaxe at a beam. "Edith's my woman, and I've had about enough of lil' snakes tryin' to steal her from right under my nose…"

"Is that right? You think I'm stealing her?" Angus asked as he chopped hard on his support beam. He tried not to laugh. Wolfgang had only ever been a pawn to her. Yet, he continued to believe that they had any sort of future together.

"Ye've been a friend to me over the years, so I'm gonna let ye know… when all hell breaks loose up there, I'm gonna attack whoever I please, and whatever happens, happens."

Before Angus could respond, the supports collapsed and the tunnel cave-in began. The group ran to the adjacent tunnel and watched as the rocks and boulders fell and filled up the tunnel. A familiar musty smell permeated the air and dust flew into their faces for some time before it finally ended.

The group then turned and walked up a new incline, lit completely by torches on the walls. At the top of the slope was a false wall. Wolfgang and Angus charged into it and pushed it open with some effort. The door revealed a corridor of the Mountain King's castle. At first, they weren't sure where to go, but then they heard the chanting:

Shah!

Shah!

Shah!

Shah!

As they walked toward the noise and commotion, Angus felt a creeping dread hanging over him. Not only had Wolfgang threatened him, but the Gold Fever-infected men were not trustworthy, either. To make matters worse, Bronrar seemed distant from him now, and he worried that the nervous miner might betray him. As Wolfgang had implied earlier, the upcoming fight was going to be every man for themselves.

CHAPTER 37
BLAZE OF GLORY

As the captured souls of the Mountain King closed in on the group of 13 like a pack of hungry wolves, Henic panted like a sick dog. His throat sounded dry. Conrad held him upright, but he could feel himself carrying more of his weight with each passing moment.

"As soon as the first blades clash, we make a run for the exit past the throne," he whispered.

"No… I'll only slow ye down. An' that Mountain King'll probably get ye if ye ain't fast enough… leave me here," Henic muttered back.

"Not a chance. We've made it through too much to let this be the end," Conrad said.

"B-but we can't-" Henic interrupted himself with a heavy cough. "Make it… through 'em all…"

"I'll have your back," Lucia whispered.

"Same here…" Dalton muttered from ahead without looking back.

"I'll clobber anyone who dares come near ya!" Alistair said, his voice as bombastic as ever.

"Great going, oaf. Now everyone knows to attack us," Lucia shot back in a harsh whisper.

"Good! Bring 'em on!" Alistair replied. Henic chuckled.

"Quit makin' me laugh… it hurts…" he said before his expression turned serious. "But in truth, I must thank ye all. If we make it through this, I owe all of ye a drink… many, in fact!"

The others only nodded in response.

~

JOEL WAS PEERING AROUND at the soul slaves, waiting for the first of them to attack, when he noticed Aldous looking back at him with curious eyes. The mute cocked his head as he detached the sheathed sword from his hip and held it out for him to take. Suddenly, despite the ever-present threat approaching, nothing else mattered to Joel. His eyes, wider than gold coins, remained on the sheathed blade, and everything nearby became silent. Off in the distance, he could almost swear that he heard faint, yet familiar, screams.

"By the way, m'boy, I believe *this* belongs to you," the old Wizard's voice echoed in his ears. "Believe me when I say that I understand your commitment to non-violence. I hold you in the highest regard for choosing peace when all around you is expressly violent… but if ever there were a time to go back on your vow, it is now. We've come this far and risked so much to help our new friends. Don't let it be in vain. Don't let them die. Not without a fight."

He tossed the blade to Joel, who let it fall into his outstretched hands. Immediately, a jolt of life shot through him, and his whole body tingled. The soul slaves were close now, yet still, he couldn't help but inspect the sword he had neglected for so long.

The sheath was made out of black leather, and upon it was a golden symbol that not many would recognize. He sighed and then shook his head at Aldous. Surely, there would be someone else who could use it, he thought. The old Wizard offered no response and returned his attention forward.

"Giving your rat friends more weapons? A useless gesture! Their fate will be the same, regardless!" the Mountain King roared.

"Watch your tongue! You speak ill of the Key Keeper," Aldous replied.

"Oh? How convenient! All protectors of the monolith will remain in one spot, then. Yes, I think that is a splendid idea!" Olivier said.

The soul slaves inched closer and closer, now within striking distance.

"Last chance to surrender peacefully… what say you, Aldous?" the Mountain King asked. Joel looked around, clutching his sheathed sword until it burned his hands. They were outnumbered, but it wasn't impossible to escape. They needed some sort of wild card, he thought.

Aldous cleared his throat and then puffed up his chest. "I say-"

Suddenly, a crashing noise echoed behind them. It had sounded like a battering ram striking wood. As creaks and groans filled the throne room, all in the group turned to see that the door had been kicked open, and standing before them was a grinning Wolfgang with 13 men in tow.

"'Ello, there! I gots a special delivery fer the Mountain King!" Wolfgang shouted as he grabbed his pickaxe and threw it forward at one of the captured souls, a man in a hiking uniform. Before he could react, the axe head plunged into his skull. He gasped briefly as blood spurted out and he stumbled back. Just as he hit the ground, the hiker exploded into many small, green balls of light; all of which shot back into the chalice on the Mountain King's right.

With that death, the battle began. The Gold Fever-infected men rushed into the throne room and spread out onto different sides while Wolfgang charged the other hiker. The captured soul had drawn a dagger and held it up in a defensive position. The blond brute licked his lips and drew his broadsword. In one smooth motion, he lunged out and stabbed the hiker in his chest.

Wolfgang continued to charge until the hiker toppled over. Then, he ripped the blade out of his chest, leaving a geyser of blood in its wake, and finished him off by bringing the blade down on his neck. The hiker's head rolled, and like his friend before him, burst into an incredible display of green light that went back to the Mountain King's chalice.

MEANWHILE, Conrad and Henic scurried toward the exit behind the throne; the latter of which was dragging his feet as he used the strategist's shoulder for support. Conrad estimated that there were about 100 paces from the throne to exit, but with the chaos of battles breaking out all around them, it may as well have been across the mountain, he thought. At first, Dalton, Lucia, and Alistair had stayed with them as promised, but one by one, each became ensnared in their own fights: Alistair remained behind to fend off a couple of slavers with his battle axe. Lucia had found herself sidetracked by two men in fur coats, while Dalton had been attacked by some trolls.

Conrad and Henic hobbled forward, and by some miracle, no one had disturbed them. The exit was within their grasp, but then, out of the shadows appeared an imposing figure: Angus blocked their way.

"Going somewhere?" he asked.

"Stand aside. He needs medical attention," Conrad replied with urgency.

"Normally, I would be sympathetic. Your friend is dying as we speak, after all. There is no hope for him to reach a doctor in time…" Angus trailed off and then pulled out a mace, the spikes of which were covered in dry blood. "But y'see, every once in a while, I get a sharp pain in my leg… a reminder of your cheap shot. You and I have a score to settle."

"From what I have been told, I should have finished you off back then," Conrad said before he walked Henic over to a pillar on their left and gently leaned him up against it to sit him down. "It seems that he will not let us through… don't worry, I'll be quick…" Conrad turned to face the giant and drew his rapier.

"You have a problem with my killing others, but what will you do? I won't allow you to pass until you've killed me," Angus said while approaching.

"Don't mistake mercy for weakness. I may have spared you before; and I may have spared Wolfgang in the tunnel, leading to Henic's injury…" Conrad said as he gripped the hilt of his blade harder and harder until it was shaking. Angus raised an eyebrow as the strategist pivoted to his side and took a fencing stance. "But now that Henic's life is on the line; now that you've shown me who you truly are… I will do what I must."

A deep-pitched chuckle escaped Angus' mouth as he continued his approach. "Your actions belie your words. You must feel guilty for allowin' Wolfgang to kill yer friend. And didn't he have his wife and boy takin' care of that dumpy farm of his? I wonder if they will be able to survive without him… but you don't need to worry about that. All of your worries will fade away once I've bashed your skull in!"

Angus' stroll turned into a charge, and in short order, he was within striking distance with the club held overhead. Conrad made a quick stabbing motion to fend him off, but the giant swiped at the blade with his mace and knocked it away.

With his great reflexes and speed, Conrad brought the blade back and attempted another stab, and the result was the same. This time, however, Angus was close enough to attack, and he swung for his head. Conrad gasped while hopping back, a great *whoosh* accompanying a slap to the face from wind created by the swipe. After narrowly avoiding the spiked ball, he planted his feet and then lunged out to stab once more. Angus attempted to sidestep, but the blade made contact with his arm as he did, and sliced across. It was a superficial cut, but it still spilled blood.

"Nice moves," Angus said as he swiped a finger across the blood and rubbed it together with his thumb. "But at this rate, you'll never win in time to save your friend. He has *moments*, not hours, to live, I'm afraid."

"If you don't think we can make it, then why not stand aside?" Conrad asked. He readied himself once more.

"It's not him that I care about; I only want to kill you!" Angus said as he took another swipe with his mace. Conrad once again hopped back and attempted a stab toward the big man's leg, but it missed.

"Henic," Conrad said as he looked to his left, out of the corner of his eye. "While I fight, do you think you can make it out of here on your own?"

Henic slowly got to his feet, which filled Conrad with hope. He had enough spirit to continue, and he'd make it, somehow-

"No, Conrad…" he said. His heart sank. "I don' much think I'll be makin' it outta here. The truth is, I can barely stand… the end is near."

"No…"

"I must agree with his assessment. It would be better to let him die in peace than struggling 'till the end," Angus said.

"No one asked you!" Conrad shot back.

"Who ever said anything about dyin' in peace?" Henic said as he began to walk around the column. "If I'm goin' out, it's gonna be in a blaze of glory!"

With those words, he disappeared behind the pillar.

"Henic! Wait!" Conrad called out as Angus took a swing at him with the mace again. The strategist leaped backward, but he offered no return attack.

"There is nothing you can do. His death is inevitable, and if you survive this day, you will have to live with the guilt for the rest of your life," Angus said.

Conrad scowled back at him. He lunged out and unleashed a flurry of attacks: First was a thrust toward the midsection, which Angus parried with his mace. However, Conrad immediately turned that into a diagonal slash, which the giant had no choice but to step back from and avoid. From that, he found an opportunity and lunged out for another stab. Angus pivoted sideways to avoid, but the blade caught him and ripped through his shirt.

This time, it was a more serious hit. Blood seeped through the cut fabric and began dripping down to his pants. Yet still the giant stood firm, and Conrad groaned. He didn't have time for this, but he also knew that taking eyes off of Angus for even a moment presented the very real danger of his skull being caved in by the mace. For now, he could only hope that someone else would give Henic the help he needed.

～

HENIC APPROACHED a stone wall of weapons. He paid little heed to the chaotic battles around him, for he was certain that his last moments were upon him either way. As his vision blurred and his stomach turned, he looked across the row of weapons. Laid out before him were a bow with arrows lying next to it, a war hammer, a broadsword, a claymore, and a spear. His eyes fixated on the spear. It had a long shaft and a fancy black blade at its end.

As Henic reached out to grab his weapon of choice, his hand froze. What was he doing? He was not a warrior, but a farmer; and *a dying farmer*, at that! The battlefield was no place for him. All of his life, he had stuck to his own business, tending to his farm while not going out of his way to trouble or help anyone. It had been the best way to stay safe and secure, after all-

The farmer gasped in realization. That had only worked during times of peace and prosperity, he thought. As Faiwell had begun to struggle, more eyes were cast on his family; his farm. They were jealous, hateful eyes. He had resolved to keep his head down, hoping to avoid those gazes, but it only got worse when Wolfgang entered the picture; and then Brice and the hooligans. No matter how much he had tried to keep to himself, trouble had found him. Now, his family would pay the price. They would be left alone to work the fields while giving away their livelihood to the men who had terrorized them.

No, he thought, grabbing the spear with newfound energy surging through his body. His vision returned to normal, his stomach ceased to burn, and his legs stiffened with life and strength. It was the last rush of energy that his body would ever give him, and for good reason: It had finally dawned on him that in times like these, trouble would find him and his loved ones no matter what they did; and in that situation, the only option was to stand and fight.

If he was going down, then he'd take more than one with him. Wolfgang was at the top of the list, for he would be sure to continue reaping the labors of his family farm if he survived this trip. Killing any others who posed a threat to his new friends would help to ensure their survival, and he hoped that they would return the favor by holding off Brice and the hooligans from his farm. It wasn't his ideal solution, but with precious few grains of sand remaining in his hour-glass, it was all he had left to cling onto. If nothing else, he hoped that the story of his final acts could be passed down to his children.

With a deep breath, Henic rushed back past the column with his weapon at the ready.

"Oi! Angus!" he cried as the giant and Conrad both looked back at him, wide-eyed. "I ain't dyin' until I take *you* with me!" He charged in with his spear and lunged out to stab, but Angus dodged.

Conrad used the distraction as an opportunity to make a quick slash in Angus' direction. He succeeded with a cut across his chest, although it didn't appear deep enough to be fatal.

"Gah!" Angus felt his chest for the blood. He then took several steps to the side in retreat and bumped into an infected miner. "Take care of them! Your Dark Savior commands it!"

The miner squealed with glee and charged in with his pickaxe over-head, aiming for Conrad.

"Fer the will of the Savior!" he cried. Conrad scrambled to prepare himself, but Henic stepped in and stuck the crazed miner in the gut with his spear.

"Don' worry about me, I'll be fine!" Henic said as he withdrew the spear from the miner's stomach. He keeled over, and despite the blood pooling around him on the floor, a grin filled his face. "Just take care of yerself, alright?" He then ran toward the throne to help the others.

"Wait!" he heard Conrad cry from behind, but there was no more time for words. He had to find Wolfgang.

To the side of the Mountain King's throne, Dalton faced down two trolls. These mountain trolls were large, hairy, and green-skinned. They wore one-shoulder singlets, and carried with them mammoth spiked clubs that had been heavy enough for him to dodge. However, with the oversized claymore, he had found difficulty in landing a decisive hit of his own.

"Oi! Hold still, ye lil' scoundrel!" one said as he swung the big club and missed. Dalton used the opportunity to swing horizontally at him, but the other troll blocked with his club.

Dalton groaned. He needed to get back to helping Conrad and Henic, but the oversized claymore was too slow, as it had been for Lucia. It was a great weapon for striking fear into untrained enemies, but a foe that was either unafraid of its size or experienced in combat rendered it all but powerless. In the case of the trolls, however, it was a matter of there being two of them to handle at a time. One always blocked for the other. Now more than ever, he needed a helping hand.

"Take this, foul troll!" A voice called out to his right. He turned to see Henic of all people, charging them. He lunged out and stabbed upward with his spear, and before the troll could even turn to see what was going on, the spear pierced into his head.

The troll shook uncontrollably as Henic pulled the spear blade out. Dark blood dribbled down to his thick neck as he fell to his knees and burst into green light. The other troll growled and rushed Henic while his spear was down, but Dalton intervened and used the mighty claymore to slice at his ankle as he ran. The troll cried out in pain and crashed to the ground. His ankle had nearly been severed from his foot, but the thick skin saved it from coming clean off. Even so, blood spurted and pooled rapidly around the troll's legs as he writhed on the floor. Dalton stood over him and stabbed his neck to finish the job. He looked back to thank Henic, but he had already rushed off to another battle.

"Give 'em hell, Henic!" Dalton called out as he turned and locked eyes with a yellow pair, filled with murderous intent. Wolfgang whirled his broadsword around, playfully.

"Everyone keeps tellin' me that yer the best warrior in all of Faiwell!" Wolfgang shouted from further down the throne room. "Let's see if it's true!"

With his blade at the ready, the blond brute sprinted in his direction, and Dalton too hurried forward, ignoring the battles around him. The claymore was down and at his side, an offensive stance meant for a quick, powerful blow. They met near the middle of the room and crossed blades with a loud *clang*.

～

IN THE CENTER of the throne room still stood Aldous. He and the Mountain King had only been staring at each other as the battles raged on around them.

Joel and a few other miners stood behind the old Wizard, unsure of what to do. There were so many battles going on that the mute felt it best to wait and see who would attack them rather than preemptively striking.

"Joel…" someone whispered from behind. He instinctively ducked his head. "It's me, Bronrar." Joel looked back at him and raised his sheathed sword in defense.

Bronrar brought a hand up and bobbed it. "No, no, I'm on your side! I see now that Edith, Wolfgang, and Angus were up to no good all along. I'm sorry about before… I only want to help, now!"

Joel lowered his sheath and smiled back at him. He then made some hand signals, and Bronrar tilted his head.

"You don't know what to do?" he asked. Joel shrugged and then signed some more. "I see… afraid to kill, eh? I understand. I'm with ye on that one. But that doesn't mean we can't lay a beating on those who deserve it, eh?"

Joel looked upward in thought. He had dedicated the rest of his life to pacifism, but what exactly did that mean? He was certain that he would never kill again, but what about violence? What if it was justified? As long as it was non-lethal, Bronrar, who himself didn't like fighting, felt it was necessary.

That was when Joel got an idea: He could still use the sword while it was sheathed. That way, he could do his part in battle while not fatally injuring another. He nodded at Bronrar and the duo made their way to the right, where some miners were being pressed by the soul-enslaved and Gold Fever-infected.

TO THE SIDE of the throne, Lucia defended against two men who were dressed in animal hides and furs. Both men wielded specialty blades that she recognized as falcatas: Midrange swords that were thickest and heaviest near the tip, allowing them to pierce armor at times. Even a glancing blow from the blades could be fatal. So far, her speed had aided her in parrying the blows, but she knew that it was not a winning strategy. One of the first things that Dalton had taught her was that you could only win a fight with offense.

Then, an idea came to her: Thus far, the fur-clad men had revealed their preference to lunge out with heavy blows of the falcata. They had every right to be confident in those strikes since Lucia was without the use of her other arm and had to rely on light, quick strikes. So, perhaps she could use their forward momentum against them. She would need to be lightning-quick to not get tagged by the second man, but sooner or later, her defense-only strategy was bound to fail. Taking them by surprise was her best option.

Lucia angled her arming sword downward and diagonal across her body. The two men looked at each other with raised eyebrows.

"So, ye've given up, eh?" one asked. He brought his falcata up for a vertical slash and lunged out as he did so. Lucia smiled. It was exactly what she was hoping he would try.

The mercenary brought her sword up in an arced motion and deflected his falcata. Then, his momentum continued forward and the lunge turned into an awkward trip. At that moment, Lucia pivoted to the side, curled her wrist, and swung her blade back around. It came down diagonally to strike the back of the man's neck as his stumble forward continued, decapitating him. Blood spilled out briefly from his spinning head before he exploded into a green lightshow like the others before him.

Lucia didn't have time to admire her handiwork, however, as the other fur-clad man was in the midst of his own attack. Now facing only one opponent, she could use the reach advantage of her long arms and blade. Before the man could come within range, she lunged out for the stab in similar fashion to a fencing technique. The sword pierced his midsection and stopped him in his tracks. Lucia smiled as she withdrew the arming sword and thought of Conrad. Tactics had won out over brute force, this time.

~

Meanwhile, Alistair had his hands full with not only the two slavers, but the avian; who soared above and occasionally swooped down for an attack.

"Get down here so I can roast ya like a chicken!" Alistair called out to the bird-man, who tweeted back at him, mockingly.

The big man also swung wildly at the slavers to keep them at bay. They wielded whips for weapons, so he needed to keep his distance.

"Doesn't anyone have tha guts ta fight me up close?" Alistair asked aloud.

Suddenly, Henic entered the fray, crying out as he hoisted his spear upward in an attempt to land a hit on the avian. The bird-man barrel rolled to dodge and then made a turn overhead for a return attack.

As he swooped down, a pair of talon-like hands popped out of the avian's wings, and each held a dagger. Henic dove to the floor as the avian soared over him. Alistair gripped his battle axe, ready to intervene; but then, out of nowhere, Joel appeared with his sheathed sword in hand. The mute wound up and swung with such fluidity and speed that it almost made Alistair go cross-eyed.

The sheathed blade struck the avian in his torso, and he squawked as a loud *crack* echoed about the throne room, rising above the weapons clashing and the battle cries being uttered. He sputtered out of control before crashing to the ground and rolling all the way to the far wall; knocking over a few weapons when he finally stopped.

Alistair's eyes wandered over to Henic, whose blood streaked the floor from his previous dodge. He panted heavily as one of the slavers approached him. The big man dashed toward them with his battle axe at the ready, but he knew that he was too far away to intercept the slaver in time.

The slaver pulled his whip back and cracked it in the direction of Henic, and Alistair gasped. He was in no shape to take a blow of any kind.

However, before the whip could reach him, Bronrar stepped in and held his pickaxe out. The whip wrapped around the shaft of the pickaxe and narrowly missed his hands. He stood firm, holding on for dear life as the slaver tried to pull the weapon from his grip. In the meantime, Henic charged and plunged the spear into the slaver's chest. He let out a choking gasp as he fell to the floor and burst into green light.

The other slaver snuck up on Henic while he was distracted, but hadn't noticed that Alistair was now within range. The big redhead swung the battle axe at full strength into his back. He too exploded into balls of green light that flew into the Mountain King's chalice.

～

NEAR THE THRONE, one of the miners had snuck up behind the Mountain King with a sword in hand. Aldous noticed, but he did not break eye contact with Olivier for fear of alerting him. As the miner brought his sword back to stab him from behind, one of the soul-captured women appeared from the shadows and screamed while jumping onto his back.

"What're ye doin'? Crazy wench!" the miner shouted as he threw her down. He turned back to find the Mountain King standing before him like an impenetrable wall.

"What's wrong? You don't like it when someone sneaks up on you?" Olivier asked. The miner only stared back, slack-jawed. "Neither do I!"

The Mountain King placed a hand atop the miner's helmet, and bolts of lightning erupted with such vigor that it made an explosive mushroom seem like child's play. Aldous had no choice but to shield his eyes as the blinding light surged about the throne room.

After a short period, he could sense that the lightning had calmed and brought his arm down. Several of the nearby combatants had been knocked down, but most bolts had gone into the Mountain King's unfortunate target and continued to do so. His entire body had been charred, yet he still drew breath, as evidenced by his pained moaning and uncontrollable shaking.

As the bolts bounced around and through the miner's body, Aldous gripped his walking stick with both hands and pressed it to the ground. He may not have been able to save him, but he could at least ensure that his death wouldn't be in vain.

The room darkened as the last bolt surged through the miner's body, now motionless. He had been fried to the point where he was smoking, and the blood that boiled from within burst out at points in his body; from his legs up to his eyes. The Mountain King released his grip from the metal helmet and the miner's lifeless body dropped like a sack of potatoes.

"Do not fear! For you will get a second chance at life, like all the others!" Olivier said with a smug smile.

The Mountain King then turned to see a giant fireball headed straight for him. Aldous had gathered flames from the torches lit around the throne room, and that was why it had dimmed.

The fireball exploded in front of the throne, creating an even more intense light than the previous eruption of lightning had. The throne room shook and cries were heard all around as the resulting shock-wave knocked the combatants down. For a brief few moments, the room fell silent. All battles had temporarily ceased.

~

DALTON HAD BEEN KNOCKED to the unforgiving floor by the force of Aldous' blast, but he knew that he'd be spared no time to rest. He shook his head in an attempt to regain his wits and did so in time to see Wolfgang wildly bringing his sword down on him. The warrior rolled along the floor and heard the *clang* of the blade behind him.

He jumped to his feet and attempted a diagonal and downward slash with the claymore, to catch him in the legs. However, Wolfgang was too fast. He hopped backward well before the blade reached him.

"Ye ain't as great as they say..." Wolfgang muttered before cackling. Dalton scoffed.

He had the same issues as Lucia: The claymore he was wielding was well over twice as heavy as any standard weapon of its same kind. A normal-sized claymore would have been enough to tag Wolfgang in Dalton's estimation, but Lucia's stubborn desire to prove her strength; to strike fear into her opponents; had seen her fight with a blade unsuitable against a skilled or speedy opponent.

"I don't suppose you would give me a moment to find a new weapon, would ya?" Dalton asked with a smirk.

"Yer complainin' about yer weapon? Everyone has an excuse when they lose!" Wolfgang replied.

"Lose? Last I checked, you haven't landed a blow yet!" Dalton said, chuckling. "But I'll have to watch out. I have heard a great deal about your techniques, y'see..."

"Oh?"

"Yeh... I'm surprised you haven't tried stabbing me in the back, or from behind in my neck while I wasn't looking... or in the dark when I can't defend myself," Dalton said and then shrugged. Wolfgang scowled back at him. "It's a shame. Underhanded tactics seem to be the only way a scrub like you can win a fight!" He laughed at him mockingly.

"Shut yer mouth!" Wolfgang bellowed before leaping out for an attack. Dalton blocked at an angle, and the blades snagged. The warrior sharpened his eyes and moved his face closer to the blond brute. His chipper demeanor vanished faster than one of the Mountain King's lightning bolts.

"It is the only way you could'a beaten Faramond, y'know. While he wasn't looking. I would know because I taught him, and I know what he could do. You're a knob compared to him, as a warrior and as a man!" Dalton said in a rush of anger as he pushed Wolfgang, sword-on-sword, to the ground. He then pointed the claymore down at him, the tip mere inches from his face.

"I did what I had to do fer the Dark Savior and fer my gal!" Wolfgang cried.

"You speak of Edith? She has no loyalty to anyone but herself. I laid with her no less than a couple of weeks ago!" Dalton said as Wolfgang's yellow eyes widened. "And then she told me that she was entangled with you… she didn't care! She was proud of it!"

"You lie!" Wolfgang shouted as he swung his sword across and knocked the claymore back enough to get to his feet. He then started to swing around wildly, and Dalton dodged all attacks. After another miss from Wolfgang, Dalton whirled the claymore around and came within a hair's length of his face. He jumped back and scowled while breathing heavily.

"I can't lose! Not with the Dark Savior by my side!"

Dalton's eye twitched. Was it possible to demoralize the Gold Fever-infected? Even after such distressing truths had been revealed to him about Edith, Wolfgang seemed as battle-hungry as ever. With an unsuitable weapon and a crazed opponent standing before him, the warrior prepared himself for a long, difficult battle.

NEAR THE CENTER of the room, Aldous watched the clearing smoke with bated breath. Without any water or lightning around to use, he had just acted on his best opportunity to harm the Mountain King. The last of the smoke faded, revealing that the steps and throne had been blown away and that the gold had partially melted from the blast. Yet, Aldous was shocked not to find the Mountain King standing before him, but a wall of thick luxmortite that had been singed and partially damaged by the blast. The dark blue metal liquefied before his eyes, giving way to an unharmed and smirking Olivier.

"Y-you can create luxmortite now? But how?" Aldous asked, incredulous.

"It took over a thousand years! But with all the free time I have, my conjuring prowess, and of course my chalice…" He looked to his right and gasped. It was missing. Panic overtook the Mountain King's expression. "My chalice! Where is it?"

"Oho! You mean this?" Aldous asked as he held the chalice out for him to see. It was Olivier's Wizard artifact, and it was often used to channel his magic. Without it, he could still perform the same feats, but they would drain him more.

"I see, now… the fireball was a distraction!"

Back when the fireball had exploded, Aldous used the magnetic fields of those around him to attract the metallic chalice to his free hand. It was another, lesser-known capability of his lightning magic.

"Your treachery shall not go unpunished!" Olivier grasped a lightning bolt in his hand, much like a spear, and threw it. In the split second that Aldous had before impact, he held out his walking stick and absorbed the bolt.

"I'll save that for later, thank you very much!"

"So, it would seem you have finally mastered lightning, then… impressive…" the Mountain King trailed off before laughing. "But you are limited to what is around you! For me, there *are* no limits!"

Olivier held a hand up, and a large stone pillar materialized over his head. However, the end of it was sharp, like a spear. He pointed at Aldous, and the massive column flew at him. The old Wizard and a couple of miners still with him dove to the side as the pillar soared overhead and hit the ground with a great *thud*.

The noise of stone dragging on stone made Aldous' shoulders shoot up to his ears. The smell of burning stone, overbearing as a lord collecting debts, wasn't much better. As he got to a knee, Aldous looked back to see that the pillar had skidded all the way to the door of the throne room. The Mountain King laughed aloud.

"You find something funny?" Aldous asked.

"As an Elemental Wizard, you have no answer for repelling *mere stone*? I can make a thousand more of those and drop them all at once if I wish! Better yet, I have a thousand *more* ways that I could kill you! Where do you get the nerve to challenge *me*?" he replied.

"Begging your pardon, but you're the one who wished to kill us!" Aldous said as he closed his eyes and clanked his walking stick off the floor. The fight was about to turn dangerous, and he needed something to get everyone out of the throne room.

Olivier laughed derisively. "Oh, my… you have something else you wish to try? This should be amusing!"

~

Henic stood back-to-back with Baltr while battling a few chainmail-clad men, but as reinforcements from other miners arrived, Dalton and Wolfgang's skirmish caught his eye. Despite the earlier surge of energy, he could feel his life waning. This was his last chance to get justice for himself; to ensure that his family would not be haunted by that ghoul after his death.

"Think ye can hold down the fort, fellas? I've got my sights set on Wolfgang," Henic said as he swiped at a man with his spear.

"We can manage. Do what you need to do!" Baltr said.

Wolfgang pushed Dalton back into a column and unleashed a flurry of strikes that were all blocked. However, with his back literally against the wall, he was stuck in perpetual defense and unable to respond with an attack of his own.

"Oi! Wolfgang! Go to hell, where ye belong!" Henic called out as he stabbed at him with the spear. The blond brute jumped back to avoid, and that distraction was enough for Dalton to free himself from the column.

"Great timing, Henic! Let's take him together!" said the warrior.

"No... I'll do this myself," Henic said as his vision began to blur and his legs weakened, nearly buckling under his own weight. He shook the cobwebs out and gritted his teeth. He just needed to land *one good hit*, he thought.

Dalton lowered his blade and nodded. "I understand."

Wolfgang scoffed. "Ye think ye can beat me? Ye can barely even stand! Why don' ye be a good lil' farm boy and go die in a corner, where ye won't be a bother? I've got better things to do."

The blond brute raised his broadsword and made a start for Dalton. Henic, however, was not to be ignored. He intentionally stabbed in a spot between Wolfgang and Dalton, stopping him in his tracks. He turned to face him once more, his eyes a solid yellow and his brow twitching.

"If I let you off of this mountain alive, you'll just go back to takin' goods from my family..." Henic said.

"That's right. It's what I deserve," Wolfgang replied with a mischievous grin.

"You deserve death!" he replied in a fiery rage. Wolfgang let out some muffled laughter. "All I ever tried to do was keep my head down so scoundrels like you would leave me alone, but ye went and troubled me, anyway! And after all of those endless days out in the fields, just to serve you, how did ye repay me? Ye gutted me like a wild boar!" The farmer pointed to his stomach wound, bleeding profusely.

Wolfgang's chuckles turned to a delirious laugh, and then suddenly, the laughs ceased, and his face turned to stone. Confusion overtook Henic. Somehow, it seemed like *he* was the angry one, now. "Ye wanna know why I decided to start collecting goods from ye? I *hate* people like ye. While I slave away in the mines all day, every day… ye get to be out in the fresh air, and with yer *stupid* lil' family. Ye never have to worry about food or wealth."

Henic snorted. "Your jealousy does not surprise me."

"No! Fairness is what it is! Men like me, who keep Faiwell alive with our work, should be treated like kings compared to people like ye! Whether it's farmers who fatten themselves off of our land," he said, pointing at Henic's sizable gut with his sword. "Or drunken fools who haven't done anything worth a damn in *years*," he continued, now pointing at Dalton. "Or some banker who is good for nothin' aside from takin' all of our damned money." This time, he pointed at an approaching Conrad. "Or least forgivable of all, people who contribute absolutely nothin' of value!" Now his sword was pointed across the throne room, at Joel.

"All of ye… worthless. Yet, yer treated far better than I ever was! But I ain't angry! The Dark Savior will treat us accordingly! He sees me for the asset that I am, and for the worms that ye all are. The world that we build together will not miss ye when yer gone, and so I have no problem endin' any of yer miserable existences!"

Conrad stepped forward with his rapier drawn, but Henic held a shaking hand up to stop his progress. "No! This is my fight. I will face him alone!"

"Very well, farm-boy! I'll finish the job!" Wolfgang howled as he suddenly lunged out and attempted a sword swipe. Henic defended with the blade of his spear and knocked the sword away. He then attempted a stab, but Wolfgang dodged with great vigor.

Next, the blond brute closed in with an even greater burst of speed than before. Now, he was too close to defend with the spear, and Wolfgang performed a diagonal slash downward. Henic ducked the attack and fell back onto one hand on the floor. As he did so, he brought his spear back with the other hand, and it sliced through Wolfgang's boot.

He cried out in a surprised pain as he fell to the ground, grasping at his foot. Henic stood as fast as he could, then pulled his spear back and up to strike a decisive blow. With sights set on Wolfgang's black heart,

Henic began the final thrust, only for his body to give out on him. His arm fell limp and a blood-soaked coughing fit began. Now, he had to use the other end of the spear's shaft to hold himself up.

As he coughed uncontrollably, Henic's watery eyes picked up on Wolfgang rolling away. In response, he attempted a few weak stabs down at the floor, but none were successful. The blond brute hopped to his feet with a new limp, but his movements remained swift, at least to Henic's fading vision.

Wolfgang swung his sword diagonally, one way, and then the other, repeatedly, as he closed in. Each time, Henic blocked with the tip of his spear, but eventually, he got too close. Wolfgang chopped down once more, but this time, it hit the wooden shaft of the spear, shattering it. Too exhausted to be shocked, Henic's eyes wandered to the spearhead bouncing off the ground. He felt a molten-hot pain stab into his chest, but his eyes remained down. He didn't need to see what had happened; he already knew.

Just as suddenly as he'd felt the burn, Henic was granted sweet release, and an odd sensation came over him. It was as if the final grains of sand in his hourglass were spilling out. He looked down and touched his chest to find his hand covered in red. The searing sting returned, and his breaths stuttered. Yet, in his mind, the pain was not from the sword that had just been ripped out of him, but his complete and utter failure.

He looked at Conrad, whose eyes were wide with rage. He took a step forward to intervene, but Henic used every last morsel of his willpower to hold a shaking hand up, stilling him. He hoped to have a final word with him before his death.

"Any last words?" Wolfgang asked between grinning teeth. Henic took hard, labored breaths. His vision turned dark, but he still wished to fight. His body was ready to embrace the end, but his spirit was not.

"Yeah..." Henic choked out as he leaned in close and spit a blood-soaked snot into his eye. Wolfgang scoffed and went to wipe the blood off with a thumb. *This is it*, he thought. His last chance. Henic closed one eye and pulled the wooden shaft back with his jittery arm. Its end was still sharp at the point where it had splintered. With his last iota of energy, he plunged the sharpened shaft into where Wolfgang's shoulder and chest met.

"Gah!" Wolfgang cried as he stumbled back. The fleshy, splattering noise of the shaft exiting the wound overtook Henic's remaining senses. How satisfying it was for *him* to feel the pain for once, he thought. Henic, too, fell backward, but Conrad rushed over and caught him before he could hit the ground.

Wolfgang grimaced at the pair down on the floor. The stab wound inflicted had torn a hole in his shirt. Underneath, spurting blood and splintered wood were apparent. Henic smiled as the blond brute switched his sword from left hand to right. Even if he hadn't killed him, he had at least weakened him for someone else to finish the bastard off.

~

"A FEISTY ONE to the end, eh? Well, now yer *both* dead! In the name of my Dark Savior!" Wolfgang cried.

Before he could make any moves toward the duo, Dalton jumped between them with a new long sword in hand. He had to have found it among the wall of weapons, Conrad thought. Its steel glimmered in what remained of the torchlight in the throne room, so clean that one could see their reflection on it.

Wolfgang, wide-eyed, attempted a quick horizontal slash, but Dalton easily parried it and returned a slash of his own. The attack came within a hair's length of the blond brute, and he soon began taking steps back with nervous, snorting breaths.

"My work here is done!" Wolfgang shouted and then cackled as he ran off for the exit. Dalton looked back at the pair with concern in his eyes.

"Go! I'll see to Henic's care…" Conrad said. Dalton nodded and ran off in pursuit of Wolfgang. "Henic… I'm sorry. I failed you…"

"Naw… ye can't blame yerself…" Henic said with a few weak coughs. "Wolfgang did this to me… there ain't nothin' ye could've done… but if yer truly feelin' guilty, then I have a favor to ask of ye…"

"Anything."

"For most of my life, I was too afraid to take a stand… I gave in to the demands of madmen, hopin' that they would just go away… but they never did… I put my family through hell to appease those bastards…" he said, his eyes filling with tears. "But everything changed on this trip. I learned that sometimes, there ain't no way to avoid trouble. You can only fight back. I believe that you are willing to fight, to take a stand! Please… by whatever means you can spare… do not allow Wolfgang off of this mountain alive… and don't allow those hooligans to take from my wife n' boy anymore!"

Conrad nodded. "You have my word."

"By the way, yer free to tell anyone about what a fearsome warrior I was on this expedition…" He laughed, but Conrad could only spare a few token chuckles, as those laughs soon turned to bloody coughs. His body shook uncontrollably. "And please… tell my family that… I fought back… *I fought…*"

Henic drew his final breath in Conrad's arms, and then he fell limp. His lifeless eyes stared back up at him, and he shuddered. While perhaps true that not taking action had led Wolfgang and the hooligans to terrorize him; it had been *he* who convinced Henic to take action; *he* who hadn't killed Wolfgang when he had the chance.

Conrad took a deep breath and then laid Henic down, running a hand over his eyes to close them. The farmer's last request was the least he could do. His expression sharpened, and then he stood while drawing the rapier. If Wolfgang knew what was good for him, he would allow Dalton to kill him quickly; for he would not receive the same kindness from Conrad. The strategist began a calmly paced walk toward the torture chamber, but his outward appearance belied the fire growing within.

CHAPTER 38
TORTURE CHAMBER

As Joel and Bronrar fought alongside Alistair, they noticed that the avian had recovered from his earlier wipeout and flew overhead once more.

"Oh, great! The turkey's up in the air again!" Alistair said as he swiped at a Gold Fever-infected miner with his axe.

"I don' think he's a turkey…" Bronrar muttered as he attempted to jump up and chop the avian with his pickaxe. The avian took evasive maneuvers and whirled around. He then swooped down in an attack attempt, but Joel swung at him with his sheathed sword. In response, the avian twirled while lowering his elevation; and while doing so, he let loose one of his daggers. In a flash, it flew into Alistair's leg.

The avian smirked as he flew back upward and out of reach. Joel and Bronrar looked at each other in shock as Alistair continued to fight the Gold Fever-infected with a dagger in his leg. Eventually, the big man pushed the miners back and looked over his shoulder to see the pair staring at him.

"What's tha problem? Are ya gonna help or wha-" Alistair's face turned red and he practically bit his tongue off before grasping his leg. "Gah!" He gazed upon the dagger in his thigh, his mouth agape. Then, he reached a rickety hand down and ripped the dagger out.

"OH, LORDY! IT HURTS!" he shouted as blood started to clot in his pant leg. "That damn chicken! I'm gonna get 'im!"

Alistair threw the dagger up at the avian, but he dodged it easily and continued to hover around the center of the throne room as the chaotic battles continued all around.

"We've gotta do somethin' about that avian. He's causin' all sorts of trouble…" Bronrar muttered to Joel.

～

AFTER MUCH PREPARATION, Aldous finally opened his eyes to find the Mountain King staring back at him with an amused smirk. Even with his Wizard's artifact taken away, Olivier was merely toying with him. Aldous only hoped that such arrogance would lead to his defeat, or at least the others escaping. However, he first needed to get everyone out of the throne room, hence the spell he had just prepared to launch.

Above, the avian had gone to the other side of the room and came around for a high-speed swoop down at Joel, Bronrar, and Alistair. The trio managed to avoid him, and at the same time, a great *boom* sounded off above; as if something had crashed into the ceiling. The avian turned around and began a new attack pattern as another crashing *boom* came from above.

As the avian flew past the middle of the ceiling, one more *boom*, the loudest yet, shook the throne room as an avalanche of snow fell through the ceiling and crushed the bird-man. He squawked before exploding into green light and returning to the chalice.

The snow piled in, and Aldous waved his walking stick around to separate it, creating an unbearable blizzard in the room. Many combatants were knocked back, but Alistair managed to shield Joel and Bronrar with his great size. They pushed their way through the blinding blizzard, along with many others, toward the exit. The snow was waist-high by the time they disappeared through the archway, and Aldous returned his focus to the Mountain King. Even as the snow pelted him, his smirk remained, and he was now crossing his arms.

Aldous smiled back. He never truly had a hope of winning, but the least he could do was trouble his former mentor.

～

THE TORTURE CHAMBER WAS A DANK, dark room with various torture devices scattered throughout it. Skeletons lay all around the floor and some hung from nooses tied to the wooden beams above. Other, fresher remains were caught up in a horrid metal device that looked to have ripped the victim's limbs off by stretching them in different directions. Another skeleton lay in a guillotine, their skull missing. There were also signs of old, dry blood on the walls and floor. Flowers had been laid all around, but they were overpowered by a putrid rotting flesh scent.

Many of the combatants had made it out of the throne room and into the chamber; the first of which were Angus and Lucia. The mercenary had stepped in to fight for Conrad, who was too concerned over Henic to continue. Because of the mace's limited range and Lucia's newfound combat speed, he struggled to fend her off, let alone land a hit.

"Not so tough without Wolfgang around to defend you, eh?" Lucia asked.

"You have the better weapon, and that is all," Angus replied in his usual monotone manner.

"Is that right? And I suppose Conrad poked a few holes in you because he had a better weapon, too?" she asked before snorting.

"That's true… both of your weapons have range over mine…" Angus trailed off as his eyes darted to his back left. Lucia cocked her head. What was he planning? "Y'know… there is no reason for us to fight…" He began to back up, and Lucia's eyes widened. The giant was headed for a discarded shield on the floor.

"That's what they all say when they're about to die!" Lucia said as she dashed at him, her sword primed and ready to cut him down.

Angus backpedaled rapidly as Lucia gave chase. Soon, she was within range and lunged out for a downward slash. Angus scooped the shield up as he knelt and then used it to block the slash. The arming sword bounced back and made a dull clunking noise on impact.

"Now, it's fair!" Angus roared with a smile before unleashing a flurry of club swings. Lucia blocked each strike with a slight tilt of her blade.

She then pointed her sword downward and diagonally across her body: The same form that she had used to kill the soul-captured men, earlier.

Angus swung the mace as she had predicted, and then Lucia brought her arming sword up in an arced motion to parry and throw him off balance. Next, the mercenary pivoted and flicked her wrist to bring the blade around and down for the death blow to his neck.

However, Angus craftily pulled his shield back far enough to block the sword. After the dull impact bounced off, he rolled away and then hopped to his feet with panicked breaths. Lucia only smiled back at him. He had come quite close to death.

"Curse you…" He gripped the mace with such force that she could hear the strain of his skin against it. She prepared herself for the next attack.

∿

FURTHER BACK IN the torture chamber were Dalton and Wolfgang, who dueled with such intensity that none of the other combatants dared interrupt. Yet, slowly but surely, Dalton began to push him back with superior technique and movement. Under normal circumstances, Wolfgang believed that he could match him, but because of his injured shoulder and a bothersome limp, he was falling behind.

Dalton lunged forward and attempted a diagonal slash to the right, and Wolfgang blocked. However, he continued to close in, turned his wrist to curl the blade over, and elbowed the blond brute in the chest as he grabbed his sword with the other hand.

Wolfgang gasped as the warrior ripped the blade from his hand and tossed it over his shoulder. He fell to his knees, reduced to a coughing, blubbering mess from the well-placed elbow to his chest. Dalton placed the tip of the blade on his neck and stared into his eyes with conviction. So close to the release of the Dark Savior, would this be the end?

"Time to die," Dalton said in an ice-cold tone as he pulled the sword back. However, before he could cut him down, a group of miners crashed into Dalton; and he got caught in the tussle. Wolfgang had been saved by complete happenstance.

He howled with laughter and scurried off to collect his broadsword. While running, he spotted Conrad heading straight for him, but before they could confront one another, more soul-captured men attacked the strategist, and Wolfgang felt that it was a better idea to leave.

While making his escape, Wolfgang's eyes locked on Joel, the quiet boy whom he'd wanted to kill since the start of the trip. The mute was attacking Gold Fever-infected miners with his blade still in the sheath. Such childish and weak behavior filled him with all the more hatred.

After all, Joel stood for everything Wolfgang was against: He did not like black gold and was therefore against the Dark Savior. He was non-violent, so others had to fight for him. He was too good to talk like everybody else. All he cared about were his stupid maps. He contributed *nothing*, yet was given special treatment by the others. The only thing he deserved was a slow, painful death, Wolfgang thought.

Like a wolf stalking his prey, he picked up speed and bared his teeth. He eyed Joel's neck and then licked his lips. *Yes*, he thought. It would be nice to see his head roll.

However, a new obstacle aimed to stand in his way: Bronrar was sprinting from the other side of Joel to cut Wolfgang off. He held his pickaxe overhead, as if ready to bring it down on him at any moment. After the initial shock of Bronrar's bravery subsided, Wolfgang smiled. *Perfect*, he thought.

~

JOEL SHUDDERED UPON HEARING A FLESHY, squishy sound. He had heard it plenty of times on this horrid trip: The noise of a blade piercing flesh. He turned to see Bronrar with his pickaxe held overhead, frozen as the peak of Mt. Couture. Wolfgang stood before him, grinning, and also still.

The nervous miner dropped his pickaxe and lowered both hands to his stomach, where he caught a pool of his own blood. Joel looked down at Wolfgang's broadsword, still in his gut. A waterfall of red was now pouring out. Next, the blond brute twisted the blade, and Bronrar gargled in pain before vomiting blood out. Wolfgang began to cackle like the maniac he was, and his laughter drowned out the light cries for help that came from Bronrar's trembling lips. In that moment, a torrent of rage came over Joel; one he'd not felt in a long time.

In a flash, Joel smashed his sheathed blade into Wolfgang's face. The blond brute stumbled back in recoil, ripping the blade from Bronrar's wound in the process. He spit out a tooth and doubled over as blood dripped from his lips.

Suddenly, Wolfgang straightened himself and smiled back at Joel. "Yer lil' friend over here can't protect ye this time! It's just you an' me!"

"Yer forgettin' about tha mightiest warrior there is!" Alistair's voice cried out. Both Joel and Wolfgang turned their heads to see the big man charging in, about to bring his axe down for a thunderous chop.

Wolfgang scrambled to block at the last second, but the combination of his injuries and Alistair's strength only allowed him to lessen the impact. The big redhead's swings pushed him back more and more, and as he did so, he laid into him verbally.

"What's wrong? Can't ya fight properly, man-ta-man? Or are yer only wins from when ya get em' when they ain't lookin'?" He wound up and unleashed his strongest cut yet. Wolfgang growled as his hand buckled from the impact, barely hanging onto the grip of his blade. "I'm gonna chop ya up to lil' bits and feed ya to tha Nightcrawler! Then again, maybe yer too vile a creature ta be eaten!"

Alistair slashed horizontally and Wolfgang ducked under instead of blocking. Now, he was too afraid to even clash blades.

Joel took Bronrar under his shoulder and stood rigidly to hold him up. The wound was deep; far worse than Henic's had been. He was wobbly and barely able to speak, but there was life in him yet; which meant that an important decision rested on Joel's shoulders.

One option was to let him perish, which was an unhappy thought. Especially after Bronrar had understood the error of his ways and redeemed himself. Simply letting him die went against the entire reason that he and Aldous had intervened with the Mt. Couture expedition in the first place.

However, the alternative had possibilities worse than death. For the waters of Resurrection Falls would save his life, but infect him with Gold Fever. He would become a ravenous follower of the Dark Savior, just as the others had. Joel had to wonder, then: Would it be selfish to try and keep Bronrar alive if it changed who he was for the worse? Or would letting him die in agony be an act of evil on his part?

CHAPTER 39
RESURRECTION FALLS

As Alistair put Wolfgang on the defensive with many heavy swings of his battle axe, Joel's eyes darted past the battles and around the filthy walls of the chamber. Across the room, he spotted the exit. Unfortunately for him and the fast-fading Bronrar, there were many chaotic skirmishes in the space between them and their escape.

"I overheard while we were hidin' behind the big door..." Bronrar trailed off, his voice faint. Joel lowered his head and focused his ears. "The Resurrection Falls... will you take me?"

Joel's heart sank. If he had overheard the Mountain King's description of Resurrection Falls' capabilities, then surely, he knew what the effects were. He shook his head and did his best to sign at him with only one hand.

"Yeh... I heard him talking about the effects..." he replied between short, raspy breaths. "But I'm tellin' ye right now... I can beat the Gold Fever... just ask Edith an' Angus... they weren't happy with me about it..."

Joel fidgeted his mouth with hesitation, for what he had said was true: Bronrar had been the only member of his group not to succumb to the black gold fully when exposed to it in high amounts. He had fallen prey to fits of greed and was happy to take more of the dark, sparkling ore, but hadn't gone beyond that. He was still of sound mind, lacked the yellow eyes, and seemed to feel downright uncomfortable around the other Gold Fever-infected. However, Joel was still nervous about the idea. The Mountain King had warned them that drinking Resurrection Falls' water would be like a concentrated dose of the black gold; plunging the drinker into madness forever. Could Bronrar's natural resistance allow him to use the Resurrection Falls, unscathed?

"Please... take me..." Bronrar moaned.

The mute balled his fists as his head spun at dizzying speeds. He needed to focus on something else; to clear his mind. His eyes wandered to Alistair and Wolfgang's fight, the latter of which had been backed into a corner. The big man took a swing at Wolfgang's head, but he ducked the attack and his battle axe rang off the stone wall like a tolling bell. The blond brute then ran toward another chaotic battle across the chamber.

"Ye'll never catch me, fat-head!" he called out between fits of uncontrollable laughter.

"We'll see about that, ya muck-spout!" Alistair replied as he started to give chase. However, he stopped in his tracks before passing Joel and Bronrar. Concern came to his eyes, and he lowered his weapon.

"Oh, that ain't no good..." Alistair said, his eyes fixed on Bronrar's torn, bloody stomach.

"Resurrection Falls..." Bronrar moaned. Now, he was white as a ghost. Joel looked up at Alistair with panic in his eyes, hoping for an answer.

"Err... didn't that Mountain King feller say that it'll drive ya mad? I don' know if it's-"

"I can resist it... please..."

At that moment, Joel realized that he could not pass the responsibility of Bronrar's fate onto someone else's shoulders. He had come to a decision: Whatever he may have believed, who was he to deny a dying man his last wish? Bronrar's confidence in his ability to resist the madness may well have been desperation, but at the end of the day, it was *his* life. Could he force someone to die simply because he felt it was for their own good? He had decided that the answer was no. Especially since he had sustained the injury while defending him from Wolfgang.

The mute nodded at Alistair and began a march toward the chamber exit with Bronrar in tow.

"Understood... I'll keep a lookout ta make sure no one attacks ya!" Alistair readied his battle axe and walked alongside the pair.

~

Dalton found himself embroiled in a fight with three other combatants: A Gold Fever-infected miner, a man draped in chainmail, and a troll. It was an odd four-man free-for-all because Dalton could attack the troll at one moment, only to defend against the crazed miner the next. Somehow, thus far, they had all managed to stay alive.

The troll had taken the most damage: He had a few cuts and stab wounds, but trolls were typically able to withstand more than a human, so long as it wasn't a blow to the head or neck. The chainmail-clad man had the advantage, not only because of his armor but the fact that he held a shield. The Gold Fever-infected worker had been a wild-card. One moment he'd mumble to himself, the next he would go on a crazed attacking spree.

"Need a hand?" Out of the corner of his eye, he spotted Baltr approaching.

"Ah! Baltr. I was worried you didn't make it outta the throne room!" Dalton said in jest as he took a swing at the troll next to him. He blocked the strike with his club.

"I can't die before you, sir. After all, who would save you from your foolish decisions if I wasn't around?" Baltr asked while swinging his pickaxe at the crazed miner in front of him. He then dodged a sword swing by the chainmail-clad man. "For instance, choosing to fight against three opponents at the same time!"

"Not my choice!" Dalton said as he parried a club blow by the troll and responded with a diagonal, downward slash at his giant leg. The troll cried out in pain as the blade chopped into his knee, and he crashed to the floor with a thundering *thud*. "I was about to finish that knob Wolfgang off, but then they ambushed me!"

He pulled the sword from the troll's knee and landed a neck blow, nearly cutting his head off, but not quite, because of the thick skin. It was enough for the troll to burst into green light, however. The soul of the slain troll traveled back into the throne room, which was practically glowing white from all of the snow and ice within.

~

Surrounded by mounds of snow and sheets of ice, Aldous and the Mountain King stood at the center of the frigid throne room as green balls of light shot into the luxmortite chalice. Aldous could be certain that if any others remained in here, they did not draw breath, for his own breaths took the form of a noticeably thick fog that was primed to freeze if the climate were to become even a little cooler.

"This is the best you can do?" Olivier asked, his nose crinkling.

"You look cold! Do you need an extra garment?" Aldous asked with a smirk.

"No, thank you… I have my own!" he replied, wiping a hand over his chest. Plated armor suddenly took shape around his torso.

Aldous raised an eyebrow. The armor was iron or perhaps steel. Why not make use of the same luxmortite that had thwarted his earlier fireball attack? Perhaps it was a sign that his vast reserves of magic were waning. To conjure no less than five thunderstorms in two days on its own would be draining, but then there were the eyes he'd used to keep watch around the mountain; the souls he had to resurrect for battle; and the various spells he'd performed since they arrived in his castle. Even worse, all of his conjurations had been instant. Despite Aldous' mastery over water, when gathering the snow and ice, he had been sure to do so slowly. It had saved him precious magic.

"Do you have any more tricks up your sleeve, Aldous? If you've tried everything you need, I can end this now," Olivier said, his yellow eyes glinting.

"A few more tricks, mayhap!" he replied while pointing his walking stick at him. Two giant hands made from snow and ice sprouted up on each side of Olivier and clapped together in the blink of an eye. An explosion of dust-like ice shavings clouded the throne room's center, and Aldous waited with bated breath for the results. He groaned as the haze cleared and the Mountain King stood in the same spot, surrounded by flame and unaffected.

"You'll have to do more than that!" he bellowed and then raised his hands. With the gesture came a great wall of fire that spread omnidirectional and faster than a speeding arrow. Aldous grimaced and braced for impact by raising his walking stick. Like the prior lightning bolt, it was an opportunity for him to absorb the element for later use, but he would have to be careful; for he was not a master of fire.

The great wave of flame encompassed the entire throne room, and the heat and strength of it greatly surpassed Aldous' expectations. While absorbing the fire, his tunic and beard hairs singed, and his walking stick shook uncontrollably in his hands; a sign that it was about to burst. Still, he gripped his artifact with ox-like strength and reinforced it with magic, weathering the portion of the blast that had hit him.

After striking the stone walls and columns all around, the fire fizzled out, but the environment had changed: All of the snow and ice had melted to lukewarm water that came up to both of their waists. The walls were covered with char marks and a harsh, ashy smell filled the air.

Yet, the Mountain King had not finished his attack just yet. He waved his hand to conjure a hurricane-like wind that pushed the water before him into a great wave. Aldous let out a panicked cry as the wave swept him up, smashed him against a column, and broke through it. He then crashed to the ground on the overlooking second floor of the throne room.

"Are you done yet?" Olivier called out and then laughed.

"Not quite..." Aldous mumbled as he rubbed his aching back. He stood and then manipulated the water below into a jet plume that he hopped onto. As he lowered on the plume, Aldous remembered the stone column that Olivier had thrown at him earlier. The old Wizard raised his walking stick and gathered all water in the room behind him.

The Mountain King tilted his head and raised an eyebrow. "You're still trying? I thought you would have understood by now..."

Aldous grunted as he pressed his walking stick down with authority. In response, the water built up to a large wave that carried the stone column, its sharpened tip charging ahead like a giant spear. The old Wizard's eyes twitched when Olivier said something, but the roar of the raging water had drowned his voice out. As the wave passed through him, he shaped it into a giant fist that grasped the column and plunged it straight onto a motionless Olivier. The pillar crashed and endless chunks of stone exploded outward while the wave splattered like high tide against the rocks. Aldous fixed his eyes on where he had aimed his attack, hoping to see some semblance of damage to his opponent.

His eyes widened, however, when he saw that the pillar had not even reached the Mountain King. Out of the receding water appeared a large pair of skeletal arms that sprouted out of the floor. Half of the column had already broken from the impact, but the other, sharper half had been caught and gripped by the protruding arms.

"A nice little trick..." Olivier trailed off as he crossed his arms. "But ultimately? Pointless." The skeletal hands gripped down on the pillar and crushed what remained of it into rubble.

Of course, Aldous thought. Earlier, the Mountain King had been muttering an incantation to perform a spell: The Dark Hands were characterized by a pair of giant, skeletal arms that held great strength and destructive capabilities. They were most notable, however, for being one of the signature spells of Wilhelm the Oppressor. *His* Dark Hands had reached the height of buildings, though.

"More dark magic, eh?" Aldous asked with a nervous laugh.

"Marvelous, aren't they? A benefit of living up here, drenched in loneliness, is that I can use my anguish as a cost for the spell instead of inflicting further harm on myself or another."

"Yes, well… there are other prices to pay for using dark magic outside of the cost. A Dark Wizard can only live in misery!" Aldous said, clenching his walking stick. "You should already know this! Come to your senses, Olivier!"

"It's sad to see you wearing such small-mindedness on your sleeve. And you would be so bold as to lecture *me*? What nonsense! I have *forgotten* more about magic than you have ever learned!" he said before gazing at the skeleton arms and smiling. "Now, let's take care of this pesky water, shall we?"

The skeletal hands opened up and approached one another, but they did not touch. A round, green light formed between them and grew exponentially in size as each moment passed. Then, like a beam of light coming through a window, the green energy shot out at a gasping Aldous.

The old Wizard hopped back and narrowly avoided the blast at his feet, but he was not hit with the expected water splash. Instead, a sizzling noise filled his ears and a cloud of vapor plumed upward. In short order, the haze lifted, and he could see that the water was draining into a deep, dark hole. The green energy returned to the chalice floating nearby.

"How?" Aldous asked, his mouth agape. "How could you fire off soul energy without making a sacrifice?"

"The answer lies before your very eyes," he replied, pointing to the chalice. "My *guests*, of course, are souls whose bodies I must conjure if they are to take a physical form. But most of the time, they are merely swimming around in my chalice. So, one day I thought, 'why not make use of them?'"

"I see, now. Taking in wayward soul energy is the reason for the

Dark Hands' cost, eh? Then, if you can simply reuse your soul-servants, it would give you unlimited ammunition, so to speak…"

"Indeed. It has also allowed me to study the makeup of the soul in more detail than I ever could have hoped for. As you know, souls contain power beyond our wildest dreams, but we are only able to tap into morsels of such power. Yet, I think that you will soon find that I've tapped into more of it than any Wizard before me!"

Suddenly, the Dark Hands shot out another energy blast. Aldous dove into the draining water and heard the *sizzle* of the beam shooting by. On a knee, now, he looked back to see that it had punched a hole in the wall.

"A well-timed hole…" Aldous said as he held his walking stick up and let out a snorting breath. In a flash, snow burst into the throne room and flurried around them. The blizzard-like conditions made it difficult to see.

"This, again? You Elementals lack creativity!" Olivier said.

As Aldous snuck through the throne room under a veil of white raging around them, more green energy blasts whizzed by him, vaporizing the snowflakes and ice shavings into little puffs of fog. Behind, he heard a loud searing noise that rose above the raging winds of the blizzard; and they were followed by what he believed to be collapsing walls and columns. If the Dark Hand attacks lasted much longer, there was a real danger that the throne room could collapse on top of him. He put his head down, and his jog turned to a full sprint.

"Come out and fight! Coward!" the Mountain King roared.

"Hello!" Aldous said from behind him as the snow died down.

Olivier turned just in time to see a lightning bolt flying out of Aldous' walking stick; the very same one that he had absorbed earlier. As he heard the crackle of the bolt striking its target, the old Wizard followed up with a fireball twice the size of the one he had fired at him before. Built of the same flames he had taken in from the Mountain King's wall of fire; it roared like a mighty dragon and lit the room to such a degree that all Aldous could see was white.

The force of the explosion rocked Aldous to his very core. Due to his temporary blindness, he couldn't see what was happening, but it felt like his whole world was spinning. Then, he landed in a mound of snow. The blast must have knocked him back, he thought as snow shot up the sleeves and down the collar of his tunic. The sudden cold shocked his body so that he snapped to a sitting-up position immediately, as if awakening from a nightmare.

His vision returned, and he could see that for the most part, the throne room had been filled with snow again. There were several holes in the walls, all having been burned with such intense heat that there was not a bump within them. One of the columns had indeed collapsed as he suspected, but thankfully, the room was well-built. It seemed there was no danger of a cave-in, yet.

At the center of the throne room, a fire raged on and a heavy plume of smoke traveled up, gathering at the ceiling. Olivier's Dark Hands had collapsed and fallen into many different bone fragments. Aldous' heart was filled with a cautious optimism. Had he truly managed to defeat a King Wizard?

"A fine attack!" a voice called out from the smoke. Aldous' stomach sank. "But not enough!"

A great gust of wind exploded outward, and Aldous shielded his eyes with a forearm as he felt the sting of the fire and the harshness of the smoke pass by him. After lowering his arm, he looked upon the Mountain King in disbelief; for he was alive and well. While his armor was tattered and he steamed from the sheer heat of the attacks that had hit him, he showed no signs of true injury.

Olivier scoffed and then reached back. He swung an open hand forward, as if slapping the air, and then Aldous gasped: In an instant, a small tornado took shape and swept him up. The old Wizard became sick to his stomach as he spun around and around. The mixture of dust and snow that had been caught up with him got in his eyes and shot down his nose and throat as he tried to breathe.

Then, just as suddenly as he had been swept up, the tornado spit him out; throwing him head-first into the bottom of the overhang of the second floor. Aldous cried out as his head struck the unforgiving stone, and then he fell back to the first floor like a sack of potatoes.

Struggling on his hands and knees and coughing now, Aldous looked up to see the Mountain King holding his hand out. With a conjured bolt of lightning, he magnetized the luxmortite chalice so that it came to him. Aldous groaned as blood from the gash on his head began to drip down into his eyes, but he did not wipe it. It would be unwise to look away from such unseemly power; even for only a moment.

"How about I show you something interesting?" Olivier asked with a devilish grin.

Back in the torture chamber, Lucia and Angus' duel was interrupted when the latter suddenly fled in the direction of the exit.

"Where are you going? Face me, coward!" Lucia called from behind. Her eyes widened upon realizing that he was headed for Joel, Alistair, and Bronrar. She began to give chase, but it may have already been too late, she thought.

Then, Alistair jumped in front of Joel and Bronrar and brought his axe down upon Angus. The giant used his shield to block and attempted to pivot around him, but Alistair stuck his boot out and tripped him up. He then swung his battle axe down once more, and Angus was forced to block with the shield again.

Squinting now, Lucia could see that Joel was holding Bronrar up under his shoulder and they continued toward the exit. It also seemed that, despite a noticeable limp, Alistair had Angus' back against the wall. So, she set her sights on a group to her left; one where Wolfgang wildly swung away at other combatants, even those on his own side. It was time for someone to put him down; time for a rematch.

"The Savior wills it!" Wolfgang howled as he plunged his blade into the gut of a Gold Fever-infected miner, who smiled back at him.

"For the Savior…" the miner said through grinning, blood-soaked teeth. Wolfgang ripped the sword out of his stomach, and he collapsed to the ground.

Lucia began the charge toward him with her arming sword out and ready to strike. As if sensing her, Wolfgang turned and his eyes lit up with an obvious joy. They crossed blades, both one-handed, and then she pushed him back.

"Well, if it ain't the big bitch! About time ye found the courage to face me! Are ye ready to die? Don' worry, yer slaughter will go toward a great cause!" Wolfgang said as he attempted a thrust with his sword.

She knocked the sword away and then responded with a speedy stab of her own. Wolfgang pivoted to his side, resulting in a near miss. He raised an eyebrow as she retracted the arming sword and resumed a long-guarded stance. Surely, he had realized a change in her speed and execution, she thought. The only question was how he would react-

Wolfgang swiftly charged forward, cackling to the tune of his own insanity, and swung his sword down and diagonal, across his body. He repeated the attack from each side, over and over, while Lucia defended each swing with expert precision.

The mercenary counter-attacked with a couple of horizontal slashes from both sides. The attacks were parried, but then she brought her sword down for a direct vertical slash. Wolfgang blocked once more, yet he had to commit to a full block: Lucia continued to push down on his blade while he held it upright. With the leverage advantage, she closed in on him and landed a thundering knee to his stomach. He doubled over and dry-heaved, giving her ample time to bring the butt of her sword down onto the bridge of Wolfgang's nose. A loud and satisfying *crack* echoed in Lucia's ears, but even better were the cries of pain from his wretched mouth. She pulled her blade back for the finishing blow, but Wolfgang wisely leaped backward.

Lucia smirked at Wolfgang, whose nose bled profusely. It had gone crooked, but not for long: The blond brute laughed as he pushed the bridge of his nose back into place.

"Yer a lot better now that ye got a new weapon, ain't ye?" Wolfgang asked as he shot a snot of blood out of his nostrils. "The Savior must be testing me before I get to meet him!" His eyes glowed yellow as ever.

"You think that I am a mere test to be conquered? All in the name of your false God?" Lucia asked. Wolfgang growled at her. "This is one test that you're going to fail, I'm afraid."

～

Down the tunnel to Resurrection Falls, Joel continued to carry Bronrar over his shoulder. Although he'd been dragging his feet and his breaths had become shorter, he was still alive, and that much filled Joel with hope.

"This is all like some sorta… crazy dream, ain't it?" Bronrar asked. One chuckle gave way to several hoarse coughs. Joel nodded back in return.

"I know that I'm dyin'… but it doesn't… feel real…" he muttered. The torches flickered on the wall, reflecting off all of the red dripping from his stomach. The path was on a decline and Joel had to take careful, rigid steps. He was certain that if Bronrar were to fall, he wouldn't be getting back up. "Do you think… there's any kinda afterlife?"

Joel looked up in thought. Aldous had once told him of a place where souls traveled after the body died, but no mortal could know for sure. At the moment, however, it didn't matter. What mattered was ensuring that Bronrar was comfortable, just in case these were his last moments. The mute nodded at him with an assuring smile.

"Ah, that's good… yer usually right about these things…" Bronrar mumbled as he became heavier on Joel's shoulder. His eyes were only half-open now, and his breaths seemed dryer and shorter with each step taken. Joel could only hope that they were nearing the falls. He could hear rushing water off in the distance, but with the cave wall acoustics, it was hard to tell how far away it was.

"But I don' understand… if there's an afterlife, there must be a God… an' if there's a God… why would he let me go? I tried to do the right thing…" Bronrar whimpered. Now, he appeared to be nodding off, and he was taking almost no steps on his own.

It got to the point where Joel dragged him along the path with all of his might. He felt his muscles stretching and sweat poured into his stinging eyes from the effort. Yet, he could still hear light breaths coming from Bronrar, and that was enough reason to push through. They could still make it, he thought. The rushing water grew louder.

After an exhaustive journey, Joel finally reached the end of the tunnel to see a new cave that was well-lit by torches all along its edges. The light mist dampening only one side of his body drew attention to his immediate left; where a great waterfall shot out from a hole in the rock wall and fell into a pool that seemed to drain from its center. They were too close to give up, now. Joel pushed the burning of his legs out of mind and continued toward the pool with Bronrar in tow.

MANY OF THE battles had spilled out of the torture chamber and into the tunnel that led to the falls. Furthest down the path were Wolfgang and Lucia, who had incorporated their respective speeds into much of the duel. The blond brute had put up more of a fight since Lucia broke his nose, but she was slowly wearing him down with superior form and a reach advantage. Now, she was biding her time; waiting for him to make a mistake so that she could strike a decisive blow.

Wolfgang swung wildly while crying out, and finally, she found a gaping hole in his defenses. She held her arming sword out at an angle, letting his blade slide off and past her injured shoulder. Simultaneously, Lucia made a stabbing motion with her sword, and with a loud *rip*, she sliced across his chest. Wolfgang hopped back as blood spurted out from the new tear in his shirt. She snorted in frustration and lowered her blade to rest her aching arm. His reaction speed had come into play yet again. As soon as she had felt the sword cutting into him, she could also feel him moving away. What he lacked in skill, he more than made up for in unpredictability and combat speed.

"That ain't nothin'!" Wolfgang shouted as he charged in and lunged out for a stab. Lucia pivoted and dodged with a swipe at the blade to knock it away. She then responded with a flick of her wrist and brought her sword around to diagonally slash at him. He brought his blade up to meet hers, and then a succession of quick-paced strikes and parries ensued.

Eventually, Lucia closed in on Wolfgang and knocked his sword upward with a strong swing in the same direction. Before he could bring it back down to defend himself, the mercenary reset her position and thrust her blade at his midsection. He attempted to dodge, but the fatigue of all the battles and injuries had become apparent, and finally, his movements slowed. The blade pierced into the side of his stomach and poked clean through.

Wolfgang gasped through bloody lips as Lucia withdrew her sword. He stumbled backward until his back hit the tunnel wall, next to a torch. He looked down at his midsection and so too did Lucia. She nearly groaned to see that she hadn't hit an organ, calling to mind another bothersome quality of this battle: Wolfgang seemed to have ungodly luck. All of those fights; all of those injuries, and he had somehow avoided a fatal battle wound.

"I must give credit where it's due: You are quite resilient. Most men would have passed out from fatigue or the pain of their injuries by now. Perhaps the Dark Savior truly is watching over you," Lucia said while pointing her blade at him and smiling. "What a shame that you will die in this tunnel before getting to meet him."

"Shut yer damn mouth!" Wolfgang shouted back with such intensity that blood spewed from his mouth and onto her clothes.

"Do you know your Dark Savior's true name?" Lucia asked as Wolfgang raised an eyebrow. "I do… should I tell it to you before you die?" Her smile turned to a grin.

"Ye wouldn't know his true name! A non-believer like ye would not be given such an honor!" Wolfgang hissed as Lucia inched closer, her sword pulled back and ready for the decisive stab.

"I won't die…" the blond brute trailed off as he looked to his left. He started to giggle. "I shall meet my Dark Savior! And you? You will burn!" He ripped the torch off of the cave wall and threw it at her.

Within sword's reach now, Lucia didn't have time to react to the surprise attack. The torch made contact with her leather armor and set her ablaze. She cried out while flailing her sword around in vain, but even more horrifying than the searing heat was that she could smell the skin cooking underneath her clothes. Out of desperation, she dropped to the ground and rolled back and forth. Eventually, a cooling sensation came over her. The flames had been put out, but within seconds, it became obvious that the damage had been done.

The flames had burned through parts of her torso armor near the ribs, and those parts of her skin had already layered down and deformed into dark red blisters. She could also feel burns even where the flames had not gotten through the armor, and the pain was immense; among the worst she'd ever felt. Even still, Lucia was prepared to fight until the end. She sat up and then looked over her shoulder to see Wolfgang off in the distance, running down the tunnel toward Resurrection Falls.

Lucia's vision became blurry and her head felt light. She started to shiver, despite the burns on her torso feeling like a glowing poker was being held up to her skin.

Suddenly, her eyes lost focus, and then time seemed to pass in an instant. When her blurry vision returned, she saw a man approaching her, and he held a blade. One of the Gold Fever-infected? She reached out for her arming sword, but her hand was too jittery to get a good grip on it.

"Lucia, it's me, Conrad."

She breathed a sigh of relief and then held her hand out. "Could you give me a lift?"

Conrad took her hand and helped her up. As she stood, he took her over his shoulder. His hand grazed her back, where the flames had seared her flesh.

"Ack!" she cried while flinching. As if a sudden jolt to her system, her vision returned to normal.

He looked up at her with intense eyes. "Your lips are blue, and you're as pale as a ghost. What happened?"

"That bastard Wolfgang set me on fire..." Lucia trailed off as she took in a deep breath, but it only made the pain near her ribs worse. "The worst part is that I had him... but I took the time to taunt him instead of finishing the job."

"Was it a good insult, at least?" Conrad asked, his expression softening. It made Lucia feel better to see him in higher spirits.

"I told him that I knew the name of his Dark Savior and that I wouldn't tell him what it was before killing him," she said as they both laughed, but Lucia immediately regretted it. She recoiled from the pain of each chuckle.

"I bet that hurt him more than he hurt you."

"And what of Henic?" Lucia asked. She already knew the answer.

"Dead. Killed by that low-life," Conrad said as his eyes sharpened and he gripped the hilt of his rapier with intensity. "First, he wounded him after we saved his life… and then he finished him off."

"I'm sorry…"

"No, I'm the one who's sorry. If I had only killed Wolfgang back when I had the chance… Henic would be going back to his family right now. His last words… he begged me to kill Wolfgang so that his wife and boy wouldn't have to work in the fields to keep on serving him. Henic worked day and night on his farm to give him free goods, but he killed him anyway without a second thought," Conrad said as he drew his rapier. "And I cannot allow that to stand!"

"Then leave me, and go face Wolfgang. I'll be fine…" Lucia said.

Conrad let out a long breath and then sheathed his blade. "I won't leave another friend behind. We shall escape these mines together."

Lucia couldn't help but smile despite the immense pain coursing through her. She hoped that he was right.

IN THE RESURRECTION FALLS CAVE, Joel had finally dragged Bronrar to the pool of water. His eyes were half-open and dull, and he had become unresponsive to any gesture made by the mute. At the edge of the pool, Joel sat him down so that his legs were submerged over the edge. He cupped the water in his hands and brought it to Bronrar's mouth. The first attempt saw it all spilling and dribbling out. On the second try, he tilted the nervous miner's head back so the water would go down.

Joel stood as Bronrar slumped over. In but a few moments, he seemed to get much better, with more alert reactions, and less sluggish movements. He went to cup the water on his own for a second drink, and then a third. Then, Bronrar miraculously stood under his own power for the first time since Wolfgang had gutted him. Joel looked down at his torn shirt to see that the wound had become little more than a scar on his belly. Both had pure joy written all over their faces as Bronrar started walking to him, his arms outstretched for a supposed hug.

Joel was ready to accept the hug, but suddenly, Bronrar held his head and doubled over while groaning.

"Ugh… Joel… I think it's the Gold Fever!" he cried while shaking his head and falling to his knees.

Joel rushed to Bronrar's side in case he needed his shoulder to lean on once more. There was little else he could do. The nervous miner writhed in pain for a little longer, until, without warning, it seemed to end. Bronrar sat there, wide-eyed.

"I-I did it! I overcame Gold Fever!" he said in a blissful tone. He and Joel chuckled. "I knew it! I knew that I could resist it! This is great! Like a second chance at life!"

"What do you say we get out of here, Joel?" Bronrar asked. The mute nodded and they both started to walk across the cave.

Joel was about to do something he thought was improbable some way through the expedition: Leave Mt. Couture alive. He was also happy to see that not only had Bronrar turned himself around, but he was alive and well after his heroic actions. Despite all of the death and destruction that had occurred, he could at least look to Bronrar as a shining example of something good coming from this otherwise disastrous mining trip.

CHAPTER 40
BETRAYAL

As Joel walked ahead, merry as could be, Bronrar started to fall behind. A brief pang of worry struck him as he looked over his shoulder. He was relieved to see the nervous miner in perfect health. Perhaps it was he who was moving too fast. But how could he not? They were about to escape the clutches of Mt. Couture; a feat not since replicated in over a hundred years! He was certain that most of his new friends would make it, too. Even Aldous would find some way out, he thought. He always found a way.

"Say, Joel?" Bronrar asked from behind. "Can I ask you a personal question?"

Joel looked over his shoulder again and nodded.

"Have you ever wondered what the Dark Savior was like?" he asked. A chill shot down Joel's spine, stiffening his legs so much that his feet began to drag. "I have'ta admit, I've found myself wonderin', lately…"

The mute shook his head no and returned his attention forward.

"Ah… no interest, eh?" Bronrar replied with a chuckle. "I think it's a shame, ain't it? We were sent here to be controlled and killed, and fer what? I was hopin' to get somethin' out of it." Joel remained silent in the hopes that he would let the topic come to an end.

"It's just a shame… a real shame…" Bronrar trailed off. Joel's ears twitched. His tone had changed from friendly to aggressive. "That you can't see the truth!"

Joel turned just in time to see Bronrar's fist collide with his eye. The punch knocked him for a loop and he stumbled back before tripping over his own feet and falling to the rocky ground. With speed he'd never seen from him before, Bronrar jumped on top of Joel and wrapped hands around his neck. Dazed from the surprise blow, Joel struggled to move under Bronrar's full weight and stranglehold. His next thought was to make use of his sword, but out of the corner of his hazy vision, he could see that it had slid away from him at some point during the attack; too far for him to reach.

"The truth is… there was a reason that we were brought to this miserable place! It was to meet our one and only Savior!" Bronrar shouted before bursting out into an insanity-filled laugh. "And I won't let you get in the way! All non-believers must die!"

Joel gazed into the yellow eyes of Bronrar as pockets of choking breath escaped his mouth. Slowly, he morphed into something else; *someone* else. He no longer saw his Gold Fever-infected friend, but that same woman from back then. Not her again, Joel thought. Anyone but her.

She glared at Joel with bulging yellow eyes and a crooked smile. Her long, dark hair was disheveled and so too was her bloodied, malnourished face. The woman let out a deafening screech and her wretched spit spewed onto him. *Just kill me this time*, he thought. He watched helplessly as a blade came to her throat and slit across. He wheezed and flailed around in vain attempts to stop it, but the blood emptied out of her neck like a pouring bucket. The sea of red splashed his face and shocked Joel back to reality.

A wide-eyed Bronrar released his grip and tipped over like a falling tree. He grasped his neck, but the blood quickly seeped through his fingers. Joel gasped for new breaths of air and shook his head to get the cobwebs out. Who had saved him?

Bronrar gurgled on his own blood and began desperately crawling in the direction of the Resurrection Falls. Yet, with each passing moment, his movements became more sluggish. Eventually, the wide miner stopped before a man. Joel's eyes regained their focus, and he was shocked to see Wolfgang looking down on him with a mischievous grin.

"I told ye that I was gonna kill ye, didn't I? I keep my promises!"

All of the color had been drained out of Bronrar's chubby cheeks, and yet still he smiled back up at his attacker and muttered, "For the will of the Savior…" before puking out some more blood. With that, his eyes glazed over and he fell face-first to the ground.

"Ye weren't *really* one of us, fool!" Wolfgang said before spitting on Bronrar's corpse. "And as fer ye…" the blond brute walked over to Joel, who clawed backward while still on his bottom. He needed to get closer to his sword. "I promised I'd kill *ye* too, didn't I?"

Wolfgang leaped forward and attempted a downward slash, but Joel quickly retrieved his sheathed blade from behind and held it out to defend. Wolfgang's sword clashed with the sheath mere inches from Joel's chest. The thick leather of the covering gave way to the chopping blade, and a light ring of clashing metal sounded off. Yet, there was also a loud *crack* that overpowered the all other noises. The blond brute stepped back and scoffed.

"It would seem that I've been usin' this thing a lil' too much…" Wolfgang said while inspecting his sword. Several small cracks had formed at the sword's edge. "No matter, I'll take yers after I kill ye!"

Joel stood and then held his sheathed sword up in a defensive position. Wolfgang raised an eyebrow and laughed.

"So, ye finally grew a spine, eh?" he asked with an amused smirk. "Well, it won't make a difference! Yer soft! Weak! Helpless! And worst of all, ye can't do anythin' right! Why don't ye make it easy on yerself and bend the knee, lil' man?"

Joel glanced at Bronrar's corpse. Blood was pooling around his head, and a lump came to the mute's dry throat. After bravely standing in Wolfgang's path to save him, *that* had been his reward? To be gutted and then sliced open by a maniac? A newfound determination flowed through Joel. The least he could do was not let his sacrifice be in vain. The time had come to stand his ground.

"Have it yer way, then! Ye'll die like all the others who've stood between me an' my Dark Savior!" Wolfgang cried as he charged full speed ahead.

"Joel!" a familiar voice called out. Wolfgang stopped in his tracks and then looked back. Conrad walked out of the tunnel with Lucia hunched over his shoulder, dragging her feet.

Not too far behind them, Angus was running away from Alistair.

"Get yer big arse back here and fight me!" he cried as Angus burst out of the tunnel. Alistair stopped next to Conrad and Lucia near the beginning of the cave and put hands to his knees while gasping for breath. Angus continued his sprint forward.

Wolfgang groaned. "What a nuisance!"

"Bronrar?" Angus asked aloud with uncharacteristic panic in his voice. "Bronrar!"

Angus rushed to his friend's side and knelt on the ground to take him in his arms. He turned Bronrar over and shuddered. Blood still poured from his gaping neck wound, but there were no other signs of life to be found coming from him.

"No…" he muttered. "How could you…" the giant stood and turned to face Joel. "How could you kill him when he trusted you? I will crush your bones, one by one, so that you can experience his pain, tenfold! Your death will come slowly!" With bloodlust in his eyes, he dashed forward while raising his mace and shield to battle positions.

The more likely killer between Joel and Wolfgang was obvious, but Angus had to have been in denial. Once again, the mute resolved to defend himself. He would not let Bronrar's sacrifice be in vain, and since his opponent held a shield, he was certain that he could subdue him without striking a death blow.

As Angus pulled his mace back, Joel stood firm. He could feel the power; the rage, that the giant was ready to unleash on him, yet some-how, his nerves steeled. Everything seemed like it was in slow motion. He slid the blade out of his sheath and its metallic, dark blue form sliced through the air with grace. Upward and diagonal the blue blur traveled, striking the shaft of Angus' mace as he brought it down with monstrous force.

Crack

The shaft of the mace, despite its fine iron craftsmanship, fractured, and then split. The club head soared past Joel, and he heard it bouncing off the rock far behind. There was a brief pause between the two, and Angus stared down at him with wide eyes. Joel pulled the sword back, telegraphing a strike. He wanted him to block.

Angus raised his shield as the slash came at him from a downward, diagonal angle. When the blow was struck, the shield groaned and its structure caved in. He let out a stuttering gasp while looking down at the shield to see a sizable dent. Joel lowered his sword. The fight was over.

The giant cried out in pain and threw the shield away to reveal a dangling, broken arm. It had shattered just as a twig would under a stomping boot. He fell to his knees and then lowered his head as if awaiting an execution. However, Joel remained motionless. After a few moments, Angus looked up at him with confusion in his eyes. He hoped that such mercy would send a loud and clear message that he hadn't been the one to kill Bronrar.

"Ah, so the quiet one can fight, but he chooses not to, eh?" Wolfgang said while approaching Angus. "That makes me want to kill ye even more! But first, let's take out the trash!" Angus, now pale and of heavy breath, looked at him, slack-jawed.

"I *did* say it was every man fer himself, didn't I?" Wolfgang asked with a knowing smile. "Ye were gettin' a little too cozy with my gal. And ye of all people should know what happens when ye do stupid things like that!" Angus let out a defeated sigh and then looked down.

"Oh, and by the way…" Wolfgang said while raising his blade. "It was I who killed yer idiot of a friend! First, I stuck 'im like the pig he was, but he was resilient… or what's the word? *Stubborn*. An' I don' like that type. So, I slit his throat and watched him bleed out like the dog he was!" Wolfgang said before bursting out with laughter. Angus was shaking, now. "But don' worry, I'll make sure yer death is quick! Ye've been a *real pal*, after all!" Finally, he brought his blade down.

Joel jumped in and blocked the vertical slash with his sword. As Wolfgang's weapon recoiled, Angus rolled and then picked up the dented shield with his good arm. Then, he charged the stumbling blond brute at full force.

Wolfgang hacked away in Angus' direction, but the shield blocked each blow, and upon reaching him, he laid a thundering shoulder tackle into his chest. Wolfgang flew back, as if a child being thrown, and landed hard on the rocky floor. He wheezed while struggling to sit up, and Angus used those moments to grab his shield by the top. He took aim with the bottom of the shield, where it was sharp, and attempted to impale him. However, Wolfgang regained his wits and pivoted out of the way while on all fours.

As Angus' shield bounced off of rock, he lost his grip. The shield spiraled away from his flailing arm, and in that time, Wolfgang had regained his footing. He slashed at the back of Angus' leg, and blood splashed out of his cut pant leg as he grunted through gritting teeth. Angus tipped over and struck the ground like rubble from a tunnel collapse. He could only look up from his side as Wolfgang stood over him in victory.

"Yer not worthy of meetin' our Savior, so it's time fer ye to die!" Wolfgang said as he raised his blade once more.

"Wolfgang!" a voice called out from behind. He turned just in time to see Conrad's rapier lashing him across the shoulder. The blond brute hopped back and then snorted. Some blood squirted out from his tattered shirt.

Joel raised an eyebrow. Conrad had the opportunity to stab him from behind, to kill him, but he had intentionally called out to him. Obviously, he wanted to best him in a fair fight, but what did that mean? Had Henic been yet another victim in Wolfgang's rampage?

"We have a score to settle," Conrad said as he took a fencing pose. Lucia and Alistair were approaching slowly, and several other combatants had made their way out of the tunnel passage and into the cave.

"I don' have time fer this…" Wolfgang muttered as he turned and ran off in the direction of a new tunnel, across the cave. "I must meet the Dark Savior!"

Conrad looked back at Lucia and Alistair. They nodded and shooed him away, respectively. He then looked at Joel, who also gave him a nod. With that, Conrad put his head down and began a sprint in Wolfgang's direction.

~

ALDOUS STOOD STILL as the night and wide-eyed in the Mountain King's throne room. Henic smiled down at him from the crumbled stairs of the throne.

"Why the long face?" Henic asked.

"He got you… I'm sorry…" Aldous replied, choked up.

"What is there to be sorry for? I feel much better, now!" he said and then slapped his stomach. "See? No more hole in the belly. I'm a chubby man once more!" The farmer laughed.

"Your soul was not meant to be captured! It was meant to fly away; to be free!" Aldous said.

"But I feel free…"

"Do you see now, Aldous? I have given this man a second chance! He had no hope of reaching medical treatment in time. His suffering has ended, and now he is one of my guests!" the Mountain King said.

"Please, let him go!" begged Aldous.

"I shall accept nothing less than you and your friends' unconditional surrender!" Olivier replied.

"It really ain't that bad, Aldous!" Henic added.

"You don't understand, Henic! You are now a slave to his every whim!"

Henic eyed the Mountain King and asked, "Is this true?"

"It is true that because I have given you a second chance, you must earn your keep!" he replied. Henic's body began to tremble. Now, he was walking toward Aldous with a pickaxe in hand.

"Whoa! Hold on… I ain't fightin' him!" Henic closed his eyes and grunted and groaned to no avail. His legs kept on moving. "Aldous… I have no control!"

"Olivier! Stop this! Face me yourself!" Aldous said. He pointed his walking stick at Henic and walls of ice shot up around him, halting his movement.

"You'll have to kill him…" the Mountain King said with a smirk. Aldous gasped. Henic was already chipping away at the ice with his pickaxe. "The choice is yours! Will you betray your friend and kill him? Or will you join us?"

Aldous tightened his grip on the walking stick. He hoped that the others were close to escaping, for he would not be able to hold out much longer.

~

Down in the Gold Pit, Edith watched on as her five Gold Fever-infected grunts swung pickaxes at the monolith. It was a surprisingly durable slab of stone, but they were starting to get to the heart of it. The issue with 'destroying the monolith' was that Edith was not quite sure how much it needed to be broken up. Breaking off small pieces hadn't been enough, so she came to believe that a complete collapse was necessary. To move the process along quicker, she had begun laying into the men verbally.

"You call yourselves miners? Pathetic! The Dark Savior will not be pleased!" she had said.

"I can't believe my father ever hired you!"

"Faster! Faster!"

Any time she had gotten the slightest inkling that the workers would turn on her, all she had to do was bring up the Dark Savior. They were all too easy to manipulate, and it filled her with joy.

"Egois sumheach voduit meais leatmea nunta anua tunun leamini thoitatum meam," Edith chanted to herself. She had remembered the incantation perfectly, for it was the key to her destiny. Soon, she would have wealth and power beyond any other, and Drake would be dealt the humiliating death that he deserved.

Then, no one would be able to stop her. All around the world, her name would be uttered with hints of fear, love, and respect. She would build an empire that put even the greatest kingdoms of history to shame, and she would amass a grand, loyal army of Gold Fever-infected so that she could bring all other lands to their knees. And while on their knees, they would bow to her; worship her as a Goddess. She would become all-powerful, and all would aspire to be just like her. But of course, all would fail to match her beauty and cunning. For there was only one Edith Dan-

Skreeeee

The Nightcrawler's shrill cry sent ripples through her body, bringing her back to reality. It had been a hollowed-out noise thanks to the thick barrier of debris between the collapsed tunnel and Gold Pit. Yet, like a battering ram slamming a door that was about to burst, she could hear it charging into the boulders with its great strength. Time was short.

"Hurry up! The Nightcrawler is coming! You want to meet the Savior, don't you?" she asked. The men began to chop away faster. Pieces of the monolith fell off little by little, but still, no portal appeared as she had been told.

Skreeeeeee

~

In the Resurrection Falls cave, Dalton lunged out and stabbed at a chainmail-clad man. The blade sliced into the side of his neck, and with it came an eruption of blood. The man cried out before falling to the ground, and the warrior turned his attention elsewhere.

Baltr had his hands full with a Gold Fever-infected man and a knocker who'd been dressed up like a jester. The stringy man threw the knocker off of his back to reveal several bloody bite marks through his ragged tunic, and as the crazed man lunged out at him, he plunged his pickaxe into his gut.

Despite his inevitable death from the blow, the miner grinned through bloody teeth and held onto the pickaxe while it was lodged in his stomach. Baltr looked over his shoulder to see the knocker running at him, arms outstretched and drooling. He struggled and struggled to pull the pickaxe out, but the crazed miner held firm.

"Die!" he said between hysteric laughter. "Die for our Savior!"

The knocker leaped forward and Baltr closed his eyes. Then, Dalton charged in with a jumping, vertical slash that clubbed the knocker out

of the air. It screeched while dropping to the floor, in two bloody halves. It burst into balls of green light that shot out of the cave and back up the tunnel to the torture chamber.

Baltr's eyes widened, and Dalton gave him a nod when he looked back. He ripped the pickaxe out of the Gold Fever-infected man's midsection and then kicked him to the rocky floor. Finally, he finished him off with a pickaxe swing to the neck.

Dalton's cheeks filled with air, and Baltr narrowed his eyes at him. "Don't say it…"

"You were almost killed by that lil' fella! That's one *deadly jester*!" the warrior said before bursting out into laughter. The stringy man raised his pickaxe into attacking position and approached him. "Come, now! I was only jokin-"

The pickaxe came down and Dalton gasped. However, it hadn't been aimed at him. The axe head went just past his shoulder, and he heard a fleshy *splat* from behind. Blood splattered onto his cheek, and the warrior looked back to see the chainmail-clad man from earlier. Baltr's pickaxe was lodged in a vulnerable spot where his neck met his shoulder. The man burst into green light that shot back up the tunnel.

"That was close! Thank you…" Dalton said, nearly breathless.

"Still feeling overconfident, sir?" Baltr asked with barbs of sarcasm.

He chuckled. "I suppose I had that one coming!"

"What should we do now?" Baltr asked.

Dalton looked around the cave. Some battles raged on near the falls, but none involved their allies. Unfortunately, six of their own, including Henic, had perished in battle. The rest of the conflicts that had spilled out into the cave were between Gold Fever miners and soul slaves. At about the halfway point of the cave, near a wall, Dalton spotted Lucia and the rest of their friends. They appeared to have surrounded someone.

"None of these other battles seem like they have anything to do with us," Dalton said.

"Yes, and I do hope they kill each other," Baltr added.

"That would make things easier, wouldn't it? But for now, we should regroup with our allies," Dalton said as he turned to face Lucia and the others. He and Baltr began a quick-paced walk toward them.

When the pair reached Lucia, Alistair, and Joel, they could see that they were interrogating Angus, who had his back to the wall and nursed a swollen, twisted arm as he sat.

"What's going on?" Dalton asked.

"Angus over here is feeling a little sore that his murderous friend tried to kill him," Lucia replied with amusement on her tongue.

"I am only sad that I did not take Edith's advice and kill him myself!" Angus outburst to wide eyes and gasps from all. "Then, at least Bronrar would be alive… and I could be with her…"

"Are ya daft, lad? Edith is doin' the same thing ta you that she's done to Faramond and Wolfgang!" Alistair said.

"He's right," Lucia added. Alistair almost looked incredulous that she had agreed with him, and Dalton had to choke back laughter so they could keep the pressure on Angus. Perhaps he would reveal more about Edith's plans if they pressed him.

"It matters little," Angus said before smirking. "Edith has all but succeeded. I don't know if you lot can even comprehend what is happening here, but she is about to open a portal to the Dark Savior; or a spawn of him, anyhow… she has learned an incantation that will allow her to control the beast, and when that happens, the world will fall before her feet."

"So, that's where she is! The clever bitch… she used all of you as a distraction while she stayed back and opened the portal!" Lucia said with clenched fists.

"Why would you willingly go along with a plan that saw you as little more than a pawn?" Dalton asked.

"I know of Edith's treacherous ways, and I knew there was a good chance that she would betray me in the end. Yet, I have fallen in love with her… or perhaps the *idea* of her. All my life, I have wanted to improve my situation; to become more than a mere worker that scrapes by on breadcrumbs. So, I began allying myself with folk that had or desired power."

"That is why I stood by Wolfgang for so long. Vile as he may be, his lust for power made me believe that he would eventually obtain it. Turns out that all he received for his troubles was heaps n' heaps of madness," Angus said with a chuckle. "Edith, on the other hand, *has* power, and she *has* a plan to obtain even more. At first, our relationship was business and nothing more, but over time, I came to admire her beauty; not just her looks, but *who she is!*"

"Uhhh, I think ya gots it backwards, lad! I think ya meant ta say she looks beautiful on tha outside, but she's pure evil on tha inside!" Alistair said with a raised eyebrow.

"No… I mean it. Edith's reckless exercise of power, her plans, her motivations… I love everything about them. I had this dream, y'see…

and it may have been foolish, but that's how I felt. I dreamed that we could rule together and exercise our power upon the people as we saw fit. For once, I would make the rules, and others would bend to *my* will! But it would seem that Edith's dreams only have room for herself," Angus said before letting out a sigh. "Ah well, it was a nice thought while it lasted."

"Says you," Dalton said as he crossed his arms. "True leaders pull their own weight and don't *need* to abuse their power. They lead by example, not by fear and intimidation. That is why you failed, and it is also why regardless of what happens today, Edith will share the same fate, eventually."

"Act high and mighty all you like. The Gold Fever-infected men respond to fear and abuse of power just fine. It's all the same to them, so long as it is for their Dark Savior. And rest assured, even if you escape this wretched place, you will be seeing Gold Fever spread outside of these mines soon enough!" Angus shot back. He started to laugh. Dalton rolled his eyes and then nailed him in the head with the butt of his sword.

Angus fell silent and slumped over. The others looked to Dalton with raised eyebrows.

"What? Did you all really wish to hear any more of his insane ramblings?" he asked with a shrug. "Or did you wanna stop Edith's spoiled arse from gettin' what she wants?" He held up his sword in triumph, as if a general on the battlefield, rallying his men.

"I'm in," Lucia said.

"I'll be joinin' in, too! I'm gonna hack away at tha Dark Savior scum an' kill 'im before he even knows what hit 'im!" Alistair added.

"I've always followed you, no matter how foolish your plans were," Baltr said before sighing. "But this time, you have a point. The fate of our village, or perhaps even all the world, is at stake!"

Joel nodded as he held his blade up and touched Dalton's in solidarity. Alistair held up his battle axe and added it to the mix, and so too did Baltr with his pickaxe. Lucia winced in pain, but she managed to raise her sword as well. At that moment, Dalton noticed her torn clothes and blistered red skin under them.

"What happened?"

"Wolfgang lit me on fire with a torch, so he could run away. He didn't even have the honor to finish our fight," she replied while shaking her head.

"Y'know, Edith may succeed and unleash the Dark Savior onto us,"

Dalton said, lowering his sword. "But if I could just plunge my blade into Wolfgang's neck, I would *still* die a happy man."

"Conrad may beat you to the punch. He chased Wolfgang down that tunnel, to avenge Henic," said Lucia.

"Oh… Henic didn't make it, eh?" Alistair asked, his spirits plunging into the depths. Joel's spirits dampened, too. He lowered his head, as if in prayer.

"Then, we do this in his name. For Henic!" Dalton called out as the group touched blades once more.

They marched toward the tunnel that Wolfgang and Conrad had run through. Even with the possibility that the Dark Savior might be unleashed on them, all were ready for a fight.

CONRAD BURST out of the tunnel to find paths going to his immediate left and right. To the right, off in the distance, were blue and green streaks of light shooting down from the ceiling of a vast cave. About midway down the path, he could make out the shadowy figure of Wolfgang, who was hunched over and gasping for breath. To his left was a sliver of natural light at the end of the tunnel. That had to be the secret exit, he thought.

Somehow, Conrad wasn't tired. In fact, he didn't feel anything as he dashed down the right path in pursuit of the blond brute. All that he was doing felt natural; effortless; like taking a breath or walking.

Wolfgang stood upright and then looked back at him from the shadows. He giggled like a maniac before resuming his sprint for the oddly-lit cave ahead.

The strategist thought to call out; to bait him into a fight, but it made no difference. He could feel himself catching up. All of the injuries and battles had taken their toll on Wolfgang's body.

In a long and brutal stretch, the two men sprinted and Conrad closed in. Within a few strides, now, he put his head down and found another level of speed. He then leaped out and tackled Wolfgang to the ground. The blond brute landed with a great thud, while Conrad rolled past him before regaining his footing. Now, they were just outside the cave. Wolfgang looked up and growled at him from the rocky floor.

"You and I have unfinished business." Conrad pointed his rapier down at him.

Wolfgang scowled as he gingerly rose. However, his annoyance soon turned to laughter. Conrad raised an eyebrow. It wasn't like his Gold Fever-induced hysterics, where he felt maniacal and antagonistic. These laughs felt *happy*.

Conrad gripped the rapier hilt until his weapon shook. "Feel free to keep on laughing all the way to your shallow grave."

"Ye don't understand… ye wanna fight me, but ye've already lost!" Wolfgang said between chuckles that tapered off. Conrad leaned in. What was he talking about? "The Dark Savior walks among us once more!"

Conrad looked over his shoulder and gasped. A dark portal had opened next to some stone rubble at the cave's center. It must have been the remains of the monolith, he thought.

"So, that's where Edith was this whole time… she was opening the portal…"

"That's right! All we had to do was distract ye fools fer a little while. My mission is complete! Now, I will be one with my Savior!" Wolfgang said with the same reverence that one might show a God. Conrad shuddered. It was exactly as Aldous had feared. "Yer fate is sealed, but ye might as well try and escape. Maybe ye can live a lil' longer that way!"

The strategist readied his rapier and then pivoted sideways to take a fencing stance. "Maybe I am going to die here, but I can tell you this much… so will you."

"Stand aside! Remember what I told ye before? I've done things that ye couldn't even imagine! I know a true warrior when I see one, and when they got the guts to do what needs to be done!" Wolfgang said as he grabbed the blade of Conrad's rapier and gripped down on it until blood came from his grizzly hand. It was just as he had done earlier in the expedition. "And you don't got what it takes…"

Conrad looked Wolfgang in his cold, yellow eyes with determination. Without a word or noise, he yanked the rapier down to slide it out of his grip. Wolfgang gasped as the slick stream of red poured from his hand. He howled in pain and held his hand up by the wrist, staring at the deep cut with an odd mix of insanity, anger, and fear in his expression.

"Fine! If ye wanna die now, then I'm happy to do the deed!" Wolfgang said before drawing his sword. "Yes… I understand now… this is my last test… before I meet the Dark Savior, isn't it?"

This is it, Conrad thought as he readied himself.

Edith and the Gold Fever-infected men gazed at the dark portal in wonder. It was larger than the monolith had been tall, and it swirled around loudly like some sort of whirlpool. The noises were haunting; like desperate souls crying out for help, or wind raging through a tunnel. Most ominous of all was that nothing had come out of it. The group of six stood in silence, waiting for something to happen.

Skreeeeeee

The cry of the Nightcrawler, louder and nearer than ever, had successfully pushed Edith's patience past its limit.

"Well?" she asked one of the miners next to her. "Go in and check on it!" The infected man stared back at her with a furrowed brow at first, but she knew how to take care of the ones who didn't obey. "You want to meet your Savior, don't you?"

The man's demeanor immediately became friendly, and he mumbled, "Savior… my Savior…" as he walked toward the spinning gateway of shadow. Despite his supposed eagerness, he trembled while approaching.

The miner reached his hand into the portal and then pulled it back out quickly. "I-it's cold…" he muttered and then chuckled.

He then stuck his hand back in, giggled some more, and pulled it back out. The infected miner took a step in, but then he halted. Edith could see ripples in the portal. Something had disturbed it.

Out of the opening burst a large, dark tentacle. Before he could react, the crazed miner found himself ensnared by it. The crowd behind him gasped and took a few steps back. He tried to free himself between nervous fits of laughter, but the grip was too tight. Soon, other tentacles came from the bottom of the portal; dark, slimy, and waving around playfully. The crowd took even more steps back, but none ran away. All looked on in awe.

Edith next observed a pair of dark arms sticking out of the portal. They were long and thin, but completely limp at the wrists, as if they were broken. Each was adorned with rotting yellow fingernails that made her scoff with disgust. Next to come out was what looked to be the body of the monster: The many long tentacles below slithered ahead and gave way to a fat lump of a torso that jiggled like gelatin and was so huge that it nearly took up the entirety of the gateway. Then came the head, which was something straight out of a nightmare. From a long, arched neck similar to a giraffe's, the beast's head hung down and reminded Edith of a human skull, albeit a pale imitation. It had a rounded scalp, but its eyes were caved in and black until the middle, where piercing yellow pupils seemed to float in pools of shadow. Its jaw was stretched low and wide, with bright white teeth that were far longer and wider than a human's. A lack of lips gave him a permanent, haunting grin. The creature opened his mouth and let a long, red tongue slither out like a snake.

"*This* is Greed?" she mumbled as he looked down upon the miner he had ensnared in a tentacle.

Greed lifted him with his tentacle until they were face-to-face. He did not speak a word, but instead stared straight into the man's matching yellow eyes.

"M-my Lord and Savior!" the miner cried out as the beast cocked his deformed head. "I-I am at your command! I live to serve yer will!"

Greed tilted his head back and let out what Edith could best describe as a hoarse chuckle. He then opened his massive jaw to an even greater length before snapping his head forward.

"Wha-" was all the miner could get out before Greed's giant teeth clamped down around his neck and ripped his head off. Blood erupted from the stump of where the man's head had once been, splattering it all over the monster's face and raining down below. Yet, Greed paid it little mind while chewing on the disembodied head.

Crunch

Crunch

Crunch

The other miners took steps back and began whimpering like scared children, but none of them could look away. Even Edith found herself repulsed by the display.

After a few more moments of chewing, Greed turned his gaze back to the dangling, decapitated body, still wrapped up by the tentacle. Out of his tentacles grew more arms that were long, thin, and filthy-looking; much like the ones on his torso. Five in total had sprouted out, and he used them to tear at the rest of the body as if it were mere finger food.

One arm pulled at the miner's leg and ripped it off with little effort. The noise seemed unbearable to the other miners. It was a certain fleshy crunch that did not appeal to human ears, but Edith was differ-ent. She was overcome with excitement. She imagined that it was her father being ripped to pieces, instead.

No, she thought, a sly smile coming to her face. Drake's death would be much, much slower.

As the monster ripped apart and gobbled up pieces of the body, the miners watched on with betrayal in their eyes.

"W-why would the Dark Savior do this to us, his faithful servants?" one asked aloud as Greed bit a gaping hole into the torso.

"Has our Savior abandoned us?" another called out while the unbearable crunching of ribs rang in everyone's ears.

"Mayhap… it's not really our Dark Savior…" a worker mumbled. Greed stuffed the miner's lower body into his mouth all at once.

They winced with each *crunch* and *splat* of the legs as Greed chewed until finally, he was finished. Nothing remained of the miner, save some blood around the monster's deformed mouth.

"Why? Why did you eat him, my Lord?" one of the miners asked. The monstrosity looked down upon him and spoke his first words of the early evening:

"I… was… hungry…" he hissed back. His voice was like a whisper directly into their ears. It pierced Edith's racing mind and echoed within. She was so excited that she couldn't help but let out a satisfied sigh. This monstrosity; this beast; was the very definition of *power*. And soon, he would be under her command.

"Yer not our Dark Savior!" an enraged miner shouted back.

"No… not Dark Savior… Greed…" he said. The monster began to crawl toward the group with his tentacles. "Join… me…"

"Kill him! He is a non-believer!" a miner called out as he charged the monster, and so too did the others.

One of the miners jumped between tentacles and plunged his pickaxe into Greed's fatty, dark torso. However, it wasn't like a conventional body: It seemed soft and squishy. The monster paid the attack little attention and continued to slither forward. Then, from behind, a tentacle ensnared the miner and lifted him into the air. Struggle as he might, the crazed man could not get loose. He then looked up and gasped to see another tentacle staring him straight in the face. It shot into his mouth and the miner grabbed his neck as if he were choking. In mere moments, his neck had swollen to nearly twice its size before he stopped struggling. The tentacle phased through the man and flipped him around, so he hung by his head with the strength of the feeler, much like a marionette.

The miner's eyes had turned black, and his body hung limp, but occasionally it twitched. It seemed to Edith that the worker had fused with one of Greed's tentacles. She watched on as other miners shared similar fates: One had a tentacle pierce his stomach and then push through, so he was held up by his spine. Another had a feeler go through his skull and fused with it from there. The least fortunate miner of the bunch had the tentacle go up through his colon. He was the only one to scream out in pain, but it filled Edith with such joy to see.

When all was said and done, Greed began his approach to Edith with four miners dangling from his tentacles like puppets. Everything about what had happened filled her with excitement. He was unstoppable, and that meant *she* would be, too. She smiled from ear to ear and then licked her lips. Her moment had come.

"I feed… on greed…" the monster whispered.

"Is that right?" Edith asked, her confident smile unfading.

"Join… us…" Greed hissed, looming over her like a predator would over its prey.

"No, Greed. I'm afraid it's *you* who shall join up with *me*," Edith replied with a snorting chuckle.

The beast cocked his head, but he did not stop. He was mere moments from reaching her, now. Edith recalled the incantation. This was what her life had led up to: The key to her happiness; the everlasting power to rule over the unworthy masses. They would come to fear, love, and respect her as she'd always dreamed. More than anything, though, she couldn't wait to see the look on Drake's face as he learned of her betrayal; while being ripped limb from limb by her new pet.

Edith held out her hands and closed her eyes. "Egois sumheach voduit meais leatmea nunta anua tunun leamini thoitatum meam."

She opened her eyes. Greed had come to a halt. Edith clapped her hands together with child-like excitement. Now, he was her puppet, her tool. A mighty tool that she would wield to reshape the world.

"You will now obey *my* command," Edith said with great poise. "First, I want you to-"

Hoarse laughter came from the beast. He resumed slithering toward her.

"What are you doing? I said you will obey my command!" Edith shouted. He remained silent.

Edith's mind lurched. Had she forgotten the correct incantation? Said something wrong? Why wouldn't he listen?

"Egois sumheach voduit meais leatmea nunta anua tunun leamini thoitatum meam," she said in a panicked tone. Greed continued forward, and now her mouth was chattering. "E-e-egois s-sumheach voduit meais leatmea nunta anua tunun leamini thoitatum meam!" she cried. Her stomach dropped. He was right in front of her.

Up to now, everything had transpired just as her father and the Dark Wizard had said. Their plan seemed strong, and it had worked in her favor even when she had changed a few things. Why, then, hadn't the incantation worked? She had spent weeks of torturous study sessions with Drake. There was no way she could forget-

Edith's green eyes grew to the size of gold coins as a dark thought occurred to her: In the weeks leading up to the expedition, it had been stunning to see what a monster her father truly was. Yet, in a twisted way, it had filled her with relief to know that someone else saw things in the same way as her. However, in that similarity, Edith now understood what the incantation failure meant. It hadn't been a mistake on her part, *but a lie entirely*. Her father had sold her out; betrayed her as she had planned to betray him.

Edith's breaths stuttered as panic set in and she realized what was about to happen. Greed had gotten too close for her to run away, and so the only option, however unlikely it was to work, was begging for mercy.

"P-please… d-don't hurt me…" Edith said as the tears rolled down her cheeks. The monster raised a tentacle so that its tip was right in front of her face. "Please! I beg you! I'll do anything!" she began to sob as the feeler closed in.

"I-I d-don't wanna die… p-please…" She wheezed as the tears flowed from her eyes and snot ran out of her nostrils in an embarrassing display. Yet, she didn't care. She would do anything to live for but a moment longer, and that was when her mind jumped to a new idea.

"W-wait! You feed on greed, do you not?" Edith asked as Greed leaned forward. He seemed interested. "I can give you so much!" she said with a nervous chuckle. "Power, sex, money… anything you desire, my Savior!"

The tentacle approached Edith's face, and she squirmed as the tip wiped the tears off of her cheek. Her jaw became slack, and her jittering body started to calm. Greed had not attacked her. She breathed a great sigh of relief and looked up at the monster with a smile.

"So, we have an agreement? A partnership?" Edith asked.

"No…" Greed hissed as Edith's mind went blank.

What did he mean, *no*? How could he turn his nose up to such a generous offer?

And then, she felt it: A darting pain where her neck and spine met. The tentacle from earlier was still in front of her face. Had it only been a distraction while another one snuck behind her? Edith felt a violating darkness course through her body, and soon she convulsed violently; flopping to the ground and bursting into tears.

"N-n-noooo! I-I don' wanna die!" Edith wailed. She tried to crawl away, but the feeler, which had begun ripping and tearing its way down her spine under the skin, wouldn't allow it. Her limbs quickly losing all feeling, she began to claw at the rocky ground in desperation. "H-help! Someone! Wolfy! Angy! Fara! A-anyone! Please…" There was no response.

As the tentacle took control and dragged her back, Edith's nails snapped and they left 10 thick trails of blood along the rocky floor. She felt the darkness take her, and in some odd way, it was a pleasurable experience; like something she wasn't allowed to do, but she did it anyway. It was unnatural, yet calm. She could feel her very existence fading, and now, she was fine with it.

GREED WATCHED on as the blonde beauty's body flailed and shook involuntarily under the influence of his oppressive tentacle. Her eyes twitched rapidly, back and forth, until they completely crossed in different directions, and remained that way. Drool dripped from her lips and her body finally went limp. The merging was complete.

"Ah… so much… greed…" the monster hissed in a satisfied tone.

Greed lifted her with his tentacle, so she was in between the miners that he'd fused with earlier. They all dangled like puppets as he continued toward a cave exit. He could see that there were two men about to engage in a duel up ahead.

CHAPTER 41
JUSTICE

At the Gold Pit entrance, Conrad and Wolfgang were set to engage in a duel to the death. The blond brute wasted little time and lunged out with a vertical slash. Conrad sidestepped and responded with a lightning-quick stab that landed near his lower rib area.

Wolfgang gasped and swung his sword to knock Conrad's blade out of his flesh. He then attempted a downward and diagonal cut, but the power and speed behind it were below standard. The strategist didn't even bother to block and instead sidestepped once more, throwing Wolfgang off balance. He swiftly followed up with a thrust into his leg. He let out a weak cry before falling to his hands and knees. Blood streamed down from his leg, and now that Conrad was really looking, all of Wolfgang's limbs had sustained damage throughout his many battles. How in the world had he lasted this long?

"I have a question for you…" Conrad said as he walked over and lashed Wolfgang on the back with his rapier. He fell completely on his face. "Do you feel helpless? Like Henic felt when you extorted him for his goods? Like the innocent miners felt when you slaughtered them?"

His nose crinkled when he heard Wolfgang's muffled laughter from the ground.

"They deserved it!" Wolfgang shouted as he pivoted to his hands and sweep-kicked Conrad, causing him to stumble. "They were *weak*! Worthless!" he said while swinging wildly at the strategist. He blocked the slash attempt, but barely; and once again he was off balance. "But not me! I am *not* weak! I am *not* worthless!" He pushed Conrad back with a flurry of swings and thrusts. "I've proven my worth! To my woman! To my Dark Savior! I kill fer them!"

After blocking several slashes in a row, Conrad became overwhelmed and Wolfgang knocked his rapier back with a sudden burst of strength. Before he could return to a defensive position, the blond brute lunged forward with the broadsword and landed a stab. Conrad gasped as the cold steel pierced his upper arm. Then, it turned warm, and soon after, searing hot. He couldn't help but wince at the pain. Wolfgang ripped the blade out while cackling like a hyena.

"Ye see that? Ye shoulda lived to fight another day! Now that I said so, yer gonna die by my hand!"

Conrad let his injured arm dangle. The blood dripped onto the cave floor, and his eyes sharpened. It reminded him of how Henic's wound had constantly bled before his inevitable death. Both the hole in Henic's stomach and the hole in his arm had been avoidable if he had only kept focus while in the presence of a killer. Back then, he'd been anxious to get information out of Wolfgang, and *not so anxious* to take a life. This time, though, something else had distracted him.

He glanced over his shoulder to see a large, dark creature off in the distance, but he didn't want to take his eyes off Wolfgang for any longer to get a better look. All he knew for sure was that it had to be Greed, and that left him with little time to finish his business here. The strategist took a deep breath. At least the stab wound wasn't on his dominant arm.

"It seems to me like you have passed the blame for your reprehensible behavior onto others. Even the Dark Savior had to answer for his crimes, and surely a day will come when Edith is forced to do the same," Conrad said as his pained expression turned into a smirk. "But you? Your trial is *now*. And I think that nearly everyone who's had the displeasure of crossing paths with you would agree: You are *guilty*."

"Don't think fer a second that a peon like ye gets to play judge with me! I have proven my worth, but ye have not!" Wolfgang cried as he charged ahead and attempted a horizontal slash.

Conrad ducked the blow and landed a stab in his right chest plate. Wolfgang's eyes bulged and he doubled over, wheezing. The strategist ripped the blade out of his chest and then smashed the butt of his rapier on the side of his skull. Without any further noise or resistance, he crashed to the ground like a toppling tree.

"Sleeping on the job?" Conrad asked as he lashed Wolfgang's back with the rapier. A loud *rip* echoed in his ears and sent a chill down his spine. However, the blond brute hardly flinched in response. "I thought that I was the final obstacle between you and your precious Savior? Surely, I can't be any harder to kill than all of your other victims." He lashed him again.

"What do ye want from me?" Wolfgang asked as he struggled to all fours. "Why don' ye just kill me?"

"I want you to understand what you have done. You called all of your victims worthless; weak. I want *you* to feel that way before the end. You never even gave them a chance!" Conrad shouted. Wolfgang chuckled.

"They *were* worthless… the lot of 'em…" he muttered between labored breaths.

"You scum," Conrad shot back as he laid several more lashes onto Wolfgang's back. He face-planted to the ground again. His swollen, beet-red back was full of tattered fabric and bloody slices. Conrad scoffed in disgust. "Obviously, someone has questioned your worth, and you are trying so hard to prove them wrong… and failing. So, you lash out in a mindless rampage, killing others who don't deserve it. Does that sound about right to you?"

"Shut up…"

"But who could it be that tortures you so? You have not met the Dark Savior. Edith has surely shown you some love in the past… could it be someone else? A family member, perhaps?"

"I said… shut yer damn mouth!" Wolfgang reached his hands and knees again.

"I'm not like you, Wolfgang," Conrad said while stepping back. "I will at least finish you off, face-to-face: a courtesy you gave to *none* of your victims. On your feet! Make your final stand…" He pivoted sideways and took a new fencing stance.

Wolfgang struggled to his feet and hunched over to rest on his sword, which stuck into the ground. He took long, hard breaths, and was bloodied all over his body: There was a gash on his head from the butt of Conrad's rapier; a few stab wounds were also present, courtesy of Conrad; there was a festering, splinter-ridden wound where his chest and shoulder connected, thanks to Henic's shattered spear; and many leg wounds from his battles in the throne room and torture chamber. Even his face had been damaged in the aftermath of Angus smashing him with the shield.

How pathetic, Conrad thought. He had wanted to take down the unapologetic, smug, and maniacal man who'd done wrong to and killed so many good people. However, looking at him now, Conrad's stomach dropped and he felt sorry for him. Before him was a shell of a man who was barely living, let alone ready for battle.

"All of the damage you've accumulated has reduced you to such a sad state. The idea of killing someone so pathetic makes me sick. Yet, your justification for killing the others was that *they* were weak? How could you possibly enjoy such a thing?" Conrad asked, angrily. Wolfgang cracked a smirk.

"So, yer still afraid to kill me?" he asked. Conrad tilted his head, but remained silent. "Why don' ye let me go, then? I ain't a threat to anyone like this…"

"I can't do that…" Conrad said as he gripped the rapier hilt until it burned his hand.

"Why not? Ye seem like a nice fella. I know ye don' wanna do this…" Wolfgang's eyes were half-open and his tone was drowsy, lackadaisical. Conrad began to tremble. He hadn't killed another man before, let alone one so helpless. It would be like killing a wounded animal. "C'mon, show me some mercy… ye believe in mercy, don't ye?"

Conrad's brief moment of hesitation faded. Wolfgang was trying to lull him into a false sense of security. He frowned back at him and said, "Not for you."

"So be it, then!" Wolfgang shouted as he charged him with a sudden burst of energy.

The blond brute swung his blade horizontally and Conrad ducked beneath it. He then transitioned the missed swing into a stab, which the strategist deflected to his right with the rapier. He did not attack back, however, and so Wolfgang's flurry continued.

With each swing missing and Wolfgang's movements slowing, Conrad prepared to strike the final blow. It was only a matter of time, and no matter how pathetic he had become, it had to be done. Wolfgang was too dangerous to be left alive.

"Ye don't have the stomach to take a life, do ye?" Wolfgang asked as his slash was parried. "After I kill ye, I'm gonna take care of all yer friends, too! Especially that burned bitch!" he continued as another stab was dodged. Conrad gritted his teeth. *Not yet*, he thought. "I bet that greedy, worthless farmer is watchin' this fight from hell! I'll be sure ta keep his wife *real busy* after I escape these mines!"

His loud and brazen laughs echoed off the cave walls as the battle moved under a beam of dark green light shining from the ceiling. Conrad's eyes widened and he stood his ground.

Wolfgang brought his sword up for a decisive vertical slash, but so too did Conrad. Their blades met overhead, but rather than push back, Conrad let Wolfgang's sword continue down along with his own weapon as he sidestepped and twirled so that he was next to him.

Then, he wrapped his injured arm around Wolfgang's sword-wielding arm and pivoted to the side. With a twist of his wrist, a loud *crack* sounded off, and Wolfgang loosened his grip on the sword. He grunted and doubled over, off balance, while Conrad windmilled his rapier along with the blond brute's snagged sword.

Conrad pointed the rapier tip into Wolfgang's neck as the broadsword soared through the air. It bounced off the rocks several paces away, and then there was a tense moment of stillness; of quiet.

"Ye don't have to do this..." Wolfgang trailed off, a noticeable sweat building on his brow. It dampened the previously dry blood on his forehead, and it began leaking down into his yellow eyes. Yet, he did not try to wipe them. He remained motionless.

"Speak your last words," Conrad said as he pushed the rapier tip harder into his neck. "You cannot talk your way out of this. This is justice for Henic and the others."

"I'm sorry," Wolfgang said.

Conrad's eyes widened. "W-what did you say?"

"I'm sorry... fer everything I've done. Please don't kill me..." he replied. Conrad shuddered and the grip on his rapier weakened. "Are ye ready fer that burden? To take another life?"

"Stop it..."

"I'm only tryin' to warn ye... once ye start, it's hard to stop..."

"Enough!" Conrad shouted.

"Please... I'm beggin' ye... I don' wanna die..." Wolfgang said as he closed his eyes and lowered his head. He began to sob.

Conrad's crisis reached its peak. It wasn't supposed to be like this. It hadn't transpired in the same way as the stories and legends he'd read about over the years; where the hero narrowly triumphed over the powerful villain. Before him was not a mighty antagonist, but a sad, broken man whom he'd easily defeated. Conrad didn't feel like a hero. He felt like an *executioner*.

In that moment of hesitation, he lowered his rapier slightly, so that the tip no longer poked Wolfgang's neck. Suddenly, the blond brute looked up and flashed his beaming, yellow eyes, along with a callous grin that struck dread into Conrad's heart. In two swift motions, he knocked the blade out of Conrad's hand and then punched him in the jaw.

The punch dizzied Conrad, and the blue, black, brown, and green of the cave swirled along with his dazed eyes as he stumbled back and fell to the ground. On his back, he looked up to see Wolfgang in the midst of a pounce. He landed on top of him and then wrapped bloody hands around his neck.

"Ye really are stupid, ye know that?" Wolfgang asked before laughing like a maniac. Conrad gagged and flailed his arms around, but it did nothing to improve his situation. He clawed deep into his air-deprived mind for something, anything, to help him escape. "Ye shoulda killed me when ye had the chance!"

Then, Conrad remembered the dagger that was tucked into the boot under his pant leg. He reached desperately for it, but the tips of his fingers couldn't even reach his knee while he was laid out flat, and he couldn't shimmy down or move much while under the full weight of Wolfgang.

As panic set in, Conrad waved his arms around and landed a few light slaps to Wolfgang's worn-out face. In response, he tightened his grip and stared a hole through him with blank, yellow eyes. Despair took hold as the strategist gurgled aloud and the scope of his failure settled in. Because of his hesitation, all of those innocent people would go without justice in their deaths, and he would soon join them. Even worse, he had broken his promise to Henic. Now, there was a very real possibility that Wolfgang would escape the mountain and continue to terrorize Henic's family.

Wait, he thought. Henic. *Henic.* Suddenly, Conrad's bloodshot eyes widened and he remembered something important: It was Henic's final act of defiance that could save him! The deep spear wound between Wolfgang's shoulder and arm! Conrad was certain that he could reach it, but did he have the energy? His arm wiggled as it rose along the blond brute's arm. His vision began to fade and his breaths ceased, but his arm continued upward, driven purely by instinct now.

"That's the difference between ye an' me! Ye weren't prepared to do what had to be done, to kill! Soft men like ye will always perish in the end! And me? I'll meet my Dark Savior and help him rule the world!" Wolfgang proclaimed as Conrad's hand reached his shoulder and gripped around it. With his last reserve of strength, he pushed his thumb and gouged deep into the wound that Henic had inflicted.

Wolfgang cried out in pain and loosened his grip around Conrad's neck. The strategist then used the shock to throw Wolfgang off of him, to his left. While taking his first breath in some time, he contorted his knee and grabbed the dagger from his boot. With the fury of all that had been murdered, Conrad plunged the blade into a stunned Wolfgang's neck as he lay next to him.

"I'm *always* prepared..." Conrad muttered before laying back out on the floor, coughing from the hefts of his breaths and dryness in his throat.

Drowning out the coughs was Wolfgang's pained gagging. Conrad turned his head while still lying to see him feeling the handle of the dagger in his neck. The realization of his death must have been setting in by now.

However, Conrad was shocked to see Wolfgang stumble to his feet, the dagger still in his neck. Blood squirted from the small gaps between the wound and blade, and his droopy eyes reflected an odd mix of insanity and desperation. His stomach dropped as the blond brute loomed. He couldn't even move his arms and legs. But then, to his relief, he hobbled past; as if he hadn't even noticed him on the rocky floor. Conrad's vision was still hazy, but he seemed to be walking toward the dark figure that was approaching them.

Either way, the fight was over, and his fate was sealed. There was no coming back from a dagger that large to the neck. Justice had been served.

Wolfgang's vision blurred, and his ability to breathe halted as the blood poured from his neck wound like a bucket with a hole in it. He knew that it meant the end, and yet, it was too soon to die. He didn't even need to see the Dark Savior, so long as he had helped him. It was only Edith that he wished to see in his final moments.

He wandered aimlessly toward the other side of the cave for a time that his blank mind could not even begin to comprehend, and then, like magic, the blonde beauty appeared before him. He smiled while trying to pick up his pace, but his legs wouldn't allow it. He stumbled forward and fell to his knees.

Wolfgang looked up to see Edith. His vision was hazy, but he could tell just from her shape. A dark figure loomed behind her.

"She wants…" a voice whispered. It bounced around in his mind as his vision went dark. Edith placed a hand on Wolfgang's cheek and slowly caressed downward. Wolfgang latched onto her hand with his own, using his last iota of strength. "She wants…"

Edith's hand eventually reached the dagger in Wolfgang's throat, and his body lost all strength. He began to slump, and his last thoughts were not of happiness or sadness; only wonder. He wondered why she would want the dagger when her lover was about to die. Mayhap it involved another one of her brilliant plans, he thought. She always succeeded in her plans. He felt the dagger leave his neck, and then he fell to the darkness.

∾

"SHE WANTS… BLOOD…" Greed whispered as Edith looked upon the crimson dagger with crossed, bloodshot eyes. Her jaw slackened, she licked the bloody blade before throwing it to the ground and pushing Wolfgang's fresh corpse over. Next, she pounced like a wild animal and pinned his lifeless arms to the ground while hovering over him. Edith plunged her mouth onto his neck and began mindlessly sucking his blood like a leech or a bug. "Sex… power… death… her greatest desires… reflect… greed…"

Edith continued her feast, the blood splattering on her dress and her face as she did. Soon, she began to rip and tear at his flesh.

∾

JOEL, Dalton, Baltr, Alistair, and Lucia finally reached the end of the tunnel and were presented with two options: The green and blue cave to their right, or the sliver of light at the end of a path on the left.

"Which way?" Alistair asked.

"Methinks the world-ending portal would be in the oddly-colored cave, no?" Baltr said.

"Makes sense to me!" Dalton said before snorting. "Are you all ready to meet this 'Dark Savior', anyway? I personally can't wait to tell him what I think of him."

"I'll let my sword do the talking," Lucia added.

"Awright, but what's that other tunnel, then?" Alistair asked, pointing to the left. "Is that tha secret exit Aldous talked about?"

"It must be. Good to know, if we make it outta this mess," Dalton said.

The group was ready for one last round of battle, and this time with the most dangerous of opponents.

CHAPTER 42
GREED

While trailing his friends on the path, Joel was hard at work, catching up on his map of Mt. Couture. In addition to the current system of tunnels that they traversed, he had yet to update drawings of the Mountain King's castle or Resurrection Falls. Part of him wondered if there was any point in finishing it. Even if they managed to escape, having such a map on his person might be dangerous. It could fall into the wrong hands, after all. The mute shrugged and continued scribbling away. It helped ease his mind, for Bronrar and Henic's deaths were still fresh in his memory, and he feared there might be worse to come.

Suddenly, he crashed into something solid and then stumbled back. His eyes glazing over and his ears ringing, Joel wondered how he had managed to stray so far from his friends that he'd collided with a rock wall. As the dizzy spell ended, he looked up from his map and inaudibly chuckled. It had been Alistair that he crashed into, just like when they first met.

This time, however, the big man remained facing forward. He and the others had stopped, and they all stared ahead in silence. Joel shuffled sideways so he could see past Alistair's large frame, and that was when he realized they had entered the cave. Upon taking in his surroundings, many things struck him: The sheer size of the area; the clashing black gold and blue light on the ceiling; the rubble of the monolith, and the swirling, dark portal that accompanied it; but most troubling was the dark beast that remained motionless toward the center. He appeared to carry several humans on his tentacles.

"I suppose that thing is Greed," Dalton said.

His eyes wandering to the left now, Joel spotted Conrad, who was on a knee and breathing so hard that he could see his shoulders moving up and down, even from a distance. He looked to be wrapping his upper arm with some fabric. The mute jumped in front of the others, who were still staring at Greed in apparent awe, and then pointed to Conrad. Without a word, they all ran over to check on him.

"What happened?" Lucia asked when they arrived.

"I did it… I stabbed Wolfgang in the neck with my dagger…" he trailed off.

She smiled and said, "That same dagger you showed me when we first met? Incredible to think it came down to that… but it makes sense. Back in the throne room, I could see that you were thinking a few steps ahead in the heat of battle. Wolfgang, on the other hand, tends to make up his strategies as he goes along. I'm sure that was the great difference."

"In a way, the great difference was *all of us*," Conrad replied, hanging his head. "After all of the fighting; all of the injuries he sustained; he wasn't much of a challenge. For some reason, I thought he would be a threat to the very end. Yet, I couldn't help but pity him while in such a pathetic state."

"Chin up, lad! If anyone deserved to go arse up in their grave, it was him!" Alistair said before slapping him firmly off the back.

"Right you may be, Alistair, but something about his death feels hollow. I thought that it would be satisfying to see him reduced to helplessness, to get justice for all of his victims… but instead, it feels like he was just another causality of this wretched mountain."

"No," Dalton said, pointing at him with authority. "I think you are misplacing your feelings. It's not supposed to feel good to kill another, no matter how vile they are. Believe me. Do not be tricked into thinking that Wolfgang wasn't responsible for his own actions. He behaved despicably and received the proper punishment. He was not a victim. When someone shows you that they are a killer, believe them. Do not spare them even a moment of mercy."

Conrad smiled and looked back and forth between Dalton and Lucia. "Good advice. Your student told me the same thing. I think that I will live by those words from now on. Not heeding them nearly cost me my life."

"Hold on. If Wolfgang is dead, then where is his body?" Baltr asked.

"I must give him credit: Even though that dagger to the neck meant the end for him, he *still* got up and went down there," Conrad said as he pointed to Greed.

"He must have wished to see his Dark Savior up close before death," Dalton said.

~

MEANWHILE, Greed watched on as Edith gnashed on Wolfgang's flesh. She combined the violent bites with kisses to his neck and then began nibbling on his ear. However, the nibbles soon turned to bites and she eventually ripped the ear off with her teeth, too. She chewed on it loudly, shamelessly, as Greed observed with a permanent grin on his warped, elongated face.

Eventually, he grew tired of the display, however, and lifted Edith back with his tentacle. At his command, her body fell limp and she stopped chewing. Bloody bits of skin, fat, and muscle fell from her mouth, which hung open. Her face and neck were covered in red.

Greed grabbed Wolfgang's corpse with a free tentacle, and from it grew several long, thin arms. Each arm grabbed one of his limbs, and with minimal effort, ripped them off like pieces of a chicken dinner. Greed's mouth opened inhumanly long and wide as he tossed a leg in, and then an arm. In moments, he crunched through the bone and muscle and swallowed. He threw the remaining arm and leg in and began chewing. Blood and bone fragments spewed out, but he paid it little mind. His glowing, yellow eyes remained fixed on the stump of a body that remained before him. *The main course*, he thought with a delighted hiss.

~

THE GROUP WITNESSED Greed's disgusting feast from afar. Even from where they were, it was hard to watch a man be ripped to pieces and eaten by a monster.

"Oh, lordy! I think I'm gonna be sick!" said Alistair.

"Is that…" Lucia trailed off, squinting. "Wolfgang?"

"It's nice to see that Greed doesn't let worshipers get in the way of a good meal," Dalton said.

"This looks bad. If he can easily rip human limbs apart, he may well be as strong as the Nightcrawler, if not more," Conrad said.

"And what of the people on those tentacles of his? Are they under his control?" Baltr asked.

"I think so," Lucia replied, squinting once more. Now, she was smirking. "And I think Edith is one of them."

"A fittin' end fer her, then!" Alistair said.

"I don't like our chances against this thing," Dalton said as he playfully swung his long sword around. "But what other choice do we have? We can't sit by while a calamity is unleashed upon the world."

Joel made hand signals toward the group.

"Joel says-" both Conrad and Dalton blurted out. They looked at each other, awkwardly.

"Oh, so translating him is *your* specialty, is it?" Dalton asked with a chuckle. Conrad shrugged in return. "Carry on, then."

"Joel says that we cannot permanently hurt him ourselves. We have to push him back into the portal, and then he can lock it with the key," Conrad said.

"That's right! It's just as Aldous said. The key can repair that monolith and seal the portal once more," Lucia said with a raised fist.

"Alright, but how can we even begin to push such a monster back?" Baltr asked.

"Don' worry, I'll push 'im back with me mighty strength!" Alistair boasted as he held his axe up and pointed it at the monster.

"The only thing that *could* push him back is your mighty stench," Lucia said, waving a hand in front of her nose.

"What?" he asked while smelling his pits. "There haven't been any opportunities to wash!"

Dalton took in a long breath through his nose and then let out a dry cough. His eyes were watering. "That ain't an ordinary stench. It's the *smell of determination*!"

"Erm…" Alistair trailed off, red-cheeked. "Th-that's right! No one, not even tha Dark Savior, can compare to my fury n' fortitude! Stand by me, lads n' lass, and I'll forge tha path ta victory!"

"I must admit that I'm a little less worried about our obstacles whenever Alistair is in high spirits," Conrad said, smiling at him. Joel nodded along before putting his map away. More than ever before on this trip, he was ready to fight.

"These could be our last moments alive…" Dalton said before taking a step forward. The others followed his lead. "If we go down, then let it be in glorious fashion. Let us live on in Greed's nightmares!"

With that, the group of six let out a cheer and marched toward Greed, who had finished feasting on Wolfgang's corpse. The monster's long tongue slithered out of his mouth while cackling at them. He lowered his puppets to the rocky floor. Soon, they reached the monster, and faced down Edith and the miners, bobbing under the influence of Greed's wriggling tentacles.

"Oh, my… Lady Edith…" Baltr said, leaning in and wide-eyed. There was blood all over her face, neck, and clothing. Her normally calculating green eyes were in a state of disarray; crossed in opposite directions. A mixture of blood and drool dripped from her slacked jaw.

"I suppose Edith now understands the pain that manipulation causes others," Dalton said before smirking. He brought his sword up and took a stance.

"I wonder if chopping the tentacles down would release his hold over Edith and the others," Conrad mused. He drew upon his rapier and took a sideways stance.

"I can try to release Edith, but my blade may slip and cut her…" Lucia said as a smile crept onto her face.

"Who cares 'bout all o' that? Let's strike this foul beast down!" Alistair called out and then raised his battle axe. Joel readied his luxmortite sword alongside him.

"Her desires… she wants… death…" Greed whispered. His voice made Joel shudder, like a trickle of cold water down his spine.

"So, he's not just a mindless monster like the Nightcrawler…" Dalton said. "I'm willing to make a deal with you, Greed," the warrior continued as he pointed his blade past the beast and at the portal. Greed cocked his deformed head. "You get yer fat arse back to the portal, and no harm will come to you."

"No deal… never go back…" the monstrosity hissed as one of his controlled miners attacked with a pickaxe swing.

Dalton sidestepped and then plunged his blade into the miner's body. However, even after ripping his sword out, the miner continued to attack and showed no signs of pain or slowing down.

"As long as the tentacles hold them, they cannot be killed by conventional attacks. We have to cut down those tentacles!" Conrad called out.

"I don't have the right tool for that!" Baltr said while holding up his pickaxe and shrugging.

"I'm afraid it's the same for me..." Conrad said, lowering his rapier.

Joel's heart skipped a beat, as the strategist hadn't noticed a miner flying at him from the left end of one of Greed's tentacles. If black gold could slowly turn a man mad, then being taken in by the monster who had created it would be a million-fold worse, he thought, springing into action.

The many colors of the cave blurred around him as he leaped forward and cut through the tentacle before they could reach Conrad. The miner, now limp, fell to the ground along with the sliced feeler. It splattered into a dark, jam-like substance when it hit the floor. Conrad stared at Joel with wide eyes. His mouth fidgeted as if he had many questions. Joel could only smile. Perhaps he would answer them if they somehow managed to escape with their lives.

"Ooooo! Tha boyo can fight! Let's see who can chop down more tentacles, then! Watch this!" Alistair cried as he dodged a miner and then hacked another feeler off. The miner fell to the ground and remained motionless, like the other.

"You lack grace in your swing. Watch and learn!" Lucia said to Alistair.

She charged at Edith, who cocked her arm, as if about to throw a punch. She smirked and then sidestepped the jab, and grabbed her extended arm while pivoting. To finish, she chopped down on the feeler with her arming sword, and it flailed while spilling more of the jam-like substance, but it had not been cut all the way through. With a second strike, the tentacle was severed, and Edith dropped to the floor below. Like the previous two miners, she did not move or speak.

"It would seem that your aim held up, after all," Conrad said with a snorting chuckle.

"Well... I couldn't be outdone by *him*, could I?" Lucia replied, nudging her head toward Alistair.

"So rude..." the big man muttered.

Dalton, on the other hand, had managed to cut down the remaining two miners on his own. The group began to celebrate the minor victory, but then, the severed feelers began acting strange. The lique-fied, jam-like substances rippled as if a stone had dropped into them, and they began swirling like whirlpools. In short order, the dark substance spilled out of its spin in streams, and they returned to Greed, to be assimilated back into his body. Each of the cut tentacles wriggled with apparent excitement as they grew back to their original states.

"Is he invincible, then?" Dalton asked as the beast swung a tentacle toward him.

He ducked the swing while simultaneously holding his sword up, slicing the tentacle from underneath. When it landed on the ground, it turned to the dark, jam-like substance once more. As it began to stir, Dalton hurried forward and squished it with his boot. It splattered all around, yet still, he and the others watched in horror as it all streamed back to and assimilated with Greed. His tentacle regenerated, good as new.

"Alright… let's try this, then!" Conrad said and then flipped his rapier around so it was held like a javelin. With a grunt, he threw it up at the dark beast's face. It was a direct hit on Greed's forehead and recoiled his head backward. The group looked on with cautious optimism as the monster stopped all movement, but then, they heard a gravelly laugh.

Greed's head lurched forward and he looked upon them with that permanent, haunting grin. The rapier slowly sank into his forehead until it had been completely consumed. With a light hiss, he opened his mouth and out shot Conrad's blade, faster than a speeding arrow. Conrad gasped as it struck the right side of his chest. With dry, stuttered breaths, he dropped to his knees.

"Hang on!" Lucia said, coming to his side. One of the tentacles swiped at them, but the mercenary held out her blade and it cut into the feeler; though not all the way through. The cut tentacle grew several arms and they took hold of her sword. Rather than attack her with it, however, they bent the arming sword, and it groaned under the immense stress until snapping like a twig.

One of the arms then reached out for Lucia, but Joel jumped in once more for the save. He swung upward and diagonally for a clean cut through the dark arm. Greed wailed, and hearing it for the first time struck Joel like a blow to the gut. It was otherworldly and unnatural; filling him with an indescribable discomfort. He pushed through his raw feelings, however, and hacked off another of the arms before it could launch an attack.

The dark monstrosity then swung two tentacles at once from each side of the mute. Joel reacted to the one on his left and sliced clean through it, but he could only turn around in time to see the feeler to his right striking him in the midsection. Hit so hard that all breath had been knocked out of him, the world around Joel spun and tumbled as he skidded across the harsh, rocky ground like a rock skipping along the water. When he finally came to a halt, Joel found himself far out of reach from Greed and his friends.

Joel got to his knees before the reality of how much damage he'd absorbed set in. His ribs were set ablaze and attempts to take in anything more than a half-breath were met with painful wheezing. He crumbled back to the ground and writhed in agony until the cries of Lucia caught his attention. He looked up through blurry eyes to see that a tentacle had grabbed her by the ankles. She was upside down now, and a struggle of strength ensued as Conrad held her wrists and tried pulling her back.

They were quickly losing the battle, as blood gushed from a pale Conrad's chest and even more came from the burn blisters that had popped from Lucia's torso due to the strain. The strategist's boots were dragged through the dirt little by little, and his trembling hands were loosening.

Dalton and Baltr fought through many tentacles in their attempts to reach the faltering duo, but Alistair was the first to come to their defense: He threw his battle axe at the tentacle, ripping through it and releasing Lucia from her torture. However, the axe was caught by one of the many grown arms, and it too was ripped to pieces with inordinate strength.

Conrad and Lucia collapsed to the floor, holding each other in their arms as they stared down a jungle of flesh-tearing hands and tentacles. On his way to help them, Baltr was knocked down by a feeler. Dalton saved him with another flash of his blade, but he was the only one with a weapon left, save for Joel, who began clawing forward as his breaths fell shorter and shorter. They seemed so far away, but he had to do something, anything, to help them. They hadn't come this far just to be slaves, or to be ripped to pieces like insects.

Despite his lack of a weapon, Alistair joined Conrad and Lucia and raised his fists, as if ready for a brawl.

The monster cackled as a tentacle approached the trio. Lucia winced and groaned while reaching down to her boot, and from it, she retrieved a dagger. She and Conrad smiled at each other, but they spoke no words.

When the feeler reached them, Lucia sprung the dagger and cut its tip off. However, from the stump, it grew some more arms. One of the ragged hands caught another swipe by the mercenary and squeezed the blade. It crumbled under the great pressure of its grip, and in the meantime, Alistair threw a thundering right hook at the tentacle. Its gelatinous form rippled from the blow, but was none the worse for wear. With a casual flick, it felled the big man and sent him crashing to the floor. The trio looked up at the vicious hands and tentacles. There was nothing more they could do.

Dalton attempted to get over to them, but he had to fend off multiple tentacles at once. Baltr was without a weapon and had taken multiple grazed blows from Greed. He stayed behind Dalton and remained doubled over.

Still in a daze, Joel had reached his feet, but with only one step, he lost balance and fell back down before he could return to his friends. He looked up, helpless, as the tentacles were about to strike.

SKREEEEEEEEEEEEE

Greed ceased all movement, save for his neck, which he spun 180 degrees and spotted the Nightcrawler. It burst out of the tunnel and galloped toward him with ferocious speed.

"The beast…" Greed hissed.

In seconds, the Nightcrawler reached him, and it leaped through the air with a claw extended for the first attack. However, Greed caught it with his tentacles, and from those tentacles sprouted some arms to counter. The Nightcrawler responded by slashing the arms off with its long claws, and then too fell the feelers that held it. When it reached the ground, the beast clawed away at Greed's large body and then took aim at his head.

It attempted a slash, but Greed caught the beast's arm by biting down on it with his long, malformed teeth. The Nightcrawler wailed in pain for the first time that Joel had ever heard, but remained vigilant. It clawed the top of Greed's head off, and the dark jam-like substance flew through the air like a bucket of water had been thrown. Greed released the Nightcrawler from his teeth, and it hopped back to observe the damage.

However, much the same as before, the part of Greed that had splattered assimilated back with his body, and his head reformed. His horrid yellow eyes met the aggressive glare of the beast's many red, glowing eyes.

SKREEEEEEEE

The two monstrosities clashed once more. Meanwhile, Baltr was taken by surprise when, as Greed simultaneously fought the Night-crawler, one of his tentacles ensnared him. Dalton immediately tried to cut him down, but in his overzealous reaction, hadn't noticed the tentacle that had snuck up behind him. He too, was taken and hung upside down as Greed did battle with the beast.

The next to come under attack were Lucia and Conrad. However, before the tentacle could reach them, Alistair sacrificed himself and he was taken instead. The pair had no time to appreciate it, as their various injuries had left them defenseless. Mere moments after the big redhead's sacrifice, they too were taken.

Joel continued to stumble forward, but couldn't make it more than a few steps without tumbling down face-first. He could only watch from the ground as the Nightcrawler began to gain the upper hand in the battle. The beast slashed through the clumps of darkness that made up Greed's body and pushed him back more and more.

Greed attempted to use his captured prey as distractions, but the Nightcrawler was focused solely on the main body. It weaved through the various tentacles and arms to land blow after blow on the dark monstrosity. Eventually, the fight got pushed back to where the portal had opened up. Joel watched on from the ground, his aching body trembling. His breaths shorter than ever and his vision fading, his last thoughts were filled with panic as he watched the Nightcrawler tackle Greed, with all of his friends in tow, into the portal of darkness. Then, all went black.

Joel awoke with a start, but he quickly regretted it when his ribs flared up. He grabbed at them and let out a wheezing cough before realizing that his head was clear once again. He looked around, but nothing had changed about the Gold Pit. Only he and the victims of Greed remained, and the blue lights of the luxians clashed with the Dark Savior's black gold, making dark green beams of light that shot down from the ceiling. He hadn't been out for long.

Feeling a great sense of energy and urgency, Joel hopped to his feet. He grabbed his luxmortite sword and made way for the broken monolith and portal. Before he got far, however, something caught his ears:

"P-please... help me..."

Joel turned to see Edith lying face-down on the ground. The other Gold Fever-infected miners remained motionless and silent. He had assumed that the process of fusing with Greed would be fatal. How could Edith have survived?

"I don't want to die..." she sobbed. Joel walked up to her and inspected for himself. Edith's spine had been completely shredded by the fusing process. It wasn't hard for him to determine. Her body was motionless and all down her back were carved-up skin and blood. Underneath the sea of red and pink, he could see the white of her severed spine.

"Please… I can give you… whatever you want," Edith said. There was little that Joel could do, however. She would likely never walk or have use of her upper body again, he thought. It was a sad turn, even for someone who cruelly sought power like her. Since she was harmless now, the mute figured he could take her along, should he manage to escape. He was sure that her rich and powerful father would at least take care of her. But for now, he had other business to attend to.

As Joel walked toward the portal once more, he heard Edith call out, "I curse you! I curse you all! All of the ungrateful miners! All of the bottom-feeding traitors! And *especially* Drake! I hope you all die miserable, painful deaths! In fact, I'll be the one to kill you all! Just watch!" She then screeched aloud like a frustrated child and returned to her sobs. After some time, she quieted down.

Soon, Joel found himself in front of the broken monolith and portal. The mute removed his necklace and held out the dark blue medallion: the key. As if taken by some other force, the key slowly magnetized and attached itself to what was left of the monolith. Joel watched on, as piece by stone piece, the great block started to repair itself.

As he watched the slow restoration of the monolith, Joel's heart sank. The repairing of the seal would ensure that his friends remained trapped in the Cold World. That was, of course, assuming that they hadn't been killed by the monstrous battle between Greed and the Nightcrawler. But what other choice was there? He and Aldous had been warned never to directly interfere if humans tried infiltrating Mt. Couture. Their roles were to warn the Wizard King and then await orders as needed. They hadn't listened, and this was the result. Not only had they failed to rescue most of the miners, but now the Greed monolith was destroyed, threatening the very fabric of this world.

Joel now understood that his and Aldous' pure intentions had unintended consequences. Normally, the first and second miner teams would have succumbed to Gold Fever, and many of them would have died while trapped in the labyrinth; or been eaten by riggits; or charred to the bone by dratagons; or crushed to death by knocker trickery; or blown to bits by the explosive mushrooms; or devoured completely by the Nightcrawler. The few survivors, if any, would return to Faiwell, warning all never to mine at Mt. Couture again.

However, Joel's warning of the black gold had altered the destinies of many, and the same could be said of Aldous' interference via magic. They hadn't directly opened Greed's seal, but they had a hand in it. Before him stood an opportunity to right that mistake. It was his mission, his duty, to rebuild the monolith before Greed could escape again.

Yet, something tugged at the back of his mind. He had only known these new friends of his for a few days, but after all they'd been through, it felt like they had a lifelong bond. He couldn't discount the fact that something nefarious had been going on in the background, either. Edith and her father somehow knew about black gold and the monolith. Perhaps this conclusion was inevitable. Perhaps it was good fortune that he and Aldous had decided to act. Perhaps it was now time to act in defiance of the rules once more.

Joel looked back and forth between the monolith and the portal, with two choices haunting his mind: His friends? Or the mission?

JOEL'S MAP
MT. COUTURE
Snow Hills
Pine Tree Forest
Mountain King's Castle
Snow Mounds
Resurrection Falls
Secret Passage
Ice Hut
Steep Cliffs
Ceiling Hole
Dalton's Journal Found
Sand Pits
Exit
Dalton Found
Cavern
Beach
Underground River
Nightcrawler Attack
Dralagon Cave
Labyrinth
Faramond Killed
Vertical Shaft
Thin Wall
Black Gold Cave
Explosive Mushrooms
Kracken's Attack
Blue Light Cave
Riggit Encounter
Tunnel Collapse
Ollie Found
Black Gold Cave
Mouth of Hell

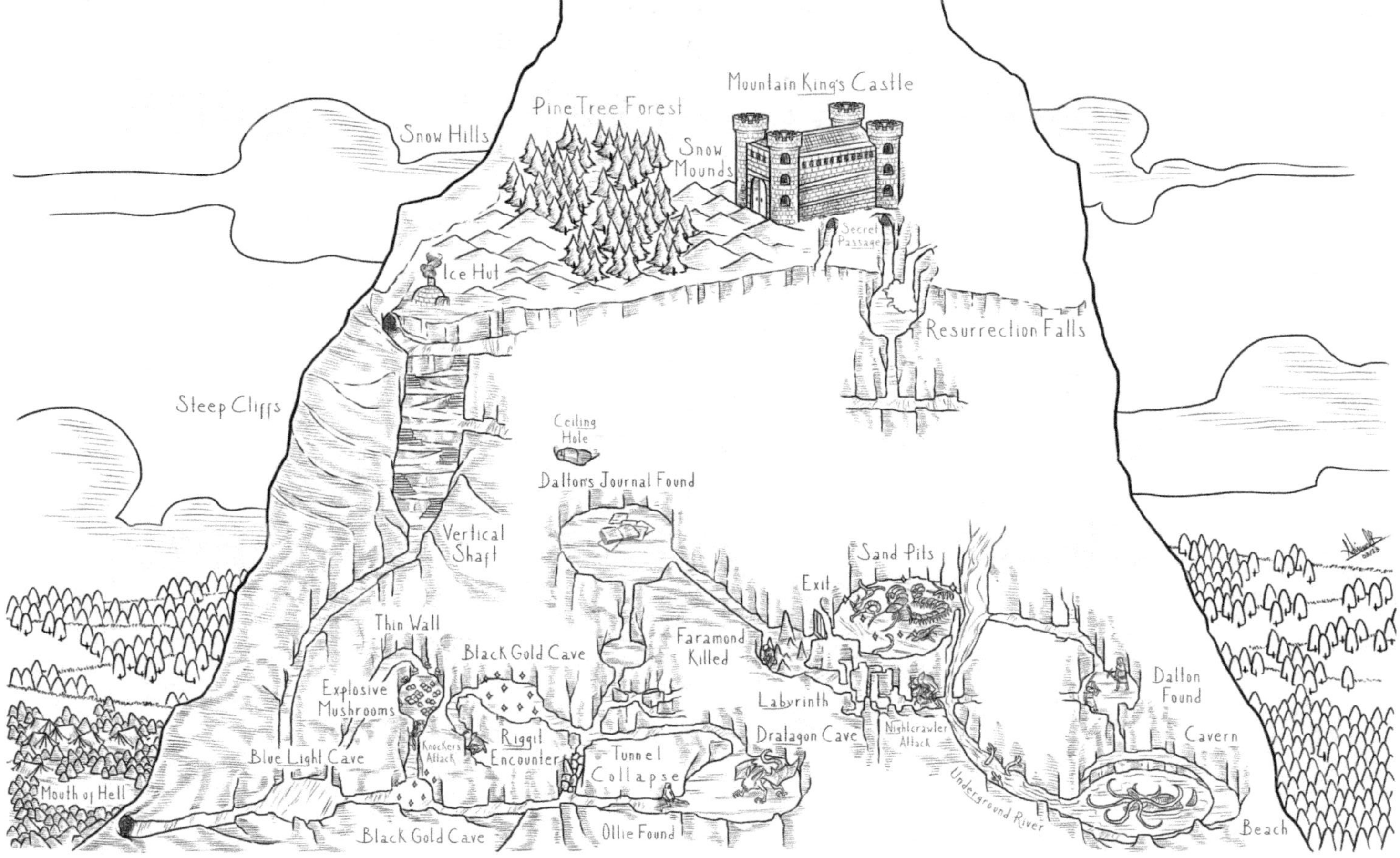

CHAPTER 43
THE COLD WORLD

Friends or the mission? Determination overcame Joel as a third option came to mind: Why not both? As the monolith repaired itself, he would plunge himself into the portal and try to rescue them. If Greed was going to escape before the reconstruction finished, there was nothing he could do about it, anyway. Whether it was trapping himself in the Cold World, dying at the hands of Greed and the Nightcrawler, or escaping Mt. Couture, Joel decided that he would share the same fate as his friends.

He turned to face the swirling portal of darkness and drew his sword. Even such a subdued motion sent a striking pain through his ribs, but he had to put that suffering aside for the time being. With no further hesitation, the mute walked up to the portal. The shadowy whirlpool shrieked at him like a feral beast, but somehow, he wasn't afraid. He continued through, and all of his senses numbed.

The world around him swirled and an array of colors mixed in his eyes until all went dark and his ears started to ring. He held his hands out, trying to get his bearings as his vision slowly faded in. And when the ringing in his ears mercifully ended, a howling wind overcame him instead.

As if he had walked into a new room and closed the door behind him, Joel found himself in another world, and it was not a pretty place. Chills pierced his trembling body and he felt tired. Just as Aldous had said, the Cold World seemed to eat away at his soul. The sky was dark and the clouds above lit up every few seconds with lightning and claps of thunder that felt contained; and with each lightning flash, he could see a little more. Protruding from the clouds seemed to be massive, black spikes, and there had to be *millions of them,* he thought with a shudder. He hoped that none of them would fall.

At that moment, Joel noticed a new sensation at his feet. The ground was pulsating every second, and looking down, he could see that it was dark red; *fleshy.* Under the howling wind around him, he could barely hear some gurgling noises coming from the organic floor. It reminded him of a hungry stomach.

Joel could see that he was in a mountainous region, but he was also inside a trench of sorts. It was not all that dissimilar to the labyrinth that he and the others had traversed yesterday, but this area saw rocky walls protruding out as opposed to cut stone. Most noticeable of all, however, was the black gold filling up the rock entirely. The sight, feel, and even the smell nauseated him. It was like he had stumbled upon the ultimate concentration of that cursed metal.

As Joel walked forward, he heard the hisses of Greed and the shrieks of the Nightcrawler off in the distance, along with explosions and bashed rock clanking together. Relief swept over him. They didn't sound close, for the time being. Soon, the mute picked up on other noises: A man was groaning down a corridor to his left. He looked that way to see Alistair with his back turned and hunched over a pile of black gold. A slack, dark red webbing was attached to his arms and back. They were coming from the pulsating ground.

He ran up to the big man and ripped the webbing off. It was sticky and unbearable to the touch, sending waves of discomfort through his body; like grinding fingernails on stone. His eyes twitched as he watched the odd material recede into the ground. Was the floor truly alive? Whatever was going on, Alistair hadn't reacted to being freed. He remained hunched over, mumbling nonsense to himself. Joel tapped him on the shoulder. To his horror, Alistair stood and turned to stare him down with a new set of yellow eyes. The concentration of black gold had to have infected him with Gold Fever faster than normal, he thought.

Alistair scowled and then asked, "Do ya follow the will of our Savior, lil' waif?"

Joel smiled back up at him and cocked his head.

"Answer tha question, lad!"

Joel continued to smile and shrugged. He didn't know what else to do.

"ANSWER THA QUESTION!" Alistair shouted as he grabbed Joel by the collar and hoisted him up. "DON'T YA KNOW IT'S RUDE-"

Suddenly, Alistair's eyes widened and the yellow in his pupils faded. He slowly lowered the mute and then let go, rubbing his forehead and scrunching his eyes; as if remembering. *Yes*, Joel thought with clenched fists. He was remembering when they had first met, and surely that would remind him of all that they had been through together on this trip. Up to a certain point, Gold Fever could be broken by one's strongest emotions; and the bond that they had forged after surviving so much together was enough to overcome it.

Alistair let out a long exhale, as if he'd come to the surface from a long dive. "Oi! Sorry 'bout that, lad! I don' know what came over me…" Joel nudged his head toward the piles of black gold ore behind him. "Oh… that'll do it, then!" he said with a chuckle and then slapped him hard on the back. The pain rippled through his spine and to his ribs, but he did his best not to show it.

"Ya know what this means, don't ya? Gold Fever can be cured!" he shouted excitedly as the cry of the Nightcrawler echoed off in the distance. "Wait… where are the others?" Joel pointed over his shoulder with a thumb and then turned to leave. They would have to do some searching.

As they walked, the Cold World continued to gnaw away at their souls and it reduced them to constant shivering. The thunder and lightning erupted from within the dark, spiky clouds above, and with each flash, Joel could swear the spikes multiplied. He could also hear what sounded like explosive mushrooms far off in the distance, but the trench walls blocked their view.

In one corridor, Joel felt the ground at his feet changing. Whereas before it had been pulsating, it now felt like it was moving in the opposite direction of him, slowing his stride. He looked down and gasped to see a hole ripping, tearing at the very fabric of the floor. He held an arm out and halted Alistair as a stream of rotten air shot out of the hole, nearly as wide as the trench path itself.

"Whoa!" Alistair cried as the horrid air from the hole continued to stream up like a geyser of water; and along with it came more odd red webbing and what Joel could best describe as dark mucus.

The foul stench of the bursting air saw Joel and Alistair dry-heaving as they shimmied around the hole. It sounded like a monster screeching at them, and Joel's body numbed the closer he got to the black gold on the walls. Yet still, they made it around and continued.

Eventually, the pair happened upon a trench to their right, where they saw Conrad. He was hunched over piles upon piles of black gold with dark red webbing attached to his arm and back.

"Aw, lordy! Did I have that gunk all over me, earlier?" Alistair asked. Joel nodded, and the big man's shoulders shot up to his ears. "I think this place might just be hell, lad! We gots ta find everyone and get outta here!"

Joel approached Conrad and ripped the organic web off before tapping him on the shoulder. He turned, and just as feared, the strategist had yellow eyes and an angry, crinkled brow.

"Only the Dark Savior can bring us true justice!" he shouted while taking a swing at Joel. His combat speed had declined greatly from injuries and fatigue, however, so the mute ducked it with ease.

"Oi! Just what do ya think yer doin', Conrad?" Alistair asked as he jumped in and caught his next punch attempt.

"We must kill the non-believers! They plunder the land and steal from hard-working men! They are the source of our problems!" Conrad said as he tried to shake his fist free.

"Fool!" Alistair boomed as he slapped him across the face. Joel's mouth hung open as the harsh noise echoed all around the trench. "What would Henic think about the way yer actin'? All like a knob n' such? He paid the ultimate price at the hands of a man who believed tha same nonsense!"

Conrad's jaw fell slack and he wheezed while grabbing the rightmost portion of his chest, where he was bleeding. Upon looking back up at the duo, Joel saw that his eyes had turned blue once more.

"Was I… just attacking you?" he asked.

"Ts'alright, lad! Yer punches had no… err… *punch* to 'em, anyway!" Alistair said with a great laugh.

"So, then… we can overcome Gold Fever with our strongest feelings and emotions… I was wondering about that. It seemed like bringing up Dalton helped to snap Lucia out of whatever trance the black gold had her in, before…" Conrad said. Joel and Alistair smiled back at him. "But what about the others?"

Joel led the trio down more trench paths as they heard the battle of the monstrosities draw closer. The mute held his sword at the ready, just in case. Over his shoulder, he could see that Alistair and Conrad were limping behind and in no condition to fight. All kept their heads down, shivering as the sparkles of the black gold beckoned them from each wall. The organic floor seemed to be pulsating faster than ever; so much that each step felt more like a bounce. Joel hated to admit it, but it was almost *fun*. It felt like if he really wanted to, he could bounce off the floor and fly away.

After traversing a few more corridors, the trio encountered Lucia, who was laid out on the ground, grasping mindlessly at piles of black gold. The red webbing was strewn about her whole body, from head to toe, and she appeared to be writhing in pain.

"It hurts…" she moaned, holding the burns on her torso with one hand while caressing black gold with the other. "Only our Savior can make the pain go away…" Her eyes had turned a piercing yellow.

"What is that red material?" Conrad whispered as they approached her. Joel made hand signals to let him know that it was harmless. "Good. Now, allow me to handle this. I think that I can snap her out of it."

Joel and Alistair looked at each other with worry, but they did not stop him. Conrad knelt and began ripping the webbing off of her. She only shivered in response. After it was all gone, he put a hand on her shoulder, and opened his mouth, about to speak.

Suddenly, Lucia's arm shot out and she grabbed him by the throat with her good hand. Joel and Alistair started toward them, but Conrad held up one of his hands as a signal for them to stop, and they obeyed.

"Remember… Dalton. He's still in danger… we must save him…" Conrad muttered as her iron-like grip loosened. "Remember what you went through… in Luneria…" He traced the red crescent-shaped tattoo around her eye with his finger.

Lucia's eyes returned to their normal brown and they became wide with realization. She stared ahead blankly as if her life was flashing by, and then she exhaled loudly.

"What was I thinking?" she asked in a daze, finally releasing Conrad's throat. "My apologies…"

"It's alright… it was the black gold. I did the same thing to them, earlier," Conrad said, pointing back at Joel and Alistair.

"Dalton? He's in danger?" Lucia asked as she struggled to her feet.

"He may well be infected with Gold Fever like we were," Conrad said as he turned to face Joel. "Can you lead us to him?"

He nodded, and with that, the group continued through the corridor-like trenches. As they walked along, they heard a hiss come from Greed. Joel prepared his blade. He was close; *too close*. Then, they saw the dark monstrosity crash through a wall of rock in front of them. Small chunks of black gold exploded in their direction, and they shielded their faces as the Nightcrawler burst through the rubble and jumped out for an attack. Greed caught the beast with his tentacles and threw it so that it soared off into the distance.

Suddenly, holes in the organic floor opened up all around Greed, and they shot out the same dark red webbing that had been attached to the others when Gold Fever had taken them. They attempted to attach to the monster, but he swatted them away with the might of his tentacles and then slithered up the rock wall and over the trenches. Mere moments after disappearing into the dark landscape, more cries, hisses, and the sound of crumbling rocks filled the air.

Joel's gaze focused on the closing holes in the ground. It seemed that they had been reacting to the black gold, and with Greed as the source of its creation, it made sense that more of the red webbing would try attaching to him than his friends. What this odd, disgusting material's purpose was, he couldn't hazard a guess, but he didn't want to find out. He was sure to wait for those holes to completely close up before proceeding, and his friends didn't argue.

After a short time of standing around, shivering, Joel continued through the trenches and soon stumbled upon Dalton. He was curled up against one of the rock walls, but unlike the others before him, he held only one piece of black gold ore in his hand, and there was no red webbing present. Lucia stumbled her way past the others and approached the dazed warrior. She sat next to him as the thunder roared above their heads. Joel looked up, and more spikes had surely sprouted from those dark clouds. He hoped that she could snap Dalton out of it quickly so they could get to finding Baltr and then leave this wretched place.

"Life is a bloody struggle, and then you die..." Dalton trailed off as he played with the ore in his hand. "Fragile... so fragile..." Lucia grabbed his hand. Dalton looked back at her with yellow eyes. However, he did not attack her as the others had done before.

"So fragile that one mistake can haunt you for the rest of your life..." Dalton mumbled as Lucia put both hands to his cheeks and looked him in those yellow eyes once more. "I don't want that burden anymore... only *he* can help me..."

"Do you remember me?" she asked. Dalton raised an eyebrow in return. "I am your foolish student, Lucia. I ran away five years ago so I could prove myself. But now I'm back because I wanted to thank you for all of those times you took care of me. I still use your lessons in swordplay to this day, in fact!" Dalton turned his head away.

"You don't need me anymore… *we* need the Dark Savior," he replied in a sad tone. Lucia wrapped her arms around him.

"There are stronger bonds than the Dark Savior could ever give you… like the bond you had with my father… or my mother, Anora. Do you remember them?" she asked

Finally, Dalton let out a long exhale.

"I miss them every day…" he trailed off as Lucia released her hold and looked back upon him. The yellow had left his eyes and he smiled back at her. "I didn't attack you, did I?" Lucia shook her head while wiping a tear that had come to her eye.

As she and Dalton stood, the warrior looked around and said, "I'm glad to see that you are all alive and well, but where's Baltr?"

"We have been searching around for everyone, and you were our latest find. I'm sure we will stumble across Baltr, soon," Conrad said as the group heard a moan from down the trench corridor.

"It seems even in this hellish realm; he continues to linger by my side!" Dalton joked as he led the group down a path that brought them to Baltr.

Like nearly all before him, the stringy man hunched over and admired the vast piles of black gold before him. The red webbing hadn't found its way to him, yet.

"So lovely… so orderly… so obedient…" Baltr said.

"What do we do to snap him out of it?" Dalton asked the group.

"Yer tha one who knows 'im best! So, it's you who's gotta snap 'im outta it!" Alistair said. The others nodded in agreement.

"Try talking to him about things that will incite strong emotions," Conrad said.

"Hm… alright…" Dalton approached the mumbling miner. "Hey, er… Baltr. Remember how you said you'd follow me to the end? Well, we are at the end now, aren't we? Let's get the hell outta here!" he said with a chuckle, but Baltr refused to turn around. Dalton looked back at the group, and they nodded at him to keep going.

"Remember how you rescued me from the Nightcrawler?" Dalton asked as Baltr shuddered. "Or how 'bout when you saved my sorry arse from Gold Fever?" he continued, but there was no response. "How about when you calmed the miners down and kept 'em under control when they got riled up?"

Baltr remained silent, and the loudest clap of thunder yet erupted from above. Joel's eyes fixated on the clouds. They looked like deadly spiked balls, ready to drop at any moment. For all he knew, that's exactly what they were. They were in a different world, after all, and he had no idea how it operated. The mere act of walking around for a while had been taxing; *foreign*. Nothing about it had felt right. Never before had he thought he'd be longing for the mines of Mt. Couture, but even that place was preferable to here. *Here*, he felt uncomfortable, and it reflected on his soul, slowly withering under the stress of the environment.

"Look… what I'm trying to say is that even though I was named leader of the expedition, there is no one here who deserves it more than you. I'm thankful to have had you by my side. If the Miner's Guild were ever foolish enough to allow me to mine again, it would be my honor to serve with you as leader," Dalton said.

"Well, it's about time you admitted it!" Baltr said as he turned around and burst out with laughter.

"W-wait! You mean to say that you were fine all of this time? I said all that nice shite for nothin'?" Dalton asked, eyes wide.

"After that first bit about staying by your side to the end? Yes," he said. Dalton sulked as the whole group laughed at his expense.

"Alright, that's enough from you lot! We need to get out of here, after all!" Dalton said.

"Joel, you were the one to start finding us all, weren't you? Can you retrace your steps?" Conrad asked. The mute smiled and nodded back at him.

The group strode through the trenches with urgency as they heard the two monsters clashing nearby. And now the thunder and lightning strikes, which had felt trapped by the great dark clouds above, were released from their supposed captivity. The next clap of thunder was the loudest Joel had ever heard, and shook the ground as an earth-quake would. A weakened Conrad fell to the floor from its effects, and holes opened up all around to shoot out red webbing at him. Lucia and Alistair helped him up as everyone else ripped the webbing apart in a panic, and then they pressed on.

Next came the enormous lightning strikes, which coiled down like a pig's tail instead of streaking as it would in their world. Each strike was a different shade of green that lit up the sky to make it look as if it were day. For those brief moments, Joel could see the clouds above were not black, but a dark red. The helix-shaped lightning gave way to dark, rotten winds of the same shape, traveling back up to those clouds.

Tornadoes? *No*, Joel thought with a shudder. Those winds made a crater in the clouds, and now they were collapsing into themselves. It was only a matter of time before-

Suddenly, the clouds burst and gave way to an eruption that sounded like millions of explosive mushrooms going off at once. Yet, even among the deafening noise that saw everyone else ducking and covering their ears, Joel kept his focus up, where the true threat remained. Those multitudes of massive spikes that had caught his attention earlier were now hurdling toward the ground, so fast that some of them burned up like a shooting star in the night sky; but some remained, and they seemed so large that avoiding them would be impossible.

As he turned to run, Joel and the others were hit by a massive shockwave. The world around him spun before he abruptly struck one of the rock walls and crashed back down to reality. His ribs throbbed and his head was hazy, but even still, he kept those spikes in mind. How long did they have before impact?

Joel got his answer as the ground rumbled from a harsh impact nearby, and a new shockwave struck him and the group. He soared through the air before striking another rock wall, and before he could even slide all the way down, chunks of the organic ground, rock, and black gold flew at his face. He quickly himself shielded with his arms, but the debris seemed endless and the impacts became more painful by the moment. By the time his bottom touched the pulsating ground, it had already ended. His ears were ringing and he could feel blood trickling down his arms and face, but he was alive, at least.

A shroud of dark red dust covered the area, but luckily, it was windy, and Joel only had to suffer through a coughing fit for a few moments before it cleared. When his vision returned, the mute looked up in awe to see a dark, enormous spike sticking out of the ground and partially collapsed. He estimated that it was taller than the Miner's Guild building, and it was shiny, as if metallic. The good news, however, was that it had struck through the trenches at an angle before landing, and it had cleared a path for them as a result.

Everyone had sustained minor injuries from the spike, but all were able to walk. They cut through the trenches and finally reached the dark portal as another coil of lightning came down nearby. Joel inaudibly gasped as the dark winds traveled up to the clouds. He looked upon what little landscape he could see ahead: Dozens of spikes stuck up from out of the trenches. It had been pure luck that they hadn't been hit. Before a great wall of wind could hit them again, the group jumped through the portal and returned to the cave from whence they came. Dalton got to his feet first and motioned to the tunnel ahead.

"This way! To the secret exit!" He and Baltr led the charge forward.

Conrad was sure to retrieve his bloody dagger before he and Lucia held on to each other for support while walking. Alistair followed behind them. Joel, however, remained still as the night.

A tingle ran down his spine. *The key was gone.* The monolith remained a pile of rubble and had stopped rebuilding itself. How could it be? His mind lurched as it explored the possibilities. Could Edith have somehow gotten it? Even when her spine had been severed so horribly? Could it have been Aldous or the Mountain King? Or worse! One of the Gold Fever-infected miners that they had left to fight the soul-captured warriors? And what about Angus? He had been knocked out, but enough time had passed that he may have recovered, journeyed to the Gold Pit, and stolen it himself.

Joel looked around frantically to see that not only was the key missing, but Edith was gone, too. She'd been completely helpless, he thought. How could she have possibly moved? None of it made sense to him, but regardless, it didn't matter. He had failed his mission. When he chose to save his friends, he had hoped that he could get away with fulfilling both duties: to the mission and to his friends. Yet, much like stepping on a well-hidden explosive mushroom, it had all blown up in his face.

"Oi! Don't just stand there, lad! We gotta get outta here!" Alistair called back. Joel snapped out of his panicked stupor and understood there was nothing he could do. He followed the others once more.

After the group walked through the cave, they trudged on straight past the turn to the Resurrection Falls. Ahead was a sliver of orange light; perhaps the beginnings of a sunset, Joel thought. With their freedom near, the group picked up the pace until they reached a rock wall with a thin passage in it.

Each member of the group slid through, although Alistair had to be yanked out by the others thanks to his large frame. After climbing some rocks, they emerged from the depths and onto a rocky platform, where they tasted fresh air for the first time in a while. Below were a series of zigzagging paths that were narrow and steep. Joel was certain that it would bring them to the backside of the mountain, where Frez Pond lay. From there, they could make their way around the rock formations and back to the Dead Woods.

Before them was a beautiful sunset which at first put Joel at ease; until its red colorings reminded him of the bloodshed and hardships that they had been through in the mines. It was a stark reminder of what they had escaped, and it made him appreciate his freedom all the more. However, questions remained: At what cost had they survived? Had they helped to unleash the world's ultimate evil? What would they do next?

One thing he was certain of, however, was that what he'd been told about the mountain was true, and it was a warning that he would echo until the end of his days: *Stay away from the mines of Mt. Couture.*

MT. COUTURE

Mountain King's Castle
Pine Tree Forest
Snow Hills
Snow Mounds
Secret Passage
Ice Hut
Resurrection Falls
Steep Cliffs
Nightcrawlers Den
Gold Pit
Secret Exit
Ceiling Hole
Dalton's Journal Found
Secret Passage
Vertical Shaft
Sand Pits
Exit
Thin Wall
Faramond Killed
Black Gold Cave
Explosive Mushrooms
Labyrinth
Dalton Found
Knockers Attack
Riggit Encounter
Dratagon Cave
Nightcrawler Attack
Cavern
Blue Light Cave
Tunnel Collapse
Mouth of Hell
Black Gold Cave
Ollie Found
Underground River
Beach

EPILOGUE

In a grassy field that led up to a busy building made of stone, Dalton Rayleigh leaned up against an old statue of a man holding a pickaxe. It was a nice, sunny day in Faiwell, but a dark cloud hung over the building like an omen. He was waiting outside the Hall of Elders, where the leaders of the village often convened to make important decisions. On this day, however, they had housed both Dalton and Baltr to question them about the disastrous expedition to Mt. Couture.

Baltr exited the hall. He looked tired, and underneath his loose tunic, Dalton could see the wrappings around his midsection, where the Nightcrawler had clawed at him. He had only been given a day of bed rest before being summoned, and so even though his questioning had ended an hour prior, he had stayed behind to ensure that all had gone well with the stringy man.

"Dalton," he said with a nod as they met amid the field.

"I hope you don't think me vain for saying, but 'sir' had a nice ring to it," said the warrior with a smirk.

Grasping his pained stomach as he laughed, Baltr shook his head. "And yet, I am almost certain that you recommended to the Elders that I become a leader on future mining expeditions."

"I had perhaps mentioned your capabilities of herding the miners into line when they weren't listening to me…"

"You'll be happy to know, then, that they took your word at some value. I am to lead a team on a new expedition, soon. Perhaps they wish to see if I am worthy of the position in the long term."

Dalton raised an eyebrow. "This new expedition-"

"Will not be to Mt. Couture, no," he replied, wagging a finger. Dalton breathed a sigh of relief. "As agreed, I told them nothing of the black gold. I told them that we found little of value in those mines."

"I'm sure that Aldous will appreciate that," Dalton said, looking down.

The old Wizard had suddenly appeared before them this morning, begging them not to disclose anything about black gold or the Dark Savior. What had stricken Dalton about the interaction was just how tired, desperate, and weak Aldous had seemed. Perhaps their experiences in the Cold World had paled in comparison to whatever the Mountain King had put him through.

"Even if I *did* foolishly believe that the black gold was to our benefit, covering for Aldous was the least I could do. If it weren't for him and Joel, we would all be dead; only meant to serve as cautionary tales for future miners."

"True," Dalton said before sharpening his eyes. "And did you tell them of Edith's treachery?"

"Erm… that was difficult to do without bringing up black gold and its effects on the others," he replied.

"Bah! I knew your soft spot for 'Lady Edith' remained!"

"She's gone, Dalton."

"No," he replied, pointing at him. "She is only missing. And that means she and that scheming father of hers might be trying to weasel out of punishment for their crimes."

Baltr sighed. "Do you truly believe that Drake will be held to account? Anyone who would have known of his plans is either missing or dead. He is still in good standing with the Guild and Faiwell as a whole. We can't touch him."

Dalton groaned. He was right, but he didn't like it. He snorted and then smiled back at the stringy man. "How about a drink? I owe you at least a few, I'd say."

~

After a few days in Faiwell's hospital, Joel was sent home with his ribs wrapped up. A few of them had been cracked from the blow struck by Greed, and being thrown around in the Cold World hadn't helped. Still, there wasn't much more the doctors could do. He simply had to get rest and let them heal. Upon entering the little shack, he found Aldous lying in bed, curled up in a ball.

He shielded his eyes from the light and said, "Who goes there?"

The mute waved, and Aldous breathed a sigh of relief. "Ah, it's only you, m'boy. I'm glad they let you out of the hospital. Sorry for not visiting, but I needed a few days to recover, myself."

Joel signed back to him. He asked how he had escaped Mt. Couture, and what had happened in his duel with the Mountain King.

"Let's just say that Olivier pushed me to my limit, but once it became clear that you and the others had escaped, I left via the back side of the mountain, just as you lot did."

With a snort, he made more hand signals.

"I'd rather spare you the details," said Aldous.

It was clear that something was wrong, so Joel decided to switch the blame around to himself. That would get him talking, he thought while signing some more.

"Yes, I am aware that the key is lost," he replied. More hand signals. "I'm afraid that I haven't a clue where it is at this time, but rest assured, the Wizard's Council is hard at work, trying to find it. In the meantime, they are probably busy keeping Greed at bay in the Cold World. I'm sure they will update me, soon."

Was Aldous' state of exhaustion affecting his thinking? Or was he simply lying? Their failure to protect the monolith likely meant expulsion from the Council, or they would *at least* be put on probation. As such, there was very little chance that they would be kept informed on the subject of Mt. Couture. Joel decided to hop into his bed instead of pressing him on it any further. Both of them needed rest.

∼

Lucia awoke with a start and immediately regretted it as the burns all about her torso flared up. She groaned in pain while wincing, but then she realized that others had joined in with her groaning. To her left was a line of beds where bloodied men lay; some motionless, others wriggling like worms that had just been hooked. The sun poked through a couple of windows across the room from her, where women in funny hats strode by while carrying medical supplies.

An infirmary, she thought, next looking to her right. In the next bed over was Conrad. He sat up, reading a book. There were bandages all about his body, but he showed no signs of pain.

She cleared her throat and then asked, "How long have I been out for?"

The strategist placed a bookmark between the pages and closed the book before smiling back at her. "Today marks one week since we returned to Faiwell, but I think you were already out on your feet by the time we reached the Dead Woods on our return trip."

Lucia looked up in thought. Her memories were hazy. She recalled the steep trip down the backside of Mt. Couture with only the moonlight to guide them. Even more tense had been the navigation around Frez Pond. Finding out that riggits had called the pond home hadn't been a pleasant discovery, but luckily, they'd been able to sneak by the rabid beasts under the dark veil of night. Her last memory of the trip back was when they had finished traversing the planes between Grimrock Plateau and the Dead Woods. They had reached a tall hill, where she got a good look at the northeastern portion of the woods and spotted a massive tree. Unlike all the others, this tree bloomed with life and strength. She remembered that it had made her smile as all went dark.

"I think that's correct."

"How are you feeling?"

"Burnt," she replied with a snort. Now that she had taken her surroundings in, Lucia could feel that her torso was wet. The nurses must have doused her in herbal water, she thought. "And how about you?"

Conrad waved her off. "I'll survive. They told me that I need to rebuild the muscle in my chest and upper arm, but that's about the worst of it."

"Then, why have they kept you?"

"Oh… erm…" he muttered, rubbing the back of his head. "Well, the others were discharged earlier, and I thought that someone should stay behind to be sure that your condition didn't worsen. We were all worried about you."

Lucia looked down and cracked a smirk while blushing, but only for a moment. She nudged her head to the left and said, "I recognize some of those men. They were infected with Gold Fever…"

"Don't worry," he replied, holding a hand out and bobbing it. "Those men stumbled back into Faiwell a day or two after us. At first, they were like rabid animals, but a couple of nights ago, Aldous snuck in. He brought another fellow along with him; I think that he was also a Wizard. Somehow, they figured out what was near and dear to these men's hearts, and used that information to break the black gold's spell over them. It was as if their minds had been read. And the miners seem to have no memory beyond the first day or two of the expedition…"

"Not that I don't appreciate the old man's assistance, but did he tell you anything about what happened with Greed and the Cold World? I have a feeling that there is far more trouble to come."

"A reasonable expectation, yet what little information Aldous has given me makes it seem like the situation is under control," said Conrad.

"I find that hard to believe," she replied.

"There is little we can do about it right now, anyway. For now, we must focus on recovering," Conrad said while rummaging through a sack at his bedside. He retrieved a couple of books. "In the meantime, can I interest you in some material on the Ancient Ones? I have been reading up on what little Faiwell has on them since Aldous told us their true story. It's fascinating to see what we got right and wrong."

Lucia shrugged. "Sure."

~

IN THE MINING GUILD HEADQUARTERS, Drake Danvers stood at the center of the great hall, where hundreds had gathered to hear his speech. Lucia snuck in with a long sword hidden underneath her heavy cloak. She had no doubt that he would talk his way out of facing consequences for planning the Mt. Couture expeditions. That was why today, she planned on killing him.

"-and I must confess that in my overzealous desires to bring this great village out of the depths of poverty, I made a mistake," he said. Lucia wanted to gag. His lies would be paid for in blood, she thought while brushing past some miners. "And that mistake cost many lives. Including my Edith-"

He held a fist up to his mouth, choked up. A tear rolled down his cheek. Lucia gritted her teeth as the crowd fell silent. Nearby, one of his assistants consoled him. If only they knew the *real Drake*, she thought while brushing past more men, who seemed to be sympathizing.

"I… I hope that you all can forgive me…" he continued, hanging his head. Some in the audience cheered encouragement as Lucia cut to about the halfway point of the crowd. She now gripped the hilt of her sword. It would have to be a quick strike.

With the next step forward, a firm hand grasped her shoulder, halting her. Lucia let out a weak gasp. Caught? Already? Perhaps she stuck out like a sore thumb amongst all of the men in attendance. *Perhaps*, she thought with a frown, it would have been wise to bring a bow and some arrows, instead.

She turned to see that it was Dalton who had stopped her. The mercenary narrowed her eyes. "What are you doing?"

"What are *you* doing?"

"What must be done, of course," Lucia replied.

"Look well," Dalton said, pointing to the far corner of the room. There, a marksman stood, his bow and arrow at the ready. He then pointed behind Drake, where several armed guards stood; and finally, to the other corner of the hall, where another marksman watched on. "You would be throwing your life away."

"I can make peace with death, so long as Drake goes down with me."

"You would be riddled with arrows before even reaching him."

Lucia scoffed. "Why are you here, anyway? I thought you would be busy courting Village Elder Ward's granddaughter."

"She has been successfully courted," he replied with a cheeky smile.

"Was she 'a fine lay', as you put it?" Lucia smirked.

"I truly regret writing in that journal…" Dalton muttered with a frown. "But unfortunately, our courtship was killed before it could truly begin. She is being arranged into a marriage with a prince from one of the western settlements. Elder Ward thought it would be beneficial to our trading. It is a shame, really. I thought that she was my one, true love."

"Right…" Her eyes were narrow with suspicion. "I'm sure you will survive. Now, if you'll excuse me-"

"Ah-ah-ah!" Dalton said, wagging a finger. "Can't let you do that. As your mentor, I have a responsibility to ensure your safety."

"*Former* mentor."

"Then, become my student once more," he said, holding a hand out. "Now that you are competent, we can complete your training."

"I have made it this far on my own. What more training do I need?" she asked.

"Take another step closer to Drake, and I'll show you..." Dalton trailed off in an ominous tone. Lucia cocked her head. "Or, you could train under me for a while longer, and recover in the meantime. Your burns are far from healed."

Lucia grimaced and stared a hole through him. Was he truly prepared to take her down in such a large crowd if she didn't obey?

He sighed. "I'll make a deal with you: Train with me for a while. We will have practice duels every day, and if you beat me even once, I will acknowledge your skill. And more importantly, we will take Drake out together."

The mercenary raised an eyebrow. It was true that she risked dying pointlessly if she rushed Drake now. With Dalton by her side, their chances of success would be far better. He was an excellent fighter, but Lucia was sure she could eventually beat him once in a while, with some practice. She cracked a smile.

"Consider it a deal."

The warrior nodded, and they returned their attention to the center of the hall, where Drake continued to drone on.

"-and that is why it has been decided that we will refocus our efforts on the nearby mountains. We are sure to find more valuable metals if we put our efforts into new digging sites."

The audience erupted with applause and cheering. Lucia tightened her fists. He was offering them a solution that had *always existed* because the Mt. Couture expedition was never meant to be a success. He had everyone completely fooled.

CONRAD WIPED a hefty sweat from his brow as he turned and waved to Henic's widow and son. They returned friendly waves before getting back to work out in the fields of Foreman farm. It had been a long afternoon, and his chest ached, but it was worth every drop of sweat and every ounce of pain to help them whenever possible. Some part of him had accepted that Wolfgang held nearly all of the blame for Henic's death. Yet deep down, he knew that it had been preventable if he had just seen the writing on the wall and killed Wolfgang when the chance first presented itself.

As he traversed a long path, flanked by old wooden fences that held farmland, Lucia appeared at the end. She strode toward him at first, but then turned and walked alongside him when he reached her. She, too, seemed to have worked up a sweat.

"Sorry I'm late," she said with a heavy breath.

"Not to worry. I don't expect you to be here every day, though your presence is always welcome," he replied.

"I don't think Henic's family expects you to show up every day, either. Yet, here you are."

"Point taken," Conrad said with a snort. "I only meant that I know you are busy with training. How goes your sparring with Dalton, anyhow? Is he as great as they say?"

"He's *even better* than they say, if anything," Lucia replied before scowling. "With every improvement I make, it feels like he improves tenfold. He's a monster…"

"I'm sure you will absorb those same skills, soon enough."

"Hopefully. Still, I can't complain. I live with him for free, and I get free training sessions. Most of the work I do is upkeep around the house, or out in the fields, with you. It's not a bad life, I must say!"

"Normally, I would agree, but a dark cloud still hangs over us all. There is some sense of dread that I cannot shake. Everything might *seem* fine, but I get the feeling that something is happening in the background. Something awful…" Conrad said, looking down.

"Well, did you have any luck contacting the miners from the base camp? The ones you were separated from?" Lucia asked.

"Peter slammed the door in my face… again," he replied, and they both chuckled. "But earlier today, I did finally manage to get ahold of William. If you may recall, he was that tall, silly fellow on the trip who liked to talk."

"William… yes, I think I remember."

"It was difficult to get useful information out of him, but he did tell me that when he and the others returned to Faiwell, they turned the black gold over, and were compensated with gold and silver coins," he said.

Lucia's eyes widened. "So, Drake has the black gold, then."

"That is likely, yes. We later found out that it was the Mountain King who'd been conjuring up those thunderstorms to stop us from leaving the base camp, but it still concerns me that both Cyriack and Aldous sensed a dark presence among us. I worry that one of the miners who returned to Faiwell is not who they say they are, but William couldn't provide me with much more on the matter that would be helpful."

"And what of the hooligans? Have they made any attempts at Henic's farm since returning?" she asked.

"No, and I was curious as to why they would stop extorting them until William spilled the beans today. While Brice and the others did return with that group of 11 the night before we got back, they have been missing ever since…"

"Not good."

"Indeed…" Conrad trailed off while looking down. The duo exited to the streets of Faiwell, which were hustling and bustling under the hot orange sun.

"I know what might cheer you up," Lucia said, putting a hand on his shoulder. "There is still time for us to climb the northeast barrier wall and watch the sunset. I think it will make for a better view than our usual spot. What do you say?"

He looked up at her and smiled. "I'd like that."

"No! Noooooo! There was still so much left for me ta doooo!" Alistair cried as the knocks at Aldous' front door became louder and more frequent.

"J-just a moment!" Aldous said, shuffling past the big redhead.

He opened the door to be greeted by two well-armored men.

"We are here for *him*," one of them said, pointing past him and at Alistair.

"Yes, yes, I know."

"Hand 'im over peacefully, old fella," said the other man.

"We plan on it, but could you give him a few moments to pack his belongings? We'll be right out," Aldous said. The armored men nodded, and he closed the door behind him.

"So…" Alistair tried to whisper, but it came out at normal volume. "How are we gonna escape these knobs?"

"We aren't," said Aldous.

"W-we aren't?" The big man started to sob, and Joel stood by his side, patting him on the back.

"There is no choice, I'm afraid. I warned you to keep your head down, but you couldn't help yourself, could you?" Aldous asked, putting hands to his hips.

Joel sighed. He had worried from the beginning that this would be the conclusion. Alistair had been bragging to anyone who would listen about his exploits in Mt. Couture's mines. Somehow, his boasts had caught the attention of the Village Elders, and, wanting to wash their hands of the disaster, they had decided to deport him. He had only recently immigrated to Faiwell, after all, and they didn't need much justification.

"Oh, lad! I'm gonna miss ya, I am!" Alistair said as he laid a bone-crushing hug onto Joel that practically sucked the soul from his body. "Yer like a brother ta me! A wee, lil', small, brother… but a brother nevertheless!"

Aldous laughed in the background, and the big man took notice. He finally released Joel from the bear hug and approached the old Wizard, next.

"Oho! Hold on, Alistair!" he said, holding a hand out. "I'm still recovering from my battle with the Mountain King, y'know!"

"Aye, a fine point, lad." Alistair gave him a firm handshake instead, and Joel frowned in their direction. That battle had been a month ago, he thought, rubbing his back. Aldous was probably fine by now.

Joel let out a deep breath. There were more important matters to address. He signed to Alistair, who focused with great intensity on each hand movement.

"Erm… ya wanna build me a home?" he asked, his round head tilting.

"Ah, so close," Aldous said as Joel let out a snorting chuckle. He had learned much about USL over the past month, but he still had a ways to go. "He asked for you to write down where you live so that we might come visit you soon."

"A splendid idea!" he cried while grabbing one of Joel's crumpled-up maps. He spread it out over Aldous' back, who tried to protest, but fell silent when the ink pen was jammed into his back. Joel laughed inaudibly. It was nearly impossible to spend time with Alistair and remain injury-free, he thought. "There ya go!"

He handed the paper to Joel, who squinted. It was difficult to make out the words with Alistair's poor penmanship at play, but he was certain that Aldous, as cultured as he was, could figure out the place.

As he packed his belongings, Alistair continued to sob.

"Tell Dalton that I'm sorry I couldn't complete tha trainin'… I know that I was his best student…"

Joel rolled his eyes. Dalton had told him that he needed 'much more training' to become a competent battler.

"And tell Conrad that I meant ta read that book he lent me, but I don' wanna take it back ta me homeland…"

Now, Joel was laughing. He had read less than a page in the past two weeks!

"Eh… and tell tha lass… erm… so long, I suppose?" Alistair muttered before his tearful eyes widened. "Oh, wait, wait! Tell her that I'm tha superior warrior, and if she wants ta prove me wrong, she'll have'ta come find me!"

As he finished packing his things, he continued, "Ah! I forgot that I was supposed ta go with Baltr on his next trip to tha mines! You'll tell 'im that I wanted ta go, but couldn't make it, won't ya?"

Joel nodded. Baltr's first expedition out as a leader had been a rousing success. At a new digging site, they had found vast deposits of gold, and there would be much more for them to mine in future expeditions. In one fell swoop, they had solved the precious metal shortage crisis. Although the more Joel heard, the more he was beginning to suspect that the shortage had been very much purposeful.

"A-are ya sure… ya don't wanna help me escape?" Alistair asked, his lips trembling. Both Aldous and Joel put their hands on his shoulders and nodded. Normally, they'd have been game for such a thing, but with their status among the Wizard's Council in question, they couldn't afford to make any more of a ruckus.

As the armed men walked to a horse and carriage with Alistair in tow, he couldn't help but break free and give Joel and Aldous one last spine-crushing hug. Instead of focusing on the pain, the mute wondered what his trip home would be like. The idea of traveling across the land and sea, making his own maps along the way, excited him. They would certainly have to visit soon.

After many tear-filled goodbyes, Alistair finally succumbed to the will of the armed men and left via the horse and carriage. Somehow, his departure felt like the last step in a return to normalcy.

Despite Joel's suspicions, neither Angus nor Edith had revealed themselves in the month that had passed since the Mt. Couture disaster. They had been declared dead by the Miner's Guild. No information, save what Alistair had been blabbering about, had made it to the general public of Faiwell. Aside from a few returning miners that Aldous had been quick to take care of, there had been no signs of Gold Fever in the village. Though it had been an encouraging sign, a sense of dread hung over both he and Aldous: The black gold was still at large, and Drake had likely acquired it. It was a matter of *when*, not *if*, he would put it to use.

In a way, a true return to normalcy was impossible, now. What they were currently experiencing was a façade; the calm before the storm. Of the 123 total miners sent to Mt. Couture, only 20 had returned alive. Yet, Joel got the sense that the nefarious minds behind the plot to unleash Greed would not be satisfied with so many still alive and knowing what had truly happened. Five men, Brice and the hooligans, had already gone missing. Had they been killed in secret? Or had they always been in on the plan?

More concerning still, the monolith that sealed Greed remained destroyed and couldn't be repaired until the key was found once more. The Wizard's Council had not provided Aldous with any updates. For all they knew, a calamity was about to fall upon them, and there was nothing they could do but sit and wait for it.

Even so, there were *some* positives to take from the expedition. Joel had gained perspective on the scale of his mission and learned that he was justified in fighting, sometimes; and without the intent to kill. He'd also gained several new friends whom he treasured dearly. In a situation that had seemed hopeless, they had given him hope. They had listened to his pleas, and accepted him, despite his quirks. It had been a long, long time since he'd felt that his word was truly taken into account. It was a disadvantage of being a mute, especially one who had been sworn to secrecy.

Joel was glad to have broken that secret. Trouble seemed to loom on the horizon, but he had gained friends that he was certain would be by his side, fighting, when the time came. He was certain now, that to have done nothing, as he was supposed to do, would have filled him with regret. And none would have survived, as opposed to 20. The release of Greed had been inevitable, but to find such a good group had not been. By taking action, Joel and Aldous had not failed, as the Wizard's Council seemed to believe. They had succeeded, and they'd all be better off for it. Soon, they would have to prove it.

THE END

If you enjoyed *Gold Fever*, join the newsletter and receive free side stories set in the Dark Savior Series world! You'll get all side stories released up to this point, including *Slaying the Beast, Ground Into Dust,* and *The Seer's Game*. As more are released, you will receive those for free as well!

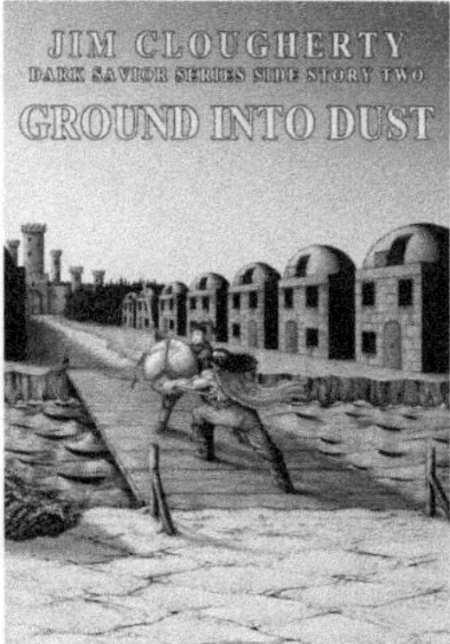

https://www.jimclougherty.com/subscribe-fantasy

What sort of devilry is afoot? Find out in Seven Seals!

For more information and updates on the Dark Savior Series, visit https://www.jimclougherty.com/

Amazon Author Page: https://www.amazon.com/Jim-Clougherty/e/B07TXCK9XZ/

Your opinion matters to me. Let me know if you enjoyed this story:

Amazon Review Page: https://www.amazon.com/review/create-review?asin=B0CPT868VK

Goodreads Page: https://www.goodreads.com/review/new/203490570-gold-fever

ACKNOWLEDGMENTS

I would like to thank Kevin McDermott, the one who got me writing this story in the first place. *Gold Fever* wouldn't exist without you! Just as much, there is no *Gold Fever* without Jean Clougherty, who always encouraged me to write, though it took me years to listen to her advice!

I'd also like to thank Ben Kibit, who helped form my writing style early on. Then there's Chris Guin, who has acted as my unofficial, unpaid creative frustration therapist over the years. Without someone to vent to, none of us can ever hope to finish stories with our sanity intact.

Finally, a thank you to all of the friends and family who supported me along the way. It has been a long, long journey, especially to this second edition. Your interest and enthusiasm for my stories truly helped me at the most difficult times.